Mary Berry

Extracts of the Journals and Correspondence of Miss Berry from the Year 1783 to 1852

Vol. 2

SALZWASSER VERLAG

Mary Berry

Extracts of the Journals and Correspondence of Miss Berry from the Year 1783 to 1852

Vol. 2

Reprint of the original, first published in 1866.

1st Edition 2022 | ISBN: 978-3-75258-833-0

Verlag (Publisher): Salzwasser Verlag GmbH, Zeilweg 44, 60439 Frankfurt, Deutschland
Vertretungsberechtigt (Authorized to represent): E. Roepke, Zeilweg 44, 60439 Frankfurt, Deutschland
Druck (Print): Books on Demand GmbH, In de Tarpen 42, 22848 Norderstedt, Deutschland

MISS BERRY'S

JOURNALS AND CORRESPONDENCE.

VOL. II.

EXTRACTS

OF THE

JOURNALS AND CORRESPONDENCE

OF

MISS BERRY

FROM THE YEAR 1783 TO 1852.

EDITED BY

LADY THERESA LEWIS.

IN THREE VOLUMES.

VOL. II.

LONDON

1865.

JOURNAL

CORRESPONDENCE OF MISS BERRY.

1796.

Miss Berry stated in her entry for this year that General O'Hara had met them at Cheltenham, and afterwards at Park Place. He was no new acquaintance to Miss Berry, for so early as the year 1784 he is mentioned in her journal as having accompanied their party in their expedition to the Falls of Terni.

General O'Hara was highly esteemed by those with whom Miss Berry lived in greatest intimacy. He is often mentioned with praise and interest in Lord Orford's letters. He was a cherished friend of Marshal Conway and Lady Ailesbury, and was on terms of almost brotherly affection with their daughter Mrs. Damer. He was for some years Governor of Gibraltar, and the following character of him, which appeared in the novel of 'Cyril Thornton,' may throw some light on his claims to the warm admiration of his friends, and to that enthusiastic love, which he inspired in vain, and never really lost:—

'It is impossible for me to recur to the period of my sojourn in Gibraltar, and yet to say nothing of the governor, General O'Hara. His appearance, indeed, was of that striking cast, which, once seen, is not easily forgotten. General O'Hara was the most perfect specimen I ever saw, of the soldier and courtier of the last age, and in his youth had fought with Granby and Ligonier. . . .. Notwithstanding the strictness of the discipline which he scrupulously enforced in the garrison which he commanded, no officer could be more universally popular than General O'Hara. . . . In his own house, and, above all, at his own table, he delighted to cast off all distinction of rank, and to associate on terms of perfect equality with even the humblest of his guests. The honours of the table were done by his staff, and the General was in nothing distinguished from those around him, except by being undoubtedly the gayest and most agreeable person in the company. . . . Before we quitted Gibraltar he died. There was no hypocrisy in the heavy looks of the soldiers, as they followed his remains to their last earthly tenement.'—*Vide Cyril Thornton*, vol. ii. pp. 159, 160, 161, 163.

How far General O'Hara was really worthy of the ardent admiration with which Miss Berry viewed his general character and his powers of mind, it is needless to enquire. She loved him with that warm and generous enthusiasm that invests its object with every human quality deemed necessary to perfection, and to the latest years of her life she firmly believed that her union with him would have given increased elevation to her own character, would have called forth the best feelings of her heart, and secured her happiness in this world. At Cheltenham she became aware of the more tender and serious nature of his sentiments towards her, and an engagement of marriage, formed during the subsequent visit to Park Place, was the result of their mutual attachment. How Lord Orford bore the intelligence of this projected change in the life of one of his 'beloved wives,' does not appear by any of his letters; but it certainly was matter of considerable anxiety to both General O'Hara and Miss Berry that the communication should be so made as to avoid giving pain to her devoted old friend. The letters which close the correspondence with Lord Orford of this year are full of solicitude for her health, and show that his interest in her welfare was unabated. General O'Hara quitted England for Gibraltar in the month of November. He proposed an immediate marriage, in order that Miss Berry might accompany him, but she conceived it her duty to decline this offer out of consideration for others. 'In submitting to this absence,' she wrote, 'I *think* I am doing right. I am sure I am consulting the peace and happiness of those about me, and *not my own.*' Perhaps she mistook her line of duty; perhaps she brought upon herself greater evils than those she meant to avert; but who will not admire the self-sacrificing spirit in which her decision was made? They never met again, and a shade of tender regret was cast upon her long life that was never effaced. Forty-eight years after the engagement was broken, and correspondence terminated, Miss Berry reopened the packet of letters that had passed at this time, and ere she closed it again, attached to it the following touching little record of the disappointed hopes and blighted affection that deepened the natural vein of sadness in her character:—

'This parcel of letters relate to the six happiest months of my long and insignificant existence, although these six months were accompanied by fatiguing and unavoidable uncertainty, and by the absence of every thing that could constitute present enjoyment. But I looked forward to a future existence which I felt, for the first time, would have called out all the powers of my mind and all the warmest feelings of my heart, and should have been supported by one who but for the cruel absence which separated us, would never have for a moment doubted that we should have materially contributed to each other's happiness. These prospects served even to pass cheerfully a long winter of delays and uncertainty, by keeping my mind firmly riveted on their accomplishment. A concatenation of unfortunate circumstances—the political state of Europe making absence a necessity, and even frequent communication impossible, letters lost and delayed, all certainty of meeting more difficult, questions unanswered, doubts unsatisfied. All these circumstances combined in the most unlucky manner crushed the fair fabric of my happiness, not at one fell shock, but by the slow mining misery of loss of confidence, of unmerited complaints, of finding by degrees misunderstandings, and the firm rock of mutual confidence crumbling under my feet, while my bosom for long could not banish a hope that all might yet be set right. And so it would, had we ever met for twenty-four hours. But he remained at his government at Gibraltar till his death, in 1802. And I, forty-two years afterwards, on opening these papers which had been sealed up ever since, receive the conviction that some feelings in some minds are indelible.'—*M. B.*, Oct. 1844.

Miss Berry's view of the blessings of married life is so beautifully portrayed in her 'Life of Lady Rachel Russell,' that it cannot be read without feeling how capable she was of appreciating the value of that happiness which it was her misfortune to have missed :—

'It was thus, surely, that intellectual beings of different sexes were intended by their Great Creator to go through the world together;—thus united, not only in hand and heart, but in principles, in intellect, in views, and in disposition—each pursuing one common and noble end, their own improvement, and the happiness of those around them, by the different means appropriate to their sex and situation;—mutually correcting, sustaining and strengthening each other; undegraded by all practices of tyranny on the one part, and of deceit on the other; each finding a candid but severe judge in the understanding, and a warm and partial advocate in the heart of their companion; secure of a refuge from the vexations, the follies, the misunderstandings and the evils of the world, in the arms of each other, and in the inestimable enjoyments of unlimited confidence and unrestrained intimacy.' *

It was at the end of April 1796 that the engagement with General O'Hara was finally broken off. The following extract from a letter of Miss Berry's to Lord Orford evidently alludes to her recent distress :—

* Life of Lady Rachel Russell, prefixed to her Letters.

May 19, 1796.

But let me assure you (though I trust you know me too well to doubt it), that whether in or out of spirits, happy or otherwise, every new occurrence of my life only seems to give me fresh instances of your consoling friendship, to increase my confidence in it, and to convince me that I may flatter myself with having inspired *one* sentiment at least as lasting as it is rare. Farewell.

From Lord Orford.

May 30, 1796. 3 o'clock.

A million of thanks for y^r letter, though with my poor scrawling hand I don't think I can have time to answer a quarter of it before the post departs. I have had people till this instant, and Kirgate is not at home, and I have been forced to get Sir Charles to write letters to Norfolk, where there is started up an opposition to Coke and Wodehouse, whom I must support.

My first object is to beg you to stay as long as it does you all good; yet to-day is most unfavourable.

I want no book but * first volume of the Thames.

The scene at the Opera on Saturday was much stronger than even the papers represented. The Princess at first retired, but the Duke of Leeds persuaded her to stand up and curtsie. She did, and then all the house rose, and then every woman as well as man, in every part, clapped incessantly, and repeated it, and it was well *two* other persons were not there, as insults were loudly declared to be intended, and on their not appearing, 'God save the King' was called for, and sung with the same view. Their Majesties were not there, or a third person might have heard something unpleasant, as the town has got a notion of too much favouring Lady J. at least.

My fingers are too bad to suffer my writing more, and I am sure you will forgive y^r O.

From Professor Playfair to Miss Berry.

Edinb., May 8, 1796.

Dear Madam,—When I took the liberty of asking permission

* The name is much blotted, but was probably Farringdon, the author of 'Britannia Depicta.'

to write to you I said I would not be troublesome by the frequency of my letters, and I have indeed kept my word with disgraceful punctuality.

The whole business of this letter, I fear, will be nothing else but to make apologies and to ask questions. How does Lord Orford? His mind has so entirely resisted the approaches of old age, that I would fain hope his body will still hold out for a long time, tho' it has not, it must be acknowledged, made so vigorous a resistance as the intellectual part. The literary world would wish to prolong the possession of one of its brightest ornaments, more especially at a season like this when it has suffered so many losses and is threatened with such unknown calamities.

Let me entreat your patience while I propose one question more. In what state is the MS. you did me the honour to show me at Twickenham?* Is it perished, or have you executed the plan that you proposed about submitting it to Lord O.? The more I think of it, and consider its superority in every point to anything that has appeared for many years, and of the dialogue, in particular, to anything that has perhaps ever appeared with us, the more I am convinced that it would have the most brilliant success. But I am doubtful how it will be brought forward if the author is resolved, at all events, to remain unknown.

In return for all the valuable information that I am thus requesting you to communicate, I wish I had anything that I could offer in exchange. The literary and philosophical world, at least such parts as I hear of, afford but little that is interesting. I waited with much impatience for the 'Life and Miscellaneous Works of Gibbon,' and if I have not been quite so much delighted as I supposed, I have yet been highly gratified by becoming more intimately acquainted with the person and character of a great man whom I had before only admired at an immense distance. Lord Sheffield has not been very discriminating in the selection of some of the pieces he has given to the public, and I wonder that his lordship should have preferred the character of an exact editor to that of a delicate friend. After all, he has suppressed, I fear, some valuable details concerning the progress of Gibbon's religious opinions, which, I think, should on no account have been done.

* This must refer to Miss Berry's play of 'Fashionable Friends.'

This, however, is but conjecture, and, on the whole, I feel much gratitude, both to the author and the editor. I have lately seen a posthumous work of Condorcet's; it is a very curious book, full of false views and unsound principles, mingled with truth and philosophy in a manner extremely ingenious and artful. But I must leave it for another letter, as this is grown most insufferably long.

I fancy to myself Miss Agnes, this time, one of the greatest metaphysicians of the age, and familiar with every argument of Locke, Berkley, Leibnitz, and Hume. At least she was setting about the study with so much industry when I saw her last, that, knowing her abilities for the acquisition of that or any other branch of science as well as I do, I cannot doubt of her having made such proficiency. She at least has not the excuse that your favourite poet has so beautifully applied to himself in the case of another science,

Gelidus obstiterit circum præcordia sanguis;

and, therefore, if she has not extended her researches as far as I suppose, I will ascribe it solely to the avocations of a fashionable winter spent in the gay circles of London, which, to say the truth, it must be very difficult to unite with the abstract speculations of metaphysics. Be that as it will, I shall have the honour of writing her a long letter of metaphysics very soon.

If I dared to ask you another question, it would be what you are yourself just now busied with—what studies of Greek verse are to be your amusements in the summer? Are you to be at Twickenham all the summer, or what are your other arrangements? . . . .

I must now make an end, for you will begin to think that I can no more measure time in writing than in not writing, and the former to one's correspondents may prove the most incommodious error of the two. I must, therefore, only add that I have committed this great packet, with the 'Life of Mr. Smith,' which accompanies it, to the care of young Dundas, who has undertaken to convey them to you in safety. The *Life* is a present from the author, who had once the pleasure to converse with you for a very short time indeed, but long enough to convince him that few people are so well entitled as yourself to a present of the kind that he now sends you. Permit me only to add that, with the utmost sincerity of esteem and friendship,

I am, dear Madam,

Your obedient and humble servant,

JOHN PLAYFAIR.

From Lord Orford.

Berkeley Square, June 2, 1796.

I hope the post will bring this to you before you set out to-morrow, which I do not write so much to answer your letter, as to remind you that you must return to-morrow if you mean to go to the exhibition on Sunday with Mr. Farringdon, who lives at *No. 35, in Charlotte Street, Rathbone Place.* I speak very disinterestedly, for I am sure I shall not be able to accompany you, as my legs are not yet well.

I am glad all y[r] improvements have succeeded so well; I wish I may ever see them!

I did not suppose you c[d] send me my commissions on Monday, it was so tempestuous that nobody who had not a rage for going abroad at the very moment she had proposed to do anything, could have taken it for a day suited for a jaunt into the country, much less was it one for y[r] crossing my lawn. *Apropos*, the 'Thames' is not in numbers, but in a volume half-bound, I think.

The crisis ripens, the universal applause was repeated on Tuesday at the Opera, but nothing offensive heard. I think *her* appearance was well advised; her absence would havefallen on her husband and been imputed to him; to suppose that she sought popularity would have offended nobody but him, which at this moment could not have made the case worse. He is said to be gone to the Grange for a month.—Oh! I must interrupt myself, I have this moment had such infinite pleasure! my dearest Duchess of Richmond * has this moment been here! and oh! she looks so much better than when I saw her in the summer. She has recovered much of her sweet countenance, her spirits are returned, and her manner is like itself—in short,

* The Duchess of Richmond died in the following November. She was the daughter of Bruce, Earl of Ailesbury.

my joy has made me shed tears! But I will resume my letter, or I shall not save the post.

——and is not to be at the birthday. Lady J—— removed three days ago to her daughter's new house, and, as her new child is dead, will probably move farther, for her present position is not tenable. Lady Harriet is gone to Nuneham for a long season, on pretence of St. Antony's fire—but I must finish.

The Dutch fleet has been found at the Canaries, nine ships, but in a most deplorable condition, and the sailors all ill. Adieu till to-morrow.

Berk. Sq., June 25, 1796.

How grieved I am at the bad account you still give of yourself, and that real summer does not mend you! My hand is better. tho' you see with what difficulty I yet write, yet I *would* positively scratch out a few words to convince you I can, and to tell you Hewetson has assured me I may go with perfect security to Str. on Thursday next, and even stay there for some days; but I shall see you on Monday.

I have been tempted to make Kirgate frank this, as his hand is so very like to mine; but I would not venture any miscarriage, when a note to you and a letter to Agnes were concerned. This attempt says more than all I would say if I had my old pen from the wing of Hercules, my ancient goosely stationer.

The following extract of a letter written by Miss Berry to an intimate friend at this time shows how much her nerves and health had suffered from mental distress, and how vigorously she resolved to combat the effects of her depression :—

London, June, 1796.

You cannot have desired more to hear from me than I to write to you, but for above a week I was really incapacitated by illness, and although the extreme irritation on my nerves has been quieted by five days of perfect retirement in the country, such has been, and is, the depression on my spirits that I have found it absolutely necessary to avoid everything likely to agitate them. But do not suppose this long period of mental and bodily suffering has been lost upon me. I have 'communed much with myself in my own chamber;' I have reflected, and seriously reflected, that, however little I have hitherto enjoyed, and much I have suffered in life from the circumstances in which I have been placed being quite inappropriated to my situation, still, that a being endowed by nature with a sound understanding, possessing a cultivated mind and a warmly affectionate heart, cannot be intended for unhappiness, nay, can never be permanently unhappy but from its own fault, and that with a conscience as clear as mine, it will indeed be my own fault if I do not make my future life less uncomfortable than my past. All this I have felt under the severe tho' *perhaps* salutary pressure of a recent and cruel disappointment.

In the months of July and August Miss Berry accompanied Mrs. Damer, first to Bognor, and afterwards to Goodwood.*

From Lord Orford.

Straw.-hill, July 25, 1796.

I have not writ to you till to-day that I was sure I was well enough; for two days I was in a strange way, yet said nothing of it. On Friday I came down to breakfast, and then attempting to dictate my catalogue for Princess Elizabeth, Kirgate perceived that I neither articulated, nor used right words, and advised me to leave off. I did, and sent for the apothecary, who found my pulse low and quick, and would have had me take æther, but I would take nothing without Hewetson. Your father and sister were with me looking over prints in the evening, but thought I was very low, tho' I complained of nothing; but at one I waked with a great palpitation, I was forced to call up my servants, and really thought I was going; but about three I felt sleepy, and did not wake till seven o'clock, since when I have been perfectly well,—such a strange constitution I have!

Lysons and Mr. Farringdon dined with me yesterday, but I

* Seat of the Duke of Richmond.

did not go down to dinner. They went in the evening to see Agnes's bower, and then came at night with her and her father hither.

I am glad you find your rocks are groves not quarries, and, consequently, that you will saunter, and not be snapped up by a privateer. I wish you could have given me a better account of my dearest Duchess; tell me when you see her again exactly how you find her.

I have made more blots than words, but they make so considerable a part of my letter, that I could not spare them, tho' they contribute nothing to the story. Both my hands and my head are much worn out, and as I cannot write with my pulse, I will set you no longer to deciphering.—Adieu!

Strawb.-hill, July 26, '96.

I received y[r] letter from Bognor this morning, and am mighty glad your rocks are not of a temper to receive vessels with open arms. It would not be pleasant to have one's betrothed turned into the *Fiancée du Roi du Gallia.* Our Tritons are humane and polite enough to have all manner of attentions for women; but the French, if they get to Rome, will be brutal even to the Virgin Mary.

You see I am piquing myself upon writing legibly, and not making a thousand blots; consequently, the Lord knows when I shall have finished my letter; besides, my pen limps, and forgets its spelling. I shall go to town to-morrow for a couple of days, but am not likely to see a soul but people on business. I sat with Agnes this evening, she is delighted with your writing to her so daily. Before I went to her, Lady Cecilia and Mrs. Johnstone came and drank tea with me, and to thank me for venison and orange flowers. They told me it is feared the French will forbid the bans with the Duke of Wurtemburg* by seizing his dominions, and that Lady A. Cumberland is appointed Lady to the younger Princesses. I answer for nothing from Hampton gazettes, nor know anything more substantial.

The living of Crostwick,—which the madam who calls herself Mrs. *Aufrere,* and I would call Mrs. *Auferre,* would have *carried off* from me, is not vacant, and if it were, and in my

* His marriage with the Princess Royal of England.

gift, I should have wished it a thousand,—is a miserable pittance of not thirty pounds a year; so you will not name it, unless it will please my sweetest to hear she was the first in my thoughts.

Wednesday evening.

I came as I have told you I intended, but I have not heard a syllable new, or seen an acquaintance, but the Churchills and Horace, and they were going with the children to Astley's; fortunately Mrs. Chatterpost had intended to bring her husband to dine with me to-morrow, which my coming prevented. I suppose she thought I should be melancholy not to know everything in the world that is not worth knowing.

I find that my memory fails in a very novel manner. I moult many of my letters; my words look like Hebrew without points. I do not recover my walking at all. In short, I advance to what I have foretold, that I should have nothing but my inside left, and then I shall be but an odd figure.

Having nothing better to talk of than my ruins, I shall not make my despatches tedious; it will be trouble enough merely to read them. Adieu.

Strawberryhill, July 29, 1796.

It is almost ridiculous for me to attempt to write with my own hand; my fingers are so maimed they stumble at every long word; my attention dozes, and I have no more imagination left than if I were forcing myself to write a new novel in five volumes. In short, my decay is so sensible to me, that I will not deceive myself, nor expect any further recovery—no change will turn quite round; I must only take care not to let it expose me.

Agnes will give you Lady Charlotte's intelligence from Brighthelm. Our villages furnish us with nothing but a reconciliation which I conclude will not be much longer-lived than the Royal one—it is between Hardinge and his wife: the separation failed for want of a wherewithal for a separate maintenance.

Mr. Joseph Banks has carried Lysons to Kew with drawings of all his discoveries at Woodchester. They made great impression, and he is to send patterns of the mosaics for the Queen and Princesses to work.

Tuesday, Aug. 2.

The post is going out, and none is come in, which is a great disappointment; and besides, writing in a hurry, my hand shakes, and I am forced to call for Kirgate. I hoped to hear of all at Goodwood, and flattered myself that I should have better accounts both of you and my dear Duchess—now I am in perfect ignorance of everything. Your sister goes to music at Udney's this evening. I shall be jealous if she has had a letter when I have not, and yet I wish she may have had, that I may be sure no disorder or accident prevented your writing to me as you had promised. I will keep my letter a few minutes longer, tho' it will be barely in time.

Strawb.-hill, Aug. 5, 1796.

As I am not much in your debt for letters, I shall not complain that I have nothing to send you in return. I do this moment receive one from Goodwood, which I am not surprised at your not admiring. The park at Halnaker is pretty, but the old part of the house was, even in my eyes, deplorable, and scarce preferable even to the vile modern part.

I am grieved that you can give me no better an account of my dearest Duchess; still, tho' slow (and slow indeed it is to me who have it so very much at heart), I am confident she will recover, tho' I may not be so happy as to see it.

Yes, I will certainly encourage any plan that may be of service to y[r] sister. I am not indifferent to the very few persons on whose affection I depend.

I do not know a tittle that is worth calling for Kirgate to write for me, and as the day is very fine, I am going to be carried down to sit in the garden. My pen, you see, can walk a little better—that is all I can boast of. Y[r] bathing, I hope, will be more prosperous. Adieu!

Strawberry-hill, Aug. 9, 1796.

I have just received such a long letter from you of the 6th that if I attempted to answer it with my own hand I should be two days engraving it. Besides, tho' I like to hear so much from you, I am very averse to your writing much, especially when you are bathing, which I am delighted to hear is of service to you. I like your drawing too, tho' not just now, as it adds to your being sedentary. I have another strong reason against your writing more than short notes to me; it would curtail your frequent letters to poor dear Agnes, which make her so very happy.

I will reply as briefly as I can to some other points of your letter. I am grieved that my dear Duchess has any additional pains.

When I saw Halnaker House there was a new red-brick apartment that had been run up by the last Earl of Derby that possessed it, but I suppose the D. of R. has pulled it down.

I am glad you have no worse new neighbours than the Pepys's, tho', as you and your companion are both so erudite, I shall not wonder if he brings some of his clan to educate under your eyes.

You may be assured that Lady I. does not go to Brighton, nor any of the connection, or disconnection. Mrs. Lisle is commissioned to search for a villa for her mistress, which she has not yet found. The Countess drives about in a plain coach without arms. The Pss. told the P. she could not let Mrs. P. wait any more, but might keep her salary; he replied that was impossible; and it is said Miss Colman, the late Maid of Honour, is to succeed as Bedchamber-Woman. The *bon-mot* in the 'Times' was certainly not mine, but perhaps was borrowed from a very ancient one: when Lord Cowper got himself made a titular prince of the empire, he wrote to England to know what place he was to take; I said I could tell him exactly—between Prince Boothby and Count Ellis.

I have little faith in an invasion at present; the unparalleled spirit, activity, and cleverness of our seamen will not tempt the French sailors much to embark; they may attempt to run in a few vessels here and there into open coasts of the three kingdoms, and they do give out that they will try one more campaign against us, *corps à corps*.

Have you heard of single-speech Hamilton's mad will? He bequeathed the landed estate to Lord Egremont, and ten thousand pounds to the young Lady Spencer, and then said he was very sorry that both land and money had been entailed by his father, and that he only made the bequest to show his kind disposition towards them.

The Duchess of Devonshire has been in great danger of losing her sight, by catching cold very indiscreetly. They have saved her eyes by almost strangling her with a handkerchief, and forcing all the blood up into her head, and then bleeding her with leeches. This is all I have to tell you but a few words on myself. I take the air every morning in my coach, and sit an hour out upon the lawn, and crawl a little about between two servants, and do think I have gained a grain of strength; nay, last night I took courage and was carried up into Lady Mendip's room, and even played two rubbers at cribbage. I found nobody there but the tribe of Agar (for I had informed myself) and Mr. Williams, and the General and Lady Cecilia. Most of the neighbourhood is dispersed; the House of Orange (which is nothing to me) are gone to Nuneham, Oxford, and Blenheim; the Murrays to make a visit somewhere for a fortnight; the Mackinzys to Brighton; and the Darrells to Cheltenham, as usual. Lady Mount brought Madame de Cambis here t'other morning; the young Mounts are upon their mountain. Dixi.

The letters of August 16th and 24th, already published, complete those addressed to the Miss Berrys during this journey. The next which has been preserved is in December, without date of day, written in Kirgate's hand, and addressed to Miss Berry at Cliveden (Little Strawberry Hill).

Berkeley Square, Wednesday morning, Dec. 1796.

Tho' I thank you for letting me hear so often, your last night's letter by the penny post was most uncomfortable. You had not grown better, as I hoped and expected. The weather is grown so much softer to-day that I trust you will recover faster, but pray take notice and remember that you are too delicate to run any risks. My horses shall certainly be with you on Friday night. I have seen nobody yet to-day. Last night I had Mrs. D. and my sister, and G. Nicol, and Cosway, whose *glibity* was very entertaining. He told us that the late Duke of Orleans had told *him* that his object was to make his son, the Duke de Chartres, king; and he said that Monsieur de Vergennes, the day after signing the commercial treaty with us, had said to him (still to him, Cosway) that he (Vergennes) must have been drunk when he signed a treaty so favourable to England—such blabs were the French!

My kin have at last had a letter from their son, George Churchill, in Jamaica, who is perfectly well, and who even does not mention having been otherwise, whence they conclude some previous letter must have miscarried. Adieu, unless I hear anything before the post goes out.

This last, dated December 15th, and already published, closes the correspondence with Miss Berry. It begins:—

[I had no account of you at all yesterday but in Mrs. Damer's letter; nor have I had any before post to-day as you promised me in hers. I had indeed a humorous letter from a puss * that is about your house which is more comfortable, as I think she would not have written cheerfully if you had not been in a good way. I would answer it, but I am grown a dull old Tabby, and have no 'quips, and cranks, and wanton wiles' left.]

An extract of a letter from Miss Berry to an intimate friend, shows the state of her mind at the close of this sad year.

Dec. 1796.

You will, I know, wish me to say something of myself. It shall be little, for who can talk of suffering to *you*, or dwell upon disappointments when they think of *yours*? After a twelvemonth passed in the most painful, agitating, and unavoidable suspense, I find myself not only totally disappointed in a plan of happiness, founded on the most moderate desires, and pursued by the most rational means, but obliged to change

* This was written by Miss Seton in the name of a kitten at Little Strawberry Hill, with whose gambols Lord Orford had been much amused. *M.B.*

my opinion of one of the characters in the world of which I had ever thought the highest, and in whose honour, truth, and affection I had ever had the most entire confidence and the sincerest satisfaction long before I considered him in any other light than that of a friend. I shall not dwell on the effect which you will easily guess all this must have had on a heart as warm and as little *generally confiding* as mine, but a heart which when once it trusts, trusts so implicitly. My consolations have been in the increased and touching affection of my sister, the kind, rational, and unremitting attentions of Mrs. Damer, and the reflection that there is no part of my conduct that I could for a moment have wished otherwise. These have succeeded in restoring me to the power of employing myself and my spirits to near their usual level.

It appears that some of Miss Berry's friends sought to alleviate her distress, and lessen her regrets at the unfortunate termination of her engagement, by endeavouring to blame and depreciate the object of her affections; but, with her, disappointment did not find comfort in resentment, and she generously defended from censure or detraction the conduct and character of one who had been to her the cause of bitter suffering.

Extract of a letter to a friend :—

. . . . Mrs. L., you say, 'observes that my affections have been more deeply engaged than I was aware of,' and Mrs. D. 'has repeatedly intimated the same' to you. Needed you any intimation that my affections *must* have been *deeply* engaged before I resolved, or even thought of marrying? Had I ever chosen to think of making what is called a *prudent* marriage, did you suppose, that I, in common with all my sex, might not have done it? Or could you suppose *this* a *prudent* marriage? Did my silence on this subject deceive you? and did you really believe me capable of the *platitude* of talking in raptures, or enlarging on the character and perfections of the man whom I considered as my husband? Now that he no longer stands in that position, it is not *my* having reason to complain of him that shall prevent my doing him justice. I know not where you have taken your reports of his character but, I know that a character 'universally highly thought of,' is the last I should choose for any intimate connection, for, (except in early youth) nothing but mediocrity can possibly attain it. I have heard O. H. called too *exigeant* and *worretting* by idle officers under his command, and too bold by the ministerial people here, after the failure at Toulon; but in my life I never heard an allegation against either his heart or his understanding, and if I had, I should not have believed it, because in a long acquaintance I have myself *known* and *seen* repeated proofs of the excellence of both. Instead of not knowing 'any real virtues he possesses,' until this unfortunate affair, in which I am still convinced his head and not his heart is to blame, I know nobody whose character united so many manly virtues. It was this, joined to a knowledge of his conduct in all the relations of life in which he then stood, that entitled him to the 'approbation and love of such a heart' as mine, and I felt and know he decidedly 'suited me as a friend,' because to an excellent understanding, great natural quickness, and much knowledge of the world, he joined an affectionate tenderness of heart which had always inspired me with a degree of confidence and intimacy, you have often heard me say I hardly *ever* felt with *any* other person. . . . I still believe that had this separation never taken place, I should never have had to complain of him, nor he to doubt me.

1797.

'I go to Lady Spencer's at St. Albans, and to Brooke Hall to meet Mrs. D. and Mr. Whitbread. *Lord Orford dies.* See much of the Starembergs.'*

The principal event of the year was the death of Lord Orford; and the account of his declining health and reason is thus given by Miss Berry† :—

Very soon after the date of this letter (Dec. 15), the gout, the attacks of which were every day becoming more frequent and longer, made those with whom Lord Orford had been living at Strawberry Hill very anxious that he should return to Berkeley Square, to be nearer assistance in case of any sudden seizure. As his correspondents, soon after his removal, were likewise established in London, no more letters passed between them. When not immediately suffering from pain, his mind was tranquil and cheerful. He was still capable of being amused, and of taking some part in conversation; but during the last weeks of his life, when fever was superadded to his other ills, his mind became subject to the cruel hallucination of supposing himself neglected and abandoned by the only persons to whom his memory clung, and whom he always desired to see. In vain they recalled to his recollection how recently they had left him, and how short had been their absence; it satisfied him for the moment, but the same idea recurred as soon as he had lost sight of them. At last nature, sinking under the exhaustion of weakness, obliterated all ideas but those of mere existence, which ended without a struggle, on the 2nd of March, 1797.—*M. B.*

* Austrian Ambassador for some years in England.

† *Vide* the note accompanying that portion of Lord Orford's Correspondence which was first published in the year 1840.

A sad picture of that decay of body and extinction of mind which forestalled the cessation of life itself, and diminished the pang of final separation; but it must always have been a touching and gratifying recollection, for those to whom Lord Orford looked for the happiness of his latter years, that, whilst his feverish fears pointed to their absence as his greatest ill, they were ever at hand to soothe his apprehensions by their presence, and to smooth the pillow of their dying friend.

It has been often a matter of speculation whether Lord Orford's great attachment to Miss Berry had ever led to any explicit declaration of a wish to obtain her consent to their union in marriage. Notwithstanding the frequent professions of equal attachment to both sisters, it is easy to see throughout the correspondence that Miss Berry herself was his first object. The dread of being thought ridiculous by playing the part of a more than septuagenarian lover, no doubt acted as a constant check upon the indulgence of such hopes as he might have reasonably entertained as a younger man; and so entirely dependent was he on the society of Miss Berry and her sister for what remained to him of pleasure in life, that even if impelled by the wish to secure to himself the absolute right to her companionship and attentions as a wife, he probably feared to lose her friendship by proffering the hand she might not accept; yet, it was admitted by those best entitled to know, that at one time Miss Berry was conscious that the choice was within her power; but she clung to his friendship too warmly and too sincerely, not to sedulously guard him from the expression of any feeling she could not fully return. She accepted his friendly affection without reserve. He was spared the mortification of ever learning from her lips that more he could never expect. The letter of the 15th December was, according to Miss Berry's account, the last received by her, or her sister, from Lord Orford. It was the close of that tender and voluminous correspondence, which, during the space of nine years, evinced a warmth of heart, a never-failing playfulness of thought, and refinement of wit, not only well worthy of the fame of the 'Prince of Letter Writers,' but leaving on the mind of the reader a still stronger impression of the genial affection and considerate kindness which marked the declining years of Lord Orford, and saved him from the chilling influence of increasing age, painful infirmities, and domestic loneliness.

By Lord Orford's will,* Little Strawberry Hill was left to the Miss Berrys, and in a codicil, a box, marked O, containing MSS., was left to Mr. Berry and his daughters, with directions that Mr. Berry should undertake the care of a new edition of his works, with the addition of all the papers contained in that box. Miss Berry acknowledges, in a letter addressed to a friend at this time, that in making her father his editor and Mrs. Damer his executrix, 'Lord Orford caused his papers being secured to *her* eye *and mine*, and made me his editor without the necessary publicity attached to the name.' Miss Berry describes herself in the same letter as labouring with incessant perseverance for nearly a twelvemonth; as neglecting all her own pursuits; never looking in a book but that was conducive in some degree to the work she had in hand; reading and *re*-reading with perfect integrity of intention, both with respect to the author and the public; and she adds that she is making all that part of the publication which depends on her selection as worthy of it as possible. It may be fairly presumed from this account that on Miss Berry devolved the chief labours of the editorial

* Will of Horatio Wallpole, Lord Orford, proved 1797. Messuage and outhouses, late in the occupation of Mrs. C. Clive, left to Mary and Agnes, daughters of Robert Berry of North Audley Street.

In second codicil:—Box marked O, containing Manuscripts, left to Robert, Mary, and Agnes Berry—to be divided 'share and share alike.'

duties bequeathed to her father. The edition published with the name of Mr. Berry was given to the public in the year 1790.

The following memorandum was written at a time of great depression as to the prospects of her own country, but with Miss Berry's usual wish to bear some part in promoting the welfare, or extending the knowledge of her fellow-creatures; it was probably the germ of that excellent work 'A Comparative View of Social Life in England and France,' which appeared many years afterwards, and was the fruit no less of study than of personal experience and personal observation.

May 7, 1797.

I am resolved for the future to make memoranda of the remarkable circumstances and characters that pass either immediately under my own eyes and knowledge, or that I can learn from such undoubted authority, and such accurate observers, as may satisfy even the steady search and unquenchable desire of truth which has ever existed in my mind. It is my unfortunate lot to pass the most reasonable years of human life--I mean from thirty upwards—in times of universal fermentation; when the minds of men all over Europe are undergoing some great change, and when some new system of social order is struggling into existence opposed by all the obstinate rancour of prejudice, and encouraged by all the heedless enthusiasm of novelty.

My own country tottering on its basis, with every means of self-correction and principle of renovation within itself, in little more than a hundred years after its complete establishment, seems to the thoughtful mind but a new assurance of the impossibility of permanence to any institution of man. In such times and such circumstances, my sex and situation condemning me to perfect insignificance, and precluding all possibility of my ever taking an active part, and then, like others, being misled and blinded by the part I have taken, perhaps I am but the more fit to record what I see. A very small fraction of the great and awful scene may fall under my cognizance; but however minute the features that I may attempt to seize, they will neither be uninteresting nor useless to those inspired with the same accurate love of truth and candid investigation of human nature with myself.

Letters of H. Walpole not yet published.

A certain number of Lord Orford's unpublished works have remained till now amongst Miss Berry's papers. The interest attached to all that fell from his pen has much increased, as fresh publications and new editions of his letters have made his readers better acquainted with his peculiar vein of thought and humour. They are now therefore given to the public; and the close of the year in which Lord Orford died seems the fittest place to which to assign these last gatherings of his miscellaneous productions.

To Mr. Gray.

From Cambridge, 1735.
In the Style of Addison's Travels.

DEAR SIR,—I believe you saw in the newspapers that I was going to make the tour of Italy; I shall therefore give you some account of the places I have seen, which are not to be found in Mr. Addison, whose method I shall follow. On 9th of Oct^r^, 1735, we set out from Lodone[1] (the Lugdunum of the Ancients), the capital city of Lombardy, in a chariot-and-four. About 11 o'clock, we arrived at a place the Italians call Tempialbulo.[2] Virgil seems to have prophesied of this town when he says—

> Amisit venem vetus Albula nomen.
>
> By Time the founder's great design was crost,
> And Albula its genuine title lost.

Here are no remains of Roman antiquity, but a statue of Marc Aurelius,[3] which the Lombards call Guglielmo Terzo, one of their kings, and some learned men,[4] St. George and the Dragon. It is an equestrian statue, and almost equal to that of Charlemagne, at the Great Cross,[5] at Lodone. The church is an old

[1] London.

[2] White-chapel.

[3] Statue of K. William at a stone-cutter's.

[4] See Addis. Trav., p. 26.

[5] Statue of K. Charles at Charing Cross.

Gothic building, and reckoned the most ancient in Italy. Here was some time ago an altar-piece of the Lord's Supper, in which the painter having quarrelled with the Abbot[1] of this church, represented him like Judas, with this epigram:—

[1] Dr. White Kennet, Bishop of Peterborough.

> Falleris, hâc qui te pingi sub imagine credis,
> Non similis Judas est tibi—pœnituit.
>
> Think not, vain man, thou here art represented,
> Thou art not like to Judas—he repented.

From thence we made the best of our way to a town, which in English we should call Stony-Stratford, and corresponds with the description which Virgil has given of it—

> —vivo præter vebor Ostia Saxo
> Stratfordi, Megarosque sinus, Tapsumque jacentem.

Those that follow are little dirty towns, that seem to have been built only to be 'knocked'[2] on the head, like

[2] Expression of Addison on this line.

> Antitheum, Glaucumque, Medontaque, Thersilochumque.

The next town of note is Arc,[3] so called from its being built in the shape of a bow—*ab Eoo curvatur in Arcum.* From Arc we travelled thro' a very pleasant country to Epino,[4] whose forest is celebrated by Virgil in these lines:—

[3] Bow.

[4] Epping.

> Sylva Epini latè dumis, atque ilice nigrâ
> Horrida, quam densi complerant undique sentes;
> Rara per occultos ducebat semita calles.
>
> Epinum's woods with shrubs and gloomy oak
> Horrid, and all with brambles thick o'ergrown,
> Thro' which few narrow paths obscurely led.—*Mr. Trap.*

We were here shown, at a distance, the thickets rendered so famous by the robberies of Gregorio.[5] Here I was met by a very distant and troublesome relation. My namesake hints at such an one in those lines of his—

[5] Gregory, a noted highwayman. See Ad. Trav., p. 1.

> Accurrit quidam notus mihi nomine tantùm,
> Arreptaque manu, Quid agis, Cosinissime, rerum?—*Hor.*
>
> There step'd up one to me I hardly knew,
> Embrac'd me, and cried, Cousin, how d'ye do.—*Mr. Creech.*

We lay that night at Oggerell,[6] which is famous for nothing but being Horace's Oppidulo, quod versu dicere non est.

[6] Hockerel.

In our way to Parvulun,[1] we saw a great castle,[2] belonging to the Counts of Suffolcia; it is a vast pile of building, but quite in the old taste. Parvulun is a small village, but formerly remarkable for several miracles[3] said to be performed there by a Welsh saint, who, like Jupiter, was suckled by a goat, whence they think it Porrum et Cepe nefás violare.—*Juv.* The wonders of Parvulun are in great repute all over Lombardy. We had very bad ways from hence to Pont Ossoria,[4] where are the ruins of a bridge that gives name to the town. The account they gave of it is as follows:—St. Bona being desirous to pass over the river, met with a man who offered to carry her over; he took her up in his arms, and under pretence of doing her service, was going to ravish her; but she praying to the Virgin Mary for help, the wretch fell into the stream and was drowned, and immediately this bridge rose out of the water for her to go over. She was so touched by this signal deliverance, that she would not leave the place, but continued there till her death in exercises of devotion, and was buried in a little chapel at the foot of the bridge, with her story at length and this epitaph—

Hâc sita sunt fossâ Bonæ venerabilis ossa![5]

From Pont Ossoria we travelled by land to Nuovo Foro[6] (the Novum Forum of Iockius), where are held the greatest races in all Italy. We were shown in the treasury of the Benedictines' Convent, an ancient gold cup which cost an hundred guineas (a great sum in those days), and given, as the friar told us that attended us, by a certain German Prince, he did not very well know who, but he believed his name was one King George.[7] The inhabitants are wonderfully fond of horses, and to this day tell you most surprising stories of one Looby, a Boltognian. I saw a book dedicated to the head of that family, intituled 'A Discourse on the Magnanimity of Bucephalus, and of the Duke of Boltogne's Horse Looby.'[8]

I staid here three days, and in my way to Pavia[9] stopped at the Palace of Delfini,[10] which is built on the top of a large barren mountain, and at a distance looks like the Ark resting on Mount Ararat. This mountain is called Gog, and opposite to one called Magog. They are very dangerous precipices, and occasioned the famous verse—

Incidit in Gogum qui vult vitare Magogon.[11]

[1] Littlebury.
[2] Audley Inn, the seat of the Earl of Suffolk.
[3] Winstanley's Wonders, or Tricks in Mechanics.
[4] Bone Bridge.
[5] Epitaph of Venerable Bede.
[6] Newmarket.
[7] See p. 78.
[8] See p. 30. D. of Bolton.
[9] Cambridge.
[10] Lord Godolphin's house on Gogmagog Hills.
[11] 'Incidit in Scylla qui vult vitare Charibd.n.'

I need not repeat the history of Gog and Magog, it being known to every child, and to be found at large in most books of travels.

Pavia and its University are described by Mr. Addison, so I shall only mention a circumstance which I wonder escaped that learned gentleman. It is the name of the town, which is derived from the badness of the streets: *Pavia à non pavendo*, as *Lucus à non lucendo.*

Till next post, adieu!

Yours ever,

HORATIUS ITALICUS.

To the Hon. Henry (afterwards Marshal) Conway.

London, October 31, 1741.

MY DEAREST HARRY,—You have made me infinitely happy, but infinitely impatient for Monday se'nnight. I have wished for you more particularly this week, and wanted you all at Sir Thomas Robinson's* and the birthday. You have already had accounts, I suppose, of the former from Lady Caroline and Mr. Selwyn, but I will say my bit about it too; I told Lady Caroline I would; besides, I made a list of most of the people, and will tell you some of the company, which was all extremely good; there were none but people of the first fashion, except Mr. Kent, Mr. Cibber, Mr. Irving, and the Parsons' family, and you know all these have an alloy. Kent came as *governess* to Lady Charlotte Boyle,† Cibber and Irving have long had their freedom given them of this end of the town, and the Parsons's ‡ took out

* In Horace Walpole's letter to Sir Horace Mann, dated October 22, 1741, he says:—'The whole town is to be to-morrow night at Sir Thomas Robinson's ball, which he gives to a little girl of the Duke of Richmond's. There are already two hundred invited, from Miss in bib and apron to my Lord Chancellor (Hardwicke) in bib and mace.' Lord Dover adds a note to explain that Sir Thomas Robinson was not the diplomatist, afterwards Lord Grantham, but Sir Thomas Robinson of Rokeby Park in Yorkshire, commonly called '*long Sir Thomas.*'

† Lady Charlotte Boyle, second daughter of Richard, third Earl of Burlington, married William, Marquis of Hartingdon.

‡ The family of Alderman Parsons, a Jacobite brewer, who lived much in France, and had been taken notice of by the King.

theirs at Paris. There were an hundred and ninety-seven people, yet no confusion; he had taken off all the doors of his house, and, in short, distributed everybody quite to their well-being. The dancers were the two Lady Lenox's* (Lady Emily queen of the ball, and appeared in great majesty from behind a vast bouquet), Lady Lucy Manners, Lady Ancram,† Lady Lucy Clinton, Ladies Harriot and Anne Wentworth, Sophia and Charlotte Farmor, and Camilla Bennet; Miss Pelham (Lord! how ugly she is!); Misses Walpole, Leneve, Churchill, Parsons, Maccartny, Pultney, Mary Townshend, Newton, and Brown. The men, Lord John Sackville, Lord Ancram, Holderness, Ashburnham, Howard, Hartington, and Castlehaven; Mr. Colebrook, Poulett, Churchill, two Townshends, Parsons, Vernon, Carteret, Colonel Maguire, and a Sir William Boothby. For the rest of the company you shall see the list when you come to town. Lord and Lady Euston and Lady Caroline did not dance. A supper for the lady dancers was served at twelve, their partners and waiting tables with other supper stood behind. Oh! I danced country dances, I had forgot myself. The ball ended at four.

Now for the birthday. There were loads of men, not many ladies, nor much finery. Lord Fitzwilliams and myself were the only two very fine; I was in a great taking about my clothes, they came from Paris, and did not arrive till nine o'clock of the birthday morning. I was obliged to send one of the King's messengers for them and Lord Holderness's suit to Dover. There were nineteen suits came with them. Do you know I was in such a fright lest they should get into the news, and took up the *Craftsman* with fear and trembling. There was the greatest crowd at the ball I ever saw. Lady Euston danced country dances with the Duke. My aunt Horace had adapted her gown to her complexion, and chose a silk all broke out in pink blotches. The Duke of Kingston, Lord Middlesex, and Lady Albemarle, are dreadfully altered. You can't think what an alteration towards old I find among my acquaintance.

Harry, you must come and be in love with Lady Sophia

* Lady Caroline and Lady Emily Lennox; the former married, 1744, to Henry Fox, first Lord Holland; the latter married, 1746, to James, twentieth Earl of Kildare.

† Lady Ancram, daughter of Robert, third Earl of Holderness.

Farmor; all the world is or should be. But I had cried her up so much before she appeared that she does not answer everybody's expectation. No more will the Opera to-night, for Amorevoli is ill and does not sing; his part is to be read. They had certainly much better have staid till Tuesday; but for fear of disappointing people, I fear they will disappoint them. I am not to be there, for Dodd has got a fever with the heat of the ball last night, so I shall not leave him. Indeed, my dear Harry, I will not scold you about the Opera, but I should have been glad, I own, that you were not in the direction. I doubt much of the success; and even should it succeed, gentlemen—and they very young gentlemen—are mighty apt not to understand economy and management. Do get out of it, if possible.

Good night! I have nothing more to tell you now, but I shall have a quantity to say to you. My loves to all your family.

Yours ever,

H. W.

To the Same.

Strawberry Hill, Thursday, Sept. 2.

Not being in town, there may be several more new productions, as the *Grubbœa frutex* blossoms every day, but I send you all I had gathered for myself while I was there. I found the pamphlet much in vogue, and indeed it is written smartly. My Lady Townshend sends all her messages on the backs of these political cards, the only good one of which, the two heads facing one another, is her son George's. Charles met D'Abreu t'other day, and told him he intended to make a great many good speeches next winter. 'The first,' said he, 'shall be to address the King, not to send for any more foreign troops, but to send for some foreign Ministers.'

Mr. Fox had a very bad sore throat, but never was in any danger. You have heard, I suppose, what an abominable will Lord Fitzwilliams left; did not mention his wife or younger children in it, but leaves all to his eldest son, tho' she is one of the most deserving women in the world, and the younger son and five daughters will have but 2,500*l.* a-piece!

My Lord Chesterfield is relapsed: he sent Lord Bath word lately that he was grown very lean and very deaf; the other replied, that he could lend him some fat, and should be very glad at any time to lend him an ear.

I shall go to London on Monday, and if I find anything else new, I will pack it up with a flower picture for Lady Ailesbury, which I shall leave in Warwick Street, with orders to be sent to you. Adieu!

Yours ever, H. W.

To the Same.

Strawberry Hill, Monday night, July 2, 1764.

If my Lady Ailesbury* does not think the little 'bull' as handsome as Jupiter himself, I shall resent it. He is accompanied by seven bantams for the Infantas.†

As Lord Frederick and Lord John are gone to you this evening, I can tell you no politics but what they know. The *Bedfords* are certainly jealous of some negotiation being on foot between Lord Bute and Pitt, but I cannot find that it is with any reason, tho' I do not desire to have them undeceived.

Lord Bath has been dying, but is out of danger, and, what I like more, Legge mends again. Your brother has sent me the Duke and Duchess of Berwick, and what upon earth to do with them I don't know. They have the grace to call themselves Lirias here, yet they do not go to Court, and say they are only come to see their relations. He looks like a cook, but does not seem to have parts enough for one. He had never heard that his great-grandmother married Mr. Godfrey; he told me to-day that she called herself Churchill, but that her family name was Marlborough. The Duchess of Lina, who is sister of the Duc of Alva,‡ is a rational civil being, not at all handsome, but easy and genteel. They have more debts than dukedoms, tho' he is Duke of Veraguez, too, and have crowded all their rich blood into la rue de Suffolk Street.

They talk of a match between Lord Middlesex and Lady

* Lady Ailesbury, daughter of John Duke of Argyll, widow of Charles Earl of Ailesbury and Bruce.

† Daughters of Lady Ailesbury.

‡ Anne Seymour Conway, afterwards Mrs. Damer.

Jane Stuart:* in the meantime, Mr. Ellis is dying for her, and Lord Holland's young Macartney † very desirous of living by her.

The fashionable diversion in town is a conjuror. We had him last night at my Lady Harrington's. His tricks are ten times more dexterous than Sandwich's.

There was last night at Guerchy's ‡ a daughter of Lord Dillon,§ just come out of a convent, who is to be the future Duchess of Norfolk. She has a fine person, and not at all a disagreeable face.

The Mecklenburgh Countess was there too, ten times more dirty, frowzy, extravagant and mad than ever. Prince William has said, 'This is the worst sample we have had yet.' I begin to think he will not command the army.

My Lord Townshend and Charles had quarrelled lately. My Lady made a reconciling dinner for them, and all was made up. As soon as they parted, George wrote the most abusive letter in the world to Charles, and they are rather ill together again. Adieu!

Yours ever, J. W.

To the Dowager Duchess d'Aiguillon.

Strawberry Hill, Nov. 3d, 1766.

One cannot repine, Madam, at some portion of illness, when it procures one such marks of goodness as I have experienced, especially from your Grace; indeed, it grew a little too serious, and I began to think that I should not live to pay my debts of gratitude. My Lady Hervey, with all her kindness to me and her partiality, her just partiality, to France, is however in the wrong to attribute any part of my illness to my manner of living at Paris. I came from thence perfectly well; and, to say the truth, I ascribe much more to the damp air of England than to any course of life. Yet I will not say too much against my

* Eldest daughter of the Minister, Earl of Bute.

† Sir George (afterwards Lord Macartney) who married her.

‡ Comte de Guerchy, Ambassador from France.

§ The Duke of Norfolk married secondly, in 1771, Miss FitzRoy Scudamore of Holme Lacy, county Hereford.

own country, that I may not destroy any little merit I may have in returning to Paris this winter. I neither deserve nor expect any sacrifice, but am ready to sacrifice anything both to your Grace and Madame du Deffand, who have both shown me so many marks of kindness and protection.

Mr. Hume has, I own, surprised me, Madam, by suffering his squabble with Rousseau to be published. He went to Scotland determined against it. All his friends gave him the same advice; but I see some philosophers can no more keep their resolution than other philosophers can keep their temper. If he has been overpersuaded from Paris, I suspect that the advice was not so much given him for his sake, as to gratify some spleen against Rousseau; and that his counsellors had a mind to figure in the quarrel; for men of letters delight in these silly altercations, tho' they affect to condemn them. It spreads their names, and they are often known by their disputes, when they cannot make themselves talked of for their talents. For my own part, I little expected to see my letter in print, as your Grace tells me it is, for I have not yet seen the book. I have neither been asked nor given any consent to my letter being published. I do not take it ill of Mr. Hume, as I left him at liberty to show it to whom he pleased; I am, however, sorry it is printed: not that I am ashamed of any sentiment in it, especially since your Grace does me the honour of approving it; but I think all literary controversies ridiculous, impertinent, and contemptible. The world justly despises them, especially from the arrogance which modern authors assume. I don't know who the publishers are, nor care; I only hope that nobody will think that I have any connection with them. Nor have I; tho' I have played the fool in print, I have not so much of the author as to think myself of consequence enough to trouble the world with my letters and quarrels. Authors by profession may, at least they generally do, give themselves such airs of dignity; but they do not become me. However, madam, I only laugh at all this, for I am no philosopher, and therefore am not angry.

I am told it is asserted that I have owned that the letter to Rousseau was not mine; I wish it was not, for then it would have been better. I told your Grace, I believe, what I told to many more, that some grammatical faults in it had been corrected for me, for I certainly do not pretend to write French well; and it ought to be remarked, too, that the letter was not written in the name of a Frenchman. I must have been vain indeed if I had flattered myself that I could write French well enough to be mistaken for a Frenchman. The book too, I hear, says that the real author ought to discover himself. I was the real author, and never denied it. But is not it amusing, madam, to hear an anonymous author calling on somebody, he does not know whom, to name himself? And are not such authors very respectable? I shall not imitate him, nor ask to hear the publisher's name: I do not believe I should be much the wiser for knowing it.

I am told, too, that my letter to Rousseau is censured in this book. It is very mortifying to me, to be sure, that, when so many persons of taste had been pleased with that letter, it should be condemned by higher authority; but it is not uncommon for men of taste and men of letters to be of a totally different opinion. Nor am I surprized that a trifle, designed as a jest, and certainly never intended to be made public, should be anathematized by their holinesses the philosophers and the enemies of Rousseau. It looked like candour to blame me, when so real an injury was meditated against him as the publication of his absurd letter to Mr. Hume. Philosophy is so tender and so scrupulous!

I beg your Grace's pardon for troubling you so long. You find I am so much of an author, that I contradict myself, and think this very foolish controversy important enough to employ two pages. Indeed it is not; and if I were not alone in the country, I should not have thought it worth two lines. Such a real genius as Rousseau cannot appear, but he causes all the insignificant scribblers in Europe to overwhelm the public with their opinions of him and his writings. But he may comfort himself; his works will be admired when the compilers of dictionaries and mercuries will be as much forgotten as your Grace's

Most obedient, humble servant,

HORACE WALPOLE.

In a letter from Horace Walpole to Sir Horace Mann, dated May 12th, 1767, the following passage occurs :—

[Nothing was ever so vexatious! I had just written you a long letter of three sides, and laid it upon the hearth to dry, while I stepped into the next room to fetch some sealing wax. A coal has fallen on it, and I find it all in flames. I have not time to write half of it again. I will just run over the heads, if I can remember them.

My chief article was a wonderful speech made by Charles Townshend last Friday, apropos to nothing, and yet about everything—about ministers, past, present, and to come—himself in particular, whom I think rather past than to come. It was all wit and folly, satire and indiscretion. He was half-drunk when he made it, and yet that did but serve to raise the idea of his abilities.]

The following account of Charles Townshend's* speech, dated May 8th, 1767, is probably the 'chief article' of the burnt letter to which he alludes. Horace Walpole sometimes preserved copies of his letters, but in this case it seems more probable, though dated the 8th, it was a memorandum from recollection of the letter he had intended sending to Sir Horace Mann.

May 8th, 1767.

Charles Townshend had come to the House with a black silk hanging over his wounded eye, which in the warmth of debate he turned aside, and discovered two very small slips of sticking-plaister over and below his eye, not amounting to more than scratches. In the beginning of the day he made a fine speech, in which he said he hoped his behaviour in the conduct of the transaction with the East India Company had wiped out the levities and imperfections of his former life; and he magnified his own firmness in having borne and overborne much reproach and contradiction, which he insinuated to have received from Lord Chatham, whom he had not seen during the winter. At

* Honourable C. Townshend, second son of Charles third Viscount Townshend, made Chancellor of the Exchequer in 1766; died Sept. 1767.

four o'clock he left the House, tho' the management of the day depended on him; and taking one or two members with him, he went to dinner. His presence growing absolutely necessary, Mr. Conway sent for him. He returned about eight, as Mr. Grenville was speaking; after whom Townshend rose, half drunk, and made the most extravagantly fine speech that ever was heard. It lasted an hour, with torrents of wit, ridicule, vanity, lies, and beautiful language. Not a word was premeditated, yet every sentence teemed with various allusions and metaphors, and every period was complete, correct, and harmonious. His variety of tones and gesticulation surpassed the best actor in comedy, yet the faltering of his pronunciation from liquor, and the buffonery of his humour and mimicry, would not have been suffered in high comedy. Nothing had given occasion to his speech, and there was no occasion on which it would not have been as proper, or, to say truth, as improper; for if anything could exceed his parts, it was his indiscretion. He meant to please everybody and exalt himself; but lest he should not enough distinguish the latter, he took care to overturn all he had done to effect the former. The whole of his speech was diverting to every man that hated any set of men; it was impertinent and offensive to all it described or seemed to compliment; and was most painful to those who had any love for him. The purport seemed to be an intention of recommending Rockingham's party for ministers, with himself at the head of them; complimenting but sneering at Grenville, and slightly noticing Conway. But lest the great families whom he adopted should assume too much, he ridiculed the incompetence of birth and high blood, cried up the sole advantage of abilities and experience, and informed those he protected that rank was not talents, and that they must wait till ripened, and not come to government as if forced in a hotbed. The most injurious part fell on the Crown, he stating the mischiefs of the late so frequent changes, calling for restitution of the first post in administration to the House of Commons, and treating the actual ministry as no longer existent. Government, he said, must not continue to be what he himself was always called, a weather-cock.

Nobody but he could have made that speech; and nobody but he would have made it, if they could. It was at once a proof that his abilities were superior to those of all men, and his judgment below that of any man. It showed him capable of being, and unfit to be, first minister. Yet tho' it was rather the tittle-tattle of a coffee-house, and the flower of table eloquence, still was it the confusion of affected and laboured oratory. Nature in him made sport with rules and meditation; and half a bottle of champagne, poured on genuine genius, had kindled this wonderful blaze.

The House was in a roar of rapture, and some clapped their hands with ecstacy, like audience in a theatre. Nor was it the least striking circumstance of this speech, that, laying his hand on his heart, he called God to witness that he had not been made privy to the business of the day. Fourteen of the ministerial managers, who then were actually sitting round him, had concerted with him the motion at Townshend's own house that very morning, and were thunderstruck at his madness and effrontery; and when Conway, the moment he concluded, asked him how he could utter such a falsehood, he thought it the most favourable way of recommending the business to the House.

In this speech, he beat Lord Chatham in language, Burke in metaphors, Grenville in presumption, Rigby in impudence, himself in folly, and everybody in good-humour; for he pleased while he provoked at random; was malicious to nobody, cheerful to all; and if his speech was received with delight, it was only remembered with pity.

The letter addressed to the Duchesse de Choiseul appears to have been written in December 1770, when Horace Walpole writes thus to Sir H. Mann:—'The Duc de Choiseul is fallen. Abishag (Madame du Barry) has strangled an administration that had lasted fourteen years. I am sincerely grieved for the Duchesse de Choiseul, the most perfect being I know of her sex.'

To the Duchess of Choiseul.

Pendant que la France entière vous marquoit ses regrets, madame, je n'osois pas vous importuner des miens. Mais le triomphe de la vertu doit-il se borner à un seul pais? La reconnoissance et la plus parfaite estime ne trouveront-elles pas un moment à se faire entendre? Oui, chère grandmaman, je perds le respect, qui vous est dû à tant d'égards, pour épancher mon cœur avec plus de liberté et de tendresse. Je me réjouis avec vous, car de quoi vous plaindre? Avez-vous été ambitieuse, avare, insolente? Sont-ce des créatures qui vous regrettent, ou des malheureux? Monsieur le Duc de Choiseul est-il condamné de sa patrie et de vous, ou approuvé et comblé de louanges? Est-il plus doux de deviner ce que la postérité dira de nous, ou de l'entendre de la bouche de sa patrie et de toute l'Europe? Oh! vraiment je bénis le ciel de m'avoir donné un père et un grand-père dont la gloire ne fait qu'accroître tous les jours, et à qui il ne manquoit que la disgrace pour fixer l'immortalité. Oui, oui, belle maman, il faut vous conter ce qu'on dit de papa Choiseul; et cela ne vient pas d'une voix suspecte. My Lord Chatham a dit en plein parlement, que depuis feu M. le Cardinal de Richelieu la France n'avoit point possédé un aussi grand ministre que M. le Duc de Choiseul, et qu'il avoit emporté les regrets de tous les ordres de l'état. Voilà comme parlent les véritables grands hommes, qui s'y entendent. Notre peuple, qui ne connoît M. de Choiseul que par la peur qu'il leur avoit faite, a une manière de louer toute différente, et se félicite de sa chûte. Ce n'est pas un éloge à mépriser.

Votre fermeté et la noblesse de votre âme, madame, m'assurent que parmi tant de sujets de gloire, vous n'oublierez pas entièrement un homme que vous avez comblé de bontés, et qui vous est attaché par la reconnoissance et par l'admiration de toutes vos belles qualités. Permettez-moi de conserver le doux titre de votre petit-fils, et laissez-moi m'enorgueillir, comme si j'étois grand prince, sans mérite des vertus de mes ancêtres. Ma foi, je ne les troquerois pas contre un Cardinal de Richelieu, trop flatté si s'ose me signer,

Madame,

Votre très-affectionné et très-fidèle serviteur,

HORACE WALPOLE *de Choiseul.*

My Answer to the Rev. Wm. Mason.

[Berkeley Square, Feb. 2, 1784.

I thank you for your condolence on the death of my brother, and on the considerable diminution of my own fortune, tho' neither are events to which I am not perfectly reconciled. My brother was seventy-seven, had enjoyed perfect health and senses to that age, did not even begin to break till last August, suffered no pain, saw death advance gradually tho' fast with the coolest tranquillity, did not even wish to live longer, and died both with indifference and without affectation: is that a termination to lament?

I do lose fourteen hundred a year by his death; but had I reason to expect to keep it so long? I had twice been offered the reversion for my own life, and positively refused to accept it, because I would receive no obligation that might entangle my honour and my gratitude, and set them at variance. I never did ask or receive a personal favour from my most intimate friends when in power, tho' they were too upright to have laid me under the same difficulties, and have always acted an honest uniform part: but tho' I love expense, I was content with a fortune far above any merit I can pretend to, and knew I should be content were it much lessened. As it would be contemptible to regret the diminution at sixty-six, there is no merit in being quite easy under the loss. But you do me honour I do not deserve, in complimenting me on not loving money. I have always loved what money would purchase, which is much the same thing; and the whole of my philosophy consists in reconciling myself to buying fewer baubles for a year or two that I may live, and when the old child's baby-house is quite full of playthings.

I am surprised that you expected me to take notice of Lord Harcourt's turning courtier. It did not astonish me in the least, as I have known for near two years that such an event was by no means improbable, and did myself try to contribute to it, when I thought it not at all irreconcileable with his former conduct: nor do I wonder at your announcing in effect the same of yourself. Were I surprised, I should contradict one of my own maxims, which I have scarce or never known to fail, and which is, that men are always most angry with those with whom they quarrel last, which generally produces reconciliations between those whose hatreds agree *in eodem tertio*. But, in truth, I concern myself with no man's politics but my own; first, because I have no more right to dictate to others, than I will allow anybody to dictate to me; and secondly, because I can see into no heart but my own, nor know its real motives of action. My own point has been to be consistent, ever since I first thought on politics, which was five-and-forty years ago; and I feel a satisfaction in having been so steady, because it seems to me, if I do not deceive or flatter myself, that it is a proof that I have acted on principle, and not from disappointment, resentment, passion, interest, or fickleness.

It made me smile, indeed, when I heard that Lord Harcourt, on his change, had given away his ring of Brutus to Lady Jersey's little boy; because I do not see how anything that has happened within this twelvemonth has affected the character of Brutus, who died seventeen hundred years before the coalition was thought on. I am glad, however, that if I change, I may keep my Caligula without committing treason.

Your distinction of *the Crown's friends* is, I own, too theologic a refinement for my simple understanding, who never conceived a confusion of two natures in one person, yet still remaining separate. Nor in human affairs should I comprehend why a pope's disgracing himself as a gentleman by the means of duplicity, should make one fall in love with his tiara. Do you think I should accept for sound reasoning, if you were capable of telling me that, tho' you vowed in a sermon that you would never be a bishop, yet your gown being distinct from you, you could see no reason why your gown might not be turned into lawn sleeves?

What miracles *the new set of men* that are to arise are to achieve, I neither know nor care; I shall be out of the question before that blessed millennium arrives; unless they are already come, as perhaps they are—and for that, too, I cannot have long to care; tho' I firmly believe that your *new* set will only effect what has often been tried before, and what you say *ought* to be tried, i. e., to prove themselves *the Crown's friends*; an act of loyalty which I dare to say the wearer will be the first to pardon.

You see, by my using the same liberality of correspondence, I approve of yours. I am above disguising my sentiments, and am too low for any man to disguise his to me. Mine, indeed, having no variety in them, must be less entertaining; and therefore, unless I take a freak of hobbling to court, you can have no curiosity to hear them. Nor should I have mentioned them now, but that I thought it respectful to you and candid, when you communicated y[r] *new* sentiments to me, to tell you that mine remain unaltered.

I cannot conceive why you think that I shall not like your tragedy: am I apt to dislike your writings? Tho' I am too sincere to flatter you when I think you unequal to yourself, I did reckon that I was one who had taste enough to be sensible to the utmost of the beauties of y[r] capital works; and tragedy is certainly not a walk in which I can believe you will miss your way—you have trodden more difficult paths with the happiest facility. I shall be glad to see your piece, when you will indulge me with it, and am

Yours ever,

HORACE WALPOLE.]

*Explanation of Mr. W.'s Letter to Mr. M.**

Mr. Mason, G. S. Earl of Harcourt, and Mr. H. Walpole were intimate friends, and agreed in condemning the K.'s measures. But at the end of the year 1783, when Mr. Ch. Fox produced his famous E. India bill, Mr. Mason and L[d] Harcourt, without even the slightest hint to Mr. Walpole, changed sides totally, and tho' Mr. W. dined with the Earl in private but the very day before L[d] H. voted against that bill, he did not drop a syllable of his intention, nor of his design of going to court, which he had not done for some years; yet he had acquainted Mr. Mason, or rather, I believe, had been persuaded by him secretly to take those steps; and when they were taken, Mr. Mason wrote an authoritative letter to Mr. Walpole approving that conduct, and presumptuously flattering himself, even without giving any reason for their total tergiversation, that he should influence Mr. Walpole to take the same part. Mr. W. thought it became him to treat such treacherous and impertinent behaviour as it deserved, and to let Mr. M. see that, with all his admiration of Mr. Mason's satiric abilities in poetry, Mr. W. neither feared his anger, nor w[d] suffer him to govern his principles. Mr. W.'s answer received none; and tho' Mr. M. continued to

* In Mr. Cunningham's edition of H. Walpole's letters, the explanation to the foregoing letter is taken from a book called 'Walpoliana;' that which is here given is taken from a MS. in Walpole's own handwriting.

visit him for a year or two, a total coolness ensued, and all correspondence by letters ceased.

Lady Harcourt, who during Ld Rockingham's short administration had overwhelmed Mr. W. with letters, two or three in a day, to get her lord a place, which he had tried in vain, was made lady of the bedchamber; and she and her lord became a proverb, even to courtiers, of the most servile attachment to their Majesties, tho' both had forsworn St. James's on the King's and Queen's neglect of them on the unfortunate death of the Earl's father; and his lordship, besides wearing a ring of Brutus with the daggers and ides of March, had given away the portraits of King and Queen, their presents to the late Earl.

Mr. Mason had preached a sermon at York against the Archbishop, in which he declared he never wd be a bishop, and was going to print it, but had been dissuaded by Mr. Walpole from making such a rash vow in print. Mr. Mason hated Lord Rockingham and Mr. Fox.

The K. had approved of and encouraged the D. of Portland and Mr. Fox on their India bill, and then commanded even the lords of his own bedchamber to vote against it.

Mr. W. has a very fine antique bust in bronze of Caligula.

The Opposition had for many years complained of that knot of devotees to the court, who affected to call themselves the King's friends; and nobody *had been* more determined against them than Ld Harcourt and Mason.

Mr. Pitt, when in opposition, had supported Mason's and Wyvill's project of altering the representation of Parl., and Mason, no doubt, expected wd promote it when become minister; but he disappointed him: and Mr. Pitt, on the contrary, gave a capital blow to the House of Commons by maintaining himself by the prerogative against a majority of that House, which proved that Mr. W. had foreseen rightly of the new set of men.

Mason's capital work indisputably was the Heroic Epistle to Sr William Chambers.

Unknown to whom addressed.

May 27, 1794.

DEAR SR,—An idea has arisen in my thoughts, on which I have a great desire to consult you, not minutely, but in general, and this for two reasons: the first, because I have not extended or weighed the idea sufficiently myself; and the second, because the season is not yet arrived to carry the design (supposing it should be proper and practicable) into execution.'

My wish is, that all who live under our present unprecedentedly happy constitution, composed of King, Lords, and Commons, should be grounded from their earliest youth in such a firm attachment to that matchless system, in such undivided ardour of patriotism for that trinitarian but one composition, that no monarchic or republican doctrines, no factious or interested views, no attachment to political leaders or dictators, may ever be able to detach them from the great principles of the constitution.

It is undesirable that we have no system of education at all calculated for impressing such essential patriotism. Parents content themselves with breeding up their children in their own principles; that is, of talking before their children with a bias towards Whig or Tory principles; and the masters or tutors appointed are probably chosen, if principles enter into the consideration, for being supposed of the same party as the parent. If the tutor or master be a clergyman, he will doubtless instill into his pupil a due respect for the Church, which, tho' incorporated by law into the general system, is not a specific part of our tripartite constitution, tho' admitted into it, and which I would preserve there for (perhaps a singular) reason. I mean, looking on the complex body of higher and lower clergy as a pin that tends to support that third part of the constitution, the Crown, which might be too much weakened if deprived of that buttress, should a contest arise between the Crown and the two other branches of the legislature, who, possessing the whole landed property of the kingdom, might be an overmatch for the third power; and since the union of the three has produced and preserved our unexampled system, and raised this country to such a summit of glory and wealth, with perfect freedom, it would be madness to shake an edifice so cemented, in order to try speculative experiments and reforms which might endanger, but could not augment, our general felicity. The happiness of the whole is not to be risked to humour a few visionaries.

After this short introduction, I will sketch my novel idea.

I would have an exposition of our triformed constitution drawn up, showing how, in its contexture and consequences, it is preferable to all systems of government yet invented. (I do not detail more on this head here), but when stated in the strongest and clearest manner, and *then reduced to a corollary of implicit faith*, I would have all schools, seminaries, colleges, universities, obliged to inculcate this creed into all the youth committed to their care, and a plan of education a little more necessary to a Briton than Greek and Latin, tho' I do not desire to exclude or interfere with the instruction into those languages —far from it. If a code of constitutional doctrine could be formed, I would have it subdivided. I would have an accidence of short aphorisms or axioms extracted for young beginners; larger grammars for the adults, and these only taught in short lessons on holidays, and without punishments annexed, that the learners might have no disagreeable sensations annexed to what I wish to have them love—the constitution. Lectures in the manner of sermons might be delivered once a week to the disciples of all ages, and the *love of our country and its beautiful constitution* inculcated by every art possible.

You, my dear S^r^, would be infinitely more able than I am to dilate these rude hints into a valuable and practicable system. My object is to raise a spirit of enthusiasm for our constitution into our young and future countrymen; and as my plan would attach them to each branch of the legislature, not one of the three can, or at least ought to be averse from adopting it by law, if it were better digested, and a patriotic code formed, which it would be the interest of all the three powers to sanction. All opposition that should tend to annihilate any one of the three powers would be baffled, if the bigotry of the nation to the established constitution were predominant.

Unknown to whom addressed.

I am not at all sorry, S^r^, for the little misunderstanding that has happened, both as it has procured me a most obliging letter from you, and as it gives me an opportunity of explaining my expressions by Mr. Bedford, which I hope you will give me leave to do, yet as briefly as I can, for your time, S^r^, is precious, tho' mine is not.

If I had the pleasure of being better known to you, you would not have been surprised at my message. Being a very subordinate officer of the Exchequer, I have always known it was my duty to receive the commands of my superiors the Lords of the Treasury with respect and obedience, and to give them any information that they please to demand within my small province. I once received a parallel order from Mr. Robinson, as Mr. Bedford can tell you, and behaved with the like deference. Allow me to add, that Mr. Bedford will always be ready, S[r], to comply with y[r] commands, either with regard to any information he can give you or in other particulars.

It is very true, S[r], that at first I did imagine that there might be a farther view in your inquiry; but I was not less ready to obey it. When the Commissioners of Accounts sent for Mr. Bedford, I gave him the most positive orders to lay before them the most minute details of my office, and to answer circumstantially their every question, as I would resign my place to-morrow rather than hold it by any subterfuge or disguise. I owe every thing I have to the Crown and the public, and certainly by no merit in myself. I should deserve to lose all were I capable of any deceit. When there has been any question on patent places, I have thought it most respectful to await the determination of the legislature in silence: and therefore resolved neither to make interest to save myself from what should be thought necessary for the public; nor, as I have great contempt for ostentation, not to affect to be willing to give up my right, as I do not believe that any man really desires to have his fortune lessened; tho' I flatter myself that nobody is less disposed to prefer his private interest to that of the public.

These sentiments, S[r], led me into the mistake which you have been pleased so obligingly to clear, for which I beg you to receive my sincere thanks. May I, S[r], entreat you likewise to offer like respectful thanks to Lord Shelburne? I am very sensible of his lordship's kind attention, to which my insignificance has no pretensions; and, therefore, my gratitude can but be the greater. I would thank his lordship myself, but he can have no time to throw away on complimentary letters; and I have taken up but too much of yours. I have the honour to be with great regard, S[r],

Y[r] most obedient and most obliged humble Ser[t],

HOR. WALPOLE.

As there are still a few persons (tho' truly very few) who are so idle and weak as to bewilder themselves in the Chattertonian Controversy,* and who would rob the poor lad of the honour of having imposed on them by his forgeries; and who having miscarried in reestablishing *his* credit, still vow vengeance on one who has aided to dissipate the delusion; it would perhaps be cruel to destroy their harmless, tho' silly, pastime, which hurts nobody; and vain to attempt to set a man right who, by inventing falsehoods to justify his mistake, shows he is conscious of being in the wrong. I, tho' invited to resume the trifling contest, am less called upon than most men to enter the lists, especially against *masked* antagonists, as, having once told my whole story simply, with unimpeached veracity, and to general satisfaction, I declared I would not waste a word more on the subject, of which everyone but two or three old and early converts, is heartily weary; for whatever pity accompanies a detected impostor, this is not an age in which his ashes raise new proselytes. When Tom Paine is hanged, his disciples will not be numerous.

If I violate my own resolution, it is not to revive the controversy but to leave a memorial behind me, that shall baffle the future aspersions that I am persuaded are prepared and meant to substantiate the exploded charge of ill-usage of Chatterton, as soon as I shall be no more. My adversaries keep back and dare not publish my letter of kind advice to that unhappy lad, tho' no doubt they are possessed of it, as well as of my first letter to him, which they have printed to show that at the first moment I was imposed upon by him. Why are they not as industrious to authenticate the other? No, it would do honour to my sensibility, and their object has been to represent me as harsh, cruel, and insolent to him, which that I ever was, they must suppress my kind letter, and forge one in a contrary style, to make believed—and if such letter is produced, Rowley will have written it as much as I did.

I will now trace the steps by which this scarce-gasping contest has been attempted to be set again upon its legs, for while a

* See Letters and Papers relating to Chatterton, pp. 205 to 239 (vol. iv. 4to. edition of Lord Orford's Works), amongst which this Memorial is not included.

spark of life remains, there is no case so desperate for which some physician or other will not be found to prescribe.

'Chatterton was too young and had too much parts to have attained that summit of antiquarian excellence, the dull accuracy of dates, and consequently his forgeries were ill-adapted to the barbarous style and narrow discoveries of the dark ages for which he pretended to model his compositions. He attributed beautiful imagery to monks who had no imagination, and antedated arts by whole centuries, in which ingenious discoveries would have been imputed to magic sooner than to genius. But as in all ages there are men of monkish blindness, Chatterton was believed when he coined the most palpable improbabilities, and a real genius of the seventeenth century persuaded his converts that his works had been the productions of the barbarous *fourteenth* in which they would have been unintelligible. A black from the coast of Guinea would as soon have understood his African eclogue because it has the names of some African rivers, as the good folks of Bristol would have comprehended the phraseology of Olla, tho' sprinkled with some English words now obsolete. Had the imaginary Rowley existed and written for the stage, he would probably have penned Mysteries, not Dramas on the Greek model, of which he could never have heard; but Chatterton had never, I suppose, heard of the Mysteries, or he would have lent some translation of them to Rowley—to the complete satisfaction of our antiquaries, who must internally be a little shocked at a classic, and consequently a heathen tragedy, issuing from the gloom of a convent at Bristol. Credulity's darling apothegm is Credo quia impossibile est, and its faith increases in proportion as it is confuted; for faith ceases to be faith, and becomes conviction when it rests upon demonstration. Faith dwells in the clouds, demonstration on a rock.

An article which appeared in the 'Sun' in October 1797, elicited a letter of contradiction from the nephew and heir of Sir Horace Mann, and which also explains Lord Orford's repossession of his own letters addressed for so many years to his friend at Florence.

In the SUN *of 2d October*, 1797.

The late Lord Orford had designed to publish his correspondence with the late Sir Horace Mann, and for this purpose ordered most of his letters to be transcribed, making such omissions as he thought proper. The originals were then returned to the present Sir Horace Mann, who will not permit the letters to be printed, alleging that having the originals in his possession the *copyright* is vested in himself. With this hiatus, however, the works of Lord Orford are likely to make five volumes in quarto.

In the SUN *of 4th October*, 1797.

SIR,—I must positively contradict a paragraph in your paper in which there is not the slightest foundation of truth. A correspondence for many years subsisted between Lord Orford and Sir Horace Mann. Whenever I returned from frequent visits into Italy, I brought with me by Lord Orford's express commands all the letters he had written to my uncle to the period of my return. They were sealed up in a packet and delivered by me into Lord Orford's own hands, who gave an injunction that no copy should previously be taken of any one of them. I cannot therefore have it in my power to withhold the publication, or have the least idea of any copyright being vested in me, as is maliciously represented, for the originals never were returned to me, nor can I have the smallest claim to them. They are by Lord Orford's will submitted to the disposal of the most honorable and intelligent persons, whose understanding will point out to them what are proper for publication.

I am, Sir, your obedient Servant,

HORACE MANN.

Egerton Farm, Maidstone, Oct. 3, 1797.
To the Editor of the 'Sun.'

DETACHED THOUGHTS.

It is said that Congreve had too much wit in his comedies. It is a pity that no comic author has had the same fault.

A Gothic cathedral strikes one like the enthusiasm of poetry; St. Paul's, like the good sense of prose.

I would never dispute about anything but at law, for there

one has as much chance as another of getting the better without reason.

* Liars are like the old writs of kings that were signed *Teste Meipso*, for they have no witnesses but themselves.

* It is wrong to dispute, as one may set out in the wrong, and then one is sure to remain so, for one not only grows heated, but partial to one's own arguments, and then one remains in the wrong.

* By the throngs at places in England where waters are drunk, a foreigner would conclude that this is the most unhealthy country in Europe; but it is a proof of the reverse, for nine in ten go thither from health and spirits, and to dance and game and be diverted, for one who goes from illness.

A dead language is the only one that lives long, and is unlike the dead, for by being dead, it avoids corruption.

* Indiscreet persons, who say all they think and tell all they know, put others on their guard not to trust to them.

In former ages men were afraid of nothing but cowardice. Even riches, which now make men fond of life and consequently timid, then made men brave, for everybody was forced to defend his own property, or the stronger would have invaded it.

* Most writers on Government make a great mistake when they suppose that laws were made for the benefit of society. More laws have been made for the interest of individuals than for the good of the community. When an individual has power of making laws, he makes them *for* himself and *against* others.

Of all the Virtues Gratitude has the shortest memory.

* Otway perhaps took the names of Castalio and Polidore in his 'Orphan' from Castor and Pollux.

There are playthings for all ages: the plaything of old people is to talk of the playthings of their youth.

Man is an aurivorous animal.

History is a romance that is believed; romance, a history that is not believed.

Montaigne pleased because he wrote what he thought—other authors think what they shall write.

This world is a comedy to those who think, a tragedy to those who feel.

* The asterisks indicate those 'thoughts' that have not been published before.

Our Passions and our Understandings agree so ill, that they resemble a Frenchman of quality and his wife, who tho' they live in the same house together, have separate apartments, separate beds, go different ways, are seldom together, but are very civil to each other before company; and then the Passions, like the lady, affect to have great deference for their husband the Understanding.

* The Reformation in England was so short of what it ought to have been, that in reality it was only a re-formation.

* The line in Horace, Quo teneam vultus, &c., might, if corrected in the stoppage, be applied to people who frequently change their principles; thus—

> Quo teneam vultus mutantem Protea?—nodo—by a halter.

It is idle to attempt to *talk* a young woman in love out of her passion. Love does not lie in the ear.

Whoever expects pity by complaining to his physician is as foolish as they who having lost their money at cards complain of their ill-luck to their companions the winners. If none were ill or unfortunate, how would physicians and gamesters get money?

Beauty after five and thirty is like a forfeited peerage, the title of which is given by the courtesy of the well-bred to those who have no legal claim to it.

Albano's boy-angels and Cupids are all so alike, that they seem to have been the children of the Flemish Countess who was said to be delivered of 365 at a birth.

* A good character is the only wealth a man can keep up which will be his after his death.

Persons extremely reserved are like old enamelled watches, which had painted covers that hindered your seeing what o'clock it was.

Many new pieces please on first reading, if they have more novelty than merit. The second time they do not please, for surprise has no second part.

An author without originality is like a courtier who is always dressed in the fashion; nobody minds the colour or make of his coat; if it is ill-made, it is criticised; if not, what can be said on it? hundreds are dressed as well. Booksellers and salesmen lay up the book or the coat the moment the fashion of it is past, till they can sell either into the country.

* Some faces change so little that they look as if they had been made once for all.

If a man's eyes, ears, or memory decay, he ought to conclude that his understanding decays also, for the weaker it grows, the less likely is he to perceive it.

* Motto for Captain Coram, who instituted the Foundling Hospital:

Coram quem quæritis, adsum.

* In the Bas Empire, the Romans had two parties, the Blue and the Green. Those colours would be very convenient in all times when men change sides so often. No two colours are so easily confounded. A man of the blue party going over to the green might pretend he had always been of a bluish green.

* It is probable that the eyes of no two persons see objects alike. Each object may appear larger or smaller, or darker or lighter, or of a different hue to one man from what it does to another. This may be one of the causes why some see more or less beauty in a woman than others do; and why some see resemblances between two faces, that to another do not seem to resemble.

Envy deserves pity more than anger, for it hurts nobody so much as itself. It is a distemper rather than a vice, for nobody would feel envy if he could help it. Whoever envies another, secretly allows that person's superiority.

* An epic poem is a mixture of history without truth and of romance without imagination.

* Old persons, who are too juvenile for their age, give no proof so strong of their loss of memory as by not remembering that they are nearer to their second childhood than to their first.

When flatterers compliment kings for virtues that are the very reverse of their characters, they remind me of the story of a little boy who was apt to tell people of any remarkable defect in their persons. One day a gentleman who had an extraordinarily large nose being to dine with the boy's parents, his mother charged him not to say anything of the gentleman's large nose. When he arrived, the child stared at him, and then turning to his mother said, 'Mamma, what a pretty little nose that gentleman has!'

* A woman in a riding habit is something between a man and a portmanteau.

Experience becomes prescience.

Nothing is more vain than for a woman to deny her age, for she cannot deceive the only person who cares about it—herself. If a man dislikes a woman because he thinks her of the age she is, he will only dislike her the more for being told that she is younger than she seems to be, and consequently looks older than she ought to do. The Anno Domini of her face will weigh more than that of her register.

Censorious old women betray three things: one, that they have been galant; the next, that they can be so no longer; and the third, that they are always wishing they could be.

* An old woman who pretends to be religious and yet propagates scandal is the reverse of charity, which covers a multitude of sins: She uncovers all she knows, or suspects, or invents.

No woman ever invented a new religion: yet *no new* religion would ever have spread but for women. Cool heads invent systems, warm heads embrace them.

* The advantage of truth over falsehood is, that the former can never be *detected.*

Posterity always degenerates till it becomes our ancestors.

It is unfortunate to have no master but our own errors. If we profit ever so much under them, the unjust public always recollect the master, more than they take notice of the improvement of the scholar.

* The heart of man would not bear to be examined in a microscope.

Men are capable, often, of greater things than they perform. They are sent into the world with bills of credit, on which they seldom draw to the full extent.

* It is possible that the pyramids of Egypt may last so long that they may come to be supposed to be the tombs of some kings who are not yet born.

Motto for Congreve's 'Old Batchelor':—

Nolito fronti credere, nupsit heri.—*Mart.*

Epic Poetry is the art of being tiresome in verse; of excluding half the passions, and most of the ingredients that constitute amusement. It is an Index Expurgatorius for wit; a monopoly of gaping, and utter prohibition of laughter. Nobody may joke in an epic poem except a god, and that only upon some occasion that is not *dignus vindice.* A hero may now and then attempt a sarcasm, but then it must be a very clumsy one. An Epic Poem must be a tragedy that does not make you melancholy. You must not be concerned for any person slain in it, except for a young man or two, who is introduced only to be killed. The action must be one: you must be as long as possible before you bring it about; and whenever the catastrophe is inevitable, you must digress to something that will make the reader forget how near you are to the conclusion. Above all things you must allow that an Epic Poem is the most sublime work that can be achieved; you must own that there are not above five or six good epic poems in the world, and you must totally forget that the men who wrote them might, in half the time wasted on such senseless productions, have produced works in other kinds ten times more worthy of immortality. An Epic Poem is like the Tower of Babel, which answered no end, and with the stones and labour bestowed on which might have been built many excellent fabrics.

THOUGHTS ON GOVERNMENT.

The world is divided into men of sense and fools, but unequally. Strength is pretty near imparted alike to all; but the majority, having little sense, would make an improper use of their strength. Self-love being equal in all, a man of sense would turn his strength to advantage. I do not know whether it was a strong fool, or strong man of sense, that first employed his sense to render others subject to him: probably the latter. But all men have sense enough to see the inconvenience of being subject to brutal force. Men of sense, who had not strength enough to resist the force of a combination of fools, or the artifices of sense endued with force, invented laws and government. For such was certainly the origin of both, and not that silly idea of patriarchal authority. It could strike the common sense of nobody, that, because a man was fit to govern his own children, he was therefore fit to govern a whole people. No man is fit for it, because no man can do it alone. He must have ministers, deputies, substitutes; and if they abuse their power, all his fitness will not enable him to correct their errors or crimes. If he punishes or removes them, he is equally liable to be mistaken in his choice of their successors.

Government being once established, and accompanied with power, made a new division of mankind into knaves and fools; in which the latter were always reduced to be imposed on and governed by the former; till ambition and self-love invented Hereditary Power; and ever since that time, more fools have enjoyed royalty than wise men; because artful men had laid the foundations of hereditary power on such solid ground, that subsequent artful men could not remove them; and the number of fools born being greater than that of wise men, there are far more foolish kings than wise.

If we believe that Government had not this origin, but was designed for the benefit of mankind, as most say they suppose, its present existence would be more abhorrent from its institution than the hypothesis above. It cannot be for the interest of a community that its chief magistrate should be maintained in an opulence and splendour that impoverishes the greater part of his subjects. It is not for their good that he should have power to put to death, imprison or banish them, at his will. It is not for their advantage that his ministers, officers, substitutes, should have like power delegated to them. It is not for their advantage that he should have an imaginary honour and dignity, in support of which he should employ his subjects in war; that he should have power to expose them in battle to revenge his personal quarrels, or indulge his ambition. All these and a thousand more are absurd prerogatives, and not only not for the benefit of the community, but to their great detriment. Prerogatives affected to the Crown, and for the sole advantage of the wearer of it, and prejudicial to its subjects, are contradictions totally repugnant to the idea of a good government, and *ipso facto* annihilate it. An army greater than is necessary to defend the country from invasion and oppression by a foreign enemy, is destructive of the good of that country; not only as it may invade its liberty, but as it employs too many men who might be more usefully employed.

Such is the nature of man, that a king had rather reign over vast solitudes than over a small free nation. Conquest is the blackest crime against society, because no man has a right to force any number of men to be his subjects: I mean by conquest, the ambition of acquiring dominions to which a king has no right. It is a crime both to the invaded, and to those whom he leads to invasion. And every man that falls in the quarrel is murdered by the king.

A king that violates the laws of his country, and is expelled or dethroned by his subjects, is not less guilty if he attempts to recover his crown by force. All nations have a right to prescribe the terms on which they choose to be governed; and if the king has sworn to conform to those laws, and does not keep his oath, he is a criminal in the highest sense of the word.

Any endeavour of extending his power beyond the laws of which he is king, is a violation of those laws, and he deserves to be punished. To support him in his attempts is treason against the community.

No nation can make laws for posterity without posterity having equal right to repeal them. No man can be born with a right to oppress others. No man is of a nature superior to other men. He is as fallible as they. A crown gives no superior virtue or wisdom; but it demands more of both; because a king, who is only a chief magistrate, ought to have virtue and wisdom not only to govern but to set an example to his people. His vices are more detrimental than those of a private man; and a vicious king weakens the laws, which are made to discountenance as well as to punish vice. An ambitious, an avaricious, or a prodigal king encourages those vices in his ministers and in his people by his example; and if he punishes those vices in others which he practises himself, he is unjust. He is bound not only to be virtuous himself, but to choose virtuous men for his ministers and servants; for as he cannot himself execute all the duties of his magistracy, he is responsible for those to whom he delegates his power. The most virtuous king is obliged to take care that he tolerates no vicious persons about him, and, if he is really virtuous, he will tolerate none. A virtuous king may have a hypocritic, but never will have a profligate court. He is a judge of men's outward professions, if not of their hearts. The appearances of virtue will have some effects; those of profligacy can have none.

PLAN FOR ENCOURAGING PAINTING.

It is a common complaint that in England there is little or no encouragement for historic painting; and it is almost as common an answer, that as historic pictures are seldom admitted into churches, and as our churches have each but one altar, there are few public places fitted to receive large pieces. The first objection might be removed in some degree by the following plan; and the second is not only not true, but proper spaces will be pointed out by the same plan.

Many funds for historic paintings might be pointed out with small inconvenience to the contributors. Suppose every Archbishop of Canterbury was obliged to pay 300*l.* within three years after his promotion to the see, or rather one hundred each year, for only the three first years, which at his grace's option should either go to a fund for furnishing historic pictures on scriptural or historic English subjects, or should pay for one picture on such a subject, which picture should be placed in the palace at Lambeth, *and always remain there.*

The Archbishop of York should in the same space of three years pay 200*l.* in like manner for the archiepiscopal palace in Yorkshire.

The Bishops of London, Durham, and Winchester, 250*l.* for the ornament of their palaces. Ely and Worcester, 200*l.* Other bishops less in proportion to their incomes.

Thence their palaces, naked as they are, and stripped on every death, would still have some decoration, and the arts would spread into the counties.

Every bishop should pay the sum allotted, if he remain three years before translated. And if translated, after three years, he should pay again, being translated to a better see.

The Lord Chancellor should in like manner pay 300*l.* if continued in office three years, or 100*l.* for each that he did remain. The picture paid for by him, or by a fund from the following years, should represent some English historic subject, some memorable æra of the Constitution, or some remarkable trial or cause; and the picture should be hung in the Court of Requests, in the Painted or Princes Chambers.

The Chief Justices, being for life, should pay 300*l.*; the Chief Baron and Master of the Rolls, 200*l.* each; the Attorney and Solicitor Generals, 200*l.* each, if remaining in place three years, or in proportion. The pictures on the subjects and for the like positions.

The Speakers of the Houses, 200*l.* each, if three years in office; the subjects like the former, or on any memorable debates.

The First Lord of the Treasury, being of very uncertain tenure, should only pay 100*l.* a year, according to his duration, and never after three years.

The First Lord of the Admiralty to contribute in the same manner.

The pictures furnished by the Treasurers, to adorn the Treasury, and when that full, the House in Downing Street. The subjects, English historic.

The Admirals, naval engagements, &c., for the Admiralty.

The two Secretaries of State, and other great officers might be taxed in proportion, and the Palaces of St. James's or Kensington be adorned by their contributions.

No contributor should be allowed to give his own portrait in lieu of an historic picture.

Perhaps it would be better to have all the contributions go to a separate fund for each class, and be laid out whenever a proper subject was fixed on, and a price agreed on of 300*l.*, 400*l.*, or 500*l.* according to the size of the picture, and merit and price of the painter.

A standing committee to fix on the subjects, and regulate the prices and dimensions. The costume of every age in every picture to be strictly observed.

The City of London might find some similar methods for decorating the Mansion House and Company Halls.

Feb. 9, 1785.

THOUGHTS ON THE REIGN OF GEORGE III.

Few reigns in our annals have been distinguished by so many changes of administration as that of George III. James I. very frequently in the latter part of his time displaced Ministers, particularly his High Treasurers; but they never were his Prime Ministers: they were promoted or removed by the caprices of his rash and presumptuous young favourite, the Duke of Buckingham. King William, as wise as James and George were foolish, was forced to change his administrations by the factious struggles of the Whigs and Tories, the latter of whom were his enemies, and the former unsteady friends. George, aiming at nothing but personal power, and sacrificing the dignity of his crown, the interest of his kingdoms, and frequently his own peace to accomplish that sole object, could bear no Minister who would not be a tool, and removed every man, when he could, who was fit to be his servant. He commenced his reign by disgusting Mr. Pitt, who had raised Great Britain to a height of glory it had never before attained, and who, tho' far more ostentatious than solid, had endeared himself to the nation by fortunate rashness, and, which was of still more importance, had struck terror into all our enemies. This great man was driven away to make room for a wretch who, with as much vanity as Mr. Pitt, and resembling him in no one essential, and whom the King himself had grown to hate, before he raised him to the head of the administration, sweeping away in the same breath that ridiculous and impotent veteran, the Duke of Newcastle, who had had the address to engross much power during the administration of Sir R. Walpole, who did not love him, and knew himself betrayed by him, and who associated himself with Mr. Pitt, during the plenitude of the latter's power. Lord Bute's pusillanimity anticipated his incapacity, and he fled from his post before he had time to show how totally he was unfit for it. A momentary triumvirate of Lord Egremont, Lord Halifax, and Mr. George Grenville stepped into the vacancy, because no system was ready, and because the King had a predilection for nobody. These men, mistaking chance for abilities in themselves, neither ingratiated themselves with the King, nor would condescend to pay court to the self-dethroned favourite, who, from habitude, retained more of the royal confidence than any other man, and who had hoped to find substitutes who might at once stand between him and the danger of responsibility, and who would submit to be actuated by his influence. Finding himself disappointed, he had the folly to fly to the man whose power he had usurped, Lord Chatham, who would not have been implacable if the King had not already conceived the idea of employing no man who would not stoop to be a cypher. The mutual intractability of His Majesty and Lord Chatham vested the sole power in Mr. Grenville, who had many ingredients that fitted him for the place of Minister, but wanted as many to make him a Great Minister, and more that would suit the temper, views, and insincerity of the King. Grenville was firm, intrepid, daring; he was also immeasurably obstinate, avaricious for himself, and triflingly penurious for the revenue. He was tedious, ungracious, implacable; and not content with seeking every opportunity of being revenged on the nominal favourite, he refused the King inconsiderable sums for his amusement, and teased him for unreasonable grants to himself. Is it necessary to say that want of judgment crowned all his bad qualities? At the moment that he had raised a convulsion in America by his offensive Stamp Act, his hatred to the favourite induced him to join in a public insult to the King's mother. Such conduct had its natural consequence. Grenville was disgraced, and Lord Chatham being betrayed by his friend, Lord Temple, who had chosen that conjuncture to be reconciled to his brother Grenville, again refused the administration, which the King, from having no choice left, was forced to put into the hands of Lord Rockingham, who, disdaining to be the lieutenant of the nominal favourite, and proscribing the King's secret tools, who in reality had the confidence which the favourite only seemed to possess, the new administration was suffered to remain but a single year, and Lord Chatham was once more called to power, and accepted it, tho' with scarce an adherent left.

Never was a greater fall! That wild intoxication which, seconded by fortune, had been so happily applied to military Quixotism, was by no means adapted to the sobriety of peaceful councils. Whether the insanity remained, when the fire of adventure had subsided, or whether, conscious of his own defects, he preferred the imputation of disordered intellects to the confession of incapacity, Lord Chatham had scarce resumed his power before he totally suspended the exercise of it, and, which indeed was rather an evidence of delirium, he retained his superintendence, tho' he obstinately refused to officiate.

The nation had for some years beheld, or thought it descried, a real Minister behind the curtain, who interposed his credit without holding an office. Here was the reverse—a Minister in whose name all business was transacted, but who would exercise no part of his function.

From so strange a position arose the authority of the Duke of Grafton. He had been delegated by Lord Chatham, who sullenly saw him grow Minister from the exigence of the moment, and who still would neither be consulted by him nor forgave him for acting without his orders.

Grafton proved a Minister after the King's own heart. No merit, no talents had recommended him; he was indolent; his bad temper created no adherents; his pride was unsocial, and he was content to be prompted by the secret Junto. His behaviour, his negligence, and the variations in his ill-humour, occasioned such universal discontent, that even the prerogative majority in the House of Commons was shaken, and, subservient as the Minister was, the King's influence grew into as great danger as if his Minister had been formidable to himself. It is probable that the Junto instilled a panic into the Duke himself, tho' they were by no means satisfied that they were provided with an adequate successor. Lord North, the Duke's second, was tried, and more than repaired the breach.

With as much indolence as Grafton, North had infinitely more parts, an excellent temper, an amiable private character, most conciliating sociability, never-failing wit, and a steady resolution of pliancy to all his Majesty's prejudices. This inveterate submission, most commonly in contradiction to his own judgment, proved his ruin. Acquiescence in all the worst measures of the American War, and negligence in the execution of them all, awakened even the prostitute majority in the House of Commons. The royal perseverance in that odious and impolitic war, and Lord North's compliance with his master's infatuation, cost the one America, and the other his post of Prime Minister.

If Lord Shelburne could have waited to undermine Lord Rockingham, or to wait for his death, which was imminent, he might have reduced the King to the necessity of submitting to the spirit of the Constitution; but Shelburne was impatient to be Minister, and liked to become so by treachery rather than by patience. He broke the party to pieces, by transacting a settlement with the King rather than with his allies, and by that means succeeded Lord Rockingham, who died in two months. But, having undermined his own ground, Shelburne had no strength but what the King should please to impart to him; nor did that weight suffice against his own folly and falsehood, which, by the beginning of next year, overset him. The King's anguish was inexpressible, not at losing Shelburne, whom he both hated and despised, but at being forced to accept an administration of honest, able men, whom he could not bend to his own purposes. He offered the Treasury to the boy Pitt, who in the compass of five days twice accepted it and twice had not courage to undertake it,—a want of spirit that it cost him nine months to surmount.

The Duke of Portland, enforced by the matchless abilities of Mr. Fox, became Minister, and commenced a system that promised reparation to many of the evils inflicted on this country by the fatal measures of the reign. But Mr. Fox daring to attack that detestable incorporation of harpies, the East India Company, and its servants, or rather its masters, the King perceived that the worst enemies of this country were now presented to him as most useful allies, and therefore, adopting their fears and vengeance, and borrowing their plunder in aid of his own exhausted treasury, he at once dismissed his new Ministers, and threw himself into the hands of Lord Temple, almost as young and inexperienced as Pitt, but, fortunately for the latter, a greater coward. Lord Temple fled the very moment that he had lent himself to the removal of the Ministers, and Pitt, whose presumption had sighed for nine months over his last faint-heartedness, catched at a third offer of power, and determined to varnish over his timidity by excess of insolence and abuse of those who had had more spirit than himself, and a much greater degree of spirit, for they knew they could not trust the King, and Pitt was sure of his support as long as he was subservient.

That ground he secured by open prostitution of his former professions, declaring himself the Minister of the Crown. On that foundation he stands at present, and finds it a pedestal which his extreme ignorance has not as yet been able to overturn, tho' defeated, forced to abandon, or to correct, every measure he has hitherto attempted.

He must continue to support and extend prerogative, or he will be sacrificed by the King. If his abilities prove equal to the task of enlarging the power of the Crown, he will have the glory of being an able Minister at the most premature age, but instead of being remembered, like his father, for glorious services, he will be contrasted with him, and paralleled with Cardinal Richelieu.

From this slight view or sketch, it is obvious that every disgrace and misfortune that has fallen on the King has proceeded from only those Ministers whom he himself approved.

By removing Lord Chatham, Lord Bute was enabled to strike up the shameful Peace of Paris, which saved France and enabled her to support the Americans. By the compliance of Lord North, war was made on America. By the courtly treachery of Lord Shelburne, the American Royalists were abandoned; and by Pitt's ambition, Mr. Fox's India Bill was prevented, which France regarded as the most fatal blow she could receive. By Mr. Pitt's dread of a Reform of Parliament in Ireland, his eleven propositions were conceived, which are likely to divest the King of his sovereignty over Ireland, almost as much as he has lost it over America.

Upon the whole, both the Crown and Great Britain have lost their dearest interests by the King's ambition of extending his prerogative. He has sunk to be a little Prince in Europe; and the loss of dominions and credit will be ill compensated to his successors by any domestic jewels he may ravish from the Constitution. When Louis XI., the most detested of the French monarchs, placed the Crown *hors de page*, he at the same time extended the bounds of his empire; and if he was an odious tyrant, was at least not a contemptible politician.

June 14, 1785.

I have extreme contempt for an anonymous writer, who betrays consciousness of guilt by concealing himself, and who has been so foolish as to take ridiculous pains to verify what I never denied, and so mean as to ascertain my handwriting and disguise his own. He shows a willingness to stab in the dark, but luckily possesses no sharper a weapon than a broom-stick, with which he has clumsily knocked himself down, to my great diversion.

LIFE OF RENÉ OF ANJOU,

KING OF NAPLES.

Feb. 1, 1779.

The courage that would constitute a hero may, if unaccompanied by proper symbols, form only a philosopher, in the eye of common acceptation. Ambition, love of glory, activity, perseverance, recommend the former. Contempt of danger, indifference to fame, resignation to misfortune, indicate as firm a soul; but courting, soliciting no applause, are seldom honoured with the suffrages of the multitude. When boundless humanity, or even success, crown the temperate hero, he attains the more amiable titles of philosopher and father of his country, but is rarely placed amongst the favourites of noisy celebrity. Marcus Aurelius is scarce known as an intrepid general, for he fought to protect his country, not to aggrandize himself. Henry the Fourth of France, as brave as the first Cæsar, is more adored as a man than as a victor, for he sheathed the sword the moment he had conquered in a just cause.

René of Anjou, of whom history has recorded no symptom of want of courage, and on whom his subjects conferred the most desirable of all appellations, the Good, from the dawn to the conclusion of a long reign; having lost splendid crowns, and retaining only a province, with which he had the wisdom to be contented, has been distinguished by no panegyrics, and is rather considered as a pusillanimous prince, who submitted to reverses, and who, without struggling against impossibilities, preferred his ease, his pleasures, his amusements, and (it should be remembered) the happiness of his remaining subjects, to the tormenting efforts of disappointed and unsatisfied ambition. He lost crowns, he lost his son, he saw his daughter dethroned,—but he never lost his temper. His people, his wives, his mistresses, his natural children, his muse, his pencil, nay, the institution of festivals, and the laws of heraldry, consoled him for the more painful duties of royalty that were torn from him, but not till he had bravely defended them; and unlike hundreds of trifling monarchs, he sank not into an inglorious prince till he had deserved to be a puissant and illustrious one. That mind is noble, which, like Scipios', can sport with pebbles on the shore after demolishing Carthage, or that, like René's, can adjust the ceremonial of tournaments after losing battles and sceptres. Never to forget the pomp of triumph nor the sting of defeat, is the symptom of pride, or of obstinacy, or of conscious shame. The true hero is satisfied with having served his country; the true philosopher with having done his duty. Their minds are then at leisure to be private men: and to be able to trifle is to prove that they are sincere.

Letter to Mr. H. S. Woodfall.

Sir,—Strolling by chance lately into a public house, the landlord showed me the following lines, with which he was much transported, and wished to get them set to music. They were written by an apprentice who frequents his house, and whom mine host extolled above Churchill and Falstaff, the latter of whom he takes for a poet. As there is something very original in this little piece—at least genuine strokes of nature—I thought it might not be unacceptable to many of your readers.

Yours, J. G.

THE JOYS OF SPRING.

A new song.

Returned is the spring,
And the nightingales sing:
My Phillis and I
To the country will hie,
Where we'll revel and love,
Like the blackbird and dove.
Nature calls us abroad,
And on one side the road,
At the Saracen's head
In a snug little arbour a napkin is spread.

Charming scenes!
Peas and beans!
Union of hearts,
And gooseberry tarts!
On cool tankard and cyder and cream we regale,
And mix kisses and squeezes with cakes and ale:
Till with Bacchus and Cupid at length overcome,
We trudge home and all night sleep as sound as a drum.

In joys like these O! let me live,
Which rural life alone can give.
Nor ambition nor riches intrigue us:
The Golden Age
Contents the sage:
His highest view
But reaches to
His Phillis, a haycock, and negus.

In Wright's original 'Theory of the Universe,' are the following lines, quoted by accident from Dryden and Pope:—

Had we still paid that homage to a name,
Which only God and Nature justly claim;
The western seas had been our utmost bound,
Where poets still might dream the sun was drown'd;
And all the stars that shine in southern skies
Had been admired by none but savage eyes.—*Dryden.*

He who through vast immensity can pierce,
See worlds on worlds compose one universe,
Observe how system into system runs,
What other planets and what other suns,
What varied Being peoples every star,
May tell why Heaven made all things as they are.—*Pope.*

The comparison of these lines shows that Dryden was a poet by nature, Pope by art. Dryden might have said in prose what he has said in rhyme, and yet there would have been harmony in his numbers. In the five first lines of Pope there is fine poetry, but no mortal could have spoken so in prose. The sixth line is mere prose, with no harmony at all. Dryden's thoughts, tho' expressed in common words, fell into music. Pope was forced to use transposition and less common words to prevent his thoughts from appearing in prose.

Letter and Verses to the Honourable H. Conway.

February, 1758.

I am this minute arrived, and going to dine at Brand's. I will come to you afterwards, before I go to North House. In the meantime I send you a most hasty performance, literally conceived and executed between Hammersmith and Hyde Park Corner. The Lord knows if it is not sad stuff. I wish for the sake of the subject it were better!

When Fontenoy's impurpled plain
 Shall vanish from th' historic page,
Thy youthful valour shall in vain
 Have taught the Gaul to shun thy rage.

When hostile squadrons round thee stood
  On Laffelt's unsuccessful field,
Thy captive sabre, drench'd in blood,
  The vaunting victor's triumph seal'd.

Forgot be these! Let Scotland, too,
  Culloden from her annals tear,
Lest Envy and her factious crew
  Should sigh to meet thy laurels there.

When each fair deed is thus defac'd,
  A thousand virtues, too, disguis'd,
Thy *grateful* country's voice shall haste
  To censure worth so little priz'd.

Thou, patient, hear the thunder roll,
  Pity the blind you cannot hate;
Nor, blest with Aristides' soul,
  Repine at Aristides' fate.

The following passage, with its accompanying verses, are all in Lord Orford's handwriting, though not signed by him :—

Lord Bolingbroke wrote these lines of Maynard, at his house of La Source in France :—

Las d'espérer et de me plaindre
Des muses, des grands, et du sort,
C'est ici que j'attends la mort,
Sans la désirer ni la craindre.

PARODIED.

Weary of hoping, and complaining,
Of kings that reign or should be reigning,
Without a wish I wait death here—
And, as I'm safe, without a fear.

Of rebel blood, and traitor in his heart,
But bow'd by int'rest to the wiser part,
Unchang'd, he shifts his principles, that burn
To sap the laws he could not overturn.
But Nature planting coward in his soul,
To Norton's hands he trusts the poison'd bowl;
Content from England's fall to count his gains,
Whether a Brunswic or a Stuart reigns.

To all the readers of Horace Walpole's letters the name of Thomas Kirgate is most familiar. He was often the humble instrument of communication, between his employer and his numerous correspondents, and gave to the world the fruits of the well-known Strawberry Hill Press; but whether from carelessness, or from an inadequate idea of his necessities, it seems to be a melancholy fact that he was not sufficiently provided for by will; and the 'Printer's Farewell' carries with it a touching reproof that thirty years' service was not better remembered. He died in 1820.

THE PRINTER'S FAREWELL TO STRAWBERRY HILL.

Adieu! ye groves and Gothic tow'rs,
Where I have spent my youthful hours,
    Alas! I find in vain:
Since he who could my age protect,
By some mysterious, sad neglect,
    Has left me to complain!

For thirty years of labour past,
To meet such slight reward at last,
    Has added to my cares:
To quit the quiet scenes of life,
T' encounter bus'ness, bustle, strife,
    Hangs heavy on my years.

Farewell! my printing-house, farewell!
Where I no more shall calmly dwell,
    Within my peaceful door:
No more in conversation free,
Enjoy my friend and sip my tea;
    Ah! no; those days are o'er.

On thee, my fellow-lab'rer dear,
My Press, I drop the silent tear
    Of pity, for thy lot;
For thou, like me, by time art worn,
Like me, too, thou art left forlorn,
    Neglected and forgot!

October 1797. T. K.

MISCELLANEOUS LETTERS.

1798.

ENTRY.

'Mrs. D. and Lady Ailesbury settle at Strawberry Hill. Become acquainted with Mrs. Howe.'*

In the month of January Miss Berry received a letter from their friend Mr. Brand.† After announcing his marriage to Miss Deborah Wharton, daughter of Dr. W., of Old Park, Durham, he adds:—

Lady Ossory, to alleviate my confinement in a very bad cold, has treated me with Lord Orford's letters to her, tho' in a very mutilated transcript, and desired my opinion about their publication. I advised that they should be kept in the family as an invaluable treasure rather than be published in this manner, but thought many of them so well written and so interesting at the present moment (some from Paris especially), that I could not help wishing to see them printed in Mr. Berry's collection. I was glad to find afterwards that Lord Ossory and most of her friends were against publishing the collection as it stood. I am to dine there on Wednesday and to bring you a message when I come to town. The message, I *guess*, may be the offer of some of the letters. Can I be of any service in this business

* The Honourable Caroline Howe, married John Howe of Branslop, Bucks; died June 1814, in her ninety-third year. She possessed an extraordinary force of mind, clearness of understanding, and remarkable powers of thought and combination. She retained these faculties unimpaired to the great age of eighty-five, by exercising them daily, both in the practice of mathematics and in reading the two dead languages, of which late in life she had made herself mistress. To these acquirements must be added warm and lively feelings joined to a perfect knowledge of the world, and of the society of which she had always been a distinguished member.—*M.B.*

† Vide Journal of 1784.

by giving any preparatory hint? Is there any particular period of his correspondence you would like to have? any chasm to fill up?

Miss Berry commences her reply by wishing that 'printer' and 'proof sheets' had left her that day a little more time to express her feelings on the approaching event.

Thank you much (she continues) for your information concerning Lady Ossory. When you come to town I shall make you laugh at her ever intending to publish anything after her declarations on the subject. Be the bearer of any message from her to us, and receive any letters she gives you for us. But we have none to ask for, and none to want, and no chasm to fill. Our volume will already, I find, be such a thumper, that unless I subtract some from those already in hand I can add none.

Two thick volumes of these letters have since been given to the public, by Mr. Vernon Smith,* and have recently been incorporated, under the editorship of Mr. P. Cunningham, into a new edition of Horace Walpole's Letters.

Miss Berry omitted, in her little entry for this year, a visit to Malvern, to which the following letter alludes from Sir Uvedale Price;† a letter truly characteristic of the great lover of the picturesque:—

Foxley, August 29, 1798.

It is impossible to say how much I have been vexed and disappointed. I had got off my engagement for Monday though

* Now Lord Lyveden.

† Sir Uvedale Price, of Foxley, co. Herefordshire, was the author of the 'Translation from the Greek of the Account of Pausanias of the Statues, Pictures, and Temples of Greece,' published 1780, 'Essay on the Picturesque,' 1794, and of other minor works; also of a 'Dialogue on the Distinct Character of the Picturesque and the Beautiful,' in answer to the objections of Mr. Payne Knight, published 1801. Sir Uvedale was born in 1747; married to Caroline, fourth daughter of George, first Earl of Tyrconnel, created Bart. 1828, died 1829.

with some difficulty, as there was a haunch of venison that would not hear of being kept. I had ordered my horses to be ready, and myself to be called before daybreak on Sunday, all which was most punctually performed; the morning was such as there is no speaking of but in poetry—

> Più bell' aurora, più lieto dì
> Dal' sen' del' onde mai non uscì.

But I rose very unlike the morning, with a violent headache and shiverings—in short, quite unable to go. So after looking wishfully at the Malvern Hills, which are on view from my window, I at last shut out the day and did not exercise the Christian virtues of patience and resignation. I hope my recording angel (I conclude there is more than one to the planet, or he has no sinecure) did not set down all my fretting and pining, but considered how severe the trial was. I never promised myself so much pleasure in any expedition; I had planned a ride across a tract of country I had never been through, parts of which I know must be full of beauties from the general view of it from the Malverns, for it is a country full of small knolls and swellings covered with wood, and in the sheltered parts between them there are a number of fine hop yards, and this is just the beginning of hop-pulling; then, to crown all, at the end of this pleasant ride I was to find you at Malvern. I was particularly glad to hear that you were to be at Malvern village, and not at the wells, for I have such a horror for that staring red house and staring view from it, that nothing less than the pleasure of your society would tempt me to stay there. Now, on the other hand, I am delighted with the view from the inn, for the rich tower of the church rises finely above the horizon, and most happily breaks the extensive distance, which is thrown off and enriched by the battlements of the body of the church; and though the face of Worcestershire is not by any means so varied as our side of the hills, yet when viewed from Malvern, it has the material advantage of receiving the full effect of the evening lights. I am very apt to consider, wherever I happen to be, what would be the best situation for a house in respect to the view from it, and I found no spot in Malvern, where all the objects were so happily combined as the inn. Not only the church, but the old archway, the parsonage covered with jasmin, the churchyard, the path through it, the cottage at the end, form a very lucky composition of foreground and distances. All this, and many parts about Malvern, I was very desirous of seeing with you, for I have never had the pleasure of being with you amidst any striking scenery, though we have talked upon the subject. I had hoped for one of those days that are passed with delight and always recollected with pleasure, but it seems to have been *écrit la haut* that we should not meet this time. I remember having received a letter from a devout old German, who was *chef de cuisine* to Lord Barrington, in which he told me that he was very happy to have been the instrument, under Providence, of procuring me a good cook. I beg you will present my best compliments to Mr. Berry and your sister.

I am, dear Madam,
Most sincerely and faithfully yours,
U. Price.

General Fitzpatrick desires his best compliments.

Some extracts of Miss Berry's correspondence with different friends, and some reflections on the different books she had been reading, close the remains of this year.

To Mr. Greathead.

Little Strawberry Hill, August 2, 1798.

The torments of an evil conscience I can bear no longer, and therefore write to you I must. If I hated writing ten times more than I do, I am sure fifty letters would have been less pain and trouble to me than what I have felt for never having written to you at all, whenever you came into my thoughts, which has been much oftener than I wished, I assure you. This time twelvemonth I fully thought and hoped that, instead of now corresponding by letters, we should have been together at Pyrnant. Lady Tancred's accounts were by no means inviting, tho' I made due allowance for a traveller whose peregrinations for several years before had been confined to the road between London and Ramsgate—never, I think, exceeded a trip to Paris in the halcyon days of French despotism. Most thoroughly do I begin to feel the want of that *shake* out of English ways,

English whims, and English prejudices, which nothing but leaving England gives one. After a residence of four or five years we all begin to forget the existence of the continent of Europe, till we touch it again with our feet. The whole world to me, that is to say the whole circle of my ideas, begins to be confined between N. Audley-street and Twickenham. I know no great men but Pitt and Fox, no king and queen but George and Charlotte, no towns but London. All the other cities, and courts, and great men of the world *may* be very good sort of places and of people, for aught we know or care; except they are coming to invade us, we think no more of them than of the inhabitants of another planet. We should like, indeed, just to know what is become of Buonaparte, because we are afraid of our settlements in India, and because we are all great news-mongers and politicians, tho' more ignorant, more incapable of any general view upon those subjects, than any other people with whom I ever conversed (the French of ten years ago only excepted). Well, that I may not quite grow to the spot on which you left me last August, I am going to begin *my travels* on Tuesday next. My sister, as she could not go to Pyrnant, was obliged to go to Cheltenham, from whence my father and I are going to fetch her home.

* * * * * * *

I am anxious to hear if Bertie has yet met with Matilda Pottingen, and if he writes odes upon her in the style of Ruggiero. I know Lysons sent you the *Anti-Jacobin*, and, in spite of its title, I am sure you would be diverted with the excellent laughable criticism upon German plays—such, I mean, as we ignoramus's see them through the medium of bad translations. Lysons I have heard of at Cheltenham, and likewise of Mrs. Siddons, who has been acting there. I improved my acquaintance with her last winter, and I need not tell you how much she gains by being known. She read 'Hamlet' to us one evening, in N. Audley-street, which was to me a great treat.

To Bertie Greathead, Esq., at Göttingen.

To the Honourable Mrs. Damer.

Cheltenham, August, 1798.

This place and everything about it recalls, in the most lively manner, scenes and recollections to my mind, which, tho' melancholy, I cannot call unpleasing. They are, thank Heaven! unembittered by reproach, and undisgraced by folly. My imagination seems to pass over everything that has happened since, and to bring me back to the calm but lively enjoyment of a society in which I delighted.

To the Same.

Brandsby, Oct. 1798.

I have not said a word to you of our glorious victory,* but *you* do not suspect *me* of not feeling it. Do you participate in some other less agreeable feelings which to me accompany this and every other success in that quarter? When I think (that under other circumstances) *we* might have been so much nearer the scene of action, and among the first to receive and congratulate the gallant conquerors! How much more appropriate to our minds, interesting to our feelings, and gratifying to our vanity, in spite of all the privations with which such a situation might *seem* to have been accompanied, than anything we are or have been doing.

Brandsby, Oct. 1798.

I rejoice to hear you say that all you have felt on our late glorious victories, convinces you that active scenes are no less gratifying than ever to your mind, and that they have roused that latent spark of heroism which I know, and which you know yourself, exists in your composition. I have sometimes feared lest the narrow circle to which you have confined yourself, and the sort of life which circumstances have combined to make you lead, for these last four or five years, should contract, not your sentiments or ideas, but your powers of acting in and enjoying more animating, active, and interesting passages of life, into which it would be your ambition, as it would be mine, to carry a mind as philosophic and sedate, as ever we enjoyed in our own gardens. For my part, I think the magnitude of objects would render easy all the difficulties, sufferings, and exertions for their attainment, and even considerably soften the

* The battle of the Nile was fought August 1, 1798. The despatch announcing the victory was dated August 3, and it appeared in the *London Gazette* Oct. 2. A length of time between the event and its announcement, that seems somewhat strange to those who have lived since the invention of steam navigation and electric telegraphs.

disappointment of a failure. The *magnis tamen excidit ausis* must, I think, have been a great comfort even to poor Phaeton.

To the Same.

Brandsby, Oct. 1798.

Do you know that I have been working as hard at Greek for this week past as you could possibly desire? The parson who I mentioned in my last, stayed till yesterday. He is a very good scholar, and has been much in the habit of teaching. He corrected a piece of Isocrates which I had done by myself, and then read on with me in the same oration, and whilst he was here I translated above two pages more, writing them down, I mean, and all the verbs and their parts in the opposite page, in our own way, you know. This young man's pertinacity about the use of accents would have *provoked* you; it *diverted* me, who was too weak and too ignorant an opponent to attempt their defence. I find that about six months' regular tho' moderate study would really make me a sufficient Grecian for my purpose, that of mere enjoyment, and that six months I am determined (as much as I can determine anything) shall be next winter, if I can possibly find an assistant.

Extract of a Letter from Miss Berry to a Friend.

Little Strawberry, Tuesday, Nov. 19, 1798.

. . . . I have been as busy as a bee in my garden and greenhouse, to which I always return with new pleasure and satisfaction, convinced that when once one likes and enters into it, it is one of the very best sources of interest and amusement; there is nothing that so agreeably fatigues the body and rests the mind. . . . . As soon as I have got *my work under* a little in the garden, I mean to set seriously into Greek, and to finish Wraxall and many other books I have in my eye; by-the-bye, don't let me forget to advise you to read the 'Natural Son,' or 'Lovers' Vows;' it is the entire and literal translation of the play which is now acting with such success at Covent Garden,* but *not* as it is acted; you can get it at Todd's, where I did, to read in the chaise. I think it quite charming, and it

* 'Lovers' Vows.' Play in five Acts, translated and adapted to the English stage by Mr. Richard Cumberland, from the German of Kotzebue.

affected me much, tho' not of the black and dreadful school of Schiller. You must allow for German manners and for the (at all times) sad disguise of a translation. I find people of taste in general disapprove of it as acted, tho' they own it affecting. This I can readily believe to be just, for I should conceive it very difficult to adjust to an English audience. We all regretted its not being acted while we were in town. Another book which I purchased at Todd's and read in my chaise was the 'Essay on Population'* which Mr. Wrangham left with you. It is uncommonly clearly thought and written, and contains much curious and uncontrovertible reasoning on the subject in question.

Extract from a Letter to the Same.

Little Strawberry, Tuesday, Nov. 27, 1798.

I think, by way of filling up my cover, I shall send you a letter of Edwards', written in answer to some inquiries I had made about the event of his friend Johnstone's trial. You will see how rationally and liberally Edwards owns Government here to have been in the right, and you will see that Attorney-Generals are not always so much in the wrong as you are inclined to think them. As to poor Tone's † case, I think judge,

* Thos. Robt. Malthus, born 1766; published in 1798 his 'Essay on Population.' A few years later he was appointed Professor of Political Economy at the East India Company's College at Heyleybury, a post which he retained till his death, in 1834. He was the author of several works on political economy, and was one of the founders of the Political Economy Club, and the Statistical Society.—*Imperial Dictionary of Universal Biography.*

† Theobald Wolfe Tone, born at Dublin in about 1763, called to the bar 1789, became a political writer, and, though himself a Protestant, was the founder of a club called the 'United Irishmen.' He was finally taken prisoner in the act of returning with the French invading squadron, in which he had accepted a commission. He was brought to Dublin and tried by a court-martial: he prayed the Court to sentence him to be shot. This request was denied him, and he was ordered to be executed, but the night preceding that of his intended execution he contrived to inflict a dangerous wound on his own throat. The next morning Mr. Curran applied to the Court of King's Bench for a writ of Habeas Corpus to bring up the body of Mr. Tone upon the ground 'that courts-martial had no jurisdiction upon subjects not in the service of His Majesty during the sitting of the Court of King's Bench.' The Chief Justice, Lord Kilwarden, ordered a writ to be made out immediately, but Mr. Tone was not in a condition to be moved.

jury and accusers, and friends, all seem to be equally *Irish mad*, and nobody to have common sense but the poor unhappy prisoner, who, I heartily hope, *will never live* to be tormented with a new trial.

Little Strawberry, Tuesday, Dec. 14, 798.

. . . During my illness I have finished the 2nd vol. of Wraxall which I had just begun at Brandsby, and which I like better and better the farther I go. I have consulted, too, one of his authorities for many things in the age of Henry the Third, Montaigne's Essays, a very curious and an *astonishing* book, considering the times in which it was written, and which one never consults without entertainment. I have *re*read, too, Condorcet's book,* and compared his ideas and arguments on the subject of population with those of the Essay we have been reading, and certainly the Essay has not only the best of the argument (upon these points) in a *philosophical* light, but is absolute *conviction* on the subject of the different ratios in which population, and the means of subsisting that population, increase. . . .

That Miss Berry should have read with interest such a work as Malthus's essay on the 'Principle of Population,' that it should have confirmed her own unassisted ideas on such a subject, and that she should have felt that she coincided with the reasoning of such an author, is no small proof that her mind was considerably in advance, not only of other women, but of the majority of the men of that day.

. . .

I cannot but feel flattered at finding my own unassisted ideas upon subjects of philosophical politics and national economy confirmed by those of some of the most enlightened authors. A pleasure of this sort I have lately received in reading Malthus's *Essay on the Principle of Population*,—his ideas on the relative greatness of two countries, the one deriving its wealth

The execution was suspended, and on the 10th he died in prison from the effects of his self-inflicted wound.—*Annual Register.*

* Mr. Malthus refers to M. Condorcet's 'Esquisse d'un Tableau Historique des Progrès de l'Esprit Humain' in his 'Essay on the Principle of Population.'

principally from trade and manufactures, and the other from agriculture—upon the high price of labour materially checking our foreign dealings—his assumption that high duties and prohibitions on foreign produce and foreign commodities is neither more nor less than giving a bounty to our own manufactures, and thereby depressing and turning away attention and capital from agriculture.

All these ideas I have long entertained, in all his reasonings on them I perfectly coincide with him; and, if I may be allowed to go on a little farther by myself, not without hopes of finding these further ideas also confirmed, in future, by some better head than my own, possessed of more data, and having that practical acquaintance with details of which I must necessarily be ignorant; I would say, then, that I can see no possible objection (in theory at least) to a country, under the peculiar circumstances that ours happens to be, receiving all the produce and all the manufactures of all the countries in Europe without any particular restriction or higher duties on the one than on the other. We are allowed on all hands to have risen to a perfection of machinery in our own manufactures hitherto unrivalled, and which allows us, in spite of the *present* high price of labour and of provisions, to undersell others in the foreign markets.

Our manufactures, in time of peace, certainly employ as many hands and as much of the capital (as the economists call it) of the country, not to say more than can be properly spared from agriculture and its improvements necessary to the welfare of the state.

Under these circumstances, what possible harm could accrue to us from receiving, for instance (and it is certainly the strongest instance that can be cited), the wines and silks of France at the same regular and moderate duties at which we should receive the produce of what are now called the most favoured nations?

Can anybody suppose, while we continue to possess superior habits of industry and commercial confidence, that we need dread a competition with France, while we have hardware of all sorts, collars and muslins, articles of much more general and necessary use than wine and silks, to bring to their market, and those of every other quarter of the world?

Our allowing an open and fair competition, which surely we could have no reason to dread, would, in the first place, remove that odium under which we too surely lay with all Europe for a spirit of mercantile tyranny and monopoly; and, at all events, it would gently let us down to our own level (a very high one it must always be) in the scale of commercial nations—it would weaken the blow that our fictitious and unnatural commercial wealth will unavoidably receive, and enable us to bear it without any violent convulsion either of public prosperity or of private happiness, by turning more of the capital of the State to the support and increase of the agricultural system—the *only* solid basis of commercial prosperity.

But on this subject, as on many others, a few simple, fundamental, immutable principles are so involved in the complex systems which are built upon them, that by the generality of mankind—nay, even by the reasoning part of mankind—they are utterly forgotten, and by few indeed received to suffice really.

Thus all possible systems of political economy, and of commercial or agricultural success, and of national prosperity, must *all necessarily* be founded on a few simple principles, which, like the truths on which rest the first principles both of reasoning and of mathematics, will, at first sight, appear *so* self-evident as to make demonstration superfluous; while the farther we advance, the more we perceive how often they require to be impressed on our minds; and that error can only be avoided by frequently rallying our wandering thoughts to the standard of their immutability.

These principles in political economy may be thus stated:—

1st. That man cannot live without food; consequently, that no greater number of people can possibly be made to exist than there is the means of maintaining; or, in other words, that no power can make the population exceed the means of subsistence.

2nd. That man will feed himself before his neighbour; consequently, that the nation which gets from others the means of subsistence, instead of having wherewithal within itself, will be the first to starve; or, in other words, that the nation which habitually imports instead of exporting corn will be subject to severe scarcities.

3rd. That in plenty, what remains to man at the end of the

year, after he has fed himself, is the only possible fund he can have, either for raising a greater quantity of food next year, or for keeping himself idle and making others work for him; or, in other words, that the surplus produce of agriculture and of labour is the only possible fund and support for commercial prosperity.

By the test of these few simple principles, all systems whatsoever, to whom related or by whom begot, must be tried; and no apparent contradictions to them in the circumstances, past or present, of any of the States of Europe, can diminish one jot from their immutability.

Extract from a letter to Mrs. Cholmeley.

Little Strawb., Tuesday, Dec. 11, 1798.

. . . On the evening of Friday we went to the play at Covent Garden. Saw 'Lovers' Vows,' and a new farce called 'The Jew and the Doctor,'* which has more real laughable fun in it, more plot, and certainly more good writing, than any *comedy* I have seen or heard of for this age: as a *farce*, it certainly is quite admirable, and, I dare say, will always maintain its place upon the stage. It is said to be the first production of young Dibdin, son to the man who writes the songs and exhibits some sort of an entertainment to the public under the name of the Sans-Souci. 'Lovers' Vows' disappointed me. The necessary curtailments which have been made from the German 'Natural Son,' to avoid *des longueurs*, and to suit it in some degree to our manners upon the stage, destroy the effect of many situations and sentiments, by having in a great degree taken away their efficient, or at least *sufficient* cause, and consequently making them appear awkward or misplaced, or more or less than enough to the minds of the spectators: in short, a good play must ever be a *whole* from which it is quite impossible to take out a bit here and put in a bit there without disfiguring and degrading the original, even when that original would not succeed in representation, as is certainly the case

* 'The Jew and the Doctor' was first performed at the Maidstone Theatre, and afterwards at Covent Garden. Mr. Dibdin says, 'though not produced in that order it was his *first*.'—*Vide* advertisement to 'Jew and Doctor,' in Mrs. Inchbald's Collection of Farces.

with the 'Natural Son,' as I read it, closely translated from the original. . . .

Roscoe * has just sent us a poem of his translation from an Italian poet whose very name was unknown to my very shallow Italian erudition.† It is called 'The Nurse,' from 'La Babia' of Luigi Tansillo. I have read it over, tho' not yet with sufficient attention; but I am disappointed in it, because I expect nothing but what is excellent from his pen.‡ The subject, which is reprobating hired nurses and exhorting all women to suckle their own children, does not do in English verse, tho' the *Ariosto-like* familiarity and simplicity of the original, makes it pretty in the inimitable beauty of the Italian language. The subject, too, never to the eye of reason and nature can admit of an argument, and therefore is a repetition of the same idea. I mean, that it never can admit of anything but a *physical* argument from some peculiar defect or infirmity of the mother, which does not and cannot do in poetry. The poem is published, beautifully printed, with the Italian on the opposite page; it is not long, and you can no doubt get it at York.

* William Roscoe, born at Liverpool, 1753. His father kept a public-house, and also carried on the business of a market-gardener. In 1774 William Roscoe became an attorney of the Court of King's Bench; in 1784 he was elected Member of the Manchester Literary and Philosophical Society. He first appeared as an author in 1796; he wrote the 'Life of Lorenzo de' Medici,' 'Life of Leo X.,' &c. &c. In 1816 he was elected M.P. for Liverpool. The Royal Institution of Liverpool owes its origin to him. Died in 1831, in his seventy-ninth year.

† Tansillo, an Italian poet of no great merit. 'La Babia,' published 1767; Roscoe's translation, published 1798.—*Watts's Dictionary.*

‡ 'Mr. Roscoe is happy in an opportunity of paying his respects to the Miss Berrys, and requesting their acceptance of a copy of "The Nurse," translated from the Italian of Luigi Tansillo. He is well aware how much his translation will suffer in the estimation of persons so fully acquainted with the Italian language by a comparison with the original, which possesses a degree of simplicity wholly unattainable—at least by the present translator: besides which, they will perceive numerous omissions and variations, the reasons of some of which will be sufficiently obvious. It would afford Mr. R. great pleasure if he could flatter himself that this trifling production could afford Miss Berrys any amusement; and should any error or impropriety occur to them on its perusal, he shall esteem himself highly obliged by their noticing it to him whenever their leisure will permit. Mr. R. incloses another copy, which he requests Miss Berrys will take the trouble of sending to the Hon. Mrs. Damer, with his best respects.

'Birchfield, Dec. 3, 1798.'

To the Same.

Little Strawb., Monday, Dec. 24, 1798.

You will see in to-day's paper the confirmation of the capture of Minorca,* which I fancy is really of very considerable importance towards maintaining our present superiority in the Mediterranean. Mrs. Charles Stuart may now, instead of 'tearing her hair for her general's departure,' go to him at Minorca, of which he is made governor. . . . The Union with Ireland may most truly be called the *Irish* Union, for it seems likely totally to *disunite* the two countries. Wrong heads, either individually or nationally, are, to be sure, the d—l to deal with! The Union with Scotland (from which she has to date the most rapid improvement and prosperity which ever took place in a country) was opposed with hardly less violence by the pride and prejudices of the Scotch; but the Scotchman will always ultimately submit both his pride and his prejudices to his *interest*, and has the sense to see what that interest is; which latter sense I can by no means allow to the Irish, after their *seriously* planning to set themselves up, in the present state of Europe, as an independent republic under the protection of the French! You will think me growing *ministerial*: nothing less, I can assure you. We have behaved like brutes and like fools to Ireland; but now they are behaving like brutes and fools to themselves; for I feel convinced that a union with this country would be the making of Ireland, tho' I by no means think it likely to be a great advantage to England: the balance must *always* be in favour of the poorer country admitted to participate in all the commerce and commercial undertakings of the richer one. I am told there is in Somerville's 'Queen Anne' a very curious and detailed account of all the opposition made to, and all the arguments *pro* and *con* the Union with Scotland. I have not yet come to it. What signifies if the idle Irish lords should all come over and live here?—their estates

* In the 'Gazette' of Dec. 24th is the despatch addressed to the Right Hon. Henry Dundas, and signed 'Chas. Stuart,' giving an account of this event, beginning—'I have the honour to acquaint you that His Majesty's forces are in possession of the Island of Minorca, without having sustained the loss of a single man.'—*Annual Register.*

would very soon be bought by great linen-weavers and other manufacturers, as all the little Scotch lairds' estates have been bought by people having made commercial fortunes, and able and willing to lay out a great deal of money in ameliorating and cultivating to the utmost their purchases. My Irish speculations are luckily interrupted by dinner. Farewell!

'Tristram Shandy,' while it diverts, always reminds me of a Dutch portrait, in which we admire the accurate representation of all the little disgusting blemishes—the warts, moles, and hairs—of the human form. Even when he affects us, it is by a minute detail of little circumstances which all lead to the weaknesses, and are often connected with the ridicules, that belong to our nature; while Rousseau, on the contrary, like the great masters of the Italian school of painting, gives grace and dignity to every character he brings forward—choosing to represent scenes and situations when every ennobling faculty of our mind is brought into action, and the greatest expression of passion and character is produced without even losing sight of decent grace, or presenting anything disgusting to the imagination.

The one degrades worth, by a thousand little mean circumstances that destroy the respect which it *ought* to inspire; while the other consoles frail human nature with the idea that even great failings are redeemable by virtuous exertion.

When I read 'Paradise Lost,' I am no more able to conceive the powers of imagination and genius exerted by Milton in the composition of that poem, than I am able to conceive the intellect of Sir Isaac Newton in the demonstration of the phenomena of the universe. Both seem to me beings more exalted above myself in the scale of intellectual perfection, than I am above the brute creation. Both serve, more than any other contemplation of nature, to raise and purify my ideas of its great Author—of that Being who has powers to delegate *such* powers! such emanations of *something* so purely spiritual! so clearly detached from all corporal properties and all animal analogies!

With gratitude, too, I bow before the Origin of all good for having placed me in that order of understandings, not disgraced by the unconsciousness of such perfections, but who, looking up to them at an incalculable distance, with pride and reverence, as to the brightest ornaments of the nature to which I belong, am yet capable of being enlightened by the philosophy of the one, and enraptured by the poetry of the other.

Mr. Knight surprised me much the other day by his sentiments of Milton's poetry: I mean, of Milton's poetry in his 'Paradise Lost.' That even the finest parts of that poem, while he admired them, should rather oppress and sink him, than exalt to that sort of enthusiasm and rapture, the true end and aim of all really fine poetry, I cannot understand in a man of his admirable taste and classical acquirements. The perfect taste, the delicacy, the divine purity of all the descriptions of Paradise, of Adam and Eve—of their happiness, their loves, &c. &c.,—*he* thinks cold and unanimating, and admires most the descriptions of Satan, and the diabolic part of the poem.

Here, again, I much wonder at and differ from him. Nothing indeed can be more impressive, more dignified, grander, or more consistent, than the character and conduct of Satan and his compeers throughout; but I must ever think such a character, and the conduct and descriptions incident to it, less original, less infinitely difficult, as to the effect produced by them, than the exquisite pictures of the undisturbed happiness of Paradise and its inhabitants before their fallen state. To represent scenes which interest, of uninterrupted happiness, without events, without distress, without incident of any kind, and, above all, to represent love—the enjoyments of happy, gratified, *human* love—without grossness, without satiety, and with a purity both of thought and of expression, for which he could have neither prototype nor example, seems to me one of the greatest possible efforts of the magic powers of true poetry, which may indeed be said, in the instance of Milton, to have formed a creation of its own.

EXTRACTS FROM LETTERS

1799.

'STRAWBERRY let, at the [no name given] at Twickenham. We go to Cheltenham to meet the Douglas' and Lady Spencer. Mrs. D. came to meet us at Malvern.'

It is in the extracts of Miss Berry's letters to her friend Mrs. Cholmeley that we best trace her occupations and thoughts during this year.

Jan. 3, 1799.

Thus late with angel grace along the plain
Illustrious Devon led Britannia's train;
And whilst, by frigid fashion unreprest,
She to chaste transports open'd all her breast,
Joy'd her lov'd babe its playful hands to twine
Round her fair neck, or midst her locks divine;
And from the fount, with every grace imbued,
Drank heavenly nectar, not terrestrial food.
So Venus once, in fragrant bowers above,
Clasp'd to her rosy breast immortal Love,
Transfus'd soft passion through his tingling frame,
The nerve of rapture, and the heart of flame.
Yet not with wanton hopes and fond desires
Her infant's veins the British matron fires;
But prompts the aim to crown by future worth
The proud pre-eminence of noble birth.

FINIS.

Here are the concluding lines of Roscoe's poem* which I promised you. Your opinion of him as a poet may be perfectly true, for I have never yet had time to read his translations of Lorenzo, and know nothing of his verses except some little insignificant trifles; but I can never agree to your idea of 'prettyness' suiting the Italian language better than English or

* 'The Nurse,' a poem, alluded to in the letter dated Dec. 11, 1798.

French. I have ever thought that the only thing to which the Italian language has been hitherto quite unapt is prettiness, *sentiment*, id genus omne, in which the French, by its continued application to them, so perfectly succeeds. The Italian language, I am persuaded, is *capable* of becoming anything; but hitherto I think you will find it to have been the language of *passion*, not of *sentiment*. . . .

I rejoice that you have such agreeable accounts from your boy. You, I trust, will experience the truth of what I have ever thought—the infinite use, advantage, and service a mother can be to a son; advantages and services which, if not neglected on the one side, I believe are rarely if ever forgotten or ill repaid on the other.

Little Strawb., Saturday, Jan. 12, 1799.

. . . Somerville's 'Anne'* is, I think, more dry than his 'William,' but clear, distinct, impartial, and wonderfully informing; his chapters upon the Union with Scotland are particularly so, and the topics and events of the present day make them doubly interesting. From the almost rebellious state of Scotland at the time, from their ridiculous ideas of an independent kingdom, and their general aversion and opposition to the plan, of none of which circumstances I had before at all a just idea, I assure you I begin to think that, *volens nolens*, we *must* have a Union with Ireland. If their potatoe heads rebel with, they most certainly will rebel without it, the moment a great military force leaves the country; and I really fancy the attempt at least of a Union is all we have for it to save them from the merciless fangs of France.

The news from Naples is melancholy beyond expression, and too plainly shows that the immortal victory of Nelson will only tend to a still greater and fruitless destruction of the human race in that devoted country; while our ignorant ministers and their pert adherents (ignorant, I mean, of foreign affairs), instead of sticking to their ships and their sailors, are talking of being the deliverers and arbitrators of Europe!! . . .

* 'History of Great Britain during the Reign of Queen Anne; with a Dissertation concerning the Danger of the Protestant Succession.' By Thos. Somerville, D.D., F.R.S., Edinburgh, Minister of Jedburgh. Published 1798.—*Watts's Dictionary*.

N. Audley Street, Tuesday, Jan. 22, 1799.

. . . . I have ever sought in friendship persons I considered as my superiors in mental endowments; indeed, such superiority must ever be the first real inducement and only real foundation for an intimate union to a thinking mind. If I afterwards found an inferiority in some points, I looked for and recognised a superiority in others. My very seeking their intimacy at all, necessarily supposed these circumstances, this balanced equality; but, certainly, the more *superior* I found them in judgment, in feelings, in opinions, in taste, the more I sought, cultivated, and congratulated myself on the conviction; the more I *took* and the less I *gave*, the more I should have considered the balance in my favour. . . .

N. Audley Street, Sunday, Feb. 3, 1799.

. . . . I hope you have read the Irish debates on the Union. I think you will have found in them much abuse, little eloquence, and absolutely *no* argument. I fancy they think they hold the charter of their constitution and independence by a *bull*; for, would you believe it, the first official accounts misstated the majority of the House of Lords for the minority, and the mistake went all over London. I myself was shown a letter by Mathew (Col. Mathew), which, from its handwriting, and the office manner in which it was drawn up, I am sure must have come from a clerk of the Parliament, in which this mistake in computation was regularly stated!! Mr. Pitt's speech on opening the business in the Parl[t] here, I really think very good; tho', in my opinion, some of the strongest arguments in favour of a Union he hardly touches upon; whether from thinking the cause too good to want them, or what other reason, I cannot pretend to say. Sheridan's answer I thought miserable, I mean in point of argument, and in his first speech he had got himself fairly into a dilemma, when he first urged the *independence* of the Irish Parl., and then its *incompetency*. The famous Irish pamphlet in favor of the Union, called *Cease your Funning*, which after much trouble I got to read, disappointed me; it is sharp and well-kept-up irony from beginning to end, on a pamphlet on the other side, by the L[d] Lieut.'s secretary;* but it is not very entertaining, and not at all instructive.

* An official pamphlet by Mr. Cooke, the Irish Under Secretary of State,

If our ministry open and discuss their plan of Union here, if that plan is a liberal one, and if they do not now cram it down the people's throats, but leave it to be considered and taken up at some more propitious moment, I should suppose they would do wisely, and *therefore* I doubt they will not do it.

Here is a long batch of politics for me. I might turn to your other favorite subject, religion; for, in compliance with your request and my own wishes, I have been and am reading with much attention Mr. Wilberforce's book, and likewise strictures on it, in a series of letters by Mr. Belsham,* a man who has, I am told, wrote several good historical tracts. When I have done, I will tell you sincerely the impression they make upon me: I can assure you it is a very deep one. My mind, always *over* serious, grows every day more so as I approach that middle age of life, when the prospect of rational beings begins to close in upon them, and the visionary distance fades from their strengthened or weakened sight.

I have not sealed with black wax to you, because I think it always alarming at a distance; but I am in mourning for my uncle (Furguson's) only daughter, who has just died of a consumption at the age of 15, with the courage of a hero and the resignation of a saint.

N. Audley Street, Tuesday Feb. 19, 1799.

. . . . Your 'Practical Education'† is a title I have long set down in my pocket-book as of a work to read, which I most certainly shall at my first leisure minutes. They, I fear, will not be many, for I am *going to go on* with my Greek, under a master recommended to me by Charles Burney, an English master. Therefore, you will no longer have reason to be (comically) angry at my supposed obstinacy about the pronunciation of Greek. I intend to have him but once a week, that, allowing for my too frequent interruptions from bad health and *necessary* idleness, I may yet be able to work a good deal by myself, without which

entitled 'Arguments for and against the Union considered.' It was widely circulated, and discussion of the subject encouraged.—*Edinburgh Review*, April 1859.

* Thomas Belsham, author of 'A Review of Mr. Wilberforce's Practical View of the Prevailing Religious Systems of Professed Christians,' published 1798, and of a variety of other works.—*Watts's Dictionary.*

† By Miss Edgeworth, published 1798.

little can be done with all the masters in the world. This will confine my reading (after I have finished what I am at present about) principally to what I call *reading up to the day*: I mean pamphlets and things of the moment, which one is left in the basket without. Poor Jerningham has just published a little thing, which he calls 'a dramatic whim.'* It is not positively bad in its way, but it is a way that you would not like. It is a scene and a frolic of Charles 2nd and some of his most distinguished courtiers at Peckham, where (it seems) he had a country-house. However, bad or good, I rejoice that a bookseller has given him 40*l.* for it, without his name to it (which, indeed, might have done more harm than good). The poor soul is just now in a distress for which one must pity him, tho' it is in fact the luckiest thing that could possibly have happened to him. . . . Mr. Sotheby† sent me his 'Battle of the Nile.'‡ The subject must ever inspire, however recounted, a degree of enthusiasm very favourable to the recounter. There seems to be a number of good lines in his poem, but the conduct of it is not to me clear; and the same want of clearness, I think, applies to some of his verses. . . . .

N. Audley Street, Tuesday, March 5, 1799.

. . . On Saturday Mrs. Damer and ourselves dined with your mother and brother; and yesterday we went with him, at his own request, to the Great Orleans Pictures which are exhibited at the Lyceum, in the Strand. It was my second visit. Among them is the Sebastian del Piombo (a Resurrection of Lazarus),§ of whose excellence, if you remember,

He talked so much and long about it,
That e'en believers 'gan to doubt it.

But he could not say too much—I give him credit for all his

* 'Peckham Frolic, or Nell Gwynn,' comedy in three acts.

† William Sotheby, born 1757; entered the army, in the 10th Dragoons, when engaged in protecting part of the Scottish coasts from the incursions of Paul Jones. In 1798 he published his translation of 'Oberon.' He also translated the Georgics of Virgil, and the Iliad and the Odyssey of Homer. He was also the author of 'Saul Constance of Castile,' &c. Died 1833.—*Imperial Dictionary of Universal Biography.*

‡ Published in 1799.

§ Now in the National Gallery.

admiration; it is one of *the fine* pictures in the world—excelling in grouping, composition, drawing, intellect, clearness, expression, and all that constitutes the perfections of the higher order of painting. Mrs. Damer, he, and I stood before it for above half an hour yesterday thoroughly enjoying it. I am heartily sorry that you do not see these pictures, for they are by far the finest—indeed, the only real display of the excellency of the Italian schools of painting that I ever remember in this country. And then one sees them so comfortably, for there are fewer people go to the Lyceum than even to Pall Mall, for the pictures are all of a sort less understood and less tasted here; and besides, they are without frames; and besides, the Lyceum is out of the way; and besides, it is not near Dyde's and Scribe's, nor Butler's, nor any of the great haberdashers for the women, nor Bond St. nor St. James' St. for the men. . . .

. . . I am well acquainted with Warton's criticism on Pope; and tho' it is certainly open to all you say of its wandering manner, it is as certainly never unentertaining, and, in my opinion, contains more candid and liberal criticism upon whatever may be the object under consideration, more enthusiasm about genius, and ten thousand times more real taste than in all the critical writings of the morose and bigoted Johnson. Whatever recommends Lucretius to your notice, recommends a source of exquisite pleasure to your poetic mind: his metaphysics are naught, but his poetry is divine. Virgil shrinks into *prettiness* whenever compared with him: but remember he is supposed to have died the day Virgil was born; therefore he is less polished, less uniformly harmonious.

I have got your critique upon Mr. Sotheby's 'Nile,' which I dare say I shall read with pleasure; but how can you (except indeed for a lesson to your boy)—*you*, who can *so* translate Gray and *may* read Lucretius, and *have* little time, condescend so to criticise a minor poet? . . .

Tuesday morning, March 12, 1799.

. . . I am quite impatient to read the song of the Nile, and shall certainly get it to-day when I am out; for, having resolved to buy, I would not borrow it. I don't know how my 'transports' may be *vis-à-vis des vôtres*, but I believe few people (with a head as prosaic as mine) read and regard poetry more in its *true* intent, as one of the chief consolations and ornaments of human life. I always read to be pleased and interested, to forget myself as long as possible in the charming regions of imagination, or to rejoice in feeling its mighty powers giving irresistible energy to the cause of truth and virtue. . . .

. . . Do you remember my speaking to you in high terms of a series of plays upon the passions of the human mind, which had been sent to me last winter by the author? * I talked to everybody else in the same terms of them at the time, anxiously enquiring for the author; but nobody knew them, nobody cared for them, nobody would listen to me; and at last I unwillingly held my tongue, for fear it should be supposed that I thought highly of them only because they had been sent to me. This winter the first question upon everybody's lips is, 'Have you read the series of plays?' Everybody talks in the raptures (I always thought they deserved) of the tragedies and of the introduction as of a new and admirable piece of criticism. Sir G. Beaumont,† who was with us yesterday morning, says he never expected to see such tragedies in his days; and C. Fox, to whom he had sent them, is in such raptures with them, that he has written a critique of 5 pages upon the subject to Sir George. I mention these two as persons of whose taste I, and I believe you too, have a very *decided* opinion. I own my little *amour-propre* is mortified that, having been honoured with a copy of the work, my humble tribute of unfeigned admiration and undictated praise had not reached the author before it is drowned in the general voice. But, whoever that author is, they still persist in

* Joanna Baillie, daughter of Rev. James Baillie and his wife Dorothea Hunter, born at the manse at Bothwell, near Glasgow. She was niece of the great anatomists William and John Hunter, and sister of Dr. Baillie. In 1798 she published her first volume of plays; in 1836 she published three more volumes of dramas; and at different times several other pieces of poetry, many exceedingly graceful. Died at Hampstead 1851, in her 89th year.—*Imperial Dictionary of Universal Biography.*

† Sir George H. Beaumont, Bart., born in 1753. His name now stands for the type of convention in landscape-painting. Married, in 1784, the daughter of Chief-Justice Willis. He was greatly admired as an actor in private theatricals; he was a professed painter, as well as professed critic. Had he been poor, he might have made a second-rate artist. It was principally owing to Sir George Beaumont's exertions, and to his promise of leaving his own collection of pictures to the nation, that the erection of a National Gallery is due. Lord Dover, Lord Aberdeen, and Lord Farnborough were his first principal supporters in this laudable design.—*Imperial Dictionary of Universal Biography.*

preserving a strict incognito, for which I honour their honest pride, which scorns to be indebted to *any* name for the success of such a work, and, with the patient sense of real merit, has quietly waited a whole twelvemonth for the impression it has at last made on an obdurate public. I fancy one of them will be acted—the least good one, in my opinion—but there are two fine characters for Kemble and Mrs. Siddons.* She (Mrs. Siddons) who was one of a little party we had last night, spoke of them with a surprise and delight that did honour to her taste. She (by the bye) was at her very best last night; had put off the *Catherine*, or rather not put it on since her return from Bath, and sang to us after supper, and was agreeable. . . .

N. Audley Street, Tuesday, March 19, 1799.

. . . I am glad to hear of you at York, and glad to hear of you at the play. 'The Jew and the Doctor,' I felt, must please you: it has true comic humour, a sufficient degree of intrigue (which, if not new, is well put together), and is infinitely better written than any modern comedy that I have seen. A comedy in five acts appeared last week at Covent Garden by the same author, which prepossesses one in its favour, but I have neither seen nor heard any account of it. Apropos to plays, be sure you read the vol. I mentioned to you in my last. There is now such a rage for them here among all, the few, people who think on these subjects, that they even admire the comedy excessively. Here, I own, my admiration stops; not that there are not many strokes both of nature and character in it; the intrigue a common one, and, I think, none of the characters very interesting. All this talking and thinking about plays brings my own long-forgotten into my head, which it had better not, for it always gives me an itching to do something with it, and it had probably better be left untouched to my executors. . . .

You, who know the activity of my mind, will be pleased to hear that I have got a man to pursue Greek with me, recommended

* Sarah Siddons, born 1755. Her father, Roger Kemble, was manager of a provincial theatre. From an early age she was accustomed to figure on the stage as one of her father's troup. In 1773 she was married to Mr. Siddons. She made her first appearance at Drury Lane in 1775, in the character of Portia. She bade farewell to the stage in 1812; her last appearance was in the character of Lady Randolph, in 1818. She died 1831.—*Imperial Dictionary of Universal Biography.*

by Dr. Chas. Burney. He is an Englishman, so that I shall soon lose my foreign accent; and he has been all his life employed in teaching, so that one might expect his method to be good. But, alas! what a difference I find between his *learning* and that of my Greek Petrachi! The one I feel and see is only a scholar more advanced than myself in the same study, and unused and incapable of taking any deep views upon the subject: the other had fathomed every depth of the language in which he first began to speak; and if ever he failed in explanation, it was only where the accuracy of his ideas went beyond my powers of perception. However, this man or any other is better than none, and will prevent, at least, my having the mortification of thinking that I have thrown away many months' time and some painful attention, to be left on the threshold of knowing, what in truth everything both in science and taste refers to, and is deduced from.

N. Audley Street, Thursday, March 21, 1799.

. . . I am delighted you like 'Basil,' with whom and with his admirable friend I am in love. Nothing to me can be more affecting than the end of that play. The *great guns* of taste, I find, all prefer the other, except Mr. Fox: I am satisfied while *convenio cum eminentissimo Carpegno.* The second tragedy you will, I think, find very affecting too; it is going to be acted. The author, applied to by the means of Cadell, still refuses to come forward even to receive emolument; says the piece is before the public, that the Theatre may do what they please with it, only desires the simplicity of the plot may not be infringed upon. Neither fame nor a thousand pounds therefore have much effect upon this said author's mind, whoever *he* or *she* may be. I say *she*, because and *only* because no man could or *would* draw such noble, such dignified representations of the female mind as the Countess Albini * and Jane de Mountfort.† They often make us clever, captivating, heroic, but never rationally superior. . . . I have just received a work in 2 vols. from H. More, called 'Strictures on the Modern System of Female Education:' ‡ when I have read it, you shall hear of it.

* Character in 'Basil.'

† Character in 'De Montfort,' by Miss J. Baillie.

‡ Hannah More, born in 1745, a popular writer on moral and religious

Thursday, March 28, 1799.

. . . . H. More's book will, I should think, to you supply everything that you want in Miss E.'s 'Practical Education;' for this should properly be called, Strictures upon the Education of Young Ladies as far as it relates to religion and morality. There are many excellent details in it, much good sense, and an infinity of wit, for which last indeed I think all H. More's prose is quite remarkable; but there is in her writings, as in Mr. Wilberforce's, a principle radically false, which in my opinion vitiates every system built upon it, and saps the very foundations of morality—nay, the very throne of God! . . . . The world in general has nothing to do with one's faith: mine is perfectly satisfactory to myself. Without disputing about or upholding our several doctrines while we 'now see darkly as through a glass,' let us both endeavour to continue acting our parts well, and we shall meet hereafter in some place where we shall both understand the subject much better, and where such a disquisition will not be attended with that human leaven of error and acrimony which they are too apt to be here. . . . My Greek, about which I am really anxious, takes me up some time, and I have often, for ourselves and others, what many women would call *business*. At present I have to talk and think a good deal, and never very agreeably, about a trusteeship of my father's to his uncle's great property in Scotland—an affair in which we are in no respect involved. . . . .

Tuesday, April 2, 1799.

. . . . In the many hours I have spent alone this last week, I have been able, though by very little bits at a time, to go entirely through Hannah More, and Mrs. Woolstonecroft* immediately after her. It is amazing, or rather it is not amazing,

themes, and of some dramas. Her father was in humble circumstances. She had four sisters; and, whilst still in their youth, they found themselves at the head of a flourishing school. Hannah wrote verse very early, and was the author of 'Cœlebs in Search of a Wife,' and of many works of a very serious character, and severe strictures on what she termed the fashionable world. She was of a most active and benevolent character. She died 1833.—*Imperial Dictionary of Universal Biography*.

* Mary Woolstonecroft, born 1759, died 1797; authoress of 'Thoughts on the Education of Daughters;' married to William Godwin, who published, after her death, many of her unpublished works, 1798.—*Watts's Dictionary*.

but impossible, they should do otherwise than agree on all the great points of female education. H. More will, I dare say, be very angry when she hears this, though I would lay a wager that she never read the book.

. . . Indeed, I have been most literally alone; for Mrs. Damer went on Friday and only returned yesterday from Brocket Hall, where she assisted in acting a play with Lady Melbourne's sons. It was 'Ways and Means,' a three-act thing of Colman's. I never saw it. Her part was only Lady Dunders, a mere fat old woman who has only a few words to say. But she put them all in the way of doing better than they otherwise would. . . .

N. Audley Street, Friday, May 17, 1799.

. . . I was much entertained by some letters which Price showed me from Sr G. Beaumont, Fox, and Knight,* containing criticisms on the series of plays which he (Price) had set them all reading. They were excellent, the ideas of three, very superior understandings and tastes, all struck with different beauties and blemishes, and reasoning upon them according to the varied medium of mind through which they saw. . . .

N. Audley Street, Thursday, May 23, 1799.

. . . I fear there is no hope for you about the criticisms on the plays: the letters were all, *de tous côtés*, addressed to Price; they were only pieces of letters upon other subjects, but he knows their value, keeps them in cotton, and went out of town for good on Monday last. . . I began Homer's Iliad on Wednesday last, to my no small delight, and felt no particular difficulty in the comprehension of the first doz. lines. . . .

Cheltenham, Monday, Aug. 5, 1799.

. . . I am in no sort of hurry to leave this place, where I enjoy a quiet in the morning which I seldom or never attain at

* Richard Payne Knight, Esq., of Downton Castle, Herefordshire; born 1750; well known for his great classical attainments, his love of art ancient and modern, and as a collector on a large scale. His collection, valued at 30,000*l.*, he bequeathed to the British Museum. He was a writer on classical subjects,—'An Analytical Essay on the Greek Alphabet,' &c. &c.; and in 1805 he published his 'Analytical Enquiry into the Principles of Taste.' Died 1824.

home, and the rest of the day lead a life as comfortably unlike a *public place* as can be well imagined. The Douglas's, L[y] Spencer,* and ourselves always meet at the well of a morn[g], and generally pass some part of the even[g] together, either walking or at the play (where we have had Kemble,) or sometimes, but very seldom, at the rooms, where, as we have hitherto none of us known anybody, we have had little temptation to go; but there are new arrivals every day, and some agreeable, conversable males will at last occur, I hope, which we much want in our society, altho' never did I see so many men in a place of this sort, but all of them unknown both to ourselves and those we know here. Did I tell you that L[y] Spencer (the Dow. I mean) had sought our acquaintance with *empressement*, and that I have become a great favorite with her and her granddaughter,† who is a charming, natural, unaffected girl of sixteen, with a warm heart and good understanding? She will never, I think, be handsome to compare with her mother, but has much of her captivating manner. She has taken to me (of whom she says she has heard so much beforehand) with all the overflowing warmth of an affectionate heart at sixteen. . . .

Letter from the Dow. Lady Spencer to Miss Berry.

Nuneham,‡ Aug. 21, 1799.

You are very good, my dear Miss Berry, to give me the proof you have done that I am not yet forgot. I should have been

* Margaret Georgiana, eldest daughter of Stephen Poynts, Esq., of Medgeham, Co. Berks; married, 1755, to John, first Earl of Spencer. Lord Spencer died in 1783.

† Lady Georgiana Cavendish, daughter of the Duke of Devonshire, wife of the late Earl of Carlisle, and mother of the present: died 1858. The interest with which this lady inspired Miss Berry, more than double her age, soon ripened into a friendship that terminated only with Miss Berry's existence. If it may be permitted here to offer a tribute of respectful admiration to the memory of one whose virtues were exercised so strictly within the pale of private and domestic life, it would be to remark how truly her opening character had been discerned, how well through life she kept the fair promise of her youth, and how in her declining years she reaped the rich reward of more than ordinary devotion from those around her, and to the last remained the centre of affection and duty to a circle of numerous descendants.

‡ The seat of George Simon, second Earl of Harcourt: born 1736, died 1765.

glad to have heard that you had found some old friends among the new-comers, that might have replaced those to whom you kindly gave up so much of your time.

We met the Duchess of Devonshire, several of my g'child^n, and Miss Trimmer,* at Oxford: this last is the governess to the Lady Cavendishes, whom I wish you to notice when you see her, because she is excellent in herself and invaluable to them; and you will therefore feel with me that the more weight can be given to her by others the better: indeed, she is in a very independent situation, and has never been on any other footing than that of a friend.

I am here in a most beautiful place; the weather is delightful, and my early rising gives me many hours to stroll about before the society I am in begin to live. But I want my sweet child, to whom I might point out a thousand striking scenes, and I often long for Miss Douglas's pencil and yours to fix them on my memory. The way of living here is in the old style, which tho' the modern world would call formal, has, like many old customs, sterling worth—great regularity, decent magnificence, and much real charity and beneficence of every kind is daily going forward, besides a little drawing-room *loisir* for general conversation, which, when there is anybody that understands what the thing means, is not unpleasant. But I forget I am only thanking you for your letter, and not commencing a correspondence, for which having neither time nor talent to bear my part, I am not unreasonable enough to request. I beg my best regards to Miss Agnes, and my compliments to Mr. Berry,

And am, dear Miss Berry,

Your faithful and affectionate,

Hum^ble serv^t,

G. SPENCER.

P.S.—Have you ever seen the 3^d vol. of Mason's Poems, published two years ago? I never did till I came here; and I have found some sweet things in them, which I have been reading this morning in the flower-garden facing the cinerary urn Lord Harcourt has erected to his memory.

I cannot help translating the end of a sonnet written in his

* Daughter of Mrs. Trimmer, the well-known authoress of children's books and works of education.

70th year, which you will not wonder at my being particularly pleased with,—but I wish you was here to mend my pen.

Still round my shelter'd lawn I pleas'd can stray,
  Still trace my sylvan blessings to their spring;
Being of Beings! Yes, that silent lay
  Which musing Gratitude delights to sing,
Still to thy sapphire throne shall Earth convey,
  And Hope, the cherub of unwearied wing.

Lord Harcourt makes me open this again, to add his very particular compliments.

From Miss Berry.

Great Malvern, Sept. 10, 1799.

. . . Never was any place better calculated than this to enjoy clear, sunny, calm weather. You heard me last year, after only a slight acquaintance, talk in raptures of it; and I assure you that now, after a ten days' residence here, and having explored both the mountains and the plain, I am quite convinced it is the most beautiful and enjoyable part of England, as to every *rural* perfection, that I have seen. The village is in itself singularly rural and cheerful. We are lodged in the parsonage-house.

. . . . We were to have gone to Lord Sommers's, at Castleditch,* in this neighbourhood, to-morrow; but their house being full, we have happily cribbed two or three more days here. On Monday we shall proceed on our peregrination by going down the River Wye from Ross to Chepstow, a navigation which is famous for its romantic scenery. From Chepstow we shall go on to the first place upon the coast in Wales, where my father thinks he can get a fortnight's good bathing. . . . . .

The Inn at Pyle in Glamorganshire,
Tuesday, Sept. 24, 1799.

. . . Of your public affairs in Holland *I* have thought wretchedly from the moment that, after the first engagement, the whole country did not rise and join the English troops, who, on the contrary, seem to have gained not an inch

* Charles Cocks, of Castleditch, created Lord Somers 1784; inherited from his mother, Mary Cocks, the seat of Castleditch, now known as Eastnor Castle.

of ground but that they fought for. . . . . The ministerial *prôneurs*, however, still maintain that everything is going on well; but the Dutch in this country, I know, are in very bad spirits.*

Miss Berry omitted, in her brief summary of this year's events, a little expedition into Wales, made in company with her father and sister, and of which she kept a journal. The following extracts will show the changes that have taken place in the mode of travelling through this part of the country, and the very different estimate now taken of the picturesque.

Monday, September 16*th.* — Left Castleditch (Lord Somers's) for Ross; the road, most part of the way, very bad—sometimes stony, sometimes deep and very hilly. The town of Ross a wretched, black-looking, ill-built place. The churchyard neat, and the spire of the church pretty, and the view fine, but, in this country of fine views, not remarkable.

Tuesday, 17*th.*—Left Ross at half-past 10 A.M. The weather precluded all idea of going on the Wye. The road from Ross to Monmouth good—towards Monmouth generally near the river, and very romantic and beautiful. Monmouth is an old, ugly, unpicturesque town, prettily situated, and with a very pretty spire to the church, in the same fashion and much the same proportion as that at Ross.

Wednesday, 18*th.*—Left Monmouth at 10 A.M.; arrived at Chepstow at half-past three, by the river. The banks of this winding river are very high, rocky, and well wooded, particularly about Tintern Abbey, which, though

* An expedition to Holland was concerted between Great Britain and Russia, in the confidence that numbers of the Dutch, opening their eyes to their real interests, would combine with them as their deliverers, as soon as they saw they could with safety act according to their wishes.—*Annual Register*, 1799.

near the water, is not seen from it. The scattered cottages of the village of Tintern, upon the side of the hill immediately rising from the water, very pretty. The approach to Chepstow upon the river, on coming in sight of Piercefield, beautiful. I recollect nothing finer than the ruins of the immense Castle of Chepstow crowning the perpendicular rock that rises from the river, and which is, as well as the river, diversified with every variety of foliage. The town of Chepstow is an inconsiderable place, with but one inn (the Beaufort Arms), a very bad one, that keeps a few post horses, all of which were engaged. The day after we arrived, we were obliged to send forward the whisky to Newport (sixteen miles), in order that horses might be sent back for us and the chaise. It was late before the Newport horses got back and were sufficiently rested to return with us; and they were all so bad, and the hill out of Chepstow so steep, that they refused to draw at all, and others had to be sent for. It was eight o'clock, and long dark, before we arrived at Newport. The approach to Newport was over a long stone bridge, now building, and left without any parapet or rail whatsoever on either side. The lamps to our carriage just showed us our situation when we were on the bridge; and I am glad I did not see more of it, for it would certainly have made me very giddy, though the danger might be little with tired horses who knew the way.

Friday, 20*th*.—Newport is a small town, with a pretty round castle upon the edge of the river. The inn is new and large, now building by Sir Charles Morgan,* only half finished and less than half furnished; *d'ailleurs* clean, and the people civil. Left Newport at eight o'clock; breakfasted at Cardiff. The road is rather less hilly; still we regretted not having taken four horses. Cardiff

* Sir Charles Gould, married Jane, daughter of Sir William Morgan, K.B., of Tredegar, and assumed, under the will of his brother-in-law, the name and arms of Morgan of Tredegar. Died 1806.

is a small ugly town, situated on the edge of the flat low country which goes down to the Bristol Channel. Cardiff Castle, belonging to Lord Bute* in right of his wife (a Windsor), has been repaired; was fitting up for a dwelling-house for the young Lord Mount-Stuart,† who died. On his death, the building, furnishing, &c., were stopped. Some of the rooms are floored and ceiled, and some family pictures of the Windsors hung up in two of them. The enclosure of the castle is turned into a lawn with shrubs, the ruined keep left as a ruin in the middle of it, and a walk round the walls. The entrance, which is the old gate, is the prettiest thing about it. There are the remains of some dungeon-rooms joining to it, in one of which they say Robert, William the Conqueror's eldest son (who is buried at Gloucester), was confined by his brother. From Cardiff to Cowbridge the road much the same—stony and hilly, but in general good. Cowbridge is a wretched little town, or rather village, with one bad inn, which keeps post horses. From Cowbridge to Pyle the road and the country much the same. The distinctive characteristics of South Wales are hills, universally enclosed and cultivated, and cottages, universally white; and these more often dropt about singly than collected in villages. The fashion of white-washing is so general in South Wales, that they whiten even the outer walls of their little enclosures and their pig-stys. This certainly gives a clean and cheerful look to everything, but, in a picturesque point of view, makes too many white spots in the landscape. Pyle is a very

* John, fourth Earl of Bute, born 1744; ambassador to the Court of Spain, 1792; created marquis 1796; married, first, 1766, Charlotte Jane, eldest daughter and co-heir of Herbert Windsor Hickman, second and last Viscount Windsor of the kingdom of Ireland—she died in 1800; and, secondly, to Frances, second daughter of the late Thomas Coutts, Esq. He died at Geneva, 1814, and was succeeded by his grandson.

† John Viscount Mount-Stuart, born 1767; died 1794, aged twenty-seven, in consequence of a fall from a horse. He married, 1792, Elizabeth, daughter of Patrick Crichton, Earl of Dumfries.

small village, composed of a few scattered houses along the roadside, with an excellent inn. It was built by Mr. Talbot, of Margam. The garden, which is a shelf of rock with a wooded bank below, is laid out with extremely good taste. There is an extensive view of the sea, and in fine weather of the opposite coast of Devonshire.

Saturday, 21*st.*—Went from Pyle to Newton, a little village at about four miles' distance, immediately upon the coast, where the landlord at Pyle has a house, and where they receive people, boarding them together as at Malvern Wells; but the house in itself is small, cold, and comfortless. It is surrounded on every side with loose sandhills, which shut out the view from the sea as thoroughly as if they were Alps. There is so much of the same loose sand, that it is impossible to stir out without getting above our shoes in it: in short, a place more destitute of beauty or comfort I never saw. We found here four Welsh ladies and an Irishman living together at a very bad ordinary; and as the company was not large enough to be entertaining, we returned to the inn at Pyle on Monday morning.

Extract of a Letter from Miss Berry to Mrs. Cholmeley.

Cheltenham, Saturday, Oct. 5, 1799.

. . . . The weather has become a most serious consideration with respect to the harvest. Not all the wheat, and very little of the barley, is housed even in this country; what you are to do in the North I have no idea. I had hoped that, from the very extraordinary lateness of the season in every respect, your harvest might not be yet begun, and that you might still have some fine weather for it in this month. Wheat is here at the same price you mention it with you, 14s. a bushel. A scarcity of bread in the winter will not mend our public affairs, which, I think, are going on as ill as possible everywhere but in India, where those who really know say that the death of Tippoo Saib for the present entirely secures our possessions, and frustrates all the designs of the French, even if they ever reach India, which, I feel convinced, in spite of the victories of that Almanzor, Sr Sidney Smith,* they will. As to Holland, if the D. of York † and the rest of them would but be persuaded to *pocket the affront*, the sooner they all come back the better, and the less disgrace will attend them; for if the Dutch, like the wife of the 'Médecin malgré lui,' *choose* to be beat and hanged and robbed and murdered by the French, it is vain that we oppose it. We may step between and receive some of the blows, but we shall never prevent them.

The only person you know here, I believe, is Mme de Coigny.‡ I never see her in London, but am very glad to meet her here, for she is very entertaining and really uncommonly clever. Mentioning her puts me in mind of a book which I am now *devouring* with delight, though no new one, and though I am now reading it for the third time. I mean Mad^me de Sévigné's Letters. Are you well acquainted with them? But I forgot

* Admiral Sir Sidney Smith, born 1764; served, 1781, during the American war; shared in Rodney's victory over the French, April 1, 1782; and was post-captain at the age of nineteen. He then entered the Swedish service, and, in 1793, as a volunteer in the Turkish marine; distinguished himself at Toulon, under Lord Hood. In 1794 he commanded a frigate, to the terror of the French coast. In 1796, he was taken prisoner at Havre-de-Grâce, and imprisoned in the Temple; was treated with great rigour, and his exchange refused. At the end of two years he made his escape; reached England in 1798, and commanded in the Mediterranean. Buonaparte was preparing to subjugate Syria. The gallant and skilful resistance then made by Sir Sidney Smith at Jean d'Acre cost the French the loss of 4,000 men, and at the end of two months they were obliged to retreat to Egypt. For this brilliant success Sir Sidney received the thanks of both Houses of Parliament. His career as a naval commander continued till the year 1814. He died at Paris, 1841.

† The Duke of York had landed in Holland the 13th of September.

‡ Madame de Coigny, daughter of the Marquis de Conflans and granddaughter of the Maréchal d'Amenthières, married to the Marquis de Coigny, son of the Duc de Coigny, Feb. 1775. 'This lady, whose figure and talents, together with the favour of her husband's family at court, conspired to place for several years at the pinnacle of fashion in Paris, was, during the early period of the Revolution, long resident in England, where the cheerfulness with which she submitted to the loss of her former brilliant existence and to the difficulties of her actual situation are remembered with hardly less admiration than was excited by the uncommon liveliness of her conversation and the quickness of her repartees.—*Vide Miss Berry's Notes to M. du Deffand's Letters.*

you don't like gossiping books, and this is certainly eminently so. But what a heart had that woman, what a capacity of affection! Then her ideas are always so lively, so just, so clear! She gives you a faithful and curious transcript of the then world, and suggests more reflections to a thinking mind than almost any book I know. Besides, I love the woman, and am intimately acquainted with all her friends, and very seldom find any society in which I pass an hour so agreeably. . . . .

Cheltenham, Monday, Oct. 14, 1799.

. . . . We go on just as we did here, and the weather goes on just as *it did*; that is to say, we never yet have two fair days together, and but once since our return one completely fair day. What you will do in the North I have no idea. Hay and corn have already risen here; and the price of bread, I fear, will be enormous, which, not only in its immediate effects, but in all its consequences to a great capital, is dreadful. We must hope to get through it as we did the last scarcity, and many other *mauvais pas* which we have seen, and which, when passed, I always wonder how we ever got over them.

. . . . Mad^me^ de Coigny is still here, and is of these parties; but they are so little in her way, that though she makes a *dépense d'esprit* that would ruin anybody else, she cannot much mend them. . . . Madame de Coigny said the other day, speaking of the possibility of a very disagreeable man finding anybody to marry him, 'Il y a des personnes si amoureuses en mariage, qu'elles ne regardent pas du tout le mari.'

Cheltenham, Tuesday, Oct. 22, 1799.

. . . . What think you of this tour of Buonaparte's? For my part, I think it very likely to be the *coup de grâce* to the affairs of the Allies; for if, as is more than probable, he has contrived to negociate a peace between France and the Turks, and now comes to head a victorious army in Europe, what have we to oppose to him but the arrogance and ignorance of our Ministers? which is certainly *quite as remarkable* as his conduct and luck. If one was not likely to be so seriously involved without a possibility of preventing them, in the misfortunes of one's country, what an interesting and entertaining age do we live in!

Cheltenham, Monday, Oct. 28, 1799.

. . . . As Mad[me] de Coigny for the last week almost lived with us, I ought to have much wit to repeat to you, which I am too unwell at present to recollect. . . . She is a cheerful-minded, contented creature, after a fall from *such* a brilliancy of situation as would have first weakened and then soured the minds of most other people. This I attribute in a great degree to an extremely religious education (the only education indeed she ever received), and which no prosperities, no dissipation, no anything has been able to obliterate from her mind. She calls herself 'l'enfant gâté de la Providence,' and has an unfeigned and uninterrupted cheerfulness about her, which she is more likely to receive from her belief in such an idea than any other circumstance in her situation. . . . .

I am too unwell to begin talking of Holland. I have long been perfectly convinced, by several circumstances that have come to my knowledge, of the entire and disgraceful ignorance of our Ministers as to foreign politics. Would to heaven, for the sake of the many brave men that have fallen, that they had not given all Europe such a convincing proof of their ignorance!—a proof by which their own country, I fear, is not in a state to profit as it ought.

. . . . Do you know, I doat on Mme de Sévigné too much to bear her being spoken even slightingly of. I have now read her over for the 3rd time with equal pleasure and redoubled admiration. I wish I could convey this taste to you, however you may think fit to despise it, because you would find it a source of great *cheerful interest*, which is a thing you want in life. . . . .

N. Audley Street, Monday, Nov. 4, 1799.

. . . . Imagine what the roads *must* be when we were 11 hours and ½ coming from Oxford with a p[r] of post horses in our own carriage. Posting is everywhere raised to 14 or 15 pence a mile, and the stage next London to 18[d]. The charges at the inns, too, seem to be encreased in proportion, so that the innkeepers, at least, will be no losers by the extravagant price to which I see everything is or will be immediately raised. . . . .

I am told the general discontent and ill-humour about Holland is great—well it may.* I could almost wish it greater, that

* This expedition to Holland was a grievous failure. On October 17, a

even sober, dull people might be convinced of the total incapacity of our Ministers for foreign affairs.

. . . . The weather is as completely wintry as it can be in December since we left Cheltenham. It has been continued cold rain and wind; wretched weather for the return of our poor troops! Most of them however, I understand, are already arrived. . . . .

Strawberry Hill, Tuesday, Nov. 12, 1799.

. . . . We mean to return here the beginning of next week. As we find our company a real comfort while they stay here, and that it is impossible to be more perfectly at one's ease and more comfortable than anybody may now be in this house, the having effected making this house, such as you remember it, both comfortable and warm, is nearly next to a miracle. The Burns, both Mr. and Mrs., you have heard me mention as very agreeable people, rational, well-informed, and cheerful; and we have besides sometimes Lady Howe * of an evening (now a neighbour at Twickenham), sometimes Lady Cecilia, and, in short, no want of *extraneous* company. . . . . Lady Ailesbury is, I think, particularly well and in good spirits, and is, indeed, the picture of what an old woman of between 70 and 80 ought to be, and so seldom is. Mrs. Damer chips away at her marble one half of the morning, and trots about the grounds the other half in all weathers, and is much the better for this variety of exercise. . . . .

Lady Howe, who was at the Drawing-room on Thursday, says all the poor officers look very thin and weather-beaten, and none of them much like talking of their adventures. Never was there such deadly fighting;—our men drawn up upon a totally exposed sandbank, where no considerable number could ever be formed together from the nature of the country (which I, who have been all over it, exactly recollect), set up as marks

suspension of arms was agreed on; and, as the price of permission to the British troops to re-embark on board their transports without molestation, 8,000 of the seamen, whether Batavian republicans or French, who were prisoners in England, were to be given up to the French Government: the combined English and Russian army to evacuate Holland before the end of November.

* Sophia Charlotte, Baroness Howe of Langar, daughter of Admiral first Earl Howe. She married, first, the Hon. Penn Asheton Curzon, and, secondly, Sir Jonathan Watkin Waller, Bart.

to be shot at by the people from their intrenchments, and from ditches, barns, and houses in the flat below them. Never was there nearly so large a portion of officers killed and wounded; in the 1st batt. of Guards six officers only escaped totally unhurt. The scene upon the parade when the Guards last week marched into town was, they say, heart-breaking; numbers of women and children running eagerly through the ranks and enquiring for husbands and fathers, of whose fate they were entirely ignorant, and many of whom they were destined never to see again! The houses of the officers of the Guards who arrived before the men were, they say, beset with women for the same purpose. Heavens! how much harder such a duty to a heart of humanity than any they had yet gone through! Lord Chatham was saved by the button of his epaulet, which turned aside a ball whose only effect was a great contusion on his shoulder. Thomas Grosvenor had half his moustache and the tip of his ear shot off. These are people not mentioned among the wounded. Grey, Sr Charles Grey's son, is still at the Helder, and, they say, cannot live, not having strength to bear a necessary amputation of leg. Colman, the maid of honour's brother, is shot through the lungs; cannot yet be turned in his bed, and is by no means out of danger. To all these people the French general and officers behave with the utmost degree of attention and kindness. . . . .

My young friend (for I cannot call her my *little* friend) Lady Georgiana Cavendish came to me in N. Audley Street. . . . She is a charming, warm-hearted, affectionate girl. . . . Lady Spencer, when we parted, *recommended* her to me with the most flattering expressions of all the service I might be to her. In this she probably deceives herself; but she shall not be deceived in me. . . .

Strawberry Hill, Tuesday, Nov. 19, 1799.

. . . . My other *adventures* in town, were going to Devonshire House to see Lady Georgiana, and become acquainted with the Duchess. Hitherto we had only known each other at second-hand. Her manner is very pleasing and unaffected. She was excessively civil to us, and asked us together next night, Saturday, to the play with her, where she has got a large private box. Poor Ag. was so unwell that she could not be of the party; but I went. The women were only the

D[ss], L[y] Georgiana, and myself. We had all the few men in London in the box, several that I knew, and it was very agreeable. There I first heard of this marvellous revolution in France, of which you will see the papers full; and, I fancy, more than the papers nobody can at present tell you. For my part, I think it will be better dealing with *one* or even with *three* rogues than 500; but it will, in all probability, shortly end in Bonaparte's assassination; for, in a country where every man thinks himself *equally able* and *equally fit* to govern, the government of one or two or three must ever be looked upon with invidious eyes, and not long *looked upon* at all, where murder is no crime.

Just before I left town, I received a note from the D[ss] about a print of L[d] Orford that I had promised her. She adds in the prettiest and most affectionate terms towards her daughter, that she must take the opportunity of telling how much she is flattered by 'the kindness I have shown to her dearest Georgiana.'* . . . .

* Saturday night.

As I am sure, my dear Miss Berry, you will not think ill of me for having a *hobby-horse*, and as I hope that you will not think me very impudent in urging its claims to you, I take the liberty of writing to ask you if, without indiscretion, I might petition for one of the private prints of Lord Orford. The Duke has given me the large-paper set; and I have the greatest wish to ornament it to my utmost with any prints, or even scraps of writing, &c., that may render it a treasure above other copies.

I have got all 'the noble authors' that Harding has engrav'd, and I shall procure drawings of the others; but, in spite of my eagerness in this pursuit, if I am guilty of an indiscretion, I entreat you to refuse me.

I must take this opportunity of telling you how very highly I am flattered by the kindness you have shown to my dearest G. I think her a very extraordinary creature, from the good qualities of her heart and mind; and how much then, loving her as I do to adoration, must I be gratified by a goodness which I must look upon as a very distinguished happiness to her!

Pray excuse this letter. Je dors debout et vous demande grâce; but I could not help writing to express my humble petition before your departure.

Pray say a thousand things to Mrs. Damer, whom I hope very soon to see at D. H. Felicissima notte.

G. Devonshire.

Dr Madam,—You have augmented the favour of accepting the print which I offered by your manner of claiming it.

Your Grace will observe that this portrait is the same as that prefixed to the works. It is one of the proof impressions which we had taken before we allowed the bookseller to make use of the plate. There are two other

Strawberry Hill, Tuesday, Nov. 26, 1799.

. . . . You will see by the papers, which contain all that anybody knows about France, that the Triumvirate have begun their government with just the same *bits of justice* that the last Revolution did, only sending a still *greater* number without a shadow of trial to Guiana. France is now to me like Caleb Williams, or some such vile interesting book, in which, tho' its principles disgust, one cannot help longing to know what will come next. . . . .

Strawberry Hill, Tuesday, Dec. 3, 1799.

. . . . Apropos to the Douglas's, they say his speech upon the Irish Union is one full of facts and information. It is directly in answer to Foster. The Irish Speaker's, the only rational one upon that side of the question. L[d] Minto's, upon the other, I have heard, too, universally praised as the clearly-stated and well-reasoned arguments of a great statesman. They are all published; and if you are curious upon the subject, I advise you to read them, which I mean to do, not by way of making up my mind upon the subject, which has long since been done, but to read some good sense and good reasoning upon it, of which the debates in the newspapers never contained a single word.

prints of Lord Orford, both of which, I think, should obtain a place in a complete copy of his works, and both of which I shall have the honour of offering your Grace when I return to town; for I cannot now lay my hand upon them.

I have likewise several other little scaps, both of prints and printing, which in the eyes of a *collector* are not without value, much at your service. I shall think myself happy in thus contributing my mite at once to your Grace's amusement, and to honouring the works of my deceased friend.

I cannot express how much I am gratified by the part of your note which relates to Lady Georgiana. I think I may venture to say that I am hardly less aware than yourself of the claims of her character, of the integrity and warmth of her heart, and the excellence of her understanding; and, indeed, the great disproportion between her years and mine makes your Grace perhaps the person in the world best able to judge of the nature of my affection for her. It is such as I shall rejoice in every occasion of proving, and such as will make me follow her happiness, her successes, her evils in life, with an anxiety and an interest which nothing but real friendship can feel, and real merit inspire.

I have the honour to be Your Grace's most obliged.

N. Audley Street, Monday, Dec. 16, 1799.

. . . . I have hardly been out of the house yet of an evening, and seen but few people in the morning: for receiving morning visits in London is the *abomination of desolation* of time, of which I never will be guilty—occupied you know I always am with one thing or another . . . . . . The Mathew Montagu's* I saw yesterday morning established in the ground-floor of the great house in Portman Sq^r, while the old lady, who no longer goes out at all and sees hardly anybody, occupies the grand-floor, an arrangement so proper and so natural that all the world wondered it was not done before. . . . . Last night we had a comfortable quiet game at whist here with only Mr. and Mrs. Burn, Jerningham, Mrs. Damer and myself, and M^dme De Coigny the latter part of the evening as a looker-on with Agnes. News there is none, French or English, public or private, or between Mr. Burn and Mme De Coigny we should have heard it. It is but too true that the French have left the support of their prisoners here to us, which in this time of scarcity is truly villainous and truly distressing. Some French people are already returning to France, and all the Royalists in high spirits. The fiction of having discovered the little Louis XVII. alive, nobody believes, and it is never hinted at in any of the French papers, tho' I own, if true after all, it would not at all surprise me; and I have ever thought when (if ever) peace and security comes, a great many of the guillotined will make their appearance again.

N. Audley Street, Thursday, Dec. 26, 1799.

. . . . . What little I could read during two days and part of two nights has been Mercier's† *Nouveau Paris*, a sort of continuation of his former *Tableau de Paris*. This last, in six vols. is one of the most stupid, unclearly thought, ridiculous books I ever saw, and yet I read it, not without entertainment and instruction; because I am sure that, without intending it,

* Mathew Montagu, Esq., born Nov. 1762; married, 1785, Elizabeth, daughter and heir of Francis Charlton, Esq., became fourth Lord Rokeky in 1829; died 1831.

† Bartholomew Mercier, a learned French bibliographer and miscellaneous writer, familiarly known by the name of the Abbé de St. Leger, was born 1734; died 1799.—*Le Nouveau Paris*, published 1799.

he gives me a better idea than anybody else of the state of mind and the habits of the people, and, consequently, of the real causes which have influenced them in the different *crises* of their revolution, and made them what they are. Yet I can hardly recommend the *lecture* to anybody else: for the facts he tells you, and the truths he lets you into, are all drowned in botherheaded arguments which don't deserve the name of reasoning, and false information, and false ideas. Of a very different nature is a little book I have lately read over again for the third or fourth time,—I mean, Mackintosh's accounts of his proposed lectures on the Law of Nature and Nations. Such a compendious syllabus of all the leading principles of truth and virtue I never met with! I mentioned it to you, I think, last year when I first got it. My approbation has now at least, none of the enthusiasm of novelty, but is the deep-felt approbation of a plain understanding and a warm heart.

G. Ellis's work will, I dare say, be very entertaining: when is it to make its appearance? he always writes neatly and well I think. Talking of works, don't let me forget to answer your question about the *Walpoliana.* If you had seen it, you would not doubt what we *must* think about it,—that it is infamous thus to make a dead man speak, and consequently say whatever his editor pleases, which is notoriously the case in many instances in the *Walpoliana,* besides repeating private and idle conversation, of which, of all other things, poor L[d] Orford had the greatest dread. I was at first almost sorry to find that the man had spoken civilly of us, for fear anybody might suppose we countenanced such a work; but I am told, which I own I did not expect, that it has not at all succeeded, that it is generally decried, known not to have our sanction, and that the bookseller has lost money by it, which last one must be glad to hear, as otherwise the editor might, and I dare say would, have made other two, or other six such vols., whenever he pleased.

THOUGHTS ON ARCHITECTURE, 1799.

The only art completely possessed by the architects of this country seems to be that of making a large building look small, in which their success is wonderful! As witness Somerset

Place, all the barracks, and indeed almost all the public buildings of this reign (George III.).

London itself seems to have been built as if by common consent upon this principle. All enormous as it is, it is only a congregation of smaller towns. Grosvenor Square, one of the largest in Europe, has by no means an imposing air in proportion to the magnitude of its space; because neither the houses as parts of that space, nor the doors and windows as parts of those houses, are at all in proportion to it. Proportion! that indefinable soul of beauty in almost all external objects!

Very different was the art of the M. Angelos, the Bramantes, the Palladios, and Scamozzis. *They* contrived, often in a very confined space, by a division of large parts in proportion to one another and to the whole (whatever that whole might be), to impress with ideas of grandeur and magnitude. A strong instance of this, among thousands that might be re-called, is the entrance into the Laurentian Library at Florence, designed by M. Angelo. It is just twenty-two feet square, from the middle of which springs a staircase; yet so far from giving an idea of anything small or crowded, it is impossible not to be struck with an idea of size and even magnificence on entering it.

EXTRACTS FROM LETTERS.

1800.

'WE are at Strawberry Hill in November. We go in the winter to Broadlands, and in our way there to the Bishop of Winchester at Farnham.'

A few extracts from Miss Berry's letters to Mrs. Cholmeley and others, together with the play-bill of the pieces performed at Strawberry Hill, and the prologue written by Lord Mount Edgcumbe,* which were treasured amongst her papers, is all that remains of this year.

N. Audley St., Thursday, Jan. 2, 1800.

. . . . To-day we are flattered with a thaw, but I fear it is too good to last. Most earnestly it is to be wished on every account, for if we were to continue to have a very hard winter, much cattle, I should fear, must absolutely be starved, to say nothing of man.

What think you of the *man Buonaparte*?† absolute King of France, quietly established in the Tuileries! For my part I admire him, and think, if he can keep his place, he does his country a service. Nothing ever gave me so desperate an opinion of our Ministers and their yet more desperate projects than the abuse which is daily vomited forth in all the ministerial and soi-disant impartial papers against Buonaparte and this new order of things. Formerly they said we were fighting and aiding the other side because it was impossible to make peace with an absolutely democratical government; now that an absolutely aristocratical government is established, what is it to us whether Louis Capet or Louis Buonaparte is at its

* Richard, second Earl of Mount Edgcumbe, born 1764; married Sophia Hobart, daughter of John, second Earl of Buckinghamshire; died 1839.

† Buonaparte was appointed First Consul. Sièyes and Roger Ducos were displaced in favour of Cambacères and Le Brun.

head? If the nation is once in a state to maintain the relations of peace and the conditions of treaties, what *have* we, what *ought* we to have to do with the means? I confess that, as a citizen of enlightened Europe, after all the various tyrannies under which the French have laboured, I should really be sorry to see them return to their old original worn-out tyranny under the Bourbons. For slaves I am convinced they can be alone fit, till their many stains, contracted in the *fange* of the despotism in which they were born and bred, have been washed out and purified by a purgatory of I know not how many revolutions; but to return so soon and after such dreadful convulsions to the point from whence they set out, even I don't wish them.

I have been reading (for the little I could read) a new novel of Godwin's, in four vols., called 'The Travels of St. Leon.'* It is an odd work, like all his, and, like all his, interesting, tho' hardly ever pleasantly so; and while one's head often agrees with his observations, and sometimes with his reasoning, never does one's heart thoroughly agree with his sentiments on any subject or in any character. He now *allows* that the social affections may be cultivated to advantage in human life, and upon this plan his present novel is formed. I should tell you, which I know from Edwards, that it was written for bread, agreed for by the booksellers beforehand, and actually composed and written as the printers wanted it. I think you will see many marks of this throughout the work if you read it, which I should recommend to you, if, like me, you have not seen a *readable* novel for this age. Lord Minto's speech on the Union is really a very clear, logical, and admirable dissertation upon federal governments and the various modes of separate and united legislatures, but I do not think his logic is sufficiently abridged, concentrated, and forcibly put, for a speech delivered in any public assembly, where one must always count upon one quarter being stupid and three parts idle. The first frank I get I will send you a copy of a letter of the K. of Naples to Lord Nelson, which I think will please.

N. Audley Street, Saturday, Jan. 11, 1800.

Mrs. John Hunter is assuredly and declaredly not

* By William Godwin, published 1799.

the author of the plays. St. Leon, when you get it, I think you will find a very disagreeable book.

Feb. 1800.

I am much more disgusted in society by the little impression made by real merit, than by the so often lamented tolerance of vice. This tolerance—for tolerance only it is—cannot *satisfy* even those who are the objects of it, and could never be borne by a mind deserving anything more. By *real merit* I don't mean partial excellence or particular talents, that make themselves useful, or desirable in this or that particular situation or circumstance, for these, I think, are always rated even above par in the stock of common esteem. But I mean general superiority of intellect and excellence of character. In what light must the steady, rational, consistent mind, which such superiority and such excellence supposes, view, not the incapacity of one-half of the world to distinguish them at all, but the very little impression made on those who *have* distinguished, and *would* be capable of appreciating them? How often will they have occasion to refer to that philosophy and knowledge of human nature which must necessarily form a part of their character, when they see that all their excellences and all their acquirements will not outweigh the most trifling object of self-interest, the most open attacks of flattery, or even the pushing perseverance of those who, conscious they have little else to recommend them, take care by being always in the way, to make it much less trouble to take notice of than to avoid them.

The false pictures given of human life in most novels, and which alone (in my opinion) makes them dangerous reading for young people, is, not that the sentiments and conduct of the hero or heroine are exalted above the common level of humanity, for there is no well-conceived novel which is not read by many an ingenuous and noble mind, who can reflect with pleasure that *they* have acted on some occasion with all the high sense of honour, the exalted generosity, the noble disinterestedness described in their author. But what they must not look for in real life, what they would expect in vain, what it is necessary to guard them against, is, supposing that such conduct will make a similar impression on those around them, that the sacrifices they make will be considered, and the principles on which they act understood and valued, as the novel writer, at his good pleasure, makes them. Among the thousands who have erred like *Julia*, how many more have resembled her in character and subsequent conduct than in possessing a friend like *Claire!*

It was during the month of November this year, when Miss Berry mentions they were staying at Strawberry Hill, that Mrs. Damer indulged in the favourite amusement of private theatricals, on which occasion Miss Berry, her sister, and her father took part.

THEATRE, STRAWBERRY HILL,

November, 1800.

Will be presented a COMEDY in Two Acts, called

THE OLD MAID.

Mr. Harlow	Mr. BURN.
Clerimont	EARL of MOUNT EDGCUMBE.
Captain Cape	Mr. BERRY.
Mrs. Harlow	Miss BERRY.
Miss Harlow	Mrs. BURN.
Trifle	Miss A. BERRY.

To which will be added,

THE INTRIGUING CHAMBERMAID.

Goodall	Mr. BURN.
Valentine	EARL of MOUNT EDGCUMBE.
Oldcastle	Mr. BERRY.
Trusty and *Col. Bluff*	Mr. HERVEY.
Slap and *Security*	Mr. CAMPBELL.
Mrs. Highman	Mrs. BURN.
Charlotte	Miss A. BERRY.
Lettice	Hon. Mrs. DAMER.

The PROLOGUE to the Performance to be spoken by the EARL of MOUNT EDGCUMBE.

The EPILOGUE by the Hon. Mrs. DAMER.

PROLOGUE,

WRITTEN BY THE EARL OF MOUNT EDGCUMBE,

And spoken by him at the opening of the Theatre, Strawberry Hill, Nov. 1800.

Noise and disputing behind the Scenes.—The Curtain begins to rise.

(*Speaks within.*)

HOLD, hold! What 's this? No prologue to our play?
Down with the curtain—let it down, I say;
Let me go forth—I must, I will have way!

(*Enters.*)

So, I 've escaped at length; with much ado,
With threats, entreaties, ay, and wrangling too,
I 've forc'd my passage, ere the curtain rise,
To mark your looks, your thoughts to scrutinize,
And read our doom, before-hand, in your eyes.
Long in the green-room was the point contested;
Scarce to my pray'r a half-assent I 'd wrested;
When, loudly summon'd by the prompter's bell,
(To young adventurers tremendous knell!)
Restraint disdaining, hastily I flew
To state the case, and plead my cause to you.
What! an unpractis'd, novice band engage,
With vent'rous step, to tread the awful stage;
Before this dread tribunal dare t' appear;
Face such an audience as I now see here;
Nor send one humble messenger before,
To court your favor, and your smile implore!
Thus did I vainly urge: they all reply,
'But who so bold will venture?' Who will?—I.
Give *me* your Prologue; let this task be mine,
Or I 'll no longer be your Valentine.*
Thus then—but soft! methinks I here descry
Smiles of good humour beam from ev'ry eye;
The gen'rous sentiment each bosom move,
That prompts to pardon, if it can't approve:
Yes, in these partial looks with pride I view
Our fondest wishes realiz'd by you.
No more, no more: I'll hasten to my friends;
Tell them, in their despite, I've gain'd my ends;
Bid them with confidence dispel their fear,
Certain to meet a kind reception here.

---

* The part of Valentine in the 'Intriguing Chambermaid.'

It was at the close of this year that Lady Georgiana Cavendish's marriage was settled with the Earl of Carlisle. Miss Berry's continued and affectionate interest in her welfare is warmly expressed in her letter of congratulation to her brother, Lord Hartington, in answer to the announcement of the intended marriage.

Little Strawb., Tuesday, Dec. 23, 1800.

Let me congratulate you upon what seems to give you all so much pleasure, and which I enter into as heartily as I can, considering how little I personally know the person in question. I hope at least he is worthy of her, that he is aware of, and will do justice to, her character. . . . She has a deep, serious, thinking mind and a warmth and integrity of heart which will constitute her happiness while doing right, and her misery if led into error. What a character to set out with! What ties upon her good conduct in every relation of life! It is he, he that is to be congratulated. May he know, and deserve his happiness, by contributing to hers!

Let us hope that, as she deserves all good, all good awaits her, which no heart but your own can invoke more sincerely, or rejoice in more thoroughly, than that of your faithfully attached

M. Berry.

PRIVATE THEATRICALS AT STRAWBERRY HILL.

1801.

THE only entry in Miss Berry's Memoranda, for this year, is, that the amusement of private theatricals at Strawberry Hill was repeated, and,for the first time, a comedy in five acts, written by Miss Berry herself, and entitled 'Fashionable Friends,' was performed by the troop of amateur actors. The Prologue and Epilogue were contributed by her friend Miss Joanna Baillie,* and are pleasing specimens of that kind of composition. The parts were cast as follows:—

FASHIONABLE FRIENDS.

COMEDY in Five Acts.

Dramatis Personæ.

Sir Dudley Dorimant	Lord MOUNT EDGCUMBE.
Sir Valentine Vapour	Mr. BERRY.
Mr. Lovell	Mr. BROWNLOW NORTH.
John	Mr. CAMPBELL.
Lapierre	Mr. BURN.
Doctor Syrop	———
Lady Selina Vapour	Honourable Mrs. DAMER.
Mrs. Lovell	Miss BERRY.
Mrs. Rackett	Mrs. BURN.
Miss Rackett	Miss A. BERRY.
Trimming	Lady ELIZABETH COLE.

* Miss Berry's intimacy with this distinguished authoress appears to have been well established at this time, and she preserved to the last a very high opinion of Miss Baillie's poetical powers, and the greatest esteem and affection for her character.

PROLOGUE TO THE 'FASHIONABLE FRIENDS.'*

BY MISS JOANNA BAILLIÈ.

IN ancient times, when harvest's yellow store,
In barns well lodged, call'd to the field no more,
And good folks sat the cheerful fire about,
And merry mummers play'd, and loud laugh'd every lout,
Winter approach'd with no forbidding grace,
And dull November wore a waggish face.
In the same season, whilst our favour'd land
Toasts Ceres' bounty and the olive wand,
We 've dight us out in guise and motley geer,
And thus before these friendly ranks appear.
As heretofore you 've been, Oh! be ye still
The gentle judges of our mimick skill!
Before you now we bring—I will aver it—
A comedy of no ignoble merit,
If wit, and sense, and unstrained nature may
Its listed pleader warrant so to say.
Such as to please had own'd no humble pow'rs,
Taste, not perhaps quite so refined as ours,
In other days, when plays, as plays have been,
Were written to be heard as well as seen,
And gleams of cheering favour sometimes thrown
On what was said as well as what was shown.
But times, like the clos'd scen'ry of a play,
With all their good old fashions, pass away.
If nought but plot and bustle can engage
(That hunt-the-slipper bus'ness of the stage)

* Hampstead, October 14, 1801.

I send you a plain simple Prologue of no pretensions, but such I hope as you will not dislike; if you do, throw it aside, and I shall not be at all offended. Whatever I have done in the way of poetry I am sure I have lied well for you, and that is all the merit I can claim. I should have sent it to you sooner, but I have been very much occupied in a great many divers ways, and of all things I hate at present to write one word more than I can possibly help.

I hope you receive pleasure from this blessed prospect of peace that is opened upon us so suddenly. I have rejoiced heartily, and paid for our clay and candles with no begrudging spirit. Perhaps it opens to you some pleasant views independent of the public good. If it does, may they prove in reality such as your imagination represents them.

Farewell! and let me hear soon how you do.

Yours affectionately,

J. B.

Your much-priz'd favour now, so let it be,
I drop my claim, and urge another plea.
This piece an outcast helpless foundling stands,
Whose uncapp'd head receives from worldly hands
No kind endearing stroke. 'Out on the brat!
'Tis harelipp'd, ricketty, and blear'd, and squat,
And squints, and halts. Away, I can't abide!'
Alas! no partial parent smiles beside.
But do the generous such sternness show
To the outcast and the unown'd? O no!
They look on such still with a friendly eye,
And in its form ev'n added beauties spy;
As left and lonely things, with wondrous grace,
Wave their neglected heads in some unbidden place.
Then to this gen'ral sympathy confess'd,
A native inmate of each gentle breast,
I'll freely leave it, with no anxious fear,
To meet the judgment that awaits it here.

EPILOGUE.

BY MISS JOANNA BAILLIE.

Whilst fogs along the Thames' damp margin creep,
And cold winds through his leafless willows sweep,
And fairy elves, whose summer sport hath been
To foot it lightly on the moonlight green,
Now, hooded close, in many a cowering form,
Troop with the surly spirits of the storm;
Whilst by the blazing fire, with saddled nose,
The sage turns o'er his leaves of tedious prose,
And o'er their new-dealt cards, with eager eye,
Pale dowagers look and smile, or inly sigh,
And blooming maids from silken work-bags pour,
Like tangled sea-weed on the vexed shore,
Of patch-works, nettings, fringe, a strange and motley store;
Whilst all, attempting many a different mode,
Would from their shoulders hitch times' heavy load,
Thus have we chose, in comic sock bedight,
To wrestle with a long November night.
'In comic sock!' methinks indignant cries
Some grave fastidious friend, with angry eyes,
Scowling severe, 'No more the phrase abuse!
So shod indeed there had been some excuse,
But in these walls, once a well-known retreat,
Where taste and learning kept a fav'rite seat;
Where Gothic arches, with a solemn shade,

Should o'er the thoughtful mind their influence spread;
Where pictures, vases, busts, and precious things,
Still speak of sages, poets, heroes, kings,
On which the stranger looks with pensive gaze,
And thinks upon the worth of other days;
Where learning's rock, the time-defying Press,
Hath oft sent forth, prankt in its wordy dress,
The new-coin'd thought, in fair and goodly print,
Sterling and bright as guinea from the Mint;—
Like foolish children in their mimick play,
Confined at grandame's on a rainy day,
Who borrow'd robes o'er stools and benches sweep,
And thro' chink'd doors and tattered curtains peep,
With paltry farce, and all its bastard train,
Grotesque and broad such precincts to profane!
It is a shame—but no, I will not speak;
It makes the blood rise mantling to my cheek.'
Indeed, wise Sir! Perhaps 'tis very true;
But lack a day! what will not woman do?
Ah! he who o'er our heads those arches bent,
And stored these relics dear to sentiment,
More mild than you, with grave pedantic pride,
Would not have ranged him on your surly side.
But now to you, who on our frolic scene
Have look'd well pleased, and gentle critics been,
Who have received, with minds from caption freed,
The better will, for the imperfect deed,
Nor would our homely humour proudly spurn,—
To you, the good, the gay, the fair I turn,
And thank you all; if, here, our feeble powers
Have lightly wing'd for you some wintry hours;
If these remembered scenes, that now are past,
Shall on some future minutes pleasure cast;
Shall still amidst your mazy fancies gleam,
Or on your pillow hang one pleasant dream;
To right good end we 've worn our mumming guise,
And we 're repaid and happy—ay, and wise!
Who says we are not; on his sombre birth
Gay Fancy smil'd not, nor heart-light'ning Mirth,
Home let him hie to his unsocial rest,
And heavy set the night mare on his joyless breast!

The following verses may be considered as a tribute to the success of 'Fashionable Friends,' written by some approving spectator, but no name is given:—

Verses sent to Mrs. Damer after the first representation of the 'Fashionable Friends' at Strawberry Hill, Nov. 1801.

Sweet be the rest and undisturbed
That crowns the pleasant toil to-night,
And long may its remembrance live,
Long, long be cherish'd with delight.

Or if the spirits, highly wrought,
Court not so soon th' oblivious hour;
If e'en in slumbers unsubdued,
Genius and Fancy yet have power;

(Since all that beauties choose to say
With faith implicit is receiv'd,
Since ladies never yet could lie,
And tales so grave are sure believ'd,)

O! may the parent of your child,
For your fond cares his thanks bestow,
Farquhar support the trembling sprite,
While Damer wreathes his modest brow.

Mark how he bends to sprightly Burn,
See how he kneels at Berry's feet,
And owns that, but for Edgcumbe's worth,
He could have punish'd foul deceit.

That youth—O'Brien is his name?
His hand the grateful Bard shall seize,
Glad on *some* stage to find again
One gentleman who moves with ease.

The vision flies—but not in dreams
Alone shall live this pleasant night,
For long shall its remembrance live,
Long, long be cherish'd with delight.

The more critical prose opinion, which appears to have been written by some other spectator, but to whose MS. no name is appended, was certainly encouraging to give a wider publicity than that of private theatricals to 'Fashionable Friends.'

The great strength of the play is witty sprightly dialogue, kept up uniformly throughout, without ever flagging in any part; and in the great skill with which one of the chief characters, Lady Selina, is drawn: the weakness, if it has any, seems to me to be this, that the plan and conduct of the plot resemble those of many plays that we have already, and the first part of the play has, perhaps, less action carried on in it than the present taste in plays may require. I think, however, that its strength will do more than get the better of its weakness, and that represented in a theatre where the dialogue may be distinctly heard, it will meet with the warmest applause.

The event of the following year unhappily proved that this prophecy was not fulfilled.

1802.

The state of the Continent now enabled Miss Berry again to indulge in her taste for foreign travel, and after an interval of eleven years, she left England with Mrs. Damer, on a visit to Paris.

A visit of scarcely more than a month's duration, to a foreign country, can furnish but little deeper than surface knowledge of its social and political condition; in so short a time, little can be gathered which does not come under the traveller's own immediate observation.

Miss Berry made notes of *what* she saw and of *who* she saw. The social habits and the persons composing the society through which she was now passing, had undergone great changes since she had last been in France, and she set down in detail whatever came before her eyes. Her Journal is, strictly speaking, a daily account of what she saw and did at Paris, and nothing more; it contains neither essays, speculations, or prophecies. She saw and made acquaintance with many whose names had already become historical, but had more opportunity of observing their personal appearance than of judging of their character or conversation; to her it was the exchange from the misty ideas associated with mere names, to the substantive reality of living men, and though the perusal of her Journal cannot impart a similar gratification to others, it tends to approximate the reader to those times and scenes, to which he is thus introduced, by an eye-witness.

Miss Berry was much impressed with the magnificence of the interior decorations of the Tuileries, and of the official houses of ministers, &c.; but so great has been the subsequent development of manufacturing power and tasteful skill, that many objects which then excited her surprise by their richness and splendour, are now within reach of moderate fortunes to procure, and the silk hangings, embroidered muslins, rich candelabra, and ornamental furniture, &c., are to be found repeated over and over again in the large country-houses of England. Some allowance must also be made for the heightened effect which novelty and fashion give to whatever is decorative. It would seem, for instance, that in 1802 the combination of mahogany and ormolu, carried with it ideas of richness and elegance, that it would not now convey, and handsome mirrors were thought to have gained in effect by light drapery, in place of the massive gold frames now again so highly prized; but Miss Berry was an experienced judge of luxury and magnificence, and the impression conveyed to her mind by what she saw of republican splendour was no doubt correct, according to the taste of the time.

JOURNAL.

Monday, March 8th.—Left London at half-past eleven o'clock, arrived at Sittingbourne at seven in the evening. The road from London to Dartford so very deep in stiff mud that four horses could hardly drag the coach (though by no means heavy) at more than a foot's pace for several miles together. The morning foggy and very cold. No great road that I know in England is so tedious to travel as this to Dover; the stages are long, the road continually up and down hills, several of which are long and severe, and the postilions in all the stages stop at a half-way house to give their horses water. To go from London to Dover in one day would at the best time of the year be a very long day's journey.*

* This once laborious day's journey is now accomplished in 2 hours and 20 min.; and that from London to Paris in 9 hours.

Tuesday, 9*th*.—Arrived at Dover at half-past one o'clock. The day bright and sunny, but cold, with a great deal of wind at north-east. The country about Canterbury pretty, even at this bare season. Saw Dover Castle from a hill six miles from Dover. The York Hotel at Dover much more cheerfully situated, looking to the sea, than the 'City of London,' and the accommodation much better. Since dinner I have walked down to the pier; though I have twice landed here before from France, I was always sick and sorry, and in a hurry to get away, and never walked about the place. It is picturesquely situated close under its high chalk cliffs, the most elevated point of which is surmounted by its fine and extensive castle, its inner and outer harbour, both crowded with shipping, which interrupts the view of a number of mean-looking houses. All this I have seen this afternoon lighted up by a bright sun, and it has struck me very much. Had we arrived here a couple of hours sooner, so as to have got our carriage on board, and to have saved the tide, there was wind enough to have carried us to Calais in two hours and a half; but having missed the day's tide, it would be useless to sail in the night, as at whatever time we reached Calais we should be kept on board our vessel till the morning.

Wednesday, 10*th*.—A clear sunny day, with hardly a cloud. Went on board the Swift, Captain Blake, at Dover quay, at eleven o'clock; got to Calais harbour at ten minutes past four, and alongside the quay in ten minutes more, the same tide carrying us from one harbour to the other. The pier and the quay were crowded with sailor-looking people, as there was another English packet just leaving the quay with a number of passengers.

A shabby custom-house officer immediately came on board the vessel (an old invalid officer or soldier, I know not which), begged to see our passports, and desired us to write down our names and nations. We were kept on board till somebody from the vessel had gone and returned to some municipal officer; not the smallest rude comment or remark was made upon us by the crowd upon the quay, and the moment the captain said we might leave the vessel, half a dozen dirty civil hands were held out to help us up the ladder. With the captain of our vessel and the old invalid (or whatever he was) we proceeded first to one of the low small houses close by the quay, where our names and nations were again set down, and then to a sort of bureau of the custom-house, where we were desired to *declare* if we had anything upon us *contre les droits*; our declaration in the negative being immediately taken, we went, still with our captain, our old invalid, and M. Quillaque (the successor of M. Dessein), who had now joined us, to the Hôtel de Ville, where the commissaire de police read our passport, and everyone answered to their names. Here we left our pass from M. Otto * with a promise from the commissaire that we should have his that evening. All these ceremonies passed without any rudeness, impertinent questions, or delays whatsoever.

From the Maison de Ville we went directly to Dessein's, and were in possession of a very comfortable apartment by five o'clock. The only thing that I remarked with surprise at Calais was that in passing from the quay through the gates and the market-place, and from thence to the inn, I did not see one single soldier except a sentinel at the door of the Maison de Ville. Dessein's inn is very clean and comfortable, but neither the cooking nor the wine good, and immoderately dear.

* Louis Guillaume Otto, a native of Baden, was the French commissioner for prisoners in England. He was born 1754; employed in early life by M. de la Luzerne, made Comte de Moslay by Buonaparte in 1805, and a Peer of France by Louis XVIII.—*Correspondence of Lord Cornwallis*, vol. iii. p. 385.

Thursday, 11*th*.—Left Calais between eight and nine o'clock. The first thing that must strike anybody who knew the appearance of this part of the country formerly, is the improved state of cultivation, all the land looking clean, well cropped, and neatly ploughed, and the cottages cleaner (on the outside at least) and infinitely more comfortable than they were. I think, too, those scattered about the country were more numerous than formerly. The people, the children particularly, struck me as looking much better, fatter, fairer, and better fed.* The only buildings that wear a melancholy and ruinous appearance in the country are the poor churches, all of which, even in the little villages, have their windows broken, the tops of their spires knocked off, and with most of them their roofs falling to pieces; at the same time I believe they are almost all used. Those belonging to abbeys, of which in the course of this day's journey we passed two or three, are, for the most part, actually pulled down. They have been sold to individuals with ground belonging to the establishment, and have been taken down piecemeal as they found means of using or disposing of the materials.

The road between Calais and Montreuil is excellent. Between every change of horses there is now one, and generally two turnpikes,—a simple bar, which would, in case of necessity, push across the road, not like our gates. The tolls are very high (for a berlin with six horses and a courier, 57 livres between Calais and Paris, 2*l*. 7*s*. 6*d*.), and I find, it is supposed, at present, that the necessities of the Government do not allow much

* Miss Berry's personal observations on this subject fully bear out M. de Tocqueville's opinions, written about fifty years later:—'La révolution d'ailleurs n'avait pas accablé le pays d'une manière égale; quelques-uns en avaient porté le faix, un grand nombre y avaient trouvé des biens très-précieux mêlés aux maux qu'elle causait. Je crois que le peuple proprement dit avait été beaucoup moins atteint dans son bien-être qu'on ne se l'imagine communément.'—*Œuvres et Correspondance inédites d'Alexis de Tocqueville, par Gustave de Beaumont.*

of it to go to the conservation of the road. However, there were many people working where it was out of repair. At Saumer, a wretched little town two posts from Boulogne, where the carriage, according to the *ancien régime*, was surrounded by beggars, I observed *the first tree of liberty* I have yet seen. It was a shabby little lime, which had been transplanted when too old to flourish, and was surrounded by a little white railing, in the *place* or market-place.

At Montreuil, where we slept, l'Église de Notre Dame, the principal church in the town, is an entire ruin, nothing remaining but a part of the walls, the broken tracery of some very handsome Gothic windows, and one or two of the Gothic pillars of the inside. On questioning the people at the inn at what time their church was *démolie*, they all denied it being demolished, and said it had fallen down. At last the maid who was waiting upon us owned that it had been pulled down—that a rich individual of the town had bought the church and meant to preserve it, but that the people of the place, *dans le temps de la terreur* (which they now all talk of as if it had taken place in the days of St. Louis), had threatened him with the guillotine if he did not allow it to be destroyed, and so, indeed, it has been most completely. But what struck us extremely, was the sort of shyness which the people had, both to ourselves and servants, of owning this, or allowing it to have been demolished, as if they considered it as a disgrace. Two convents were likewise destroyed in this little town. It possessed no less than seven churches; the one I have mentioned is the only one destroyed, but of the seven there are but two open for worship. All the châteaux (of which we passed several small ones in this day's journey) in part or in whole shut up and visibly neglected, but not defaced or pulled down.

Friday, 12*th*.—Left Montreuil. The road sandy and the country near it very open, but everywhere well cultivated. Much wood about a long straggling village through which we passed, all the houses thatched, and every one having a garden or an orchard belonging to them.

At Namport, the first post from Montreuil, a wretched village, a shabby wooden cross is still subsisting, placed against a bank, the first I have seen in France. Of a large château very near the road, in a village near Nouvion, the windows were broken and shut up, and the woods and walks neglected but not cut down. Abbeville, which is a large town, struck me as looking very wretched; indeed, it is the appearance of the country, its culture, and its inhabitants, not of the towns and little bourgs, that is improved. The fortifications of Abbeville seem quite neglected, and in some places pulled down. I observed fixed against the gate a *Défense aux Citoyens*, in the name of *liberté* and *égalité*, to pull down or injure the walls, &c. There is a small barrack near the gate, at the entrance of which I saw a dragoon, absolutely the first soldier (the sentinel at Calais excepted) I have seen in France. While our horses were changing, observing a church very near the post-house less mutilated than usual and open, I ran over to see it. It was in tolerable good order inside, with some pictures remaining, and the brass candlesticks of the principal altar. In each of the side aisles was a priest standing at a table and surrounded by above a hundred poor ragged children of both sexes, whom he was hearing their catechism. Road beyond Abbeville planted with apple trees on each side for several miles, all of which are in good order, and many young ones neatly and carefully planted.

Flexcourt and Pecquigny are wretched villages in the old style, full of beggars. At Flexcourt we were detained twenty minutes for horses. Near Pecquigny, on the bank of the Somme, is the very large Abbaye du Garde.* The

* The Abbaye du Garde is occupied by monks of the order of La Trappe. —*Murray's Handbook*, 1844. The present proprietor of the Abbaye du Garde is M. Bocquillon de Genlis. 1860.

church is entirely pulled down. The Abbaye, which looks like a large modern-built château, is purchased by a negociant of Amiens, who inhabits it as his country house. Immediately above the village of Pecquigny is a large château of the Cte. D'Artois's,* with half the roof off and otherwise quite ruined.

Arrived at Amiens, through a very long, straggling, dirty faubourg. The town itself looks well, and has wide and good streets. The cathedral here has not been touched, and the people boast they have heard much more than they have seen of the Revolution. We sent a note to Lord Cornwallis to enquire after him, asking his orders for Paris. Mr. Merry † knew of our coming, and was with us in an hour after we arrived. The account he gave of the way in which the negotiators pass their time at Amiens was curious. Lord Cornwallis riding every morning, and Joseph Buonaparte not getting up till one or two o'clock. The conferences, which are very

* The Castle of Pecquigny was built at the end of the fifteenth century. Madame de Sevigné thus describes it in her letter, dated April 27, 1639:—'C'est un vieux bâtiment élevé au-dessus de la ville comme Grignan; un parfaitement beau chapitre comme en Grignan; un doyen, douze chanoines; je ne sais si la fondation est aussi belle, mais ce sont des terrasses sur la rivière de Somme qui fait cent tours dans les prairies; voilà ce qui n'est point à Grignan. Il y a un camp de César à un quart de lieu d'ici, dont on respecte encore les tranchées.'

The castle of Pecquigny was sold by Jean d'Ailly, in 1774, for 500,000 frs. to M. de Ber, who resold it the following year to the Jew Calmer; finding his religion deprived him of the power of appointing to the dependent livings, he resold it to the Comte d'Artois, who kept it till the Revolution. The castle was then sold as national property. It belongs now to the Baron Adrien de Morgan, Membre du Conseil Général de la Somme, who bought it twelve or fifteen years ago from the post-master at Pecquigny.

† Lord Cornwallis, in writing to a friend, says of his mission:—'My family on this occasion is circumscribed, and, exclusively of Mr. Merry, who has been negotiating at Paris, and Mr. Moore, of the Secretary of State's office, who is to act under him, consists only of Lt.-Col. Littlehales, and Lt.-Col. Nightingall.' Mr. Andrew Merry married, in 1803, the widow of John Leather, Esqr., was Minister in France, the United States, Denmark, and Sweden, from April 1802 to April 1809. He died 1835.—*Correspondence of Lord Cornwallis,* vol. iii. p. 384.

frequent; never begin till three or four, and last till dinner, which is never sooner than six, seven, or eight o'clock. These dinners are confined to a round of four or five houses, of which the Prefect and the Mayor of the town are two, and they are all heartily tired of always seeing the same faces. These dinners, however, last a very short time; the carriages are kept waiting, and then they all go to the theatre, except our good Lord Cornwallis, who sits on quietly drinking a glass of wine with anybody who will sit with him.*

Saturday, 13th.—Left Amiens. In the very open country I observed some women for the first time working in the fields. Beyond St. Just, for a quarter of a mile, the road so bad that I think in wet weather a heavy English berlin would not have been able to pass, but everywhere a quantity of materials are to be seen ready collected for repairs. At Breteuil a large new château more than half demolished. At Clermont is a large park of the Duc de Fitz-James.† The house is entirely

* This account is fully confirmed by the following extracts from a letter of Lt.-Col. Nightingall:—'Nobody need envy us; the only thing like comfort is on those days when we dine quietly at home by ourselves, and as for amusements, there are none of any kind. . . . . We meet every day the same people, and always the same formal parties at dinner. The company consists of Joseph Buonaparte, who is rather the best among them, though he has not at all the manners of a gentleman; he means, however, to do well and to be civil. His wife (Maria Julia Clary, m. 1794) is a very short, very thin, very ugly, and very vulgar little woman, without anything to say for herself. The Dutch Ambassador is, I think, above par, and his wife, who has been pretty, has more the manners of a gentlewoman than any one here. The next in the list is the Prefect (Nicholas Marie Quinette, afterwards Baron de Rochemont). He is a very ill-looking scoundrel, and was a member of the National Convention . . . This man is not likely to become a bosom friend of ours. . . . The next are the Mayor and his wife. . . . We have generally one or two great dinners a week—dine once at Joseph's and once at Schimmelpennick's, and sometimes with the Mayor or Prefect. As there is no variety whatever, you are now in possession of our style of living at Amiens. . . . I forgot to mention that when we dine out we get nothing fit to eat or drink, which does not add much to the pleasure or satisfaction of the party.'—*Correspondence of Lord Cornwallis,* vol. iii. p. 436.

† The park and château, formerly the property of the Duke de Fitzjames, are passed on the right (from St. Just) shortly before reaching Clermont

pulled down,' and there are breaches in the park wall every here and there, but the trees are untouched and flourishing. The country about Clermont and Lingueville, and between it and Chantilly, very pretty.

Sunday, 14th.—Not a single tree cut down in the road between Chantilly and Paris. The château at Chantilly totally demolished; the stables remained, and have been used as dragoon barracks. The town through which we passed (for the inn, a new one, is beyond the town) looked, I thought, much worse than formerly. At a village between Lusarche and Ecouen, where there is a large stone church undefaced, many people were going to church. At another village, upon another undefaced church the words *Temple de la Raison* were painted over. Most of the churches between Chantilly and Paris are less injured than any that we have yet seen. I wish I could say as much of the venerable and beautiful church of St. Denis, now christened *la Franciade*, but universally *called* St. Denis. Its roof is more than half off, that is to say, nothing but the broken *charpente* left, which has the most melancholy appearance possible, and one of its spires is quite destroyed, down to the tower, from which it rose. The corresponding spire seems to have been spared, and the portail and the beautiful Gothic tracery of the east window appeared to me, as I saw it (*en passant*), not much injured. The entrance to Paris this way was never striking, and we had got into the Chaussée d'Autin, now called the Rue du Mont Blanc, and stopped at Perrégaux's* door, before I knew where we were. The Boulevard struck me, as it always did, with its appearance of gaiety, though I think the large

sur Oise.—*Murray's Handbook*, 1834. The present owner is M. de Beaumesril. 1860.

* Jean Frederic Perrégaux, Senator and President of the Bank at Paris, was born at Neufchatel, in Switzerland. He established one of the first banking houses in Paris, and was much favoured by Napoleon.—*Dict. des Contemporains.*

houses looked less well painted, and less well kept up than they used to be. From Perrégaux's door we drove to the Hôtel de l'Empire, Rue Cerutti, a street above the Boulevard where we had taken an apartment. The salon was adorned with great glasses and expensive pieces of furniture, but was by no means as comfortable as any apartments I ever occupied before in Paris, and is at the enormous price of eighteen louis for fifteen days, or thirty for a month. After a little consideration, a little murmuring, and a good deal of regret at losing time in getting settled, we sent the maid and the courier in search of another in the Faubourg St. Germain, the quarter of Paris to which we were both most accustomed. After a tedious absence they returned, having been in more than half-a-dozen hotels which were all full, but saying that we might have the first floor of the Hôtel d'Orléans, Rue des Petits Augustins, for the next day, at the rate of five louis a week. The hotels in the F. St. Germain are no longer the fashion, as they used to be. The brilliant *quartier* is the one we left, and is so far convenient that it is now near all the theatres, and in the Hôtel de l'Empire there are certainly most elegant apartments, and indeed they ought to be so, for Mr. Caulfield, a young Irishman, was occupying one for which he paid ninety louis a month. The rest of the house was full of English. We hoped, in spite of our unsettled state all the morning, that in the evening at least we should be able to go to some one of the theatres in some *loge grillée* of Perrégaux's, as in former days. *Mais, point du tout*, Perrégaux never came; and we spent the evening in posting our journals, not without often complaining, with Titus, *diem perdidi.*

Monday, 15*th.*—Left the Hôtel de l'Empire in a fiacre, of which, by-the-bye, there are more than ever at Paris, and certainly better than they used to be, though by no means 'good carriages,' as in England we heard they were. There are as many chariot-fiacres as coaches, and, in addition to these, there are long stands of cabriolets to hire in the same way, in almost every *quartier* of Paris, and both the horses, the harness, and the carriages are much neater and better-looking than one could possibly expect. They have all a number painted upon them, as the hackney coaches, and are obliged at night to have lamps lighted and at all times a *grelot* under the horse's neck or somewhere about the harness. So have *all* the cabriolets belonging to individuals, and all are under the same obligations with respect to lanterns and *grelots*. In our chariot-fiacre (chariots seem to be considered as the genteeler of the two) we arrived at our Hôtel d'Orléans, where I found not one pin had been altered since I knew it sixteen years ago; consequently, it was not a little dirty as to hangings, painting, and furniture.

Received a visit from Barrois, the son of a great bookseller here, whom we knew formerly with Edwards* in London, and whom Edwards had desired to come to us as soon as we arrived. From him, a very sensible, unprejudiced young man, we learnt a number of things by no means favourable to the present state of affairs in this country, and from him and his sentiments could pretty well guess at the opinions, the fears, the prejudices, and the prospects of the far greater part of the better order of people, if not in France, at least in Paris.

At one o'clock went to the Gallery of the Louvre. To strangers it is open every day (except the Decades) from ten till four, by merely showing their passports at the door. To give any idea of this gallery is quite impossible. You ascend to it (at present) by a commodious plain staircase, and first enter a large square room about twice the size of the exhibition room in Somerset House, lined with all the finest Italian pictures, very well placed as to light. Out of this room you enter

* A well-known bookseller in London: shop in Pall Mall.

a gallery—*such* a gallery! But *such* a gallery!!! as the world never before saw, both as to size and furniture! So long that the perspective ends almost in a point, and so furnished that at every step, tho' one feels one must go on, yet one's attention is arrested by all the finest pictures that one has seen before in every other country, besides a thousand new ones. The small pictures, and all those taken from palaces, are in their own handsome gilt frames, but the large ones and those taken out of churches are, for the present at least, only in flat frames of yellow wood. The first half of this gallery contains the Flemish, Dutch, and French schools; about the middle there is a recess on each side, from whence commences the Italian schools. All I can *say*, and, indeed, all I could *see*, of the pictures was, that each of these general divisions contained all the noted and exquisite pictures that one had formerly admired in their separate countries. They appeared in very good order, and not as if they had been varnished or worked upon.* The light, too, is by no means bad, and if they had blinds to the windows, as is intended, would be as good as could be expected for such a multitude of pictures. In the same immense gallery, on the ground floor, are the statues, but here the space is divided into several different rooms (called by the different names of salle d'Apollon, salle des Muses, &c. &c.) or rather divisions made by columns, all open one to another. The walls are stucco, painted to look as if incrusted with red and green granite, in a fine, simple style, worthy of Italy, and at the same time very advantageous to the statues, which are all a thousand times better placed than ever they were in Italy, not excepting the Apollo, which stands in a niche at the end of the rooms, and admirably

* Upon further examination, I am sorry to say, we found this not to be the case with the Italian pictures of the old schools, which their reparations are destroying. I mean destroying the identity of the picture and the touch of the master.—*M. B.*

lighted. Of the statues, their numbers, their beauty, the feelings they excited as old acquaintance, &c. &c., like the pictures, I shall say nothing. In the gallery we met Mrs. Cosway,* who is etching a general view of it, with a little sketch of each of the pictures. She introduced us to a secretary or keeper, M. de la Vallée, a modest quiet man who seemed really to have taste, and showed us many things.

In the evening we had intended going to the Théâtre François, now called the Théâtre de la République, but finding no places either in the first or second row, we enquired of our valet de place (who in Paris are sort of cicerones, and used to be extremely clever in their office) in what other good theatre we were likely to get in. He carried us to the Théâtre de Vaudeville close by. We were shown into a box *au premier rang*, where only one man of very ordinary appearance was sitting in the front row. We supposed he would offer us his place, *mais point de tout*, he did not even look towards us; he never even made the least movement by way of inviting us to sit beside him. *This* is indeed a *revolution* in France, and such a one as I could not have believed if I had not seen it! We found ourselves in a good-sized theatre, rather dirty but prettily ornamented, and filled by people whose appearance certainly promised very little; but it is now quite as impossible to judge from appear-

* Maria Cosway, daughter of an innkeeper of the name of Hadfield, at Leghorn, wife of the English artist of that name, and artist herself. After her husband's death she went to Paris with the object of drawing the Gallery of the Louvre, and accompanying each separate drawing with a history of the picture and its painter. This intention was not fulfilled; but she remained at Paris, and became the devoted admirer of David the artist. After some years' residence in Paris, tired of the pleasures of the world, she retired to a convent near Lyons, of which she became the Superior.—*Dict. des Contemporains.* Mrs. Cosway was no new acquaintance of Miss Berry's. As early as a letter dated June 8, 1791, Horace Walpole says, 'I am glad Mrs. Cosway is with you. She is pleasing; but surely it is odd to drop a child and her husband and country all in a breath.'

ances in France as it was formerly, though from directly opposite reasons. We sat for a time behind our man, who, to complete the business, chewed tobacco, and at every instant spat into the empty place beside him! In time, we obtained from the *ouvreuse* a stage-box, and were thus relieved from the neighbourhood of the spitting man, which had really made us sick. The appearance of the men in this theatre was still worse than that of the women—I mean more dirty and slovenly. More of them were powdered than would have been in England, but in great-coats, boots, and had in every way a neglected appearance. The women were none of them indecently dressed, but few smart, and all unbecoming. The *sortie* of this little theatre is convenient, under cover, and one carriage only, being able to come up at a time.

Tuesday, 16*th.*—Went to deliver some letters of introduction to Madame Chabot de Castillane, to Madame de Beauvau, and Madame de Mortemart, to Madame Louise de Talleyrand Périgord, to Madame d'Audenarde, &c. It used to be a necessary etiquette at Paris to deliver your letters yourself, and even ask to be admitted before the people knew you, and when they were to read the letter in your presence, that was to tell them who you were. But now sending them by a servant with a ticket would, I believe, do quite as well. Went to Madame le Roi, at present *the Mademoiselle Bertin* of Paris.* She is lodged in a ground-floor of a magnificent hotel in the Rue de Richelieu, now the *Rue de la Loi.* She was very civil, and not at all pert; but if she *had* anything pretty, treated us *en dames étrangères*, and showed us nothing that I should have liked

* The well-known Mdlle. Rose Bertin was dressmaker to Marie Antoinette. During the Reign of Terror she was visited by commissaries of the Government, desiring to know the amount and details of the queen's debts to her; but apprised of their intended visit, she destroyed her accounts, and declared with unshaken firmness that the queen owed her nothing. Mdlle. Bertin died in 1813.—*Dict. des Contemporains.*

to have worn, not on account of its singularity or youthfulness, but of its common vulgar look. Mrs. Damer ordered a bonnet (at the price of two louis) to be made on the model of one entirely of lace, which was to cost *seventy-two* louis. The furniture of Madame le Roi's apartment was elegant in the extreme, purple lustring, festooned *à l'antique* with a deep orange fringe. The chairs, &c. &c., mahogany, with the same furniture. Mahogany furniture is, I find, become very general at Paris. In the evening went to the Opera; in a box *au premier*, containing six places, for which we paid the enormous price of 57 livres. But the crowd is always great there, and on the *beaux jours*, of which this was one, no possibility of securing places in any other manner.

This theatre, built in the Rue Richelieu, is new and handsome. It has three rows of boxes, and some near the stage, for the people of the theatre. The ornaments are all in pale browns, and bronze, and gold, not very gay. The lustre or circle of Argand lamps by which it is lighted, in perfect taste. The pieces given were 'Anacréon' with a long dance introduced; and, at the end, 'Télémaque.' Laÿs,* the first man of the opera, who was Anacreon, has a very fine voice, and the music very pretty, and they were all *perfectly* well dressed *à l'antique*. The head of Anacreon was perfect: but a French opera is always a dull thing. The dancing is certainly more *marvellous* than ever. I do not think it more pleasing. In the first ballet there was only one *entrée* of men, three together, all the rest were women, of whom six were capital dancers; but the women now dance in the style of men, that is to say, with all the difficult steps and *tours de force* possible. A long *pas de deux* was performed with such a perfect *ensemble* and precision, that

* Francis Laÿs, born 1757, was originally destined for the Church; but in 1779 he appeared on the stage, and continued a favourite with the public till his retirement in 1822.—*Dict. des Contemporains.*

one was obliged to rub one's eyes to feel sure it was not two machines moved by the same strings. 'Télémaque' was not half so well given as by D'Egville in London. Vestris * was Télémaque—that style of dancing never was what suited him best—he is still marvellous and has movements that nobody else ever had, but he is grown so much thicker that his figure looks *écrasé* and his head too large; his wig was bushy light hair, curled all over. Mdlle. Clotilde was Calypso, † and at first I did not much admire her figure, which is remarkably tall, but when she came in dressed for hunting, she was the exact copy of the statue called the *Diana Caciatrice*, the drapery of which is open just above the knee, and in my life I never saw such perfect legs, nor legs so perfectly resembling those of the Apollo, into the attitudes of which they fell a thousand times. All the other women dancers were dressed in one petticoat of white muslin, or something as thin, with another drapery of the same stuff arranged in various ways about half as long as the first, but both allowing the whole form to be fairly perceived up to the waist, covered with flesh-coloured *tricot*. Some of them had no covering above the waist but flesh-coloured *tricot*, with some little strap on one shoulder. The company at the Opera, though *everybody* was there, did not appear brilliant; the women all wrapped up in their frightful shawls, with heads by no means looking dressed, and the men, even at this most favourite spectacle, have a neglected, dirty appearance. Indeed, it is at the *sortie* of the theatre that one of the wonderful changes that have taken place in Paris is very decidedly

* Auguste Vestris, son of the celebrated dancer known by the name of Dieu de la Danse, and who retired from the stage in 1781. Auguste Vestris, like his father, was considered the best dancer of his time.

† Clotilde Augustine Malflattrai, born in 1776. She was pupil of the elder Vestris, and appeared first in 1793. In 1802 she married Boildieu, the composer, but her misconduct was such that in 1808 they were finally separated. She quitted the stage 1819, and died 1826.

visible. That of the Opèra, where one used to see brilliant groups of all the young people of fashion, and all the fashionable *filles* who rivalled and surpassed them in appearance, is now the strangest collection of odd, blackguard-looking people that can be conceived. We stood for some time waiting for our carriage, and had leisure to remark them. I did not see one woman who had the appearance of a gentlewoman, though there was one standing next me for some time who had a lace veil over her hat which could not have cost less than sixty or eighty guineas, and a large *real* shawl nearly as costly. The order in going away is still very good in these great theatres; if one stays to the last, one is obliged to wait some time for the carriage, but it is sure to come up and get away without interruption or accident.

Thursday, 18*th*.—Went with Barrois to the Préfecture de la police générale. The passport given at Calais (or anywhere else on entering France) obliges you to show yourself at this office as soon as possible, after your arrival; so people go within three or four days, as it suits them, and *say* they arrived the day before. The two men-servants went with us, as they are much more difficult about men than about women. We passed up a very dirty back stair into a large room full of as dirty-looking clerks, into another partition of a large room, where two or three other people were waiting for the same business as ourselves. The man to whom we spoke was very civil, and after detaining us about a quarter of an hour, copying our names into half-a-dozen books, allowed us to depart; but the servants were detained nearly an hour before they made out the paper which is given in lieu of the passport whilst staying in Paris. In this office (where, if they do the business they are appointed to do, it must be immense), all the papers are kept in bandboxes on shelves round the rooms. One might have fancied oneself at a millinér's instead of an office of police.

In the evening to the Theâtre de la République, formerly called Français. This, too, is a new *sàlle*: the beautiful one in the Faubourg St. Germain was burnt down, and another was built before this, which did not please. This has no right to better success, for it is both ugly and inconvenient. They have had the rage of making everything *à l'antique* lately, and this house is quite spoilt by too many columns and too small apertures for boxes. There is an amphitheatre, called *la galerie*, of two rows, entirely round the house, in which, when people stand, they prevent those in the side boxes from seeing, and when they speak, from hearing. The piece, 'Bazazet,'* acted by the four actors of the theatre. Mdlle. Raucourt,† now a great fat red-faced woman, acted Roxane in the worst taste possible—violent inflexions of voice, and sometimes speaking three or four lines together entirely in a whisper, which was meant to have great effect, but which in fact only prevented her being heard. Mdlle. Vanhove,‡ in Athalie, much better: her figure is not dignified for tragedy, but her acting natural and impassioned. The Vizir Acomat well acted by Duprés—a fine figure, clear enunciation, and much spirit without rant. The dresses handsome, and scrupulously exact in costume. It was followed by 'Défiance et Malice,' acted by Saint Val § and Mdlle. Mézeray.‖ She copied Mdlle.

* Racine.

† Françoise Marie Antoinette Sancerotte Raucourt, born 1756. She made her *débût* at Paris 1772, and was enthusiastically received. In 1776 she lost favour with the public, and travelled abroad. In 1779 she returned to Paris, and recovered her former popularity. In 1793 she was, during six months, a prisoner in the Temple; and afterwards, with other actors, reopened a second Théâtre Français, and fortunately obtained the protection of Bonaparte in 1799. In 1806 she opened a theatre at Milan. Died 1815. —*Biog. Univ.*

‡ Afterwards married to Talma. Retired from the stage 1810.

§ Saint Val first appeared with great success in comedy. In 1793 he was imprisoned with the other actors till 1794. He was afterwards much admired as a tragic actor. Retired from the stage 1818: died 1835.

‖ Josephine Mézeray, born 1772; appeared at the Théâtre Français 1791. Her personal attractions and admirable acting in the parts of coquettes,

Contat, but *haud passibus equis.* He is a stumpy ignoble figure in comedy. Had I never seen the piece admirably acted in society in England, I don't know that I should ever have been as much pleased with it as I was.

Friday, 19*th.*—In the morning at shops. Vaché, a great silk mercer, is lodged in a vast hotel, Rue Vivienne, under the same roof with Lignereuse, the successor of d'Aquerre, and likewise with a considerable depôt of Sèvres china. These sort of shops being in great hotels is quite a new thing at Paris. Vaché's magazin is in a very large apartment, and consists of everything that has to do with silk mercery, trimmings, &c. &c.; it is reckoned the first magazin in Paris. Lignereuse's disappointed me. There were fewer things than I expected; all in the most expensive, and very few, if any, in real good taste. Of mahogany and ormolu mixed together almost everything is now composed; and the ornaments of the candelabra, the pendules, &c., in a minute frittered style. The new Sèvres china, too, is not in pretty taste: tortoise-shell, steel, and all sort of odd dark colours form the ground of the cups, with gold borders upon them.

Dined at Madame Chabot de Castellane, to whom Madame de Staremberg had given us a letter. We were appointed at half-past five. A prettyish house in a garden, Rue Plumet, Faubourg St. Germain. The lady herself looking cross, but civil and sensible. Company consisted of nine persons, of whom ourselves and the master and mistress of the house and the *instituteur* of their children (who dined at a side table) made five; the others were Madame

secured her success. In 1704 she was imprisoned; on her release she joined Mdlle. Raucourt. The theatre was closed at the revolution of the 18th Fructidor, on the ground of being a reunion of royalists. She reappeared at the Théâtre Français, but a professional jealousy disturbed her mind, and she was found one night in a ditch full of water behind the Invalides. The piteous cries of her little dog attracted attention to the spot, and she was rescued, but died a few days later in a state of raving insanity, June 1823.—*Biog. Univ.*

de Staël, Mat. de Montmorency, M. de Crillon (a very gentlemanlike Frenchman of the best sort of middle-aged man). The dinner all served at once, except a remove of fish and four plates of vegetables, which made more meat on the table than ever I saw before in a French house. The dinner lasted a still shorter time than formerly.

Saturday, 20*th*.—Went to the Paper Magazin on the Boulevard—formerly Arthur's, now Robert's Papers. All flock, of one colour, to look like casemir, with flock borders; very good effect. But here again the taste less good than I expected.

In the evening went with Mr. Jackson to make visits to some of the Ministers' wives—to Madame Luçay, the wife of the Préfêt du Palais, and Madame Fouché, of the Minister of Justice. We sat out on this business a little before ten. Got to Berthier's,* the War Minister, who received on this day. He is lodged in a great hotel, called the Hôtel de la Genèvre; the staircase dirty, and no appearance of servants or attendants. (At all the Ministers' houses there are sentinels, not only at the door but in the antechamber.) The apartment very handsome. In the second room were a number of men only; in the third, where Berthier received (for he has no wife), about a dozen women, and a great many men

* Louis Alexandre Berthier, born 1755; brought up as a soldier, he remained faithful for a time to the Bourbons, and assisted the escape of the aunts of Louis XVI. Under the republic he was made chef d'état-major to the army in Italy. In 1798 he commanded at Rome, when the Pope was deposed. It is said he unwillingly accompanied Buonaparte to Egypt, having fixed his affection on an Italian lady. On the downfall of the Directory, 1799, he became Minister of War. In 1806 created Prince de Neufchatel; and married Princess Elizabeth Marie of Bavaria-Birkenfeld. After the campaign against Austria he was created Prince of Wagram. He accompanied Napoleon to Russia. In 1814, he returned to his old allegiance, and in 1815 accompanied Louis XVIII. to Ghent. Wishing to remain neutral, he retired to Bamberg. Here he was murdered by six men in masks, supposed to be emissaries of some secret societies, who, suddenly entering his room, thrust him out of window into the street, from whence he was taken up dying.

in uniforms of some sort, either military or of the constituted authorities. Berthier received us very civilly. He is a little rather ill-looking man, with a crop curled head of dark hair; his dress the uniform of a Minister d'Etat—blue cloth, with a broad silver embroidery. But a greater revolution seems to me to have taken place in the race of tailors than in that of any other set of men. Nobody's coat is now well made, and more especially the uniforms of the constituted authorities—they all look too long and too big; in short, like coats made by a village tailor. Cambacères,* the Second Consul, was among the company: he came late, and was received without any sort of distinction. He is an uncommonly ill-looking, shortish, thick man, with his eyes sunk in his head; his hair badly dressed; his dress the undress uniform of the Consuls—blue velvet, with a broad gold embroidery, fustian breeches, and common turn-down boots. General Macdonald† (he that commanded in Italy), neatly dressed in uniform, like a soldier, and with a very intelligent though not a noble countenance; the hereditary Prince of Orange, in his uniform; the President of the Tribunât, in *his* uniform—blue cloth, embroidered with gold, pantaloons, and hussar boots bound with gold tassels. We

* Jean Jacques Regis de Cambacères, born at Montpelier Oct. 1783; died at Paris June 1824. He served as a deputy in the Convention 1792; became President of the Assembly, and afterwards President of the Committee of Public Safety. He lost the confidence of the Directory, having refused to vote 'La Mort du Tyran.' He was chosen by Buonaparte as Second Consul. When Buonaparte became Emperor, Cambacères was appointed 'Archi-Chancelier,' in which office he remained till the fall of Napoleon.

† Stephen James Joseph Macdonald, Maréchal of France, Duke of Tarentum, born at Sedan in 1765, of a Scotch family long settled in France. He distinguished himself at Jemappes, and, in 1795, at Menin Commines and Courtrai, he passed the Wahl on the ice, and captured the Dutch fleet. At Wagram, created Maréchal on the field of battle, he bore his part in the Russian campaign, and fought at the battle of Leipsic, 1813. He attended Napoleon at Fontainebleau, and urged his abdication. He afterwards adhered to the Bourbons. He died in 1831.

found ourselves almost immediately surrounded by a number of acquaintance whom we had met elsewhere—the *old original* Princess Sta. Croce, looking quite as young and well as ever she did in Italy, and quite as uncovered as anybody in France; Madame Doria from Genoa, &c. &c. We were presented to a number of French women—Mesdames de Semerville and Joubert,* Madame Le Conteuse, Madame de Marmont, Perrégaux's daughter (married to General Marmont, a favourite of Buonaparte), Madame Visconti, a very handsome Italian, the mistress *en titre* of the master of the house; Madame de Staël too there. Most of the ladies loaded with finery of shawls, laces, and a good many diamonds, and abominably ill-dressed; Madame Visconti well dressed in black velvet, with only diamonds in her head. The servants who served refreshments were in boots. The ladies sat all round the room, as in a small assembly in London; and the men stood in the middle. Here we remained till near twelve o'clock, when the rooms began to be very thin.

Two people, a man and his wife, who kept a little shop upon the Pont Neuf, were murdered last night at half-past six, that is to say in daylight, with hundreds of people passing every instant, and a Corps de Garde upon the bridge; these shops, too, being only the recess formed by the top of the pier of the arches of the bridge, one hardly conceives how it is possible for two people to let themselves be *égorgés* without calling for help, which must have been near.

Sunday, 21*st*.—Walked in the Tuileries from the Place de Louis XV. to the door at the Pont Royal. The day was not fine, and threatened rain; however, as the Decade

* Mdlle. de Montholon was married to General Joubert on the 16th of July 1799, at the moment when he was ordered to take the command of the army in Italy. He left his bride, according to some, the day after the marriage; according to others, a few days after; they parted at Pont-de-Vaux, never to meet again. On the 15th of August he was killed at the battle of Novi.

and the Sunday happened to meet, a good many people were walking in the alley next the Terrace des Feuillans; but there exists now little of that charming variety which used to distinguish the public walks of Paris. All the men are about equally ill-dressed; and among the women the old costume of different *états* has almost vanished. The parterre before the Palace is much prettier than it was: in each former division of parterre they have made a grassplat surrounded by borders, which divisions are enclosed with a sort of rough treillage and very pretty shrubs and plants growing well within. Several of the statues have been removed from other places to the terrace immediately before the Palace.

In the evening at the Théâtre du Louvois, by far the prettiest I have seen in Paris, both as to *coupe* and decorations: the *coupe* is that of the burnt Théâtre Français; the decorations, a pink or dark buff-coloured ground, with arabesques, griffins, &c., in bronze colour; the backs of the boxes painted as if hung with blue cloth or silk. The pieces given were 'Les Provinciaux à Paris,' followed by 'La petite Ville;' both most laughable comedies, or rather successions of scenes written by Picard,* himself an excellent actor in both pieces—indeed, all the characters were represented with that perfect *naturel*, that *ensemble* only to be found on the French stage. In the morning called on Madame de Staël. Found her in an excessively dirty *cabinet*—sofa singularly so; her own dress, a loose spencer with a bare neck. The shops, between its being both Decade and Sunday, were nearly all half shut, and many altogether.

Monday, 22nd.—In the morning, Statue Gallery

* Louis Benedict Picard, dramatist, born at Paris 1769; died in 1828. His first production was 'Le Badinage Dangereux,' followed by a long succession of clever comedies. 'Le Contrat d'Union,' 'La Petite Ville,' and 'Les Marionettes,' are considered the best. He was also a writer of poems and of novels.—*Rose's Biog. Dictionary.*

and some brocantines. These shops at present contain treasures of old Sèvres china and rich ornaments of all sorts, which have been bought for nothing out of the great hotels, and are selling now for a fourth of their original price.

In the evening to Madame de Luçay's, the wife of the Préfet du Palais. This again was an assembly about as numerous as that at Berthier's, but less well composed as to women; here again, was all the Corps Diplomatique: Cardinal Caprera,* the Nonce du Pape, in his regular cardinal's dress, Cardinal Erskine,† in that of a monsignor; he is as yet only a cardinal in petto as it is called, consequently has no right to the dress. The same Italian squad of women and some French, but dreadfully vulgar-looking.

The apartment was too small for an assembly, but arranged prettily enough, painted to look like panels of satin-wood and mahogany. The mistress of the house a pretty and very civil little person; the master very civil too, *bien coiffé* and not in uniform. To this meeting we went at ten o'clock, came back to our hotel a little before twelve to supper, and then started for a ball at what is called the Circle des Etrangers; it is given in a large and very handsome hotel near or upon the Boulevards, in the Rue Grange Batlière, and I believe the expenses are defrayed by a club of men. We were told that here we should see *les nouveaux riches.* If all the company consisted of them they are numerous indeed! It was a meeting of many

* Cardinal Caprera, born 1733; was sent to France in 1801, when the First Consul solemnly re-established the ordinances of religion. The Cardinal led the Te Deum that concluded the ceremony on this occasion; and in 1805 he crowned the Emperor Napoleon King of Italy. He died in 1810.—*Dict. des Contemporains.*

† Charles Erskine, born at Rome 1753; descendant of a Scotch family who followed the Stuarts into exile. He was made Cardinal by Pius VII. and was well received by the First Consul. He died in 1811.—*Dict. des Contemporains.*

hundreds, I think not less than three hundred or four hundred persons. There was a file of carriages of nearly a quarter of a mile long on the Boulevard, another in the street by which we came. In London this would have been the means of breaking a dozen carriages; here, some soldiers stationed on the Boulevard allowed one carriage of each file to come up successively. Of the *dress* and the *undress* of the women in the ball, and the appearance of the men, and indeed of the whole company, I can give no idea. The little coloured prints of the Paris fashions are exact unexaggerated representations of their dresses, but in reality they are seldom exhibited upon as handsome figures. Loads of finery in gold and silver, excessively fine laces, bare necks and shoulders more than half-way down the back, with the two bladebones squeezed together in a very narrow-backed gown; arms covered with nothing but a piece of fine lace below the shoulder; and trains that never ended: in short, an endless variety of bad taste, without one single figure that one's eye could repose on with pleasure. Such were the women. Among the men, in vain I looked for *les merveilleux et les incroyables*. A general unsmartness of appearance pervaded them all; even those who we saw dance (and excessively well) a French country dance. We left the ball between one and two o'clock, with people still coming in. It continues all night, and the company sup at any time they like in separate rooms. I must not forget to say that these extraordinary figures of men and women *waltzing* together, in the slow and deliberate manner in which in France they think it graceful to perform this dance, was ludicrous in the extreme. From every circumstance, both of the meeting and of the people composing it, it was nearly impossible to believe oneself at Paris; but then I should add we were told that the principal part of the company was what they call the second order of the *nouveaux riches*.

Tuesday, 23rd.—In the evening went to the Princess de Beauvau's (Mdlle. de Montemart's sister), to whom I carried a letter from Mrs. Harcourt: as I did not even know that it was meant as one of introduction, their civilities to us were the more marked. They are lodged in a small house, the apartment more like an English than a French one in size and furniture. Indeed, having been all long in England, (Mdlle. de Montemart from a child) they are much attached to English manners, habits, and fashions, and speak English better than any French persons I ever heard. We were the first of the party; after us came Madame de Bouillie (wife to the son of the Marquis de Bouillie, an uncommonly pretty, fair, quiet-looking young-woman), Madame d'Hennin, Madame de la Rochefoucauld (widow of the Duc who was assassinated*), the Duc de Rohan-Chabot, his nephew the Chevalier de Chabot, Mr. Jackson, Lord Cowper, Mr. Luttrell †, and Lord Henry Petty.‡ We sat

* Louis Alex. de la Rochefoucauld supported warmly many of the doctrines of the Revolutionary party, but was not prepared to go the lengths of its most violent partisans. He openly disapproved of the conduct of Péthion and of Manuel in 1792. The friends of these men becoming the dominant party, the Duke was insulted and persecuted. He left Paris; but his retreat was discovered, and assassins were sent to Gisors, where he was murdered, Sept. 1793, aged circ. sixty years. His mother narrowly escaped a similar fate.—*Dict. Univ.*

† Henry Luttrell, Esq., was distinguished through life by his conversational powers; he had a fund of anecdote at command and a ready flow of epigrammatic wit; but his satire, though pointed, was seldom calculated to wound, and he was a favoured guest in every society in which he lived. He was the author of 'Letters to Julia,' published 1822. Mr. Luttrell died at an advanced age in 1851.

‡ Lord Henry Petty, second son of William, first Marquis of Lansdowne, born 1780, succeeded to his brother's titles and estates, 1809; married Louisa Emma, daughter of second Earl of Ilchester; died 1863. Miss Berry's mention of Lord Henry Petty in his early youth, can hardly be passed over without a word of tribute to one who afterwards filled for so many years a most prominent and useful position, both in public and social life. His political career began at the age of twenty six, when he was appointed Chancellor of the Exchequer. As a statesman, his sound judgment and consistent principles secured him the confidence of those who acted with him, and the respect of those who were opposed to him. His liberal encouragement

round a very small room in conversation, these people dropping in at different times till twelve o'clock, when a cold supper was served in one of the coldest dining-rooms I ever felt; we returned up stairs in about half an hour, and were at home by half after one. The supper, I believe, was for us and the other English, for few or no suppers are now given here, either by the new or the old set.

Wednesday, 24th.—In the morning to St. Roc, the church in the Rue St. Honoré. This church and Notre Dame are those which suffered the most in the days of devastation, and, *nota bene*, it is now the most fashionable church in Paris next to the Carmes de la Rue Vaugerard. The side chapels are entirely *dégarnie*, the altars and everything taken away from them ; the sides of the church and the basement which support the columns of the aisles, were formerly lined with marbles; this lining is in many places taken away, and all the pictures, and all the fine frontispieces of even the remaining altars. There are two chapels behind the great altar in this church, and in the farthest they have placed a marble crucifix bigger than life, and very well executed; it was formerly in the church of the Mont Calvaire; here it is lighted from above, and seen through two recesses, and the effect is admirable. In this church there were a few shabby-looking people saying their prayers, and one woman I

of art, and his taste for literature, made him the Mæcenas of his day, and those who benefited by his generosity, or whose society he sought, for their merit, though often cheered by his kindness, were never oppressed by his patronage. Lord Lansdowne had seen much, and heard much; he had read much; he had observed much; his memory was retentive, and his power of collecting facts and amalgamating the knowledge derived from experience, made him, not only a valuable leader and adviser in the affairs of state, but also a most agreeable and instructive member of society; he died in the fulness of years, and there are few whose death was ever regretted by so wide a circle of persons, who could proudly and gratefully claim the right to mourn him as a friend and a patron. Miss Berry's acquaintance with Lord Lansdowne probably dated from this visit to Paris, it continued with warm unvarying friendship and intimacy to the close of Miss Berry's life.

saw at confession. The children of a number of different parishes are sent here to say their catechism, and by the multitude of chairs piled up in every part of the church, one must suppose that it is often very full.

In the evening, Comédie Française: 'The Philosophe sans le savoir,' and 'La Gageure imprevue.' The first is a piece of Sedaine's,* much admired and very frequently given now, perhaps because perfectly well acted by Molé,† Fleury, and Mdlle. Contat.‡ It is in itself one of the flattest pieces of nothing but *comings in and goings out* that I ever saw. Whether *for* or *against* duelling one don't know. The 'Gageure' is an old *petite pièce*, in which I have formerly seen Preville.§ It is now admirably acted in every character. Molé is still super-excellent, though old; Mdlle. Contat, whom I have seen in her brilliant days, seen grown fat but still brilliant, is now still fatter and no longer brilliant, but has a lovely countenance, and in the *rôles de tantes*, which she has now adopted, is as excellent as she was formerly in those of the coquettes. Nobody ever to my ears pronounced her language so prettily.

* Michael John Sedaine, dramatic writer, born at Paris 1717, died 1797, author of 'Rose and Colin,' 'Wife Revenged,' &c.—*Watts's Dictionary.*

† Francis Reni Molé, born 1734, appeared on the stage in 1754; his politics saved him from sharing the fate of his comrades in 1793; he was considered one of the best comedians of his time, and enjoyed a reputation as a tragedian. He died in December 1802, and was followed to the grave by all the actors of all the theatres in Paris, and by a deputation from the Institute, of which he was a member.—*Biog. Univ.*

‡ Louise Contat, born at Paris, 1760. She was the pupil of Madame Preville, and made her appearance on the stage at sixteen years old. Her first great success was in the part of Suzanne in Beaumarchais' Mariage de Figaro, 1784; and she became a distinguished performer at the Théâtre Français. Her immense size obliged her to change her line of characters. She quitted the stage three years before her death in 1813.

§ Pierre Louis Dubus, commonly known by the name of Preville, was born in 1721. After a brilliant career of thirty-five years on the stage he retired, appearing only twice again—in 1791 and in 1794, to celebrate the restoration of himself and his colleagues to liberty, after the Reign of Terror in 1793; he died in 1800.

It was near eleven o'clock before we got to Madame Fouché, the wife of the Minister of Police, who had an assembly that night, and to which Mr. Jackson had announced our coming. All the company were leaving when we entered the room; luckily we found Mdlle. de Contuela, whom we knew, and who presented us to a fair vulgar-looking woman in a yellow wig, with a very fine gold-muslin gown with a border of gold, and a very fine lace handkerchief, which fell down like an apron before her. This was Madame Fouché.* Our visit lasted less than ten minutes; we had not half time to admire the beauty of their most splendid apartments. They inhabit the Hôtel de Mazarin, upon the Quai de Voltaire, which has been *remis-à-neuf* for its present inhabitants; the salon is hung in panels with the most exquisite Gobelins, and surrounded with such a profusion of carving and gilding in admirable taste as I never saw in any palace. Son of a grocer at Nantes, he (Fouché †) was of the religious society called *Oratoriens*, which they could quit when they pleased. He was a Deputy to the Convention (that is to say the Third General Assembly), and was sent as a Deputy or Pro-Consul to La Vendée, where he *distinguished* himself as aide-de-camp to Carrier, Ministre de la Police Générale, before the return of Buonaparte. When the Jacobin clubs were opening again, he, though supposed a violent Jacobin, had them

* Madame Fouché's maiden name was Guoico. 'Des femmes titrées devinrent les amis intimes de Madame Fouché, femme de beaucoup d'esprit, qui les traitait sans cérémonie.' Madame Fouché died 1813.—*Biog. nouvelle des Contemporains.*

† Joseph Fouché, afterwards Duc d'Otranto, born 1763. He was twenty-five years old when the Revolution broke out; was married, and settled in his native town. He voted with Danton for the death of the King, and was sent with Collot d'Herbois to Lyons, 1793. In 1799 he was raised to the office of Minister of Police. He married, in 1815, a lady of the family of Castellane. His well-known history is too long and too much involved in the history of the time to be comprised in a biographical note. He was exiled in 1816, and died at Trieste in 1820.

shut up to keep his place, and was maintained in it by Buonaparte, though known still to be a Jacobin. Fouché himself was in the anteroom, and we only just made our curtsies *en passant.* His figure is not prepossessing; a little man, with a pale flattish face and small grey eyes; his dress that of a minister of state, blue velvet embroidered in silver, hussar boots.

Thursday, 25*th.*—In the morning, to the Musée des Monuments Nationaux, which occupies the whole emplacement of the Convent des petits Augustins. Here they have brought together all the figures of their kings, from St. Denis and every other place; all the tombs and monuments of their great men and women; in short, all the spoils of their churches and convents from almost every part of the country. Everything of former ages in way of sculpture, which the Vandalism of the present time in the moments of effervescence left undestroyed. These are partly arranged and arranging (for there are a vast number of workmen now employed here by a M. Le Noir) in large *salles*, some formed by the church, and others by the cells and dormitory of the monks, and everything is thrown together according to their centuries,—that is to say, all the sculptures and tombs of the thirteenth century together, then of the fourteenth, and so on. We had only time to give a rapid *coup d'œil*, but M. Le Noir gave us tickets to revisit the Musée when we pleased. It is curious to observe the rapid decay of the art from the days of Francis I. to those of Louis XIV. The admired tomb of Cardinal Richelieu, which happens to be placed in what was the Capucins' Church, and surrounded with a number of tombs of the former period, will not bear any comparison with them. In the garden surrounded by the cloisters are hundreds of figures yet unplaced: a beautiful one of Ignatius Loyola, in marble; a whole-length bronze of Louis XIV., a boy, very clever. At all these museums and collections one must be an artist, and *only* an artist, to admire without regret or often without indignation. In the large garden of the convent, which is prettily planted, M. Le Noir is arranging tombs and cenotaphs to all the great geniuses of France. Here he has (or says he has) the heart of Molière and the bones of Racine, &c. &c.; in short, he calls it the Champs Elysées. This said M. Le Noir, the only violent Jacobin (in conversation) that I have heard, is the only person who *viséed* in his discourse, towards the abuse of religion, &c.

In the evening we were presented by Mr. Jackson to the Second and Third Consuls; we went first to Cambacères', who inhabits the Hôtel d'Elbœuf: we found him in the second room of a large apartment on the ground-floor, lined entirely with Gobelin tapestry, Turkish stories, after designs of a French painter; when admiring its freshness, he (M. Cambacères) said, it had been up above sixty-four years, and is certainly still more brilliant than even pictures for furniture.

The company consisted of a circle of men all standing as at a levée, in the middle of which we were presented to the consul, and led by him to a row of chairs, where were ranged about eight or ten other women, all of them the wives of some of the constituted authorities; they were only in demi-toilette, as this is not called an assembly. Most of the men in uniforms, military or civil. M. Cambacères' manner is very civil; he spoke as much to us as in such a meeting one can expect, and asked us to come to his next assembly on *Septidi* (Sunday).

From hence we went to Le Brun's;* he is lodged in

* Charles François le Brun, Duke of Piacenza, born 1739; deputy to the States-General 1789; appointed Third Consul Dec. 1799; Arch-Treasurer of the Empire 1804; Governor-General of Liguria, Duke of Piacenza, in 1805. Signed the constitution that recalled the House of Bourbon, and created a Peer of France by Louis XVIII. After the return of Napoleon in 1815, accepted the peerage from him, and the place of Grand Master of the University, which rendered him incapable of sitting in the new Chamber formed in Aug. 1815. He died in 1824.

that part of the Tuileries called the Pavillon de Flore, entered from the corner of the Great Cour. The apartment is small, not magnificently furnished like the others, but containing some good pictures. Here was just the same sort of meeting as at Cambacères, indeed many of the same faces who had followed or preceded us there; amongst the rest General La Fayette* was announced; he was in no sort of uniform—a plain blue coat, round hat, and cropped head; he is rather a gentlemanlike, sickly-looking man, but as I never happened to see him before, I am no judge how much he is changed. I observed that two young men, the one General De la Roche, the other the general who commanded at Porto Ferrajo; neither of them spoke to him. Cambacères has no wife or lady who does the honours. At Le Brun's (who is a widower), there was an old vulgar-looking housekeeper woman, some relation, to whom everybody made a bow; she came civilly and sat by me, but she was so entirely ignorant of everything around her, that she did not even know the names of anyone in the room. Le Brun was the son of a farmer of Vire, in Normandy,

* Marie Jean Motier, Marquis de la Fayette, born 1757, at the Castle of Chevagnac in Auvergne. As a general and as a politician he occupied a prominent place in three great revolutions, and acquired fame in both hemispheres. The history of La Fayette is too well known and too closely interwoven with the history of France, to be attempted in a short biographical note. He was married at the age of sixteen to a daughter of the Duke of Ayen. In 1777 he sailed for America. He sat as deputy for the nobles of Auvergne at the Assembly of the States-General in 1789. In 1790 he swore on the 'Altar of the Country' in the Champ de Mars, fidelity to the King, the law, and the nation. A year afterwards he was denounced by Robespierre, and accused by Collot d'Herbois, but not condemned by the Assembly. In 1792 he took refuge in flight into Austria; he endured five years' imprisonment at Olmutz; set at liberty by Napoleon's intervention, in 1797; re-entered France on Napoleon's becoming First Consul. His conduct in 1830 decided the fate of the old dynasty, and established that of the new. He was Commander of the National Guard. He declined negotiation with the King's party, by publicly replying: 'Il n'est plus temps,' and on the same day giving a public reception to the Duke of Orleans. He died May 1834.—*Imperial Dictionary of Universal Biography.*

secretary to the famous Maupeou, for whom he wrote all the edicts and proclamations; called by Maupeou 'Mon Bijou;' was of the Constituent Assembly; then of the Conseils des Anciens, from whence, when Buonaparte came from Egypt, he was made Consul. He has the manners and appearance of a clever man; he recollected Mrs. Damer, from having seen her as long ago as when the Prince of Conti's pictures were sold here in 1775. He is a man of letters, has translated 'Tasso's Jerusalem' and the 'Iliad of Homer' into French prose.

After staying about half an hour at Le Brun's, we returned where Barrois was to meet us, and changing our dress, that is to say, making ourselves *less* smart, we were conducted by him to one of the many public rooms open most nights for dancing in this great town. The one we chose, as the nearest, was called the Hôtel de Longueville, in the Place de Carouzel. It is a very long low room, painted in arabesques, very dirty, but very well lighted by the patent lamps suspended from the ceiling. We found this place at eleven o'clock about half full of shabby-looking people; masks were admitted that night, so that a third of the company were in masks, which I regretted. After all the repeated histories one has heard of the indecency of the dress and manners of Paris, I felt some degree of uneasiness before I went in, for fear of seeing somewhat too much. My fears were quite superfluous. I never was in a more quiet decent assembly; there was not one woman dressed the least indecorously, not one half as naked as those at the Bal des Etrangers. Nor was there any impropriety of manners; there was indeed much less gaiety than I should have expected in such a meeting, much less than I have formerly seen in dances of this order of people in France. The dances were principally waltzes, for which there is such a rage at present, that in every society they have in a manner superseded their own pretty country dances, in which they excel, while they don't waltze half as well as the Germans. All the women who dance in the sort of balls I am now speaking of, are *sensées* to be of bad character, which made the decency of their dress and manners the more remarkable. There were several *bons bourgeois*, both men and women, walking up and down the room, for it is only dancing which is forbid *à des honnêtes femmes* in these places. There were several women in men's clothes, a fashion now very general in this order of people, sometimes for convenience, and at other times, I dare say, for less excusable reasons. There were likewise several men in women's clothes, but these wore masks, or intended to do so. We remained at this ball near an hour, and left the room much fuller than when we entered. It was to continue all night.

Friday, 26th.—In the morning, walked in the Champs Elysées from the Place de Louis XV. quite up to the Barrière. It was between three and four o'clock, and there was almost a string of carriages then going to the Bois de Boulogne—so much are the hours of Paris altered. The Bois de Boulogne is more than ever the fashionable rendezvous of all the world that have horses and carriages. Saw three women on horseback, well mounted, with hats and habits exactly like English women. The road upon each side of the *pavé* through the Champs Elysées very rough, and the walks between the trees are by no means in good order. There were not many people walking, though the day was fine and warm. Dined at Mr. Jackson's (our Minister). He is well lodged in a *rez-de-chaussée* apartment in the Hôtel de Caraman, Rue St. Dominique. The company consisted of Madame Brignole, Madame de Staël, the *ci-devant* Abbé, now M. de St. Phar, the Prince Auguste d'Aremberg, called formerly the Comte de la Marche, Baron Amfelt, Adrien de Montmorency,* the Swedish Minister

* Anne Pierre Adrien Montmorency, born 1769, succeeded to the title of Duc de Laval on his father's death, 1816. He served in the army as a

(Baron Ehrenswerd), the Marquis of Douglas,* and General Marmont's † wife (Perrégaux's daughter), a pretty little woman, but with airs and graces and certain careless impertinence of manner which *réncheried* upon all the *ci-devant* duchesses and marquises; her husband is an *affidé* of Buonaparte's; is one of the five who returned with him from Egypt, and now much in his confidence. He is rather short, with black hair out of powder, and much beard; a sensible, intelligent, grave countenance: he put me something in mind of the second daughter of the Archbishop of York.‡

While we were dressing, between five and six, to dine at Mr. Jackson's, the cannons of the Invalides announced to us that the long-expected peace was at last signed. It seemed to make very little impression on the company with whom we dined. Our Minister seemed much in the dumps, for which probably he had reasons of his own. The news in no way occupied any part of the conversation or attention of the rest of the company. At the Opera or in the streets, I expected to see some lively demonstrations of some sort or other. *Mais point du tout!* in the streets there were no crowds, or groups, or bonfires, or anything; the public offices were illuminated with little *pots-à-feu* upon the outside of

young man, but giving up his profession he returned to France in 1801. In 1814 he was roused again to take part in the Royalist cause; the same year he was sent as ambassador to Madrid; he filled the same position afterwards at Rome and in London.

* Alexander, Marquis of Douglas, born 1767, succeeded his father as Duke of Hamilton, 1819; died 1852.

† Auguste Frederic Louis de Marmont, Duc de Ragusa, was born in 1774, of an ancient and respectable family. He entered the army in 1789. In 1796 he was first aide-de-camp to Napoleon, when commanding the army of Italy, and was from that time engaged in constant military service and commands, and generally with distinction, till defeated by the Duke of Wellington, at Salamanca. On the return of the Bourbons he gave in his adhesion, and accompanied Louis XVIII. to Ghent. Died at Venice, 1852.

‡ Dr. William Markham.

the walls, but hardly any private houses were lighted—nothing *like* a general illumination. The Tuileries were beautiful with straight lines of fire along the immense extent of the building, and again upon the iron rails and gates of the *cour* in front. At the Opera, where we did not arrive till near nine o'clock, the announcement of the peace had taken place immediately after the curtain drew up, and was received, we were told, with loud applause by a crowded house. But this first applause over, there was no return, no allusions, no anything that could lead one to suppose a great event had taken place. I am told that the people of Paris have now for long been so fatigued with emotions and changes and great events, that they are grown perfectly indifferent, and that all those events that have happened in their own history for these last three years, have been received with equal indifference.

The opera was 'Edipe à Colonne,' the music very pretty. The ballet 'Paris,' admirable; but unfortunately, in the midst of it, Jackson announced to us in a very unqualified manner, the death of ——, which he had just heard from England! Of the ballet I saw little more!

Saturday, 27*th*.—I had a bad night, and woke with such a violent attack of nervous headache, that I was confined to my bed all day.

Sunday, 28*th*.—Drove through the Bois Boulogne to Bagatelle. It is now open to all the world upon paying sevenpence a-piece for people walking, or fifteen pence for a carriage. The first *corps de bâtiment*, through which we drove to the little pavilion itself, is inhabited by a traiteur, who, I fancy, is a considerable proprietor of the whole, and I dare say makes it answer very well, for on this fine Sunday there were above half a dozen cabriolets and other carriages in the *cour*, and a number of people walking about the grounds, which are kept in very tolerable order, though very different from what I saw it when we breakfasted there with the Duke of Dorset* in 1785. The Pavilion, too, is open to all comers. The arabesques upon the walls, the ceilings, and the chimney-pieces remain the same, only much less clean. Some of its Sunday visitors were playing in the billiard-room. The grounds are pretty, though the trees have ill-thriven, and, I think, the evergreens and firs have positively not grown an inch in the last fifteen years. The water, too, is ridiculous, conducted in little narrow winding channels, with half-a-dozen bridges of all sorts and sizes over it, and half-a-dozen different rock-works and caverns on its banks. In the Bois de Boulogne were numbers of people walking and sitting in groups under the trees. On our return, between three and four o'clock, all the carriages of Paris—bad, good, and indifferent—were drawn up in the great alley of the Champs Elysées, opposite the garden of the house formerly belonging to the Duchess de Bourbon, now a public garden, and called the Hameau de Chantilly, from whence a balloon was just going off. We saw it inflated and appearing above the wall of the garden, and soon after our return home saw it passing over our heads at a vast height. This day has convinced me how much Sunday is now kept by the Parisians. Most of the shops were shut, everybody in the streets or in the public walks, in their best clothes; in short, a *dimanche bien constaté* of the *ancien régime.* The gaiety of Paris and its environs in a fine day of this sort must strike every mind agreeably, even one as little disposed to cheerfulness as mine is at this instant.

In the evening at Cambacères' assembly. It is excessively entertaining to us to see there the figures of a number of persons whose names one has been reading of in newspapers for these last ten years. Among those we saw was a *garçon imprimeur*, who became the editor of a

* John Frederick, third Duke of Dorset, appointed ambassador to France December 1783. He married, 1790, Arabella Diana Cope, daughter of Sir Charles Cope, Bart. He died July 1799.

journal, which he composed, printed, and distributed himself,—General Brune* (who commanded in Holland); he is one of the very tallest men I ever saw, between thirty and forty, rather awkward, with a sensible but not agreeable countenance. Massena † was there, not in uniform; a crop, with thick black hair; a vulgar-looking intelligent countenance, and rather a short thick figure. There were several whose name we could not learn, in general's full-dress uniforms, which is extremely rich: blue embroidered in gold, with scarlet cuffs, a monstrous high scarlet collar, both covered with embroidery; white pantaloons flourished all over with embroidery in the front, and likewise down the seams, to hussar boots bound with gold and gold tassels; a broad scarlet belt, covered with gold ornaments, and fastened with a large *plâque* in front; a large and highly ornamented sabre. Cambacères received us in the great apartment on the first floor, consisting of I know not how many rooms. As in London, the first room only was full. This hotel (the Hôtel d'Elbœuf) is a specimen of the fine old ones, *remis à neuf*, and some new furniture, such as bookcases, &c., and beautiful carpets, to which one's attention was every minute disagreeably called by all the men indiscriminately spitting upon them. There were many

* Maréchal Guillaume Marie Anne Brune, born 1763. He was sent to Paris to study the law; wrote pamphlets on the state of public affairs, and in 1790-91 was editor of the *Journal de la Cour et de la Ville*. He aided Danton in forming the Club des Cordeliers. He commanded in Belgium, 1799, when the Prussian-English army capitulated. In 1800 he commanded in La Vendée, and in 1803 was sent ambassador to Constantinople. In 1814 he gave in his adhesion to Louis XVIII.; joined the standard of Napoleon on his return from Elba, and repeated his submission to Louis XVIII. after the Cent Jours—but was murdered at Avignon on his way to Paris.—*Rose's Biog. Dict. and Biog. Univ.*

† André Massena, born 1758; in 1793 he commanded the right wing of the army in Italy; his constant successes obtained for him from Napoleon the title of 'L'Enfant chérie de la Victoire.' In 1810 he replaced Soult in Spain, and was repulsed by the Duke of Wellington. In 1814 he gave in his adhesion to Louis XVIII. After Waterloo he was Commander-in-Chief of the National Guard; died 1817.

more women at this meeting than I have seen at any of the others—all of the *new world*, or foreigners. Many of them strange, uncouth figures, all meaning to be smart loaded with finery.

Monday, 29*th*.—I never even in England experienced such a violent and sudden change in the temperature as took place between yesterday and to-day. Yesterday it was oppressively hot in the sun, without a breath of air. To-day, the wind having got into the north, it was so cold that snow fell in the morning. Called at Madame de Boufflers (the wife of the Chevalier) and Madame de Castellane, whom we found at home. Her account why the two present societies cannot easily amalgamate is curious and very true by what we have seen.

In the evening at the Opera. 'Astyanax' was the opera, and 'Psyche' the ballet. All French operas are so like one another that it is only of the decoration that one can speak. The last scene, of Pyrrhus going on board a vessel with Astyanax and Andromache, and sailing away with all his fleet, was very good; but *au reste*, it is always the same scrambling and violent exertion of voice, always the same exaggerated action, always a scene which we have called *the tearing scene*, where, from sorrow, or joy, or fear, or entreaty, *ils se jettent l'un sur l'autre*, and after half pulling one another to pieces, are always either torn asunder, or go off in one another's arms. The bodily fatigue of these *grand rôles d'opéra* is so great that the people must have monstrous strong constitutions, as well as monstrous strong voices, to support them. Mdlle. Maillard, a great fat woman, acted Andromache not without some dignity; but there is no fine female actress at the Opera at present. The ballet of 'Psyche,' as they give it here, is a long pantomime, little dancing, but admirable in its way. Madame Gardel*

* Marie Anne Elizabeth Gardel, wife of a favourite dancer of that name, born 1770. She appeared in 1786, and from the year 1792 was held in high

was Psyche, and is lightness and grace itself. St. Amand was Amour. The scene of Psyche ascending the rock, of her being carried off in the clouds by Cupid, and of her torments in Tartarus; of her toilet and her lesson of dancing given by Terpsichore, charming. In all the ballets here, even when there are not many *entrées* of the principal dancers, the *remplissage* of figurants, &c. is never tiresome, because it is done with a grace and a perfection of execution which exists here, and here only.

Tuesday, 30*th*.—In the morning to the Abbé Sicard's* Institution for the instruction of the deaf and dumb. Every decade, I believe, he gives a public lesson, or rather exhibits some of his pupils in public. Lord Henry Petty, who recommended us to go, procured us some tickets. It is a seminary (formerly a religious one), called St. Maglaire. We entered a large room, with circular benches filling it up, to a sort of estrade, where the abbé stood, and about twenty of his pupils, in uniform of pepper and salt faced with blue, seated on each side of him. The most entertaining part was when he gave a first lesson to a very pretty little boy of eight years old, and when he allowed his most advanced pupils to prove how thoroughly they understand both language and grammar, and how clear and just are their ideas. This was done by one deaf and dumb reading (by signs) out of a quite new pamphlet to another deaf and dumb, who, as fast as anybody speaking

estimation by the public. She retired in 1816 but reappeared in 1819 on the occasion of her husband's benefit.

* Roch-Amboise Cucurron Sicard (Abbé), born 1742. In 1791 the Constituent Assembly adopted his establishment for the instruction of the deaf and dumb as a national institution. In 1792 he was seized whilst instructing his pupils and thrown into prison; he appealed to a Protestant friend, M. Laffon de Ladébat, from the chambre d'arrêt of L'Abbaye St. Germain-des-Près, saying he was the only priest the people had not yet sacrificed; his appeal was not in vain, and he was rescued from a most perilous position. He afterwards endured two years of exile, but was restored to his labours and his institution by the revolution of the 18 Brumaire. He died in 1822 at the age of eighty.—*Dict. des Contemporains.*

could dictate, wrote down word for word what was contained in the book upon a large slate tablet, exposed to the eyes of all the spectators, and afterwards making upon another slate tablet by the side of it, a grammatical analysis of what he had written; that is to say, taking out all the propositions or assertions made in the phrase he had written, and placing them one after the other in their grammatical construction, and without their connecting prepositions, conjunctions, &c. This was both curious, satisfactory, and amusing; but when the master talked himself, which he did in a proportion which more than made up for the dumbness of all the others, he proved that if he had the powers of giving others clear ideas he had not left a single one for himself. He *embrouillèed* himself in systems of general grammar, of mind, and of logic, till he became so excessively confused and tiresome, that after sitting there from eleven till past one o'clock, and finding there was no hope of his ending, we contrived to get away, resolving never to trust ourselves to the eternal Babel of a teacher of deaf and dumb till we had become the *first* ourselves, and had no objection to remain the *second.*

From this we went to the Tuileries, to see the apartments occupied by Buonaparte. Sandos, a Swiss tailor, settled here and much employed by Madame Buonaparte, procured us this permission, which is only obtained by favour, as it is by no means shown to all the world. It is well they are not. *Republican simplicity* might well be excused for being startled at such magnificence. I have formerly seen Versailles, and I have seen the Little Trianon, and I have seen many palaces in other countries, but I never saw anything surpassing the magnificence of this. The apartment was that in which they actually live; it is the lower range of windows looking to the garden from the Pavillon de Flore to the centre. It consists of a large antechamber; a *salon*, hung and furnished with blue-lilac lustring embroidered in the honey-suckle pattern with maron, in the best taste possible. The curtains had the same pattern in an *appliqué* of cloth. In this room is the beautiful St. Cecilia with a turban, playing upon the harp, by Domenichino—I think from the Borghese Palace. The second *salon* was furnished with yellow satin and brown and *sang de bœuf* fringes, and nothing can be more magnificent than this room; the glasses were all *drapés*, and not framed, which has a much handsomer effect; beneath the glasses stood beautiful porphyry and other fine marble tables, and upon these tables magnificent vases of Sèvres and of granite, &c., mounted in ormolu, and very fine candelabra; in the middle of the room hung a lustre of English crystals, mounted with a great deal of ormolu; the chairs, exquisite tapestry. The next room was the bedchamber, the one where they actually both sleep in one bed. The furniture here was blue silk with white and gold fringes—the bed, in a recess *drapé*; it is of mahogany, with rich and rather heavy ormolu ornaments. The room is hung with some small old pictures; beyond this a small *salle des bains*, without any particular ornament; here Buonaparte shaves and makes his very short toilet; and from hence an *escalier dérobé* leads up to his *cabinet de travail* above; beyond this room (the *salle des bains*), from which a passage is taken off, is a *cabinet de lecture*, that is to say, a smallish room, with bookcases all round about the height of a chimney-piece, shut up, of rosewood inlaid *à la Grecque*, with satin-wood, the walls above hung with green; and in this room is placed the 'Madonna della Sedia,' but it immediately struck both Mrs. D. and myself to be a copy, or if the original, painted over so as to be no longer itself—I hope and believe it is a copy. Beyond this is Madame Buonaparte's dressing-room, fitted up with the same elegance—a low room—white muslin embroidered, and white lustring curtains with white and gold fringes. Here was a rosewood cabinet, or rather large *nécessaire*, containing everything for ladies' work, all in cut steel, the outside much ornamented with the same; it was brought from England to Madame Buonaparte by General Lauriston.* Beyond this dressing-room is a small bedchamber, inhabited by Mademoiselle de Beauharnois† till she married. It contains a very large cabinet lately brought from Versailles, and meant to be placed in one of the large apartments. It was originally made to contain the queen's jewels, and is by far the richest *meuble* I ever saw, though neither pretty or in good taste, but covered with ormolu *naçre-de-perle*, Sèvres china, and painted cameos. From hence we went up stairs, meaning to see the great apartment, but it was locked. The next day we made another attempt under the auspices of Mr. Sandos, a personage seemingly in high favour at the Tuileries. I fancy seeing this is attended with some difficulty, owing to no one being admitted into Buonaparte's *cabinet de travail*, which was indeed what we principally wished to see.

In the evening went to Berthier's. It was *novidi*, his day, and he had made it a ball. There were benches placed all round the first room, which was empty when we arrived; but in time the rooms were occupied by women, while a wide passage was left behind them for the men to move about. We got places upon these benches, and I saw a great deal of excellent dancing. The dress much less naked and extravagant than at the Bal des Etrangers. Madame d'Hamelin one of the best dancers, but she is not pretty, and has a heavy figure. M. de Chatillon the best among the men,

* General Lauriston, born at Pondicherry, 1764, was employed on various missions by Buonaparte when First Consul; he was sent to England with the ratification of the preliminaries of the Peace of Amiens.

† Hortense, born 1783, married to Louis Buonaparte, afterwards King of Holland, January 5, 1802.

though many danced admirably; but I never saw any dancing like his off the opera stage, and his figure made for it. They all wore crops, and very few *bien peigné* or looking clean. There was a supper for above a hundred people. Among the company at Berthier's was General Moreau* and his wife.† He is a middle-sized, quiet-looking man, who at a distance gave me a little the idea of Sir G. Beaumont, though shorter and blacker; but I was not near enough to see his countenance. His wife is a very pretty, very modest-looking young person, prettily dressed, and dancing very well. Young Beauharnois was among the dancers; he is rather good-looking, but by no means distinguished. Monge,‡ who was once the Minister of Marine and was afterwards at the head of the Egyptian Institute, was likewise there,

* Jean Victor Moreau, general of the French Republic, born 1763; he took up arms at Rennes, where he had gone to study the law, in 1787. He assisted Pichegru in the conquest of Holland, and opened the campaign of 1796 by the defeat of the Austrians. The discovery of the secret correspondence carried on by Pichegru with the Bourbons involved him in that disgrace, and he retired from the army. In 1798 he was again employed. At the close of 1800 he won the battle of Hohenlinden. In 1804 he was again charged with being implicated in the Royalist conspiracies; he was condemned to prison, but allowed to go to America. In 1813 he returned to Europe, and was induced by the sovereigns of Russia, Austria, and Prussia to aid in the direction of the allied armies against his own country. He was dangerously wounded on the 27th of August, in the attack on Dresden, and died in consequence on the 1st of September. He was buried at St. Petersburg; the Emperor of Russia provided for his widow, who received the title of Maréchale from Louis XVIII.—*Rose's Biog. Dict.*

† Madame Moreau was the daughter of General Halot d'Osery.

‡ Gaspard Monge, born 1746, one of the founders of the Polytechnic School. He was employed, at the age of sixteen, to teach natural philosophy in the College at Lyons. In 1796 he accompanied the army in the invasion of Italy, and afterwards in the expedition to Egypt; and to him, with Bertholet and Fourier, all the scientific fruits of that expedition are due. An intimacy sprang up there between Monge and Buonaparte, which made the former so zealous an adherent of the latter, that he was expelled from the Institute at the final restoration of Louis XVIII. Monge was the author of various scientific works of great reputation. He died in 1818. —*Rose's Biog. Dict.*

and La Place,* the great mathematician, a smooth, sickly, ordinary-looking man. To him we were introduced by Sir C. Blagden,† and to Monge by Madame de Staël. But a ten years' separation of the two countries seems to have made them entirely forget England and English people, and everything that concerns them. They have not, thank God, had emigrants during this period to keep up their acquaintance with us!

Wednesday, 31*st*.—Made some visits. To Madame de Coigny; found her at home. She lives in Rue d'Agnesseau, Faubourg St. Honoré, and has a comfortable apartment in the house that was her mother's, the Marquise de Conflans. In the evening to the Opera, in the box of the Swedish Minister. 'Les Mystères d'Isis.' The music is really beautiful, by Mozart; but all music becomes nearly alike by the manner in which they sing it, except just the two or three airs given by Laÿs. 'The Mystères d'Isis' is remarkable, even here, for its decorations and *coup de théâtre*. A view of Tartarus upon one side of the stage, and the Elysian Fields upon the other, showed in succession to the hero; admirable tableaux. The last scene, of a vast palace (I know not where) where the hero (I know not who) is rewarded with the hand of his mistress, very good, but not sufficiently lighted. This, I understand, always happens after the first three or four representations of a new piece; they economise upon the lights and so spoil a part of the effect.

After the opera, went to M. le Comte de Crillons,

* Pierre Simon La Place, the celebrated mathematician and astronomer, born 1749, was son of a farmer in Normandy. D'Alembert procured for him a chair of mathematics at the Military School in Paris. In 1799 he was made Minister of the Interior by Buonaparte, afterwards removed to the Presidency of the Conservative Senate. In 1814 he voted for the deposition of Napoleon. He was created a count by the Emperor, and a marquis by Louis XVIII. He died in March 1827. He was the author of a long list of works on mathematics, astronomy, &c.—*Rose's Biog. Dict.*

† The author of several works on subjects of natural philosophy and medicine.

with whom we had dined at Madame de Castellane's. Madame de Crillon gave a little ball, or, as it was called, a *souper dansant*, to which Madame de Coigny was told to ask us. I sent in my name from the antechamber to Madame de Coigny, who presented me to Madame de Crillon, a civil woman of about fifty, who it seems had a considerable fortune *aux îsles.* The party was very select, some of the best *danseuses* of the *ancien régime.* The company, consisting of about seventy or eighty people, were of that party. Mdlle. de Coigny's dancing, much as I had heard of it, did not disappoint me; it is as excellent as Madame Hamelin's. The dress, too, of these people was as simple as the others were *recherché*—plain chemises of muslin, short for the dancers, with their hair *coiffé en cheveux*, with a bunch of flowers, was the general costume, and no bosom more displayed than it would have been in England. There was an excellent supper served in a fine *sallè à manger*, at one o'clock, with room for every one to sit down. M. de Crillon is the youngest son of the Duc de Crillon, who commanded against Gibraltar. By prudence and by remaining at his post, he has got through the Revolution less shaken by the general convulsion than almost anybody else that can be quoted. He inhabits the same house (one of the noble ones in the Place de Louis XV.), is served even by the same servants, and in short, except by taxes and the loss of seigneurial rights, &c., is much where he was. I had remarked him at Madame de Castellane's dinner as a particularly gentlemanlike man.

Thursday, April 1st.—In the morning went with Mrs. Cosway to be presented to Buonaparte's mother. On arriving at her house in the Chaussé d'Autin, I immediately recognised it to be that which belonged to the family of Montfermeil, of whom we saw so much when we were for the first time at Paris. Of them I can learn nothing but that they emigrated, and my informer said he believed M. de Montfermeil had died in Germany, but he seemed to know little of the matter. The house suffered much during '*le temps de la terreur*' (as it is always called). It was a *maison d'arrestation*, and has since been sold three or four times over, and a great part of the beautiful garden turned into a *potager*, and the rest badly laid out *à l'Anglaise*. The house for its present possessor has been newly painted and furnished magnificently. The beautiful *salle à manger en coupole* is painted as if incrusted with porphyry and other marbles, which they imitate now at Paris in the greatest perfection. In the *salon*, chairs of crimson velvet laced with gold and crimson lustring, curtains with gold open fringes. The room in which she received us was lined with Italian pictures and furnished with purple-striped satin, with deep gold-coloured fringes. Madame Buonaparte walked with us over the whole apartment, all furnished in the same style, all covered with magnificent carpets, and all full of fine candelabra, &c. She herself is a woman turned fifty, with large dark eyes, an intelligent mild countenance, and great remains of having been very handsome. She has a civil quiet manner, but no mark of particular cleverness either in her conversation or in her manner. She is said to be in all the heights of Swedenborgism, or at least what used to be called *quietism* here; and I should fancy it was true by her partiality for our introductress, but I hardly see that she has influence or interest with anybody. Her son, when she is ill, comes to see her, has lodged her well, takes good care of her, and I fancy has little more to do with her. All the family of Buonaparte, however, live very much together, and as there are five brothers and three sisters, they constitute no small society. She endeavours, I believe, to protect the quondam convents of women and their attendant priests in the conquered countries; how far she succeeds I know not.

Dined at Madame de Staël's with twenty people. General and Madame Marmont, Madame Recamier, Mr. and Mrs. Neckar, Saussure, Lord Archibald Hamilton, Comte Marcoff (the Russian Minister), Benjamin Constant, M. de Chauvelin, Lord Henry Petty, Le Marquis Lacchesini, Comte Louis de Narbonne,* General Dessolles,† Mr. Girandin (now President of the Tribunal, son of the proprietor of Hormononville), and two other men whose names I don't know. Luckily I got seated next Comte Louis de Narbonne, who is uncommonly sensible and pleasant in conversation; on my other hand was General Dessolles, who was at the head of Moreau's état-major, and wrote the account of the battle of Hohenlinden, supposed here to be the best military despatch that ever was penned. He

* Count Louis de Narbonne, Minister of War in the reign of Louis XVI., was born in the Duchy of Parma, 1755. His mother was dame d'honneur to the Duchess of Parma (daughter to Louis XV.), and his father first gentilhomme de la chambre. After the death of the duchess, he was brought up at court, where his mother was dame d'honneur to Madame Victoire. Though attached by duty and gratitude to the house of Bourbon, he shared in many of the more liberal opinions of the revolutionary party. He assisted the King's aunts in leaving France for Rome in 1791. He emigrated to England in 1792, and was settled with Madame de Staël and her party at Juniper Hall, Surrey. He accepted employment under Buonaparte, and was created a lieutenant-general. He accompanied the French army to Moscow, and died in the retreat, at Torgau, 1813. Miss Burney gives a more romantic and scandalous account of the parentage of Count Louis de Narbonne. (*See* Madame D'Arblay's Journal.)

† Marquis Jean Jos. P. Aug. Dessolles, born 1767. Accompanied Bonaparte in his Italian campaign, defeated the Austrians in the Valteline, and was engaged in military service till the peace of Luneville, and was then named 'commandant en chef, provisoire de l'Armée du Hanovre.' He was replaced by Bernadotte, and sent, in 1808, to Spain. He accompanied Prince Eugène in the Russian expedition, but his health obliged him to return. In 1814 the Provisional Government appointed him to the command of the 'Garde Nationale,' at Paris, and he declared in favour of the Bourbons. In 1815 he appealed to the Garde Nationale to stop the progress of Napoleon, and accompanied Louis XVIII. After the battle of Waterloo resumed his command of the Garde Nationale, but disapproving of the conduct of those in power, he resigned. In the Chambre des Pairs he continually raised his voice against the infringements of the 'Charte,' and was one of the firmest supporters of public liberty.

has a mild quiet countenance and manner. The little conversation I had with him was on the subject of fine climates, for which we were both equal enthusiasts. Switzerland, by accident, was touched upon; he regretted what had been done there, believed it to have been the cause of much evil to the French. We left Madame de Staël's early, and felt ourselves so thoroughly fatigued with the *veilles* of the night before, that we indulged ourselves in staying quietly at home.

Friday, 2nd.—This was the day that our friend the Swiss tailor assured us that Madame Buonaparte was, by her own appointment, to receive us at his recommendation, as two ladies who had come from England particularly desirous to see the Grand Consul, and to make her acquaintance. We were to have gone at mid-day, but as they only returned from Mal-Maison at twelve o'clock the night before, our tailor brought us word that at three o'clock she would see us. I own I doubted it to the last moment,—however, at three o'clock we went to the Tuileries, and, after some enquiries for our tailor, we were shown into one of the *salons* we had before seen. Here we waited for about ten minutes, examining the picture of the 'Battle of Marengo,' which still remained in the room, while several people (four or five ladies) were ushered through it: at last our tailor came, hoping we did not mind a little *détour*, and then led us through a passage at the back of the apartment to the door of the little waiting-room between the dressing-room of Madame Buonaparte and the little red chamber beyond it. Here we found two or three little black boys in waiting, and a Mameluc (as they are called), that is to say an Asiatic black, in a sort of Turkish dress, keeping the door. Our tailor conducted us to the door of Madame Buonaparte's dressing-room, where she met us, and the tailor disappeared. She crossed the room to the chairs that were ranged along the wall, and, sitting down first herself, begged us to be seated also. She is a thin, dark, very genteel-looking woman, about the size, and not unlike, Lady Elizabeth Foster, but with a more sensible and less *minaudière* countenance; in her manners, without assuming those of a queen, she unites much protection and dignity with much civility. I think *elle se tire d'affaire* (and it is no easy matter) very cleverly. We talked of the taste of her apartment, of Mal-Maison, of her garden there, of the plants she was getting from England, from Lee and Kennedy's, of those she wished to have, &c. She asked us if we had places for the parade; when we mentioned those we had, she said they were not good ones; that she would place us better, and then rising went to the door, and calling to Sandos, said, 'Vous amenerez ces dames le jour de la parade, je les ferai bien placées;' upon which we curtsied, and with many thanks took our leave. Who she took us for—whether the tailor had ever explained who Mrs. D. was—Heaven knows! But it is certain she had no idea of Mrs. D.'s talent, or at least did not take the least notice of it, though I gave her a fair opportunity by asking if the little bust of Buonaparte, which stood upon a coin in the room, was like; she said it was very little like, but without *relevéing* the subject at all. In short she, like all the rest who have not emigrated, seem to have totally forgotten all the very little they ever knew about England or English people. All Buonaparte's servants, and we saw several in the antechamber and on the staircase, are in a livery—a lightish blue coat, waistcoat, and breeches, with a silver lace round the collar.

Before we went to Madame Buonaparte's, we had called on Madame de Beauvan and her sister: they are two particularly amiable people, and I regret not seeing more of them. I received a long visit from M. Frégeville,* whom we knew long ago at Montpelier. He is become a *général de division*, their highest military grade; was at

* Charles, afterwards Marquis de Frégeville.

one time deputed to the legislative body; in short has, as he said himself, had a very successful career. He is married again and has one child living; he has purchased a *terre* in Languedoc, and I fancy is very well off there.

In the evening went to the Théâtre de Montansier, at the upper end of the Palais Royal. This theatre is almost entirely filled and supported by the *filles* of the Palais Royal and their amateurs. The theatre is not of a pretty *coupe*; there are some boxes, *grillés* or not *grillés*, as you please to make them: by taking one of these one can go to this theatre just as well as to any of the others, for there is no noise, no squabbles, no indecorum, either on or off the stage. The *mauvaise compagnie* here (and I have now been twice among them) are quite as decently behaved, and *more* decently dressed, than that which call themselves *la bonne compagnie*. At this theatre they give four and sometimes five little pieces. Those we saw were, 'La Guérite,' 'La Jolie Parfumeuse,' and 'Cadet Roussel aux Champs Elysées.' The first entirely supported by the acting of Brunet, the hero of this theatre and a very good actor in the low comic. The drollery of the third depended upon *slip-slop* speaking, modes of pronunciation, which to us was not very entertaining.

From the theatre we came home, supped, changed our gowns, and between eleven and twelve went to the great ball given by M. Demidoff, a young Russian, who has been here all the winter, and spending more than anybody. He is lodged at the Hôtel de Montholon on the Boulevard. The house is in itself much ornamented, and was now decorated with much pink and silver drapery, and artificial flowers for the fête; but the rooms are not large, nor many of them, so that the company was too large for the house. The first person I met here was my old acquaintance the Duc de Richelieu. He looks much better than when I saw him in England, and is an uncommonly gentlemanlike man. He seemed really glad to see me. Indeed, nothing can be more striking upon all occasions than the manners of the *old* and *new world*: the first are all *prévenances*, attentions, and politeness; the latter seem not to know or totally to neglect all common forms, returning visits, &c. It is impossible that these *two worlds* should ever amalgamate in society: their children may. Till I saw them both I blamed the *old* world; but it is still more the fault of the *new*. All the *jeunesse de Paris* were there of the new *régime*, and very many of the old; all the Foreign Ministers' wives, and a good many strangers. Vestris, who was there, danced a quadrille, which was composed of the very best dancers of society; he danced with Madame Hamelin, M. de Lafitte* (the supposed best dancer of Paris), with Madame Ferval; the other two ladies were Mdlle. Carlot and Madame ——. Vestris's figure was curious; his *coiffure* was one of those bustling, frizzed and powdered heads which were worn about twenty years ago, and in dancing showers of powder came out of it, and it flapped up and down in the most ridiculous manner. M. de Lafitte was likewise frizzed and powdered, while the other two men, and indeed *all* the other men, wore crops. This took much from that sort of similarity of dress which certainly adds to the effect and beauty of a dance. The women were in general well-dressed, all *coiffées en cheveux* with flowers, and all the young ones dressed in white, trimmed with bunches of flowers. In the antechamber was a *bouquetière*, who gave every lady as she entered a large bouquet of beau-

* Jacques Laffitte, the well-known banker at Paris, was born 1767; he was placed in Perrégaux's bank in 1788; in 1804 became a partner. He was distinguished by his knowledge, his conduct, and his principles in all matters of finance. In 1814 he was appointed governor of the Bank of France. He took an active part in political and economical questions in the Chamber of Deputies, and acquired the respect of all parties. He was well known for his liberality when charitable contributions were needed. He died in 1844.

tiful forced flowers, roses, carnations, &c., such as at Paris at this season could not cost less than twelve or eighteen livres a piece. These bouquets were changed as often as you pleased. The liveries of this Russian are more covered with gold lace than *anyone* ever saw *anywhere*, upon a *fond* of dark green; and there were besides *chasseurs* and *coureurs*, and *jockins*, and blacks, and little boys *habillés à la Tartare*, but all equally *gallonés* upon scarlet and black; and besides all this, the persons who served (out of livery) were all in brown coats with a gold embroidery, comically like that of the tribunes here: yet, with all this magnificence of servants, they were not properly ranged and placed, and did not make the effect they ought. The supper was served as people desired it, and in any room where it was called for. To have the whole honour of this ball, Demidoff received himself, and did not allow his wife to do the honours; but people just gave their tickets at the door, and half the people in the room I am convinced he did not know.

Saturday, 3rd.—In the morning took a walk upon the *quais*, and poked into a number of *brocanteur* shops. In the evening went to Madame Fouché's assembly—very few people—as all the world had gone to Molé's benefit. We saw there Barbé de Marbois,* the one of the *Déportés* to

* Count François de Barbé Marbois, born at Metz, 1745, where his father was director of the Mint. He began life as tutor to the family of M. de Castries, Minister of the Marine, was afterwards Consul-general in the United States, and then Intendant of St. Domingo. He returned to France in 1790, in 1791 was named ambassador to the German Diet, and the year after to Vienna. In 1795 he attacked the conduct of the Directory; and was sentenced to transportation, but survived the influence of the climate of Guiana, and returned to France after the 18th Brumaire, became a counsellor of state in 1801, director of the Treasury, and finally Minister. As a senator, in 1814, he pronounced the fall of Napoleon, and he received from the Bourbons similar situations to those he had held during the Republic and the Empire. In 1815 Louis XVIII. made him Garde des Sceaux, and he swore allegiance to Louis Philippe in 1830, and continued in office till 1834. He was the author of several works, and died in the year 1837, aged ninety-two.

Cayenne, who would not escape with the others, but remained conformably to the orders of his country, till recalled by Buonaparte. He is now Ministre du Trésor public. He is a tall thin man of past fifty; not handsome, but with an uncommonly fine head, and a great deal of character about it; in short, he is the only man that I have yet seen wearing the uniform of a *Ministre d'Etat* who had the look of a gentleman. Mme. de Staël, who one is sure to find talking or endeavouring to talk to the most distinguished man in company, brought him near us, and was asking him questions about Guiana, and his manner of passing his time there, &c. &c.; which, without affectation or reluctance on his part, led to several curious and melancholy particulars of their life there. This man I find has the reputation of being one of the honestest men in France, and of having no equal in probity among his *confrères* in the present government.

From Madame Fouché's we went to an assembly at the Duchesse de Luines'—one of the very few houses among what I call the *old world* that still receive company, and the company is confined exclusively to the old world, for of the new I saw only Madame Visconti there. Four rooms were open; in the first a table was spread with refreshments, at which sat Madame de Luines and most of the ladies. In the *salon* they were playing at bêribi, in another room at crêpes, and in a third at whist. I fancy a good deal of play goes on at this house. The *old world* is certainly much better-looking as well as much better and more simply dressed than the *new world*. There were at this assembly a number of very pretty women. Madame de Bouillie, Madame de Chevreuse (the *belle fille* of the house), Madame de Montmorenci, and many others. They were none of them more *décoltée* than they would have been in England—*coiffées en cheveux* with flowers. Madame de Beauvan presented us there; we remained in the antechamber till she led us up to Madame de Luines.

Sunday, 4*th*.—Many of the shops are open to do business here of a Sunday, though certainly more are quite shut than on the Decade.

Went to the Gallery, which the more one sees the more it astonishes; and it would be very long before I should sufficiently get the better of this astonishment to be able to fix my mind quietly to one picture or one set of pictures, and really enjoy them as I used to do when there were not above half-a-dozen of the most exquisite in a collection.

Dined at Mr. Jackson's: the women were Madame de Brignole, Madame Recteren, a Spaniard, wife to a Count Recteren, formerly Minister from Holland to Spain, a lively-looking woman, and Madame Récamier,* a rich banker's wife here, who has *the* finest house in Paris in the *new* style, and is herself *the* decided beauty of the *new* world, for if she can be called handsome, it is entirely a *figure de fantasie*. She has a clear complexion, is young, tall, dressed with much affectation of singularity in the extravagance of the mode; her manners are *doucereuses*, thinking much of herself with perfect carelessness about others; for, besides being a beauty, she has pretensions, I understand, to *bel-esprit*. They may be as well-founded, and yet not sufficient to burn her for a witch. The men of our dinner were nothing remarkable. General Dessolles sat by me at table. He is *doux* and *facile* in his manners,

* Madame Récamier, the daughter of a notary at Lyons, named Bernard, was born 1777. At the age of fifteen she was married to M. Récamier, forty-three years old. Her career as a beauty, exercising a large amount of social influence, has been recently the subject of more than one biographical sketch. At the age of seventy she is said to have received an offer of marriage from M. de Chateaubriand, then near eighty, but which she did not accept. She died of the cholera, May 1849.

M. Récamier was formerly a hatter at Lyons. By successful operations in the course of the Revolution, he has acquired, I was assured very honourably, a large fortune.—*M. B.*

but I fancy is rather a good general than *un homme d'esprit.*

We left Mr. Jackson's before nine—came home—changed our gowns, and went with Barrois to the Hameau de Chantilly, one of the many public gardens open most nights for dancing, &c. This was formerly, as said before, the hotel and garden of the Duchesse de Bourbon. The entrance is by a large court from the Faubourg St. Honoré. The garden goes back to the Champs Elysées. It is extremely well laid out with many little intricacies, a large alley that goes round it, a broad terrace by the house, and a large sloping lawn before it. All this is well lighted with patent lamps, placed in large square glass lanterns hung across the walks and fixed in the *bosquets* and under the trees. Nothing can be prettier than both the general effect and the details of this garden. Under the trees was an excellent orchestra, led by the same man (a creole) who conducted the music at M. Demidoff's, and there were, I know not how many, sets of French country dances; we saw two danced by different sets extremely well. The dancers were *ouvrières*, mantua-makers, &c. &c., or *filles*, mostly the latter and shopmen, &c. &c. In the intervals of the dancing they spread themselves about the garden, where at every step are placed little green tables with two or three chairs, and every here and there little rooms like cottages on the outside, and the lower part of the house is open. All the gilding and painting upon the walls, and the glasses remain just as they were in the time of Madame de Bourbon; and in one of the rooms are still the fine tapestry *fauteuils* that originally belonged to the house; we were struck also with the locks and fastenings to the doors and windows being much handsomer than usual, and found that the arms of France were carefully obliterated from every one of them. All these rooms are well lighted, and full of little tables and chairs; and here refreshments are to be had, with prices affixed to them in a long paper called *la carte.* But this is not all. The entry of this garden is 24 sous, of which 15 are allowed *en consomation*, as it is called, that is, 15 sous worth of anything you please in food or in amusements; three country dances cost 5 sous a-piece, or three turns of a *jeu de bague* or three *courses* upon the little lake, on which there are about a dozen little boats, ready for anybody who pleases to paddle about; in summer, they say, they are never empty.

A large *salon* for dancing was arranged with treillage paper, treillage columns and painted flowers and trees with the perspective of a garden and avenue at the end, and green boxes for real flowers all round it, and a recess painted like a forest. Not the least remarkable part of this evening was that we were walking about at ten o'clock at night on the 4th of April and sitting in the open air, without feeling cold, with the green buds all bursting over our heads and the almond trees in full blow: the warmth was rather that of the end of May than the beginning of April.

Before I quit this place I must again take notice of the extreme decency and propriety of behaviour which reigned here, as in all the meetings of the lower orders where I have been. This was a garden where everybody was walking about in pairs or in parties, and everybody seeming very well disposed to amuse themselves, but one never heard an improper *propôs*, or saw anything that marked the smallest *dérèglement.*

While looking on at the dancing a man came up and very civilly asked me to join—thanking him I said, that I did not dance; he made me a bow and retired as civilly as he had come forward.

Monday, 5*th.*—At last I have seen this famous parade, which all the Parisians have been talking of for a month past. I was not disappointed in it, because my great object was to see Buonaparte, and I knew beforehand how little one could possibly see of him upon such an occasion, although, whenever we complained of not having seen him, everybody referred us to the parade, as if that was to give us *entire satisfaction.* We were unfortunate in weather; it rained hard the whole time he was on horseback. We were conducted by our friend the tailor to a window in the *entresol* of the Tuileries looking into the Court, the best situation possible, as it is above the lines of infantry and not much above the level of a man on horseback. There were several people at the same window with ourselves; Madame B. herself, and a party of people with her, occupied other windows in the same range of rooms.

Great part of the troops marched in by the centre door of the *grille* which now divides the large space before the Palace, from the Place de Carousel and this space, though large, is small for a review. Buonaparte mounted his horse (a light-coloured dun with a white mane and tail) before one o'clock, at the great centre door of the Palace accompanied by the generals of the different divisions of infantry, cavalry, and artillery; they then rode along the lines, so that Buonaparte twice passed our window, once near enough to see what one can see of a man on horseback gently trotting by with his head much *enfoncé* in his hat. I saw enough to convince me he is not much like his busts. But all I saw was a little man, remarkably well on horseback, with a sallow complexion, a highish nose, a very serious countenance, and cropped hair. He wore the dress of some infantry regiment, blue with a plain broad white lappel and a plain hat with the very smallest of national cockades in it. After riding along all the four lines, he and his attendant generals placed themselves beyond the second line, exactly opposite our window, while all the troops—first infantry, then cavalry, and then artillery—marched before him with their music playing and colours flying; none of the officers saluted but their colonel. After passing Buonaparte they filed off, and when the last had passed, he came again to the same door of the Tuileries, dismounted and disappeared. This is all that those who best see the parade can see of the mover of the whole machine. I am quite unacquainted with military details, and therefore shall not pretend to give any opinion about the troops: all I could observe was that they never marched in straight lines, and that their muskets were carried in various directions; any of our colonels of militia would have been ashamed of their men so marching before the king. The dress too of these troops, particularly of the consular guard, of which I had heard much, struck me as much less smart than *any* of our regiments of dragoons or light horse. It is a dark blue coat with a red cape, and a long large gold-coloured worsted shoulder-knot, part of which is always tucked up to the button-holes in front of the coat. Their hats are looped up with the same coloured worsted, and a very high plume of green and red, or blue and red, or red and white, like those they have lately given our troops; their hair *en queue*. The consular guard, both horse and foot, are allowed to be *l'élite* of the armies in point of size and appearance. The other regiments looked very small. The regiment of hussars, commanded by the young Beauharnois, was the next best—the dress of the officers is pretty, and the trappings of their horses, all of *peau de tigre*, with the *muffle* of the tiger embroidered, or rather *plâqué*, upon the housing that covers the back of the horse, had a very pretty effect; but half-a-dozen officers thus accoutred has nothing to do with the dress of the troops.

Although it was such a bad day, there were a great many spectators in the Place de Carousel looking through the *grille*, and at all the windows in all the houses; but not the smallest applause or shouting or notice taken when Buonaparte was riding along the lines quite near them, though this is the first time he has appeared in public since the peace. It was raining hard as we waited for our carriage, and the arcades of the Tuileries were full of all sorts of people; a line of grenadiers kept a passage up the staircase, and prevented people coming in; but they struck me as doing their duty in a much *gentler* manner than I remember by the Garde Suisse and Française doing formerly upon similar occasions.

In the evening to Madame de Staël. It was a sort of concert. When we arrived, somebody was playing on the pianoforte, and the servant begged we would wait in the outer room till the piece was over. To this we readily consented. The Prince of Orange arriving soon after, the same injunction was put upon him, and we laughingly remonstrated against keeping the Prince of Orange in the antechamber; but the servant stuck to his orders, and the Prince remained very quietly with us, and others who followed till the piece of music was finished, when we all entered together. Garat,* a public singer, allowed to be the first voice in Paris, performed. He first sang an Italian air abominably, with the most violent and forced expression. He has a good and flexible voice, and seems to understand music, but his taste is a thorough French taste. The Chevalier de la Cainea† was there too, and sang better than ever. I really began to pity poor Garat, although the greatest coxcomb in appearance that ever was beheld. But one need never pity a Frenchman where self-conceit can bring him off: he is on all such occasions invulnerable. At last they sang a duet together, in which

* There were two singers of the name of Garat—Pierre-Jean, and Joseph Dominique Fabry—brothers. It was probably the elder brother to whom Miss Berry alludes, as he appears to have enjoyed a high reputation at Paris as a concert-singer. In 1795, not having a *carte de sureté,* he was arrested as a *suspect.* He amused himself by singing, till the commandant of the fort, together with the soldiers, crowded round to listen to him, and like another Orpheus, he so enchanted his audience that they carried him in triumph to his home.

† The Chevalier de la Cainea, a Neapolitan nobleman, afterwards married to Sophia, daughter of Sir Richard Mill, of Mottisfont, Hants.

Garat did not spoil the effect of La Cainea's exquisite singing, and he afterwards gave us two French opera airs with much taste. The company consisted more of the *old* than the *new* world. Ice and cakes were carried about, and afterwards punch; no supper.

Tuesday, 6th.—Walked about upon the *quais* to a number of shops; dined at home, and went in the evening to the Théâtre de Louvois: the pieces were 'Le Père Supposé,' 'Le Vapoureur,' and 'Le Voyage Interrompu.' The second was most tiresome—all sentiment and nonsense; but a *pièce à sentiment* is here always applauded, particularly where a child is brought on the stage, which is a means of interesting to which of late they for ever resort. The children (*par parenthèse*) all act their parts admirably. The 'Voyage Interrompu' is one of Picard's, in which he himself acts a chattering *notaire* to perfection: it was very amusing and laughable.

Wednesday, 7th.—Went in the morning to meet Mrs. Cosway in the Gallery, to see David's picture of the 'Rape of the Sabines;' but it happened to be the day of the Decade, on which it is shut to all the world, to be swept and cleaned—certainly very necessary in so public a place. We went on with Barrois to see David's picture, which is exhibited, for his own profit, at one shilling and sixpence a-piece. Barrois said many other painters in Paris had attempted thus exhibiting their works, but nobody had found it worth their while but David; and I dare say very few people indeed except strangers go and see this picture. It is in a room by itself, and a glass so placed as to reflect it. It is worth seeing, as a picture in which the artist has done his utmost, and that utmost is something considerable. It is well drawn, and, generally speaking, well composed; the details well executed; the colouring of the two principal male figures *too* good—I mean out of harmony with the rest. Of mellowness it has *none*: it gave me the idea of a finely-coloured basrelievo more than of a picture. The old French school rises greatly indeed, placed as it now is in the Gallery, not only by comparing it with other modern schools, but still more by the modern French.

Went afterwards to the great Bibliothèque du Roi, in the Rue de Richelieu, now converted into the Bibliothèque Nationale, Rue de la Loi, and enriched with all the spoils of Italy. We had a letter to the librarian, but as *seeing* a library beyond a general *coup d'œil* is, in my opinion, of all wastes of time the greatest, we did not deliver our letter, but just walked through. The library is open every day to the public. It occupies an immense apartment round a court. The books are in wooden cases with wire doors, and are the height of the rooms. The cases and their arrangement are in no respect altered from what they were, but new shelves are placed between the windows, with the shelves still empty, because (it is said) the carpenter has never been paid for making them, and won't let the books be placed till he is! One immense long room is entirely filled with tables, each for about eight or ten people, and nearly every seat was occupied by persons reading or transcribing from books.

Dined at Perrégaux's with twenty-six people, more than half of which were English. Among the French, the only person of *marque* whom I had not before seen was the Minister of the Marine—General (Admiral?) Decrès. He is the same who defended so gallantly the 'Guillaume Tell'* when she was taken by us coming out of Malta. He is one of the fattest, vulgarest, ugliest black men I ever

* March 30, 1800. The 'Guillaume Tell,' Captain Saulnier, bearing the flag of Rear Admiral Denis Decrès, came out of Valetta; she was chased and attacked, but defended herself most gallantly against the 'Foudroyant,' 'Lion,' and 'Penelope,' though at last compelled to yield to such superior force. 'A more heroic defence than that of the "Guillaume Tell" is not to be found among the records of naval actions. She became, under the name of the "Malta," the largest two-decker in the British navy, except the "Tonnant."'—From James' *Naval History*, vol. iii. pp. 23–27, edit. 1826.

saw. I had no opportunity of judging more of him than his appearance. Madame Marmont, to keep up her character of fine-ladyism, was among the last of the company who arrived. Five was the hour on the card; we dined about six. Perrégaux still inhabits (as before the Revolution) the famous Pavilion built by the Prince de Soubise for Mdlle. Guimard;* it has been new carpeted and new furnished, but the decorations of the walls are the same. In the evening to the Théâtre de la Rue Feydeau: it is the only one in Paris which is the same as I remember it, and very pretty it is. The piece we saw was 'Une Folie,' a French comic opera; the music was extremely pretty and well sung.

Thursday, 8*th*.—Went at three o'clock to the Tuileries to be presented to Madame Buonaparte. It had been announced some days before by the Préfêt du Palais, M. Du Luçay, to the Foreign Ministers, that she would on this day receive the Foreign Ministers' wives, and *les étrangères de marque qui désiraient lui être présentées.* We went in at the door in the corner of the court of the Tuileries which leads to Madame Buonaparte's apartment, and were ushered into the yellow *salon* which I have before described. In the antechamber were half-a-dozen servants in Buonaparte's livery. The door *à deux battons* was opened for every person by a man not in livery. Here we found already about half-a-dozen ladies and as many gentlemen, all Foreign Ministers, or their wives, or foreigners. They continued arriving till there were about forty women and about as many men.

There was a range of *chaises-à-dos* placed all round the room, upon which the ladies were invited to sit down by

* Marie Madeleine Guimard, celebrated dancer, born 1748. She was plain, dark, thin, and pitted with the small-pox, but much admired for her extraordinary grace in dancing and pantomime. She became the *maîtresse en titre* to the Maréchal Prince de Soubise. In the Rue de la Chaussée d'Antin a house was built for her, called the Temple of Terpsichore, and a theatre holding 500 persons. She died 1816.

Madame de Luçay. We all placed ourselves, and the men remained in a *peloton* before the window at the bottom of the room. Buonaparte himself and Madame B. entered at the same time from the door of the bedchamber. The moment of their entry I did not see, happening to have turned my head another way; when I looked round again she was already in conversation with the first lady on her right hand, and the Consul, in his undress uniform of Consul, between the two Préfêts du Palais, in their dress uniforms (scarlet and silver), in conversation with the Princess Sta. Croce. He went regularly round, speaking to every lady for about two or three minutes—M. Luçay, the Préfêt, having a sheet of paper in his hand, on which was written the name and nation of each lady, which he announced to Buonaparte as he approached her. We, standing at the further part of the circle from whence he began, had the opportunity of observing his manner and address—it is very simple and unaffected. He asked one lady if she could ride on horseback, another if she had been long in France; to the Italians, of which there were several, he spoke in Italian, saying much the same sort of royal nothings. My turn happening to come before Mrs. D.'s, he asked me if I had been long at Paris. 'Plus de trois semaines.' 'Comment trouvez vous l'Opéra;' or, 'Etes vous contente de l'Opéra?' 'Oh! bien beau, mais nous avons tant vu l'Opéra.' He seemed to feel by my answer that he might have addressed us better; but totally ignorant of who either of us was, he knew not how to change the subject, and continued it with Mrs. Damer, by asking: 'Si nous avions d'aussi bons danseurs en Angleterre?' 'Oh non, nous en faisons venir d'ici.' 'Cependant vous avez une bien belle voix, c'est Madame Billington,* je l'ai entendu en Italie.' 'Oui, assurément,

* Mrs. Billington was the daughter of a German of the name of Weichsal; married to James Billington, of Drury Lane, to whom her father had

elle a une très belle voix, et c'est une Anglaise.' 'Oui, c'est une Anglaise, mais elle a épousé un Français et étudié en Italie, de manière qu'elle appartient aux trois nations.'

And so he passed on to the next person, who happened to be a Russian, and repeated the same royal enquiry, si elle montait à cheval—which put me laughably in mind of the '*Do you get out?*' of St. James's. One could not but regret in every way that Mrs. Damer's talents had never reached his ears, nor the principal object of our journey to Paris, or he would certainly, had it only been *pour change de thèse*, have addressed us upon some other subject, of which many might have immediately offered themselves, and have reserved the opera for younger women.*

While he was thus going round the circle, Madame Buonaparte followed him, leaving always a distance of two or three persons in the circle between them. She in her turn spoke to everybody, but had no attendant upon her, nobody to tell her who anybody was, so that the

partly confided her musical education. She came out at Dublin, and in London, and afterwards at Paris, where she had lessons from Sacchini. Her singing was much admired in Italy. In 1799, her husband having died, she married M. Felessart, a Frenchman. She reappeared at Covent Garden in 1801; died 1818.

* The object of Mrs. Damer's visit appears to have been to offer the First Consul a bust of Mr. Fox, but through whom the offer was made does not transpire. It is to be presumed that neither the First Consul nor Madame Buonaparte could have been aware of Mrs. Damer's intentions before this reception; at any rate, this bust was more graciously acknowledged when received years after.

The following account, which appears in a work entitled 'Queens of Society,' by no means accords with Miss Berry's simple narrative of all that *really* passed during Mrs. Damer's interview with the First Consul. 'After the Peace of Amiens, *Mrs. Damer set out to Paris, and was presented to the great man, who charmed her with his conversation.* She was known to be a friend and warm supporter of Charles Fox, and the First Consul expressed his anxiety to have from her hand a bust of the "Man of the People."'—*The Queens of Society*, by Grace and Philip Wharton, vol. ii. p. 203.

presentation was in fact one in form to Buonaparte and none at all to her, only that *he* received and had the ladies presented to *him* in *her* apartment.

After he had thus gone round to every woman, he came to the group of men, spoke *par-ci et par-là*, to about six or seven of them, and then slipped out by the same door at which he entered. Madame Buonaparte in the meantime had made her round, and had stopped at the *fauteuil* by the side of the fire. As soon as Buonaparte was gone she sat down, and invited us to do so likewise; she spoke two or three words across the room to two or three ladies, among others to Lady Caher, * and was surprised at her going away so soon, and hoped she would have stayed till autumn. We observed this, as it seemed as if she wished it publicly to appear that she had no particular intimacy with Lady Caher, which by their having met at Plombières last summer had been supposed. She then spoke to two or three of the men nearest her, and amongst others to the Hereditary Prince of Orange, but without rising or making any difference in her address to him. After ten minutes of this circle she rose, bowed *à la Française* to all the company, and went out at the same door as Buonaparte had done, into her own bedchamber. We remained talking to one another for ten minutes more, and then marched off as fast as we could.

Madame Buonaparte struck us both still more like Lady E. F., *en répresentation* than even she had done before in private: but did not gain as much by being more dressed, as I expected. She wore, by way of being in a smart *demi-parure*, a pink slight silk gown, with a pink velvet round spot upon it, a small white silk or satin hat, with three small white feathers, tied under the chin; a handkerchief, and no fan, in her hand; in short,

* Daughter of James St. John Jeffreys; married to Lord Caher (afterwards created Earl of Glengall) in 1793. Lord Glengall died in 1819.

a decided half-dress; while we were all as much dressed as the present fashions (without any decided *robe de cour*) admits of. Buonaparte himself, as I have already said, was in his undress consular uniform, but with silk stockings and small buckles. His hair is very dark, and cropped much shorter than it appears on any of his busts, and it does not lay well or smoothly upon his head. He, by no means struck me as so little as I had heard him represented, and as, indeed, he appeared on horseback. His shoulders are broad, which gives his figure importance. His complexion, though pale and yellow, has not the appearance of ill health. His teeth are good, and his mouth, when speaking, as I saw him in good humour, has a remarkable and uncommon expression of sweetness. Indeed, his whole countenance, as I saw him in this circle, was more that of complacence and quiet intelligence than of any decided penetration and strong expression whatsoever. The Man of the Parade and the Man of the Circle has left a totally different impression on my mind, and I can hardly make the two countenances (one of which I saw so imperfectly) belong to the same person. His eyes are light grey, and he looks full in the face of the person to whom he speaks. To me always a good sign. Yet, after all I have said of the sweetness of his countenance, I can readily believe what is said that it is terrible and fire-darting when angry, or greatly moved by any cause.

In the evening to the Théâtre de la République. The pieces were 'Tancrède' and 'La Réconciliation malgré soi.' Talma was Tancrède.* He acts with fire and just expression, but his voice is rough, hoarse, and very disagreeable. His countenance, too, is against him, for he

* François Joseph Talma, born at Paris 1766; brought up in England, where his father practised as a dentist; returned to Paris, and made his débût in 1797, at the Théâtre Français, in the character of Seide in Voltaire's 'Mahomet.' He became the first tragedian of his time, and effected a reform in the costume of the stage. He was greatly favoured by Buonaparte. He married Mdlle. Vanhove, a distinguished actress. Died in 1826.

squints. Were he better endowed by nature, I think he would be a very good actor; as it is, he is reckoned one of their best. A *débutante* (Mdlle. le Court) performed Amenaide very badly indeed. Her gestures were so singularly awkward, that the *parterre* laughed. When this begins at Paris, it is generally followed up in a very painful manner, everything being taken in a ludicrous light, and all efforts of the poor unfortunate actor to restore gravity are in vain. However, this was not quite the case on this occasion, for though a repetition of the same awkwardness occasioned the same laugh, it was each time hushed by applause. The *débutante* was considered (as she, indeed, deserved) to have totally failed. When they succeed tolerably they are always called for after the piece. The curtain draws up, and they appear to make their curtsey to the audience, and receive new applauses.

Friday, 9*th*.—In the morning called to take leave of Madame de Castellane, Madame de Coigny, Madame de Staël, and Madame de Beauvan. We found most of them at home, and all very curious to hear the details of our presentation at the Tuileries, which we recounted from beginning to end two or three times in the course of this day. In the evening visited Madame d'Haussenville (a daughter of M. de Guerchy,* formerly ambassador in England) and Madame de Brignole.

Saturday, 10*th*.—In the morning to Mdlle. Martin's to buy rouge. I thought, from having heard all my life of the fame of Mdlle. Martin's rouge, that her receipt must by this time have descended to her great-grandchildren. *Mais point du tout.* The original Mdlle. Martin herself, now a large fat old woman, with a very intelligent countenance, served us. She was dressed in a large bonnet, long powdered hair, the costume of twenty years ago.

* Count de Guerchy, frequently mentioned in Horace Walpole's letters. Came to London October 1763.

Afterwards called at Madame de Fleury's and at Madame Le Conteulx, whom we found in one of those charming houses in the Faubourg St. Honoré, where the gardens go down to the Champs Elysées, and the windows down to the ground opening into these gardens. Went to the house of Madame Récamier. We were resolved not to leave Paris without seeing what is called the most elegant house in it, fitted up in the new style. It is that formerly inhabited by Necker in the Chaussée d'Antin, close to Perrégaux's. There are no large rooms, nor a great many of them; but it is certainly fitted up with all the *rechérché* and expense possible in what is now called *le goût antique.* But the candelabra, pendules, &c., though exquisitely finished, are in that sort of minute frittered style which I think so much less noble than that of fifteen or twenty years ago. All the chairs are mahogany enriched with ormolu, and covered either with cloth or silk, those in the salon trimmed with flat gold lace in good taste. Her bed is reckoned the most beautiful in Paris—it, too, is of mahogany enriched with ormolu and bronze, and raised upon two steps of the same wood. Over the whole bed was thrown a great coverlid or veil of fine plain muslin, with rows of narrow gold lace at each end, and the muslin embroidered as a border. The curtains were muslin, trimmed and worked like the coverlid suspended from a sort of carved *couronne de roses*, and tucked up in drapery upon the wall, against which the bed stood. At the foot of the bed stood a fine Grecian lamp of ormolu, with a little figure of the same metal bending over it; and at the head of the bed another stand, upon which was placed a large ornamented flower-pot, containing a large artificial rose-tree, the branches of which must nod very near her nose in bed. Out of this bedroom is a beautiful little *salle de bain.* The walls inlaid with satin-wood and mahogany, and slight arabesques patterns in black upon the satin-wood. The bath presents itself as a sofa in recess, covered with a cushion of scarlet cloth embroidered and laced with black. Beyond this again is a very little boudoir entirely lined with quilted pea-green lustring, drawn altogether in a bunch in the middle of the ceiling.

Sunday, 11*th*.—Left Paris at three. When we had got upon the *Quai*, just opposite the Collége des quatre Nations, one of the wheel horses stumbled and fell from the slipperiness of the pavement, and threw the postilion. By the manner in which he lay on the pavement, it was easy to perceive that he was more stunned by previous drunkenness than by his fall. A crowd in an instant gathered round him, each one making him out worse than the other; one declaring his legs were broken, and another his head, and everyone advising different cures. He was presently seated upon the kerbstone of the pavement, and wanted to remount his horse again, which we did not allow. However, the delay occasioned by this, and going slowly over the pavement for the rest of our *trajet* through Paris, made us nearly two hours getting to St. Denis. It was dusk by the time we arrived at Chantilly. Lord and Lady Caher, and a party who had left Paris with them, had taken possession of the inn there; we proceeded therefore to Clermont. The weather had entirely changed in the course of the night; a violent wind came on due north, and there were alternate showers of hail and sunshine.

Monday, 12*th*.—An iron having been broken at Clermont, we could not get away till ten o'clock, and by the time we arrived at Amiens at five o'clock, I was so ill that we remained there all night.

Tuesday, 13*th*.—Left Amiens; when we had got about a mile beyond Pecquigny we found that the iron of the carriage had not been properly repaired; were obliged to get out at a little village called the Chausseé de Pecquigny. We went into the house of the blacksmith of the village, who was employed in examining the carriage. It was a mere thatched cottage in as inconsiderable a little village of a few thatched houses as one could anywhere see, and yet a more comfortable peasant's house I have nowhere met with. It was clean too in the inside, though the good woman of the house was in the midst of her *lessive*. They had plenty of plates and dishes set up above a dresser, good bacon hanging up in an adjoining bedroom, and behind their house much poultry, the eggs of which the woman said they lived upon and seldom sold; they had also a bit of garden: in short, I much doubt if in *any* cottage in France, ten years ago, belonging to the same order of people, one could have spent three hours as comfortably, and left it with the same feelings we did that of the blacksmith at the Chaussée de Pecquigny. From this and other delays we did not get to Montreuil till past eleven, and then found all the best rooms in the inn occupied by the Duchess of Cumberland* and her *suite*, and a French *général de division* into the bargain; however, they took us in.

Wednesday, 14*th*.—Left Montreuil; arrived at Calais in about ten hours. Found Madame de Vaudreuil lodged in the same inn, and waiting for letters from Paris to continue her route thither.

Thursday, 15*th*.—The wind so contrary that Captain Blake, whom we found waiting for us, could not sail. Called upon M. Mengaud, the *commissaire-général de police*, to enforce the letters we carried him from Mr. Jackson and Mr. Merry, begging to be allowed to return in an English vessel, which he agreed to, though to nobody else would he grant it.

* Anne, eldest daughter of Simon, Earl of Carhampton, and widow of Christopher Horton, Esq., of Catten in Derbyshire, married, in 1771, to Henry Frederick, Duke of Cumberland, brother to George III. He died 1790.

Friday, 16*th*.—Went on board the 'Swift;' sailed from Calais Pier a quarter after eleven: fine day, but the wind fell almost entirely. At seven o'clock in the evening we were within five miles of Dover in a dead calm; got into a Dover boat, were rowed into the harbour, and arrived at the York Hotel at a quarter after eight, having been just nine hours on our passage. Gave a passage in our vessel to Lord and Lady Caher, whom Mengaud would not allow to have another English vessel.

Saturday, 17*th*.—Slept at Rochester.

Sunday, 18*th*.—Arrived in North Audley Street at three o'clock.

A month after Miss Berry returned from France, she had the mortification of finding that the play which had been acted in private with such flattering success the preceding year at Strawberry Hill, did not receive the sanction of the public voice. It was brought out at Drury Lane with a cast of parts, comprising names which must greatly have conduced to its success, and the cause of its failure cannot be attributed to the want of ability on the part of the performers.

Damatis Personæ.

Sir Valentine Vapour	Mr. King.
Sir Dudley Dorimant	Mr. C. Kemble.
Mr. Lovell	Mr. Barrymore.
Dr. Syrop	Mr. Suett.
Music Master	Mr. Maddocks.
Shopman	Mr. Evans.
La Pierre	Mr. Weurtzer.
John	Mr. Chippendale.
Servants	Messrs. Gibbons, Fisher, & Webb.
Lady Selina Vapour	Miss Du Camp.
Mrs. Lovell	Mrs. Young.
Mrs. Racket	Miss Pope.
Miss Racket	Mrs. Jordan.
Trimming	Mrs. Harlowe.
Lappet	Miss Tidswell.

The Prologue* was written by William Robert

* HARD is the chase poor authors now pursue,
In this old world, to hunt out something new!
Where can the modern poet turn to find
One undiscover'd treasure of the mind,
One drop untasted yet in Learning's spring,
Or one unwearied plume in Fancy's wing?
Our grandsire bards, with prodigal expense,
Squander'd the funds of genius, wit, and sense;
Annuitants of fame, they took no care
How ill their beggar'd successors might fare:
Each thought exhausted, all invention drain'd,
A selfish immortality they gain'd,
And left no spot in all Apollo's garden,
No farm in all Parnassus, worth a farthing!
Some keen observers, on Dame Nature's face,
The crow-foot marks of time and sickness trace;
No wonder, then, if our poetic sires
Felt for her youthful bloom more genuine fires;
Nature to *them* her virgin smiles display'd.
They woo'd a spotless, *we* a ruin'd maid!
For she was won, if chronicles speak truth,
By many a Grecian, many a Roman youth;
But still the lovely libertine retain'd
Charms yet unview'd, and favours yet ungain'd;
For one immortal boy! to him alone,
Her beauties and her failings all were shown.
Heedless of time, or place, or mode, or fashion,
Disorderly she own'd her glorious passion,
What time all rules of critic prudery brav'd,
In Avon's hallow'd stream her angel form she lav'd!
Her fading graces *now* less transport move,
We feel for Nature artificial love,
Though, for her age, the dame looks passing well,
Six thousand years' hard living still must tell!
E'en for the satirist few themes remain,
Folly herself has long been in the wane;
Folly, though here immortal still she dwells,
In Strulburg palsy shakes her rusted bells!
Is Folly then so old?—Why, let me see,
About what time of life may Folly be?
Oh, she was born, by nicest calculation,
One moment after woman's first creation!
This night our unknown author will produce
Old subjects modernis'd for present use;
If you 're displeas'd, be cautious how you show it,
Perhaps your nearest neighbour is the poet;
But if you 're pleas'd and anxious to befriend us,
Like Fashionable Friends, in crowds attend us.

Spencer,* Esq., and was spoken by Mr. C. Kemble. The Epilogue† was written by the Hon. Wm. Lamb, and

* Son of Lord Charles Spencer, translator of 'Leonora,' author of 'Urania,' and other poems.

† SURE, had our author, whom in vain we seek,
Compos'd the play, you just have seen, last week,
He would not now have sent me to attend,
In Italy, the death-bed of my friend;
To throw away this gay auspicious year,
And lose the prospect which is opening here.

Is this a time for me abroad to roam?
Now Peace will send so many lovers home;
Sailors victorious still on every sea
O'er every foe, who yet must strike to me;
And captains, cover'd with hard-earn'd renown,
From Eastern climates beautifully brown;
Peace, which in every face throughout the isle
Has spread a heart-felt, universal smile,—
Peace, which in all most variously excites
New views, new thoughts, new fancies, new delights.
Some think on pleasure, some alone on gain,
On price of stocks, or plenty of champagne—
Exports and imports trading men engage,
Cloth for new marts, new dancers for the stage—
Forward the epicure with transport looks
To a fresh troop of revolution cooks,
And o'er the pie exults, whose precious store
Has been denied him ten sad years before;
While the gay nymph, who lures a crowd of slaves,
Prepares her charms, resolv'd to cross the waves;
Resolv'd the beaux of Paris to invade,
And flirt with whisker'd generals of brigade.

Amidst these different tastes, may I advance
The grounds on which I vote for peace with France?
Then—though through all this time of woe and fear,
We have not suffer'd much in England here,
Yet now, I own, new hopes within me rise,
Oft times more great, more happy, and more wise—
Now London shall appear herself again,
Adorn'd with fresh supplies of handsome men,
No thought of business now shall e'er invade
The nightly ball, and frequent masquerade;
Now luxury again on wealth shall thrive,
And pleasure rule, and usury revive.
Exulting fashion hails the happy league,
Hence love of cards, and leisure for intrigue;
Credit and curricles and dice increase,
Racing, and all the useful arts of peace.

spoken by Miss Du Camp.* Miss Berry's own account of the causes of condemnation forms the preface to 'Fashionable Friends' in the last edition of her works.

PREFACE.

'This comedy was acted for three nights in May 1802, and then withdrawn. In addition to its inherent defects of wanting the bustle and intricacies of a popular plot, and all the exaggerations of character which such plots often make necessary, it was believed at the time to be the production of some of a certain Pic-nic Club then existing much addicted to theatrical amusements, to which the *pit-filling* public (ignorant of its harmless dulness) had endowed with a supposed power of propagating loose principles and profligate wit. This piece, therefore, emanating as they believed, from such a focus of evil, they indignantly determined to stifle in its birth, and came to the first night determined to damn without hearing it. The real author, living in the midst of the world described in the comedy, was particularly anxious to avoid all suspicions of authorship; so that the piece, being entirely unprotected by its natural friends and attacked by prejudiced enemies, must have possessed much greater merit than it can boast to have secured such a fair hearing as might have *fairly* condemned it. The abuse which the newspapers of the day lavished upon it, made the Advertisement, which is here prefixed to it, necessary to its first publication.'

The Morning Post may now display unfurl'd
Four columns of the Fashionable World,
And not confin'd to tell of war's renown,
Spread all the news around of all the town:
While gay Gazettes the polish'd Treasury writes,
Of splendid fashions, not of vulgar fights,
Proud to record the tailor's deeds and name,
And give the milliner to deathless fame,
Who first shall force proud Gallia to confess
Herself inferior in the arts of dress.
Oh! join to pray my hopes may not be vain,
Commence, gay Peace, a long and joyous reign,
May Europe's nations, by my counsels wise,
Learn e'en thy faults to cherish and to prize,
And shunning glory's bright, but fatal star,
Prefer thy follies to the woes of war!

---

* Afterwards Mrs. C. Kemble.

Advertisement.

'This comedy, found among the papers of the late Earl of Orford, and remaining unclaimed in the hands of his executors for two years, was brought forward at the request of Mr. Kemble on the Theatre Royal, Drury Lane. After the extraordinary abuse that has been lavished upon it, the executors considered it as a duty to the unknown author to publish it.'

It is often difficult to judge, from reading only, what may be the effect produced by any dramatic work when placed on the stage. Miss Berry's explanation of the condemnation of her play may be correct, and it may have owed its rejection to the prejudices entertained by the public against some supposed author, for it is certainly not deficient in skilful arrangement of dramatic position, in stage intrigue, or in pointed and epigrammatic dialogue, but, on the other hand, it must be confessed that no such play would be written by a lady of the present day, or be performed in private theatricals, or be offered to the public as the representation of fashionable manners. A greater proof of the happy change that has taken place, in the course of the last sixty-three years, in the manners, the morals, and the refinement of the higher classes could not well be adduced. The plot, the characters, and the dialogue all turn upon the most undisguised love intrigues of married couples; and though the author's purity of intention is to be seen in making virtue gain some triumph over vice, and her love of truth is to be traced in the way she exposes, in all its odiousness, the false professions of a hollow friendship; though there is no intended propagation of loose principles, no confusion of right and wrong in the mind of the author, yet there is a tone of easy license with which criminal attachments are treated, little creditable to the taste and morality of that society which the author professes to describe from personal acquaintance, and which certainly could no longer be accepted as a representation of the habits and manners of 'Fashionable Friends,' and which would not now be borne either in private theatricals or in the public stage.

JOURNAL.

Tuesday, October 26th.—Left North Audley Street. A very fine sunny morning.

Wednesday, 27th.—Arrived at Dover; found Captain Blake waiting for us, too late to save the tide.

Thursday, 28th.—A south wind so directly in our teeth, that it was impossible to sail. Walked about Dover and to the Parade upon the beach about half a quarter of a mile to the west of the town, where a whale no less than eighty-seven feet long had, about three weeks before, been towed ashore by two fishing-boats. It had at first been seen by the Deal boats lying upon the Goodwin Sands, and was taken for a vessel; it was then floated nearer this way, and was dead and much wasted before they brought it in here. When I saw it, the enormous backbone, with a quantity of shapeless flesh and skin about it, was lying within water mark, and looked exactly like a large irregular shelf of rock. The jawbones, both upper and under, had been pretty well cleared of flesh, and were lying on different parts of the beach, likewise the tail with all the flesh still upon it, cut off from the fish at the lowest vertebra of the backbone. The length of the under jawbone of this stupendous animal I measured 6¼ yds., and the length between the fork of the tail, 18 ft. The length of the upper jawbone must have been much greater, but it lay inconveniently for measuring. I much regret having missed seeing this enormous creature while it was entire, for from the mangled remains of its body no idea could be formed of its shape. The farmers in the neighbourhood have been ever since employed in carrying away cartloads of its flesh to manure their ground. A Greenland captain, who happened to be here at the time, said that he had hardly ever seen a longer whale, but that it was a young one and much wasted.

Friday, 29th.—The wind still south, we could not sail. As the morning was very fine, walked up to Dover Castle. Beautiful views from every part; a great deal of money lately expended in making a road up to it on which the heaviest artillery can be dragged with ease. The whole castle apparently kept in very good order; two regiments, consisting of about 500 men each, now there.

Saturday, 30th.—The wind changed, and we went on board in a boat from the beach. The wind fell so entirely, that we lay motionless on the water. After much *whistling* for a wind, a little breeze sprang up which carried us to Calais Harbour, time enough to save the tide and land, after a passage of seven hours and a half: on deck the whole time.

The pier at Calais was less crowded than when Mrs. Damer and I arrived in the spring; I suppose they are no longer curious, after the infinite number of English faces they have seen in the course of the summer. Took possession of the very apartment I had left in April.

Sunday, 31st.—The Custom House was shut at five o'clock. Money was also to be got from a banker, who had the *modesty* to take *only* at the rate of 7 per cent. from us. Got to Cormont that night.

Monday, November 1st.—Arrived at Amiens.

Tuesday, 2nd.—Reached Chantilly. At the Posts at Clermont we found General Andreossi,* the French am-

* Count Antoine François Andreossi, born 1761, a distinguished French officer and scientific writer, served in all the revolutionary campaigns, accompanied Napoleon to Egypt, was appointed ambassador to the English Court after the Peace of Amiens. He was at the battle of Austerlitz and of Wagram. Afterwards ambassador at Constantinople, but superseded in 1814. On the return of Napoleon from Elba, he joined his cause, but was

bassador, on his way to England; he was travelling in a handsome new French coach *à l'Anglaise*, and a post-chaise *à l'Anglaise* accompanied it, which, *à la Française*, had something about it broken.

Wednesday, 3rd.—Arrived at the Hôtel d'Orléans, the apartment upon the first floor ready to receive us; and finding everything just as I had left it six months before, I could hardly persuade myself that I had been away at all. Sent to Barrois and Mr. Merry, both of whom we saw in the evening, and Mr. Jerningham, who we found lodged in the same hotel, as well as Mr. William Throckmorton * and Mr. Robert Clifford.

Thursday, 4th.—In the morning to the Musée and to shops, and to call at Madame de Vaudreuil, at l'Hôtel de Caraman (her father's house). In the evening to the Théâtre du Louvois, Mr. Moore † and Mr. Throckmorton of our party. The pieces 'Le Mari Ambitieux,' and 'Les Conjectures,' both by Picard, and in both he acted very well; but the first is a satire upon the *intrigant* and *ambitieux* of the present day, whose means and whose ends were both too ignoble to be interesting.

At the Musée the large square anteroom to the gallery, which I had seen in the spring lined with all the finest Italian pictures, was now filled with the exhibition of works of their modern artists, and I am sorry to say many more historic pictures, and many better than our own Exhibition can boast. The one which everybody

instrumental in moderating the decree against the Royal Family. After Waterloo, was one of the five commissioners to negotiate an armistice. He died 1828, leaving many works written on different subjects.—*Rose's Biog. Dict.*

* Mr. William Throckmorton, father of the late Sir Robert Throckmorton, born 1762; married Frances, daughter of Thomas Gifford, Esq., of Chillington. Died 1819.

† Francis Moore, brother of General Moore, born 1787, died in Ischia, 1854; married Frances, daughter of Sir William Twysden. He was in the Foreign Office from July 1784 to Jan. 1802; then Deputy-Secretary at War to Dec. 1802.—*Correspondence of Lord Cornwallis*, vol. iii. p. 382.

agreed in extolling as a *capo d'opèra* was a Phædra and Hyppolitus by Gérard, a young artist, of whom there is an extremely good portrait by a brother artist just under his great picture. He is evidently of the school of David, but seems likely to avoid his defects—that high finishing and hardness which makes his great pictures all foreground. In short, the French now are evidently forming themselves upon the Roman school, while ours have taken the Venetian, which, though a Sir Joshua Reynolds ennobled, I think has been the bane of all our artists.

Friday, 5*th*.—In the evening the Opera. Mr. Moore, Mr. Throckmorton, and Mr. Pigou of our party. The opera 'Tamerlane.' The story is Voltaire's 'Orphelin de la Chine,' but all French great operas are so exactly alike in their make, that it is never any matter what they are called. This opera was over unusually early. We were waiting nearly half an hour for the carriage. I thought the company in the lobby had decidedly a better appearance than in the spring, but I believe principally from there being a vast number of foreigners there.

Saturday, 6*th*.—In the morning called on Mdlle. de Mortemer, and on Lady Mount Edgcumbe. In the evening on Lady Elizabeth Foster.

Sunday, 7*th*.—Went with Barrois to the Pantheon. The whole *bas-relievos* of the *façade* have been altered from those of St. Geneviève to emblems of liberty, and between the six large columns which support the pediment, are four colossal figures in plaster, meant as models to be executed in marble, of Strength, Genius, the Republic, and another figure which I did not make out. The

* François Gérard, born at Rome in 1770, in the house of Cardinal de Bernis, his father a Frenchman, and his mother an Italian. His first works were exhibited in 1795. He was considered as the rival of David, and held in the highest estimation in France as a portrait and historical painter. Died 1837.

inside, while intended for a church, was never finished. It is a Greek cross of very fine proportions. Each division of the cross would have made a very beautiful modern church. One of the great piers which support the cupulo had given way (I think before the Revolution), and the whole arch between pier and pier is now filled up with a great *charpente* to support it. In the lower church, or what in a Gothic church one should call the crypt, supported by Tuscan columns without bases, are the tombs, or rather cenotaphs, of Voltaire * on one side, and Rousseau on the other. In the middle had been placed Marat, but no trace of him now remained. They are both enormous sarcophagi, of plaster or wood columns like red granite, in which I suppose they are *intended* (*ad Græcas kalendas*) to be executed. On Voltaire's are inscriptions on every side, telling what he did *pour l'esprit humain.* On Rousseau is only written on both sides 'À l'Homme de la Nature.' From the Pantheon we walked through the Luxembourg garden, great part of which has been newly planted, and is one of the finest public gardens in the middle of a large town that can possibly be seen. The Luxembourg palace too has been whitened and refreshed since it was the palace of the Directory. It is now that of the Conservative Senate, and some of them, I understand, have apartments there, and charming they must be. In the evening to the Théâtre Feydeau. In the 'Concert Interrompu' and 'Le Calif de Bagdat' † Ellevieu ‡ acted. He has a good voice, and is

* On the tomb of Voltaire are the following inscriptions:—'Poëte, historien, philosophe, il aggrandit l'esprit humain, il lui apprit qu'il devoit être libre.' 'Il défendit Calas, Serven, de la Barre, et Montbuilly.' 'Il combattit les Athées et les fanatiques, inspira la tolérance et reclama les droits de l'homme contre la servitude et la féodalité.' The remains of Voltaire and of Rousseau were removed to the Pantheon during the first Revolution, but were secretly taken away during the Restoration.—*Galignani's Paris Guide.*

† By St. Just.

‡ Ellevieu, born 1770, became so popular an actor, that he gave his name

by far the genteelest actor I have seen upon the French stage of late years. Madame du Gazon acted the mother in the 'Calif de Bagdat,' and though, as the French say of her, 'c'est une ruine que le temps n'a pas respectée,' she acted so well, that she made something of what would otherwise have been nothing. The house was very full, as all the theatres generally are on Sunday, and the *parterre* very noisy. They were somehow or other (I never could make out why) particularly diverted with a shawl and a fur tippet hanging over the side of a box on the same row in which we were, full of English people. This shawl and fur tippet were pulled in and put over again, always to the redoubled amusement of the *parterre*, who all talked, and laughed, and roared at once to the box, and this lasted at two or three different *reprises* for above half an hour. The quiet better sort of people in the *galerie* under our box were shocked at the behaviour of the pit.

Tuesday, 9*th*.—In the morning at the Musée. In the evening at the French theatre to see Mdlle. Duchenois,* *débutante* in 'Phédre,' who has appeared in a variety of characters in tragedy this autumn with the greatest success. She is a tall, very plain young woman, and has not yet acquired (if she ever is to acquire) grace

to a certain number of characters, and it was said of other actors 'on débute dans les Ellevieu,' or 'on étude, on joue les Ellevieu.'—*Dict. de Contemporains.*

* Catherine Josephine Duchenois, whose real name was Rafin, born near Valenciennes in 1786. The effect produced on her mind at eight years old by the acting of Mdlle. Raucourt determined her future profession. At thirteen she appeared at Valenciennes, in the character of Palmiras in 'Mahomet,' acted for a charity, astonishing the audience with her dramatic power. On the 21st July, 1802, she made her *débût* at the Théâtre Français in the character of Phédre, and never lost the favour of the public. In her last moments she was attended by the Archbishop of Paris, a circumstance without example in the annals of the French stage. She died 1835, and is buried near Talma, in the cemetery of Père la Chaise.—*Dict. des Contemporains*, and *Rose's Biography*.

and action. Moreover, she has an inexpressive countenance. Yet with all this, she is certainly a good, though an unequal actress. She enters thoroughly into the spirit of her part, seems to understand it, and has often admirable touches of nature, which the French begin to admire, even in that least natural of all compositions—a French tragedy. With Mdlle. Duchenois they are enchanted. As soon as the curtain dropped, a crown of laurel was thrown upon the stage from some upper box. The *parterre* then insisted upon the actress making her appearance, which she did, still in her stage dress, for an instant at the back of the stage, and made her bows to the audience. Still they were not satisfied. The second piece was attempted to be begun. They obliged the actors to retire. At last, upon reiterated noise and confusion, a manager, or director of some sort, came forward, and said:—'Messieurs, si c'est la lecture des vers que vous désirez, vous me permettrez de vous observer que nous l'avons en commande de ne jamais lire des vers quelconques sur le théâtre.' This message was well received. The verses alluded to were some fastened to the crown of laurel. But the noise still continuing, the actress again appeared at the back of the stage, her stage-dress off, and led in by the manager. She again made her bow, and again retired. Still the noise continued, and the farce was again in vain attempted. The audience wanted to see the actress crowned by her companions. At last, after this violent noise and bustle had lasted I know not how long, the actress a third time appeared at the back of the stage, led in by the same man, who put the crown upon her head, which she instantly and very modestly pulled off, and disappeared. The noise then ceased, and the second piece was allowed to begin. It is remarkable that now that the theatres at Paris have no longer, as formerly, soldiers in the *parterre* to keep everything quiet, that though they often make a great noise in a body about the entertainment, an actor or actress, &c. &c., yet they maintain a better police than ever they had before, in allowing nobody to talk too loud, or to disturb in any way the performance.

Wednesday, 10*th*.—Left Paris. The Forest of Fontainebleau, with all the beech trees turned into gold by the season, and all its birch trees still in leaf, hanging over those odd masses of rock, was beautiful beyond expression.

Thursday, 11*th*.—Left Villeneuve. At Sens is a fine church (where the last king's father and mother were buried), the outside of which does not seem much *dégradé*.

At Joigny, upon the stone bridge which crosses the river, is a wooden *arc de triomphe*, with a plaster bust of Buonaparte upon it, with this inscription: 'Au Restorateur de la Paix, le Peuple reconnaissant;' I suppose, erected at the time of his journey to Lyons, when he must have passed through Joigny. All the little towns upon this day's journey have those sort of picturesque old gates which one sees so often represented in Sylvesties' prints. Reached Auxerre.

Friday, 12*th*.—Between Vermanton and Lucy les Bois passed a large abbaye, with the church entirely pulled down to the façade. At five o'clock, on a very rainy foggy November night, we found ourselves only at Rouvray, a poor village, where we determined to stay. The inn was one of those large, cold barns of houses, with half-a-dozen beds in each room, and a great open smoking chimney.

Saturday, 13*th*.—Left Rouvray. In this day's journey passed a good deal of common, the first I have seen in France. The people hereabout look very wretched, though there are many little scattered cottages, and all the valleys much enclosed with corn, and vines, and wood. Arrived at Autun at three o'clock, but the people gave us so bad an account of the two intermediate places that we thought it best to stay where we were. Autun is a considerable town, with a large cathedral.

Sunday, 14*th.*—The road from Autun to Emeland continues mountainous till reaching the great plain in which Chalons stands, and which is all pasture and corn. We slept at Tournus.

Monday, 15*th.*—We hoped to be at Lyons between four and five o'clock, but we were detained at St. George de Renand by finding postilions and no horses, and at Ause by finding neither the one nor the other. At three different posts we found neither the master nor mistress at home, and at two they did not even live at the post: one can easily suppose what frequent vexation and delay this must occasion to travellers. At Ause we set out with four wretched sick horses, mounted by I know not whom; before the long *montée* we all got out and walked, from the impossibility of their dragging us up. At Limonest again no horses. These delays prevented our arriving at Lyons till late. At Lyons we went to the Hôtel de l'Europe, which was formerly the house of an individual of large fortune.

Tuesday, 16*th.*—It rained last night, and continued all this day without a moment's intermission, so that, however curious we were to see the ravages of the Revolution upon this magnificent city, we could not stir out. My father found out a Mr. Fels, a little Swiss *négociant*, long settled and married at Lyons, to whom we had been recommended long ago when we were first here, a civil, little, quiet, intelligent man, who came to us in the evening.

Wednesday, 17*th.*—The rain continued with unceasing obstinacy, but we were so afraid of leaving Lyons without seeing anything of its present condition that we sent for a hackney coach, and after going with Mr. Fels to two or three shops, drove round the Place de Bellecour and along the Quai du Rhône. Two sides of the Place de Bellecour are reduced to a heap of ruins, and bring forward, instead of its handsome façades, the fronts of the two streets that ran at its back. Of the arsenal upon the bank of the Saône nothing remains but the outward walls, and in many parts of the town similar ravages are visible. But the destruction of buildings in this unfortunate city is nothing and not worth mentioning in comparison to the destruction of men, of industry, and of commerce, which it will be years before they can re-establish, if ever. It is impossible to walk through the streets of Lyons and not be struck with the miserable appearance of the greatest part of the people, and most especially of the women, nor to enter their shops and magazines without being struck with their altered and reduced state, their small stock, and the absence of all appearance of their former affluence. The whole town seems yet *terrassée* with the dreadful blows it received; and careless, volatile, and thoughtless as French people are, at Lyons, and Lyons only it is, that I have seen the Revolution has left a deep and lasting impression of horror upon the minds of all orders of people. Well it may! Such particulars of horror as Fels gave us, himself having been eye-witness to such as one had before hoped only existed in exaggerated accounts. This little quiet man, after remaining at Lyons on account of the person whom he has since married much longer than (as being a Swiss) he need, was at last obliged to seek his personal safety by concealment in a village near Lyons, where he worked for six weeks as a journeyman carpenter. All those young men who had taken up arms to preserve the tranquillity of their town against the Terrorists were, without any other *forme de procès* than reading their names, shot, and all the older men who were of the same disposition guillotined by dozens in a day. Two hundred and nine of the young ones were chained together and fired at with grape shot in the Place de Belle-cour, till nothing was to be heard but the cries of these miserable people, requesting any friendly hand to put them out of their pain.

'Oh Francia, Francia, vituperio delle grate!'

Thursday, 18*th*.—The rain had at last ceased, but from the bad account we heard of the roads and my father's wishing to go by water, we determined to go down the Rhône, and to start the following day. We took a long and dirty walk in the streets and upon the *quais*. Lyons is certainly a most beautifully situated town; the views from all the bridges of the high and rocky bank of the Saône, covered with all sorts of picturesque stone buildings, intermixed with trees and vineyards, surpasses anything I know elsewhere. The streets are in themselves very narrow and nasty, but the two great rivers passing through the town prevent it from being close, and all the *quais* are handsome.

Friday, 19*th*.—We went on board our boat from the Quai du Saône at seven o'clock in the morning, with the sun breaking through a fog and gilding in the most beautiful manner in the world the buildings and the banks of the river. It was an hour before we got clear of Lyons and fairly into the Rhône, at a wooden bridge called De la Perrache, just below the confluence of the two streams. The fog cleared away, and it was a fine sunny day, but between eleven and twelve a wind suddenly rose from the south, which made the water rough and retarded the motion of our loaded bark. Besides the carriage on board, it had what they call a *chambre*; the *chambre* is a space covered over with rough boards like a tilt, and a piece of gauze-like canvass thrown over, and in some degree keeping the air out; this with a plank put all round by way of bench, and a good deal of straw in the bottom over the loose planks, forms the whole furniture and accoutrements of these most awkward barks. Nothing but their being in constant use, and accidents seldom happening, could persuade one they were not the most dangerous of all conveyances; but they never attempt to cope with any difficulties. The moment the wind blew our boatmen pushed to shore, and there we lay till between two and three, when the wind lowered; we then pushed out, but we had hardly got into the current of the stream before we found the wind as high as ever, and again, therefore, came to the bank on the other side of the river near Givors, and opposite a little wretched sort of ale or wine-house, used only by the men and horses who drag boats up the river. It was now three o'clock, and no appearance of the wind lowering, we despatched the courier to Vienne to get a carriage of some sort to convey us thither. My father, tired of sitting in the boat, accompanied the courier Gibaud, and they were nearly two hours and a half getting there; and so by the time Gibaud returned to us in the cabriolet it was eight o'clock, an excessively dark night threatening hard rain, the road so bad, so narrow, and so near the Rhône that he had walked with a *fallot* at the horses' heads all the way. We therefore resolved to remain quietly in the coach all night, and to send Peter in the cabriolet to my father with a note. We lighted our lamps, ate some of our cold provisions, and then composed ourselves for the night, that is to say, resolved two of us to sleep and one to watch. Gibaud and the two boatmen slept upon straw in the *chambre* of the boat. It rained most part of the night.

Saturday, 20*th*. — We all slept very quietly till four o'clock in the morning, when, it being perfectly calm and not very dark, I persuaded the men to set out again, and we arrived at Vienne at half-past five, long before it was light. One of the coach lanterns lighted us to the inn near the waterside. Here we woke my father, who had gone late to bed, and passed an anxious night, as Peter and the cabriolet had never arrived. This circumstance began now to make us all uneasy, from the badness of the road he had to pass, its nearness to the river, and the extreme darkness of the night. As soon as it was light we despatched a postilion to look for him: the postilion returned about eight, and relieved us; he had found the cabriolet and Peter. The night had been so dark that the driver would not go on, and they had stopped at some little auberge. About nine the cabriolet arrived, but why the driver would not start earlier this morning with poor Peter, who was up at four o'clock, his entire ignorance of French prevented our ever knowing. Vienne is most picturesque from the water; a high stone *quai* or embankment to the river, which is ascended in the middle and on each side by a flight of steps under large stone arches. A great Gothic cathedral, rising above the town, and mountains covered with vines and picturesque buildings rising again above that. The banks of the Rhône are beautiful, well peopled from Lyons to this place, and yet I hope never again to see them from the water. St. Vallier Tain is a little village close upon the Rhône, with the far-famed hill giving its name to the Vin de l'Hermitage rising close behind it; on the top of the hill is a small building which was a hermitage. Opposite Tain is a much larger town, Tournon, with a picturesque old château belonging to the Prince de Soubise,* and now a barrack for soldiers, and another very large building, formerly a college of Jesuits,† and now a place of education, where they pay about 40*l.* a year (according to the information of our boatmen). Soon after we landed

* The old castle of the Counts of Tournon and Ducs de Soubise is now converted into the purposes of a mairie, tribunal, and a prison.

† The Collége Royal, originally founded by the Cardinal de Tournon, a favourite of Francis I., 1542, and a few years afterwards, 1561, delivered over to the Jesuits, in order to extirpate the seeds of Protestantism. They maintained their post here, until the suppression of the order in 1766. It next became an *école militaire*.—See *Murray's Handbook.*

at Tain it blew a hurricane from the south and rained most part of the night.

Sunday, 21*st*.—Up early, hoping to have got to the Pont St. Esprit to-night. At our vilest of all auberges the people of the house squabbled with our stupidest of all couriers about his bed, and they all went together by the ears in the kitchen below with a noise enough to deafen one, which prevented our going to bed for an hour, and recommenced at four o'clock in the morning. At six o'clock, when we were hoping to be off, the wind and rain continued so violently that our boatmen said it was impossible. We felt it was impossible to stay where we were, and therefore set out to reconnoitre the other inns. The Hôtel de l'Assurance had been the house of the seigneur of the village, and to this the boatman objected, saying the host was *un coquin*, and *qu'il ne fallait pas aller là*. It was a large melancholy, *dégarnie* looking house, the worse for the signs of having seen better days, and a very bad-looking host, with two young girls (his daughters), and a strange ill-looking man who officiated as cook, were its only inhabitants. But, as we found an apartment of three rooms opening into each other and shut under one door, we ventured to remain there, hoping to go on before night. But the wind continued high in our teeth, and torrents of rain fell, so that not only proceeding further was out of the question, but we literally could not stir out of our melancholy abode. We opened the windows, and, when the rain allowed us to see anything, sketched the Montagne de l'Hermitage from our windows. At night I made Peter sleep in my father's room with his pistols, and we met with no disturbance. The beds and scanty furniture were wretched.

Monday, 22*nd*.—At last we left Tain at seven o'clock in the morning. We heard with regret that the Duchess of Cumberland's boat had passed us about half an hour before we set out. Thus what I had been so particularly anxious to avoid, knowing the inconvenience it would occasion us, these delays, and the roguery of our boatmen's master, who, I believe, desired them not to get before the boat in which he was himself, brought to pass; we did not succeed in getting to the Pont St. Esprit, with good light, which is necessary there from the rapidity of the stream under its arches. Stopped, therefore, at Bourg St. Andiol, a little village on the same side of the river, about four o'clock; bad as the inn was, we were certainly more comfortable than at Tain. At this and at all these little towns and villages upon the banks of the Rhône, I have observed a large cap of liberty hoisted upon the end of a high Maypole, or on a church steeple, or some other height.

Tuesday, 23*rd*.—The banks of the river near St. Andiol low and not interesting; the Pont St. Esprit and its town most picturesque from the water, and a charming view of both and of an old ruined fortress upon a hill. On each side of the river, between the Pont St. Esprit and Avignon, there are a number of most picturesque ruined castles, and near the edge of the water some fine trees. Arrived at Avignon: a fine warm November day. The Duchess of Cumberland's boat had arrived about a quarter of an hour before us, and she had not yet disembarked.

Wednesday, 24*th*.—Walked about the town: it looks much the worse for the Revolution. The people look poorer, the shops worse, and the great houses shabby. A most beautiful view from a rock in the middle of the town, which rises abruptly from the Rhône, and on which was situated the Legate's palace,* the cathedral,† and the prison. The palace is totally gutted, the cathedral made

* Besides what it suffered at the Revolution, this edifice was, in 1814, made the receptacle for some hundred Spanish prisoners. It has lately undergone repairs, and has been modernised with bad effect.—See *Murray's Handbook*.

† The palace of the Popes is now degraded into a barrack.

a ruin (a most picturesque one it is); the prison remains, and is probably more inhabited than ever. From this height is to be seen the whole town below, the Rhône, and the Durance, winding for many miles through a rich and well-wooded valley bounded by fine mountains; the broken bridge of Avignon, and the fine castle, which was a convent of Benedictines, upon an eminence at Villeneuve, on the opposite bank of the Rhône.

Thursday, 25*th.*—Finding the Durance (a post and three-quarters from hence) was not passable, that is to say, the *trail* (the rope and pulley from two poles) was not re-established, and the sky threatening more rain, we determined to go the same way the Duchess of Cumberland had taken the day before, though it makes a difference of no less than five posts in going from Avignon to Aix.

Crossed the two branches of the Rhône *à la trail* without any difficulty. There is a low island between them, much covered with trees, which had been all under water two or three days before, and consequently this passage of the Rhône could not then have been passable. There is a rough paved road across the island from the one boat to the other; a high *montée* after passing Villeneuve, all covered with olives (the first we have seen), and from whence there is a fine extensive view. It is well for us we had crossed the river, for it rained more or less the whole way to La Foux (the little village opposite Remoulin). Determined to go round by the Pont du Gard, though a little out of the way, but well worth while, for I know no ruin more imposing and more beautiful.

Friday, 26*th.*—Left La Foux at seven; they would not start sooner, pretending the roads were so bad they must wait for daylight, but in fact because the posts upon this road are so badly served that there are only horses and men enough to carry the mail, and that travellers can never be sure of getting the number wanted. For about a league, near the banks of the Rhône, the road had been three or four feet deep in water two days before, and had deposited such oceans of mud and water and sand, that in some places it was almost up to the naves of the wheels. From Beaucaire to Tarascon the Rhône is crossed over a bridge of boats, which leads to a causeway, and then over another bridge of boats, all of which are dreadfully jumbling, without any sort of railing, and would be positively dangerous in the dark. At Tarascon we arrived by ten o'clock. Here again found no horses; they were to be back by twelve o'clock: we waited till twelve, till one, till past two before they came, and it was three before they were ready to set off with us. When we saw the road we could not wonder at the delay: for the first hour we went continually through water, sometimes up to the horses' knees, sometimes up to their fetlocks, but continually walking through water—the road and the whole flat country near it on both sides had been overflowed by the Rhône. Arrived at St. Remy with the last rays of light: it is a good-looking open village, with large trees in the street, which, after the little stinking walled towns of this country, is remarkable.

Saturday, 27*th*.—Orgon is a walled village, beautifully situated on a rock, at the bottom of which there is a rich valley watered by the Durance. The road here bore marks of having been overflowed, as well as all the adjacent fields, by the river, which the people of the country call *très méchant*, as it loads their fields with nothing but gravel and stones, while the Rhône often fattens them with mud. The whole country hereabout is undone with the quantity of rain they have had within this last month, after a long drought of nearly seven months. Between Orgon and Pontroyal the road is scarcely passable at a footpace, and portions of the road entirely impassable between Pontroyal and St. Canat. At this place the postilions are obliged to drive out of the road into the fields; and a great deal of rain having fallen just before we passed, in one of these drivings off and on the road, our carriage stuck entirely fast up to the nave of the wheels in stiff mud, the middle having hit upon the root of an olive tree. We all got out, and we soon found it was vain for the postilions and their horses to endeavour to move it: in the first attempt they made they cracked the pole. Agnes and I therefore trotted away as hard as we could to the village, luckily not above a mile and a quarter off, for the road was monstrously muddy, and it rained hard before we got half way there. We immediately took possession of a very miserable little inn, sending fresh post-horses back to the carriage to help it out of its scrape; in the meantime a muleteer passing with a couple of mules had done the business. The carriage arrived an hour after ourselves: the cracked pole had to be mended. It rained hard, and we determined to stay here at St. Carnal all night.

Sunday, 28th.—Arrived at Aix; the road so bad that we were obliged to walk the horses the whole way. Country very pretty. Aix, like all the rest in the southern part of France, bears melancholy marks of the neglect and poverty into which it has fallen during the Revolution: the pavement is so neglected that a carriage would with difficulty get along some of the narrow streets; many of the handsome houses are quite untenanted, and others look quite neglected, their proprictors (where they still exist) living only in a corner of them. We had a letter to M. d'Albertas, possessing one of these houses, and who, not having emigrated, still possesses all they have chosen to leave him of his fortune. His account of the situation of all the upper order of people in the provincial towns most melancholy: they live *chacun de son côté* as they can, but sociability and comfort seem banished from among them. The préfêts and sous-préfêts who are appointed to the governments of the departments are for the most part low, and all of them poor, and think of nothing but enriching themselves while they can, and neglect in the most shameful manner the districts they are appointed to look after; thus roads and bridges and towns are all degraded, and nothing done to repair the neglect and the ravages of ten years' Vandalism.

Monday, 29*th*.—We heard so bad an account of the roads to Nice, that we sent our trunks by a carrier to lighten the stress upon the carriage.

Tuesday, 30*th*.—The road from Aix to La Grande Pugère very picturesque and beautiful; but from thence to Tourves (two posts and a half) so excessively bad in the way of mud, of stones, and of holes, that we walked above half the way; and, I believe, the carriage would never have passed some of the *mauvais pàs* but for the aid of soldiers, who, being quartered all over the country for the surety of the roads, accompanied us from one of their posts to another, and supported the carriage and helped it forward in any difficulty. When at last we got to Tourves* it was four o'clock, and beginning to rain. We were so heartily tired, *corps et âme*, with the road we had gone through, and the thoughts of what remained to us, that we put up for the night at the very dirtiest Cheval Blanc that I ever encountered, and where I was kept awake the whole night by a storm of wind and violent rain beating at the window, every drop of which I knew would count against us on the road next day.

Wednesday, *December* 1*st*.—Left Tourves, the most miserable village I have yet seen, at half past six. Having found how useful the soldiers were, we took a party of four with us from this place, and continued so to do during the whole route. There was no difficulty in this, as we found them at every change of horses, and they have lately been accustomed to this business, and are very

* Tourves, a wretched town of 2,800 inhabitants in the Département de Var. No inn.—Vide *Murray's Handbook*.

serviceable. When we arrived at Brignolles by ten o'clock, the postmaster told us we should find a little torrent between that and Flassans, so swelled by the last night's rain as to be impassable for several hours. Perhaps his advice might be somewhat influenced by wishing to detain us. But we resolved to stay here for the day. It was well we did.

Thursday, 2*nd.*—Left Brignolles at seven o'clock. Very fine morning. We had our side-saddle put on a bidet of the poste, and rode and walked alternately the whole way to Flassans. Being in the carriage was out of the question, for after the first half league the road was one continued broken-up pavement, or rather heap of rocks,—how any carriage gets over it, I have no idea. From Flassans to Luc we continued to ride and walk. The day was delicious, the country beautiful, and had it not been for the worry of having a carriage that one expected to see broken every moment, I should have thought the journey delightful. On leaving Luc the road passes through a wood of olives, with a high mountain on the left crowned by a romantic village and a castle belonging to a M. de Corbel (or some such name), who possessed a large estate around it. The castle was made an entire ruin, and the property taken from him, in the Revolution. The postilion, my informer, added that he had returned into the country, and had got back some small part of his estate. Beautiful hills just before entering Vedauban, covered with pines and evergreen oaks, which, in a sunny day like this, makes one entirely forget winter.

Friday, 3*rd.*—We left Vedauban at six, in a drizzling rain, continuing more or less the whole way to Muy, nearly half of which we rode and walked. From Muy to Fréjus the road had been described as very bad and difficult, and it justified its reputation, for worse to be passable *at all*, I never saw. A stone bridge having been carried away, the carriage was obliged to make a *détour* of above a league across the country. We walked and rode almost the whole way to a village within a league of Fréjus, from whence the carriage was to turn off the road; and here, taking one of our escort of soldiers to show us the way, my father, my sister, myself, and Peter, by the advice of our postilions, proceeded to Fréjus on foot. The road we had to go was, they said, a short league. When we came to the broken bridge, we were obliged to leave the road and pass along a bank with water on each side, so narrow and so slippery with the rain, that it was with great difficulty, and with laying hold of the bushes or trees on one side of the bank, that we kept our feet at all; added to which, at certain distances, we had to pass over a sort of heads, made to keep back a strong stream of water which was running below our bank on the right hand from flowing into the fields on our left. These heads were certainly not more than twelve inches wide, and the water was on both sides of them! How I passed I know not, except that I knew I could not remain where I was, and that it rained hard, and that we were wet through shoes and boots. In something less than an hour we arrived at Fréjus, the inn, luckily, near the gate of the town. We were soon comfortable again, and the more so, that the carriage arrived safe, and sooner than we expected. Fréjus is a wretched-looking old town, with an old ruined gate to it, and situated about half a mile from the sea as the bird flies.

Saturday, 4th.—Here we had intended to embark our carriage to avoid all further risk on these impassable roads; and this can only be done at San Rafaelle,* a little village upon the edge of the sea about a mile from Fréjus; but there were no tolerably-sized vessels, no quay, nor con-

* Napoleon landed at this small port 1799, on his return from Egypt, and embarked hence, 1814, for Elba. This is the birthplace of the Abbé Siéyes. *Murray's Handbook.*

venience for embarking anything. So, finding the Duchess of Cumberland's two coaches had safely passed the mountain two days before, we determined to venture also. Walked to Fréjus. Just without the town on the Aix side, a very complete ruin of a Roman amphitheatre,* the upper rows of arches only being entirely destroyed. On the other side of the town are great remains of an aqueduct,† which brought the water from the mountains, and is very picturesque in the landscape. Fréjus, like all the other towns in the South of France, having had its convents, its seminaries, and its public buildings destroyed or shut up, its pavement, streets, &c., entirely neglected, and its inhabitants reduced, exhibits an appearance of wretchedness unknown in former, and, perhaps, worse times.

Sunday, 5*th*.—The morning threatened rain, but tired with the delays of our journey, and knowing that every drop that fell would make the rest of it more difficult, we ventured to start early. The road flat for about a league before ascending the Estrelles Mountains. It has been a well-made mountain road, as it winds round several hills and was not *very* steep; but ten years' neglect, and the *dégât* which mountain rains always make, have in many places rendered it hardly passable. In some places nothing but having men to support the carriage would have prevented it from overturning. The hills are everywhere green with pines and rich underwood of a thousand beautiful shrubs, such as arbutus loaded with fruit and flowers, cistus, myrtles, and a variety of heaths, all growing perfectly wild, but no houses or huts, or marks of habitation near, not even distant villages upon neighbouring

* Outside the walls of this small and dirty town, of less than 3,000 inhabitants, is the once-celebrated Forum Julii, founded by Cæsar; on the west are the remains of a small circus, recently cleared out, far inferior in size and preservation to those of Nismes and Arles.—See *Murray's Handbook.*

† The most considerable Roman remains here are those of an aqueduct; it has been traced for more than twenty-four miles up the valley of the Ciagne, whose clear water it conveyed to the town.

hills. The post, upon the descent of the mountain, is a single desolate-looking house, but surrounded by magnificent chestnut trees. Everybody avoids sleeping there, the accommodations are so wretched. It was occupied by the French soldiers—a sergeant's guard of foot and three gendarmes on horseback. We took with us no less than seven men and a corporal to help us on the road, and, Heaven knows! they were no more than necessary at the broken bridges. The descent of the Estrelle, I understand, was always rough; it is now nothing better than a heap of rocks, over which *by habit* the horses pass, and *by chance* may pull a light carriage after them without breaking it, and this was luckily the case with ours; but in many parts we could not even ride, but got off and led or drove on our horses. On reaching the bottom of the hill we got into a sort of marshy bed of a small river, which, like all the rest, has overrun. Arrived at Cannes,* a town, or rather open village, prettily situated upon the sea-shore, with fine wooded hills rising behind it. The inn, a little new-built place, so immediately upon the sea that its noise kept me awake. L'Isle de St. Marguerite,† to be seen from the descent of the Estrelles, seems here close by, and is, I believe, not above a league and a half from the nearest part of the shore. It is a picturesque object with its castle and a number of flat-topped pines, which look actually growing out of the sea. In spite of being a good deal tired with our day's journey, and our little inn chimney smoking abominably, I could enjoy from the window a brilliant red sun, setting in the Mediterranean and colouring all the objects near the horizon with that purple and blue peculiar to the South of France.

* Napoleon landed from Elba 1½ miles east of Cannes, in March 1815, with an army of 600 grenadier guards, 200 dragoons, and 100 lancers without horses.—*Murray's Handbook.*

† In one of the group of two isles called Lérins, is a fort, once a state prison, where the 'Man in the Iron Mask' was imprisoned (1686–1698). The dungeon in which he was confined is still pointed out.—*Ibid.*

Monday, 5*th*.—Left Cannes very early. The road, though good through the village along the coast, when flat and sandy and requiring no repair, soon became too bad to remain in the carriage. At every little ascent from the level of the sea, the rain had made gullies that had as usual carried away half the road, and in other places it passed over rocks; but while I live I never can forget the charm of my walk about seven o'clock this morning, with the same clear, glorious sun of the night before rising again out of the sea, giving the most vivid colours to the beautiful vegetation covering the rocks on which we were walking, and lighting up with the most exquisite roseate hue the sunny side of the distant snow-covered mountains of the Col de Tende. This scene, the freshness of the morning, the beauty of the plants, the colour and sound of the Mediterranean, gently lashing against the rocks below me—however ill I describe it—will remain for ever on my mind, and has added one to my, alas! too small stock of agreeable recollections. The whole road from Cannes to Antibes is charming. On descending an eminence towards Antibes, one sees, at the same time, Nice on the other side of a beautiful bay, backed by its wooded hills, white villas, and high mountains. Antibes is a regular fortified town upon a promontory which forms one side of the bay. The inside of the town, like the others—narrow streets, with all the best houses ruined. As it is no longer a frontier town, there are few soldiers here. From Antibes to Nice is four posts round this beautiful bay. The road for the most part flat, and fortunately not requiring much attention, for it has been just as much neglected as all the rest. About a league from Nice is the wide and stony bed of the Var, a great mountain torrent running in I know not how many streams to the sea. At the beginning of the Revolution, the French built a wooden bridge over this to facilitate the passage of their troops. It was a work of no great difficulty, and certainly of great use, but it was done in a prodigious hurry, with wood cut down in a forest close by, and used immediately. Little wonder, therefore, that the violent rains of this last month, and the very violent storm of wind and rain (which detained us on the Rhône the 21st of November), broke it down in two or three places. Repairing *it*, or anything else, is now out of the question, though this is *talked of*, which is more than can be said of the roads. Within this week three planks have been laid over the broken places, upon which foot passengers, with steady heads (for there is no sort of rail or guard to them) may pass, and upon which we all did pass, each taking hold of a man's arm. The carriage was obliged to go down nearer the sea to pass where the currents were more spread and shallow, and then to be dragged over loose stones and shingles. The view of Nice, the high abrupt rock round which it is in a manner built, its long faubourg stretched out along the bank of the sea, and the wooded hills behind it, looked beautiful. At last the carriage arrived, and with it above half-a-dozen men, with poles in their hands and barefooted. They had helped to pass it across the river, and not being satisfied with the courier's offers of payment, followed him to demand more, and at last took what we offered. We continued our journey. Entered Nice by this long scattered faubourg on one of the finest days I ever saw. Lodged at the Hotel de York, in the Place St. Dominique.

The deep impression made on Miss Berry's mind by the walk of this morning and the wretched night at Tourves, is thus spoken of by her many years afterwards :—

When we look back to the disagreeable circumstance in which we have often been placed, and the painful sensations to which we have often been exposed, and then recollect how many comfortable or, at least, easy hours we have passed since, when the memory of these painful moments have been entirely obliterated, it ought to be a great motive of fortitude and patience in those to come. I can call to mind a night passed at Tourves, a miserable village between Aix and Nice, in the worst inn I ever inhabited, after a day of much fatigue on the worst road I ever passed, and when I expected every minute to see our carriage broken to pieces;—my companions both sadly out of sorts and depressed by the prospect before them; myself necessarily uncertain how the journey, when once accomplished, would turn out to any of us. I can never forget arriving at this wretched inn, in a still more wretched village, on a melancholy rainy evening, the 30th of November 1802, and actually lying awake all night, in spite of my fatigue, from mere vexation of mind. This was not quieted by the rain beating in at my window, every drop of which I knew would count against us in our next day's journey. I could think of nothing cheerful, nor fancy any future pleasure; and yet three days afterwards, on the same journey, the charms of an early morning walk, between seven and eight o'clock, upon the rocky edge of the Mediterranean between Cannes and Antibes,—the sun rising unclouded from that glorious sea, and tinging the distant snowy mountains with the most beautiful roseate hue,—the vivid green of the pines on the nearer hills, the beauty and variety of the vegetation immediately above me, the mild freshness of the morning air in the middle of winter,—made an impression on my mind, which at the time totally obliterated, and is certainly now much oftener recalled than, the remembrance of the night passed at the miserable Cheval Blanc at Tourves.

NICE.

Thursday, 9*th*.—Saw a sort of bustle in the Place St. Dominique from our windows, and three coaches, all *voitures de remises*, came out of our inn, and drove into the *Place*; and after making some short tour in the town, the first coach, with two gendarmes on horseback trotting in advance, then stopped at a house in the *Place*. I enquired what this might mean, and found that the house at which the carriages stopped was the Mairie; that the mayor's wife had lain in, and that the carriage preceded by the two gendarmes contained the préfêt, who was going to stand godfather to the child. I saw him get out in his préfêt's embroidered coat, and he was shortly after followed into the house by a number of trays carried by *traiteurs*, which, I suppose, contained the collation that was given him. This was between four and five o'clock. Before six o'clock, the same three carriages proceeded up another street to some church. There were a number of little ragged boys about the door, who shouted when the carriage drove off, because some money was thrown to them. These little *polissons*, a few idle people who happened to be upon the Place, and a few soldiers from the caserne which is next door, were the only spectators of this *no show*. And this was all the ceremony of the magistrate of one of their principal towns going in state to the second magistrate! This will not do: oppressed as the towns are, more than ever with taxes, their public concerns and conveniences, such as roads, bridges, and buildings shamefully neglected, and their church and their nobles having nothing to assist them, they have not even the amusement of those shows, and that sort of public pomp, of which everyone, when its cost did not fall immediately upon himself, felt proud, and which served to amuse and gratify an idle people. They are now without their old amusements, and with no new industry, ten times idler than ever.

Tuesday, 14*th*.—Took possession of our house in the faubourg. It had been furnished and inhabited by General Morgan, who gave it up to us on our paying the rent which he had agreed for, viz., 90*l.* till the 1st of May. The rent was enormous, considering the house, the style of its furniture, &c.

The following letter, addressed to Mrs. Damer, gives a somewhat more detailed account of the Miss Berrys' first settling at Nice for the winter.

Nice, Thursday, 16 Dec., 1802.

I remember your telling me that you thought you should feel comfortable and pleased at Strawberry if you could fancy me quietly settled, or taking a quiet walk at Nice. Be comfortable and be pleased then, dear soul! *car enfin m'y voici.* After all our scruples and regrets about the 90*l.*—and *mine,* I assure you, were many,—we have been obliged to give it. We found we were eating up our heads (as they say of horses) at the hotel. . . . Everything here in the house way is unfurnished; the people always offer to furnish them for you, but they do it very badly, plague you to death, and 'tis weeks before you can get into them. This Genl and Mrs. Morgan were still willing to let us have their house. . . . *Graces à ses soins,* this is much better furnished than any other house here. Mrs. M.'s idea was to make it as like an *un*comfortable English house as she could, and Agnes and I have had a world of rummaging, and twisting, and twirling all the things about to make the sitting-room and the rest of the house look comfortable, and I think at last we are very well lodged. . . . The Chev[l] de Chateauneuf, to whom the D[ss] of Devonshire gave me a note, is not here, but as she likewise gave me the name of his sister, a M[de] de S[t] Agathe, I sent a civil note to her, with the D[ss's] compliments, &c., which soon brought her to the hotel; and she turns out a prettyish, agreeableish sort of a young woman, without affectation, and apparently not without cleverness, and she brought a Mons. Reynardi and her *belle sœur*, and two other demoiselles; in short, *nous voici faufilées* in any society there is at Nice. But these poor people have been all *émigrés,* are but lately returned, have lost more than the half of the little they had, and can do nothing for anybody. However, we shall like their society sometimes, if we can get them to come to us, which I suppose in time they will. I spend my mornings most agreeably; the beauties of this place rise upon me every moment. I really think that for *one's own eating* (as poor L[d] Orf. said) it is the *very* prettiest place I ever saw. The weather, for the most part, since we came has been delicious; it is now cold, that is to say in the early morn[gs] and even[gs], for in the middle of the day nothing but the almanac calling it Dec[r]. could possibly persuade me it was anything but May. I am so glad to find that tho' my enthusiasm is gone, I am still *animal* enough to feel this, 'in ogni fibro il sangue.' I continue most comfortably well. . . . Would I could give half as good an account of the other poor sick souls! for Mrs. Ellis * nothing more can be done. If she recovers it will be a miracle; her inflammation baffles all attempts to reduce it, and she is now too weak to admit of *any*. I sat with L[d] Hervey near an hour yesterday; and he seems to have little or no hope! The poor Miss Francis, too, I think is going on very ill. The D[ss] of Cumberland is, they say, well except being lame. She is glad to see anybody after two o'clock, and we shall go some of these days, as I suppose she will like to see all the English. The walks here are delicious, and I am going to get an ass's legs to save my own. The worst of the place is everything being abominably dear, which makes my father groan and think it less pretty than he otherwise would. As for me, I am very sorry we cannot save money here, but am resolved at least to enjoy it as much as I can, and trust to you and Hoper † letting Strawb. well. The last part of our journey f[r] Avignon here cost *enormously*, f[r] being so long about it and having an escort, and our baggage carried, &c.; otherwise my calculation of 250*l*. for the journey would have been considerably within the mark.

* Elizabeth Catherine Caroline Hervey, only daughter of Lord Hervey and Elizabeth Drummond of Quebec, married Charles Rose Ellis, Esq. (afterwards Lord Seaford); died 1803.

† Mr. Hoper is frequently mentioned in Miss Berry's journals as the person on whom they relied for transacting business for them.

JOURNAL.

1803.

Entry for 1803.—Lady Ailesbury dies: we return to England, September.

Nice, January 29*th*.—In the night of December 31st, a violent storm of thunder, lightning, wind, and rain took place here; from that time to this, now above three weeks, we have not had more than four or five days free from heavy and continuous rain. It is not cold, and the few sunny days which we have enjoyed were such as to make the shade agreeable. The night before last (January 23rd), the clouds that fell in rain in the plain fell in hail or snow upon the nearest hills. To my feelings a sudden and extraordinary degree of cold in the finest days always takes place here about four o'clock,—that is to say, just before the setting of the sun.

February 2*nd*.—On January 27th the weather cleared up, and we had then four or five dry days.

In this month Miss Berry received the intelligence of Lady Ailesbury's death. As the wife of Marshal Conway and the mother of Mrs. Damer, her name is so familiar to the readers of Horace Walpole that her daughter's touching description of her own feelings on the occasion may claim a place in Miss Berry's correspondence.

Tuesday morning, Jan. 18.

. . . My dearest, kindest of mothers expired yesterday morning without a groan, even without a sigh; her countenance instantly became placid, and her fine features made her beautiful in death! Such, I am convinced, can be the end only of one possessing a virtuous mind and a conscience without reproach; and such a one, I am proud to think, was my mother! A scene more affecting, more impressive, than her end, it was not possible to see. My grief is extreme, and much as I ever thought I should regret this dear mother, I find that regret deeper and more painful than I expected. All the arrangements—every little improvement at Strawberry Hill—this house—all (sometimes imperceptibly at the moment to myself) tended wholly to procure her amusement and comforts; and all these have lost their value to me. But never more to behold that benign countenance brightening up at the sight of me! this does give me the feeling of an almost broken heart!

Thursday, 10*th.*—A long course up the valley upon the mountains above the préfêt's house, with Colonel Smyth and Baron Trip.

Friday, 11*th.*—To St. André. The road beautiful and picturesque, but such as none but those used to scrambling and narrow mountain paths could go. Colonel Smyth and Baron Trip our guides, with the help of an ass, we walked in all better than twelve miles.

Thursday, 24*th.*—To the Vallée Obscure. It is a valley with a small stream of water running through it, and narrowed to a mere passage of the water between the hills. These often rise on each side more than a hundred feet above the stream, and in some places are not much more than six or eight feet apart. We rode on through this little stream about half a quarter of a mile, winding between the perpendicular hills almost united at top by trees and brushwood. The intention of our guide, General Reynardi, was to take us out at the other end, which opens into a beautiful *riant* country; but the peasants of the environs said that the heavy rains of this winter had brought down such large masses of earth and stones from the sides of the hills that it was quite impassable. It is about two hours' walk from Nice, the whole way beautiful, by the villa of the Contessa da Casta and the Capucins'

Church. The day was delicious. In the Vallée Obscure, between the hills, where the sun can never penetrate, the cold was striking. Pretty little blue apaticas growing upon the sides of the rock.

Sunday, 27th.—Every Sunday during Lent there is a sort of fair held at the different churches near Nice—it begins with Cimia. The road up to it was crowded with people, and the *Place* before the church full of people selling all sorts of gilt gingerbread, figs, raisins, wine, &c., &c., but no other sort of commodity. There was a function in the church, which was full, and the people dispersed themselves about in groups in the fields and under the olive trees, drinking the wine and eating the figs, chestnuts, &c., they had brought with them. We observed but one party who were eating meat, although there is a general *dispense* for the whole country. The *beau monde* of Nice all take a walk to these *festins*, as they are called, upon the Sundays in Lent, and generally take that opportunity of calling on the way at the different churches, and upon such of their friends as have country houses. The proprietors are always there at these times, though very seldom at any other. The weather delightful—but one cold or rainy day from the 11th to this date, March 2nd.

Sunday, March 27th.—These *festins* ended to-day with one again at Cimia, very crowded, although the day was unpleasant. *Festins* had been held at St. Bartlemi, before the Capucins' Convent, on the Villafranca road; and that was by far the prettiest, as the people spread themselves in little parties all over the rocky hill of Mont Alban, and singularly enlivened the whole scene.

The weather this month dry, and till the 24th warm and enjoyable.

Friday, April 8th.—Went to Falicore; were above two hours getting there. It is a cleaner little village, or bourg, than any other I have seen; view beautiful on every side.

As we got off our horses and walked about the *Place*, the whole town came out to look at us, and among them the three principal persons of the place,—the mayor, the curé, and his nephew, the avocat. The curé turned out to be an old acquaintance of General Reynardi's, who was with us; and he insisted so much upon our coming into his nephew's house, and our taking a glass of wine, that we were obliged to comply. The house was clean and comfortable for this country, and the wine, produced in a bottle (containing at least half-a-dozen common-sized bottles), most excellent white Muscat. We stayed with them about half an hour; it was impossible not to be pleased with their hospitality. It was Good Friday, so that there was no eating going on among them. About a mile and a half from Falicore, upon the bare and rocky side of the hill immediately under Mont Can, they have lately discovered a considerable cavern or grotto. One descends into it by a ladder from the aperture on the side of the hill; it is lined with stalactites, which in several places form little Gothic tabernacles, which, with a lamp placed in or behind them, were really very beautiful, though the colour of the stalactites was not very clear-looking, and there is but one great detached column; so that I suppose to those much accustomed to visit grottos (which I am not) this would be considered as but a middling one. The proprietor, however, a Piedmontese, who bought some of the *émigrés'* land, and possesses a house at the foot of the hill, thinks far otherwise, and is having stairs cut in the rock, and thinks, I believe, that he is to make money by showing it to the strangers who come to Nice. Our party consisted of General Reynardi, Colonel Smyth, Prince Louis Lichtenstein, and ourselves.

Saturday, 30*th*.—After uninterrupted fair weather for eight weeks, a violent thunder-shower fell in the night of the 27th. To-day distant thunder was heard, and a vast congregation of heavy black clouds hanging over the mountains seemed to pour down rain, but on clearing off they left Mont Cań and all the lower mountains whitened with hail. The cold in the plain here was almost as great as we have ever experienced during the winter.

Tuesday, May 3rd.—Left Nice. Madame de St. Agathe and General Reynardi accompanied us to the further side of the Pont du Var. It is now passable for light carriages, but the reparations have been made in a slight and slovenly manner—the gardefoux on the part that has been repaired might be pushed down with a stick. Before we had got above half way to the Pont du Var the two Princes of Lichtenstein* and Comte Attems joined us. When we had passed the Pont du Var, Madame de St. Agathe bid us adieu, and, I really believe, with sincere regret. She is an amiable, unaffected creature, with a good natural understanding, and had she seen more of the world she would be very agreeable. At Antibes, we drove to the inn, thinking the Lichtensteins would go no farther, but they kindly proposed accompanying us to Cannes.

At Cannes we arrived at half-past three. The road near the edge of the sea, from which the view struck me so much in the winter, I again made on foot. The day was an unlucky one for distant views, and for a last look at the beauties of Nice; heavy clouds hung upon the distant hills, and the prospect was much involved in mist; but still this part of the road charmed me.

At Cannes the Lichtensteins bid us a most kind and hearty farewell, and returned on their post-horses to Nice, leaving upon our minds the impression of their being two of the most agreeable, well-informed, unaffected young men that we have met with for an age, to say nothing of their distinguished military merit and all they have both

* Prince Louis died, unmarried, in 1833. Prince Maurice died in 1819, leaving three daughters now living—Princess L. Schwartzenburg and two Princesses Lobkovitz.

suffered, for their Emperor and their country in the late war. They constituted our constant every-day society for the last fortnight of our stay at Nice; for though they both occupied themselves much in the morning, they took long rides with us in the afternoon, and came to us every evening. Never idle, *desœuvrés*, or wanting to get rid of time themselves, I never lived in intimacy with any young men so *never à charge* as with them. I quit Nice with a regret, with a feeling of melancholy, which I hope I shall ever experience at leaving any place where I have spent five months quietly and comfortably, to say nothing of regretting its exquisite natural beauties, which gained upon me the more I became acquainted with them. To cease *to be* in any place where one *has been* for five months together, always appears to me a sort of death. One's resurrection in the next place to which one means to go, is uncertain as to its equal comfort, and has seldom (except under very particular circumstances) the charm, the ineffable charm, of *intimité*.

A few extracts from Miss Berry's correspondence at this time have been preserved. The two following are from letters addressed to her friend Mrs. Damer, with Mrs. D.'s reply to the first:—

Nice, Jan., 1803.

. . . In spite of my headache yesterday, I contrived to read nearly three volumes of Madame de Staël's Delphine. As I conclude it is long before this time in London, I need not tell you what it is. It is certainly interesting—the great *sine quâ non* of a novel. It is well written, too, and there is much nice observation of the affections of the human heart; but much false and incongruous, and still more, which has only been drawn from, and only applies to, the corrupted and *factieux* societies of Paris. What chiefly diverts me is the portrait of herself (of her character, I mean), under that of Delphine, which she herself, I dare say believes is a striking likeness, and likely to do her immortal honour! The attempt, nobody who knows her the least can avoid seeing; but were it as like, as it is ridiculously dissimilar to her life and manners, it would be, by no means, I should think, a portrait that one should choose to expose of oneself. Such pictures of the passions I think hideous and fearful, instead of touching. Of all the passions, I consider love as that which the least admits of an exaggerated description. It is itself an exaggeration, and the only method of profoundly interesting *les âmes vraiment sensibles* is to keep the expression of it subdued, and to leave much to the mind of your reader. How differently has Rousseau treated a great passion, and a passion which leaves a ten times deeper impression of its violence on my mind, than all the so-often repeated struggles of Leonie and Delphine; while the perfect and admirable friendship which he contrasts with it, speaks peace and consolation to the suffering mind, and points out the true and only resource of a *cœur aimant* against the delirium of passion.

London, Feb. 1803.

. . . You will see how much we agree about Delphine, and how much we have both thought it worth occupying a portion of the alas! small sides of paper a letter can consist of, or time be found to fill it. Delphine is certainly not an exact portrait of Madame de Staël in all senses; but I think it quite curious to see the soul (as I think it here does) of a person, certainly one of genius, pervading a whole book, for so it is,— ideas, opinions, passions all.

You do not know how much I admire what you say on love, her love, I mean. I have ever with you thought such descriptions of that passion put me in mind of the wrong end of a magnet being placed to the point of steel. But Delphine and Leonie will clatter through the world and carry crowds in their vortex. The more they are abused, the more they will be followed and studied, and even admired.

The following extracts from a letter of Miss Berry's very young correspondent, Lord Hartington,* then only thirteen years old, will not be without interest as to passing events:—

* William Spencer Cavendish, Marquess of Hartington, born 1790, succeeded his father as sixth Duke of Devonshire, 1811.

Devonshire House, Jan. 30, 1803.

You cannot think, my dear Miss Berry, how much pleasure your letter gave me; everything you can say about Nice will be news to me, as I have never had any correspondent there. . . . I envy you very much upon your *tall personable* beast on the mountains, whilst we (poor souls!) are shivering in great coats by the fireside. We are *certainly* to go to Paris this summer. Perhaps we shall meet you there on your way back. . . . I will, if you like it, write a *newspaper* for you every week. You can stop them as soon as you like. . . . . Lord and Lady Abercorn have had a play at the Priory. It was 'Who's the Dupe?' and 'The Wedding Day.' It was very well acted. Lady Cahir * acted Lady Contest. The other actors were Pen † and George Lamb, ‡ Lawrence, § the two Mr. Maddocks, ‖ Lady Charlotte Lindsay, ¶ Miss Butler and Mrs. Kemble. ** Mamma and my sister were there. There was no room for poor me: I should like to have been there very much. . . .

Andreossi came here the other night, and talked a great deal about Bonaparte, and defended his cruelty in Egypt, which is mentioned in Wilson's book on the war there. He said that it was not true that he had ordered all the wounded to be killed, for they took away numbers, and those few who were killed, were past recovery, and that he did it out of humanity. My aunt Besborough is to set out from Paris the 6th of next month. Moreau has been to see her; he makes no scruples of disapproving of the present government. My aunt asked him if he was not afraid of Bonaparte killing him, upon which he said—'*Bonaparte est un tyran mais pas un assassin.*' He said that

* Lady Cahir, afterwards Countess of Glengall.

† Hon. Penistone Lamb, son of Penistone, first Lord Melbourne, and Elizabeth Milbanke, daughter of Sir Ralph Milbanke: died 1805.

‡ Hon. George Lamb, his brother, died 1834.

§ Lawrence (Sir Thos.), the celebrated artist.

‖ The two Mr. Maddocks (brothers), Kentish gentlemen, well known in society at this time. The name is preserved in North Wales, where, near Bethgellert, a harbour was constructed by the elder brother, called Port Maddock.

¶ Lady Charlotte Lindsay, daughter of the second Earl of Guildford, eighth Lord North; married Lieut.-Col. the Hon. John Lindsay, 1800; died 1849.

** Mrs. Brereton, daughter of Mr. Hopkins, prompter at Drury Lane; married to John Kemble, the great tragedian, 1787.

he was not afraid of his banishing him, for he had the hearts of all the army, and that he did not dare. . . . I am afraid you will be sadly tired with this long scrawl: I will write something more substantial when I get some news; in the meantime, I remain yours, ever affectionately,

HARTINGTON.

Extract of a letter from Sir Harry Englefield to Miss Berry.

Feb. 18, 1803.

. . . I have lived in town now over a month, as if I had been at Nice or Pekin, and knowing little more of the world here than you do. I have seen Lady Hertford once, but heard very little, except that General Andreossi asked Lady Anne B—— who Miss Gibbes was, and was answered—'*C'est la sœur de loi du grand parleur.*' * Some good French is also told of the Duchess of Gordon,† who is giving continual balls and fêtes at Paris. . . . I hear that Lady Palm.‡ is in very good health, and when she sees her friends, which is but seldom, very tolerably cheerful. Lord Minto saw her the other day at Broadlands,§ which, by-the-bye, has had a narrow escape from fire. The furniture of one bedchamber was quite burnt. Sotheby meditates a religious poem, with a reasonable spice of metaphysics in it. As your roads are bad, I shall not attempt to send it except by sea, and then I rather apprehend it may bring the ships into a scrape, like Lord Elgin's brig which went down near the Island of Cythera, laden with marble from the temples of Minerva and Theseus, and all the journals and drawings made in the Morea by these gentlemen who had surveyed the Thermopylea and Platea, and a thousand places untrodden by European Christian feet for many centuries; the event is really a calamity to all lovers of art and science. We Grecians have a new feast, however. A play of Euripides or Sophocles or of their time (really and truly) has been discovered at Moscow, and parts of it are

* Miss Gibbes was sister-in-law to the Right Hon. Charles Abbot (afterwards first Lord Colchester), Speaker of the House of Commons.

† Jane Maxwell, Duchess of Gordon, called by Horace Walpole one of the empresses of fashion.

‡ Mary, daughter of Benjamin Mee, Esq., married Henry, second Viscount Palmerston, 1783; died 1805. Lord Palmerston died 1802.

§ The seat of Lord Palmerston, in Hants.

already arrived here. Dr. Burney has seen it, and has no doubt of its authenticity.* Then a Mr. Clarke has collected most curious MSS. in the Levant, and brought them safe home. A Plato of the ninth century, and several ancient songs with their music.† I suppose the street organs will soon be playing Sappho's 'Lamentation,' Anacreon's 'Fancy,' Tyrtæus' 'March,' and Erinna's 'Hornpipe.' *A propos* of this, I suppose you know that in the 'Mystères d'Isis,' at Paris, there is an entire ballet copied from the 'Obelisks' — all the dancers are
 &c.

You know how I respect Agnes' pencil. I am most happy to hear that she continues to work; I am sure she will improve, for every touch gives power to the next. I wish you would lay aside your chalk, and take to black-lead; for chalk is a grimy business, and at best is bad, and at worst is detestable. If you would take pains, you would do extremely well. . . . My neighbours here ‡ go on most lovingly. Their affection seems to grow with their growth, and fatten with their fat. He and

* No trace of this play is to be found. Whether the MS. which Dr. Burney saw proved to be a fraud or a mistake must now be doubtful. Miss Berry's correspondent was not likely to have been misinformed as to some such supposed MS. having been in the hands of Dr. Burney, with whom Miss Berry and her friends were well acquainted. The highest authorities at Oxford, Cambridge, and the British Museum, to which may be added the name of Mr. Grote (all powerful on such subjects) declare that no such play exists to their knowledge, and no record of any such discovery at Moscow. In 1782 an Homeric Hymn to Ceres was discovered at Moscow; and a large fragment of a play of Euripides was found at Paris by Bekkar in 1821; but neither of these discoveries throws any light upon the work supposed to have been sent here in 1803.

† In a letter addressed by Dr. Edward Daniel Clarke to the Rev. Robert Matthews, dated 1802, he enumerates the various MSS. he has got:—'In Greek I have the works of Plato, the Lexicon of St. Cyril, a volume of Greek poems, and two works on Ancient Music.'—*Life of Edward D. Clarke*, by Wm. Otter, p. 517. In a letter from Dr. Clarke he says, 'Porson is all rapture and joy about the Plato . . . he says it may be considered as equivalent to the combined authorities of any two known MSS.'—*Ibid.* p. 560.

It was in the Monastery of St. John, in the Isle of Patmos, that these MSS. were discovered, and are now deposited in the Bodleian Library, Oxford.

‡ Prince of Wales and Mrs. Fitzherbert.

old Q——* attended a lecture the other day, read by a Professor Aldini, on a hanged house-breaker. Galvanism made the dead man open his eyes and grin extremely: they had a noble end in view, but alas! the doctor gave them no hopes.

Extract of a letter from Miss Berry, but no mention of the name of her correspondent:—

Nice, Feb., 1803.

All general principles of government of moral conduct, of *all* species of reciprocal duties, must all be referable to the instincts of nature and to *moral truth.*

These general principles, immutable, invariable as the Being from whom they emanate, are to be modified in their application to general use, or individual commerce. Thus in governments, or associations of men, the safety of the whole is to be purchased by the loss or danger of some individuals—that is to say, a power of protection, and consequently of punishment is to be placed *somewhere.* From the nature of man, punishment will be sometimes misplaced, and protection will be sometimes abused, but still the *principles* upon which both act may be true, consequently just. For justice is nothing else but *moral truth.*

Try all human institutions, the principle of all governments, all commercial regulations by this rule, and it is easy to convince oneself of its certainty, not by what *may be* built upon it, but what *has been* experienced from it. Try by this rule the English government, the former French government, the present. The principle of the first (the English government), both in its civil and criminal administration, will be found in perfect consonance with the above rule. See then, in spite of the perversity of human nature, the incapacity of ministers, the nullities of kings, the contagion of neighbouring corruption, *what* it has resisted! how it has survived the general stroke of Europe! what powers of self-preservation and regeneration it has within itself!

The former French government, in its original principles, in its tacit agreement between the *governors* and the governed, was in opposition to every point of moral truth. In vain were

* Duke of Queensborough.

its natural advantages—in vain the character of some few brilliant princes—the virtues of many distinguished citizens—with everything that could, in fact, contribute to its natural *tout-puissance.* By the falseness of principle in all its institutions, and in its whole organisation, its former history presents nothing to the eye of philosophy but a wretched combat between depravity and folly. Look at its present history, that marvellous page now open under our eyes, the same negligence of moral truth in all the various pretended constitutions.

Extract of a letter from Miss Berry to a friend.

Nice, March, 1803.

I am reading over for the fiftieth time, I believe, the letters of Madame de Sévigné. They always improve on me, and are *here* particularly interesting. *Here,* where her immediate descendants still remain; *here,* in the neighbourhood of so many of her scenes of action, her Provençal phrases, and the things to which she so often reverts. Do you know her as much by heart as you ought to do? It is amazing how constantly her *âme aimante,* and all the various expressions it dictates, puts me in mind of yours. It is the same manner of thinking and feeling for everything that has to do with what she loves. In short, it is the true pre-occupation and interest of real affection, that first and best of sentiments! more tender than friendship, more sure, more composed, more satisfying than love.

Letter from Miss Berry to Mrs. Greathead at Paris.

Nice, Tuesday, March 22, 1803.

. . . I have the pleasure of receiving your letter of the 11th, which makes me forget everything but a wish to hear and see more of friends for whom, believe me, no silence, nor no absence can ever cool our affection, or even lessen our interest.

The account you give of Paris is such as I expected from what I myself saw of it last year. Had we been all there together, I venture to flatter myself, you would have liked it much better than either of us should separately. As it is, we have given up all thoughts of it when we leave this place. . . .

I am always desirous to enjoy any part of what remains to me of life by passing it in the society of such friends as yourselves. Do, then, think of spending a part of the summer with us in Switzerland. I have only mentioned Lausanne or Geneva as the two places we all best know. But anywhere, where you think you could be comfortable, I am sure we could make ourselves so. I think I may venture to say we are not *bad* at this, and at *living* that sort of society, the only really enjoyable to rational people. I think we have in some degree proved this here, where we found nothing but a parcel of English, none of whom we knew, never meeting of an evening, nor in any other way than in giving each other English dinners at English hours, and declaring, and positively *believing*, there was no society of any kind to be had at Nice. We could not believe this, and soon found out the contrary; made some very agreeable Nice acquaintance; declared off from the very first the English dinners, which my father's age and habits of life enabled us without offence to do. Made a *soirée* about once a week for our Nice friends, some of whom are musical and all play cards; gave them a good supper, and soon found all the English most willing and pleased to be asked to our parties, which have certainly been the best thing here in the way of society, and have been once or twice gay enough to end in a little *impromptu* dance.

I have now only to add, that my health is so improved by the winter I have passed here, that I am a different creature from what you have seen me for the last two years in England, and am capable of enjoying not only society, but long courses in the exquisitely beautiful mountains which surround this place. Agnes has been drawing a great deal. We long to see Bertie* and all his wonderful works. . . .

To Mrs. Greathead, Paris.

* Mr. Bertie Greathead (junior) evinced in boyhood an ardent taste for pictorial art, portraits, and historical pieces of great merit. He visited France during the short peace, for the purpose of improving his judgment in his favourite pursuit; and when others were made prisoners, Napoleon permitted him to retire to Italy; he was there seized with a fever, and died in the twenty-third year of his life.

Extract of a letter from Mrs. Howe.

March 10, 1803.

. . . Another very great death happened on Tuesday morning—that of the Duke of Bridgewater. What I am going to write will show what an immense property he has left behind him. He has given about 30,000*l.* a-year landed estate to General Egerton (now Earl of Bridgewater), and 600,000*l.* in money, all this in his own disposal; and 40,000*l.* to his brother, who is, I believe, a clergyman. To Lady Louisa Macdonald and Lady Ann Vernon each 10,000*l.* To Lord Gower he leaves the navigation, that is, the income of it; the management of the concern being put in trustees' hands; his house in town all strictly entailed (but to him for his life), the pictures, library, &c., as heir-looms, and then to his second and younger sons successively, and their sons, excluding whoever may be Marquis of Stafford; his intention being to make a new family, for whoever has it is to take the name of Egerton. Lord Gower's sons failing, it goes through a long specified entail to the sons of his three nieces. . . . Besides Lord Carlisle's and Lady Louisa's younger sons, Lady Ann Vernon has eight or nine. The navigation is reckoned a clear 74,000*l.* a-year; the last year it produced 80,000*l.*, and is supposed to be improving.

The same.

April 10, 1803.

Lord Gower sells his present habitation, and makes the late Duke of Bridgewater's his town residence; first building a fine drawing and eating-room, &c. to the park, raised to the height of the picture gallery and library, and moves the stables to Cleveland Court; then over the coach narrow way called Katharine-wheel Yard he throws a bridge, which leads to his garden in the Green Park; it will be a very complete business when finished.

The same.

Thursday, May 19, 1803.

In our present situation with France, my dear Miss Berry, an impatience to run over the papers relative to all that has passed between the two (alas!) adverse kingdoms since the treaty of Amiens, which were laid before the House of Commons yesterday, is a natural impulse. . . . As a war is now in a manner begun, I guess it may cause you and yours to leave Geneva very quickly, therefore am unwilling to defer till next week writing my grateful thanks for your last finished the 29th of April; and calculating I have half-an-hour to spare, before I need dress for the Queen's ball (her natural birthday), I am glad to seize it, and thus make a beginning. . . . Lord Whitworth arrived in town last night, and probably General Andreossi landed at Calais several hours ago. The King was at the little theatre in the Haymarket Tuesday evening, and was received in the most flattering manner — 'God save the King,' 'Rule Britannia,' and every allusion to the present moment that could be seized upon, met the highest applause.

4 o'clock, Friday, May 20.

I need not say I am very well, my dear Miss Berry, when I tell you I was not in bed till five this morning, and not in any manner discomposed or too much tired; but of course not up by cock-crow. . . . Lady Douglas was at the ball, but neither of her daughters; no one below the rank of earl's daughters and peeresses were there, except myself and one living in the house, and the attendant upon the Princess Sophia of Gloucester.

JOURNAL.

Wednesday, May 4th.—Left Cannes for Muy. The morning, rain fell before we began to mount the Estrelles. The new-fallen rain had laid the dust, and refreshed all the beautiful shrubs with which the sides of the road are covered; the air was mild and calm, heavy clouds hung upon the tops of all the mountains, and a solemn stillness pervaded the whole landscape, which, together with the wild and uninhabited look of these hills, gave it a most impressive character.

Thursday, 5th.—At Flassans they gave us five miserable, weak horses, which, on a hill by no means steep, absolutely refused to draw. In vain the postilions swore they would go on very well; in vain they strove to make them move, and, while they were half murdering them with blows, wished us to sit in the carriage. That was impossible; we all got out, in one of the most pouring rains I ever saw or felt. There was a wretched peasant's hovel a little way off the road, to which we made as fast as the wind and rain would allow us. Here, in a sort of stable, I wanted to stay till the horses were up the hill. They moved on a little, and the postilions hallooed to us to get in. Again the horses would not move; again they were *assommés de coups*; again we got out, and again we made for our hovel, where we in vain endeavoured to make the peasants lend or find some horses to help us. They had none themselves, and the moment they knew it was the post, nobody would interfere or stir a foot. At last the wretched beasts moved up the hill, and we were obliged, dripping wet, to follow them, the wind and rain more violent than ever. The people told us there was an inn on the top of the hill; we insisted on the postilions stopping there, meaning to change our wet clothes, warm ourselves, and again try to persuade them to seek other horses; but in none of these points did we succeed. The inn was a wretched *grenier*, with one fireplace, round which a great number of noisy, strange, low sort of men were sitting, who seemed very little disposed to make room for us,—one man especially, who seemed a friend of the postilions, was particularly anxious to assure us we could get nothing there, and to force us out of the house. We were literally wet to the skin, and our dripping great coats made the bottom of the coach so wet that no partial change could be of use. The postilions positively refused to go on to Brignolles for other horses, and nobody else would stir, though we offered to bribe them all. At last, after losing three-quarters of an hour, we were forced to get again into the carriage, with small hopes of being dragged over the very bad road before us, when fortunately we met the cabriolet of the post, with which we changed horses, and at last arrived at Brignolles, and were not the least the worse for this thorough wetting, and sitting in wet clothes, which is so often supposed to be an unavoidable cause of all sorts of ills.

Friday, 6th.—It rained all night, and continued with very short intervals the whole day. Between Brignolles and La Grande Pugère my father and I walked a great part of the way. One part was the worst and most dangerous of the road from Nice to Aix, not excepting the Estrelles. Arrived at Aix in a pouring rain, at seven o'clock.

Saturday, 7th.—The incessant pouring rain determined us to stay at Aix all day. We never stirred out of the hotel, and amused ourselves in the evening, when it began to grow fair, with drawing from the window.

Sunday, 8th.—Left Aix. We saw a cart *embourbé* when we passed St. Cannat in the winter, and we found another one in the same situation now. The people complain of their roads, but are firmly convinced that the very next week they are to be thoroughly repaired,—and so they were six months ago. Bonaparte's government is not one to repair roads for people who can do so well upon the promise only of better ones.

Between the Pont-National and Orgon is a large handsome château and park, belonging to a Mr. du Lubron (or some such name). The park; which is very large, has been laid open in the days of the Revolution, and many fine trees have been cut down and are still lying there. The postilion was anxious to tell me that the owner lived at another château in the neighbourhood, probably of a very different sort from this, which is really a fine country-seat. We arrived at Avignon on a very fine evening; it was Sunday, and all the public walks upon the outside of the walls were full of gay, cheerful-looking people; but I lost all the pleasure I should otherwise have received from such a scene, by Agnes being extremely unwell.

Avignon, though situated in a plain, presents itself well from the number of high buildings, towers, &c., enclosed within it, and from the extraordinary beauty of its walls, which are in as perfect repair and look as new as if they had just been built.

Monday, 9th.—Left Avignon. The road to Douzère is along the valley of the Rhône, and often near its banks, but the country on both sides looks much less beautiful from the road than from the river,—and from the river I sincerely hope never to contemplate its beauties again! There are no olives north of Avignon; from there to Lorques the road is through rich pastures and comfortable looking villages. On this great Lyons and Marseilles road I observed that between every post we had three stops, one to change horses with some other carriage, and two for the breaking of traces. Between Mornas and La Palisse we met the Turkish Ambassador and his suite, in two carriages with six horses each, upon whom our postilions in vain exerted all their eloquence to allow them to change horses, and then revenged themselves by declaring 'qu'ils étaient des coquins, des voleurs, des Turcs;' though it was two Frenchmen in the first carriage, with the Ambassador, who absolutely refused changing; for the Turks, as may be supposed, knew nothing about the matter.

At Orange we were detained, and employed our time most agreeably in examining the Arch of Triumph,* which stands on the right-hand side of the present road, just out of the town. It is much more beautiful than I had formerly thought; and though it may have been overcharged with ornaments, they are so beautifully worked, the Corinthian columns are in such beautiful proportion, and the end which has not been built against

* The date and destination of this arch are unknown; the received opinion at present refers it to the reign of Marcus Aurelius and to his successes on the Danube and in Germany.—See *Murray's Handbook.*

gives such a high idea of the sculpture of the Dacian and other captive figures with which it was adorned, as makes it still a fine example of Roman, or rather Grecian, architecture.

A part of the wall of the amphitheatre* appears on entering the town, but all beauty is now destroyed by its being filled and built up with poor mean houses.

Tuesday, 10*th*.—Came in sight of the Rhône; continued for the most part along its bank. At Valence I thought I had remembered the *fronton* of a very fine Gothic church, and went in search of it, but in its beauty I was quite disappointed. It is a plain, unornamented, large Gothic church, with no fine front; but in a side chapel of the middle aisle, hung with black cloth or paper, all dropped with tears, are deposited the heart and entrails of Pius VI., the poor pope who, after being expelled Rome by the French, and dragged about from one town to another, at last died at Valence, 1799. Over the door of the chapel is written, 'Ici repose le cœur et les entrailles du Pape Pie VI.' They are in a box set upon a high stool in the middle of the chapel, the whole covered with black velvet, and a triple crown embroidered upon it. Upon examining the church we found they had at first been placed in a less conspicuous situation, in a retired, out-of-the-way chapel, and in a sort of wooden painted sarcophagus, still bearing an inscription which marked what it had been: 'Ici sont deposés le cœur et les entrailles de Pie VI.' †

As soon as we turned off the great Lyons road at Valence, and took that of Grenoble, the surrounding

* The interior has been cleared of the miserable hovels which filled it, and whose tenants in some instances, burrowing like moles, had formed cellars in the thickness of the walls, regardless of the risk of undermining it and of being buried in its ruins. The removal of a hundred of these cabins now enables the spectators to judge of the arrangement of the scene on its inner face.—*Murray's Handbook.*

† The church contains a bust and bas-relief by Canova, to the memory of Pope Pius VI.—See *Murray's Handbook.*

country became much more beautiful. The cultivation between Valence and Romans is remarkable; the vines for the most part are on espaliers, round cornfields, and sometimes in a double row, which gives to every field the look of what used to be called in England a *ferme ornée*.

Romans* is a largish town, prettily situated on the Isère, with a stone bridge. It has a great appearance of commerce, bustle, and comfort. Tanning seems to be the principal trade here. Upon a small stream running into the Isère live a whole row of tanners; many, I fancy, employed in preparing the skins which are to be manufactured into gloves at Grenoble.

Wednesday, 11*th*.—From St. Marcellin the road beautiful along the valley of the Isère, with magnificent and varied shaped mountains on each side, immense walnut-trees close by the road and in the fields, and the richest cultivation throughout the valley of corn and vines, everywhere trained upon *échalas* from either cherry or maple trees, planted at regular distances, and allowed to grow only to a certain height.

At a village beyond, Tullins, close to a stone bridge, is the largest growing tree I ever saw. It was an elm, of the sort general in this country, but not the same as that in England. Between Tullins and Voreppe, at a large village, is a fine French garden belonging to the house of a M. de la Mothe, of Grenoble.

Before I leave the neighbourhood of Romans I must take notice of an anecdote relative to its present manners, or rather *morals*, told me by the maid of the inn, an active, clean, intelligent peasant woman. There are always

* At this place the last native prince of Dauphiné, Umbert II., having lost his only son, who leaped from his nurse's arms out of the window of the castle of Mezard into the Isère, and was drowned, signed his abdication 1349, by which he resigned his domains to Philip de Valois, on condition that they should be an appanage of the heir to the French crown, and that he should bear the title of Dauphin.—See *Murray's Handbook*.

a good many soldiers at Romans, being in a plentiful country. When the last demi-brigade of a regiment, whose number I have forgotten, left the place to make room for those we saw there, no less than eighty young women went and declared their pregnancy to the municipality (which by the present laws they are obliged to do), '*non compris* (as my informer said) *les femmes qui appartenaient aux chefs et aux officiers.*' One need no longer wonder at the immense armies of France! She added that numbers of women accompanied them above a league out of the town, weeping and wailing at their departure, and carrying wine and eatables for them.

Thursday, 12*th*.—Grenoble is a very cheerful, well-built, busy-looking town, and all the streets that end towards the river seem *bouchée* by the mountain which rises directly behind the faubourgs, covered with vines, and crowned by an old castle which formed part of the former fortifications; the wall of the castle was up the steepest part of this mountain. On the other side of the town, from the ramparts of the more modern walls, is the most extensive view, and is equally romantic and beautiful, bounded by high mountains of an endless variety of outline, and on which some snow always lies, but finely wooded and cultivated to a great height.

In the interior of Grenoble considerable improvements are making; such as the pulling down a number of buildings near the bishop's residence and near the prisons (an old castle-like building) to enlarge the spaces around them. The intendant's house, now occupied by the préfet, faces a large garden in the middle of the town open to the public. The Palais de la Justice, formerly occupied by the Parliament, and now by the present courts of justice, is a very old building (with a façade of about the time of Francis I.), once the palace of the Dauphins, the ancient sovereigns of the country, annexed to the Crown of France in 1349. Why or wherefore these sovereigns were called *Dauphins*,* no tolerably rational or probable account is given: it is said that in the Middle Ages one of their leaders, who had united and possessed himself of several neighbouring little barbarous baronies or states, first called the country Dauphinois and himself the Dauphin of it, in memory of a wife called Delphine, whom he passionately loved. Be this as it may, there are at present in the museum at Grenoble four or five curious heads carved in marble, with a sort of crown or cap of state upon them, said to be portraits of the Dauphins, and taken from the inside of the gateway to their palace.

In the same *Place*, of which this palace forms a part, is a very old church, called their chapel. It was with many others shut up at the Revolution, and has not been opened since. The Revolution, however, was never carried to its most frightful excesses here. Most of the families who had emigrated are returned. They are much satisfied with their préfet, and it is certainly, of all the towns I have seen in France, that which bears the least marks of any change for the worse. The great commerce of the place is gloves, of which I fancy more are made here than in all the rest of France. There are few glove-shops, they being almost all wholesale dealers. The one to whom we were addressed, however, a Mr. Morans, had a great choice of every sort and colour; indeed, I never saw so many made gloves together before. We paid (and I suppose we were treated like *English*

* Dauphin was originally a title assumed by the Comtes de Viennois, from which their territory was called Dauphiné. The Count who first bore the title was Guigues IV., who died 1142 A.D. It is *conjectured* that the name arose from the figure of a dolphin as the crest of his helmet or device on his shield. In 1349 Humbert II., the last Count Dauphin, by treaty with Philip VI. of France, sold his rights in favour of Philip's eldest grandson Charles, afterwards Charles V. Charles V. made his eldest son, Charles VI., Dauphin, although there was no stipulation on the subject in any treaty. His example was followed by successive kings of France.

strangers) 33 livres a-dozen for long gloves, white or coloured, and 18 livres for habit gloves. It must, I fancy, be a good trade. They give to the women who sew the gloves (in almost every house in Grenoble you see women thus employed) half-a-crown a dozen. For long gloves it seems very little; but, what is much more astonishing, a very good workwoman will sometimes cut out and make six pairs in a day, and commonly three or four pairs.

The museum at Grenoble, one of those established by Government, is in the former convent and church of the Jesuits. The pictures and statues have been but lately brought, and are all finally arranged. The library is that which belonged to the Jesuits. It remains in the same room, and a very noble one it is. The pictures in another large room, lighted by sky-lights, are few of them good. Two curious portraits of Henry IV. and the Constable de Lesdiguières and his son, a little boy, afterwards killed by a kick of a horse, brought from *Vizille*,* his château, about three leagues from Grenoble. They are evidently of the day. The statues are chiefly casts from the antique sent from Paris, as were likewise most of the pictures. There is another room fitting up for natural history, and another for bronzes and antiques. We saw the museum on a day that it was open to all the world, and there was a number of common people and soldiers walking about; and what entertained me not a little was an invalid soldier, who was a sort of guard in the room to prevent children, &c., touching things, without stockings, and in very shabby regimentals, descanting as learnedly upon the pictures, which he called Raffaelle's, Guido's, &c., as the best-dressed connoisseurs could have done, and seemed to give perfect satisfaction to his hearers. The weather so cold that we had fires in all our rooms.

* Château de Vizille partly destroyed by fire in 1825, was built between 1611 and 1620 by Lesdiguières, the Protestant commander and governor of Dauphiné, under Henri IV.

Friday, 13*th*.—Left Grenoble. From thence to Lumbin. On the left is a finely-cultivated bank, which rises to the foot of a ridge of abrupt mountains; and on the right is the Isère, winding in various doubles along this rich and much-wooded valley, the woods ascending about a third part up the craggy and snow-covered mountains of the Upper Dauphiné, which exhibit the greatest possible variety of outline. An excellent road passes through a number of well-built comfortable-looking villages, and by a number of country-houses with uncommonly pretty gardens. Higher up upon the bank, and nearer the abrupt wall of mountain, is a continued line of villages and country-houses, almost touching one another, for a distance of two posts and a half from Grenoble. The picturesque cultivation of the vine, which I have already described, the quantity both of fruit and walnut trees, the great population, the habitable look of the houses, joined to the romantic mountains, which everywhere meet the eye and bound the view, makes the whole way from Grenoble to Lumbin one of the most delightful succession of landscapes I remember to have seen. This route from Grenoble to Chambéry, has during the war been so little frequented, except by persons travelling *en voiturier*, that the postmaster told us he and the other postmasters had given in their dismission six months before, and only remained till they could do better, or see how matters would go after the peace. Between Lumbin and Chaparrillan is a very pretty small pentagonal fort, upon the former confines of France and Savoy.* Throughout Dauphiné a number of new houses are building in all the villages, and it is impossible for any country

* Fort Barreaux, built by Charles Emanuel Duke of Savoy, in the presence of a French army commanded by Lesdiguières. On being reproved by Henri IV. for allowing this to happen, he promised to capture it when finished. He kept his word, surprising the fort by moonlight, 1598. It was afterwards strengthened by Vauban.—*Murray's Handbook*.

to bear more evident marks of thriving, of great population, and of admirable cultivation. Chambéry seemed neither the better nor the worse for its '*Frenchification.*' The palace, which I had seen formerly, was burnt down a few years ago by an accidental fire (1798). Arrived at Aix-les-Bains. The building of the baths is kept up in tolerable order; all inscriptions of how, and when, and by whom it was erected having been carefully effaced. It contains a number of separate baths for the douche, but none of cold water, nor even the means of lessening the heat of the natural temperature. The Romans made use of these waters, and considerable, though not very interesting, remains of their baths (now subterraneous) are to be seen in the garden and under the floor of a room in the house of a physician of the place. These remains have been very lately discovered. They consist of a passage terraced for the water, and very neat tile pipes through which the vapour passed. Under the floor of the room enough remains to prove the baths had been lined with marble.

On our return from our walk, we found our servants in serious council over the carriage, yet standing before the inn door. They had found the axle-tree cracked and the fore bed quite split through. No time was to be lost. A *maréchal* was sent for. He examined it in presence of, I believe, the whole town of Aix; for in France everybody is willing, indeed insist, upon giving you their company and their advice upon all occasions. He wanted, as usual, to make a job for his neighbour, the *charron*, as well as himself. However, after much useless conversation, he agreed to do it for a louis, to which I added a promise of a trifle more, if the carriage was ready to set off at ten o'clock the next morning.

Aix is a poor little town, and the waters now little resorted to. But I should think in peaceful times it would be likely to be otherwise, for their efficacy is considerable; there are neat public walks planted with that attention which the old Government of Sardinia showed in all its public concerns.

Saturday, 14*th*.—By the help of my bribe we contrived to get away from Aix before eleven o'clock. The road to Douey through a green enclosed country, with pasturage very like England. Beyond Rumilly it is upon a fine *levée* round the side of a steep hill down to a bridge over a torrent, the whole of which has been made within late years by the French. The appearance of the country of Savoy strikes me as much better, and in an improved state of cultivation and comfort to what it was formerly. From Douey the road has been neglected, and in winter the postilions said it was almost impassable for such a carriage as ours. They are so little accustomed to people travelling post, that we had a world of plague at every posthouse. We did not arrive at Geneva till ten o'clock at night.

Sunday, 15*th*.—Walked to Sechecon. The situation disappointed me, though with a garden down to the lake; but this end of the lake is much more tame than the other.

The following extracts from Mrs. Damer's letters to Miss Berry, show the anxiety now felt at the state of affairs between England and France, and the solicitude of those at home lest communication should be cut off from their friends abroad:—

From Mrs. Damer to Miss Berry.

London, Saturday, May 14, 1803.

At last the courier is arrived, and the long doubtful business decided which you will have known before this can reach you. War is now inevitable, and to-morrow Andreossi leaves London. There was no Parliament sat to-day. I have seen many other wars begin—none, in my opinion, under such bad auspices!—remedy there is none. As to myself, you may depend on it, that if I can come to you I will; I shall learn by your letters where you are to be, when you have settled your plans.

Strawberry Hill, Monday, 16th.

. . . A message was sent to the Lord Mayor on Saturday to announce war. Yesterday Andreossi still had not left London: this, tho' some have drawn a favourable inference from it, means nothing, by what I understand, and at this moment I doubt not but that he is on his road. The communication, they say, is to be made from the King to Parliament this day, and made public immediately. I hope this post, at least, letters will still go to Calais; but how it *will be* in future *no one knows*; and I am sorry to say that this difficulty appears to me very serious. I do not like to name all the ports that will probably be shut to English vessels. You talk of going by Holland if I come to you; but Holland is so entirely united at this time with France, that it is a thing understood here, that when the French Ambassador leaves London, the Dutch Minister will follow, of course, &c. &c. I feel, like my old friend, '*I wish I was asleep!*' I do not mean wholly on the score of public matters, for war is always interesting, and, tho' for the sake of humanity and for every good reason, I wish it avoided, it is to me never *dispiriting*. . . . The matter of letters, I do fear, will be a certain and immediate evil on which one must count. I mean this altered and lengthened course, for one cannot flatter oneself that packets will be allowed to sail from Dover to Calais, tho' our Captain Blake has such a thought, and talked of preparing such a plan, if the two Governments could agree upon it for mutual convenience; but I expect no such thing.

London, Saturday, May 28, 1803.

. . . Letters positively now no longer come by Calais, and the first accounts were true. They, however, will probably come before long by Hamburg, and I may hope to hear from you, tho' of later dates, and more irregularly, I conclude. This being the case, and at this moment little chance indeed, by any interference, of your obtaining leave to go by Calais and Dover, either at Paris or here, I shall not be sorry to know that you mean quietly to remain where you are till you hear what turn things take; and by what passed yesterday in both Houses concerning a motion of L[d] Fitzwilliam and one of Mr. Fox's, do not still wholly despair of peace being restored—in which case I need not say I should join you wherever you may be. What I allude to is the very unexpected turn and tone of Mr. Pitt's speech, tending to approve of the interference of Russia, and *portending* (joined to other circumstances), if it portends anything, his coming into power with peaceable views. This, together with what struck me this morning on reading the debates, was what Ld Dover told me (who, poor man, is more than ever tormented with his gout, but still keeps up his spirits), and is, as you may guess, the receptacle for news, but it is really, in the political way, news *de la première main*, and I believe him very little prejudiced on either side.

Sunday morning.

To be sure my two brothers-in-law are sad cripples! and to save the D. of Richmond, who so kindly, when he can, comes to me, I went yesterday and dined with him; he repeated what I told you above, and had seen Mr. Fox himself, who had called upon him; on which I made no remark, but was glad to hear the Duke spoke in favour of peace, &c. You have no idea of the sensation what passed in Parliament has made; it was wholly unexpected, and has certainly revived the hopes of peace. I wish only all this may not have come too late. Yet Pitt, Fox, both nations and Buonaparte for peace, it will be hard if a useless, cruel, and unjustifiable war should be continued. Should this be the case, however, and that you still, after proper deliberation, think you could with comfort and sufficient absence of anxiety as to events that most certainly may take place in this country; for on that subject there is but one opinion, and it can be no secret, I mean an invasion; much as I dislike a long sea passage, I will come to you, and with you take all chances. . . . Since I wrote this I have heard (I know not how true) that letters still go by Calais, but that none are allowed to come from France. . . . It is reported that all English are stopped and confined that are now in France.

The same.

Strawberry Hill, Sunday, June 5, 1803.

. . . You must, in a very few days after the date of the last letter, have heard that English are not all to be sent out of France, but those of a certain description detained prisoners at war: this news was known here by the 1st of June. . . I regret your not having heard from our *Chevalier*, who could certainly from Paris have given you intelligence as to what was going on. I do not pretend to say that events, as they have turned out, could by any have been entirely foreseen, but I think you have not yet seen the political state of Europe in the light in which it will shortly appear to you—and this I account for from your having been so many months away, and wholly removed from all means of forming your own judgment of things. The shutting up ports against English vessels being a wise and political measure, will, you may depend on it, be adopted to the *utmost possible extent* by Bonaparte; official notice to this effect is already come from Holland, where Mr. Lister is detained prisoner, and within reach, as one may call it; at this moment only Hamburg remains to us. This train of ideas, which my mind pursues with peculiar anxiety from your being absent, and the difficulties in which, though perhaps not likely, it is possible you may be involved, makes me earnestly wish you were returned. . . .

The little remaining shadow of peace I mentioned has, I think, wholly vanished. Mr. Pitt spoke yesterday against Ministry—thought them in many things wrong, but that the confusion, a change by loss of time for preparations, &c. &c., would now make war not advisable. Lord Hawkesbury was in great anger. Mr. Fox spoke—I believe it was little—and did not (nor I conclude his friends) divide.

London, Sunday, June 12, 1803.

I hope you did not put your letter, as you intended, into the German post, as our packets now do not go to Cuxhaven, nor can you, consequently, as things are, return that way. The French army is at Bremen, with an intention, as it appears, of occupying Hanover, and even Hamburg, tho' it is expected some other arrangement, at least as to the latter, and the passage of the Elbe, &c., will take place between France, Prussia, and Russia; but at present travellers are allowed to go through France by applying to Paris for passports (such, of course, as do not come under the late restriction), and to pass from Calais to Dover. Vessels for the mails, which are allowed to take in passengers, go regularly to and from these ports with a flag of truce. On this you may depend, and take your measures accordingly, for *this moment*; but for the *next* it is impossible to answer. . . . I always fear you may be influenced in your plans by a natural disbelief of what often must appear to you (as it would to me) idle stories, though they are, may be, real and certain facts. Should you determine to return, and through France, I think you ought yourself to write to Perrégaux for a passport, and the moment I know you have made this determination I shall take care that he shall also be written to from hence, to back your request and take every precaution for you in my power. I think, also, in this case you would do well to write to Mdme. Visconti, who was so kind and obliging to us; she very probably might assist you, were there any difficulty, and I am persuaded would do it with pleasure. . . .

Tuesday, June 14.

Events crowd on faster even than I expected, and I grow seriously uneasy about your not being here. Hanover is taken, without resistance, and the Elbe shut up. This intelligence came yesterday, by the first consul's own particular courier (called Moustache), who also announced that the communication by Calais was to end on the 28th of this month. This is not newspaper intelligence—it was told me last night by the Duchess of Devonshire, who, either herself or Lady Elizabeth, had seen Lord Hervey. The Duchess says that a *voiturier* comes in eight days from Geneva to Calais; this, could you be in time, and have your passports from Paris, would be very easy, as you are only two perfectly unexceptionable women in every way, and your father above sixty; and to return home I could certainly obtain a passport for Dover here for you. What other intelligence the courier brought it is not known—possibly some propositions of arrangement, but nothing has transpired. The King came to town, and there was a council in consequence of the arrival of this courier.

I wish to God you may have taken the advice I sent you in my letter immediately after I saw Edwards, and now be on your way through France; but this I no way expect, and now things change, and may change so rapidly, there is no giving advice but in a general way. Would your reluctance to returning to England had not been so great!—not but that this reflection is suggested, I fairly allow, by *events* I perfectly knew you could not foresee—nor could I. . . . Do not trust this or that person, but write yourself to the persons I mentioned above, to Paris, and any others there you think of; and take notice that neutral powers may not long continue so.

Supposing the passage from Calais to be actually shut for English vessels by the 28th, I cannot see at all which way you can return. For Heaven's sake, take the very best and surest advice, and do not either hurry or delay, but act as prudence may direct.

JOURNAL.

Saturday, May 28th.—Left Geneva by half-past eight, in a hired carriage with three horses, leaving Gibaud behind to get our coach from the coachmaker's, our clothes from the washerwoman, and our gowns from the mantua-maker's, and to wait till he received orders to follow with them to Lausanne. At past twelve o'clock, the night before, when we were all in bed and asleep, we had been waked by Lord John Campbell * to communicate intelligence he had received from some of the English at Secheron, viz., that by a letter which Lady Donegal † (who lodged there) had received from Lyons, they learnt that the English were arrested there, and it was believed the same order was to be received by the post the next morning at Geneva, in consequence of which he, Lord John, and his companion Mr. Robertson, meant to leave

* Lord John Campbell, second son of John Duke of Argyll, born 1777; succeeded his brother George William, sixth duke, 1839; died 1847.

† Barbara, daughter of Dr. Godfrey, born 1790; died 1829.

Geneva, and the rest of the English Secheron, before the arrival of the post, that is to say, before eight o'clock the next morning. I own, when my sister came up and woke me, I was little inclined to credit intelligence coming in so roundabout a manner, and advised her, without waking my father, to return quietly to bed and let us talk of it next morning; to which she unwillingly consented, but went to my father early the next morning, when she communicated it to him; she was so uneasy and anxious to be gone, that soon after six she was again with me. We directly sent up for the master of the house, told him *de quoi il s'agissait*, begged him immediately to get us a carriage (for there was no time to enquire if ours was finished), made our maid stuff what things she could into one of the trunks, and with much hurry and much uncomfortable bustle got off at half-past eight from the door of the Balances, not indeed before the post had arrived, but before any order it had brought to the Préfet was communicated to the sentinels at the gates, so that we passed without interruption of any sort, either at Geneva or at Versay, the limits of the French territory, about a league and a half from the town, where there is a *barrière* and a *douane*, although in the hurry of setting out the servants left my letter-case behind, in which was our passport. We stopped at Rolle from twelve o'clock till three, and arrived at Lausanne by six o'clock. As no less than three English families had left Geneva and Secheron on the same day, and upon the same account as ourselves, we found all the inns full, and got very bad rooms on the third story of the least good of the two bad ones at Lausanne. I had a violent headache by the time I arrived, which was perhaps lucky, as it took from me almost the power of every other thought but that of getting a room and to bed as fast as I could, instead of the melancholy *retour* one should necessarily have made upon oneself returning to a town after an absence of nearly nineteen years, which one had left in the heyday of life, with a thousand brilliant prospects, hopes, and ideas before one, all cruelly failed in a *manquê'ed* existence, and which at sober forty can *never* be renewed!

Our old friend Miss Cerjat came to see us the instant she knew of our arrival. Seeing her was a relief to me from finding her so much less changed than I had been led to expect from the various family distresses in which she has been lately involved.

Wednesday, July 6th.—Went to the library of Mr. Gibbon;* it still remains here, though bought seven years ago by Mr. Beckford, of Fonthill, for 950*l.* It consists of near 10,000 volumes, and, as far as I could judge by a cursory and (from its present situation) a very inconvenient examination of it, it is, of all the libraries I ever saw, that of which I should most covet the possession—that which seems exactly everything that any gentleman or gentlewoman fond of letters could wish. Although it is in no particular walk of literature a perfect collection, in the classical part perhaps less than any other, and in the Greek less than in the Latin classics, still there are good editions of all the best authors in both languages. The books, though neither magnificent in their editions nor in their bindings, are all in good condition, all clean, all such as one wishes to read, and could have no scruple in using. They are under the care of Mr. Scott, a physician of this place, who made the bargain for Mr. Beckford with Gibbon's heirs in England, and are placed in two small and inconvenient rooms hired for the purpose, and filled with rows of shelves so near as scarcely to admit of look-

* The house of Gibbon and the garden have been much changed. The wall of the Hôtel Gibbon occupies the site of his summerhouse, and the *berceau* walk has been destroyed to make room for the garden of the hôtel; nothing but the terrace overlooking the lake and a few acacias remain.—*Murray's Handbook.*

ing at the books on the back side of them. Mr. Beckford, when last here in 179–, packed up about 2,500 vols. of what he considered as the choicest of them, in two cases, which he then proposed sending to England directly, but which still remain in their cases with the others.

11*th.*—Mr. Glayre had a good house in Lausanne, with a beautiful view, a good house in the country at Romain-Motier, about twenty miles from Lausanne, both well furnished according to the ideas of the country, had frequent company to dinner in Lausanne, besides evening parties, and very often people staying at his house in the country for weeks together; gave foreign wine at his table whenever he had company, lived in every respect well and at ease, kept four carriage horses (occasionally working on his farm), having a library, buying some books every year, denying himself no reasonable fancy, and having a wife and two young children. He spent 800*l.* sterling a year!

N.B.—To this must be added the taxes to be imposed by the new Government since the independence of the Pays de Vaud from Berne, which cannot make a difference of 30*l.* a year.

This independent canton of Vaud, thinking itself so happy to have escaped from what some silly heads of it were pleased to call the *tyranny* of the canton of Berne, will, I feel convinced, in a very short time, be united to France by the general consent and desire of the rational and thinking part of the community, and I think they will do well for the real happiness and prosperity of their country in desiring such union. The peasants, I believe, have really gained by the abolition of the feudal and seigneurial rights; in short, by *their* revolution, made exactly upon the model of the French as to putting down arms, burning family papers, abolishing titles, liveries, &c. &c. But the inhabitants of the towns, who were formerly an industrious, sober, and (for the age they lived in) simple set of people, are grown at once idle, insolent, and corrupted, which sits infinitely worse upon the dull *grossièreté* of the Swiss character than upon the pert *légèreté* of the French. The men, instead of thinking of their trade, are hardly ever in their shops, but loitering about in groups, talking the politics of their country, and all looking after some place or some participation in their government, for which their former lives have not qualified them, and which their present duties, unless neglected, must prevent their fulfilling. The women consider *liberty and equality* as an equal right for everyone to read *novels from morning till night, which they do*, from the lowest *servante* to the first *citoyenne* in the town. If ever anything could persuade one to consider being taught to read as a disadvantage to the lower order of people, it would be here, from the often vile, and always absurd, use which is made of it. The frequent passage and residence of French troops in their towns have introduced much profligacy in their manners; and as they have looked up to the French as their models in everything, so like them they seem to expect the monstrous and impossible combination of well-ordered liberty in government and idle profligacy in manners.

Their commerce, which was formerly considerable in books, is falling to nothing, in spite of every living soul in the town reading. They no longer print any good works here, but draw their books from Paris, which, greatly increasing the price, and everybody but the peasants being impoverished by their revolution, nobody buys, the novels go from hand to hand from the circulating library with almost as little advantage to those who let as to those who hire them. All the tradespeople complain of having little to do, and yet they are neglectful and dilatory in executing the smallest commission, and have lost entirely all that *prévenance* of manner and wish to oblige which most commonly exists where trade really flourishes or is increasing. Everyone being a burgess of the town, he has certain pecuniary rights, amounting to about five or six pounds sterling a year, such as so many loads of wood furnished to them from the estates of the town, which are considerable—about five thousand pounds a year, and what was called *la bourse des Pauvres*, about 1,400*l.*; and when old or incapable of working, being provided for by the town (that is to say, placed at its expense in the hospital, or receiving their sustenance, fuel, clothes, &c., from the town in their own houses), they count too much upon this resource, and probably are more anxious about the direction of their public estate than their private affairs.

Their criminal justice was formerly administered by the Supreme Council at Berne, and from the infrequency of crimes and the emptiness of their prisons, one may justly suppose was well administered. Now that their justice is in their own hands, their prisons are full. Nobody, indeed, is punished, because means are always found to let the malefactors, whatever their crimes, escape out of prison by the command of their friendly judges. Their civil justice must grow still worse, and the degree of partiality which was formerly supposed to interfere in causes where anything Bernois was a party, must have been nothing in comparison to what must take place now, when *Jacques* judges *Jean*, with all the little partialities, little prejudices, and little piques, which it is not in the nature of man to avoid in a small society of which he himself forms a part. Add to this that the Government of Berne was rich, and assisted its subjects in a variety of ways (such as lending money to individuals for any considerable undertaking, at one, one and a half, and two per cent.; having their granaries always full of salt and of corn, which in case of scarcity were retailed at a moderate price, &c.), while the Government of the République Vaudoise, having nothing, can have neither public munificence nor private charities, and consequently the number of poor, of real mendicants, I mean, among the labouring classes, both in the towns and the country, is unexampled in their former history. All these inconveniences, which time seems more likely to increase than to diminish, convince me that Buonaparte's moderation with respect to this country (I mean the Pays de Vaud in particular) has been merely giving them *rope enough to hang themselves.* The inhabitants of the towns will rapidly fall into decay, if not into discord, and there not being territory enough for them all to become cultivators (to say nothing of contrary habits), the wisest among them will find it best to associate themselves to a country more fertile in resources than their own, and to give up their troublesome independence for leave to participate in the brilliant prospects of France. Nor, indeed, do I believe it possible in the present age, in the present political order of things, and with the present habits, wants, and wishes of mankind, to establish a small independent government without any other means of aggrandisement than the progression of national industry, particularly in a country like this, close to France, and not locally separated from the contagion of its manners, its errors, and its corruption, like the little mountainous cantons of Switzerland, whose various democracies were all settled in an age when a total absence of the occupations of foreign commerce and foreign relations, and the simplicity and paucity of their own wants, made it no very difficult matter to be at once a judge, a soldier, and a farmer, to have wit enough to settle such differences as were likely to occur, strength enough to till the field, and valour to defend it.

Saturday, 23rd.—Went to see the cathedral—a very handsome large Gothic church, much enriched with figures of no very good sculpture, but as perfect as the day they were put up. The middle aisle of this church is deformed with pews. Behind the choir are several old monuments of their Catholic bishops, and one only of a chevalier in a shirt of mail.* There are besides several modern monuments to strangers who have died at Lausanne. A handsome sarcophagus to the Princesse d'Orloff, a simple tablet to the memory of poor William Legge, and another to that of Mr. Ellison, who died when we were first at Lausanne in 1785. A monument, intended, judging by the pedestal, to have been very magnificent, to the memory of the first wife of Comte Walmoden; but before the monument was finished, he married again, and it has never been put up at all. There are, besides these monuments, simple tablets, with arms, to many families of the Pays de Vaud. At the time of their revolution, in their ridiculous *Patriotic Society*, as it was called, the servile and contemptible ape of all revolutionary follies of the French, they more than once proposed destroying these monuments. They, however, escaped everything but the rapacity of the French soldiers, who, in some of their visits to Lausanne, took away all the copper-gilt letters of which some of the inscriptions were made.

Sunday, 24*th*.—Left Lausanne without the regret that I could wish to have experienced at leaving so beautiful a country, in which I had formerly spent many cheerful days. But the disagreeable uncertainty in which we have been living here for these last two months has been such, that I felt rather glad it should come to an end, even by the alternative of a long and tiresome journey. The road between Lausanne and Meudon is a continued ascent up the Jura.

Monday, 25*th*.—Road from Payerne to Avenches, along a pleasant cultivated valley. Avenches is an old walled town. A Roman marble column, with a part of its base

* Otho of Gransom, whose ancestor, Otto de Grandeson, held several important offices in England, under Henry III. and Edward I.—*Murray's Handbook*.

and entablature, remains in a garden on the right side of the road.* No other Róman remains appear, but the *books* say there are several. There is a pretty view of the Lake of Morat before coming to Avènches. Morat, situated on an eminence, is a good-looking old town, with arcades in the streets like Berne. On the side of the road formerly stood the nobly simple monument, erected to the bravery of the Swiss in the defeat of the Bourguignons [1476]; but the French regiment de la Côte d'Or being unfortunately quartered at Morat in the year 1798, *nobly* destroyed it entirely, instead of, like real heroes, respecting valour of every country. Nothing remains but a few scattered bones among the weeds which mark the place of the former enclosure. The approach to Berne is marked by innumerable farm and country houses, scattered over the hills, many guinguettes and gardens near the roadside, and long avenues of trees up to the gates. Our passport here was left in the hands of the police. There seemed to be no French soldiers at the gates.

Tuesday, 26*th*.—Went to the cathedral. A very fine Gothic building. Of the four windows of the tower, three are of beautiful painted glass in mosaic patterns. The fourth was destroyed by lightning about 150 years ago, and has been replaced by plain glazing. Monuments there are none whatsoever. There is an immense organ, loaded with gilt ornaments in the very worst taste, put up in a circular gallery of Grecian architecture at the west end of the church, which takes off considerably from its length. From the terrace, of which the cathedral forms the boundary, on one side there is a fine view of the river running almost immediately under it, the well-wooded and cultivated hills of the environs, all dotted over with villages and single houses, and beyond them Alps on Alps rising in the distance. I cannot say how

* Corinthian column 37 feet high, on which the storks now build.

much I was struck with the appearance of the streets and buildings of Berne. Everything that belongs to the public is well executed and well kept; and all the private houses in the principal streets are handsome. The peculiar beauty of the stone walls with which the whole town is built adds to this effect, as certainly do the arcades under the houses. The piers also sloping outwards give an appearance of regularity and solidity extremely pleasing, while the superstructures are sufficiently varied in their forms and ornaments to prevent sameness.

On leaving the town, after crossing the bridge over the Aar, a long ascent from the other side is protected with headstone parapets, executed in the most solid manner by the Government between the years 1750 and 1758, as a sort of stone monument upon the top of the hill records. The view from hence beautiful, and the Aar is seen winding almost entirely round the town, and placing it on a peninsula. This happened to be market day at Berne, and the great street in which the Faucon is situated was, from before six in the morning, a perfect fair, with a row of booths completely down both sides outside the arcades, besides the herb and fruit market, which began the business of the day. The booths were shops of all sorts, but principally of wearing apparel, many with all the ribbons and velvets, and bits of embroidery, which enter into the composition of a Bernoise dress. Nothing, indeed, can be more picturesque than the variety of female dresses from the different cantons and districts of Switzerland, to be seen in this market—more of them odd than graceful, but all serving to make that interesting variety, the absence of which one regrets in the appearance of a people where there are no regular dresses for different classes. Left Berne. The road through a cultivated country with fine woods. The houses all constructed *à la Bernoise*, which gives a great idea of comfort to a farm-house.

Tuesday, 26*th*.—Arrived at Soleure in the afternoon. Our passport was taken at the gate by the French troops upon guard there, with a promise to bring it to us that evening. I wished to send for it, fearing any delay next morning, but the waiter assured me no mistake could be made, that the son of the landlord was one of the municipal officers who would *viser* the passport and send it. Still the passport did not arrive, and in spite of the waiter's assurances I began to be uneasy. I had seen in our walk about the town more French soldiers, hussars, and infantry, than in all the rest of Switzerland beside, and I began to suspect that their will, whatever that might be, would here be law. About nine o'clock, when my father had already retired to his room, the municipal officer begged to speak to me upon the subject of our passport; it had never been brought by the soldiers to his office, but had been carried to the French commandant; that we were entirely in the power of the French military, who, he added, were unfortunately *his* masters as well as ours. Upon this I desired immediately to speak to the commandant de la place, who luckily happened to be at supper in the house, and I prevented my father from going to bed, as his presence would be necessary to *constater* his age. At last the commandant made his appearance. He was a young man of about twenty-six or seven, with a mild, gentlemanlike countenance, and quiet composed manners. But never did I see such a thorough concentrated hatred, such a deep settled desire of revenge, expressed with such perfectly undisturbed calmness, and by an apparently cold character, as by this man against England. For once in my life I rejoiced at the helplessness of my sex; for the calm composure of this young man in uttering the most abominable lies about his treatment in England did so make my blood boil in my veins, that nothing *but* my sex could have prevented me being guilty of the signal folly of chastising him as he deserved, and consequently of making myself the aggressor. The scene ended with his first accompanying my father to the French general (Eppler), with whom he said he must *se combiner* about the passport, and then signing and sealing it himself, which, indeed, I believe, neither he nor the general could avoid doing (though they said otherwise), as my father was *non compris* in the decree of arrestation in France.

Wednesday, 27*th*.—We left Soleure at five o'clock in the morning, too happy to get out of the hands of General Eppler and his commandant de la place. After leaving Soleure, the country is less interesting and less well cultivated than any part of Switzerland I have yet seen. The town of Soleure has always been more *montée à la Française* than any other in Switzerland. The houses and the people, particularly of the better sort, have more a French than a Swiss air. It was always the residence of the French *ambassador*, the only ambassador with which the cantons were honoured. It is now the depôt of all the French military in Switzerland, amounting to seven or eight hundred. From here, as the centre of the country, they can send out bands to dictate to any other part. Indeed, here they seem to have established themselves, and I believe it will be long before the poor Swiss will be able to unkennel them from this burrow. They will always find some reason for keeping here a body of troops, and till such troops be removed, the Swiss will never be able to call those reasons bad. Upon a prominent rock, in the narrowest part of the valley, and just above a village,* is a very picturesque old ruined castle, which probably in former days commanded the country on both sides. The approach to Basle is through a long avenue of poplars. After taking possession of our apartment,

* Aussere Klus. Above it rises the ruined castle of Bipp (Castrum Pepini), built by Pepin, Maire du Palais.

we were much pleased to see Peter enter the room. He had arrived from Neufchâtel, sent by Mr. MacCulloch with a *voiturier* on a *char-à-banc.* He had put on the man's clothes, and had slept at Soleure the night before, as well as ourselves, but at another inn, and had luckily known nothing of our being there; for most assuredly, had the vindictive commandant known of him as an Englishman, or as one of our party, he would have been stopped as a good exchange for a French grenadier.

Thursday, 28*th*.—The weather was now excessively hot, and admitted of very little exercise. Determined to stay at Basle till the next morning.

Went to the principal bookseller—a very good one; to Michel's great print warehouse, always entertaining; to the cathedral, a large handsome Gothic building, containing the tomb of Erasmus, who died here—a plain marble tablet, with an inscription in gilt letters. It is of a nasty reddish coloured stone, which much diminishes its effect.

After dinner, in spite of the heat, we went to the public library, where, in several rooms under those containing the books, are preserved a number of fine drawings and some admirable pictures of Holbein. A portrait of Erasmus, and another of his friend Amerbach (a jurisconsult of this place), to whom a large volume of Erasmus's MS. letters have been preserved; a portrait of a Swiss merchant in London, which, after being in various different hands, has returned to the native country both of the painter and of the person represented; a portrait of his own wife and two children—admirable. Among other valuables are some very fine cinque-cento editions: a book of devotion of Fust in the year 1464; of Cicero's Epistles, without name of printer, in 1469; Erasmus's seal, device, and many little remembrances of him are here preserved together with the letters I have before mentioned, and a MS. of the 'Moria Encomia' with Holbein's drawings upon the margin in pen and ink. An edition of this has been published, with the drawings on wooden plates, which give a very poor idea of the spirit of the originals.

Friday, 29th.—Left Basle. In spite of the assurances of our commandant at Soleure, that without his permission we should not be allowed to pass from Basle, not a question was asked us, either on entering or on leaving it; nor, indeed, on the German side, did I see a creature to ask it, except a few poor-looking Invalides, whom we overtook in the street, going to take possession of the gate. French troops and a French officer there certainly are in Basle, but they are few, and take no direction of, or interfere with, the municipality. Freyburg, the capital of the Breisgau (the country by the late arrangements ceded to Modena), is a small town, like most German towns, with very wide streets, which *sounds better than it looks.* The heat was so excessive that we were glad to pass the rest of the day in the inn.

The following extract of a letter from Mrs. Howe belongs to this period, though it is not said at what place Miss Berry was able to receive her letters during their homeward journey:—

July 11, 1803.

. . . Many fine folks have left town, but hitherto there has not been a dearth of grand meetings; and the three or four balls at Devonshire House have kept the young people in motion; there have been, also, there several morning dances, followed by a breakfast, by way of practising quadrilles. Lady Eliz[th] Foster brought some pretty music from Paris, and some of the young ladies just come forth proved themselves excellent dancers. The two Miss Monks * are counted the first

* Two daughters of Mr. and Lady Elizabeth Monk, the one afterwards married to Sir Charles Paget, the other to Lord Oranmore.

performers; and Caroline St. Jules,* though not quite such a neat figure, is one of the best; these three all got some lessons at Paris. Lady Constance Maria Stanhope,† Lady Georgiana Cecil,‡ the two Miss Lowthers,§ Lady something Saville,‖ Miss Fitzroy,¶ Lady Maria Fitzroy,** and Miss Conyers, all belong to the set, and some more, whom I have forgot.

I trust your next letter will tell us what expectations you have of returning to England: if you can procure passports from Paris to bring you through France, it would be welcome news indeed. I doubt that is not a reasonable supposition, especially during the absence of the First Consul.

Saturday, 30*th*.—Left Freyburg between four and five, to avoid the excessive heat. The country to Emendingen is more interesting, and Emendingen is a gay-looking little open town. Near Fresenheim is to be seen an immense large building, a convent of Benedictines given by France in the late arrangements to the order of Malta; but the Emperor, it seems, disputes the gift, and the right of giving. Offenberg is a large bourg, quite as uninteresting as the country in which it is situated. One is taken to the churchyard to see an immense distant view of the plain of the Rhine, and in it a spot which they tell you is the Cathedral of Strasburg, just as I have seen a Yorkshire squire show you with pride and delight the plain of York, and assure you that in such a part of the cloudy atmosphere which overhangs the whole he can discern York Minster. On the outside of the walls—for all these little towns in Germany have walls—we found a very pleasant grass-walk, with little gardens coming down on

* Married to the Hon. George Lamb.

† Daughter of the Earl of Harrington, married to the late Duke of Bedford.

‡ Daughter of the Marquis of Salisbury, married to the late Lord Cowley.

§ Daughters of Lord Lonsdale.

‖ Daughter of the Earl of Mexborough, married first to Lord Monson, secondly to Lord Warwick.

¶ Miss Fitzroy. (?)

** Daughter of the Duke of Grafton, married to Sir William Oglander.

each side, very refreshing in the evening of a hot summer's day.

During the late war, Offenberg was sometimes in possession of the French, sometimes of the Austrians. Sometimes one was posted at one end of the place, and the other at the other, and they more than once fought in the streets.

Sunday, 31st.—From Offenberg to Rastadt the same sort of flat uninteresting country, rich in corn and vines. The numerous villages, one and all, abominably paved, looking neither comfortable nor picturesque. We arrived at Rastadt by half-past ten in the morning, for the heat was now so excessive that it was impossible to travel above two hours after the sun was fairly up.

Rastadt is a small deserted town in a great plain, with an immense palace, to which the town seems merely an appendage; and how or why anybody placed an immense palace in such a situation without the previous inducement of a great town, is difficult to imagine.* As the palace is no longer inhabited (the Elector of Baden residing at Carlsruhe), it is not much furnished; indeed, in the many visits paid by the French in the course of the war, they took away almost everything that was takable, so that when the French deputies and those of the Elector of Mentz were lodged there at the time of the Congress, furniture was sent from Carlsruhe. There is some good tapestry from Flemish pictures, and the room remains untouched which contains in glass cases the Turkish spoils (saddles, daggers, scymitars, &c. &c.) taken by Prince Louis of Baden from the Turks.

* It was built by the eccentric Margravine Sybilla, wife of the heavy Louis of Baden, who fought against the Turks along with Prince Eugène. Two congresses have been held under its roof: one in 1714, when Marshal Villars and Prince Eugène signed a treaty of peace; and the other 1798–99, terminated abruptly by the murder of the French envoys.—*Murray's Handbook.*

There are, besides, in a gallery, and scattered over all the apartments, a number of portraits of margraves and margravines, to me excessively entertaining as the perfection of bad taste. Among other happy conceits of some court painter, is that of representing some margrave's family under the figures and composition of Le Brun's 'Tent of Darius.' One must have seen the picture to conceive its ludicrous effect, or the taste of the prince who could order, or of the painter who could execute, such comical ideas. The entrance to this neglected palace is guarded by a few soldiers, and the apartments are shown by a housekeeper whose dress and appearance is more old-fashioned than her palace.

Walked to a manufactory of carriages, where one of the partners spoke perfectly good English, although he had not been in England for thirty years. The carriages were neatly made as to the iron and wood work; but the springs awkward, the *coupe* bad, and taste entirely wanting; the price about half ours in England.

The yet unexplained and inconceivable murder of the two French deputies,* sent to the Congress in 1798, took place within a quarter of a mile of the town, just at the entrance into a wood through which the road to Strasbourg lies. The exact spot was shown to us from a sort of look-out at the top of the palace.

Monday, Aug. 1st.—We got to Carlsruhe before nine o'clock in the morning, from Rastadt, three German miles. The road is bordered the whole way with Lombardy poplars, one of the most fatiguing and tiresome pieces of

* At the end of April, 1799, Bonnier, Jean Debry, and Roberjot left Rastadt for Strasbourg. A short distance from Rastadt, they were surrounded, attacked, and dragged from their carriage. Bonnier and Roberjot were murdered, Jean Debry escaped slightly wounded. All the papers relating to their mission were seized by the assassins, who were suspected to be the very hussars sent as their escort; but the affair is wrapt in mystery to this day.

German pomp that I know, and which rather adds to than amends the insipidity of a flat country. About a league and a half from Rastadt, the road in the poplar avenue being very sandy, the postilion left it and went across fields. This, in winter, would not have been practicable. Carlsruhe is a pretty clean-looking town, with many new buildings going on. Like all German towns (in this part of the world), the houses are low and the streets wide, and they almost all have a reference to the Château, for Carlsruhe is said to be in the shape of a fan, the Château being at the point where the sticks unite—the sticks the garden before the palace, the building in the *Place* opposite the edge of the mount, and the streets the different folds of the mount. The *Place* is formed by a circular façade of buildings supporting a colonnade, and the space between is occupied by a parterre divided by high cut hedges, making alleys wide enough for a carriage, the largest alley exactly opposite the centre of the palace. The apartments are handsome. Pictures there are none but family portraits, much in the Rastadt style. From the top of the tower, which the man who shows the apartments will by no means allow you to escape, is to be seen the forest behind the garden, cut into thirty avenues, all *à perte de vue*, and all diverging from the palace as their centre. The garden is pretty, in the English style, and is open to the public; in a little low sort of pavilion at the edge of the wood there is a polisher of agates and other hard stones, established under the immediate protection of the court. Strangers are carried there; the agates (which, I believe, come from Bohemia) are really beautiful. We saw many good-looking carriages in the streets, attended by clean servants in handsome liveries, and were sorry that our impatience to get to Frankfort prevented us from staying longer, delivering our letter to Madame d'Edelsheim, the minister's wife, and seeing the *monture* of a

German court, which is allowed on all hands to be one of the most agreeable of its sort.

Tuesday, 2*nd*.—The road to Durlach, for three English miles, is one uninterrupted line of poplars. Bruchsal is a large thriving town, with an immense palace, now belonging to the Elector of Baden, but formerly to, and (I believe) the residence of, the Bishop of Spire.* The country from hence has much corn and vines, with pretty wooded hills on the right hand, while the great flat valley of the Rhine continues on the left. From Weisloch to Heidelberg the country begins to be less uninteresting. Heidelberg is the only finely-situated town I have yet seen in Germany upon this route. The Neckar, a pretty clear rocky stream, runs through it, and the ground rises both immediately behind the town and upon the other side of the river; the lower part of the hills clothed with vines, the higher with extensive woods.

The old castle, the residence of the Electors Palatine, is in every point of view remarkably picturesque. Some arched substructures supporting terraces give it at a distance the appearance of a Roman ruin. But it is in fact a building of the sixteenth or beginning of the seventeenth century, and many parts of it more modern. The whole is now in ruins, and without roof or windows, except the chapel, which is still used for service. This magnificent palace, which was added by different electors to the old fortress that crowned the rock above the town, is certainly one of the finest situations I ever saw. From a stone terrace before the principal front, you look down to the beautiful near ground and to the valley of the Rhine towards the left; from another front you look up the winding course of the Neckar. The masses of building are curious and elaborate in their external ornaments. That on the

* This inanimate town of 7,200 inhabitants formerly belonged to the Prince Archbishop of Spire, whose vast palace, now empty, stands near the gate leading to Frankfort.

front towards the court is covered with the sort of pilasters, friezes, and flat-worked ornaments of the age of our James I., and indeed was not unlike what I remember of old Somerset House. The other, which faces the town, has the same style of ornament, but in the piers between each window is a large niche containing a whole-length figure in stone of the different Electors Palatine, with their names and dates on a tablet underneath. The execution of some of these statues is excellent. They are portraits not only of the persons, but of the dress of their times, and are as such extremely curious. One part of the building joins on to a fine octagon tower of the old fortress, which has been twice struck and is half destroyed by lightning, together with a large portion of the more modern building attached to it.

In a cellar of this château is the far-famed tun of Heidelberg, constructed by the Elector Charles Theodore; the initials of his name are in gold letters upon an escutcheon on each end of it—for what purpose one can hardly conceive. It was never full but once, has long been quite empty, and will in all probability never contain anything again, as it is out of repair, and would cost I forget how many thousand florins to mend. When the great King of Prussia once visited it, they put a small cask of exquisite hock within, and piercing the great tun drew out the wine, pretending the whole filled with the same. There is a railing round the upper part of it, within which twelve persons have dined. From its immensity, and its not being hooped, but ribbed like a ship, it gives one no idea of a barrel, and is more like the bottom and stern of a vessel. Heidelberg, and the country immediately about it, was the scene of some of the hottest actions between the French and Austrians during the last war. At different epochs they alternately occupied the town and disputed the possession of the stone bridge over the Neckar. The gate which opens upon this bridge, its two towers, the statue of the Elector upon the bridge, and every part of its balustrades, &c. &c., nearest the town, are still covered with the marks of bullets for the most part at the distance of a very few inches. It was upon this bridge that Prince Maurice of Lichtenstein was wounded, and his faithful dog Diane wounded and lost. Heidelberg is a populous town with a number of good-looking shops. The great church, used now both by Protestants and Catholics alternately, is quite bare. The quantity of grapes upon all the vines in this neighbourhood, and indeed in all the wine country through which we have passed, is something wonderful, and far exceeds any remembered year of plenty.

Wednesday, 3rd.—Left Heidelberg at four o'clock; reached Darmstadt soon after eleven, even then overcome by the excessive heat and dust. The inn afforded us but little relief, with the sun basking upon it—no shutters, no blinds, no anything but a white linen curtain to defend us from its power. Here we sat panting till the evening, when we sallied forth with a guide, who, as usual, could speak nothing but German, and our interpreter, to walk about the town. The residence of the Landgrave is a large old ugly melancholy-looking building, with a small irregular court, and a large clumsy body of modern buildings, not finished, but left in that most dismal of all states, which, without appearance of habitation or comfort, does not even promise to become a picturesque ruin, but remains with all its windows boarded up, a sad monument of the palace-building mania of German princes. They do not show the apartments inhabited by the Prince, therefore I conclude they are not worth seeing. Everywhere in the town are to be seen a number of clean well-dressed troops. They are the principal *trade*, if not of the town at least of the Landgrave, with whom as well as with his cousin of Cassel, we have had many subsidiary treaties. The garden of the palace is public; it is laid out *à l'An-*

glaise, with a shrubbery here, a winding walk there, and a temple at every turn. I never saw a cut walk and a parterre I should not have preferred to it. The theatre of the court opens into it, and the interior of this is really pretty; and there are besides several rooms lately fitted up with much simple elegance, used for suppers and cards, &c. &c., when the theatre is turned into a ball or concert room. There is a French bookseller here, with a very good collection of French books. At Carlsruhe the principal bookseller had very few but German and the classics.

Thursday, 4*th*.—Left Darmstadt, passing through a number of large farming villages, which looked neither clean nor comfortable. They are all execrably paved, have generally a dirty green standing pool, or some stream of water not confined within proper bounds, and are always the worst bits of road the carriage has to go over. The roads within the domain of the Landgrave of Darmstadt are excellent, the barriers very frequent, but they are cheerfully paid by all distant travellers. It is to be observed that from Basle to Frankfort one does not pass one single château or gentleman's country-house of any sort or kind, or any country habitation in any of the villages above that of a common farmer; this could not be the case in any route in France, Italy, or Switzerland, and very much takes away both from the beauty and interest of the country—open, flat, and generally sandy roads through oceans of corn, often as far as the eye could reach, diversified only by the culture of hemp, and near the villages, with plantations of poppies, compose no very charming prospects, and supply no very interesting recollections to eyes and minds fresh from the beauties of Nice and of Switzerland. Frankfort is a large populous German town, with wide streets, and large houses having often twelve and fourteen windows in front. The street in which are the two great inns, the Maison Rouge and the Empereur, may really be called magnificent from its length, its breadth, and its being entirely composed of large houses, one or two of which, recently built by rich merchants, have handsome architectural fronts ; the older houses have in general heavy grotesque ornaments about the door (generally a *porte cochère*), and finely-flourished and ornamented water-spouts projecting far into the street, sometimes in the shape of dragons, lions, &c. ; for instead of concealing this necessary appendage to the roof, they seem to consider it as a happy occasion for enriching and distinguishing the front. In other parts of the town there still remain many old houses, with their first stories projecting over the ground floor, and painted on the outside so as to conceal their being constructed only of what is called in England post and pan.

Frankfort is a regularly fortified town, with a broad ditch full of nasty stagnant water. Immediately without the fortifications is a road for carriages planted with trees on one side, and on the other side bordered with country-houses of all sorts and sizes, many guinguettes, &c. &c., just about as rural, as picturesque, and in as good taste as the environs of Islington ; this road is full every evening of people airing in carriages and on horseback. Frankfort has every appearance of an opulent place.

The banker Betteman has a very pretty country-house, with a large garden, outside one of the gates. Here we were invited two days after our arrival at Frankfort to pass the evening. We went about eight o'clock, and found between thirty and forty people assembled in the garden. The women were, for the most part, great fat heavy-looking persons, much overdressed, civil in their manners, but not particularly *accueillante* to strangers. The men, too, smacked prodigiously of a trading city ; and as their conversation, when not addressed to us, was always in German, we were not much the better for it. In about an hour's time, most of the people retreated from the garden into the house. The principal apartment was lighted up. Before we went away, between ten and eleven, we walked over the house, and found I know not how many rooms elegantly furnished, and quite full of card tables. This house is the first in Frankfort. Young Betteman himself has the air of a *grand seigneur*, giving dinners and suppers to all the foreign princes and foreigners of distinction passing through Frankfort.

Sunday, 7*th*.—Called upon Comtesse Degenfelt, to whose husband we had a letter from Prince Maurice of Lichtenstein. He is a very gentlemanlike, good-humoured young man, at the head of the military in the Emperor's service at Frankfort, for the purpose of recruiting, which both the Emperor and the King of Prussia have the right of doing in this free imperial city, which is guarded by troops of its own—very clean, well-clothed men in a uniform of blue, faced with white. With Comte and Comtesse Degenfelt we took a drive along the bank of the river, bordered the whole way with country-houses.

Monday, 8*th*.—The heat was so excessive in our Hôtel de l'Empereur. The noise so great, being at the corner of a street, we changed our apartments to a quieter situation, and close to the principal bookseller's (Eslinger).

Thursday, 11*th*.—Finding it impossible to get any satisfactory information at Frankfort as to what route we were to take towards home, and where we could cross the water, and not receiving the letters which we hoped before now would have followed us from Lausanne with a permission to pass through France, we most unwillingly set out before five o'clock this morning, to continue our pilgrimage to Cassel. We made a marvellous long day's journey—five German posts, or about fifty-five English miles, in thirteen hours to Marbuurg, where we slept. It is for the most part *chaussée*; and the villages still more comfortless-looking in Hessia than elsewhere. At

Birsbach a great deal of black dyeing is going on, and some appearance of business. Geissen is a fortified town, with a garrison of Hessian troops. About Marbourg the country is beautiful, and the town itself situated on the side of a hill, the top of which is crowned by a château,* part of it modern, part more ancient. There is here a university † or public school. The town consists of narrow streets, of odd old, post-and-pan houses, built up-hill and down, very picturesque in situation, and seen at two leagues' distance on this road.

Friday, 12*th*.—At Wabern, an insignificant village, there is a country palace of the Elector of Hesse for shooting herons, which he never shoots, and where he never comes. This one country-house, like a hunting-box in England, is, however, the one only country-house of any sort or kind that we have seen since we left Basle.

We found here a tolerably clean little inn, where, as it was a rainy evening, we resolved to stay. A young woman, some relation of the house, spoke English by no means ill. Her father had been a Hessian sergeant, and, serving in America, had married an American. The inns in the little villages of Germany bear no proportion to the badness of those in the great towns.

Saturday, 13*th*.—The road from Wabern to Cassel is an excellent *chaussée*. The country very pretty. There is a steep ascent before entering the town of Cassel; its neat, broad, well-built streets and large *Places* are very striking.

Sunday, 14*th*.—Mr. Brook Taylor, the English Minister, whom I knew a little in London, called upon us. I asked his advice about sending a messenger to Hanover, to beg

* The ancient castle of the Landgraves of Hesse, a structure of the chivalrous ages, now a prison, commanding a fine prospect.—See *Murray's Handbook*.

† The University was the first founded in Germany after the Reformation, 1527.

permission from General Mortier* to pass through that country to Hamburg, from which Mr. Taylor rather wished to dissuade me; but finding he had no other reason for so doing but the dislike to ask anything of a Frenchman, I resolved to despatch our courier the next day with a letter I had already written.

Monday, 15*th*.—Went to the parade between nine and ten o'clock. In the summer it is always in the park behind the Orangerie, and the Elector comes there himself every Monday, and often twice a week. This morning he reviewed the 1st and 2nd Regiments of Guards. Nothing can exceed the clockwork regularity of their movements; no firing is ever allowed except at the great reviews for about a fortnight in the spring, when all the military are collected from the different small towns in Hessia, in which they are usually quartered. Their regimentals are very handsome (blue, with red facings and with orange facings and silver Brandenbourgs), and their whole appearance very clean and military. In short, their Prince does nothing else, and thinks of nothing else, and is, I believe, one of the greatest adepts in every branch of the art of what is called 'German discipline.' Nothing can exceed the fitness of the *locale* for such a parade; a large plain of fine short grass, bounded by a high wood at one end, and by the gay buildings of the Orangerie at the other: it really is one of the prettiest military scenes that can be seen. The Elector himself

* Edouard Adolphe Casimir Joseph Mortier, Duc de Trevise, born at Cambray 1768. He took part in the wars of the Revolution in 1791; he accompanied General Marceau in the passage at Neuwied, in the campaign of 1796, and continued to serve with distinction throughout the whole reign of Napoleon. In 1803 he was sent to Hanover, to command the French army against that of England—an expedition which ended so unfortunately to the arms of England, and placed Hanover into the hands of France. In 1814 he gave in his adherence to the Bourbons. In 1815 he was named by Napoleon one of the newly created peers; and on the second Bourbon restoration he was excluded from the Chamber of Peers, but reinstated in 1819.

was on foot the whole time, and in every part of the line followed by one or two aides-de-camp and one *garde-du-corps* in an odd buff uniform, made something like what *we* call 'an old English dress.' The Elector is a short stumpy man of nearly sixty years old, with a very hard ungracious countenance. In the evening drank tea with Madame Butlar, wife to the Electress's chambellan, to whom we had a letter from the Comtesse L. de Werthem, Madame Butlar being a Saxon. We afterwards walked with her in the park and through the Orangerie, built by the present Elector's father. It is never now inhabited by the large orange-trees (which are placed on the terrace), but is used as a sort of summer palace, sometimes by the Elector, and at present by the Electress. The Orangerie consists of two enormous galleries suited to the purpose for which it was built, with a high arched passage forming a sort of hall in the centre, and a *pavillon* in which are bedrooms at each end. One of the long galleries is divided at present by large screens, making the dining room and the salon. Balls, too, are often given in one of these galleries, and supper in the other.

From hence we walked to the garden of Comte Malke, the Grand Chambellan de la Cour, a small slip of ground just above the bank of the river Fulda, laid out in little serpentine walks and clumps of flowers *à l'Anglaise*, pretty enough.

Tuesday, 16*th*.—Went to Madame Butlar's in the evening; walked with her, Mr. Butlar, and Comte Stotheim to see the *bain de marbre*, in one of the pavilions of the Orangerie. It is magnificent of its kind—a large square room panelled entirely with marble, and in each panel a large bas-relief executed in white marble. They were all done by an Italian,* whom the present Elector's father brought with him from Italy. The bath

* Monnot.

has a cupola over it, supported upon coloured marble columns—marble, in short, from beginning to end. From hence we walked up the steep wooded bank of the park by a very pretty winding path, to Bellevue, the house inhabited by the Elector when he resides in Cassel. It is much more like a country than a town house, with a pretty small English garden and a beautiful view of the park, the Orangerie, and all the surrounding country.

Wednesday, 17*th*.—In the morning to the picture-gallery. It is itself a palace; one room is entirely lined with and contains a fine collection of Japan manufacture; the rest are hung with pictures, and there is also a long gallery hung with pictures on both sides. It contains many fine pictures, particularly portraits by Rembrandt and exquisite works by Teniers and P. Potter; a large picture of Teniers, full of small whole-length figures—the reinstating the Magistrature of Antwerp after they had got rid of the Spanish yoke—the most graceful and interesting of his works that I ever saw; an exquisite Vandeveldt, the Sands at Scheveling at low water, with figures, &c., quite perfect in its way; the finest flower pieces by Van Huysen; an excellent portrait of a woman in white satin, by Titian.

Dined with Mrs. Taylor; nobody but ourselves, his secretary Mr. Heathcote, and a Mr. Dewer, an English gentleman long resident here. Afterwards drove with Madame Butlar in the park; fine shady alleys and winding drives for carriages near a large piece of water, and from thence to the pheasantry, where there are above 200 gold pheasants and as many silver ones. It is said that the Elector, who does not like that anything should be *wasted*, has them killed from time to time and sends them to market.

Thursday, 18*th*. — To Williamshohe with Madame Butlar. It is two English miles and a half from Cassel. Nothing can be more magnificent than the appearance of the palace, the Château d'Eau, with its pyramid crowned by the colossal Hercules, upon the top of the finely wooded hill rising above the palace. In the midst of this extent of wood the Löwenburg presents itself as a half-ruined old German castle, standing upon an abrupt heap of rocks; it is approached by a winding drive through the woods. On one side of the small court within is the chapel, and on the other the apartments; they are, except two large round ones in the great tower, little odd-shaped rooms, but all comfortable. The Elector lived here while the palace below was building, and now is here some part of every day in summer. The view from the windows is very extensive, looking over all Cassel and the surrounding country, but still the Löwenburg is more beautiful to look to than to look from.

The walk over these rocks to the menagerie, and from thence to the palace, is extremely pretty, through what *they* call an English garden, and what *we* should call *grounds.* The château, with its two wings, is entirely built by the present Elector, is of Grecian architecture, the furniture in modern French taste. One wing is inhabited by the Comtesse Stotheim and her children, and the other contains a magnificent apartment for the reception of any foreign prince when on a visit to the Elector; but during this Elector's life there is little danger of the furniture being sullied by use; it has never been occupied but once; and the same parsimony which leads him to avoid the expense of making his Court attractive, leads one to conclude his pavilion for foreign princes will not often be occupied. The other pavilion is more fully and constantly inhabited—the Comtesse Stotheim having had no less than fifteen children by the Elector, four only of whom, however, are alive. Immediately at the back of the château and its wings is a large lawn with a broad gravel walk for carriages, and it is surrounded by a large English garden or grounds, and to my eye has the same fault of rising immediately, like many of our bald English modern country-houses, from the grounds, without sufficient architectural substructures and approaches to accompany and announce the building. After seeing the Löwenburg and the château, and sitting under the trees of an open grove, we were joined by Mr. Taylor, Mr. Heathcote, and Mr. Marescotti, and dined at the inn together. After dinner, Mr. Taylor having obtained permission for the waters to play, we made the tour of the grounds to see them. Carriages and horsemen are allowed to go all over the grounds at Williamshohe, keeping to the gravel road; a permission that in England, I fear, would be too much abused to be long admissible, and which speaks well for the good behaviour of Germans, considering that this Williamshohe is entirely a public garden. The water sets a playing two or three stone pipes in the Château d'Eau, of which I have heard much better in Italy. The cascatelles falling in a thousand little streams, gushing out from every part of a high woody bank, formed upon the idea of the cascatelles at Tivoli, are well contrived and have a good effect, as the scene is wild and analogous. The Devil's Bridge, a humble imitation of that in the Alps, is pretty enough seen at a distance; the broken aqueduct very good, the situation well chosen, forming the only artificial ruin I ever saw successful.

Sunday, 21*st*.—Madame Butlar, Mr. Heathcote, and Mr. Marescotti dined with us. In the afternoon Madame Butlar, Mr. Heathcote, and I, drove again to Williamshohe and walked about parts of the gardens I had not before seen; they are really beautiful. The waters played as they do every Sunday afternoon, and there were a good many middling-looking people wandering over every part of the grounds. The Comtess Stotheim was in the gardens with two of her children, their governess, and an officer with her. Madame Butlar went up to her, and I had half-an hour's conversation with her. She is a large good-looking woman, between thirty and forty, speaking better English than French, but not much of either, with very simple unaffected manners, and looking heartily weary of the wretched *métier* of mistress to a dull prince. She was a woman of no birth, to whom, at a very early age, the Elector took a fancy and to whose wishes her parents sacrificed her, with extreme reluctance (it is said) on her part, She has since conducted herself well in never interfering or doing mischief, or taking upon herself in any way. During the residence of the Elector at Williamshohe, which is the whole summer, she occupies one of the pavilions; when he comes to Bellevue (the small palace at Cassel), she has a house near it on the terrace.

Monday, 22*nd*.—One of the two yearly fairs at Cassel began this day. I was anxious to see it. When we had got as far as Madame Butlar's, I felt so ill as to be obliged to return home. Every symptom of a high fever showed itself, and was increased in the course of the day by the noise in the streets incidental to the fair, parties of music playing eternally either before the door or in the house. Anxious not to delay our journey, I beseeched my sister to ply me every quarter of an hour with saline draughts, and though the fever continued so high all that day and night as to make my mind wander, yet the next morning it was so much lowered that I was able to be put into the coach and pursue our journey by Göttingen to Hanover. Our courier, whom we had despatched to General Mortier at Hanover, requesting his permission to pass by that route, had returned with a passport in full form, signed by Mortier for us and our servants *se rendant à Hambourg*. We went from Cassel by Munden to Göttingen. In cultivation, in villages, and in the appearance of the people, the dominions of Hanover have a decided advantage over every part of the north of Germany that I have seen. Göttingen is a large town, with straight, wide, uninteresting streets. I know not if there is anything fine about the university; I was too ill to attempt seeing it, but as all the young men are in private lodgings in the town, and attend the professors at their own houses, there are no fine architectural buildings for lodging either the one or the other as in the English universities. In the principal street is a handsome stone riding-house, erected, as the inscription says, by George II., for the use of the students at the university.

Wednesday, 24*th*.—Eimbeck, a very oddly built town, with all the roofs projecting one over another, and ornamented with much carved wood. Within about a league of Bruggen, the spokes of one of our fore-wheels became loose, which obliged us to proceed at a foot's pace to the Post, a single house half a mile from the village of Bruggen. Here is a large country seat (the first we have seen in Germany), belonging to M. de Steinberg, who was Hanoverian Minister in London for a few months before M. de Leuthe. He is now dead, but his widow inhabits the château, unmolested by the French, not a single one of whom we have seen, nor are to see (as they assure us) till we reach Hanover. A vast deal of tobacco is cultivated between Cassel and this place.

Thursday, 25*th*.—Our broken wheel detained us till two o'clock the next day. The two posts from hence to Hanover are quite flat and good road. The appearance of Hanover is not imposing at a distance; it is situated in a boundless plain, and presents nothing to the approaching traveller but two or three brick towers of churches. The streets through which we passed contained few fine houses, or marked buildings of any sort.

The drive about the town in search of lodging was the only opportunity we had of seeing anything of Hanover. It was dark by the time we got settled, and I don't know that it would have been thought prudent, as English travellers, to have exhibited ourselves much in the streets, full of French soldiers. At the gates, surrounded by French soldiers, not a question was asked. The carriage was never even stopped, as is common in all German towns, to enquire one's name and whither one is going. We drove into Hanover in an English coach as we should have driven into York or any other town in England. At the inn no enquiry for our passport, no sending it to the municipality. It was never taken out of my letter case from the time we left Cassel till we arrived in London. I thought it right, however, to send a note to General Mortier from the inn, thanking him for the permission he had given us to pass through Hanover, and accounting, by my illness, for our not having used it sooner. We heard there were a large number of French troops; the streets were full of them, but the most exact discipline was maintained, and that, and that alone, preserved the inhabitants from ruin. General Mortier was lodged in the Duke of Cambridge's house; Leopold Berthier,* the *Commissaire Général* in the king's, which, it seems, nobody but the king when at Hanover ever inhabited.

Immediately opposite our Hôtel de Strelitz was a handsome stone hotel, built round a court, which they occupied as some public office. I cannot say that we saw at Hanover any marks of devastation, of houses abandoned, or any irregularities; and all the horrible stories put into our papers of the conduct of French troops upon their first arrival, had not the smallest foundation of truth.

Friday, 26th.—After a very bad supper and paying our bill—the very highest I have ever known in Germany—we left Hanover before seven o'clock in the morning, and were probably the last English who passed through it. I own I regretted being obliged to leave it

* Victor Leopold Berthier, brother to the Prince of Neufchâtel and Wagram, born 1770. He was a distinguished officer in all the important campaigns from 1793 to 1806. He died at Paris in 1807.

without seeing something more of a place of which all English people have heard so much, which is connected with so many stories in the latter part of our history, and which certainly by its natural attractions would never induce a traveller to return to it. All the French infantry were on foot, and the *générale* beating before we left the town to collect them to attend the execution of three soldiers who were to be *fusillés* that morning, at eight o'clock for having in a squabble murdered a servant girl in the street. The execution was to take place without the town, and we saw numbers of the townspeople trooping out to see it.

An excellent hard chaussée between a row of bricks and limes, on the road to Celle, ends at about a league and a half from the town, and leaves one in sand literally more than half way up the spokes of the wheels. An avenue of wretched little birches is continued the whole way to Schilderslage; but the postilions avoid the road as much as possible, and keep on one side upon a sort of black heath. The whole road to Celle is through the same unfathomable land, marked by two rows of birch-trees, which alone distinguishes it from the rest of the country; and their white shining bark must be very useful in winter to guide wretched travellers on this immense plain, for the most part deep black boggy earth, through which carriages are always dragged at a foot's pace, and those within may think themselves lucky that its unjolting nature allows them to take refuge in sleep from its most tiresome sameness and slowness. About a league from Celle the bog changes into a wood; but the sand continues on every side, and the road in a straight line continues also. But *upon* the road one never is for an instant, and often half a mile from it. The town of Celle is approached by a pretty, gay-looking open faubourg; 1,600 French soldiers, cavalry and infantry, are now quartered there. The horses of the cavalry are in the manège of the château; and the officers and men in the château and in all the private houses. The château is a more picturesque and castle-like building than most German palaces; we did not go to see it, as it was the head-quarters, and full of officers. In the principal church are seen the monuments of the Dukes of Celle and of Brunswick-Lunenburg—curious enough, being whole-length marble figures of them and their duchesses, standing upright in niches round the upper part of the choir. In the vault beneath it, where are all their metal coffins, is that of our poor Queen of Denmark,* who passed the last years of her short and unfortunate life here. It is covered with crimson velvet, and richly ornamented with ormolu; the whole as fresh as the day it was deposited. In the public garden there is a marble monument to her memory; a wretched thing both in idea and execution, and now, though enclosed within a rail, much degraded; the copper letters of an inscription on a shield having been taken away, and the crown broken. The design of the group is a figure descending upon clouds, and embracing an urn, on which is a bas-relief head of the queen. A little boy (her son, I suppose) is stretching up to throw flowers upon it; and another female figure holding an infant (I suppose her daughter) to look at it—the whole miserably executed.

Saturday, 27*th*.—Left Celle; passed through Bergen Ville.

Sunday, 28*th*.—Wille; Haarburg to Hamburg, a two hours' passage by boat.

Tuesday, 30*th*.—Hamburg, Pinneburg, Elmshorn.

Wednesday, 31*st*.—Itzehoe, Hohenhorn, Heide.

Thursday, *Sept.* 1*st*.—Heide, Friederichstadt, Huscom. The inns are clean, and, without exception, fit places for a night's lodging; but tea, coffee, and bread and butter are often the only things to be had.

* Matilda, sister of George III.

Monday, 19*th*.—Left the 'Lark' packet in a pilot-boat, which landed us in about an hour between two little jetties a mile from the village of Southwold, to which we walked.

Tuesday, 20*th*.—Southwold is three miles off the great Yarmouth road. No post-horses nearer than Yoxford, near Southwold. Appearance of Ipswich very pretty on descending towards it.

Wednesday, 21*st*.—From Ipswich to London. Road very good the whole way. We had left our coach on the other side of the water, and came up in two hack chaises. At Rumford, as usual near London, the horses execrable, and quite knocked up by the time we got to town.

1804.

THIS year appears very barren of either letters or journals. One sad entry appears in the little diary: 'Col. —— engaged to marry Agnes. Engagement broken off in the spring. Agnes dangerously ill.' The following letter from Professor Playfair, addressed to Miss Berry, belongs to this year:—

Cambridge, Sept. 28, 1804.

MY DEAR MADAM,—. . . . I have been going about all day looking at the curiosities of this ancient seat of literature and science. Tho' I have no great fondness for English universities (owing, you will say, to my hyperborean prejudices), yet I cannot approach a place that has been so long the residence of learning and philosophy without much veneration, and without reflecting that I am now on one of those sacred spots, where the light of truth was kept alive when it was nearly extinguished over the whole earth. One must, however, regret that the institutions which have answered so noble a purpose have not kept pace with the improvement of knowledge, and do now not unfrequently retard the growth of sciences, which in their infancy they served so happily to nurse. In going into a great library, it often occurs to me to take up some remarkable book, open it by chance, and observe what turns up, as the truths that thus casually are suggested to the mind often live long in the memory. To-day, in the University library, I took up a book on the history of astronomy, called 'Theatrum Cometicum,' that is very scarce and very famous, and opened it to try the above experiment. The chapter that turned up was 'De Causis Cometarum,' and the first sentence was, 'Causa cometarum maxime universalis est Deus.' This truism was all I had for my pains, and is the only piece of instruction that I am likely to carry away from Cambridge. Some have perhaps gone away with less. Such as it is I send it to Mrs. Damer and you, who will be at no loss to appreciate the voluminous compilation in which it is contained. . . . Now that I am going far from you, and for a long time, allow me to express to you the sense I have of my good fortune in being permitted to rely on you in the number of my friends, and after so many and so long intervals to have met you always the same, or rather with a kindness that time and distance seemed even to have increased. This certainly is not *fashionable friendship*, and it must be acknowledged that one of the persons who has delineated *such* friendship the best, has practised it the least. Among my obligations to you I must not forget the acquaintance of Mrs. Damer, the liberality of whose mind, the good sense and sound reason that dictates her opinions, are not less remarkable than her elegance and taste. May I entreat you to present my respects to her.

I am, my dear Madam,
Yours sincerely,
JOHN PLAYFAIR.

1805.

Entry.—Went to Scotland with Mr. Lockhart. At Bothwell* for three months. Return to London in December with Robert.

It would appear by the following letter addressed to Mrs. Cholmeley, that Miss Berry had at this time conceived the idea of engaging herself in some regular employment that from its very labour would have given repose to the over-activity of her mind; but it is also clear that the plan did not receive the sanction of those friends whose opinion she valued, and that it was consequently abandoned :—

North Audley Street, March, 1805.

First let me thank you, which I do most sincerely, for the lively interest you take in my happiness and concerns, and for the early consideration you have given to my plan. Your first objection as to the light in which such a step would be considered by the world, and its consequent example to others, had already presented itself to my mind, and is, alas! rendered so forcible by the statements both of Mrs. Damer and yourself, who see it exactly in the same light, that I fear I need not (which would be easy) overcome your other objections. You do me the justice to believe that regular and useful employment would greatly increase my happiness. Be assured it would constitute my happiness, such as alone at my sober time of life I can hope to experience, and what, if I may judge from the description of others, I never knew when young. But I have neither a discontented nor a capricious mind. Regular employment, however mechanical, and what many people would

* The seat of Lord Douglas.

call tiresome, provided always that it left me time for the uncontrolled cultivation of my mind, would be to that mind repose, restoration, and comfort, after the manner in which my time is now frittered away by myself, because I have no sufficiently strong motive to oppose to any intrusion on my attention by others, because everyone seems to think *they* have an equal right to what I don't appear to make any decided use of myself. I was not born for indecision, and feel myself capable of making an entire change in the disposal of my time and of my habits of life, provided such change was satisfactory to my reason. Passing day after day, therefore, between a garden, which has ever been my favourite and my undiminished taste, and writing accounts or letters of business, which would occupy my hands only; engaged in the regular performance of duties, which would be neither difficult nor irksome, and with a rational motive for meeting and overcoming any inconvenience that might occasionally occur—believe me, I should see nothing either dull or dreadful in passing evening after evening uninterruptedly, trimming my lamp, and recurring to and unravelling the many pursuits after which my soul has thirsted, and of which, in fact, I have never had but a hurried, imperfect, and unsatisfactory taste. With this *taste* in the early part of my life I endeavoured to content myself, because I felt my situation imposed on me many duties, superior to learning languages, or indulging in an unrestrained love of reading, because I hoped I was then labouring for future repose and comfort. I have gone on sacrificing the present for the future till no *future* remains to me. Still I have spirit enough left, you see, to resolve that no uncomforts of situation, no sufferings, shall ever tempt me to any step that should throw me on the mercy of the world, or add my name as an additional motive for preaching up ignorance and meanness to my sex. Farewell! You will see, at least, by this letter that I am not obstinate in my own ways of thinking; and if you could know how much my mind requires some resting-place in perspective, you would, perhaps, regret even *this* being taken away from it.

Among Miss Berry's many literary friends was Miss Catherine Fanshaw, the well-known authoress of the riddle on the letter H., and of many other poems.

The following letter, with the playful verses that accompanied it, show that they were on terms of intimacy as early as the year 1805.

The ode, *supposed* to be written by Miss Berry, was of course the composition of Miss C. Fanshawe,* and the receipt of it is acknowledged by Miss Berry in the same spirit in which it was written:—

I return you your Ode, my dear Miss Berry, with many thanks, and with all due apologies for having detained it so long. Believe me, I no longer marvel at your enthusiastic admiration of Gray, whose spirit you have most happily infused into your admirable poem. Indeed, his own works could never charm me so much, for you have had the art to compress into a small compass his most valuable passages, and to give them an interest, a decision and a dignity of subject which was wanting. But it is where you venture to depart from your illustrious model that you rise to the highest excellence, and acquire an elevation and originality that, in my humble opinion, place your Muse on a higher form in Parnassus than ever his could claim.

The 'Price of the Hat' is a figure absolutely new in poetry; and as to individual character, he could never have rendered it with that truth and delicacy which we acknowledge in the portraits of yourself and Mrs. Clinton. If in so splendid a work I could search for blemishes, perhaps one might be found in the parody of two lines, which after all must ever remain inimitable:—

And they that creep, and they that fly,
Shall end where they began.

I little thought, when first suggesting to you the idea of composing an Ode on the model of your favourite Gray, or when

* Catherine Fanshawe, co-heiress with two other daughters of an ancient gentleman's family. The three lived together. Besides her talent for graceful pleasantry, whether in prose or in verse, admirable as a letter-writer, a reader of Shakspeare, and as a designer in almost every style. A first-rate judge of art says her drawings and etchings are those of an artist, &c. Too few of her poems have been published; some appearing in a volume, consisting of miscellaneous pieces by many authors, edited by Joanna Baillie.—Vide *Reminiscences of a Literary Life*, by Miss Mitford.

you lamented at the Institution the delay occasioned by the choice of a new bonnet, I little thought that you were going to immortalise your name at my instigation. This glorious circumstance gives me a sort of property in the work, by which I feel entitled to request that you would show it sparingly to the few who may be worthy, and on no account distribute any copies without the licence and authority of her who has the honour to be, with sentiments of the most profound admiration, dear madam,

Your obliged and obedient

C. M. F.

Ode, by Mary Berry.

Lo! where the gaily-vestur'd throng,
  Fair Learning's train, are seen,
Wedg'd in close ranks her walls along,
  And up her benches green!

Unfolded to their mental eye
Thy awful form, Sublimity!
    The moral teacher shows—
Sublimity! of Silence born,
And Solitude, mid 'caves forlorn,'
    And dimly-vision'd woes.
Or stedfast Worth, that inly great,
Mocks the malignity of fate.
Whisper'd Pleasure's dulcet sound
Murmurs the crowded room around;
And Wisdom, borne on Fashion's pinion,
Exulting hails her new dominion.
Oh! both on me your influence shed,—
Dwell in my heart, and deck my head!

Where'er a broader browner shade
  The shaggy Beaver throws,
And with the ample feather's aid
  O'ercanopies the nose—
Where'er, with smooth and silken pile,
Lingering in solemn pause awhile,
  The crimson velvet glows—

From some high bench's giddy brink,
With me my Friend begins to think,
As bolt upright we sit—
That dress, like dogs, should have its day,
That beavers are too hot for May,
And velvets quite unfit.
Then Taste in maxims sweet I draw
From her unerring lip—
'How light! how simple are the straw!
How delicate the chip!'

Hush'd is the speaker's powerful voice,
The audience melt away;
I fly to fix my final choice,
And bless th' instructive day.

The milliner officious pours
Of hats and caps her ready stores,
The unbought elegance of Spring;—
Some wide disclose the full, round face;
Some, shadowy, lend a modest grace,
And stretch their sheltering wing.

Here clust'ring grapes appear to shed
Their luscious juices on the head,
And cheat the longing eye:
So round the Phrygian monarch hung
Fair fruits, that from his parched tongue
For ever seemed to fly.

Here early blooms the summer rose;
Here ribbons wreathe fantastic bows;
There plays gay plumage of a thousand dyes!
Visions of beauty! spare my aching eyes!
Ye cumbrous fashions! crowd not on my head!
Mine be the chip of purest white,
Swanlike, and as his feathers light,
When on the still wave spread:
And let it wear the graceful dress
Of unadorned simpleness.

Ah frugal wish! ah pleasing thought!
  Ah hope indulg'd in vain!
Of modest fancy cheaply bought,
  A stranger yet to Payne!

With undissembled grief I tell
  (For sorrow never comes too late),
The simplest bonnet in Pall-Mall
  Is sold for 1*l.* 8*s.*

To calculation's sober view,
  That searches ev'ry plan,
Who keep the old, or buy the new,
  Shall end where they began.

Alike the shabby and the gay
Must meet the sun's meridian ray,
    The air, the dust, the damp:
This shall the sudden shower despoil,
That slow decay by gradual soil,
    Those envious boxes cramp.

Who will, their squander'd gold may pay,
  Who will, our taste deride;
We 'll scorn the fashion of the day
  With philosophic pride.

Methinks we thus in accents low
  Might Sydney Smith address,—
'Poor moralist!—and what art thou?—
  Who never spoke of dress!
Thy mental Hero never hung
Suspended on a tailor's tongue,
  In agonising doubt:
Thy tale no fluttering female show'd
Who languish'd for the newest mode,
  Yet dared to live without!'

May, 1805.

To Miss C. Fanshawe.

North Audley Street, Sunday, May 19.

MY DEAR MISS CATHERINE,—You should know how much I love parody, as well as how much I admire Gray, to know how much I am delighted with my *own* Ode. The little criticisms you make upon it, you must allow me to say, I consider as dictated by that *jalousie de métier* from which the best of us are not entirely exempted. But, however, I shall be very anxious to communicate to you any of *my* future productions, provided you return them to me speedily with as entertaining a comment as accompanied this Ode.

During Miss Berry's residence with her friends at Bothwell she took the opportunity of visiting a cotton-mill established in the neighbourhood. The following detailed account, as showing the regulations and arrangements in force more than half a century ago in such establishments, may not be without its interest; more particularly as, through the courtesy of the present owner, a detailed account of its present state (1860) is subjoined, thus marking the progress and improvements in the mode of conducting its operations:—

Tuesday, November 8th.—Walked to the cotton mill upon the Clyde, just above the grounds of Bothwell, on the opposite side of the river. Nine hundred persons employed about it, of which about 100 are artificers of various sorts, smiths, carpenters, &c., &c., to keep the buildings and machinery in repair. The remaining 800 all employed in the various operations of making the cotton ready for the weaver from the rough state in which it comes home in bales. Of these 800, nearly 500 are children from six to twelve or fourteen years old, and of the remaining 300 there are many more women than men. The children are for the most part apprentices, bound to the manufacturer for six or seven years according to their age, for their food and clothing. After this time is out, they either continue on to receive wages or go to some other business. I am sorry I did not ask what proportion of them continue on at a business of which they must have had such a melancholy experience, for all these children, as well as all their fellow labourers, are employed fourteen hours a day, from six o'clock in the morning to eight at night, of which time they are allowed an hour for breakfast, from nine till ten, and an hour for dinner, from two, till three; after which, they continue uninterruptedly at work till eight at night. I need not commemorate their in general forlorn and squalid looks; they are, God knows, painfully enough impressed on my mind. What a beginning, gracious heaven! for the dawn of human animal life and human intellect! A number of these children are sent from the parishes in London. They have just now thirty-six or forty from the parish of St. Martin's-in-the-Fields. God help them, poor souls! Never to be blessed with the fond endearment of any creature caring for anything but their mere existence and their labour, and condemned to pass the playful years of childhood in a wearisome sameness of employment, to which childhood is so particularly averse. This subject has been so often enlarged upon, I did not mean to have allowed my pen a line upon it; but it is impossible to have had it brought immediately under one's eyes this very day, and not express one's feelings somehow. In the mean time all such care is taken of these children as perhaps in such a situation is possible. They have a building where the parish children and such as come to them from a distance are lodged, girls and boys separately; they have porridge of oatmeal at breakfast and supper, and broth and beef for dinner. They have a master to teach them to read and write, which is done after their work is over at night, and they are carried to church of a Sunday. But what an idea of that religion must these poor souls have, which coops them up in a church for three hours to hear a (to them) unintelligible Scotch sermon, on the only day they are allowed the 'common air and common use of their own limbs.' Oh man, man, man! what ugly things in detail are most of thy finest contrivances! The men and women are in general all at piecework. The carders and reelers—I mean those who attend the carding and reeling (for everything here is done by machinery), are all women; they earn about ten shillings per week, the spinners from fifteen to sixteen shillings per week; these too are almost all women, and have two children attending the particular machine that each belongs to.

The women and girls that are at weekly wages, such as those who tie up and sort the hanks of cotton thread when spun, receive from six to seven shillings per week. The men make from a guinea to two pounds per week. I cannot say that in general the women looked unhealthy; they were for the most part young girls about and under twenty, and some of them good looking. Some, on the contrary, objects sadly disfigured by nature. They all work, as in all manufactories, in large lofts, heated by a large tin tube of steam, going the whole length of the room, and giving any required degree of warmth; it was to-day most oppressive, when joined to the smell of the cotton, of the oil of the machines, and of the people working them. This, however, might certainly be avoided considerably by letting in fresh air at the windows on both sides, all of which open, but which the overseer said they seldom used, and which were almost all shut to-day, though the air was uncommonly mild without, and most oppressingly hot within. I have said that the whole operations here are done by machinery; the whole is moved by one great water-wheel 18 feet and 21 feet in diameter, which turns several vast iron spindles, communicating motion to all the endless wheels which spin six thousand pounds weight of cotton thread in a week. A fifth part is lost in the manufacture; that is to say, to produce a thousand pounds weight of cotton thread, a fifth part more of the raw material is required. Part of this refuse, however, is not perfectly useless, but is sold to be used up in coarse yarn.

The only operation done by the hand is picking the cotton as it comes out of the bale quite clean; after that it is beat, carded, and spun, all by machinery, undergoing six different operations before it is ready to be spun into thread. The various multitude of leather straps upon all the wheels of this immense machinery costs them between three and four hundred pounds yearly in leather, and the oil and candles consumed in lighting the lofts four hundred pounds a-year. They are now going to have it lighted by the new contrivance for consuming coal smoke. They likewise at this manufacture dye cotton of a most beautiful colour with madder; they say such is the demand for it that they could use twice as much madder as they can get. The cotton yarn undergoes forty different operations before it is made ready to receive the colour. The number of people, which I have stated to be 900, employed in this great work, together with their wives and children, the place to lodge them, and the persons necessary to feed, clothe, and wash for them, compose a little town—and so it is, in fact, becoming, with a row of houses, two or three shops, &c. &c.—the only real foundation of towns which the Empress of Russia, with all her greatness, in vain commanded, and Frederick II., with all his abilities, in vain coaxed.

The factory thus described is called Blantyre, situated on the left bank of the Clyde, about four miles below Hamilton, and continues to be worked by the same firm as in 1805, viz. Messrs. Henry Monteith & Co.

The numbers at work in May, 1860, amounted to 1,061; their ages and employment as follows:—

	Males		Females		Total
	under 18	above 18	under 18	above 18	
Spinning-mills	27	32	32	169	260
Weaving factory . . .	1	20	41	289	351
Dye works	18	133	42	201	394
Mechanics and labourers . .	1	55	—	—	56
	47	240	115	659	1061

The above numbers include only twelve children under thirteen years of age; the employment which required so many of that class in 1805 having been long since discarded. The system of binding apprentices was given up about 1809, and the services of that class expired altogether about 1816 or 1817. While that system continued it was observed, when terms of service expired, that females generally remained in the factory working on wages and binding themselves, while the males more generally went forth into the world. This factory appears to be considered a home by all who have been employed in it, for they are free to come and free to go; there is no engagement of any kind on entering; a worker is permitted to leave without giving notice of any kind—he has only to state his wish to the manager, who gives him a line to the clerk to make up his wages, which is paid immediately and no questions asked.

No children are now received from any parish workhouse, school of industry, nor any charitable institution of any kind.

The hours of labour are now those prescribed by the Factory Act, viz.:—

From 6 A.M. till 9 A.M.	3 hours		
„ $9\frac{3}{4}$ „ „ 2 P.M.	$4\frac{1}{4}$ „		
„ $2\frac{3}{4}$ P.M. „ 6 „	$3\frac{1}{4}$ „		
5 days .	$10\frac{1}{2}$ „	$52\frac{1}{2}$ hours	
Saturday.			
From 6 A.M. till 9 A.M.	3 hours		
„ $9\frac{1}{2}$ „ „ 2 P.M.	$4\frac{1}{2}$ „ —	$7\frac{1}{2}$ „	
		60 „	

The buildings in which the cotton-spinning was carried on in the year 1805 have remained very much as they were, but by this introduction of improved machinery the work in those buildings, as well as keeping the machinery and buildings in repair, is now efficiently carried out by 260 workers, of whom 201 are females and 59 males.

The building of four stories, called the picking-house, which existed in 1805, was destroyed by fire and has been replaced by one not so high for other purposes, as picking by hand has long been discontinued. The cleaning of cotton is now all done by machinery. The buildings in which the apprentices of former days were lodged are now converted into warehouse stores, counting house, and an armoury for the rifle-corps.

In 1809–10 a large building was added, capable of holding 350 power-looms.

A gas-making apparatus was erected in 1814, by which all the works are lighted; and since 1843, all the dwelling houses in the village, as well as the streets, have also been lighted with gas.

In 1845 mechanics' shops and stores were erected.

A good school-house is kept up and efficient teachers provided; nearly two-thirds of the expense defrayed by the company, and the remainder by the children in school pence. Parents not connected with the works send their children that they may participate in the advantages of this school.

The children are taken to church by their parents to whatever church they please. There are two Established churches, two Free churches, one United Presbyterian within twenty minutes' walk of the village; besides which the Methodists meet in the village school, and one of the Free Church ministers delivers a sermon every Sabbath in the school-house, and from five to seven o'clock the schoolmasters, assisted by the heads of families and others as monitors conduct a Sabbath evening school in the school-house, which is attended by 180 to 190 children. About two-thirds of the inhabitants attend the Free and United Presbyterian churches, the remainder are divided betwixt the Established Church, Roman Catholics, and Methodists.

The village belonging to the works in 1851 contained a population of 1,280; there are now about 1,400, every available house being occupied; and were there a fourth more houses added, they would be occupied as fast as they could be built.

A considerable number of the workers come from Bothwell, High Blantyre, and other adjacent places; they come in the morning and return again in the evening. There are also a large proportion who come from all the coal and iron works, but at a greater distance. They lodge in the village during the week, going home upon Saturday, and returning again upon Sabbath evening.

There are occasionally a few who having natural physical defects could not otherwise gain a livelihood, can do the light work of the mill very well.

1806.

EXTRACTS FROM JOURNAL.

Jan. 13*th.*—I had determined immediately after seeing it, to mark down the effect *Lord Nelson's funeral* should have on my mind, and that of the people about me. I had certainly hopes that it would have been more considerable than it was, although I had little hope of its being conducted with any real taste or solemn effect, knowing that its conduct had not been entrusted to any persons of approved taste themselves, or who would have summoned artists to their assistance. On the water it was a crowd of boats, in which the immense city barges only were conspicuous. It is much easier to set down upon paper the regulations of a ceremony, such as that the boats of the river fencibles are to line each side of the procession, &c., than to give the effect of a procession so lined on the water in the foggy atmosphere of the Thames. The distance of time between the minute guns fired by these river fencibles was too long to command continued attention, and therefore, I think, failed in their effect. The music, too, was not sufficiently loud to have any effect at all; and the barge which contained his honoured remains was neither sufficiently large nor sufficiently distinguished to command the eye and the attention of every spectator, which by some means or other it ought to have done. I was looking over the wall of Lord Fife's garden, which forms one side of Whitehall Stairs, so that I saw the coffin in the very act of being landed; saw it placed on the bier on which it was borne to the Admiralty. The only really impressive moment was that in which the coffin first touched the ground. At that instant the sky, which but a few minutes before had been clear, poured down at once a torrent of rain and hail, and a sudden gust of wind arose, the violence of which was not less remarkable than the moment at which it took place. In ancient Rome, or in later days of modern superstition, such a circumstance would have been recorded as the moment in which his spirit sought its native sky, or as an omen of future bad luck, from the instant his last remains quitted that element on which he had so often triumphed.

On shore the whole ceremony was still less calculated to gratify the feelings it naturally inspired, and in which (to do them justice), not one of the thousands collected as spectators but seemed to participate. Never was there so decent, so quiet, so serious, so respectful a mob. Instead of presenting to their eager eyes the surviving heroes of Trafalgar, following the corpse of their illustrious leader, the naval officers were all put into mourning coaches, which immediately became equally uninteresting to the spectators, whether they contained a vice-admiral or a herald; indeed the heralds, from their dress, were the only conspicuous persons. The sailors, too, of the 'Victory,' the immediate witnesses of their Nelson's glory, who had indignantly opposed the idea of transferring his corpse to a frigate, and who had insisted on its remaining with them in the ship, on whose deck they had seen him fall —these sailors, instead of being allowed to surround the coffin from which they had proved themselves so unwilling to separate, were marshalled by themselves in another part of the procession, without music, without officers, without any naval accompaniments whatsoever. Although few in number, and thus separated from everything that would have added consequence to their appearance, such was the impression that their serious, quiet, decent deportment made on the multitude, that they were repeatedly and almost continually cheered as they passed along. What a deep and lasting impression would the whole of this ceremony have made on the minds of the spectators, had the naval part of the procession, as well as the military, been conducted on foot; had the companions of his glory and his danger, exposed to the regards of their grateful and admiring country, immediately surrounded the car which bore his remains; had the whole been accompanied by appropriate music—one band taking up the melancholy strain when another dropped it; and had the passage of the procession been marked by the solemn tolling of the different bells. I will not talk of the disproportions and perfect bad taste of the funeral car, because good taste in forms I never expect here; but I *did* expect sufficient good taste in moral feeling, not to have entrusted the conduct of such a ceremony, the tribute of such a nation to such a chief, as a job to the Heralds' office and their hireling undertakers! The only moment in which the mind the most disposed to enthusiasm could for a moment indulge it (I speak not of the ceremony in St. Paul's, which I did not see), was that in which the funeral car passed Charing Cross. Here nothing could be seen on every side but pyramids of heads, and every head uncovered, from respect to the object, on which every eye was entirely bent. One general feeling pervading a great multitude must ever tend to the sublime.

* * *

Thursday, Jan. 23rd.—It was universally believed that Mr. Pitt had died to-day, and everybody was talking and reasoning upon his death as a fact. At seven o'clock in the evening I stopped at Dr. Baillie's door to enquire if he was returned from Wimbledon. He had left Mr. Pitt there between three and four still alive, and Dr. Reynolds was to return there to-night. Baillie having left him, proved to me that he thought the case past all hope.

Friday, Jan. 24th.—Mr. Pitt died this morning at four o'clock. This is certainly a great event for the country in the present posture of affairs. Much curiosity and anxiety was excited to-day and yesterday to ascertain the fact—more, I think, than what may be called tender concern or great regret for his loss. And yet I know not what politics, or what party, can justify the not regretting the loss of such a superior intellect, and such great talents, for superior and great they were, although on the important subjects to which they were applied it was not always possible to approve either his principles or his conduct. Perhaps his greatest errors originated from his early and constant immersion in public business, and from his having been always an actor, never a spectator of affairs. This, perhaps, prevented his sufficiently recurring in his plans and in his measures to those great first principles never to be lost sight of by a really great statesman, and to be deviated from as little as possible; expediency and necessity will always make that little enough.

In Miss Berry's work on 'England and France' will be found a far more detailed review of her opinion respecting the character of Mr. Pitt and of the influence he exercised on the politics of his country and the pursuits of his contemporaries.

The following extracts from Miss Berry's MSS. show how strongly she felt the disadvantage of the light and frivolous education she saw bestowed upon the youth of her own sex, and with what bitter regret she witnessed the mortifying discouragement which then, far more than now, appears to have been given to all intellectual exertions in women, whose leisure and abilities afforded them the opportunity and means of mental cultivation and of literary occupation and distinction.

Extract from a Letter to a Friend.

London: Dec. 1806.

Desultory and heterogeneous reading is the great evil of all young women. Our education (if education it can be called) is nearly ended by the time that our minds begin to open and to be really eager for information. When you men are sent to college we are left (such of us as are not obliged to gain our bread, or to mend our own clothes) to positive idleness, without any object, end or aim to encourage any one employment of our mind more than another. Our imaginations are naturally more lively than yours, our powers of steady attention, I think less than yours. What would you have us do? Entire frivolity, or any and every book that falls into our hands, are our only resources; and though nobody is more aware than myself that this sort of desultory reading during the first years of (mental) life does often much mischief, and is attended always with a great waste of time, yet it has at least this good effect, *et scio quod loquor*, that a love of reading thus natural and thus indulged is often a happy preventive in future life, against more serious follies, more pernicious idleness, and it is to be hoped may be counted upon as a real resource in those days when the attractions of the world and of society fade as much in *our* eyes, as our attractions fade in *theirs*.

EXTRACTS.

Considering the education given to women, and (according to the present system) the subsequent and almost necessary idleness both of mind and body, I am only astonished that they are not more ignorant, weaker, and more perverse than they are.

All English women think it necessary to profess loving the country, and to long to be in the country, altho' their minds are often neither sufficiently opened, nor their pursuits sufficiently interesting, to make such a taste rational.

A woman who is proud of being what is generally called a *woman of business* is proud of endowments that would not distinguish a banker's clerk. They are what every woman should be ashamed of *not* having, because every woman must have sufficient leisure to acquire them; but of the possession of which an intelligent mind can no more be flattered than with the knowledge of the pence table.

The wrongs or the neglect which women of superior intellect almost universally receive from men, are revenged by the various evils which men almost as universally suffer from the weakness, the folly, and the meanness of those whom they commonly prefer in the characters of their wives and friends.

On Imagination.

O for the power of involving myself in fiction and throwing aside (for the time at least) all the dull realities of life! O for the power of creating to myself a society of fancied beings, with and for whom my soul might exert all its energies, and indulge in all its enthusiastic affections. O for the power of surrounding myself with faultless friends, faithful lovers, informed minds, and elegant manners! Rousseau possessed this power, felt this desire, and it produced his Héloise.—To purchase it at the price of *his* morbid feelings on every subject connected with social life, would be paying too dear for it. But to what delicate mind would it not be a treasure when separated from the few, on whom it depends for comfort and support?

1807.

Little Strawberry, April 29, 1807.

WHY do I feel a desire to register my feelings while sitting quite alone in a deliciously warm sunny spring-day, at the window of our drawing-room, looking up the beautiful reach of the Thames which it commands, while all nature is bursting into life around me, and the whole landscape is becoming more and more vividly green every hour? I admire this lovely season as much as ever—I enjoy it perhaps more. But how different are the feelings it generates, the thoughts it induces, the ideas it inspires, from those which the same scene, the same window, the same season, produced ten years ago. It is not that I regret them as more happy. On the contrary, my mind at present enjoys a degree of calm (the first ingredient of happiness) to which it was then a stranger. But it is a calm purchased at the price of every animating hope, of every desire of exertion, and it is secured by expecting *nothing* from the future, and remembering *much* of the past. What frustrated hopes, what unavailing exertions, what fruitless sufferings, does that past recall! Unembellished even by any of those gay thoughtless moments of youth, which, though often severely paid for, yet, when viewed through the medium of distance, become agreeable remembrances; their folly or imprudence duly expiated, their gaiety and the energy they excited remain to cheer and animate the sober dulness of advancing life. But to me these moments never existed; to me all was continued and never-ceasing exertion. Still

I laboured on, still every returning spring found me with some plan of present exertion, or (still more difficult) of present patient endurance, for the hope of securing future comfort, future independence, future repose. But no future exists to me now. I may idle away whole summer suns, as I have done this, in reverie, without neglecting any duty, overlooking any pleasure, or foregoing any advantage.

JOURNAL.

Monday, August 10th: — Went from Guy's Cliff to see Warwick Castle, distance a mile and a half; entrance through a new low Gothic gate in the outer wall; from thence to the castle, the road winds through the solid rock, making a wall on both sides, overhung with trees and shrubs; the inner enclosure of the castle bursts upon one, beautifully presenting a double gateway (the real old one) and two towers. That called Guy's Tower is, both as to proportion, form, and colour of stone, one of the handsomest I ever saw. It is a duodecagon, but the angles so obtuse as not to be striking till near observation. The other tower upon the bank of the Avon is singularly picturesque from the odd irregularities of its construction, being part of it angular, part of it segments of circles in scallops, with strange projections on the battlements, above which a part of the tower rises considerably. The ground about the walls and towers, and the space between the outer and inner court, is left rough with broom and other wild plants, making an excellent foreground to such a building. In the inner court all is smooth turf. The hall is magnificent in size, but the panelling, newly painted like boxwood, in bad taste. A fine suite of rooms, the whole length of the castle towards the river; a number of very fine pictures, chiefly portraits by Vandyke, Rubens, and Rembrandt.

The furniture extremely massive, and appropriate to the place; many old cabinets and tables of *pietra dura* and other precious materials, besides the greatest quantity of *boule* in all sorts of commodes, cabinets, candelabra, tables, &c. &c., that I ever saw collected together; the chimney-pieces are all modern, all expensive high marble, in the worst taste, of about thirty years ago. The windows are large recesses, admitting a vast deal of light; an armoury is fitted up with a vast number of old and curious arms of all nations, and all times, very handsomely and well arranged. There is a broad walk round the walls, still very passable, and a good staircase in Guy's Tower. I am to visit Cæsar's Tower another day, as we had already spent nearly five hours, poking into every creek and cranny of the rest of this noble castle. The Avon flows immediately under its walls; the walls connect with the mill belonging to the castle, and in the same style of building with itself; this has a weir upon the river, forming a pretty though too regular a cascade. Immediately above are the picturesque remains of an ancient Gothic bridge, the middle arch entirely carried away, and the side ones remaining overhung with shrubs, furze, and other vegetation. About a quarter of a mile's distance the river is crossed by a new Grecian bridge of one arch, which, though not ugly in itself, is misplaced, and destroys the harmony of the scene.

I see no place in this country of which the scenery is to be compared with that of Guy's Cliff. Guy's Cliff is so odd, so romantic, so cheerful, so enjoyable! The singular appearance of the various arches, caves, and apertures of all sorts and sizes, in the perpendicular wall of rock which forms the courtyard and faces the entrance, contrasts so well with the open cheerful scene from the drawing-room. The flowing Avon winds round a turfy peninsula immediately below, while its course lower down is bordered with alders and overhung by a group of picturesque ash-trees, and higher up the stream is arrested by a mill, and forms a cascade; there the three arches of the wheels peep out from under weeping willows and occidental planes; one fine poplar towers above the rest, and marks the farthest projection of the stonework into the river; and a foot-bridge over the water to another group of trees, finishes the landscape, and gives it all the charm of a beautiful foreground. Behind, the country is seen rising into sloping fields, and tufts of wood, and a most happily-placed country church backed by one of these tufts, forms the horizon of a lovely tranquil scene, and one most *characteristically English.*

Tuesday, 18*th*.—I am going in future to write a journal—the entertainment I have received from those of my friend here * has set me upon it. And yet why begin a journal when more, *much* more, than half one's probable life is past, 'and all the life of life' certainly gone for ever! I have hitherto avoided it, because I felt ashamed of the use, or rather the no-use, I made of my time—of the miserable minute duties and vexations which at once occupied and corroded my mind—of the manner in which I have let life slip by me, and missed its present enjoyments, by always aiming at and acting for some indefinite future.

But now that *no future* remains to me, perhaps I may be encouraged to make the most of the present by marking its rapid passage, and setting before my eyes the folly of letting a day escape without *endeavouring*, at least, to make the best I can of it, and, above all, without making impossible attempts to mend or alter anybody but myself.

Friday, 21*st*.—I have said that I am to write a journal—why not then begin? I shall have to record few days spent more agreeably, more peaceably, more rationally than during this last fortnight with our friends here, who,

* Mr. Greathead.

without fuss or bustle, or interfering with the use one may wish to make of one's time, have every kind and thoughtful attention to the amusement of their guests; without pomp or pretension, they have every comfort, luxury, and elegance for enjoyment; and their conversation, habits, minds, and manners are free from affectation, and not only please and satisfy, but attach.

Well, then, to begin. An effort it must always be, and, therefore, the sooner it is got over the better.

Yesterday (Thursday, August 20th) I went with Mr. Greathead to Warwick Castle. I soon found my friend Mrs. Hume, the housekeeper, who was so much pleased with this second visit that she left two other visitors to accompany me everywhere. First, she would show me the offices—fine arched vaults in the solid rock towards the river. The ale-cellars require about 500*l.* worth of malt to fill them. They are not quite empty, but it is long since the lord of this castle, from his various schemes and extravagancies, has been able to live in any style becoming it, or indeed to live here at all. After seeing the offices to please Mrs. Hume, I went through the dungeon at the bottom, to the leads at the top, of Cæsar's Tower, to please myself.

This singularly irregular and odd-shaped tower is unquestionably the oldest part of the castle; it is that which must have guarded the passage of the river. There is an excellent stone winding staircase from the bottom to the top, besides a smaller one, which goes up to the battlements only. Below the battlements, the tower contains two rooms and two closets, with windows upon each floor, and above the battlements is one large round arched room, with four windows in it. The view from here is very extensive. Lord Warwick wishes it fitted up as a morning sitting-room for himself, and indeed, save the number of steps, he could not have one more agreeable. A few stone steps lead from it to the leaded top of the odd little scalloped tower, which grows out of one side of the large tower, and divides its angular from its developed side—for so it literally is—though nothing but a drawing can give any idea of it.

I went all over the leads of the double gateway. The two towers contain eighteen rooms. By this time Mr. G. joined me, and we walked through a gate to look at the face towards the river, which is beautiful, the lower part being all native rock, overgrown with vegetation of various sorts. Then went up the mount to what is called the keep; but it is, in fact, nothing but the outer wall of the castle, carried over a high artificial mound of earth, made by the scooping out the ditch with two small watch-towers at the top.

The real *keep* of this castle must have been Cæsar's Tower. After going up and down so many stairs, we enjoyed sitting in the porch of the castle, and eating some excellent fruit sent by our friend the housekeeper, who with much difficulty was induced to accept the accustomed fee at this place.

After dinner strolled with Mrs. Damer by the river side, where the whole scene is deliciously inducive of quiet, calmness, and repose.

After tea, Mr. Greathead, at my request, read to us his translation in verse of Boccaccio's 'Lisabetta and her Brothers.' I had once heard it before, eleven years ago, at their house in Bryanstone Street, on an evening memorable to me, for it was that on which I had at last relieved my own mind and scruples, by confiding to my second father, to Lord Orford, that in a few months, as I then thought, I was to leave him for a still dearer friend and a nearer connection; and satisfied with having acted up to the most scrupulous, the most romantic ideas of the duties of friendship, I was indulging myself in all the rational hopes and fair prospects which seemed then to open to my still enthusiastic mind. Alas! alas!

all too soon cruelly crushed, and since levelled with the dust.

But whither am I roaming? from Greathead's tale to my own!

Friday, 21*st.*—Wrote to Agnes, scribbled a little in this book, read a little of the 'Lamento di Cecco,' which, having often heard of, I had never seen before. It is a beautiful, simple, but not vulgar pastoral, in the Tuscan patois; but after the first three or four stanzas, not very difficult to understand. If it were, there are notes, which swell a poem of forty stanzas into a tolerable-sized quarto volume! Thank heaven, one is not obliged to read them, for they seem to me the very model, or rather the caricature, of those voluminous notes, corrections, first readings, and comparings of *all* similar passages, in *all* possible authors, which encumber without enlightening half the best books one knows.

In the evening, conversation inexhaustible between the Greatheads and us.

Saturday, 22*nd.*—Went with Mr. Greathead to Kenilworth. I was resolved to go there again, and have another look at the castle and the beautiful village. The village is above a mile long, and I went in search of Charles's * mother, whom I found in a poor little cottage, her three children just returned from gleaning. I have a good opinion of her, from all her children (no fewer than eleven) being able to read and write. We went to the castle by the outside of the village. The approach to it this way by far the most picturesque, and the best for a general view. The largest rooms in Leicester's building (those which Queen Elizabeth occupied), I measured. They are only twenty-four feet by twenty-six feet, as they now stand from wall to wall, but must have been pleasant rooms with large shallow bay

* Probably one of Miss Berry's servants.

windows.* The great hall, built by John of Ghent, must have been a magnificent room, with two fireplaces yet remaining, large windows in a recess, with a step up to them, and a seat round them; and at one end of the room a large bay window on one side, and a smaller one on the other. The panelling of stone remaining in all the recesses of the windows and on the sides of the fireplaces is of very neat masonry.

From the castle we returned, through the village, to a manufactory of combs,† which is here carried on to a considerable extent, and the refuse of bone, horn, &c., goes to a sal-ammoniac and hartshorn manufactory in the neighbourhood.‡ Curious operation of cutting open the horns and flattening them, by holding in tongs to a wood-fire, and then putting them between thick iron plates, which are heated and pressed together, with the pieces of horn between them. The man we saw at this business, which is very hot and fatiguing, will earn better than four shillings per day, working fourteen or fifteen hours.

The horns for lanthorns § (after being cut open like the others) pressed by a machine worked by a horse.

* There are differences of opinion as to Queen Elizabeth's apartments; some which *now* bear that name seem more like the apartments of attendants. At the southern angle of the eastern side of the banqueting hall, the oriel window with its little fireplace gives the appearance of a small room, and this is by some called Queen Elizabeth's boudoir. This can be entered, and is a favourite seat for the visitors to the castle. The roof of the cellarage under the banqueting hall formed the foundation for its flooring; this is now gone, except under the oriel windows. One or two of the old timber beams are all that remain to testify of floors in the other apartments; there are a few wooden stairs in an inaccessible part of the large projecting staircase, and over some of the doorways the remains of lath and plaster; but this is all the woodwork now remaining, except in the gate-house or stable.

† No longer there.

‡ The comb trade is daily decreasing and has almost ceased to exist. An old inhabitant of Kenilworth, married to one of the most wealthy of the traders, can remember when her husband paid 100*l.* weekly in wages to about thirty or forty workmen, including boys.

§ The horn was prepared for lanthorns, but sent up to London to be made up.

From the comb manufactory we traversed the green scoop of a valley, round which a great part of this extensive village is built. In this valley is situated the church and the remains of the abbey, which consists only of a much-ruined gate-house and two or three pieces of rough stone.*

The tower and great door of the parish church are of the very oldest Saxon style, and from the wasted appearance of the stone in comparison of the other ruins of the place, must be very much older. Indeed, the door of the church, both from its ornaments and from the soil being raised full two-thirds of its original height, must be of high Saxon antiquity.

The pastures into which this valley is divided are still called the Abbeys, from having belonged to the abbey, and are now traversed by a neat gravelled path, and adorned by the largest and most picturesque wych elm † I ever saw, and a noble ash ‡ against the line of houses.

Everything about this village, and among other things the alehouse signs, prove its antiquity. The 'Bear and Ragged Staff' § certainly dates from the days of Leicester. But the 'Two Virgins' is of much greater antiquity. The tradition of the place says that the house *always* has been an alehouse; and as the 'Two Virgins' mean the Virgin Mary and her mother Elizabeth,|| we must certainly suppose it established before the Reformation.

* There are still some remains of an abbey, a very beautifully arched gateway, and two strong pieces of wall, standing in the Abbey fields. Part of the old vaults was discovered in the new portion added to the churchyard, which the Bishop of Worcester consecrated as new ground a few years since. There is also a building close to the arched gateway supposed to have been the hospice; and the handsome west door of the parish church, which is evidently an insertion, is supposed to have been rescued from the abbey ruin.

† Still standing. ‡ No longer there.

|| St. Ann. § Still there.

¶ It has been supposed that this sign does not refer to St. Ann, but that the second virgin is meant to represent Queen Elizabeth.

After visiting the house of which Mr. Greathead is directing the alteration for Mr. Lake,* we returned to Guy's Cliff.

Sunday, 23*rd*.—I remained in my room the whole morning reading Mr. Greathead's Journals, which let me more into their every-day life, where they went, and what they did while abroad, than a month's conversation could do.

Monday, 24*th*.—Took leave of our kind friends here, after having spent nearly three weeks with them, greatly to my own satisfaction. Before breakfast, I had, in a quiet solitary walk by the river side, taken a sort of leave of the tranquil scene, and promised myself to return to it whenever I could; but this indefinite future has something solemn in it; and ceasing *to be* in one place, and rising again in another, always gives me the idea of a sort of death.

The day was showery, and a nervous headache prevented my enjoying the set of postchaise ideas which always take possession of my mind whenever my body is set a-going upon wheels.

The inn at Woburn dirty and forlorn-looking, and our sitting-room damp and cold.

Tuesday, 25*th*.—We were half an hour from the inn at Woburn Abbey through the park. The approach very handsome. At a sufficient distance is a great body of building, low and like a pavilion, with two wings, consisting of stables, a riding-house, tennis-court, &c. &c. The whole appears like what it is, the complete establishment of a great lord in this country, without any ostentatious display of ornament. The house within excellent; two complete apartments for summer and winter, both looking equally inhabitable, though the family were not there. Some remarkably fine pictures. Those in the

* This house was afterwards sold to Sir Charles Clifford, and subsequently to William Amherst, Esq., since dead.

gallery we did not see, as the room was painting. Some very fine Teniers, an exquisite Both, an admirable picture (called by Rembrandt, though not at all in his usual dark manner), 'Joseph interpreting the Baker's Dream;' the 'Countess of Bedford,'* mother to the beheaded Lord Russell—charming whole length, by Vandyke.

Magnificent greenhouse. A space in the middle, in which is an antique marble vase of monstrous dimensions, supported by four antique marble columns, of which two are beautiful Cipollina.

At the end of the greenhouse, a cabinet, elaborately lined with marble and gilding, called the Temple, and containing Nollekens'† bust of Mr. Fox, on a white marble pedestal, with an inscription, surrounded by six other busts of his most particular friends upon brackets—Lord Howicke, General Fitzpatrick, Lord Lauderdale, Lord Robert Spencer, Lord Holland, and Mr. Hare.

One could have wished, for the honour of their public principles, that the private characters of some of them had been different. An inscription over the door says that this temple to friendship, planned and begun by the last Duke, was finished at his dying request by his brother. A covered way of a quarter of a mile in length leads to a Chinese dairy, much ornamented with china. It is in Holland's showy but unchaste taste. Indeed, in most of the things he has done here, I discovered the model of all he since executed upon rather a smaller scale at Mr. Whitbread's.

We were above two hours and a half at Woburn with-

* Anne, daughter of Robert Carr Earl of Somerset and Frances Howard the divorced wife of the Earl of Essex, married William Lord Russell, afterwards fifth Earl and first Duke of Bedford, 1637. She died 1684, aged sixty-four.

† Joseph Nollekens, born 1737. A sculptor of some eminence, he was much employed in the 'restoration' of ancient sculpture. His best works were his portrait-busts—he made 74 repetition marble busts of Pitt, and 600 plaster casts. His bust of Fox had scarcely inferior success. Died 1823.—*Imperial Dictionary of Universal Biography.*

out seeing what is called the pleasure ground, which, in almost all fine places, I have long discovered is the least pleasing part of the whole.

We drove for about two miles through the park to the entrance from the Dunstable Road, which is now building, and from the scale on which it seems planned promises to be magnificent.

Arrived in North Audley Street. London does not appear to advantage on returning from the country on a fine summer's evening. I had the comfort of finding Agnes looking well, and happy to get me back.

Saturday, 29th.—In the evening read a good deal of the last Scotch Review. What they say of Mr. Hope,* though he lays himself open to ridicule, is ill-natured and often in bad taste. An excellent criticism upon Cobbett's weekly journal, exposing, in the clearest manner, his shameful inconsistencies, or rather direct contradiction of his own opinions, both of men and measures, within this last five years, and holding up upon true Whig principles our real defects and real misconduct, without seeking to palliate or defend either the one or the other, and only wishing them to be considered as they are, and not confounded with preposterous exaggeration in the minds of the people. But alas! the people read Cobbett, and will never read the Scotch Review.

I have felt uncommonly well for these last two days. The good effects this health, which I so seldom enjoy, has upon my temper, my spirits, and my views, can only be equalled by my gratitude to Heaven for it.

Sunday, 30th.—Windham † extremely admires the

* Household Furniture and Internal Decorations executed from Designs. By Thomas Hope. Folio.

† William Windham, of Felbrigg, Norfolk, born 1750, one of the distinguished statesmen and orators of his day. In 1788 he was one of the managers of the impeachment of Warren Hastings. He continued to act with the Whig party till the division in their ranks caused by the opinions on the French Revolution, when he took part with Burke. In 1794 he

Scotch review of Cobbett, with whom he says he is out of all patience; although, by the bye, Windham is the only one of his violent favourites that he has not as yet violently abused. Horner supposed to be the author of the review. I don't doubt he is.* Went at half-past ten to Mrs. Bouverie's. Lord Clifden, arrived from Ireland the day before; Mr. Falkner and one of his daughters, Lady Julia Howard, Sir F. Vincent, Mrs. Spencer, and Mr. Rogers. Everybody anxious for news from Copenhagen, and few liking entirely to speak out their sentiments. My fears I own are great.

Monday, 31*st.*—Began to clear out that Augean stable, our lumber room. From the accumulated dust of fifteen years I came out like a chimney-sweeper, and almost choked with dust.

Tuesday, *September* 1*st.*—Drove with my father to Hogmore Lane to make enquiries after the Princess Sophia, upon her mother the Duchess of Gloucester's death.†

Tuesday, 8*th.*—Mr. William Robertson called. He was at Lisbon during the earthquake in June last. He had experienced two before in the East Indies—this by far the most violent. The old people at Lisbon who remembered that of 1755 all agreed that this shock was as violent; but not being repeated, nor of long continuance, did little damage. No lives lost but by those whose terror made them jump out of windows, &c. &c.

Wednesday, 9*th.* — Set off for Coombank.‡ Lord

joined the ministry of Pitt, as Secretary of War, till 1801. In 1804 he again united with Fox, and took office with 'all the talents' till their ejection in 1807; and during the remainder of his career sat on the Opposition benches. Died June 1810.

* It was Lord Jeffrey, and not Mr. Horner, who wrote the article.

† Maria Walpole, second natural daughter of Sir Edward Walpole and of Mary Clement, married in 1759 to the Earl of Waldegrave. Lord Waldegrave died 1763. Lady Waldegrave married in 1766 Prince William Henry Duke of Gloucester, who died 1805.

‡ Coombank, in Sandrish parish, was anciently possessed by the *Islays*,

Frederick Campbell received me with his usual cheerfulness of manner. It was a bad day, and the house, in spite of the many good pictures and other things in it, struck me as more uncomfortable than ever. Dr. Vyse, the Bishop of Peterborough (who married his sister) and Mr. Cayley, a lawyer from London, dined with us. In the evening came the Bishop's wife and four other women; good sort of dressed-up country-town ladies, of whom in a single evening one can make nothing. So I sat and worked and listened to the Bishop, who, though by no means brilliant, amused me with recounting a circumstance which happened to him very soon after he took orders, while reading the service before a large congregation in Hartingfordbury Church. The lesson for the day was the fifteenth chapter of the first book of Samuel where, reproaching Saul, he says, 'Wherefore do I hear this bleating of sheep and lowing of oxen?' At the moment he uttered the words 'bleating of sheep,' a great bellwether began *baaing* just below the pulpit, to the irresistible diversion of his audience. Sheep were feeding in the churchyard, and one of them had strayed unobserved into the church.

Thursday, 10*th*.—Went in the morning to Tunbridge to call upon the Bishop, Mrs. Madan, &c. at Dr. Vyse's parsonage, a thoroughly comfortable and indeed elegant house of the kind, and appears to advantage in going to it from Coombank, which I think unites every possible discomfort. I went at Coombank with the housekeeper

and afterwards by the Ash family, who, about fifty or sixty years since, sold it to Colonel John Campbell, afterwards Duke of Argyle, whose third son, Lord Frederick Campbell, is now owner; his father having given him this estate during his own lifetime. The house, which consisted of a centre, with square projections or wings at each angle, was partly destroyed by an accidental fire, when Lady Frederick Campbell was burnt to death. Philipott says that 'not many years since, in digging near Come Bank, were discovered many Roman arms of an antique shape and figure.'—*Beauties of England and Wales*. By Edward Wedlake Brayley, vol. viii. p. 1310. Published 1808.

into the bedroom where Lord and Lady Frederick slept before the horrible catastrophe of the fire.* Nothing can be more frightful and curious than the aspect it presents. Without being actually burnt in any one part, except about three or four feet of the floor, just near the dressing-room door, the whole is perfectly black and scorched and shrivelled up with the effects of the fire, the turpentine all sweated out of the paint.

The fatal dressing-room must have been on fire above four hours, but the *flames* only burst through the, at last, consumed door of the dressing-room when the maid at a little before five o'clock in the morning made a draught of air by opening the door of the bedchamber.

The miracle of this poor soul Lady Frederick† having been thus actually burnt to ashes in a house of which one single room alone was destroyed, is only made the more wonderful by examining the spot and hearing the report of everybody who was there, and can only be accounted for, by her having fallen into a fit with her head in the candle, and thus having been perfectly insensible before the fire attacked her. Both her sisters having died in fits makes this the less unlikely.

Saturday, 12*th*.—Returned to North Audley Street.

Tuesday, 15*th*.—I went with Mrs. Damer to Wedgewood, where I had not been for three or four years. His blue and white ware, made in imitation of china, better than the Colebrook Dale of the same sort; the patterns in better taste and the white clearer.

Wednesday, 16*th*.—Left North Audley Street for Tunbridge Wells, with our own horses; arrived at Tunbridge by the finest of moonlight nights, after one of the finest of

* The fire took place the 25th of June in this year.

† Lady Frederick Campbell was sister to the late Sir William Meredith, and had first married Earl Ferrars, from whom she was divorced for ill usage, and who was afterwards executed at Tyburn for the murder of his steward.—*Beauties of England and Wales.* By E. W. Brayley, vol. viii. p. 1319.

bright autumn days. We drove to our house under Mount Zion, and walked to Lady Donegal's. Charles Moore* there, and Lord Ellenborough† and his son.

Friday, 18th.—I dined at Lord Ellenborough's; carried with us Mr. Moore and Miss Godfrey; ‡ the party besides, Lady Donegal and General and Mrs. Ross.§ Lord Ellenborough quick and clever in conversation.

Sunday, 20th.—After dinner strolled on the common; it is the charm of this place to be able to do this at any hour of the day, without hat or gloves, and in any way you please, without observation or comment. Lady Donegal, Miss Godfrey and C. Moore drank tea with us.

Monday, 21st.—Drove out with Miss Godfrey and Agnes to Eridge Green, and then walked to the bank of rock just behind it. It is a continuation of the shelf of rock which forms all the variously denominated rocks in the neighbourhood of Tunbridge, by peeping above the soil in different places. These are very picturesque; they are a rabbit warren, with trees dropped in all the fissures of stone, and a birch wood at the top of the bank.

In the evening to a party at Mrs. Jones's: two card-tables of old women at play, and a room full of girls, with a thin sprinkling of boys, not knowing what to do. We carried Lady Donegal and her sister with us, and had C. Moore and Lord Ellenborough to talk to. But my head was heavy and oppressed, and I felt, and often now feel, my former exertions in society perfectly intolerable to me.

Thursday, 24th.—In the evening a small party at the Horsleys. Lord Ellenborough's conversation very lively

* Charles Moore, son of the Archbishop of Canterbury.

† John Law, born 1750; Attorney-General, 1801; Lord Chief Justice, and created Baron Ellenborough, 1802. He married in 1789, Anne, daughter of Captain George P. Towey, R.N.; died 1818.

‡ Sister to Lady Donegal.

§ Daughter of Sir Robert Gunning, of Horton, co. Northampton; married, 1795, to Major-General Ross.

and amusing upon law matters; curious anecdotes on Lady Strathmore's subject.

Friday, October 2nd.—Drove out with Lady Ellenborough, Lord Ellenborough and Lady Donegal. In returning, I saw a whiskey break down, a woman fly out on one side, and a man dragged from under the wheels, as I thought, on the other. I mentioned as quietly as I could, not to frighten poor Lady Ellenborough in the weak state in which she is, that I thought a bad accident had happened, and that we had better stop. She was instantly for turning about, which I was much against, believing that she would certainly see what might be too shocking to weak nerves. Lady Donegal and I got out of the barouche and ran as hard as we could to the broken carriage, about 500 yards behind. The lady, who was Mrs. Montolieu, had escaped entirely unhurt, and the young man, who was her son (a cripple both in arms and legs), had only a cut lip and a bleeding nose. He is at all times incapable of moving without two men to help him, which made me suppose I had seen him dragged a stiffened figure from under the carriage. They were put, after many refusals and apologies, into the barouche with Lady Ellenborough and Lady Donegal, and Lord Ellenborough and I walked back to Tunbridge together. The day was very fine and the walk very pleasant; Lord Ellenborough has plenty of conversation, and, though his mind is a coarse one, his language and expressions are sufficiently free from that fault.

Sunday, 4th.—Expected Prince Staremberg to breakfast. Instead of him came a special messenger despatched from town at six in the morning, to say that a courier had arrived and he could not come. I could not regret it, for my head was very unfit for the sort of exertion which his gaiety requires.

Went with Lady Ellenborough and party to Harrison's Lake, a very pretty piece of water, surrounded by wood and having a sort of low pavilion in which are two good rooms built on its edge for fishing. It was a place I had never seen or even heard of before.

The weather delicious; a warm sunny summer day from morning till night.

Wednesday, 7th.—Drove out to Rusthall Common; walked across to Lower Green, a hamlet of a few houses, picturesquely situated, where Agnes and I drew till rain came on.

In the evening we went to Lord Ellenborough's, where were collected almost all the company in the place, and among the rest Lord Erskine,* who had arrived the night before at the rooms. Lady Donegal and I played whist with Lord Ellenborough and Lord Erskine. I don't know which of the four plays worst.

Tuesday, 13th.—Went in the morning to Stoneland Park,† the old seat of the Dorset family, and where the Duchess ‡ and Lord Whitworth are now living. We were on a drawing expedition with Lady Donegal.

Wednesday, 14th.—Went out again upon a drawing expedition with Miss Godfrey on a fine autumn, or rather summer, day; beginning with a misty morning, it was quite hot at mid-day, and the beauty of everything seen in such weather quite enchanting.

Mr. Amsinck, the master of the ceremonies here, dined with us; the only one of his kind I ever saw very like a gentleman, and not at all a coxcomb.

Thursday, 15th.—Went again on a drawing expedition with Lady Donegal. Went to Langton Green and looked at the cold bath, where there are the remains of hewn

* The Hon. Thomas Erskine, second son of Henry David fifth Earl of Buchan, became Lord High Chancellor in 1806, and created Baron Erskine; died 1823.

† The former name for Knole.

‡ Arabella Diana, daughter of Sir J. Cope, Bart., married the third Duke of Dorset, who died 1799; and afterwards Charles late Earl of Whitworth (extinct), and died 1825.

stone steps, and yew hedges of an old public garden, which this was in the days of Charles II.; the cold bath beautifully clear; it is in a large, half-ruined room; a peasant's family now inhabiting what was the dressing-room.

Saturday, 17*th*.—In the morning I walked with Lady Donegal. Some serious talk with her. Whenever she talks *en tête-à-tête* upon serious subjects, she shows an excellent right-thinking mind and a kindly affectionate heart, without any affectation either of sentiment or talents, while in both she is far above the common order of women. Had she lived more in intellectual society, she would herself have been superior; as it is, she is more, she is amiable and beloved, and has the gaiety of mind which proceeds from a consciousness of deserving it.

Monday, 19*th*.—Finest autumn day possible. Left Tunbridge Wells. Lady Donegal and Miss Godfrey sat with us at breakfast, walked up the hill with us, and then took leave with a kind, hearty, and, I believe, on all sides, sincere farewell. Arrived in North Audley Street; our house looking very clean and comfortable, and most spacious after the nutshell we have been living in.

Saturday, 24*th*.—I saw Dr. Baillie, which my now long indisposition induced me to do before I left town. He is very rational, kind, and sensible—pities my complaints, but is by no means sanguine in his hopes of removing them.

Strawberry Hill, *Tuesday*, 27*th*.—Lord and Lady* Glenbervie, Miss Stirling, and Mr. North dined here. I began looking over Madame du Deffand's papers.

Wednesday, 28*th*.—Went in the morning to Richmond. Called on Mrs. Dundas; her daughter, whose foot had been cut off exactly six weeks before, was sitting cheerful and happy upon the sofa, a different creature both in

* Catherine Anne, daughter of Frederick second Earl of Guilford and eighth Lord North, married, 1786, to Sylvester Douglas Lord Glenbervie; died February, 1817.

appearance and in spirits, from what we had seen her in the summer. The operation has been performed at her own earnest request, and her behaviour was so heroic as quite to overcome Home, the surgeon who performed it.

Friday, 30*th*.—I began sorting and looking over Madame du Deffand's papers. In the evening began reading the 'Life of Clarendon.'

Tuesday, 3*rd November*.—I worked at Madame du Deffand's papers the whole morning, without walking out. I never can tear myself away from what I am about.

Saturday, 7*th*.—Sat still reading Madame du Deffand.

Sunday, 8*th*.—In the evening Lady Petre and Lady Glenbervie, Mr. North, and Miss Sterling. We played chess against Robert in a laughing manner. Mr. North, as usual, very agreeable.

Tuesday, 10*th*.—I was too unwell to dine down stairs. Prince Staremberg dined with Mrs. Damer and my father. He read to them, for the first time, his little piece 'Melcom,' and another little piece, a monologue, called 'Le Parleur Eternel,' which he had received from Paris.

Wednesday, 11*th*.—At Madame du Deffand's letters, and did not stir out. In the evening I read aloud 'Clarendon's Life.'

Monday, 16*th*.—Alone all day. Read 'Clarendon's Life' aloud in the evening.

Thursday, 19*th*.—After dinner read aloud some of Madame du Deffand's letters.

Saturday, 21*st*.—Went into Pope's back-garden, and saw the devastation going on upon his quincunx by its now possessor, Baroness Howe.* The anger and ill-humour expressed against her for pulling down his house and destroying his grounds, much greater than one would have imagined.

* Sophia Charlotte Baroness Howe, of Langar, daughter of Admiral Earl Howe, widow of the Hon. Penn Ashton Curzon (who died 1797), and afterwards married, 1817, to Sir J. Wathen Waller.

Sunday, 22nd.—At two o'clock Prince Staremberg came. He came immediately into my room, and we sent for Mrs. D. We had not seen him since the arrival of the messenger from France. He spoke to us in detail, and in perfect confidence, of everything that had been proposed *de part et d'autre.* As far as it has hitherto gone, he has conducted himself as well as possible, and had such a commission been sent to any one (whatever his abilities) less well acquainted with England than himself, he would be already gone, and all hopes over. If our Ministry* don't embrace with openness and sincerity this offer of negociation, they will never have another made them. Pray Heaven they may be sufficiently aware of the state of Europe to be convinced of the truth of this, and all the dreadful consequences that hinge upon it! I own I doubt and deprecate the extravagance of their demands, so much have our brilliant naval successes, and our factitious commercial prosperity hitherto blinded all middling heads as to our *real* situation.†

Monday, 23rd.—A dismal, rainy, and to me melancholy day, for I was out of humour with myself. A number of little circumstances lately have served to convince me that my manner is often *tranchante*, my voice

* The Duke of Portland's administration was at this time in power. Mr. Canning was Secretary of State for Foreign Affairs from March 1807 to October 1809. Amongst the principal members of the Duke of Portland's cabinet were Mr. Percival, Lord Eldon, Earl Camden, Lord Hawksbury, Lord Castlereagh, Lord Mulgrave, and Earl of Westmoreland.

† Offers of mediation on the part of Austria had been made during this year; and at this time Prince Staremberg had received orders to get the British Government to pledge themselves to a desire for peace. Early in 1808 he received instructions to urge the British Government to send two plenipotentiaries immediately to Paris to arrange the preliminaries of a peace. This proposal was, for various strong reasons, rejected by Mr. Canning, and the Prince was therefore obliged to immediately ask for his passports. Prince Paul Esterhazy, afterwards for many years ambassador in England, was at this time First Secretary of Legation in London.

often too loud, and my way of meeting opposition unconciliating. All these circumstances are exactly the contrary from what they ought to be, to make me what I wish, and what alone I can be, at my time of life. It is odd that I, who have been always thinking of growing old, and have such clear ideas of what alone can make a woman loved and amiable after her youth is past, what her views and manners should be, and what can ensure her any degree of consideration—it is odd, I say, that I should fall into the very faults I am the most aware of, and put myself into the situation I have always deprecated; but it is not too late, and at least I am not too old to mend.

In Madame Neckar's ridiculous Remains, published by her husband, are some of the very best rules and advice for the manners and conduct of a woman no longer young in society. I will read them again. They always strike me as most justly conceived.

Thursday, 26th.—Walked about the garden at Little Strawberry Hill. My greenhouse looks well. Read Madame du Deffand's letters in the evening.

Friday, 27th.—Spent a part of the morning at Little Strawberry Hill in my greenhouse. Read Madame du Deffand in the evening.

Monday, 30th.—In the evening, Madame du Deffand's letters.

Tuesday, December 1st.—Left Strawberry Hill, after spending five weeks there very comfortably and quietly. North Audley Street for the first time felt cold after the great logs and extreme warmth of Strawberry.

Sunday, 6th.—Prince Esterhazy sat with me a long time, and we had a very rational and interesting conversation about Staremberg and his present situation; Esterhazy's sentiments always marking a good understanding and an excellent heart.

Sunday, 20th.—Sir Edward Carrington, Mr. Turner,

and Mr. Churchill called, and the two Lords Balcarras and Lady Charlotte Lindsay.

Thursday, 24th.—I was obliged to keep our long-promised engagement to a *messe de minuit* and a *reveillon* at Prince Staremberg's. Agnes was unequal to going; so with a fatigued mind, very ill-disposed towards gaiety of any sort, I went between ten and eleven with Mrs. Damer. We found there of womankind only Madame de Pompies and Madame de Lapé, two Frenchwomen, whose names I have so often heard from him, but whom I never saw before, or have any great inclination ever to see again; though as Frenchwomen there was no sort of awkwardness in our thus first meeting and passing an evening with them in a small society. Soon after arrived Victorine, dressed, and looking her very best, and soon after her Catalani * and her husband, who filled up the time before the *messe* began with singing in high spirits anything that came into her head. The *messe* was said in a room below, and we two *mécroyantes*, Mrs. D. and I, remained in the drawing-room with four of the men, who had not finished their party at whist. Afterwards we had supper, at which we all assisted, to the number of about sixteen or seventeen, and I was not at home till half-past two.

* Angelica Catalani, born near Rome 1783. Her voice was remarkable even at twelve years old. She made her début on the stage at Venice in her fifteenth year. Her first appearance in England was in 1806, and she remained here till 1814. Her last appearance in England was 1824, and in 1827 she retired altogether. Died at Florence, 1849.

1808.

Saturday, January 9th.—In the evening went to Drury Lane. 'The Wonder.'* Elliston very poor in Felix, and Mrs. Jordan bringing out too often her oyster-woman notes in Violante, which destroys all the effect of her otherwise captivating voice.

Tuesday, 19th.—M. de Starlimburg called to say that the messenger he expected on Thursday next had arrived yesterday, having left Paris only on Saturday—that he brings him positive orders to leave the country immediately; that he sets off to-morrow, and war, interminable war, is the consequence.†

Wednesday 20th.—Came home early, expecting M. de Staremberg, who had promised to see me before he went, between five and six. He came, and a very melancholy few moments we passed together. He is a good, honest, honourable man, whom one cannot know intimately without being attached to. I sent a little Scotch pebble ring by him to dear Madame de Staremberg.

Thursday, 28th.—Mr. Whitbread‡ called on me. Read my paper while he sat with me.§ Praised it as extremely clear and succinct. We talked over the subject. Curious

* 'Wonder! A Woman keeps a Secret.' By Susannah Centlivre. Born 1667; died 1722.

† Vide note to Nov. 22, 1807.

‡ Samuel Whitbread, Esq., son of a wealthy brewer; born 1758; married Lady Elizabeth, daughter of the first Earl Grey, 1789; came into Parliament the following year; was a zealous adherent of Mr. Fox, and continued a steady supporter of the Whig party; conducted the impeachment of Lord Melville; died by his own hand, July 1815, during a fit of mental derangement.—*Rose's Biog. Dict.*

§ To what paper Miss Berry refers does not appear.

details about the influence of poor Mr. Fox's illness upon the latter part of the last negociation.*

Went to the play. 'The Wanderer' (the story of the Pretender), under Swedish names. Very interesting from situations, but very poorly written.

After the play, went to Lady Donegal's, where came Colonel Eustace,† Lord Hutchinson's‡ aide-de-camp, who has been with him constantly at the Prussian and Russian head-quarters since he left England, in November, 1806. Curious details of the Russian army—never able to collect more than seventy thousand men—opposed by a hundred and seventy thousand French. The Russians totally without surgeons, hospitals, or drugs. Duke of Brunswick, received the wound in his eyes which killed him, in his coach.

Sunday, 31*st*.—Read through Roscoe's pamphlet and Spence's § 'England Independent of Commerce.'

Wednesday, February 10*th*.—At past eleven o'clock went to Devonshire House. Catalani singing in the saloon, Sapio accompanying. She had all her diamonds on, and entirely eclipsed Lady Harrowby, who was standing by her at the harpsichord.

Friday, 12*th*. —Went to dine at Mr. Knight's, in Soho

* 'In 1806 some pacificatory messages were interchanged between the French and English Governments, but it is probable that on neither side were they were very sincere.' Fox died at Chiswick in September 1806.—*Imp. Dict. of Univ. Biog.*

† Lieutenant-Colonel Henry Eustace, son of General Eustace, was on Sir Ralph Abercrombie's staff and accompanied him to Holland; he went with Lord Hutchinson afterwards to Russia, and followed the Russian army during the whole of the campaign of the French invasion of Russia. He was in constant employment for many years, and became secretary to the Duke of York when commander-in-chief. Died at Geneva, 1844.

‡ John Lord Hutchinson, brother of first Earl of Donoughmore, a distinguished general officer in the army, succeeded Sir Ralph Abercrombie in the command of the army in Egypt, and created Baron Hutchinson for his services in 1801; he died unmarried in 1825.

§ William Spence, author of a work on the 'Causes of the Distress of the West India Planters,' 'Agriculture the Source of the Wealth of Britain,' 1808; 'The Objections to the Corn Bill refuted.'

Square.* The party: Lord and Lady Oxford,† Mr. Lyttelton,‡ Mr. C. Moore, Mr. Rogers, and Mr. Lawrence,§ the painter,|| and Mrs. Damer. Looked over drawings, &c. &c. till near eleven o'clock.

Monday, 15*th*.—Dined at Mr. Angerstein's, with Mr. and Mrs. W. Locke, General Moore, &c. General Moore very entertaining in his account after dinner of the Queen of Naples at Palermo, and his conversations with her, by which I find that neither time nor misfortunes have altered her from what I knew her twenty years ago.

The following letter from Lord Erskine must relate to his pamphlet, written in 1797, 'On the Causes and Consequences of the Present War with France.' 'This pamphlet had an unprecedented sale, there being no less than forty-eight editions of it printed within a few months.' (*Watts's Dictionary.*) It is probable that the recent failure of Austrian intervention had produced some conversation between Miss Berry and Lord Erskine, which gave rise to his sending her a copy of his pamphlet, with his interesting account of the manner in which it was composed.

February 21st, 1808.

My dear Madam,—I send you the Pamphlet I alluded to last night; it was written on slips of paper in the midst of all the business which I was engaged in at the time—not at Home, but in open court whilst the causes were trying. When it was not my turn to examine a witness or to speak to the Jury, then I wrote a little bit; and so on by snatches; as there was not a moment to be lost in the crisis of *folly* which characterised,

* Payne Knight, Esq.

† Edward Harley, fifth Earl of Oxford; married, 1794, Jane Elizabeth, daughter of Rev. James Scott.

‡ Hon. William Henry Lyttelton, afterwards third baron Lyttelton, born 1783, married Lady Sarah Spencer 1813, died 1837.

§ Samuel Rogers the poet, author of 'Pleasures of Memory,' 'Italy,' &c.; born 1763, died 1855, in his ninety-third year.

|| Afterwards Sir Thomas Lawrence, the first portrait-painter of his time; born 1769, died 1830.

almost as much as at present, our unhappy country. You will not be surprised, therefore, at its incorrectness. I had not a moment to amend the text, much less to correct the press in the different editions; and since I have had leisure to look it over, I have only remarked that I have no more merit in my observations as a politician, than would belong to a medical man who should pronounce that a person under an unremitting course of a slow poison would come by it infallibly to a premature dissolution.

I have the Honor to be
Your faithful Humble Servt,
ERSKINE.

JOURNAL.

Tuesday, 23*rd*.—Went to the play. 'Kair; or Love in the Desert'—perfect, complete, and unintelligible nonsense from beginning to end, with some pretty painted scenes. The farce was Bannister and Mrs. Jordan in Jobson and Nell.* Her Nell is incomparable, but she was not in high spirits.

Thursday, *March* 3*rd*.—Dined at Mrs. Blair's with Mrs. Fox, Mr. Rogers, Mr. Brougham,† Mr. Mercer,‡ Mrs. Blair's own family, &c.

Agnes and I went to Catalani's, where was a party of thirty or forty; I think, except Mr. and Mrs. Trevor, Miss Tate, and ourselves, there was not another commoner in the room. While the music was going on, a supper was preparing below stairs, which we eat *by the nose*, each separate dish, and the whole together, in the room above.

Friday, 4*th*.—In the evening went with Lady Shaftes-

* 'Devil to Pay.'

† Afterwards Lord Brougham.

‡ George Mercer, afterwards George Mercer Henderson, Esq. of Fordel in Fifeshire, a property which he inherited from his aunt, the wife of Sir Philip Durham Henderson.

bury and Lady B. Ashley,* to Lady Abercorn's†—a great drag-net assembly, twenty women to one man.

Saturday, 5*th*.—Mr. Gell, Mr. Mercer, and Colonel Murray dined with us. In the evening came Mrs. D. and Sir H. Englefield. We had a great deal of drawing, talking, and laughing.

Sunday, 6*th*.—Went after church to Mrs. Damer's. Found Lord Dorchester‡ had died of an apoplectic fit that morning at ten o'clock. Went to Lady Elizabeth Whitbread's, where was a meeting of a great many of the party.

Tuesday, 8*th*.—In the morning I had a long and interesting conversation with Mr. Thornton§ about the principles of the Methodists, and about his father and education.

Wednesday, 9*th*.—I went in the evening to Mrs. D. Read 'Marmion,' just come out, to her.

Thursday, 10*th*.—Read some more of 'Marmion.'

Monday, 14*th*.—Began reading the 'Odyssey' of Homer in Pope's translation. Delighted with it.

Friday, 18*th*.—Breakfasted at nine o'clock with only Mrs. Benwell, Dr. Hind, and Mr. Loveday. Went before ten, we three in our carriage, and the three gentlemen in

* Barbara, Countess of Shaftesbury, daughter and heiress of Sir John Webb, Bart., of Oldstock House, co. Wilts. Lady Barbara Ashley, daughter of the above and of Anthony Ashley, fifth Earl of Shaftesbury, married, August 1814, to the Hon. William F. Spencer Ponsonby, third son of Frederick third Earl of Bessborough, created Lord de Mauley in 1838; she died 1844.

† John James, ninth Earl of Abercorn, married, 1800, his third wife Anne Jane, eldest daughter of Arthur second Earl of Arran and widow of Henry Hutton, Esq.

‡ Sir Guy Carleton, first Lord Dorchester, aged eighty-five, a distinguished general in the American war.

§ Mr. Henry Thornton, second son of John Thornton, a merchant, one of the leading characters of the 'Clapham Society;' for more than thirty years a member of Parliament; a voluminous writer on moral, religious, and political subjects; a man of universal liberality and benevolence.—Vide *Edin. Rev.*, July 1844.

another, to St. George's Church. Got out at the vestry door. Here the ceremony of registering the marriage was performed by the clerk, who then assisted Mr. Loveday in putting on canonicals. We went immediately into the church, where there was not another creature but ourselves and the clerk. The ceremony over, we returned to North Audley Street, where a second breakfast, &c. was set out ready for us in the back drawing-room. At Pen's earnest desire, nobody but themselves were asked to partake of it. Soon after twelve they set off for their own future habitation at Tendon, in Sussex.*

Monday, 21st.—In the evening with Lady Charlotte Campbell† to the Argyll Rooms. Got there near twelve. The concert was just over. Dancing soon after took place in the long room, fitted up with boxes at the end, and meant to be used as a theatre. All the rooms prettily fitted up. A long debate in both Houses made a great scarcity of men. The supper, upon tables for about eight people each, in a large low room below stairs.

Wednesday, 23rd.—In the evening, a large party at home. Gow, the Scotch fiddler, a second fiddle, and a harp, came to us at half-past nine, and played some Scotch airs to my father. Afterwards, when more people came, I proposed a reel to Lady Charlotte Campbell, and began with her myself, to set the others a-going, and then, in the same way, a country dance; but the English people, as usual, were shy, though there were four or five excellent couples standing by. Fifty people—nineteen women and thirty-one men—came; twelve supped in the back room, and six or eight in the front room; everybody seemed pleased, and some men who came late were not

* The bride was Mrs. Benwell; the bridegroom Dr. Hind.

† Charlotte Susan Maria, daughter of John fifth Duke of Argyll; married, first, Colonel John Campbell; secondly, Rev. Edward Bury. Lady Charlotte Campbell was attached to the household of the Princess of Wales, and is known to the literary world as the author of several works of fiction. Died, 1861.

gone at two o'clock in the morning. Gow's music cost me three guineas.

Saturday, 26*th*.—Dined at Mr. Samuel Turner's with Mr. Alexander Baring * (the author of the pamphlet on the Orders in Council), Mr. Sharpe the M.P. and twelve other people. I sat between Mr. Baring and Mr. Sharpe. Mr. Baring is rather a heavy-looking young man, with a hesitating manner; but seems very clear in his ideas and unassuming in his manners. Mr. Sharpe I have often seen before; he is clever, but I should suspect of little real depth of intellect.

Sunday, 27*th*.—Went in the morning after church to Mr. Gell's † house in Chapel Street. Found there Mr. Morritt, Sir J. Hall,‡ and Lord Selkirk.§ Looked over some of his drawings and plans of the Parthenon. All went together to Lord Elgin's Marbles. A second view delights one still more than the first, but the cold excessive.

Thursday, 31*st*.—Went in the morning to the British Museum with Lord Frederick Campbell and Mrs. D. to

* Alexander Baring, born 1774, second son of Sir Francis Baring, succeeded his father as head of the great commercial house in the city; created Baron Ashburton, April 10, 1835; died 1848.

† Afterward, Sir William Gell, a well-known archæologist, born 1777. He was sent on a mission to the Ionian islands in the beginning of the century, and knighted on his return in 1803. His first work was the 'Topography of Troy,' published in 1803; his next, 'Geography and Antiquities of Ithaca,' in 1807; and in 1810, 'The Itinerary of Greece, with a Commentary on Pausanias and Strabo.' Sir William Gell accompanied the Princess of Wales, as one of her chamberlains, when she left England in 1814; he quitted her service on account of his frequent attacks of gout, as he alleged when examined as a witness on her behalf in the House of Lords in 1820, but continued to reside in Italy. His other works were the 'Itinerary of the Morea,' 'Pompeiana: the Topography, Edifices, and Ornaments of Pompeii;' in 1823, the 'Narrative of his Journey in the Morea;' and lastly, in 1834, 'The Topography of Rome.' He died at Naples, 1836.

‡ Sir James Hall, Bart., of Douglas, born 1761; married a sister of the Earl of Selkirk; wrote a work on 'Gothic Architecture;' rendered great services to geological science. Died 1832.

§ Thomas fifth Earl of Selkirk, born 1771, died 1820.

see the new wing and the disposition of Mr. Townley's Marbles,* and the things taken by our army in Egypt. I think them, on the whole, well placed; some of Mr. Townley's are exquisitely beautiful, though much less wonderful and imposing than the battered remains at Lord Elgin's. The sarcophagus brought from Alexandria, and covered outside and inside with figures and hieroglyphics, called, I know not why, the, 'Tomb of Alexander,' by far the most beautiful and stupendous piece of Brescia I ever saw, with the most vivid colours in the largest pieces.†

Dined at Sir P. Francis',‡ with Lord § and Lady Keith,‖ Miss Elphinstone,¶ Mr. Elliot, Mr. Trevor, &c.

In the evening Miss Tate and Catherine Frances sung two or three songs beautifully.

Friday, April 1st.—Went to Mr. Knight's and Naldi Libboni, the Chevalier, and some of the Cornewalls,** sang, and admirably well. A much larger party than usual, but it is impossible to warm that room, with its iron roof and skylights.

Saturday, 2nd.—Took a long walk. Met Mr. Windham, who accompanied me, and was very agreeable. In the evening at a pleasant party at Lady Donegal's. Anacreon Moore sang a great deal—his old things, all the prettiest.

Sunday, 3rd.—At eleven I went to Mrs. Villiers's,††

* Mr. Townley's collection was bought for the British Museum in 1805 for the sum of 28,200*l.*—*Cunningham's London.*

† Parliament granted 35,000*l.* for the purchase of the Elgin Marbles.

‡ Sir P. Francis, the supposed author of the Letters of Junius; born 1740, died 1818.

§ Lord Keith. The Hon. George Keith Elphinstone, created Baron and Viscount Keith for his distinguished services as a naval commander, died 1823.

‖ Lady Keith, eldest Miss Thrale.

¶ Afterwards Countess de Flahault; daughter of Lord Keith.

** Daughters of Sir George Cornewall, Bart., of Moccas Court, Herefordshire.

†† Hon. Mrs. Villiers, daughter of Admiral and Lady Mary Forbes, married to the Hon. J. C. Villiers, afterwards Earl of Clarendon.

where was an assembly in the lower apartment—like all her parties, a great many fine ladies, and all the fine men. A man in boots and a round hat, very drunk, walked in from the street to the middle of the first room, and was turned out by the gentlemen, and pushed out by the servants from the hall. At the street door he drew a sword from a stick, and was poking about with it, when Henry Bouverie broke it short off, and the watch carried the man, whoever he might be, to the watch-house.

Thursday, 7*th.*—I went to Lady Caroline Lamb's.* An immense assembly. We came away at half-past twelve, and walked beyond the Admiralty to the carriage. Many of the company were not away till near three, and the Prince of Wales and a very few persons supped below stairs in Lady Melbourne's apartment, and were not gone till past six. Sheridan of the number, who was completely drunk.

Saturday, 9*th.*—Went to the play, 'The World;' less bad than most modern comedies, because *aiming*, at least, at character, and Elliston acting admirably a character evidently taken from Belfield, in Miss Burney's 'Cecilia.'

Monday, 11*th.*—Went to Harcourt House. Saw both Lord and Lady Harcourt.† The latter quite amusing in her attempts at being *easy*! In vain; she never can, in spite of all her endeavours, for a moment drop the hoop and lappets! The house an exact French hotel, but dirty and wanting to be brushed up, and looking no more comfortable, than its inhabitants.

Tuesday, 12*th.*—Went to Little Strawberry.

Wednesday, 20*th.*—It froze last night hard, and some of the snow still lies upon the ground. At night finished

* Lady Caroline Lamb, daughter of third Earl of Bessborough; born 1785, married to the Hon. William Lamb 1805, died 1848. Author of a novel called 'Glenarvon.'

† George Simon Harcourt, second Earl and Viscount Harcourt; born 1736, succeeded his father 1777; married, 1765, Elizabeth, daughter of George Lord Vernon; died 1809.

Miss Warren's novel * by galloping over half the pages; human patience could not regularly wade through a series of adventures without *ensemble*, of violent situations without interest or probability, and of characters all equally pious or equally profligate. The author is, I dare say, an excellent good creature, but she had better do anything than endeavour to pourtray her fellow-creatures.

Thursday, 21*st*.—Worked at my French Letters most of the morning. In the evening began reading Ashe's † 'Travels in America,' in the north-western settlements, behind the United States.

Friday, 22*nd*.—The weather continues cold, stormy, and rainy. Worked at the Letters. In the evening Ashe's Travels again. They are, I think, very entertaining in spite of an abominable style, which aims at being *fine writing*, without being grammar and without being English. But the wonderful country he describes makes every account of it which one sees and feels is written on the spot, very interesting.

Saturday, 23*rd*.—I began botching out some sort of preface to the Letters.

Sunday, 24*th*.—Worked at my preface in the morning. A cold wet day. Not at church. Sir Thomas Liddell ‡ called. In the evening, after dinner, I read aloud the sketch of my preface, and finished the evening with Ashe's Travels, which are very entertaining.

Tuesday, 26*th*.—I watched the gardener sow all the annuals in all the flower-borders, which kept me out with my wheelbarrow in the garden till past three o'clock; then stuck to my French Letters.

* 'Conrade, or the Gamesters.' Novel by Caroline Matilda Warren. Published 1806.

† Thomas Ashe, Esq., travelled in America in the year 1806 for the purpose of exploring the rivers of Alleghany, Monongahela, Ohio, and the Mississippi, and ascertaining the produce and condition of their banks; published 1808. He was the author of many other works.—*Watts's Dictionary*.

‡ Afterwards Lord Ravensworth.

Wednesday, 27*th.*—Very cold. Worked at the French Letters. In the evening Mrs. D., and Ashe's Travels. Letters as usual.

Sunday, May 1*st.*—A beautiful warm sunny May day. Went to P. Staremberg's to see poor Cliff, little George's nurse, who remains in the house. I know few things more melancholy than to visit the empty house of intimate friends, where one has passed many many days in cheerful company. A thousand recollections immediately rise to one's memory, from which everything tiresome, or dull, or disagreeable, has vanished with the intermediate time, and nothing but what is charming (and consequently the more to be regretted) remains, But recollections of past comforts or pleasures may certainly be reckoned, however melancholy, among the pleasures of this life. I never shun them.

In the evening, Ashe's Travels as usual.

Tuesday, 3*rd.*—Dined at Lady Melbourne's. Went up to the top of the house with Lady Caroline Lamb to see her little boy asleep, who a very few hours after was seized with fits and his life despaired of. He is too big of his age—only eight months.*

Thursday, 5*th.*—Saw Lady Harriet Cavendish.† She brought us the first report of the horrible shipwreck of poor Lord Royston in the Baltic.‡ From that instant one could think of nothing but Lady Hardwicke having arrived in town late the night before to meet such dreadful intelligence, and perhaps still more dreadful doubt, for some doubt there was of the names of all the persons

* George Augustus Frederick Lamb, only son of the late Lord Melbourne; born August 1807; died 1836.

† Daughter of the Duke of Devonshire, afterwards Countess Granville.

‡ Lord Royston was shipwrecked at sea on the 7th of April by the stranding of the ship Agatha, of Lubeck, in a storm, not far from Memel. Lord Royston would have been twenty-four years old had he lived to the 7th of May. He had been four years absent from the country.—*Annual Register.*

that had perished. I instantly sent a note to Lady Charlotte Lindsay. She had not a ray of hope. At two o'clock I left town again. I felt quite glad to be here. Of my former vivacity and eagerness I have not a tithe part, though quite enough for my age and situation; the world, when one knows it well, is a dull business. Whereas the dull business of the country, particularly at this season, has something quiet, soothing, and at the same time occupying, in it. At least I feel it suits me more than ever it did before.

Friday, 6th.—Read my French Letters. Mrs. D. and I finished Ashe's Travels.

Saturday, 7th.—I worked in my greenhouse all the morning. Agnes arrived from town. She had seen Lady C. Lindsay, and heard from her everything that was to be heard of the poor Hardwickes. God help them!

Tuesday, 10th.—I began reading aloud Gell's 'Ithaca.'*

Wednesday, 11th.—In the evening, Gell's 'Ithaca.'

Saturday, 14th.—My plants moved out of the greenhouse, and I, as usual, heartily fatigued with helping to place them. Walked in the evening into the meadows by the river-side, and did nothing all day but enjoy the beauty of the season.

Sunday, 15th.—Another delicious day. Walked to church. Called at Sunbury—Sir John Legarde's—a remarkably pretty villa, close upon the bank of the river. Walked round the shrubbery and garden with Lady Legarde, and Mrs. Grant† (the writer of 'The Letters from the Mountains'), who is at present their guest. Her figure and manners awkward, but not the least vulgarity

* Published in 1808.

† Mrs. Grant, of Laggan, Inverness-shire (her maiden name was Campbell), the author of various poems and other works; 'Letters from the Mountains' being the real correspondence of a lady between the years 1773 and 1803.—*Watts's Dictionary.*

in her manners or conversation. She had heard of us somehow or other, and said she was much pleased to make our acquaintance. We saw Sir John just before we were going away, in his wheeling-chair. His legs are perfectly helpless, and this before he is fifty years old! He has a handsome lively countenance.*

Tuesday, 17*th*.—My day spent as usual—a good deal of gardening and idling, and a little reading of my French Letters. Read in the 'Times' the confirmation of the wreck and positive loss of Lord Royston.

Saturday, 21*st*.—Went to Richmond. Sat half an hour with Madame de Cambis. She happened to be in good humour, and I made her talk of Madame du Deffand and old French times, and she was very entertaining. From her I went to Lady Di Beauclerc,† and carried her the novel I promised her. Heard that Ronald would certainly set out for Portsmouth that night. In the evening read my French Letters.

Sunday, 22*nd*.—Wrote something that will serve either as preface or *avant-propos* to the Letters.

Thursday, 26*th*.—Finished Madame du Deffand's voluminous correspondence with Lord Orford, having marked such letters as I might select to re-select for publication. From so many, enough, and more than enough, may certainly be taken from each year.

Friday, 27*th*.—In the evening began selecting the first year of the Letters, and marking passages.

Thursday, June 2*nd*.—I began reading aloud Mr. Fox's historical work, in the beautiful large-paper copy which Robert Ferguson has given me.

Friday, 3*rd*.—I continued reading Fox's work. It is

* Sir John Legarde, Bart., married, 1802, Jane, daughter of Henry Aston, Esq. Sir John died two months after this visit, and was succeeded by his brother.

† Lady Diana Spencer, daughter of Charles Duke of Marlborough, married Topham Beauclerk, 1768.

very well to read it once out; but it suggests so much thought, and so many new views of things, that I shall read it over more than once to myself in a very different manner from what I am now doing.

Thursday, 9*th*.—Dined at Lady Donegal's with Agnes. Philippa (Godfrey), Charles Moore, and Anacreon Moore at dinner. I praised highly the two poems ('Corruption' and 'Intolerance') that I had been reading in the morning, before the author (little Moore), without knowing it. After dinner he owned the fact, and was much pleased with my unsuspicious praise. Moore sang.

Friday, 10*th*.—Between eleven and twelve I walked to Grosvenor Street to see Joanna Baillie; then to the Hardwickes. I saw them all, literally all, except little Charlie, who is returned to school: first, Lord Hardwicke, who controlled himself, but soon left me; then Catherine * and Caroline.† With Catherine I was much affected, for I was very unwell, and unable to contain my feelings; nor was it necessary with her. With Lady Hardwicke I feared it would; but this was not the case. As soon as I came up to her, she threw herself into my arms, and wept as heartily as myself. It is a great relief to me having seen them all; but I left them with my eyes swollen out of my head, and quite unfit to go anywhere but to Lady G. Morpeth, to whom I could say what I had been doing.

Saturday, 11*th*.—In the evening I read 'Corruption' and 'Intolerance' aloud.

Sunday, 12*th*.—Drove with Phil. Cayley to Rayman's Castle; walked through the meadows, crossed the Richmond ferry, and straight up the hill, which Phil. Cayley had never seen, and which has always new beauties even to those much accustomed to it. The door of the Star and Garter (now shut as an hotel), being open, we

* Lady Catherine Yorke, afterwards Countess of Caledon.

† Lady Caroline Yorke, afterwards Countess of Somers.

walked in, and a civil quondam servant of the house showed us the rooms. Dismal history from the woman of the foolish man who made these great additions to the former house;—ruined himself and died in prison; his wife, seeing that all was going wrong, became insane, and died before him.

The following extract of a letter from Mr. Greathead to Miss Berry belongs to this date. This is the first mention of the infancy of Leamington. Its present state has fully justified Mr. Greathead's sanguine views:—

Guy's Cliff, June 13, 1808.

. . . . . I ought to tell you that if you have a mind to make a fortune by speculations at Leamington Spa, I am your man: by the foot, by the yard, by the rood, or by the acre. I will let you land for garden ground, sell you stone, or sell you clay; you shall have salt water, or fresh water, anything you please; for if we could but get you and Agnes into the undertaking, what a place should we make of it! Cheltenham should expire with envy, and Bath itself turn pale . . . .

Tuesday, 21*st*.—Went to Lady Shaftesbury's ball—a very fine ball. The first quadrille began soon after twelve.

Lady B. Ashley
and
Mr. Delme.

Miss Di Bouverie
and
Mr. Mercer.

Miss Doyle
and
Mons. de Barblanc.

Miss Johnston
and
Mr. Keppel Craven.

The ladies were uniformly dressed, and very prettily, in white and silver. They danced admirably, without mistakes or *boggle* whatsoever. Lady Barbara really danced better than anybody I ever saw, either here or at Paris. The second quadrille was —

Lady M. Lowther
and
The Marquis of Tweedale.

Miss Cholmley
and
Mr. Mildmay.

Miss Pigou
and
Edward Montague.

Lady C. Lowther
and
The Marquis of Hartington.

It was less well danced, but without mistakes. Every creature was standing up upon chairs and benches to see these quadrilles. There was a most magnificent supper for 400 people below stairs.

Friday, 24*th*. — Mr. Thornton's breakfast at three o'clock. The Duchess of Brunswick and the Duke of Gloucester there; dined with about eighteen in a separate tent. The Duchess of Brunswick not so like either to the King or late Duke of Gloucester as I expected. They say the likeness is more in her manner of speaking.

Thursday, 30*th*.—In the evening I read 'Barillon's Letters' in Mr. Fox's Appendix.

Saturday, *July* 2*nd*.—Between two and three o'clock set out for Wimbledon. A fine sunny day; scene beautiful; all the London world there. Dined in a tent. Lady Rosslyn, Mr. Rogers, Lord Erskine, Price (father and son) *, and Charles Stuart (Blantyre), &c. joined us; Mr. Windham came, and had a talk with us.

The Spanish Deputies † were at the fête, and Lord Holland, who speaks Spanish, was doing the honours to them. The Viscount Materosa, on whose subject our

* Sir Uvedale and Sir Robert Price.

† In May 1808, deputies were sent from Spain to England to solicit succour, and to arouse the popular sentiment in favour of the Spanish cause.—*Art. from Ed. Rev.*, p. 306.

newspapers are so fertile, a little fair, fattish lad. One of the others Don — de Vega, a good olive-coloured looking Spaniard, with large grave black eyes; but none of them seem to have at all the *tournure* of people of rank. They are probably provincial nobles, or what we should call country gentlemen, who perhaps have never seen Madrid in their lives; but not the less enemies to the French and the affronting usurpation of Bonaparte.

Sunday, 17*th.*—Spoke to General Moore in Bond Street; welcomed him from Sweden*, and sent my hearty wishes along with him to Spain, whither I believe he is going immediately.

Tuesday, 19*th.*—Arrived at Guy's Cliff; received at this prettiest of places with the hearty welcome that particularly belongs to the owners. I felt only sorry I was going to quit it so soon. In the evening, Frederick North†, and with him Frederick Douglas, arrived from Wroxton, in their way to a tour through Ireland. Frederick North is always entertaining to the head, but less gratifying to the heart; and in this is much inferior to his sisters, who are often quite as agreeable as himself.

Wednesday, 20*th.* — Walked before breakfast alone, entirely round Guy's Cliff, into every hole and cranny of my last year's haunt, sitting down several times near the river, and I admired it more than ever. Mr. Greathead was making the same round at the same time with F. North; but I avoided them, and indulged in solitude, particularly grateful just now to my mind, which, either from the weakness of my late illness, or 'glooms congenial' to it, is much depressed,— and I enjoyed the sort of tranquil quiet melancholy which crept over me at Guy's

* A land force of 10,000 men, under the command of Sir John Moore, was sent in the month of May to assist Sweden against a combined attack from Russia, France, and Denmark. On the 17th of May this army reached Gottenburg, but was not permitted to land.

† Frederick North, afterwards fifth Earl of Guildford.

Cliff. I left it this day with the very agreeable impression of a place to which no one unpleasant remembrance is attached, and where I wish to find myself again.

Mr. Greathead went with us as far as Kenilworth, to show me Sir J. Lake's house, with which he has indeed done wonders, and much more than ever I expected. Here we parted. We continued our route to Coleshill, seventeen miles from Warwick, to Mr. Palmer's. Their house is the vicarage at the end of a large village-town. Inside it is comfortable, but horrible red-brick and very ugly on the outside.

Thursday, 21*st.*—Walked in the morning with Mr. Palmer and Miss de Visme to Coleshill Hall, a very old house belonging to Lord Digby. It came into the Digby family in the reign of Henry VII. [? Henry III.], being part of the confiscations of Simon de Montfort, and was mentioned then as an old house. It has, according to the fashion of those days, a large hall on one side the entrance, with a buttery-hatch and a gallery over it, communicating to the upper part of the house. At one of the entrances to the hall hangs, by a chain, a large whetstone, which has been there time immemorial, and certainly proves great antiquity in that part of the house. The rest consists of small uninteresting rooms, and a gallery of no imposing dimensions, now entirely falling to decay, and uninhabitable, though there are still some remnants of furniture. The park, from which all good timber has been cut down, is let to a farmer for grazing; and Lord Digby, to whom it belongs, lives entirely at Sherborne Castle, in Dorsetshire.

Friday, 22*nd.*—Left Mr. Palmer's, and took the route of Lancaster and the Lakes. Stopped at Lichfield to see the Cathedral. Its front is fine, with its two spires, and with the number of figures and tabernacles for figures with which it is ornamented, and a very handsome window of tracery over the great door. The inside of a

Gothic cathedral with three aisles must always be fine. This is less beautiful than Lincoln, though about the same size, and has few old monuments in it. The choir is the longest I remember to have seen. The whole presents itself well from the Close, which is well kept, and has handsome houses in it.

In the Cathedral are two cenotaphs exactly alike, and in no very good taste, to Johnson and to Garrick, with inscriptions in gilt letters so put on that one cannot read them ; and another, executed by some Staffordshire lady, to Lady M. W. Montague, celebrating and thanking her for bringing inoculation into Europe.

From Guy's Cliff to Lichfield is a very flat uninteresting country, with no fine trees or any outline of horizon. After Lichfield it improves, especially about Wolseley Bridge. Then come a number of noblemen's seats, with woods, which much ornament the face of the country. The road winds about Trentham* for a considerable time. In going to Newcastle-under-Lyme, we turned a mile out of our road to see one of the great potteries, of which this part of the country is the centre. It was Spode's—a very great one—above 400 persons employed. We saw all the various operations of common and fine porcelain, and amongst others that most curious one of stamping on the blue and white patterns—done by applying to them a print upon very thin prepared paper, which, after it has left its impression upon the cup, saucer, &c., is rubbed off entirely with common water, without deranging the impression. The country from this side Wolseley Bridge, where the manufactures commence, is very populous, and all the villages and towns black with the coal-smoke of the number of furnaces. Between Wolseley Bridge and Stone, at Rugeley—a very pretty neat village—is Lord Curzon's house, prettily

* Seat of the Duke of Sutherland.

surrounded by wood *; and further on, Lord Anson's† and Lord Talbot's more extensive grounds and woods ‡ make a fine appearance. At Sandon, between Stone and Newcastle, Lord Harrowby has nearly finished a column to the memory of Mr. Pitt, on an elevated sort of terrace near the road. Stone is a dirty-looking little town. Newcastle little less black. The whole of this manufacturing country, and particularly about the potteries which lay between and about Stone and Newcastle, is prettily waved and wooded, dotted all over with houses, and would be pretty, were it not disfigured by the smoke of the furnaces, and the ugly shape of the houses—little new square boxes of the reddest brick, with roofs just fitting them like the lids of snuff-boxes. They are building everywhere, and all the towns and villages increasing.

The roads through Staffordshire and Cheshire, which we entered at Congleton, and left at Warrington, are good, and this part of Cheshire is a rich enclosed pasture country, well-wooded, with comfortable-looking villages and fine cattle, neatly-thatched cottages and well-cultivated farms. At Warrington one again enters the manufacturing regions; and Warrington is a large, dirty, black, bustling, narrow-streeted town, with a number of canals on all sides. Wigan and Chorley are of the same description—full of furnaces, cotton-mills, steam-engines, and foundries.

Saturday, 23rd.—Left Newcastle in the morning. The road from Warrington to Chorley is a positive *chemin ferré*, paved with round stones. At Wigan, much coarse muslin and much of the Lancashire sheeting is made. At Chorley, got rid of red brick; and an immense number of new small houses, and almost villages, built and building, all stone. Fine views, bounded by an horizon of hills, and intersected by canals. Arrived at Preston.

* Hagley. † Shugborough. ‡ Ingestre.

Sunday, 25th.—Preston is a handsome town, with a wide, well-built street and a large square market-place, in which are two curious old houses, one of wood and the other of stone, both, I should think, dating before Elizabeth.

Preston is much blackened, like all the towns of this part of the country, with coal smoke.

Garstang is a small town, and near it a number of manufactures, smoke and black. The castle (the fortress of John of Ghent's ducal capital) stands nobly on a height at the end of the town. The gateway tower is very fine; the keep and two other square towers remain, and are united together and with the gateway tower by modern buildings in the same style of architecture. It is the county gaol, and admirably clean and well kept. The arrangements made on Mr. Howard's plan—sixteen prisoners the greatest number that can be in any one division, that division having a yard to itself, water in the midst of it, and each prisoner having a separate clean whitewashed cell and bed. No irons put on to any, even felons, that are not refractory. There are in the prison now, including debtors and those undergoing the punishments of imprisonment for different lengths of time, no fewer than 260 persons, of which above a hundred are felons, including eighteen women. Of this hundred, forty-five are to take their trial at the ensuing assizes next month. Of this amazing number for a county gaol, the neighbourhood of Manchester and Liverpool is given as a reason, and, I fear, a very sufficient one. The late riots among the manufacturers have likewise increased it, as six or seven of the principal ringleaders are there for trial. Still, the number is sad for a single county.* We went all over the prison with a very civil, intelligent

* The number of prisoners in Lancaster Gaol in May, 1860:—Debtors, 79; untried criminals, none; tried criminals, 58: making a total of 137.

gaoler. Among the prisoners for trial next month is a merchant worth above seventy thousand pounds, for the supposed poisoning of his housekeeper. He was (by the equality of our laws) in one of the above-mentioned yards with several other felons, but remains always within, and carefully avoids showing himself.

At Burton, a clean white village; it being Sunday, the Volunteers of the place were drawn up before the inn, and very good-looking, clean, stout lads they were.

Kendal is a picturesque town of white rough-cast houses, scattered about a green valley, with a fine horizon of hills. Took an evening walk upon a sort of quay to the stream, from whence is seen a view of the old castle situated upon the top of a green knoll. Being Sunday, the whole scene was enlivened by groups of people walking about.

In the principal street, all houses on the left side have large open entrances, through which one sees gardens climbing up the sides of a hill, very like many small towns in Switzerland.

Monday, 25*th*.—Left Kendal for Ambleside. The road winds through a variety of highly cultivated valleys, and a constantly changing horizon of distant mountains. About eight miles from Kendal we first came in sight of Windermere, with its beautifully curved shores, green cultivated banks, and wooded islands. It is pretty, excessively pretty, and if it had never been compared to the lakes in Switzerland would be more so. But this comparison has just a similar effect to declaring some well-written modern play to be very like Shakespeare—it recalls all the sublime perfections of the model, and all the weakness of the copy. We passed through the village of Bowness, and continued our route five miles along the borders of the lake, sometimes intercepted by trees, sometimes, as at Lowood, close to the shore, and uninterruptedly beautiful. The inn at Lowood is a single house. The valleys and rides about Ambleside must be delightful, and the mountains at this end of the lake are much more considerable than at the other.

In the evening Miss de Visme and I took a little scrambling walk up the glen to a mill for turning bobbins for the manufacturers of Manchester, &c.

Tuesday, 26th.—Miss de Visme and I took advantage of a fair gleam to walk up to a very pretty fall of water, called Stockhill Force. The glen is well wooded, and the fall is finely broken into two streams by a large mass of rock covered with trees, and fantastic roots making their appearance on every side.

Just as we were stepping into the coach to go to Keswick, a chaise with Mr. Law and his friend Mr. Pakenham (Lord Longford's brother) drove up to the door. We invited them to follow us as fast as they could. At Rydal went to see the waterfall near Sir Daniel Flemming's. There, caught in such heavy rain that we were forced to seek shelter in some cottages near Sir Daniel's gate, and a more comfortable scene than the inside of all the cottages exhibited I have not seen in this part of the world. The one we now entered was that of a mere labourer, with a young wife and three children; it had every necessary comfort. The good woman was making girdle-cakes of oatmeal (here the bread of the poor) over a fire of fern, by which we dried our clothes. We were nearly half an hour in her house, occupying her fire and in the way of her work, and yet she and her sister-in-law would hardly accept a trifle for their hospitality. Here Mr. Law and Mr. Pakenham came up with us. The rain was unabating, so we continued our route to Keswick, passing round the side of Grasmere.

I was more pleased with Leathe's Water, another small lake which had a singularly quiet and pastoral character. Perhaps on a fine sunny day I might have preferred Grasmere; but the solitary unenlivened character of

Leathe's Water associated itself better to the grey quiet wet evening in which I saw it.

Before we came to Leathe's Water, in a valley under Helvellyn, down the side of which many torrents were tumbling, one was so impetuous that on arriving at a little roadside alehouse, we found the people all watching the violence of this *gill*, over which a water-spout (no uncommon thing among these hills) had burst, and brought down such a quantity of water, that the bridge, some hundred yards off, was entirely covered by the torrent that was flowing *over* as well as *under* it, that the parapets were forced down, and they knew not if the bridge had not given way. Here two travellers in a whiskey were already stopped, and here Mr. Law and Mr. Pakenham again came up to us. I did not think there was a chance of our passing for many hours, if then; but the two men in the whiskey having got over, and the landlord and five or six other men promising to help us, we sent the coach first, and our three selves followed in Mr. Law's hack chaise; he and Mr. Pakenham wading through the water by us. We all arrived safely on the other side the torrent, and reached Keswick soon after 8 o'clock P.M.

Wednesday, 27*th*.—Between nine and ten o'clock went upon the lake with Mr. Hutton, the guide, in his boat. We were rowed down the side of the lake, by Mr. Pocklington's house, in whose ground is a beautiful cascade, called the Barrow Fall. The water falls in two lengths; and as one can see it from below, at the middle, and from above, and can approach quite close to its edge, it is particularly *enjoyable*.

Mr. Pocklington's taste in architecture is certainly much less perfect than in waterfalls. He has built no less than three houses on the borders of this lake, all, one uglier than the other.

The island at the Keswick end of the lake he bought

some twenty years ago for 300*l.*, and sold within these ten or twelve years for 1700*l.*—so enormously is the value of land raised upon the borders of these lakes; two acres of pasture were sold last year in the neighbourhood of a gentleman's cottage for 320*l.*, and land in the same circumstances is sometimes let for seven and eight pounds an acre.

We rowed to Lodore, first passing close to one of the wonders of this lake, the Floating Islands, which occasionally come up—literally come up, for its appearance is of two or three acres of coarse short grass which had been long submerged. The surface is just above the water, and its sides under water seem in places as if rent away from a steep bank of earth, the water being several fathoms deep immediately at its edge.

For twenty-five or thirty years none of these had appeared, till within these last three or four years. The one we saw had come up only just a week before. They talk of the lake being in great agitation without any wind at the time of the production of these islands, and that they are always the forerunners of broken bad weather. A strong mephitic smell, too, is said to issue from the ground, if pierced when it first makes its appearance.

Lodore is an occasional torrent, falling between the very high cliffs, beautiful, half covered with wood and vegetation, and having deeply worn the great masses of rocks over which it falls. We saw it luckily with a very sufficient quantity of water. It never falls in a sheet or large body, but bounds from rock to rock in a most striking and picturesque manner.* A chaise was waiting

* Here it comes sparkling,
And there it lies darkling;
Now smoking and frothing
Its tumult and wrath in,
Till in this rapid race
On which it is bent,
It reaches the place
Of its steep descent.—*Southey's Fall of Lodore.*

to carry us up Borrow Dale, whose jaws, as the rocky hills at its entrance are called, form a principal part of the beauty of this end of the lake. Borrow Dale is really grand. It is the first of this scenery that I have thought so. A very passable mountain road leads to the Bowden Stone, a great mass of rock, which at some distant period the frost and wet have detached from the left-hand hill. Here there is a cottage or two, and a very fine rugged mountain view on every side. Let nobody who comes to the lakes miss Borrow Dale, nor the fine view of the lake with the background of Skiddaw.

It poured of rain before we got back to the alehouse at Lodore.

We continued our row along the lake, passing by the little bay which Lord W. Gordon has beautifully ornamented, but which is shut out from the rest of the world. Nobody is ever allowed to land, under all sorts of penalties to the boatmen. Set off for Penrith.

Thursday, 28th.—Mr. Law and Mr. Pakenham breakfasted with us, and we started in two hired chaises for Ullswater. A boat was in readiness for us, and in about two hours and a half it carried us the whole length of the lake. Here, at the commencement of Patterdale, we found another little country inn. Two carriages were already before us. A neat clean bedroom was all they had to offer us, and it was well we got possession of that, for there arrived afterwards no less than four other carriages full of people. Some were obliged to walk in the garden, while others dined in the rooms; and yet, in spite of all this, the good woman of the house gave us an excellent dinner, without hurry, confusion, or ill-humour. I am much pleased with what I have seen of the character of these peasants. They are civil and obliging in their manners, willing to enter into discourse, intelligent about the scenes around them, and, I think, by no means imposing in their demands.

The chief beauty of Ullswater is the abruptness with which many of the fells go into the lake, but is much better seen from the shore than from the water itself. We arrived late at Penrith, and I had the comfort of hearing from my sister.

Friday, 29th.—Breakfasted at Carlisle, and arrived at Moffat between eight and nine in the evening.

The enormous long stage of twenty-one miles between Longtown and Lockerby is now divided into two. It is quite remarkable the great difference in the appearance, habits, and manners of the people, and of their houses between Carlisle and only twenty miles from it in Scotland, and this without any wide river or chain of mountains to separate them. The division is only by a little insignificant stream about three miles from Longtown.

Saturday, 30th.—Left Moffat. Took the road to Lanark. The road by the fall of Corra Linn is three miles out of the straight road to Lanark, and is a steep descent into the glen, where runs the Clyde, and where stand the great cotton-mills. We then drove into very beautifully-wooded grounds along the high bank of the river, belonging to Lady Ross. The whole river precipitates itself into a rocky sort of recess, well overgrown with wood on all sides, and is well worth seeing, though much less romantic than Lodore. In the Glen we passed the enormous cotton works, where above 1,500 persons are employed, and which of itself, with the habitations and shops necessary for the workpeople, make a town.

Lanark, about a mile or two distant, is small and insignificant, with a large dirty Scotch inn.* The descent on leaving Lanark, down to the bridge over the Clyde, is beautiful, and the whole road for seven or eight miles afterwards along the high bank of the river, a most charming drive. Lord Glencairn's house is most happily

* The population of Lanark (burgh), is now calculated at 5,305.

placed on the opposite side of the stream, and its little turrets and half-Gothic appearance admirably suited to its situation. It is a new house added to an old one, and I admired its effect, illumined with an evening sun, throwing light and shade on all its little projections, and shining on its gilded vanes. It was nine o'clock when we reached Hamilton, and I felt impatient to get on to Bothwell,* where I knew I should be anxiously expected, though I hardly flattered myself I should meet with so warm a reception as that I received from every individual of the family.

Friday, August 5th.—In the evening, loitered near the house, in admiration of the moon, most singularly beautiful at this place, where it silvers the whole reach of the Clyde, is again caught through the trees, and most picturesquely reflects on the towers of the old castle.

Monday, 8th.—Went to Hamilton Palace with Lady Douglas † and party to see the house. Some of the portraits (whole lengths) are admirable, and this duke and his son have brought there a considerable collection of really good Italian pictures. Amongst those in the gallery is one of the late Duchess of Argyll ‡ (I believe by Gavin Hamilton), which, without being a good picture, gives an exquisite idea of her beauty. The head greatly resembles that of the Venus de Medici, not in adjustment, but in features. It is, of all the ill-arranged, awkward, melancholy great houses I ever saw, the very worst.

Sunday, 14th.—Sat till dinner-time in Lady Douglas's dressing-room, reading old letters to her grandmother, the Duchess of Argyll, from *her* mother, Mrs. Warburton, and to Lady Greenwich § from the Duchess of Queensbury

* Seat of Lord Douglas.

† Lady Douglas was sister to Harry third Duke of Buccleugh; married, 1783.

‡ Elizabeth, daughter of John Gunning, Esq.

§ Caroline, daughter of John second Duke of Argyll, created Baronness of Greenwich, 1767; married, first, Francis, son of Duke of Buccleugh;

and several other persons. Remarkable form and expressions of respect in the letters of Mrs. Warburton to her duchess daughter.

Friday, 19*th*.—In the morning, drove to Douglas Park, between four and five miles from here, belonging to a Mrs. Douglas, a young widow. The place uncommonly pretty. The grounds and garden are a peninsula, round which the river Calder, a mountain stream, runs over shelves of rock, and through high well-wooded banks. A bowling-green, surrounded by very tall fine old limes, which, from the growth of trees in this country, must be 200 years old. No remembrance is preserved of their being planted. In the evening Lady Douglas proposed a walk, though all the colours of the prospect were buried in one, twilight tint. When we came in sight of the cottage, the reason for our walk was cleared up — its little pediment was prettily lighted up with coloured lamps, among the fresh green fern-leaves with which the front of the pediment was tastefully covered, and joining on to the honeysuckles which flaunt up its pillars and about its sides. The inside, too, was lighted with pretty little transparent lamps; upon the table two large flower-pots, and the tea set out with the cottage tea-things. It was very pretty, and well suited to the place. I should not forget that in the middle of the little pediment, over the porch, was my cypher, in a flowery transparency, which Caroline * herself had traced.

Colonel Cadogan †, who had been fishing here all day, joined us at tea. I regretted for the young ones that there was not more company, both to admire their taste and add to their gaiety; but they seemed not to want it,

secondly, Charles Townshend, second son of William Viscount Townshend. She died 1794.

* Hon. Caroline Douglas, daughter of Lord Douglas; married, 1810, to Captain, afterwards Admiral, Sir G. Scott.

† Colonel Cadogan, probably Hon. Henry, Lieutenant-Colonel 71st Foot; born 1780; killed in the battle of Vittoria, 1813; son of first Earl of Cadogan.

and for myself, I was as much pleased and surprised as any child could have been.

Saturday, 20*th*.—Walked on the other side of the water to my little favourite ravine, just under the remains of Blantyre Priory; again admired its singular beauty, and the grandeur of its parts, though the whole thing is only a narrow gully. The day and the spot were so delicious for loitering about, that I began cutting my name on the bark of a tree in the ravine, while the others sat by. The view of the Bothwell ruins from the Priory is beautiful.

Joanna Baillie was born at the Manse at Bothwell, which explains the allusions in the letter addressed to her by Miss Berry, dated August 23rd, 1808: —

Bothwell Castle, Tuesday, 23rd August, 1808.

DEAR JOANNA, — You and I have crossed over and figured in, in an odd way this last year. I wish there had been any *setting and footing together*, in the course of our jigging about. —I now in Scotland, and you in England — I yesterday at Millheugh, and you perhaps at Little Strawberry Hill. What a pretty place Millheugh is! I walked all down the rocky bed of the river below the bridge, and crossed over the *stepping stones* and back again, merely for the pleasure of doing it— and then went all round the house at Millheugh and to the wooden bridge which looks at the little cascade up the green walk by the side of the stream. We saw not a human creature either to welcome or forbid us their premises, which being all open, we committed no trespass. I tried the echoes with some lines of Basil; but they were dumb, and only muttered in return for your name something about muslin at Glasgow, a pattern of a handkerchief, and some stories of the poor in the village. Your heroic muse should have taught them better in such a romantic spot.

I have been over, too, at my own dear little ravine at Blantyre; and if you go there again, you will see Berina (my name in Arcadia) cut upon one of the largest trees by my own fair hand on the 20th August, 1808.

To J. Baillie.

The following letter from Miss Berry is addressed to her cousin, Robert Ferguson, Esq.: —

Letter on Spain.

Bothwell Castle, August 26th, 1808.

. . . . . I cannot say that I dare, even yet, allow myself to be very sanguine about the Spaniards. Could we hope that their present enthusiasm would last, were it in its nature to be permanent, I should be certain that they were invincible. But I dread its wasting away, and being worn out before the innumerable hosts and the *atrocem animum* of Bonaparte, undirected as their feelings are by any great superior intellect, and unconcentrated on any one really interesting object. For nothing but a first burst of sentiment in a people, moved almost to madness by insult, can possibly elevate any of their own wretched royal family into such an object. If they assemble immediately a general Cortes, and if there is a sufficient dose of intellect and a public spirit in the nation to adapt their old separate forms of liberty, to their present situation, and to consolidate them in a mass, whose momentum may prescribe any terms to the chief, who or whatever he may be, that they shall set over them, they may certainly succeed in so neutralising monarchical power as to make it a harmless, if not a useful, instrument in the hands of a Ferdinand. But all this seems to require peace and leisure. How they are to bring it about amid the din of arms I know not, and I tremble to think. Yet after all the political wonders of every sort, which we have seen in our day, nothing will surprise me; and perhaps this violent shake is necessary to bring forward those thinking heads, as well as active arms, that, nursed in the shade of obscurity, have been preparing themselves for situations to which they will be found equal.

To Robert Ferguson, Esq.

Saturday, September 3rd.—In the evening Mr. Morritt* read to us one of Massinger's plays ('The Duke of Milan').

Monday, 5th. — A letter from Mrs. D. told me of

* John B. S. Morritt, Esq., owner of Rokeby, and the friend of Sir Walter Scott.

the victory gained by our troops at Lisbon over the French, adding to it some melancholy recollections which such news was sure to recall to her mind as well as mine. I was occupied with it all the day, but perhaps such recollections, when time has softened the bitterness, ought to be counted rather amongst our pleasures than our sorrows.

We drove with Lord Webb Seymour * to Douglas Park to see the bridge, said to be Roman, which crosses a small river at the bottom of the garden. It is a single arch, and much too narrow for any sort of carriage. Mr. Morritt thought that it was really a Roman work; I would rather bet that it was not. In the evening Mr. Morritt continued reading the 'Duke of Milan.' He reads very well, and Massinger is not easy to read.

Tuesday, 6*th*.—We went, the same party as yesterday, to Hamilton, to see the pictures. Lord Archibald had arrived the day before, and wished to see us before our departure. In the evening Morritt began reading another of Massinger's plays, 'The Fatal Dowry,' from which Rowe has taken the story of 'The Fair Penitent.' The characters of the father and the husband in 'The Fatal Dowry' are infinitely more interesting than in 'The Fair Penitent;' but the events and the catastrophe are badly drawn, and the wife detestable.

Wednesday, 7*th*.—In the evening there was dancing and music, and they had all sorts of ridiculous dances. They played at false acting, Morritt reciting Antony's oration upon Cæsar's body, and I making the gestures; all which made us laugh not a little. Then they played all sorts of other ridiculous tricks, and in all this Lord Webb is as eager, as amusing, and as entirely occupied as

* Lord Webb Seymour, son of the tenth Duke of Somerset; born in 1777; died, unmarried, in 1819; held in high estimation and regard by the literary and political society of that day.

he would be in the deepest discussion. He dances, he performs antics, and plays the fool with great vivacity, and at the same time with imperturbable gravity.

Extract of a Letter from Miss Berry to the Hon. Mrs. Damer.

Bothwell Castle, September, 1808.

. . . Lord Webb Seymour staid with us till Friday last. He is a charming creature, from the perfect and elegant simplicity of his manners and the liveliness and activity of his mind upon *all* subjects; for he dances, and plays conjuring tricks, and plays the fool with the same interest and eagerness that he has in science and philosophy; *only* if he would not *so* doat upon disquisition! upon mental *dissections*, and above all, upon *accounting* for everything which it is only necessary to *feel*, and feel he does, on all the great subjects of politics, taste, &c. exactly as he ought.

Saturday, 10*th*.—Lord and Lady Rosslyn* arrived at four o'clock, accompanied by Mr. Brougham and two brothers of Lord Blantyre—Charles, the advocate, and William, who is in the service—and the aide-de-camp, Captain Morland. Lord Rosslyn gave me a letter to read from Captain Adam to his father, praising the conduct of Ronald at Vimeira in the most satisfactory manner. I went away to read it, which I did not do without tears.

Sunday, 11*th*.—I wrote to my father with the account of Ronald.

Wednesday, 14*th*.—Had a long conversation with Playfair. He seems to take a lively interest in all that relates to us.

Friday, 16*th*.—A walk with Lady Douglas and Playfair. He examined and brought home some pieces of stone, from the environs of the cotton mill, upon which he made experiments in the evening with

* Sir James St. Clair Erskine, second Earl of Rosslyn, a general officer in the army, succeeded his uncle in 1805; married in 1790 to Henrietta Elizabeth, eldest daughter of the Hon. Edward Bouverie.

Lord Douglas. It appears to me that Playfair has succeeded very well here, both with the lady and with the lord of the mansion.

Monday, 19*th*.—There was a servants' ball in the evening, when everyone danced except myself and Caroline, who played upon the tambourine or the triangle all the evening. The ball lasted till midnight. The news of the Convention* at Lisbon has arrived.

Thursday, 22*nd*.—I read to Lady Douglas my sketch of a preface for the Letters, with which she seemed well pleased. Finished reading 'The Tale of the Times,' a novel which, like most other novels, begins better than it finishes. In the evening, Caroline, Fanny,† Miss Robertson, Mdlle. de Lally, &c. &c. and I went to the farm, where in the granary was a fête, that they call in this country a 'keam,' in England a 'harvest-home dance.' I expected that the peasant men and women dancing the dances of the country mixed together with the servants of the house, would have pleased me more, but they have no grace whatever, nor the men even any choice with whom they dance, provided they could run about and make themselves hot in executing a thousand steps of a 'reel;' it seems perfectly indifferent to them who is their vis-à-vis, and the spectators are only occupied in looking and watching the moment when they could join in it themselves. This ball is given by those whose harvest is all carried, and I think that Lord Douglas's granary ought to have been better arranged, and less ill-lighted for a fête, which these poor reapers expect from every proprietor. The great and rich ought to take a pride in making it a little more brilliant than others.

Thursday, 29*th*.—Walter Scott came to dinner.

* Convention of Cintra, signed and concluded at Lisbon August 30.

† Hon. Frances Elizabeth Douglas, daughter of Lord Douglas; married, 1826, to William Moray Sterling, Esq., of Ardoch.

Friday, 30*th*.—I had a long conversation with Walter Scott at breakfast. I sat for the last time for my portrait.

October 3rd.—Miss Berry left Bothwell for Edinburgh.

Thursday, 7*th*.—Stopped at Melrose. The ruin is only a few steps from the inn. It is of great beauty, but now spoilt by the parish church, which is built into a part of the interior, with a modern roof placed against the fine Gothic columns, and supported by arches constructed upon a different plan to the ancient arches. They are now building a new church on the other side of the town, and as soon as it is finished they are going to pull down the modern edifice in the interior of the ruin. It is in this Abbey that Walter Scott imagined that the Enchanter, Michael Scot, lived, and where he makes him consulted by Deloraine, in his poem, 'The Lay of the Last Minstrel.' The cicerone, a very intelligent man, showed us Alexander III.'s tomb, upon which the poet supposed that the Enchanter and Warrior sat.* I was very glad to have seen this very ornamented Gothic ruin.

Arrived at Minto. Found Lady Minto† and her sister in the library. The gentlemen were Playfair, Walter Scott, Mr. Eliot of Wells, The Castle Spectre, and three young Scotch lawyers and reviewers, by name Erskine, Murray,‡ and Thompson,§ and the eldest son of the house Gilbert. We talked agreeably enough afterwards. Walter Scott, as usual, narrating, whilst Playfair and Lady Minto and I listened.

* They sate them down on a marble stone,
(A Scottish monarch sleeps below)
Thus spoke the monk in solemn tone.—*Canto* 2, v. xii.

† Anna Maria, eldest daughter of Sir George Amyand, sister to Sir George Cornewall, Bart., and to the Countess of Malmsbury; married, in 1777, Gilbert Elliot, first Earl of Minto.

‡ Afterwards Lord Murray, judge of the Session.

§ Thomas Thompson, Esq., Keeper of the Records in Edinburgh, and well known there in literary society.

In the middle of October 1808 Miss Berry returned to London, and her Journal for the rest of the year furnishes little worth extracting.

On Poor Marriages.

October, 1808.

I found my old friend and playfellow in a small uncomfortable house, surrounded by a number of ugly, ill-mannered children, and a silly, idle husband. The smallness of their fortune depriving her children of those means of education which she has not in her power to supply, and depriving her husband of those means of expense which can alone hope to conceal and make passable in the world, a character like his. The same smallness of fortune, crowding them inconveniently altogether, makes their manners hardly amiable to each other, and not at all so to their friends. This is a sad picture of what is commonly called a *love marriage* upon a small fortune, but which *I* call an ill-judged, inconsiderate union formed between two persons incapable of the invigorating influence of a really great attachment, and perfectly unequal either to meet, or to make the best of the ills they entail on themselves, and on their children —persons who would both of them have been much more really happy in a connection where their transient taste had been less consulted, and their permanent convenience more. Life must not be considered (as I have known many willing to consider it) as a party of pleasure, in which, if your companions can contrive to make themselves entertaining and agreeable for a few days, while engaged in the same pursuit, it is all that can be required of them. In the acceptance of a companion for life, attention must be had to the many days of difficulty, distress, and sickness which 'flesh is heir to,' and from which *no* situation can be exempted. M. B.

A Letter from Lord Webb Seymour to Miss Berry.

Edinburgh, November 7, 1808.

You must neither expect a witty letter, though you are a lady to whom I *would* write one, if I could; nor a pretty letter, though you are a lady to whom I *could* write one, had I time; but this is to be a plain matter of business letter.

Sheldon, the Professor of Anatomy to the Royal Academy, is lately dead, and an active canvass for the situation is going forward. Among the candidates is Mr. Charles Bell,* a person for whom I feel considerably interested, from the manner in which I hear him spoken of by some friends, whose good opinion I think a strong recommendation. Now, though you are not a painter, or a sculptor, or a Member of the Royal Academy, yet, as you have a good deal to say among painters, and sculptors, and Members of the Royal Academy, and Commissioners in the Fine Arts, I must believe your favour and support to be of importance to Mr. Bell. As to his good life-actions, I understand that he bears a high reputation as a surgeon and anatomist, as he has made the connection of anatomy with the fine arts his particular study. Of his attention to this point, you may have had an opportunity of judging, if you have met with a work he published a few years ago on 'The Anatomy of Expression in Painting.' As the production of a young man, it may be in some respects deficient; but I believe it to contain many ingenious and just observations. Mr. Bell appears to be a deserving man on every account, and I conceive that any service you might do him would not be misplaced. If, upon enquiry, you find there is another candidate better qualified, I should no longer beg your assistance in the cause of Mr. Bell.

The post is going, so I must say adieu.

Yours truly,

WEBB SEYMOUR.

* Afterwards, Sir Charles Bell, an eminent physiologist and surgeon; born at Edinburgh, 1774. In 1806 he removed to London; in 1811 he published his celebrated work on the 'Anatomy of Expression.' He made important discoveries on the physiology of the nervous system, and is considered to have laid the sure foundation of all subsequent knowledge of nervous physiology. Married, 1811, Marian, daughter of Charles Shaw, Esq., of Ayr; died, 1842.—*Imp. Dict. Univ. of Biog.*

1809.

Saturday, January 7th.—Mr. Longman, the publisher, came to speak about my French Letters. We settled about the number of volumes, their size, and the arrangement of the subject. I read my preface and parts of the life to him. With both he appeared much pleased—more than I expected. As to the price he would give me for the MS., we agreed he should speak to my friend Edwards, and that I would be satisfied with whatever he arranged for me.

Friday, 20th.—It snowed again in the night. I went to the City to Mr. Longman's, to take him the Letters to be transcribed for the printers. Paternoster Row, where he lives, and all the small streets in the City, are almost impassable from the quantity of snow, which lies in heaps. With much difficulty, I approached his door in the carriage.

Saturday, 21st.—I was awoke by the drum announcing a fire in our neighbourhood. Notwithstanding cold and illness, I could not resist going to the window, where I saw that the fire was neither very large nor very near. I heard in the morning it was St. James's Palace,* the side which looks upon the park. I heard by a letter that Sir John Moore's army in Spain was re-embarked.

Monday, 23rd.—This morning, whilst at breakfast,

* The fire broke out in the apartments of the Duke of Cambridge, at St. James's Palace, the whole interior of the south-east angle, fronting Marlborough House, was entirely destroyed.—*Annual Register.*

General Abercrombie * came in, in an agitated manner, to ask if we had heard any news; that it was said that there had been an affair in Spain, and that Moore † was killed. He left us to ascertain the truth, promising to let me know what he heard. In a quarter of an hour I received the confirmation of the sad news in a bulletin, sent to Mrs. Damer by one of her neighbours, and which she forwarded to me. In less than an hour, Abercrombie himself returned, his lips quivering with agitation, and drops of perspiration standing on his temples, notwithstanding the intense cold. The deep and manly grief with which he felt the death of his friend, and the disasters of our forces, though victorious, affected me extremely.

Wednesday, February 1*st.*—In the evening, met Mr. Thornton from the House of Commons, where they begin to deal with these strange affairs of the Duke of York.‡

Tuesday, 21*st.*—This morning I went to the Temple to Mr. Lysons',§ to see some very ancient MSS. of the time of Henry IV., Edward IV., and Richard III., &c. &c., of which he is the depositary, as 'Keeper of the Records in the Tower.' All these papers he has brought to light, and is going to arrange and explain them in a very satisfactory manner. They are of great interest, both for the history of the country and for the character of the kings.

* General Sir John Abercrombie, second son of Ralph first Lord Abercrombie, died, unmarried, 1817.

† Sir John Moore was the son of Dr. Moore, author of 'Zeluco,' 'Edward,' and various other works, born at Glasgow in 1761; entered the army at the age of fifteen; he was wounded in Corsica 1790. In 1796 he was Brigadier-General in the West Indies, under Sir R. Abercrombie. In 1797 he was employed in Ireland during the rebellion. In 1799 he went on the expedition to Holland, where he was severely wounded. Was sent to the Mediterranean, and again wounded at Alexandria. On his return to England, he was made a Knight of the Bath. In 1808 commanded an army in Spain; fell under the walls of Corunna, January 16, 1809.

‡ Charges concerning Mrs. Clark.

§ Samuel Lysons, a writer on British Topography and Antiquities, born in 1763, student in the Middle Temple, and his brother Daniel published the earlier volumes of the 'Magna Britannica.' Died 1819.

Friday, 24th.—In returning from Mr. Bouverie's in Grosvenor Square, we first perceived the burning of Drury Lane Theatre, which began to light up all the windows on the opposite side of the Square. From the third story at home we could see the flames, though we had not the least idea from whence they came. Behind our house it was so light that we could see to read, and the whole atmosphere was so red with flames, that everybody thought his neighbour on fire; and what was still more extraordinary, people thought the same at Twickenham, twelve miles from the fire. Our gardener woke up in a fright, and thought, from the light, that it was from some part of the new house. Between twelve and one o'clock, Mr. Cholmley arrived from the scene of action, to tell us all he had seen.

Tuesday, March 2nd.—We passed an agreeable evening at the Argyll Rooms. At eleven o'clock there were but few people; but before the end of the burletta, which was very well sung, the theatre was well filled. Afterwards, at past midnight, everyone took their places at the round tables, arranged in two rooms for a cold supper, and after supper some people began to dance in the room where the theatre is, and which is cleared of the benches the moment the *petite pièce* is over, and makes a very pretty ball-room. We found there some ladies and a good many gentlemen of our own acquaintance.

Wednesday, 8th.—We stayed at Mrs. Bouverie's till midnight, to hear news from the House of Commons, where they were discussing the Duke of York's affairs. Received a note from Ronald and Whitbread. Not the least hope of a division this first night.

* The flames burst out at eleven o'clock at night. In less than a quarter of an hour it spread in one unbroken flame over the whole of the immense pile, extending from Brydges Street to Drury Lane, so that the pillar of fire was not less than 450 feet in breadth.—*Annual Register.*

Saturday, 25*th*.—Dined at Sir John Stanley's. After dinner arrived the Miss Fanshaws, Ways, and some other people. Went to Mr. Knight, where we found Catalani, the Cornewalls, and Mercer singing. Catalani *prédonnéed* several airs delightfully with Mercer.

Friday, April 28*th*.—In the morning I saw Joanna [Baillie]. She stayed nearly an hour with me. I read to her my 'Notice upon Madame du D——'s Life,' with which she was so pleased that I could not but feel very much flattered. I afterwards went to Walter Scott's, where I saw his wife for the first time.

Wednesday, May 3*rd*.—Went to Mrs. Montague's ball. The large drawing-room making a very good ball-room.† Everybody *comme il faut là*, except the opposition.

Tuesday, 9*th*.—This morning I had a very satisfactory visit from the Bishop of Rodez.‡ He will come to me one morning in every week, that I may consult him upon my difficulties. . . . Went to the Exhibition of Water Colours, where I stayed till nearly five o'clock. These artists in water colours, in my opinion, have not made much progress since last year. There is one (Reinagle) § who surpasses all the others. After him comes Varley || in landscape, and Hopley in figures.

Wednesday, 10*th*.—Called at Lady Donegall's. Soon after Agnes arrived, saying that there was a Mr. Long who wished to speak to me upon business, and that she had brought him with her. I went to the door to see

* Created Lord Stanley of Alderley, 1839; died 1850.

† Montague House, Portman Square.

‡ Colbert, Bishop of Rodez.

§ Philip Reinagle, born 1750, and his son Ramsay, born 1772, both artists of German origin, and of some eminence as painters in landscape, portrait, and animal painting. They both exhibited in the Royal Academy as early as 1787. It was probably Ramsay Reinagle who exhibited in water colours.

|| John Varley, an eminent water-colour artist, born about 1777. He was a man of eccentric character, and made no secret of his pretensions as an astrologer. Died 1842.—*Rose's Biog. Dict.*

who it was, and found it was Prince Staremberg, but so disguised * that he could hardly be recognised. He had rather a long beard below his chin and a black wig. In this disguise he had crossed Holland, and had come over in a fishing-boat, which brought him to Aldborough in Suffolk, where he landed between one and two o'clock this morning, and he was with us between two and three o'clock in the afternoon. He stayed till four o'clock, when he was to see Mr. Canning. In the evening he returned, after having dined with Mr. Canning, in the same travelling costume.

Friday, 12th.—This morning I had the Bishop of Rodez with me for nearly two hours. I read to him my preface and my 'Notice on the Life, &c. &c.,' with which he was well pleased, saying it was impossible to give a more faithful picture of the person whom he had known during the latter years of his life in great intimacy.

Tuesday, 30th.—Dined at Sir George Beaumont's. Sat by Sir George. Lamentable the manner in which a man of his turn of mind and great accomplishments speaks of the character and genius of Buonaparte, the distressing circumstances of Europe and ourselves in the present moment making him perfectly blind to the capacity which has wrought such wonderful changes, which, whether ultimately for the better or the worse, has very little to do with the argument—thinks Cromwell a greater man.

Wednesday, 31st. — At half-past ten went with my sister and Miss Godfrey to Mr. Hope's.† The Princess of Wales had dined there, and stood godmother to his second son. She was holding a circle in the first drawing-room when we came in. Soon afterwards all the world

* This disguise must have been rendered necessary by the difficulty of crossing Holland, and not that Prince Staremberg had come on any secret mission to England. His credentials were presented in due form on his arrival, and he resumed his post he had quitted the preceding year as Austrian Ambassador to the Court of England.

† Henry Hope, Esq., the author of 'Anastatius.'

went to the statue gallery, where was dancing, late in beginning, as usual. Princess of Wales desired Lady Sheffield * to present me to her. Talked for a minute or two of the Lockes. I stood by her chair till somebody else came up, and I got away. I don't think she was taken with me, as she saw, when I did not suppose she did, the mien which I made to Lady Sheffield when she first proposed it to me—the presentation—which I changed for a proper Court face the moment I saw her looking, and the thing inevitable. The last dance before supper she danced herself with Lyttelton.† Such an exhibition! but that she did not at all feel for herself, one should have felt for her! Such an over-dressed, bare-bosomed, painted eye-browed figure one never saw! G. Robinson said she was the only true friend the Prince of Wales had, as she went about justifying his conduct.

Thursday, June 1st.—Went with a party to the ball in Argyll Street for Mr. Amsinck's benefit. The ball very full, and much like a race ball, with a number of people one knew, and a number more one never saw before. Went into one of the low boxes. Sir H. Englefield and Lord Webb Seymour with us. We sat at our ease the whole night, looking on upon the world.

Saturday, 3rd.—Went between two and three o'clock to Lady Glenbervie's ‡ breakfast at the Pheasantry. The day was very fine, and the breakfast pretty. The Princess of Wales there, and the party she named. The rest of the company all Lady Glenbervie's neighbourhood. The Princess had a hot dinner in the library. The rest of the company a cold one, under two large tents or

* Lady Anne North, second daughter of Frederick second Earl of Guilford (Lord North, the minister of George III.), married in 1798 to Lord, afterwards Earl, of Sheffield. She died in 1832.

† Afterwards Lord Lyttelton.

‡ Lady Catharine Ann North, married to Sylvester Douglas, Lord Glenbervie, 1789.

tarpaulins, which had a pretty effect in the wood. Slept at Strawberry Hill.

Wednesday, 7th.—Mrs. Cholmley and two of her daughters and Walter Scott breakfasted with us. Shortly after came Sir G. and Lady Beaumont, Robert Walpole and Lady Louisa Stuart, and Sir W. Pepys and F. Cholmley. Somebody was to read Joanna Baillie's tragedy, 'The Family Legend;' this somebody was obliged to be me, as nobody else knew her hand, or had ever seen the play. I read the first three acts, Cholmley the fourth, and I again the fifth. It had a vast effect upon Walter Scott, and one that was very pleasing, from the evident feeling of one poet for another.

Thursday, 8th.—In the evening I dressed myself like an old peasant woman—a dress and masque which I had possessed some time—and went with Mrs. Bouverie to a masquerade at Mrs. Chichester's, in Harley Street. We went at half-past twelve, and got in easily, but the noise and vulgarity of the masques, and not seeing one face unmasked that we had ever seen before, made our party immediately pull off ours and give up the idea of any amusement. The crowd, which at first was not great, increased, but it was impossible to increase the noise. We were, in less than an hour's time, joined by Agnes, as a housemaid, Miss Godfrey in my monk's dress, and Lady Donegall unmasked, from Lady Lansdowne's,* where they had left many masks, much company, and plenty of room. We were all introduced to the lady of the house by Lady Donegall. It was the dullest thing of the kind at which I ever assisted, though certainly the noisiest and fullest of *characters, such as they were.*

Wednesday, 14th.—Dined at Mrs. ——'s; a dinner of fifteen people, of whom my only acquaintance was Skef-

* Wife of John Marquis of Lansdowne, relict of Sir Duke Gifford, of Castle Jordan, Ireland.

fington,* who I found afterwards was the wit, the *bel-esprit, l'aigle de la société*!! Two ladies joined after dinner in extolling the endowments and even personal appearance of Skeffington.

Friday, 16*th*.—In the morning went to the Exhibition with Lady G. Morpeth. Portrait of Sir G. Beaumont's mother excellent. Wilkie's two pictures, and another by Bird,† a man who follows his steps, all that I remarked as very good.

Thursday, 22*nd*.—Went with Lady Georgiana Morpeth to George, the silk mercer's, through all the dirtiest streets of London, and round by Covent Garden Theatre, of which the immense walls, but more immense scaffolding, is really curious. After dinner walked with my father and sister to the fields between Paddington and Bayswater. The haymaking, a beautiful warm quiet evening; we sat for some time on the cocks of hay, which I really enjoyed, but in how melancholy a manner, Heaven, who sees within my soul, alone can know!

Monday, 26*th*.—Went to Mr. Hope's, at the Deepden, near Dorking. The place pretty, with great capabilities, from the irregularity of the ground, but wants much doing to it. A narrow glen or hollow, with high banks and fine trees; excellent place for a flower-garden, where the present one is ill-arranged. Looked over drawings in the evening.

Tuesday, 27*th*.—Drove with Mr. and Mrs. Hope to the

* Afterwards Sir Lumley St. George Skeffington of Skeffington Hall, County Leicester. He was the author of some dramatic pieces. None of his writings were published, but the songs in the 'Sleeping Beauty'—a melodrama of his composition—the eccentricity of his dress and appearance (black ringlets, cheeks covered with rouge, peculiar hat and coat, top boots, &c.) furnished to Gilray a subject for caricature. From some cause or other, he lost his fortune, his property was sold, and he was forced to live within the rules of the King's Bench.

† Edward Bird; born 1772, he began as a painter of tea-trays, but soon rose to some eminence as an artist in subjects of low life. He afterwards attempted, with much less success, great historical pictures. Died 1819.

Rookery, a place belonging to Mr. Fuller (a banker), about four miles off. There is a considerable lake, and a very pretty walk round one side of it, through noble beeches, and the wood on all sides hanging picturesquely over it. At the farm, the largest and finest witch-elm I ever saw. Again looked over drawings in the evening.

Wednesday, 28*th*.—Drove with Mr. and Mrs. Hope to Wotton Park, Sir Frederick Evelyn's.* Pretty retired place, situated in a bottom, where two finely-wooded little valleys meet, a small stream running in each of them. An old brick in-and-out country gentleman's house, the outside covered over with all sorts of different verdure, and among the rest with an apricot-tree. A fine display of flowers, from whence the ground had formerly risen in the regular stages of an old garden, quite up to the wood. A beautiful *jet d'eau* yet remains, and above it steps of green turf. The family were all walking in the garden when we stopped to look at it from the barouche. They invited us in, and we walked round a most luxuriant flower-garden, which was in all the gorgeous display of the present season.

Thursday, 29*th*.—Left the Deepden.

Saturday, *July* 1*st*.—Mr. Playfair dined with us; afterwards drove with him and Miss Godfrey to the upper gate of Kensington Gardens, and walked entirely round; the evening was delicious, the walk very enjoyable. Just in front of us was Lord Paget,† four of his children, and his brother, the General, who lost an arm at Oporto.‡

Friday, 7*th*.—Went to Lady M. Fordyce's. The Princess of Wales there, and a great assembly above stairs. Lady C. Lindsay met us on the staircase, and made us go into the room below, where the Princess was surrounded

* Sir Frederick Evelyn, married a daughter of William Turton, Esq., of Staffordshire. Died 1812.

† The late Marquis of Anglesey.

‡ General Sir Edward Paget.

by her usual court—Sir W. Scott,* Windham, Lord Henry Fitzgerald,† Brownlow North‡ Lewis,§ Sir H. Englefield, Gill, Craven, &c. &c. We sat in a corner talking to such of them as were not employed and Lady Glenbervie pleasantly enough for above an hour. The Princess very graciously bowing and smiling to us both, and, luckily, no more.'

Saturday, 8th.—At near three o'clock went in Lane's carriage with him, Lord W. Seymour, and Mrs. Lockhart, to Lady L. Macdonald's ‖ breakfast. It was a fair day. The place is small, and not very pretty at East Sheen, and there were too few people, which made it dull. Our party was conducted to breakfast by Miss Macdonald into a summer-house, where the other convives were the Duchess of Beaufort, Lady Harrowby,¶ Puységur,** Lord A. Hamilton,†† Edward Montague,‡‡ Lady Anne Hamilton,§§ and the eldest Beckford. Before six we had had enough of the breakfast. Lady Donegall and Mr. Windham joined us in the evening at home. Had some very agree-

* Afterwards Lord Stowell.

† Son of first Duke of Leinster.

‡ B. North, son of the Bishop of Winchester.

§ Mathew G. Lewis, familiarly called Monk Lewis; born 1775. 'The Monk,' a novel, was written when he was only nineteen, in ten days, at the Hague, where he was residing as attaché. He was the author of the well-known ballad of 'Alonzo the Brave,' and of the 'Tales of Terror,' 'Romantic Tales,' the 'Bravo,' &c.; and of the dramas of the 'Castle Spectre,' the 'East Indian,' and 'Timour the Tartar.' His Journal of 'A West Indian Proprietor' was published after his death. Died at sea in 1818.

‖ Lady Louisa Macdonald, daughter of Granville, second Earl Gower, married 1777 to Right Hon. Sir Archibald Macdonald, Chief Baron of the Exchequer. Died 1827.

¶ Daughter of Earl Gower, by his second wife, Susannah Stewart, daughter of Earl of Galloway.

** Puységur, probably the Chevalier de Puységur who came to London in 1806, and remained till 1815. Well known in English society.

†† Lord Archibald Hamilton, son of Archibald ninth Duke of Hamilton, born 1769, died 1827.

‡‡ Edward Montague, eldest son of Mathew Montague, Esq., afterwards Lord Rokeby, born 1787, died 1847.

§§ Lady Ann Hamilton, sister to Lord Archibald.

able conversation with Windham. Just after I went to bed, the drums beat for a great fire in Conduit Street, which so waked and hurried one's spirits, that I slept little. Mr. Frederick North's * house completely burnt down.

Monday, 10*th*.—In the morning Miss Murray called. I went with her to Bath House.† Curious the state of perfect neglect in which Sir William Pulteney had lived in it till his death. All in disorder now, and it will be long before the present Sir James gets it furnished by the way in which he goes on. The dining-room is done, and very handsomely fitted up by Morell. Mrs. D. came in the evening from Strawberry Hill; and Mr. Price, Lord Webb Seymour, and Prince Staremberg. Lord Webb leaves town to-day. His going is a loss. He is rational and conversable, a lively fresh mind, and, in short, very unlike other people.

Tuesday, 18*th*.—Went in the morning with Mr. Playfair to see the two panoramas of Cairo and of Dublin. That of Cairo admirable. The sandy arid look of the country so well given, and contrasting so remarkably with the green fringe of land on each side the course of the Nile. The near buildings—many of them picturesque and well painted. The interior of the city of Dublin is an ugly subject, but extremely well done, and giving a perfect idea of a meaner dirty-looking London.

Monday, 24*th*.—Mr. Thornton drove me in the morning to Thompson's nursery ground at Mile-End, where we spent a long time going over the whole garden. From there we went to Lodige's nursery at Hackney. More

* Hon. Frederick North, afterwards fifth Earl of Guilford.

† Sir William Pulteney, created Earl of Bath 1742; died 1764, s. p. His niece, Henrietta Pulteney, married Sir James Murray, who took the name of Pulteney. She was created Baroness and Countess of Bath, died 1808; Sir James died 1811. The house was afterwards bought and rebuilt by Alexander Baring, first Lord Ashburton. It still retains the name of Bath House.

fine plants there than at Thompson's. Returned with two enormous nosegays.

A letter from Lord Webb Seymour to Miss Berry belongs to this month :—

Worthing, Sunday, July 16, 1809.

Though the cliffs and the olive groves and the mountains of Nice are strongly contrasted with the beach at Worthing, the recollection of the coast I *so lately visited,* does not prevent me from finding considerable delight in this. I am feeding on the purest air and on pleasing dreams, inspired by the sea-breeze and the murmur of the surge. Even after having seen the Mediterranean, you must have admired some of the seas that we have had within these few days, just ruffled by a gentle breeze, and reflecting the brightest azure of our climate.

On Friday I was at Brighthelmstone (I hope you like its long name), to pass a day with Mrs. Spencer, and found her as agreeable as ever. One day with a friend in that way is worth a hundred scraps in London. In London one page of *the book* is forgotten before we have an opportunity of looking at the next; and you and I must meet at Bothwell or Tunbridge, or some other place in the same style, before we can hope to put *the mark* much farther forward.

Mrs. Spencer returned to London on Saturday. She is very anxious to see Mr. Playfair, and I promised to request you to make them acquainted.

I hope you will congratulate Playfair for me and for yourself, upon his late grand publication—*a Peerage,* in five volumes, at ten guineas a volume. Lord Galloway, whom I met at Brighthelmstone, makes it a rule never to subscribe to any book, but an application some time ago from a person of the name of Playfair—a name, too, followed by sundry scientific titles and dignities—induced him to relax his rule in favour of the *celebrated Edinburgh Professor,* who declared that he was going to enlighten the world by his speculations on gules argent and lions rampant, and addressed himself to different peers for their patronage, as well as for private sources of information. At length the work appeared, and I found Lord Galloway grievously disappointed by the trifling stuff and fulsome flattery with which the production of this profound man abounded. His brother, Edward Stewart, had indeed ventured to raise a doubt whether it was the Edinburgh Professor who was the author of this work, and I was appealed to for the decision of the question. The book, it seemed, was a bad one, so I denied that our friend had any concern in it; but had peers and pedigrees been properly treated, of course I should have felt it *a point of delicacy* to refer to better authority before I stripped off at a blow the reputation to be derived from five ten-guinea volumes. I saw the Lockes of Norbury at Brighthelmstone. Mrs. S. regretted that their absence from Norbury deprived her of the pleasure of seeing you there. Did you ever see that wonderful beauty of a little girl of hers?

Yours ever sincerely,

W. S.

Remember me to all friends.

August.—I have been reading a strange poem—the 'Columbiad' of Poet Barlow.* Who or what he is I know not, except that he is an American, deeply imbued with all the bad taste and all the prejudices which belong to his nation, in its present state of society. His language is not English—at least, is full of words which the English language, in its Eastern domain, does not acknowledge. His verses are full of obscurity, and still fuller of the most ridiculous alliterations and the roughest cacaphonias. Yet I have been amused at this first American attempt at an epic, with all its faults, all its vulgarisms, all its barbarous names, all its prejudices, and all its false reasoning. It is full of ideas, embraces an endless variety of subjects—past, present, and to come. Sets one a thinking, sometimes justly, but oftener to detect and wonder at its

* Joel Barlow, an American poet, born at Reading, Connecticut, in 1755; he was the son of a farmer. In 1787 his greatest poem, 'The Vision of Columbus,' appeared, and was dedicated to Louis XVI. In 1808 he enlarged and republished it under the title of 'Columbiad.' In 1811 he was appointed Minister Plenipotentiary to the French Government. Died near Cracow 1812.—*Imp. Dict. of Univ. Biog.*

commonplace mistakes, and the conceit with which so many false and romantic doctrines are brought forward and dwelt upon. Among others, that of the perfectability of the human race, the approach to which is supposed to be advanced and hastened by the cultivation and improvements of America! The country at present perhaps the lowest in the scale of moral education, the farthest from that intellectual character and perfection which such a system supposes. Still, represent this idea of the perfectability of our nature as you will—even in the uncouth alliterative verses of Joel Barlow—still it is a beautiful dream; still it is a reverie in which benevolent and intelligent minds will delight to indulge; still the supposition of an *indefinable*, though not an *interminable*, perfection must conduce to raise, dignify, and ameliorate man.

Sunday, 6*th*.—After church I went to Lord Howe's, and sat some time with Mrs. Howe, carrying her Playfair's problems, with which she was delighted. She goes to-morrow to Sir William Pitt's, in Hampshire, for three months. I always part with her with regret for so long a time. Go when she will she leaves not her fellow behind her, at past eighty-seven, which she is.

Strawberry Hill, Monday, 7*th*.—Princess of Wales, attended by Lady Charlotte Lindsay, came here to see the house at three o'clock. Mrs. Damer had received notice two or three days before, that she was to be thus surprised—for a *surprise* it was to be, and no trouble given. She knew we were here, and asked for us. We joined the party in the Holbein room. The Princess talked a great deal more than she looked at anything, and seemed pleased to have more people to talk to; the pictures, &c., of the house, and observations on them, came merely to fill up gaps and give new matter for discourse. She was in her very best manner, and her conversation is certainly uncommonly lively, odd, and clever.

What a pity that she has not a grain of *common* sense! not an ounce of ballast to prevent high spirits, and a coarse mind without any degree of moral taste, from running away with her, and allowing her to act indecorously and ridiculously whenever an occasion offers! Were she always to conduct herself as she did here to-day she would merit the character of having not only a remarkably easy and gracious manner, but natural cleverness above any of her *peers* that I have seen, and a good many have at different times fallen under my observation. After walking over the house, she was carried into the library, where refreshments were prepared. Of these she did not taste, but proposed our all sitting down, which we did for about half an hour, then departed with a thousand thanks to Mrs. Damer, and shaking us all by the hand. She had with her the little boy whom she brings up. Some poor body's son at Deptford,* and whom she would do well to put to school, but does very ill to take about with her during his holidays. She is not of a disposition to want either the amusement or endearing tenderness of a child; and, after all that has been said of her, one may easily guess what may be said of this little boy about seven or eight years old. She talked much of Gell, who seems at present in high favour; much of Jeuzie,† whom she really seems to value as she deserves.

Tuesday, 8th.—Lady Glenbervie called in the morning to propose to Mrs. Damer from the Princess to share a box at Covent Garden Theatre with her; that is to say, have it on opera nights. This is an arrangement nobody will make with her. But how ridiculous, how ill-managed and mean in this extravagant and spending country, that a Princess of Wales should not be able to have a box at the national theatre to herself—that the King should not give a sum yearly, and have so many boxes for the use of

* Austen. † Mrs. William Locke.

his family! The evening was fine, and I went through Twickenham churchyard, and settled in my own mind upon the place where I should like a stone to be placed, and myself deposited near it. It is a cheerful churchyard, and the place I have chosen near that beautiful view of the river, the group of poplars, and the opposite bank, which I have always so much admired, and at which I stood this evening for nearly a quarter of an hour in quiet and solitary enjoyment, gilded as it was by a beautiful evening sun. To-day I have felt better than for months past, and considered the churchyard and every idea connected with it just as I could wish to do, and as every rational mind ought to consider everything connected with their release from this existence, whose prolongation after the middle of life nothing but particular circumstances can render desirable.

Monday, 14*th*.—I worked at my French Letters all the morning. In the evening read aloud the account of General Moore's campaign in Spain. What an account it is! What an idea does it give one of his character in every respect, aud what treatment did he receive—what a situation was he put in! What abilities did he exert to rescue himself and his army! What suffering he underwent, and, after all, to seal them with his blood!

Wednesday, 16*th*.—Agnes and I went to Lady Stuart's Lodge, in Richmond Park, by appointment, to see her son Charles,* and to hear his accounts both of Spain and Austria. For, since I saw him at Lady Spencer's breakfast on the 2nd of July, last year, he has been over almost all Spain, and a very considerable part of Austria. He gives me a melancholy account of the wounds of poor Louis de Lichtenstein, in the battle of Ratisbon. He must now,

* Son of Lieutenant-General the Hon. Charles Stuart, K.B., and of Louisa, daughter of Lord Vere Bertie, and grandson of Lord Bute, the Minister; born 1779; married Lady Elizabeth Yorke in 1816; created Lord Stuart de Rothsay, 1828; died 1845.

in all human probability, be for ever incapacitated for serving, and this to a hero at twenty-nine! When we lamented to Charles Stuart how much he must have suffered within this last twelve months, he owned he had been very well amused too; that the two flights which he had witnessed and shared in, from Madrid and from Vienna, were very entertaining. His is an active, penetrating mind, which, I dare say, while busily employed, does not feel too much to be prevented treating the world like the French philosopher, 'avec le sarcasme de la gaieté et l'indulgence du mepris.'

Friday, 25th.—We all three drank tea at the Duchess of Montrose's.* Nobody there but herself and three daughters—fine, civil, and cheerful-looking girls—and the only boy, much younger than any of them. They are in Prince Staremberg's house, and the room in which we have all spent so many evenings and so much time! with a work-table in the middle of it, so much the same, and so much altered, made us all melancholy.

The following letter from Professor Playfair belongs to this date. The extraordinary energy and clearness of mind possessed by Mrs. Howe, at the advanced age of eighty-seven, seems to have interested and surprised him greatly:—

Edinburgh, Aug. 25, 1809.

My dear Madam,—I am sure, from the way in which Mrs. Howe has set about resolving the problem, that she will succeed in it easily. I have hardly met with anything more singular than the ardour and acuteness of this lady at so advanced a period of life. It is a phenomenon worthy to be recorded in the history of the human mind, the more that it

* Caroline Maria Duchess of Montrose, daughter of the fourth Duke of Manchester. The three eldest daughters were Lady Georgiana Graham, married the late Earl of Winchelsea, 1814; Lady Caroline Graham; Lady Lucy, married, 1818, the late Lord Powis; Lord Graham, present Duke of Montrose, b. 1799.

throws a cheerful gleam over that portion of life that is so 'dark and unlovely.'

To Mrs. Howe's impatience to be set right, and my own mistakes in setting her wrong, I have great obligation, as they have procured me the pleasure of hearing from you sooner than I should have otherwise have done. I only wish that in addition to what you have said, you had mentioned your health; there is no subject whatever in which I feel more interest: nothing in which I should rejoice more than to have good accounts.

As to myself, I stood the journey very well, and continue to get stronger every day, but I shall always have great pleasure in recollecting that I am to date my recovery from my visit to Strawberry Hill.

No wonder that your politics, as you say, are gloomy; the nation is in that unfortunate situation that the success of its arms do no service either to itself or its allies. Of what use is Sir Arthur W.'s very brilliant and dear-bought victory, but by the honour it reflects on British valour? The taking of a small smuggling town is accompanied with neither glory nor advantage. And the breaking of the armistice by Austria portends, I fear, the total annihilation of that power. The Pope has excommunicated Buonaparte. Does Austria trust in the effect of what was once so terrible to herself, or does she trust in the effect of our great expedition? They are weapons nearly of equal force.

Lord Frederick is here, in perfect health, activity, and spirits. Sir William Scott, who is living also at Dumbridge, is much with him. I am going with them to-day to see the bones of the sea-snake, which are now here; and likely to create a good deal of dispute among anatomists, as to the species of animal to which they belong.

I must entreat to be remembered to Mrs. Damer and Miss Agnes.

Yours, with sincere attachment,

John Playfair.

Saturday, September 2nd.—Went at two o'clock, by appointment, with Lord Webb Seymour and with Miss Coleman, to Bow Street, Covent Garden, to see the front of the new theatre—very handsome, plain Grecian doric, but the pediment in the centre strikes me as not sufficiently extended for the extent of the front; the basso-relievos not sufficiently large for the large flat space in which they are placed, and the statues in the niches at each end of the front too small, both for their niches and for the place of those niches. The composition of the two basso-relievos do not tell their own story, and are not well grouped, although particular figures are good. Then to Russell Square to look at the Duke of Bedford's statue. I like it much. The head is admirable, both in the manner in which it is treated and its extraordinary likeness. The drapery, his robes, managed without affectation as well as any Roman toga. The drapery of the legs only I did not like; they have a sort of thin twisted trouser all round them, exactly like what belongs to the Phrygian dress, and which has certainly nothing to do with the robes of an English duke. The pedestal is granite, with bronze basso-relievos — handsome. The basso-relievos and the figures of the Seasons at the corner of the pedestal are ill seen, from not being able to walk round the statue.

Thursday, 7*th.*—Went with Sir H. Englefield to Fogg's, the china shop. Some of the finest pieces of Indian china I ever saw, and two beautiful dessert services of old Sèvres. Both sold as well as most of the other pieces of Sèvres in the same room to Lord Gywdyr—one of the sets for 600*l.* Two China pagodas in this shop, most splendid pieces of porcelain, at least seven feet high, standing on the ground.

Saturday, 9*th.*—Went with Prince Staremberg and Mrs. Damer to Astley's. Well enough entertained. 'The Arab,' a pretty set of scenes, with a combat at the end, in which twelve real horses appear upon the stage. Were the stage larger, it would be a better spectacle; as it is, it is very well managed.

Tuesday, 12*th.*—In the evening went to the Haymarket

with Prince Staremberg and Mrs. Damer. Pieces: 'The Voice of Nature,' 'Of Age To-morrow,' and 'Killing no Murder.' The first is neither more nor less than the judgment of Solomon enacted by a king of Sicily. The hero (not King Solomon) was well acted by Mr. Young, and the heroine not badly by Mrs. Gibbs. The house was very full, and with very good company.

Sunday, 17*th*.—In the evening Lord Webb Seymour came to bid us farewell. He sets out for Scotland to-morrow morning. He parted with us kindly, almost affectionately. How my heart thanks anybody for this sentiment, and how much more from one so distinguished by his intelligence and amiable simplicity of manners!

Monday, 18*th*.—Breakfasted early with my father and sister, who set off for Tunbridge.

Tuesday, 19*th*.—Prince Staremberg gave an accurate and amusing account of the opening of the new Covent Garden Theatre the night before. Not a single word of either play or farce heard.* The actors all went on as if

* In consequence of the expense attending the building of the new theatre, it was found necessary to augment the prices of admission. One shilling on the boxes, and sixpence on the pit. After five nights of noise and riot, Mr. Kemble shut up the house, and submitted the accounts to a committee of gentlemen. On reopening the theatre, however, the disturbances recommenced, and in addition to the other noises was an accompaniment of coachmen's horns, trumpets, dustmen's bells, and watchmen's rattles. Many came with the letters O.P. in their hats and upon their clothes, and joined in the notable O.P. dance, as it was called, which consisted in an alternate stamping of the feet, accompanied with the regular cry of 'O.P.' in noisy and monotonous cadence. The proprietors lost their temper. A pugilistic corps was imprudently introduced into the pit, and disgraceful fights ensued. Mr. Clifford, a barrister, appeared in the pit with the letters O.P. in his hat. Brandon, the boxkeeper, procured his apprehension as a rioter, and carried him before a magistrate, by whom he was discharged. Mr. Clifford indicted Brandon for an assault and false imprisonment, in which indictment Brandon was cast. The proprietors were now obliged to make a compromise that the boxes should continue at 7*s*., and the pit be restored to the old price, 3*s*. 6*d*. The dismissal of Brandon was loudly called for and complied with. He was afterwards reinstated in office, and the customary routine restored.—*Annual Register*.

to an attentive audience. No serious damage done to the house. Walked at six o'clock to dinner at Mrs. Buller's; Cosway, and Robert Clifford the company in the evening. The *modest pomp* of ——— about politics, the state of the ministry, his anger with Robert Clifford about Lord Chatham, and his confused bothered arguments to me, very amusing for a single evening.

Wednesday, 20*th*.—Mr. Mathew Montague called upon me. More than half an hour's conversation with him on politics and the curious state in which his friend Percival and the rest of his associates in the Ministry find themselves at present—Mr. Canning * declaring he will be Prime Minister, and lead the House of Commons or nothing, and wanting Mr. Percival to be Chancellor, and go up to the House of Lords, Mr. Percival declaring that his conscience and his attachment to the King prevent this, as it would be throwing the King into the power of Mr. Canning, whom he (the King) hates. To what is this poor country reduced from the mere lack of superior abilities! At three o'clock set out for Lady Sutton's, Moulsey Hurst.

Thursday, 21*st*.—Walked to Lady Tancred's,† which joins this place. It is a pretty small house, which she

* It had been for some time apparent that the Duke of Portland could not remain at the head of the Ministry, and Mr. Canning had put forward his claims for that post. He laid a foundation for this arrangement by affirming the principle that the head of the Ministry ought to be in the House of Commons. This, as he considered, reduced the question to a choice between Percival and himself, and he asserted his claims to a preference over Percival. The King and the Cabinet did not concur in this view; and, therefore, on the receipt of the Duke of Portland's answer, Mr. Canning having failed in procuring the removal of Lord Castlereagh and in becoming the successor of the Duke of Portland, lost no time in resigning his office.—*Administration of Great Britain from* 1783 *to* 1830. By Right Hon. Sir G. C. Lewis. From this state of things arose the quarrel between Lord Castlereagh and Mr. Canning, that occasioned a hostile meeting on Putney Heath, on the 21st Sept., 1809.

† Henrietta Lady Tancred, wife of Sir Thomas Tancred, daughter of Rev. Offley Crewe; married 1805; died 1837.

has fitted up very elegantly. Her sons lives with her. Dined with Sir Thomas* and Lady Sutton. His conversation always remarkably sensible, and liberal-minded, and to the purpose.

Saturday, 23rd.—Walked with Lady Tancred to the church of the village of West Moulsey, and from thence to a house on a common, which, upon enquiry, I found inhabited by my old acquaintance Thomas Pitt,† whom we met when first in Italy. He is now a widower, with a daughter grown up, and three tall sons. I made Lady Tancred call with me upon him, but he was out. In the evening, he and his daughter and sons came and drank tea at Sir Thomas Sutton's. He is just what he was—a quiet, regular, sensible man.

Extract of a Letter from Professor Playfair to Miss Berry.

Eleg House, Oct. 5, 1809.

. . . I have been much delighted with Mrs. Howe's solution of the question about the bees. That which is contained in her second note is a perfectly accurate and scientific investigation. It is not a little wonderful that a lady leading a fashionable life should in the most active and vigorous state of her mind have acquired such a skill in the abstract methods of algebra as to be able to solve such a question. That at Mrs. Howe's age she should be able and inclined to take the trouble of doing it, is no less surprising than it is pleasing to observe. I must request you to transmit her the enclosed note. This must be a time of great agitation, I think, with you in London and its neighbourhood; the concussion reaches us at this distance very forcibly. The misconduct of all our expeditions and the duel of two Cabinet Members have filled up the cup of the iniquity of the present administration. I hope Lords G. and G. will not think of a coalition; that would only weaken and disgrace them. You ask me about the author of the article 'Reform' in the last number of the 'Edinburgh Review.' The article is by Jeffrey

* Sir Thomas Sutton, Bart., of Moulsey. Baronetcy extinct 1813.

† *Vide* Journal of 1783.

himself, and is in all respects, I think, worthy of the praise you bestow on it. 'Lord Valentia' is not in this nor will be in the next, unless Miss Agnes, whose idea of the book was perfectly just, will favour us with a critique on it. I have got a report on the progress of science for the last nineteen years made to Buonaparte last year, that I intend to give some account of it in the next number.

Monday, October 2nd.—Returned to London.

Sunday, 8th.—Went to Wimpole.

Wednesday, 18th.—Set out with Lady Catherine and Lady Elizabeth Yorke* in the chariot and four, and Lord Hardwicke on horseback, soon after ten, for Cambridge. Walked to King's College Chapel. The small towers on the outside very light and beautiful. The inside struck me much more than it did in the year 1786, when I first saw it.† I did not feel so much the want of the intersecting arches of aisles as I remember I did then. It is disfigured by an organ-loft of the worst style of Henry VIII.; sort of sprigged pilasters. The painted glass windows very fine. The east window, though very large, not remarkable for the beauty of its tracery. Walked through the two squares of Trinity; the first from the street, with the fountain in it, large, spacious, cheerful, and, I think, as striking as the Wolsey Square at Christ Church, in Oxford. In the chapel on one side of this square is the statue of Sir Isaac Newton.‡ The head and the thoughtful expression of the whole figure really admirable. One regrets that such an artist was confined to the representation of such drapery as a silk gown. The hall of Trinity a fine building. The servitors still dine there. Sir Isaac Newton's picture at the head of the hall, and again in the combination room. Saw the kitchen, in which seven

* Married, 1816, to Sir Charles afterwards Lord Stuart de Rothsay.

† In Horace Walpole's letter of June 30, 1789, he reproaches Miss Berry with not sufficiently admiring King's College Chapel.

‡ By Louis François Roubillac, a native of Lyons. He died in 1762.

persons are employed. Immense roasting apparatus, but did not look altogether very clean. Second square of Trinity a more modern building. One side of it entirely library, with windows both ways. This library is supported upon four rows of Tuscan pillars.

Thursday, 19*th*.—Set out at nine o'clock in the coach with Lord Hardwicke, Lady Catherine, and Lady Elizabeth, for Newmarket, twenty-three miles from hence. The whole way from Cambridge the road passes through the ugliest country that can be imagined. Newmarket Heath is entered by a turnpike at what is called the Devil's Ditch, a high mound, with a deep ditch of turf below, extending for several miles, of which no account is given, and which is in fact a curious antiquity. The Heath is equally bare and open upon all sides, with nothing to break the horizon but Ely Cathedral, seen at the distance of ten or twelve miles. The inn is almost opposite what are called the rooms, where men only meet, and which have rather a handsome entrance of three arcades from the street, and in this street Tattersall was selling horses by auction, and all the young men, whose faces one knows in London, were walking about, as well as all the fathers of the turf, such as Sir Frank Standish, Sir Charles Bunbury, &c. &c. It had the oddest effect possible to see so many figures one hardly ever sees out of London, walking about in a sort of village-town, for Newmarket is no more, with the exception of some good houses. About one o'clock all these men mounted their horses, and proceeded towards the Heath, half a mile from the town. We followed them in the carriage, with many other carriages, and Lord Hardwicke on horseback. The scene of so many horsemen and a good many people on foot, all trooping the same way, very gay and pretty. When they got upon the Heath, it is so vast that they seemed only like small groups upon it. It was said to be a day of little sport. But four races were run: two subscriptions, for each of which six horses started; and two matches. But the style in which all this is managed here, the rapidity with which one race follows another, though on different courses—that is, on different parts of the Heath—the scene at the betting post, one of which belongs to each course, and is the only permanent thing upon it, for the ropes are immediately moved, and the winning post (a little machine upon wheels) is moved from one to the other. All this was new and entertaining to me. Between each race all the men and all the carriages are collected at the betting-posts. Just before the horses start, the carriages take their places near the ropes, and the crowd on horseback disperse from the post. As soon as the horses are past, all the men follow them to the rubbing-house to see them rubbed down, and their clothes put on. These rubbing-houses, stables, &c. &c., are little insignificant buildings, which occupy no space and take off nothing from the extreme bareness of the Heath. Stand there is none. The ladies are all in their carriages. There were more than I expected to see there. The fashionable custom at Newmarket is, to have the plainest carriage and liveries possible, and the gentlemen all to be mounted upon shabby-looking rips of horses. The races were over between three and four, and we returned to Wimpole much pleased with our day.

Wednesday, 25*th*.—Another beautiful day. At eleven o'clock the country people of the two neighbouring parishes of Wimpole and Arrington came trooping across the park to the kitchen-door to receive the portions of beef, mutton, cold baked meat pies, bread and ale, which Lord Hardwicke gave to every family upon occasion of the day, the king having reigned fifty years, which very unwisely Government chose to make a jubilee. A jubilee! in the present situation of the country, both externally and internally! Lord and Lady Hardwicke had intended that all the peasants should have been feasted together before the house, for as every person was to do something to celebrate this *sad jubilee*, it would have been very wrong, thinking, as he does, of the Ministry to have been behindhand. The report of the Princess Amelia's death made them change this intended festival for the distribution above mentioned. It was done in the most regular manner. The cook having made allotments of the bread and meat, according to the numbers in the family, one from every family came up, and received not only enough to give one hearty meal, but enough to essentially better the diet of the moderate ones all the week. The Lady Yorkes and I were on the lawn before the door, seeing the people coming and going with their portions, and their cans and pitchers, and pails of ale. The appearance of the people *in general* was comfortable, though some very ragged and dirty. It was curious to observe the great and decided difference of industry and sobriety in exactly the same situation in life, some labourers with wife and two children upon twelve shillings a week, perfectly tidy, and, though darned and patched, clean and comfortable; others, on the same wages, hanging in dirty tatters. By one o'clock it was all over, and the people enjoying the bounty at their own fireside. In the evening there was a supper in the kitchen for all the workmen employed about the house; and in the housekeeper's room, for the bailiffs, gardener, their wives, &c. &c.

Friday, 27*th*.—Waked at last free from fever, and with a feel of health which I have not experienced for these ten days past. The weather a positive summer day. Drove with the Lady Yorkes to two villages. In the first, Harleton (called Alston), is a pretty old church with handsome windows and an old little tower, besides the great tower, of which the use is not apparent. A very good monument in this church of the family of *Fryer*, in Charles I.'s time, containing three large kneeling figures and one cumbent, all well carved in alabaster and coloured, the whole within an arch, supported by two posts of caryatides, and in perfect preservation. At the other village, Haslingfield, we went over the old manor house, for the last sixty years inhabited by farmers, but which had been the manor house of the *Wendys*, a family extinct in the male line in 1637; there are several good monuments of them in the church, especially of the last of the family, a Knight of the Bath, in the dress of Louis XIV.'s time. The manor house was surrounded by a moat. There is a date cut on stone in one of the chimney-pieces of 1555, which belongs to Queen Mary's time.

Friday, November 3rd.—The Lady Yorkes and I drove in the jaunting car down the avenue, two miles and a half long. Never was there such an unmeaning avenue; it ends in nothing, not even in a gateway, for the entrance to it from the road is on the side. The trees, of which there are two rows on each side, and between which is the road, are none of them good, though planted in the days of Lord Oxford, and half way down is a round piece of water (five acres), which can only be perceived from the garrets of the house as the ground rises between. It is no longer used as the approach to the house, and is separated into fields by hurdles and gates.

Saturday, 4th.—Went with Lord Hardwicke and his daughter to Cambridge. Stopped at the public library, a separate building between the schools and the Senate House, contains about 100,000 vols., rich (they say) in Bibles—not so, I think, in early printed books—the first in 1460, but there are few of them very perfect, and in fine condition. The oldest MS. of the fourth century, given by Theodore Beza,* 'The Four Evangelists.' Some

* Theo. Bezas, or de Bèses, born 1519, in Nivernois, of considerable eminence as a writer. At the instigation of Calvin, he continued the version of the Psalms in French, begun by Calvin; and in 1559 a Latin version of the New Testament, and was the author of many other works. He was a distinguished advocate of the Protestant faith. Died at Geneva 1605, aged 87.

good prints, fine impressions of Rembrandt, but not a complete set. The library of Trinity, a fine large room, with a hideous modern-painted window, contains about 30,000 vols., with a small fund for buying more; but all these libraries are without fireplaces or any means of warming them, and seem but inconvenient places for real study, without paper, pens or ink, or anybody to look for the books wanted. Masters of Arts are allowed to take any they may want to their own rooms, or even out of Cambridge. In this library is a very curious dried man, from the cave in the Island of Teneriffe, which has the property of thus drying up the human body. It is in a glass case; the skin appears completely tanned upon the bones, the hair is still on the head, and the teeth in the jaws.

Monday, 6th.—Returned to North Audley Street.

Letter to Joanna Baillie.

Wimpole, Nov., 1809.

My dear Joanna,—What are you doing? and where are you doing? Troth, say you, if you had wanted to know, you would have enquired sooner; and troth, if I had been doing better myself, so I should, answer I.

I have been here a month with people that I love, in a comfortable family-circle, surrounded by every comfort and every luxury of life, and sitting in a library—such a library! as would—

Make those read now, who never read before;
And those who always read, now read the more.

Yet even thus situated, with the perfect command of my own time and nothing to fatigue me; if I were to tell you how little use I have been able to make of all these advantages; if I were to reckon up how many days in this month I have enjoyed the free and unembarrassed use of my own faculties; I should make you, as well as myself, melancholy, and therefore, as this is a good day with me, I will say no more about it.

My last and only letter from you was on the 8th, from Cotswold. You had been seeing Oxford, which I was delighted to find had impressed your mind, exactly as it had always done mine. During my stay here I have been to Cambridge, which I had seen in a slight manner so long ago as to have almost entirely forgotten. It cannot vie with the magnificent groups of Oxford. But it has *one* College which may rival, if not surpass, Christ Church in picturesque beauty, and one point of view in which it appears singularly adapted for the seat of calm contemplation and learned ease. I fear the evil-minded will say, the calm is often unaccompanied by contemplation, and the ease unaccompanied by learning. Still I must ever love to see such great means brought together, and such assistance offered to both, and must ever feel a degree of exaltation of mind in places dedicated for so many centuries to the cultivation of the noblest and most distinguished faculty of human nature; perhaps, too, a little spark of sexual vanity creeps in with the wonder one cannot help feeling at *men* enjoying such advantages and doing so little, and women labouring under such disadvantages doing so much. This, my dear Joanna, regards *you* more than any other female now living. Go on then and prove to them, that poetry, at least, is as independent of sex as of rule; that it is a spark of ethereal fire kindled on earth once in an Age, which Shakspeare alone has described, and with which you are enlightened.

M. B.

To Joanna Baillie, from Wimpole, Nov., 1809.

Sunday, 19*th*.—Looked over all the three vols. of Madame du Deffand's letters, published at Paris, which I got yesterday; sketched the little alteration necessary to be made in my preface and life.

Monday, 20*th*.—In the evening Charles Stuart (Bute) sat with me till twelve o'clock. We talked over politics, on which, particularly foreign ones, he is better informed than anybody, has seen more, and judges better.

Wednesday, 22*nd*.—Saw Mr. Orme, Longman's partner, with whom I settled several particulars about my publication.

Thursday, 23rd.—Worked hard at my 'Life,' and the arrangement of the notices to be taken of the Paris publication.

Saturday, 25th.—I spent the whole day in my garden and greenhouse, completely enjoying myself and forgetting everything but the pots I was arranging and the roots I was transplanting, my mind in repose and my body in activity; but I never regret a day like this.

Wednesday, 29th.—In the morning saw J. Baillie, afterwards worked at my Letters. Before ten set out for Kensington. When we arrived the Princess had not come out of the dining-room. In about ten minutes she appeared with Lady Charlotte, and no other ladies. Her manner very gracious and civil; announced her appointment of Lady Charlotte Campbell to us as her Lady of the Bedchamber, in place of Lady Sheffield. The gentlemen soon followed her from the dining-room; they were Lord Henry Fitzgerald, Mr. Ward,* Mr. Gell, Mr. de Puységur, and Colonel Lindsay. The only break in conversation was looking at Colonel Lindsay's model of a new sort of telegraph. At twelve we supped in her own little morning room, looking full of litter, and very comfortable. Conversation flagged a little; however, the Princess sat until half-past one, then rose, wished us a good night, and we were at home before two.

Monday, December 4th.—A long visit from Stuart. Advised him to go into Parliament, where his great knowledge of foreign affairs is so much wanted. He does not wish and has no thought of it from feeling no talent for public speaking, and thinking (falsely, I think) that it would take him away from his profession, which he likes.

Tuesday, 5th.—A long talk with Mr. Orme (Longman's partner) about the printing, the quantity, and the form

* Hon. John William Ward, afterwards Lord Dudley and Ward.

of the French Letters. Soon after, a long visit from my bishop, with his notes to another cahier of the said Letters. Read to him my additions to the 'Life,' &c. &c. Interrupted by the arrival of Lord Hartington, to whom I had promised to be at home. His happiness at his sister's * marriage quite charming.

Saturday, 9*th*.—Dined with the Princess of Wales at Kensington at seven o'clock. Company, only Lord Henry Fitzgerald, Mr. Gell, ourselves, and Mrs. Lisle, in waiting. Mrs. Lisle a sad aid to the Princess in entertaining her company, not having a word to throw at a dog—but the Princess wants no aid. Dinner went off very well; servants sent away and dumb waiters. Dinner and dessert good, but plain, served upon the magnificent plate of the Prince of Wales. In the evening, nobody else came. The Princess talked of the apartments above stairs, and proposed our looking at them. Luckily not a very cold night. We all wrapped up, and, taking two candles only with us, sallied up-stairs. The royal apartment very handsome, both in size and fittings up; furniture, properly speaking, there is at present none. In the first room, some of the finest cork models I have ever seen, of all the principal ruins of Rome, and in all the rooms very fine pictures, as far as we could judge by the light of our two glimmering candles, carried in different hands. Supper on the table when we came down, and nearly one before we got away.

Monday, 11*th*.—At home all the morning. In the evening, at ten o'clock, we went to the Princess of Wales'. Meant to be an assembly. Princess Sophia of Gloucester there. Some eight or ten old women and Lady Harrowby, Lady Shaftesbury and her daughter, Mrs. C. Locke and the two Churchill girls. The only men Lord Westmore-

* Lady Harriet Cavendish to Lord Granville Leveson Gower, afterwards Earl Granville.

land, Mr. Manners Sutton, Lord H. Fitzgerald, and the two Churchills, father and son. Much later came Mr. Edward Montague * and Delme. Princess played at a round table with Princess Sophia, &c. &c. Delme and Lady Barbara, Mrs. Locke, and the Churchill girls danced reels, &c., in the saloon. The *table de jeu* in the dining-room.

Monday, 18*th.*—Busy all the morning. Saw Mercier, the printer, and gave him the first two years of the Letters to print.

Tuesday, 19*th.*—Went to Covent Garden. In Prince Staremberg's box. This was the first night of the theatre's being quiet after the late disturbances. Between the play and farce one man in the pit produced a placard, the object of which was to restore Brandon, and he was supported by a man who spoke from the upper boxes; but both their voices were soon overpowered, and all was perfectly quiet again. The house full. Play, 'Merchant of Venice,' abominably acted, except Charles Kemble, who did Bassanio well.

Wednesday, 20*th.*—Out in the morning in the carriage. Great crowd in St. James's Park, seeing the first audience of the Persian ambassador at the Queen's house.

Sunday, 24*th.*—Lady Harriet Cavendish married this evening at Chiswick. *Quod felix faustumque sit!*

The following thoughts on language; and the melancholy reflections on time gliding on, belong to this year:—

On Language.

Oct. 30, 1809.

Mitford, in his 'Enquiry into the Principles of Harmony in Language,' decidedly advises adopting the Italian mode of pronouncing Latin, and the Athenian mode of pronouncing Greek, as that most nearly approximating the ancient mode, and most

* Son of Mathew Montague, Esq., afterwards Lord Rokeby.

likely to make us sensible of the harmony of their verses. (*See page* 270 *et passim.*)

He notices the marvellous critical and grammatical learning of the modern Greeks in their ancient language, which has been uninterruptedly cultivated and taught to all persons pretending to education, ever since it was actually the common language of the people. (*See page* 276.)

In confirmation of what he says as to the acuteness of the modern Greeks in those perceptions of meaning, independent of reasoning, I remember with astonishment the depth and metaphysical niceties of a certain *Petrarchi*, a modern Greek, who gave me in some months' teaching, the few, and now almost forgotten, ideas I ever had of that exquisite language.

This *Petrarchi* was, in all other respects, a singularly slow, dull, stupid man, holding in contempt all other languages and their literature, and above all others the Latin, to which he never would allow my ignorance to help itself with an allusion or a reference. But in reply to my enquiries as to the use of the different parts of the Greek verb, what wonderful and profound application of the action of the mind in thought, or the powers it meant to express! What nice disquisition of the different tenses! What feeling, imperceptible to others, of the exact measure of passion, or of action expressed by those tenses in which no English scholar, no Porson, no Parr, no Knight, could follow him, and in which, to say the truth, I much doubt if the organs of perception of a northern people, either of mind or body, would ever have allowed them to be sensible!

Time gliding on.

The stream of time seems now to carry me along so rapidly, that I already approach the brink of the great ocean of eternity into which that stream is hurrying to lose itself. I feel so near disappearing with it, that I would fain catch at some idle weeds as my bark glides by, to mark my passage.

How heartily do I and my fireside shake hands, when we meet alone at night after an evening passed in any sort of company; for alas! however agreeable that company may be, to *have been* in it, is now, to me, much more enjoyable than being in it. Solitude broken by a book, and reverie when I can indulge in it, are very real enjoyments. The rest is merely desirable to give a zest to these. And so life glides by me! I no longer make an attempt to mark its course, and aware of the extreme rapidity with which it passes, feel the consolation of knowing that I shall not long be oppressed, even by the painful sense of my own insignificance.

JOURNAL.

1810.

January 4th.—In the evening, Mrs. D. and Mr. Stuart, whose conversation was most entertaining on the history of Spain. His information, clearness, memory, and judgment on matters of history are quite admirable.

Sunday, 7th.—At ten o'clock went to the Princess of Wales; Princess Sophia of Gloucester there. *C'est tout dire* as to the dulness of the party. The Princess knows not what to say to her, nor she to the Princess, who at the same time cannot indulge in her usual flights and conversation. The only women were (besides Mrs. Lisle and Lady Carnarvon in waiting) Duchess of Leeds,* Lady De Ros,† Mrs. C. Lock, and ourselves; the men—Lord Grey, Brougham, Lord W. Somerset, and half a score more young ones, who could have not thought it *royal sport.* The Princess asked us to stay supper, but not being well I got off.

Monday, 8th.—Waked, feeling well—a feeling for which no creature that walks this suffering earth can be more thankful nor more prone to enjoy than myself. Worked hard at my Letters all the morning.

Thursday, 11th.—Went to Strawberry. Walked over to Little Strawberry: found everything out of doors in excellent winter order and looking quite pretty; but everything at Twickenham now wears, to me, a melancholy

* Catherine, daughter of Thomas Anguish, Esq., widow of Francis Godolphin, fifth Duke of Leeds; married 1788; died 1837.

† Charlotte Fitzgerald Baroness de Ros, daughter and heir of the Hon. Robert Boyle Walsingham, wife of Lord Henry Fitzgerald; died 1831.

aspect: its charms are no longer for me. Well, this, however, is not a *real evil*: the mind, if otherwise unencumbered, will get the better of these feelings, and turn to other sources of amusement or occupation; while the memory of Twickenham will perhaps afford more unalloyed pleasure than its actual possession.

Of the publication of Madame du Deffand's Letters at Paris, to which Professor Playfair alludes, Miss Berry gives the following account, in her preface to the work she edited:—

'Madame du Deffand bequeathed to Mr. Walpole the whole of her MSS. papers, letters, and books of every description, with a permission to the Prince de Beauvau to take a copy of any of the papers he might desire, before he conveyed them to Mr. Walpole. This permission Mr. Walpole suspected he had extended to the substraction of some of the original papers.'

'To this permission,' Miss Berry adds in a note, 'was probably owing the publication of three volumes of Madame du Deffand's Correspondence, which lately appeared at Paris; the originals of almost all of which are in the Editor's possession.'

JOURNAL.

Saturday, 13*th*.—Worked at my French Letters all morning; at five o'clock set off for Chiswick.

Sunday, 14*th*.—Sat with the Duchess and Lady Georgiana: an interesting conversation, in which her excellent heart and plain unaffected good sense shone forth.

Sunday, 21*st*.—Went to dinner at Kensington. Not one of the intended party but ourselves could come: instead, we had Lyttelton, Douglas, Kinnaird,* Sir Robert Wilson,†

* Brother to the late Lord Kinnaird, banker in Westminster; died 1830.

† General Sir Robert Wilson was the son of Benjamin Wilson, the painter, born 1777. He was engaged in active service in the army from 1793 to 1812, and was then appointed British Commissioner at the head-

Lord H. Fitz-Gerald, and ourselves—Lyttelton always a host of spirits and conversation; the party by no means dull. Supper ordered at half-past eleven; we came away at one.

Wednesday, 31*st*.—Called on Lady Harriet,* whom I saw for the first time in her *own house*: it is beautifully fitted up in real comfort and much good taste.

The following letter from Professor Playfair belongs to this period:—

Edinburgh, 11th January, 1810.

My dear Madam,—I long very much to hear how you are and what you are doing, and must entreat that you will have the goodness to tell me as soon as you conveniently can. A publication which I have just seen gives me a good deal of solicitude, as I know not how far it may interfere with your intentions. I mean the letters of Madame du Deffand, just published at Paris, containing letters of D'Alembert, Montesquieu, Henault, &c. You have no doubt seen it; many of the letters are extremely interesting, and some of them, I think, can hardly fail to be the same that are in your collection. I feel very much interested to know how this matter stands.

I suppose you are now in town *en famille*. Much interesting discussion about public affairs must soon take place. What think you is to be the result? Will the inertness and apathy of the public prevail over all other considerations, and support an administration unparalleled for ignorance and weakness: or is the nation to be at length roused to a sense of its danger?

I shall write to Mrs. Howe in a day or two, and send her some problems.

John Playfair.

P.S.—Lord W. Seymour, in whom I know you to take an interest, is now here; he is much better, but I think has not recovered his former strength or activity.

quarters of the allied armies. In 1816 he was concerned in the escape of Lafayette. His conduct at the funeral of Queen Caroline led to his dismissal from the army in 1821, but he was reinstated in 1825. From 1818 to 1831 he was M.P. for Southwark; from 1842 to 1849 Governor of Gibraltar; died in London, 1849. He was a writer of several interesting works on military subjects.

* Lady Harriet Leveson Gower.

Tuesday, February 13th.—At home all the morning, working at my Letters.

Friday, 16th.—In the evening we went at half-past ten to Lady Cholmondeley's. A great assembly, with the Persian Ambassador.

Friday, 23rd.—Went to the play; in Mrs. Kemble's box. 'The Free Knights,' and 'The Budget of Blunders.' The first a sort of Sadlers Wells pantomime, but interesting, and Young's acting admirable. 'The Budget of Blunders' all old blunders, but laughable from being well acted. Got the first proof from Juigné, the new printer.

Wednesday, 28th.—Finest spring day that ever was felt, which was lucky, for it was the fast day appointed, and consequently a day of feasting and rejoicing to all the lower orders of people. After church, Agnes and I walked in Hyde Park. In my life I never saw it so full of walkers.

Saturday, March 3rd.—I dined at Lord Ellenborough's. Company almost the whole of the former ministry: Lord and Lady Grey, Lord and Lady Lansdowne, Lord Grenville, Mr. Thomas Grenville, Lord John Townshend, Lord Holland, Duke of Norfolk, Lord Hartington, and Lord Ellenborough; himself the greatest speaker.

Sunday, 4th.—At one o'clock went with Mrs. D. to Mr. Hoper's, to stand godmother, with her, to his little girl. Clergyman kept us waiting till near three, from the number of communicants there had been at St. James's Church—above 300; this accounted for by the number of people obliged to qualify, as it is called, for offices, and commonly doing so at this church. In the evening a party at home, which turned out more numerous than we expected, for we had forty-three people.

Sunday, 18th.—Went at half-past eleven to Kensington Chapel, to hear Sydney Smith preach.* The sermon upon

* The Rev. Sydney Smith, born 1771, died 1845. He was one of the

'Toleration;' very excellent in its general principles, and in the light in which Christianity ought to be considered.

Saturday, 31st.—Mr. Sydney Smith with me in the morning, looking critically over my Preface and Life. Much mended by his observations, upon which I am to work, and I set to it as soon as he was gone.

Tuesday, April 3rd.—Lord Aberdeen, the two ladies, and myself, went to their box at Covent Garden. The play, 'The Beggars' Opera,' not only most execrably sung and acted, but the best parts cut out; but whether from carelessness or propriety I am at a loss to know.

Wednesday, 4th.—In the morning called on J. Baillie, to whom I gave a good lesson, which she will *not* profit by. Sat a long time with Mrs. Hope; always good-humoured and unaffected. Hope and she the image of domestic comfort and good understanding.

Thursday, 5th.—Lady Ellenborough called for me to go to Mrs. Hope's. An enormous assembly; the whole house open, and the Princess of Wales there. Very civil to me, although I had excuses to make. All the men at the House of Commons, which sat till half-past seven o'clock, and voted the commitment of Sir F. Burdett to the Tower.

Friday, 6th.—Went at eleven o'clock to Brook Street, to Mrs. Bouverie's. Found the whole of Berkeley Square and Bruton Street illuminated; several windows having

three or four literary friends who first started the 'Edinburgh Review.' His eminence as a writer upon various subjects was great. His kindness and charity were a blessing to the poor by whom he was surrounded; his warmth of heart, the clearness and depth of his understanding, and his brilliant conversation, made him the most genial of social companions, the most cherished guest of every society he entered. His abounding wit and playful humour were always founded on good sense and on practical wisdom, and he was often apparently so amused himself with the comic combinations that sprang from these sober foundations, that, as the bright thoughts came bubbling forth in words, he enhanced the amusement of others, by his own frank mirth. To have enjoyed the society of Mr. Sydney Smith must be regarded as a privilege never to be forgotten, but stored with other memories of departed joys.

been broken. On my return to North Audley Street, between twelve and one o'clock, every house in Grosvenor Square likewise illuminated, and a few boys and rabble at the corners of some of the streets, calling 'Hats off,' and 'Burdett for ever.' All quiet in North Audley Street, and no lighting. Sir F. B. not gone to the Tower, and resisting the order.*

Saturday, 7*th*.—Soon after two o'clock went out with Agnes. Drove down Berkeley Street into Piccadilly, and passed Sir F. B.'s house twice. The Horse Guards were now patrolling before it, and the people, and for the far greater part very decent people, in peletons only in the street. From Piccadilly we went to St. James's Square, and passed Lord Castlereagh's house, in which there was not a pane left, and one or two of the lower window frames broken in. The window shutters were all shut, and many people looking at it. After sitting some time with Lady Hardwicke we came again into Piccadilly, but the crowd had become so great, both of carriages and people, that we turned up Dover Street. No passage was now allowed by the Horse Guards up Berkeley Street, and the people were crowding down to Piccadilly in every direction, and every window and the tops of the houses crowded with people, in expectation of seeing him pass to the Tower. But his resistance continued obstinate, and the Government, with a folly, improvidence, and weakness worthy of them, had never supposed resistance

* Veneris, 6° die Aprilis, 1810.—Whereas the House of Commons has this day adjudged that Sir Francis Burdett, Bart., who has admitted that a letter, signed 'Francis Burdett,' and further part of a paper entitled 'Argument,' in *Cobbett's Weekly Register*, of March 24, 1810, was printed by his authority (which letter and argument the said House has resolved to be a libellous and scandalous paper, reflecting on the just rights and privileges of the said House), has been thereby guilty of a breach of the privileges of the said House. The House of Commons hath thereupon ordered that the said Sir Francis Burdett, for his said offence, be committed to His Majesty's Tower of London.

possible, and were totally at a loss how to meet it. The whole of Saturday the people again pelted everybody in Piccadilly, and in the evening, in various parts of the town, betrayed a disposition to rioting, and to insisting upon lights; why, or wherefore, neither themselves nor any mortal could tell. Our street and all above it remained quite quiet. At half-past nine we went to Lord Dunmore's. Here we sat till past eleven, when I went to Bruton Street, where I found them again illuminated, though all was quiet; and in Grosvenor and Berkeley Squares detachments both of Light Horse (the 13th) and Foot Guards, and three pieces of artillery were stationed —in the south corner of Grosvenor Square and the north of Berkeley Square. Everybody saying that now it was impossible Sir F. B. could be touched till after Monday, when the House would meet and come to a decision.

Sunday, 8th.—Saw Mr. Hatchet, who lives at the corner of Clarges Street; he reported Piccadilly to be full of people, but free from outrage, owing to the presence of the Horse Guards; the people, however, getting into the Green Park, had pelted them through the iron rails, upon which a troop was dismounted and marched by with their bayonets fixed on their carabines, through the little gate into the Green Park, and driving the people without mischief to the walk on the other side of the pond, and keeping that next the street clear. I walked to Lady G. Morpeth's, with whom I sat an hour; it was a cold dry day, and the streets were uncommonly full, but no apparent disposition to rioting or anything more than general curiosity, and a general fabrication and belief in lies at the corner of every street.

Monday, 9th.—A hard rain, which continued all night, had helped to disperse the mob and keep all quiet in the streets last night. The rain continued the whole of this day. The first thing we heard in the morning was that Sir F. B.'s house had been broken into by the civil power, that is to say the police officers, at six o'clock in the morning, and that he was then on his road to the Tower in a hired coach-and-four, escorted by a strong party of cavalry and Light Horse. He was carried up Bond Street so far, and along Conduit Street and by Portland Street to the New Road, the Lord Mayor having declined admitting his passage with troops through the City. The crowds in Bond Street, Oxford Street, &c., were great, in spite of the continued rain, but no mischief ensued, and he was safely lodged in the Tower, and received there by Lord Moira at half-past eleven o'clock. Lord Moira got quite safe back, the crowd in the streets pulling off their hats, and being civil. But the cavalry on their return, especially the Horse Guards, after long bearing the insults of the people in the most exemplary manner, at last, in the narrow lanes of the City, fired some of their pistols and carabines, which killed two persons and wounded several others. It continued raining hard and continually the whole day, which considerably helped to drive home the idlers and the lookers on, of which every great mob in a great town is half composed. Sir Thomas Sutton called in the morning to inform us of Lord Moira* having got to the Tower quietly at half-past ten before his prisoner, and then again to tell us of his safe return. In the evening the town was quite quiet; there were some patrols of soldiers in the streets, but the cannons were moved out of the squares, and everything at the west end of the town was tranquil, to which the continuous rain in some degree contributed.

Wednesday, 11*th*.—Saw Mr. Sydney Smith in the morning; went over again my Preface and Life; adopted almost all his corrections; expressed with much warmth and sincerity my thanks to him. I believe he was pleased, but I have not known him long enough for him to know

* Afterwards Marquis of Hastings, constable and chief governor of the Tower; died 1836.

me. In the evening to Mr. Whitbread's; a large meeting of all the party, and very agreeable.

Sunday, 22nd.—Walked off to St. George's Church; the church very full, and the sermon by Mr. Hodgson, whom I went to hear, excited my attention.

Sunday, 29th.—Saw Dr. Baillie in the evening; he had been sent for to Wimpole, and was going next morning at five o'clock.

Monday, 30th.—Soon after eleven arrived the fatal letter from Agnes, brought by Dr. Baillie, announcing poor Charlie's* death at Wimpole the day before. The Lord have mercy on his mother! few things out of my own family could, on her account, more heartily affect me. While Agnes's melancholy letter lays before me, and my mind is full of what at this moment the wretched parents of this poor only boy are feeling, the carriages are rolling by in hundreds to Lady Hertford's music and Mrs. Beaumont's ball! But this is human life! I know it, and have had enough of it.

Thursday, May 3rd.—About nine o'clock Mr. Montague told me he had left Wimpole that day, and had persuaded them all to come to town, and that they would certainly arrive that night.

Friday, 4th.—In the morning went down to St. James's Square with Agnes, and the poor afflicted souls had intended seeing me as well as her, but I thought it better not to-day.

Saturday, 5th.—We went again down to St. James's Square in the morning, and I saw and sat with them all. It was a sort of relief to my mind, for I found them better than I expected, that is to say, their grief of that tender saint-like kind, which it is a comfort to share and to be shared. This evening they are to go to Lady A. Barnard's little place at Wimbledon, merely to avoid the

* Hon. Charles Yorke, died in his thirteenth year.

number of people who would want, and whom they could hardly refuse seeing them.

Friday, 11*th*.—In the morning went by myself to Wimbledon. Much more comfortable than I expected it; was a *good* day with Lady Hardwicke; both she and he had been occupied with the sheets of the French Letters I had sent them, and with my Preface. They both talked to me a great deal about it; had made little corrections, &c.

Thursday, 17*th*.—At home all morning; saw Mr. Longman; perfectly content with what I have been doing, and very civil about everything that depends upon him. At ten went to Lady Liddell;* few people there; poured in by hundreds, all the north, and many from every other point of the compass before twelve, when we went to Lady Shaftesbury's, luckily almost next door in Portland Place. The dancing began immediately: first, an English dance; then two quadrilles, admirably well danced; high benches round the room, upon which everybody mounted. Then another English dance; and then Miss Montgomery danced a Bolero, and Lady Barbara immediately afterwards the Tambourine dance, which was really admirable. The ball, upon the whole, both with respect to numbers, lighting, company, dress, and dancing, one of the most brilliant I ever saw in London.

Friday, 18*th*.—Went to Barthelman's concert with Lady Ellenborough. The party, Lord and Lady Ellenborough, Lord and Lady Dunmore, Lord Sidmouth, sat together very comfortably. The Handel part of the concert fine. The Hanover Square Rooms quite full of persons, not one of whose faces I had ever seen before. At the end of the first act I went away, and walked down the whole length of the room with Mr. Rogers, through rows of people, all well or expensively dressed, who had paid half a guinea for their tickets, such a place is London!

* Wife of Sir Thomas Liddell, afterwards Lord Ravensworth.

Tuesday, 22nd.—Soon after one o'clock went to Sloane Street, to call for Lady Charlotte Lindsay, to go to Lady Buckinghamshire's* *Venetian breakfast.* We went on by ourselves to Lady Hood's† house, next door to the breakfast, from whence we proceeded with her. The house, spacious, clean and pretty, the garden looked pretty, filled with young and gaily-dressed people dancing, some of them in masks, and many in dominoes, for this was the notion of a Venetian breakfast! The eating part of it was luckily quite à l'Anglaise, good bread and butter, tea and coffee, &c.

Thursday, June 21st.—All the streets full of common people, moving about in all directions to see Sir Francis Burdett's coming out of the Tower. Went in our carriage down to Piccadilly just as the procession, with its innumerable attendants, were passing, and therefore turned directly into the court of Devonshire House, and, going up a ladder from the stable to the roof next Sir F. Burdett's, saw at our ease the enormous troops of 'unwashed artificers' who accompanied on foot a long train of shabby carriages, and squadrons of people on horseback, which formed the procession, in which Sir F. Burdett was *not*, having gone quietly from the Tower by water to Putney, and from thence to Wimbledon, to the great disappointment of his followers; a third part of whom, it is said, left the procession before it left the City. The numbers that remained, joined to the spectators, certainly could not be less than 150,000 people; I mean the number that we saw in the whole length of Piccadilly. There were three shabby open carriages, drawn by men, and filled with other men, who were violently applauded and huzzaed. We none of us knew any of them by sight, but were told Mr.

* Albinia, daughter of Lord Vere Bertie, and granddaughter of the first Duke of Ancaster; married Earl of Buckinghamshire, 1757; died 1816.

† Wife of Sir Samuel Hood, afterwards married to Stuart Mackenzie, Esq.

Waithman was in one of them. After they had passed and huzzaed before Sir F. Burdett's house, they dispersed by the other streets of Piccadilly.

Tuesday, July 17th.—Went to Lady Ellenborough's. Soon after eleven we set out for Deptford; Lord Ellenborough, myself, and Mr. Pakenham, in their coach and four, and Lady Ellenborough and the rest of the party in two other carriages. An almost perpetual string of carriages of one sort or other the whole way to Deptford. We had cards to go into the Victualling-office Yard. From thence we walked into the Dockyard; the crowd on foot there excessive. With all our gentlemen, and Mr. Towey, a Commissioner of the Victualling-office, at our head, we could with difficulty make our way good, into the covered seats set apart for tickets from the Lords of the Admiralty and the Commissioners, on each side the slip where the ship was.* We were at last placed very near the end. The ship went off five minutes before two most majestically, though we were too near her to see much of the effect in the water. The river was crowded with boats, and when this enormous ship drove for a minute or two with the tide, before her anchors held her, she must have sunk some of the boats, which were as thick as they could lay around. But one person, that I could hear, was drowned. The Princess of Wales was upon the water in a green-covered barge, steered by a post captain. Sir William Rule, one of the Surveyors of the Navy, took us on board the King's yacht (that has always been at Weymouth); it is now in dock. A fine mahogany and gilded thing, really very handsome; but gilt blocks look somehow so inappropriate for use, that they seem too misplaced to please. The crowd of common people and their wives and children, upon the deck of this vessel was great, and nothing but authority and great

* The 'Queen Charlotte,' 120 guns.

names in the yard could obtain leave for the cabins being opened to our party.

Friday, 20th.—Sat to work, and transcribed all the many errors the accurate eye of Lord Hardwicke had discovered.

Monday, 30th.—Went by appointment with Robert to Grafton Street, to consult with Mr. Thornton about the library he proposes adding to his house. The architect with him—a Mr. Hopper; his ideas in some respects good.

Thursday, August 2nd.—Received my copies of the Letters from the bookseller.

To Mrs. Cholmeley.

Strawberry Hill, Tuesday, 7th August, 1810.

I have just been writing a line to Mr. Sydney Smith to inform him that a copy of Madame du Deffand's Letters awaits his orders, and to beg that as soon as he has cast his eye over the vols., that he will lend them to you. . . . The preface and life you will, I hope, be curious to read as my writing. You will tell me truly how they strike you. Even Sydney Smith said he never knew any one who bore cutting and slashing so well. . . . You mistake in supposing both our houses on our hands. Little Strawberry has been let ever since the 1st July, to Dr. Bell, a Prebendary of Westminster. But these yearly lettings answer so ill, and are such a continual source of trouble and vexation to me, that I mean to seek letting it upon lease. . . . If we obtain not as much for the year, as we now get for six months, we shall be rich by the change, and every such change is absolutely necessary to be made in these days, when *our* privations are at least as great as other people's. The term of our yearly job horses being out, we have none at present, and heaven knows when we shall be able to take them up again, while horse-hire and everything else augments in price every day. In spite of all my determinations not to allow money, or considerations about it, to wrong the remainder of my life, it is impossible not to be sometimes plagued, and sometimes melancholy both with what one does, and what one does not do. We have at present the happiness of having with us our friend and cousin, Mrs. Bannister (Basleton), whose husband has kindly allowed her to fly up for a month to see Agnes. The rational cheerful happiness of her well-ordered mind, in her union with a sensible man who knows her value, and who *doats* upon her, is really quite a consoling view of existence, and her having so well deserved the quiet comforts she enjoys by all her former life and sufferings, allows one reasonably to hope they will last.

JOURNAL.

Tuesday, 14*th*.—Received the two notes for a hundred pounds each for my book, from Longman, payable six months hence.

Thursday, 16*th*.—I worked hard at restoring all the Du Deffand papers into their original box, which is to be left here.

Saturday, 18*th*.—Walked over with Bab and my father, after breakfast, to Little Strawberry. The garden full of small fruits, which the tenants do not seem to destroy. My flower-garden overgrown with weeds. I was begged to go in and see Dr. Bell, which I did, and found the poor little deaf old man sitting in the drawing-room, unable to take exercise, and starving of cold because he could not think of having a fire in August!

Saturday, 25*th*.—The Princess of Wales had announced herself to Strawberry Hill at five o'clock; she did not arrive till half-past six o'clock. She had with her only Lady Charlotte Campbell, though she had said she meant to bring with her two or three gentlemen. She had waited for Mr. Gell and Mr. Craven,* who had mistaken the day. We had a cold dinner, as it was supposed to be luncheon only. The Princess was very lively, though the company was certainly not very amusing for her. She remained long at table, then walked and sat in the garden, and afterwards looked at some books of engravings; and

* Hon. Keppel Craven, son of William Lord Craven; born 1779.

was sufficiently amused to remain till twelve o'clock, instead of leaving at half-past nine when the carriage was ordered. The Princess talked a great deal to me, and, as the company was so small, I exerted myself to keep up the conversation, and to respond to her gracious manner.

Tuesday, 28th.—We went to Ham House. The house and the gardens are in the old style; that is to say, the style of Charles II., and belonged to the Duke of Lauderdale,* who married an heiress, Countess of Dysart, in her own right. There are a great many portraits, some of them very good, and several charming little pictures of the Flemish school; much old furniture, and some candelabras in silver, chased to perfection. I was much pleased with the house and its situation, surrounded as it is by large avenues of trees, with its terraced gardens, and its great bowling green; and it needs only to cut down a few trees to enjoy a most smiling scene, yet as perfectly quiet and secluded as if the house were placed in the furthest county from London.†

Friday, 31st.—During the night there was a clap of

* John Maitland, second Earl of Lauderdale, was created Marquis and Duke of Lauderdale 1672. He married first, Ann, daughter of Lord Home, secondly, 1671, Eliza Countess of Dysart, relict of Sir Lionel Tollemache, Bart.; died 1682.

† The description of a visit to Ham House from the pen of Queen Charlotte, addressed to one of her own family, may be of some interest to the reader. The spelling, capital letters, &c., are retained, as in the original letter:—

'I am to thank My dearest . . . . for a very Kind Letter I received yesterday, & wished to have answered it immediately, but was prevented doing it by a Visit to L[dy] Caroline and M[rs] Damer at Ham, where we were received most kindly in Every Sense. This little retreat is quite a little Earthly Paradise, The House stands in a Green Field Incircled by Most Magnificant Trees all Planted by the late G[rl] Carpenter, A Gravel Walk goes all Round the Shrubbery and also round another Field which goes to the end of Ham walks, there they keep three Cows the produce of their Milck is sufficient for their Establishment. The House consists below Stairs of a Small Hall, Drawing Room & Dining Room & a Small Parlour which is Lady Portarlingtons Painting Room when she inhabits the House. The Drawing & Dining Room are entirely furnished with Lady Portarlington's Paintings Consisting Chiefly of Copies after the Old and most Famous thunder which awoke and frightened everybody, and I above all, who am always, to my shame, afraid of thunder. It was a single clap, which seemed to be immediately over London, but which really fell at Kensington, near the palace. Several panes of glass were broken by the percussion of the air; and a large tree, near the entrance to

Masters. A Picture of Her Mother in a Turkish Dress, one of the Present Lrd Bute, & one of Sr Charles Stewart are those not done by Her. From the Salle de Companie You go into the Gardens where under the Shade of the finest Trees possible You may save Yourself from the Violence of the Sun. Above Stairs there are upon the Best Floor four excellent Bed Chambers, & Mrs Damer assures me that the Attics are good & the Offices also. We Dined at three & had to the Honour of Mrs D.'s Housekeeper & Cook as Elegant & good a Dinner as if a Cordon Bleue had directed it, we were very Chearfull & a little after four we drank Coffé; the Rain having ceased L^{dy} Caroline wished to shew me from Ham walks the View of the River & likewise that of Lord Dysart's Place & as She has been favoured with a Key She offered to carry us there, we walked & most delightfull it was there, & saw not only the House, but all the Beautifull Old China which a Civil Housekeeper offered to show us. It is so fine a Collection that to know & admire it as one ought to do it would require many Hours, but when all the Fine Paintings, Cabinets of Excellent Workmanship both in Ivory & Amber also attrack Y^{r} Notice Days are required to see it with Advantage to oneself. The House is much altered since I saw it by repairing & tho' the Old Furniture still remains it is now kept so clean, that even under the Tattered State of Hangings & Chairs One must admire the good Taste of Our forefathers & their Magnificence. The Parqueté Floors have been taken up with great Care, Cleaned & relaid & in order to preserve them the Present Lord has put Carpets over them, but of Course not Nailed down. I saw this time also the Chapel which is so dark & Dismal that I could not go into it. Upon the whole the Place remaining in its old Stile is Beautifull & Magnificent both within & without, but truely Melancholy. My lord is very little there since the Death of His Lady for whom He had the greatest regard & attention. We returned by six to Ham, and left Our Hostesses & L^{dy} Cardigan immediately, we were back time enough to Dress before the K^{g} returned from London, & I had before that a Visit from Augustus [Duke of Sussex], who sets out to Day to join the Prince, but means to see Oxford & Blenheim in His way. And now my dearest . . . . . I know of no more to entertain you for to Day, & if I have succeeded in giving You but a Quarter of an Hours Amusement I shall be amply rewarded, but the greatest reward You could give me, & the best News from Y^{r} Part of the World would be that of Y^{r} being better which I hope will soon be attained by Fresh Air, and inhailing the Soft Sea Breathe. This is the Constant Prayer & wish of

Y^{r} affectionnate . . . . . . & Friend,

'the 7th Sep^{tbr} 1809.' 'CHARLOTTE.

the Princess of Wales's apartments, was half torn up. Sir Harry Englefield, Rogers, Gell, and Keppel Craven, who went out the instant supper was over at the Princess's, were surrounded with a blue flame, which serpentined in a thousand little zigzags of fire; and the noise of the thunder afterwards sounded like the largest pieces of artillery fired off in their ears. They all felt deafened for a time, and then quitted their carriage, and, expecting the continuance of the storm, re-entered the Princess's apartments; but in less than an hour the sky was perfectly clear and covered with stars.

Saturday, September 1st.—Notwithstanding the storm last evening, the morning is hotter than ever. The thermometer yesterday and to-day was up to 86 and 89.

Saturday, 8th.—I went to Kensington, to Lady C. Campbell, to take Madame du Deffand's Letters to the Princess. The Princess, who came into her ladyship's room, thanked me in the most gracious manner possible. She remained talking with me for more than an hour, and invited me to dine with her to-day, but I was furnished with an excuse, which she accepted; I was going into the country, and she took leave of me, saying a thousand amiable things, and begging me to remember her, and to preserve her in my '*good graces.*'

Wednesday, 12th.—I saw Mr. Hope, to whom I had to talk upon the subject of the decorations of Mrs. D——'s theatre, and to ask his advice about Mr. Thornton's intended library.

The following letters, from Colbert, Bishop of Rodez, Professor Playfair, Mr. Cambridge, Mr. Hope, and Mr. Roscoe, bear testimony to the impression made on them by the manner in which Miss Berry had executed her arduous task as editor of Madame du Deffand's Letters, and as author of the preface and notes, which added so much to the interest of the work :—

Londres, le 3 d'Août, 1810.

J'ai reçu hier au soir, Mademoiselle, un gros paquet avec une petite lettre attachée à l'enveloppe. J'ai ouvert l'un et l'autre avec l'empressement de la curiosité, et en présence de plusieurs personnes.

La petite lettre étoit de vous, et m'annonçoit le magnifique présent que vous m'avez envoié. Elle étoit charmante cette lettre, pleine de bontés; j'en étois confus, et cependant ma modestie n'a pas résisté à la tentation de la montrer à mes amis. Ils l'ont tous jugée, comme moi, digne de toute ma reconnoissance. Je ne mérite pas la centième partie de tout ce que vous m'y dites d'honnête et de flatteur. Et pourquoi m'avez-vous offert ce magnifique don? N'étois-je pas déjà assez honoré, assez heureux d'avoir pu manifester un peu de zèle et de bonne volonté pour le succès d'un objet qui vous intéresse et qui est intéressant par lui-même? Reprennez donc vos remercimens; mais je garde l'ouvrage comme votre bienfait, une marque honorable de votre bienveillance et de votre amitié.

En parcourant les volumes, j'ai été en général content de l'impression, quoi que le nombre des *erratas* soit considérable, et je ne doute pas du succès de l'ouvrage. Je m'attens de la part des imprimeurs à plus d'exactitude dans une seconde édition. Quant à l'ouvrage même, je regrette que l'on y ait laissé subsister quelques tâches. Je ne releverai que les *épigrammes* qu'on lit dans le 2 volume, pages 385, 386, 515, et 516. Elles peuvent faire de la peine à des personnes bien chères aujourd'ui à tout bon François. Mais il est trop tard d'en faire à présent l'observation.

Quoi qu'il en soit, Mademoiselle, recevez mes respectueuses actions de grâces, disposez de moi dans toutes les circonstances de ma vie où je puis vous servir utilement; ne pensez jamais à me remercier, et songez que je serai toujours flatté que vous daigniez m'employer à promouvoir vos louables vues. Ce sont les sentimens bien sincères de votre fidèle serviteur

F. S., Ev. de Rx Z.

Edinburgh, 22nd Sept., 1810.

My dear Madam,—I have had the pleasure of your letter, and since, of the Letters of Madame du Deffand, which last arrived safe by the mail three days ago. Accept my best acknowledgments for both. I have had little time yet to look into the Letters; the preface is excellent, very well written and very judicious. The notes bespeak that great familiarity with the characters and persons who figure in the book, which cannot be acquired by reading, and are the result of living and conversing in the first circles both in France and in this country. I find a great deal of amusement and interest in the few letters I have yet read; yet I am not sure that the book will be so generally interesting as it deserves to be; its popularity, I think, is likely to be confined to a part of the fashionable and a part of the literary world, the part of each that takes a particular concern in the society and literature of France, or of what *was* the society and literature of that country. You do not, I am persuaded, expect more than this, and this I think you cannot fail to have.

I have been a great wanderer this summer, though my route has not lain far to the south. I made a visit to the Giant's Causeway, with which I was extremely delighted; though from description and drawings, I found I had conceived a tolerably exact idea of the structure; yet the impression from the greatness and magnificence of the objects could not be anticipated but by an imagination much more powerful than mine. From the Giant's Causeway I went to Dublin, and returned much delighted with all that I had seen, and with most of those whom I met in Ireland. Since that, I have been in the north of Scotland on a short excursion, and have now begun to prepare seriously for the academical winter, which begins unfashionably enough in November. If all is well, I hope to see you in May.

Some weeks ago I saw Miss Phil. Godfrey, who was here on her way to Ireland with Lady Kingston. She is very agreeable; I hardly ever had an opportunity of hearing her speak before, but her conversation is very pleasing.

I will say nothing of public matters, which seem to go on as bad as possible, but in the affair of Walcheren we have witnessed the utmost degradation that the country ever experienced, and anything short of that infamy, is to be reckoned a kind of prosperity. Among private evils, the death of Lady Rosslyn is one of the most melancholy I have known. How does Mrs. Bouverie bear up?

A most amiable and charming woman, Mrs. Apreece,* who

* Jane, daughter of Charles Kerr, of Kelso, Esq., married, first, to Shuck-

has been with us in Scotland for near a year, is just returning to the south, greatly to our sorrow (to mine certainly very much); she is extremely desirous of becoming acquainted with you; she is a great friend of some of your friends—Mrs. Clifford particularly—and so I hope you will early be able to meet. She will not be in London till February.

What shall I say about Mrs. Howe? nothing but that I am to write her in a post or two a letter full of problems and apologies. I wish you could sometimes, especially now that you are relieved from the duties of publication, find time to write me a line or two in the winter. You do not know what a treat your letters are to me. Be kind enough to remember me to Miss Agnes, Mrs. Damer, and Mr. Berry.

Yours, with the most sincere and affectionate attachment,

J. PLAYFAIR.

Extract of a letter from Mr. Cambridge to Miss Berry.

Twickenham Meadows.

. . . . I was about to take up my pen to you to express the pleasure and satisfaction we have just experienced in the perusal of your 'Life of Madame du Deffand,' which does great credit to your judgment and feeling. The plain and clear representation you have given of the mischiefs of French manners, and the sufferings she endured from the want of those consolations which religious impressions are so well calculated to furnish, to infirmity and old age, will do more to recommend religion to your readers, than any more direct argument on the subject could do. This sketch of yours reminded me strongly of some of Sir Joshua's single heads, so much and so justly admired for their simplicity and truth. I only regret you have not taken a larger canvas and introduced a greater variety of figures and objects. But it was the success of his single figures which led that great painter on to his Ugolino.

Extracts of a letter from Mr. Hope.

MY DEAR MISS BERRY,—Your preface I devoured the moment I got it. I have since not *despatched*, but finished your life, with the highest relish for the ease of its style, and the pro-

burgh Ashby Apreece, Esq., and afterwards, April 1812, to Sir Humphry Davy. Sir Humphry died May 1829.

found reflections and just estimate of Madame du Deffand's own character, and that of her age and society which it contains. I now feast upon your notes, and a delightful treat they are. *Avec une telle sauce on mangerait.* . . No matter what, I read all out to Louisa, who owes you the whole of the few moments of enjoyment she feels at this period of anxious expectation, and desires me most warmly to thank you for them. I regret your wire-wove copies having been spoilt, because it is a disappointment to you. To *me* the two lines inscribed on the title page render my little copy what no sheets of gold could equal. . . .

What a labour those notes must have cost you, notwithstanding *il y paraît si peu*, and yet they preserve the true character of notes—subordinate to the text; explaining, sometimes correcting, and never eclipsing it by a disproportionate length.

From Mr. Roscoe to Miss Berry.

Dear Madam,—It was not possible that your obliging note of the 26th could have arrived at a more welcome moment; in fact, I may almost be said to have past the last ten or twelve days in your society; for having been confined to the house by indisposition, my chief pleasure has been the perusal of Madame du Deffand's Letters with the notes, together with Lord Orford's correspondence, which, of all the books in our language, is the best calculated for the study of a convalescent, and I really believe is better than most of the physic in the pharmacopœia. On the table before me lay the beginning of a letter intended to thank you, for the four elegant volumes which I some time since received, although I have scarcely till this interval of leisure, had time to look into them. These letters seem to me to be curious and interesting, but they open the way to other reflexions than the author herself was ever aware of. What these are, I need not inform you. The judicious and excellent notes which accompany them show that you have considered them in their proper light, and that you are as well aware as I am, that the horrible depravity, selfishness, insincerity, and licentiousness, which, under the example of the French monarchs, had infected all the higher ranks of society, and impoverished and enslaved the nation at large, could have no other result than that which has actually taken place.

As to Madame du Deffand herself, I have some doubts whether we shall so nearly agree. She is a true Frenchwoman, with great penetration and shrewdness, but little discretion; great pretence to sentiment, but wholly without a heart—witness her conduct with respect to Voltaire, whom she professed to esteem and admire above all her other friends, but whose death she has noticed with the utmost indifference, and whose yet warm ashes she insulted with a wretched witticism.

Mad. du Deffand was sick in mind all her life, and could never discover the cause. Mr. Walpole, her true friend, seems from time to time to have given her some good advice, which she had the philosophy to take in good part, as a patient receives a bottle of physic, the contents of which he resolves never to swallow. Her disease was vanity; her opiate, admiration; and as this, like other opiates, requires an increased dose, she became miserable when she could not obtain it. How happy it would have been for her if, instead of depending on the opinion of others, she had relied on herself; chastised her mind; improved her understanding—naturally so capable of it; viewed the present and the future, not through the glass of fashion, but with the eye of reason; and whilst she enjoyed the calm and temperate pleasures which even her situation afforded, have looked forwards with hope and confidence to a better state. But retirement was not fashionable; good sense was not fashionable; sincerity was not fashionable; religion was not fashionable; and morality still less so; in short, it was the fashion to turn everything that is truly estimable in public and private life into ridicule; and Mad. du D. had the assurance to sing, in the presence of the King of Sweden, her *Chanson des Philosophes*, little thinking that such outrages upon decency were only the dreadful notes of preparation for those horrible calamities, which were so shortly to ensue.

It would however be unjust to Mad. du D. not to acknowledge that the easy and unaffected style of her letters must ensure the approbation of the admirers of the best models of French composition, and that the succession of important personages who pass in review before her, will amuse those who like to contemplate the shadows of fallen greatness.

If I have been pleased with your notes on Mad. du Deffand, I am delighted with the favourable opinion you have so kindly expressed of my collection of tracts on the war. In proportion as those who avow such opinions are few, the approbation they express is dearer to the feelings of an author; besides, the ladies of the present day are so warlike, that it is really extraordinary to find one, who has retained the clear and unprejudiced use of her understanding amidst the attempts that are made on all hands to confound right and wrong, and to persuade us that no other nations have either a right to think for themselves, or to be happy in their own way.

To talk over these subjects with you, and for once in my life to visit the real 'Castle of Otranto' before I go to meet its late possessor, would, I assure you, give me great pleasure—a pleasure which I do not yet wholly despair of obtaining. Lord Orford's character improves upon me every time I read his works. His wit is universally acknowledged; of his political sagacity and foresight he has left many very striking proofs; but, above all, there are so many instances of a kind and beneficent disposition, and such an enlarged and impartial solicitude for the good of others, without the least affectation or pretence, that I cannot but venerate his memory; and in this sentiment find an additional motive of assuring you how truly I am,

Dear Madam, your obliged and faithful friend,
And very obt. sert.
W. Roscoe.

Allerton, 30th Dec., 1810.

JOURNAL.

Monday, September 24th.—Arrived at Guy's Cliff. We received the heartiest of welcomes from our two friends here. Nobody staying in the house.

Tuesday, 25th.—Walked all round the place after breakfast, and Mr. Greathead showed us all the alterations he has made in the house, which render it one of the most comfortable gentleman's houses I know. The outside, too, is managed with great taste; and a little excrescence is a beauty instead of a deformity. Mr. and Mrs. Wilmot dined here—two young people living within two miles of this place; she a very pretty woman.

Wednesday, 26*th*.—At one o'clock we went to Leamington, to see the new houses building and to be built on Mr. Greathead's land—land of which he has sold three acres for 1,200*l*. an acre, or 5*s*. a yard. The houses are all building by an associated company of people at Warwick, who have subscribed and are expending 50,000*l*. here. The houses now building are in rows, like any street in London, and are in the very worst taste possible, though upon land gently rising from the old village, through which the high road passes, and which might be very pretty. Our friend has nothing to do with the building; he can lay no such restrictions or commands as his excellent taste would dictate, without losing the opportunity of making that money of his land which he has expended to his more solid comfort at Guy's Cliff. Other land, still nearer the old village, has been sold for building at 15*s*. a yard, or at the rate of 3,500*l*. an acre, at this place, which is fast rising into a considerable town and watering-place.* The two Misses Williams and their brother dined and slept here. They are the son and daughters of the clergyman in this neighbourhood. One of the daughters is entirely blind; she is very cheerful and handy, and consequently interesting, and they all seemed well informed.

Friday, 28*th*.—Mr. Greathead and Mr. Williams rowed Agnes and me down the river to Warwick Castle. The navigation down the Avon is very agreeable; a quiet stream overshadowed with broad alders, and flowing through a country of quiet sylvan beauty.

Sunday, 30*th*.—Went to Milverton Church. An excellent sermon from Mr. Lane, (?) *on* the true spirit, and *in* the true spirit of Christianity.

Monday, *October* 1*st*.—We all dined at Kenilworth with Sir James and Lady Lake. Sir James Lake's house

* The population of Leamington at the last Census was estimated at 15,724.

very pretty of its size, entirely of Mr. Greathead's contrivance; to me, who saw it as it was bought, it is wonderful. The purchase-money for it and fourteen acres of land, was 2,000*l.* The house, its alterations, and fittings have cost 5,000*l.*

Wednesday, 3rd.—Waked low and ill, and would willingly not have dined out, but Mr. Greathead wished it. I went with them to Mr. Parke's, at Warwick, a great worsted-spinner, who is likewise a sort of agent and banker to Greathead, and one of whom he has a high opinion; seems a sensible intelligent man, is a dissenter, and much in the Whig party at Warwick. He was cruelly persecuted at the time of the Church-and-King riots at Birmingham. I liked the plain unpretending manner of living of the Parkes.

Saturday, 6th.—Greathead, my sister, and myself went to Stoneleigh, about four miles from hence. We passed the house or abbey, as it is called, from an abbey formerly on the site of the present clumsy house, and drove on to the park. Before we entered we met our acquaintance Mrs. Leigh (whose husband* is to succeed to this place after the present incumbent), and the old incumbent himself, and Mr. Repton, planning future improvements; very probably, like the Irishman's, for the worse. They gave us a key to the park, but we continued on foot, and were led by Greathead to the most beautiful parts of the most beautiful woodland scenery. The Avon, which runs through it, is here in some parts a pretty rippling trout stream, with such magnificent oaks hanging over it as mine eyes never before beheld; and in others it has steep sandy banks, covered by the same magnificent trees, which in this park are in every state and stage of growth, of full vigour, and of natural decay, producing every

* James Henry Leigh, Esq., of Adelstrop, afterwards of Stoneleigh; born 1765; married, 1786, the Hon. Julia Judith Twisleton, eldest daughter of Thomas Lord Saye and Sele; he died 1823.

possible accident of woodland scenery. Many of the oaks measured by Mr. Greathead are twenty-seven and twenty-nine yards round. If this park shows some marks of neglect, it is, at least, unspoiled by improvement. After our walk we returned to the house, and saw the principal rooms on the ground-floor of one of the worst-contrived large houses of fourteen windows in front I ever saw; most of the rooms are oak boxes, floored and lined with oak, of which one *may* have too much, though I love it. We met Mrs. Leigh and her party on our road home. Mr. Repton (whom I had never seen before), fired off an exceeding fine complimentary speech to Agnes and me from the window of the carriage. The Leighs possess 12,000 acres, in the parish of Stoneleigh alone, of excellent land, much under-let at 30*s.* an acre, and in the county of Warwick, not less than 22,000 acres, upon which, certainly, 50,000*l.* worth of wood might be cut down—I don't say without injuring, but positively doing good to the estate. What a magnificent possession of real wealth! It has been long thrown away upon people who have done no good, encouraged no improvements, employed no fine arts, collected nothing; there is not even the pretence to a library in the house; and the present possessors, an old clergyman and his old sister, are perfectly encumbered with the wealth, to which they succeeded at a late period of life, and which obliged them to leave a comfortable parsonage, where they had passed their best years.

N.B.—The *whole* of the timber on the Leigh estates in Warwickshire has been valued at 1,000,000*l.* sterling.

Tuesday, 9*th.*—Agnes and I walked with Mr. Greathead, after breakfast, to Warwick, to see Mr. Parke's manufactory, which he had offered to show us, and which I visited rather out of compliment to him than from any pleasure to myself; for machinery I never comprehend except in a model; and manufactories, upon a near inspection, are always disagreeable. This is for spinning worsted, for knitting and weaving. It differs but little from cotton-spinning; the fleeces are cleverly washed between rollers. About 500 people, men, women, and children, are here employed; and the whole machinery all over the building moves by a steam-engine of 24-horse power, which can be stopped at once by pulling a single string like a bell-handle.

After seeing the manufactory in all its detail, we went with Mr. Parke and his sons to Warwick Church: I wished to see the spot where poor Bertie* is deposited. There is, as yet, no memorial of *him* on the stone which covers the family vault, and where mention is only made of Samuel Greathead, his grandfather, and Peregrine Greathead, his father's elder brother, who died when a lad.

The Lady Chapel, as it is called, in this church (the only part that escaped fire some years ago), is beautiful, and kept almost in too good repair, for it and all its monuments are gilt and coloured up, perhaps too much; 40*l.* a year is left for this purpose. A very fine tomb, with figure in complete armour of brass, and covered with a sort of cradle of the same metal, of Beauchamp,† Earl of Warwick. A fine and much-ornamented tomb, with cumbent figures of Leicester, Queen Elizabeth's favourite, and his wife; and a little cumbent figure of an eldest son of an Earl of Warwick, called upon the inscription, 'an Illustrious Impe,' admirably sculptured.

In the middle of the old chapter-house is the tomb of Sir Fulke Greville, erected by himself during his life, with the inscription upon it of 'the friend of Sir Philip Sidney.'

Saturday, 13*th*.—We took a long scrambling walk, over

* Bertie Greathead, Esq., son of Mr. Greathead, of Guy's Cliff.

† Beauchamp, Earl and Duke of Warwick, died in 1445, when the dukedom became extinct.

hedge and ditch, and turnip and stubble fields, to a shepherd's cave, cut in the rock, and to the drooping well upon the edge of the Avon, to which, three years ago, Greathead had carried me by water. The blind Miss Williams, who was one of our company, got marvellously over everything, with no more assistance than the rest of us, and with much cheerfulness.

Sunday, 14*th*.—I went to Melverton Church with the Greatheads, and stayed and took the Sacrament with them, which I always prefer doing in a quiet country church, than in the bustle of a London one.

The blind Miss Williams played much of Handel's music, and afterwards Greathead read Clarke's travels to us.

Sunday, 21*st*.—In the evening the two young Parkes came up, and we traced upon a map the route of a brother of Mrs. Parke (a captain of a coasting vessel, who has just escaped out of a French prison at Auxonne, and came round by Prague, and then by the Baltic home). He and his companion were forty-six days on their journey, walking on an average thirty miles a day, and, till they got far out of France, sleeping in the fields.

Monday, 22*nd*.—At ten o'clock we took leave of our kind friends. We have spent a month with them most agreeably, with the additional charm of fine weather. Before breakfast I had gone to Greathead in his room, where he always reads before breakfast: here we had a little serious talk about his affairs and prospects, which he considers in the most rational, manly, and respectable way. He then in the most kind and flattering manner recommended some stiff theological reading, as occupation worthy, as he said, of my active mind. I gave him simply and entirely my creed, and the only reason why I feared such reading might not sufficiently interest my mind, viz., because I have no doubts to solve, and my entire and perfect confidence in the dispensations of an all-merciful Creator, makes all lesser points, all subsequent arrangements, wonderfully indifferent to me. I cannot much interest myself in the truth of this or that dogma, or the authenticity of this or that story. Whether true or false, they can in nothing shake my faith, my hopes, and my conviction. He entirely entered into, agreed, and was satisfied with what I said, but still repeated his wish I should read upon that subject.

Saturday, 27*th*.—Went to town.

Sunday, *Nov.* 4*th*.—Called on Mrs. Howe; found her looking thin and in very low spirits about the melancholy state of the Royal Family, but otherwise quite herself and well. Met Lady Donegall, her sister, and mine, going down to the Queen's house to make enquiries.

Monday, 5*th*.—The post brought us a letter from Ronald, with the account of his father's death on Wednesday morning last.

Miss Berry's feelings on this occasion are detailed in her letter to Mr. Greathead, who had recently lost a friend.

North Audley Street, Sunday, 11th Nov., 1810.

My dear Friend,—I was intending to write to you when I received from Anne Turner,* two days ago, the account of your poor old friend's sudden decease. . . . My trust and hope in yours and Mr. G.'s rational minds convinces me that as soon as the first shock is over, you will both feel with what a singularly enviable exit this good old soul, full of years and honour, has been blessed, out of this suffering world. In the house of her friend and adopted child, with every possible attention, kindness, and comfort about her, she enjoys life to the last moment, goes to bed in perfect health, and awakes (for waking only one can call it, when her appearance does not justify even the supposition of a struggle at parting) in another state of existence, for which her conduct in this had duly prepared her. Such is indeed the enthusiasm so beautifully described by Pope—

* Anne Turner, daughter of Dr. Turner, of Curzon Street, an intimate friend of the Miss Berrys.

May death *answer*, that tender frame destroy
In some soft *dream*, or ecstasy of joy;
Peaceful sleep out the Sabbath of the tomb,
And wake to rapture in a life to come.

This I am sure will, after a short time, have its due effect upon you, but it can neither alter the feelings nor raise the depression of the moment . . . Alas! my good friend, you needed not all this, in addition to the worldly cares which have lately so unmeritedly fallen upon you. Would to heaven I could in any way contribute to the alleviation of your feelings! You know that death has lately visited our family, but with a very different aspect from that he put on to your good old friend. My uncle was seized yesterday fortnight, suddenly, while dressing for dinner, with an attack both of palsy and apoplexy together; from the first the medical people said there was no hope; he remained all Sunday totally insensible, and as if asleep. On Monday he recovered, in a degree, his speech and senses; he did not know that Sunday was passed, but asked much for Robert, spoke kindly of him, and was anxious to see him. This happiness he was denied, for he expired on the Wednesday morning. . . . Ronald was with him at the time of the seizure, but the express he sent for his brother only got to him in Yorkshire on the Tuesday, so that the news of his father's death met Robert in Edinburgh . . . The state of public affairs, and the melancholy situation of the Royal Family, were it not for one's own private concerns, one should think sufficiently agitating. The King's determined illness, its probable event, and all its consequences, must, in one way or other, interest every mortal, and either by oneself or one's friends, cast a degree of uncertainty over everybody's plans. A regency, in all cases the worst possible edition of the government it administers, hangs over our heads, in circumstances of particular difficulty and danger, and certainly without a single countervailing advantage to meet them.

The letter from Sir Wm. Gell, at Lisbon, was on its way to Miss Berry at this period.

From Sir W. Gell to the Miss Berrys.

November 9, 1810.

MY DEAR LADIES,—Though I am not aware that I can say anything which will entertain you on the very dark and gloomy day on which you receive this epistle, yet I have a fancy for writing to you; so pray call for a candle, for 'tis too dark to see without, and try to get through it. You have, as I am just informed, heard from my companion the events of our voyage, and your imaginations can easily supply the horrors attending it, as well as the delight of getting on shore with a fine clear air and roasting sun after the operation. Lady Charlotte will also give you some hints which I sent to her on my first arrival. Since that time I have been to the wars—if wars they can be called, for at present the situation of our army is that of country gentlemen in houses which look as if the inhabitants had built them on purpose for the occasion, and kindly left them to us. I went with Captain Beresford, the brother of the grand marshal, in one of those delectable carriages which I have described to my Lady Charlotte. A person in a large cocked hat, in royal livery, drove, and another was mounted behind. The distance may be about twenty-three miles, and about half way we had a relay of more monsters and fresh mules. Here, in justice to the Portagooses, I must stop to say that they are by no means the monsters represented by your friend 'the black-eyed,' for he would be a fright even here. On the contrary, the 'Guese have fine eyes, very intelligent countenances, and the most beautiful teeth in the world; besides which, they are very civil and obliging, and all the horrors related of them and their persons belong only to the rich and great. After this episode, I must tell you that such a system of ups and downs never was undergone. Take a newspaper and crumple it in your hand—that is a map of the country. Then the roads are large stones with large holes between them, and sometimes a descent between two rocks not wide enough to admit the carriage, yet with all this, and more horrors than can be described, the mules crept along very well, and the carriage jumbled after them just as if it had been ever so good. In about six hours we arrived at Capateria, Marshal Beresford's, twenty-two miles. It is a lone house by the road side, covered with tall trees, and remains a lone house in appearance, though there are fifty people in it and around it, from the nature of the place. It was my good fortune to meet with Lord Wellington, the greatest man in his day, at dinner, the very first day. He is no other than a Bonaparte, so strong a likeness, but with better colour; and more animation and merriment I never saw. He has none of the airs of a great man at the head of 100,000 men—all life and good humour. I also met El Marquis Romana,* whom I very much wished to see, and was quite astonished to find how well, first of all, he talks English, and afterwards, what a fund of information, not to say learning, the little wretch has. I talked a great deal to him, and called on him the next morning. As to his figure, such a gig was never seen—a little yellow tailor, smothered in waistcoat lapels, with a blue coat bordered with broad gold lace, very full at top, and coming below to a very narrow waist, the picture of one's great-grandfather. He is very lively and good-humoured, and entirely without humbug. In the morning the Marshal lent me a nag on which I visited the lines and fort, for, be it known to you that our people are invisible to the French, having ridges in front, and occupying in general villages and quintes or garden-houses on the west of it, some miles distant. These ridges are so high that we overlook the French in all parts, but they lie dispersed in tents, generally in different parts of the country below. Junot's camp is, as I think, five or six miles distant, though our advanced sentries and theirs speak. The consequence is, that they cannot attack us without several hours' previous notice, in any force. Our people are quite confident, and this is certain, that the French are at least twice outnumbered by the allies for the present. Their communications are and have been long entirely cut off, and they have no means of sending any intelligence of their situation, as the messenger has always been intercepted. The last, a Portuguese, who spoke Spanish well, and who agreed for the promise of a colonelcy to undertake to carry a despatch. What is singular, a deserter told us this at Marshal Beresford's, and yesterday I heard just such a man had been taken with a letter about his commission to that effect. Upon the whole, the situation of things is quite the reverse of what is imagined in England. You would think Lisbon as quiet as any place could be with operas and plays every night; but the camp is a still more

* Marquis de la Romana, general in the war of the Spaniards against Napoleon. He was the first to suggest the idea of arming the peasantry, and forming the guerillas. In this way, as well as by his personal services in the field, Romana played an important part in maintaining the independence of Spain. Died 1811.—*Popular Encyclopædia.*

curious species of tranquillity; everybody seems to do as they like; people ride all over the country; many officers come to Lisbon. Lord Wellington goes to Mafra and gives a grand dinner and ball, and in short all seems like peace; but, I believe, underhand, everything is so well settled, foreseen, managed, and planned, that every one knows what is to be done at a moment's warning, and under all possible circumstances. I returned on horseback, and had an opportunity of seeing the wonderful strength which nature and art have united to form our system of defence, should even our first line be broken. Not a turn of the road but you find two or three hills, each mounted with guns, placed in forts bearing upon you in all directions. Lisbon is certainly a better place than Madrid or any city in Spain, and more like Italy. The language is too shocking a corruption of Spanish 'os Reis de Portugal *não são tão* (*non sono tanto*) absolutos como os de Hespanha.' In this specimen *não são tão* are pronounced nawn sawn tawn, as much like a cat as possible, and your friend Sousa is called Soysa. The plays are very entertaining, and the singing in them very good. The grotesque dancing, too, I really believe the best in Europe; we go almost every night to something of the kind. To-night 'Il Barbiere de Sevilla,' a most capital buffo, Varancio, or some such name. The Queen of Spain had a passion for him, so we are persuading him to come to England to try his fortune. Pray tell Mercer it is very absurd of him not to come, as both his brethren are here. Douglas Mercer, by-the-by, who ought to be at Cadiz, chose to come here, and got two fingers broken; but he is now almost recovered of that, and looks very well; we see him almost every day. Adieu.—Most truly and affectionately yours,

ANACHARSIS.

Adml. Berkeley saw a play, 'The death of Captain Cook,' in the Isles of the Hottentots.

Monday, 12th.—Walked with Lady Donegall and her sister through the park to St. James's, to enquire after the King; the names written down in the presence chamber, and the Lord in Waiting (Lord C. Spencer) sitting in the room. Nobody with him when we went in, and not a great crowd in the other rooms.

Tuesday, 13*th*.—Walked to St. James's: the crowd great in all the rooms, and a stream going up and down stairs, chiefly men. Saw a number of people I knew.

Thursday, 15*th*.—Accepted Mr. Hope's proposal of going with him to Brighton.

Saturday, 17*th*.—Mr. Hope came soon after eleven. It was a fine sunny day, well calculated to raise one's spirits when travelling comfortably in a chaise and four. But I was out of spirits with myself. My companion, always acute and intelligent in a *tête-à-tête*, was another circumstance in my favour; but all did not do. We arrived at Brighton in the dark and the rain at half-past five.

Tuesday, 20*th*.—We drove to the West Cliff. The extent of Brighton along the cliff to the Crescent, the furthest houses on the East Cliff, cannot be much less than two miles. Went to the play ('The Rivals,' and the 'Agreeable Surprise'), which had been bespoken. The house was more than three parts empty; and the company in the Prince's box, which is always given to the lady who bespeaks the play, talked so loud by way of being so *very genteel*, that one could hardly hear the players.

Friday, 23*rd*.—Walked with Mr. Ward;* his observations are always acute, often droll. But there is *nil grande* in that man; and with a keen and *too* accurate observation of the littlenesses and vanities of others, he is, if I am not much mistaken, overcharged with both himself.

Sunday, 25*th*.—In the evening had some conversation with Mr. Grattan. His manner is singular, with much action, and his pronunciation, without being Irish, so very foreign that nobody at first could possibly take him for a native of these islands; his language is good, however, and his choice of words figurative, and out of the com-

* The Hon. John William Ward, son of Viscount Dudley and Ward; created Earl of Dudley in 1827; died 1833.

mon way; but his manner upon the whole in society is much more odd than pleasant.

Monday, 26th.—Went with Mrs. Hope to the church on the hill above the town. It is crowded with tablets and monuments within, and tombstones without; in short, the town and its inhabitants have fairly outgrown their church,* for there is but one here.†

Wednesday, 28th.—Had a long talk with Lord and Lady Conningham on horseback, and met Du Cane, just arrived. Questioned him about the King of Sweden, who, immediately after his landing, had been brought to his father's house. Went to Mrs. Grattan's,‡ where there was music by the Miss Burgoynes and Miss Grattans, and all the people assembled, who I have seen here, and the Trevors, who are just arrived. Mrs. Grattan, from lameness, is always seated, but a more pleasing woman of past fifty, both in appearance and manner, I never saw. She has been a beauty, an expressive beauty of that sort of which age never can obliterate the traces, and has a manner of speaking particularly sweet and interesting, without the smallest tincture of affectation. As to her husband, from having seen him only in company, which does not draw him out, the singularity of his manner is still with me more prominent than his agreeableness in conversation.

The Princess of Wales's kind letter of enquiry after her

* The Rt. Hon. Henry Grattan, born 1746. In 1772 he was called to the Irish bar. In 1775 he took his seat in the Irish House of Commons, and from that time his life was identified with the history of Ireland. In 1805 he sat for Malton in the English House of Commons. He died in 1820; his remains were interred at Westminster Abbey. On moving the writ to fill the vacancy occasioned by his death, Sir James Mackintosh described Mr. Grattan as one of the few individual men whose personal virtues were rewarded by public favour, and as one as eminent in his observances of all the duties of private life as heroic in the discharge of his public obligations.

† There are now at Brighton eighteen places of worship connected with the Established Church.

‡ Henrietta Fitzgerald, descendant of the Earls of Desmond, married Henry Grattan, 1782.—*Imp. Dict. of Univ. Biog.*

friends, Mr. and Mrs. Wm. Locke, who had just sustained the loss of a child, was received and answered by Miss Berry at the close of her visit to Mr. and Mrs. Hope.

From the Princess of Wales to Miss Berry.

Kensington Palace, Nov. 26, 1810.

My anxiety is so great on account of the poor Lockes, since the melancholy event of the death of their youngest child, that I am induced to commit, perhaps, an indiscretion in intruding on your leisure hours, my dear Miss Berry; but trusting to your usual good nature, and our sentiments concerning them being so congenial, you will comprehend my solicitude. I intrust into your hands, and to your sound judgment, the manner how best to convey from my part everything that is kind and soothing to them: consolation it is impossible to offer them on such a painful occasion, but it is time alone that can cure so great an affliction.

Let us waive this melancholy topic, and rejoice together at the happy prospect of our beloved Monarch's recovery. We may now trust that that storm which passed over our heads will be dispersed for a number and number of years; it must be the fervent wish of every individual, but especially that of one of his first subjects.

I look forward with great pleasure to the period which will enable me again to enjoy your agreeable society.

I wish to be remembered to Mr. and Mrs. Hope; and do me the justice to believe me, for ever,

My dear Miss Berry,

Your very sincere and affectionate,

C. P.

P.S.—I am much shocked and grieved at the melancholy event of poor Lady Aberdeen.* I trust that she will feel no bad effect from this sad disappointment, for nobody deserves more respect and admiration than she does, by those who have the happiness of being intimately acquainted with her.

* Catherine Elizabeth, eldest surviving daughter of John James first Marquis of Abercorn. She died February, 1812.

From Miss Berry to the Princess of Wales.

Brighton, 27th Nov., 1810.

MADAM,—I have conveyed to Mr. and Mrs. Locke * the sentiments of which your Royal Highness has honoured me with being the interpreter. They must themselves express their gratitude, and the high sense they entertain of your Royal Highness's benevolent solicitude. I confess I could use no words at once so impressive and so soothing as those of your Royal Highness. I am happy to say that Mrs. Locke's health has not suffered by her constant, painful, and unwearied attendance on her children, and that the remaining two† are entirely recovered. This I have been obliged to content myself with hearing by report, and by notes that have passed between us, for I have been under such strict quarantine here by Mr. and Mrs. Hope, from the dread of a possibility of infection to their children, that I have only had two short interviews with William, and that in the open air. . . . I have had the happiness to find myself here, Madam, surrounded by some of your Royal Highness's most devoted admirers. Mr. Ward, Sir W. Drummond, Mr. Rogers, Lord and Lady Aberdeen, are those with whom I have been living; and, though last, not least, my kind hosts Mr. and Mrs. Hope, who desire me to express to your Royal Highness their gratitude for the honour of your enquiry after them. Mrs. Hope has, I think, quite recovered her health here. Her best comfort, under the loss of her little girl, is the daily improvement of your Royal Highness's little godson, who is really one of the finest children of his age I ever saw. Lady Aberdeen, I am happy to say, is going on as well as possible, after her very unexpected confinement. . . . Lord Aberdeen certainly bears his disappointment remarkably well. . . . The sentiments which your Royal Highness expresses upon the prospect of his Majesty's recovery, must be those of everyone worthy the happiness of being his subject, by having a due sense of the blessings of his reign. . . .

I have the honour to be, Madam, your Royal Highness's most grateful and most obedient Servant,

M. B.

* Mr. and Mrs. William Locke, of Norbury.

† Mr. William Locke, drowned in the Lake of Como; and Elizabeth, married, 1822, to the Lord Wallscourt.

JOURNAL.

Thursday, Nov. 29th.—Returned to London.

Tuesday, Dec. 4th.—Went to Wimpole.

Wednesday, 5th.—Walked to the garden, and to the dairy and the farm. Somehow or other, the garden is never in very nice order here: the dairy is not much more finished than when I was here last year. Poor souls! no wonder that everything has been at a stand lately, and that nothing goes on with the same heart as formerly!

Saturday, 8th.—Began cutting down the trees, and clearing away about the reservoir, the only building in real good taste about this place. It is like a Roman sepulchre, and will look well when no longer choked up with trees—two beautiful yews behind and a fine cedar in front excepted.

Thursday, 13th. — Left Wimpole, and returned to North Audley Street. In the evening Mr. Thornton came, at ten o'clock, and told us what had been doing in the House of Commons.

Saturday, 15th—Lord Hardwicke brought the news of Lucien Bonaparte and all his family having landed at Falmouth* from one of our frigates, which brought them from Malta.

Sunday, 16th.—Walked with Lady Donegall down to the palace. Very few people there, and still fewer women.

* If Lord Hardwicke's information was right, Lucien and his family must have re-embarked for Plymouth: — '*Dec.* 18. —Lucien Bonaparte, his family and suite, landed this afternoon at the Victualling Office, Plymouth, and proceeded to the "King's Arms," accompanied by Sir Robert Calder (the Port Admiral), General England, Lord Boringdon, and several naval and military officers. Lucien is described as a man about fifty, of pale sallow complexion, intelligent countenance, and gentlemanlike appearance, accompanied by his wife, "a stout handsome woman," and by his five daughters and two sons.'—*Annual Register.* It was on this occasion that they visited Saltram, the seat of Lord Boringdon, afterwards first Earl of Morley.

Thursday, 27*th*.—Lady Charlotte Lindsay called. We walked down to the palace; no crowd there. Lord St. Helens in waiting, and giving up almost all hopes—of senses, I suppose, was meant.

Monday, 31*st*.—Lord Aberdeen called upon me in the morning, and promised to come from the House of Commons and tell us what was doing; which he did, but at past twelve, when we were all gone up-stairs. He wrote down the divisions in his carriage, and sent them up. I felt quite well all day, which I have not done since my attack at Wimpole, and blessed Heaven that the last day of the year ended in health and cheerfulness.

It was in the course of this year that Miss Berry lost her friend and correspondent Mrs. Cholmeley. The following extract from some reflections on the year thus alludes to that event, though without the precise date of its occurrence.

Mrs. Cholmeley's death recalls to me in a melancholy manner many passages in my own past life, and forcibly reminds me how little of that life probably remains to me. This, God knows, I call not melancholy, but consoling. . . . I became acquainted with her in the year 1785, when I was twenty-two, and was just returned from having been plunged for two years into the great world of Europe, from the most perfect retirement in England.

JOURNAL.

1811.

Tuesday, January 1st.—After we were gone up-stairs, Harrot * brought me up a paper, with the division in the House of Commons of thirteen against the ministers, on the proposed restrictions of the Regency,† and said Mr. Thornton was in the drawing-room. I went down; the fire was out, and he looked, in his great coat, the picture of cold and fatigue, yet we had a talk on politics of near half an hour. The Duke of Cumberland, that arch intriguer, has been tampering with him, and persuaded him to vote against the ministers, those very ministers which this Duke of Cumberland intrigued to bring in.

Extract of a Letter from Miss Berry to Charles Stuart, Esq., H.B.M.'s Minister Plenipotentiary at Lisbon.

London, 2nd Jan. 1811.

The enclosed might have gone under cover to Adml Berkeley, or might have found its way without any cover at all; but I have chosen to plague you with it, that I might at the same time recall myself to your memory, and tell you that if your presence is as much wanted in Portugal as your absence is regretted here, we shall never get you home again.

* Harrot was the name of Miss Berry's maid.

† Mr. Percival (first minister), Mr. Ryder, Lord Castlereagh, Lord Sidmouth, Lord Westmoreland, Lord Melville, Lord Eldon, Lord Liverpool, &c. This defeat of ministers was on an amendment, moved by Earl Gower, to the Fifth Resolution respecting the Regency, being that which gave to the Queen the care of the King's person, and the power of appointment and removal of persons in the several offices of the household, and proposing also that a Council should be appointed to advise and assist her Majesty.—*Hansard's Debates.*

Perhaps you think (considering only the importance of the business) that we are here all intent on the affairs of Portugal, impatient for the arrival of a mail from Lisbon, and hanging with fearful expectation upon the event of this last struggle for the expiring liberties of Europe—upon this last stand against the conqueror of the western world, &c. &c. You are quite mistaken, we are thinking of nothing but regencies and restrictions, whether by bill or by address, and one half of us are as triumphant this morning at having beaten the ministers last night by a majority of thirteen, as we should have been if you and Lord Wellington, *tam arte quam marte*, had beaten Massena.

To say the truth, I have a notion that this defeat of ministers is somewhat of a *ruse de guerre* on their part. I know that the Prince of Wales three days ago intended to keep them all in, and I rather suspect that this knowledge prevented what the sailors call a long pull, a strong pull, and a pull altogether. However, they have managed their matters very ill, as usual, for the Prince *is* now, or pretends to be, much affronted. They are all to resign as soon as the bill is passed, and they say their resignations will be accepted. But, at all events, these delays, whether intended or not, may very possibly put an end to *any* regency and *any* restrictions.

By what I hear to-day, I expect that just as the Prince is ready to step into his new title, the King will be ready to govern us just as he has done before, and will be declared by his physicians well enough, that is to say, mad enough, to wish to retain the government.

Saturday, 5*th.*—Before dinner, Matthew Montague, Sir John Sebright, and Lord Hardwicke met here. Matthew's account of one of the divisions in the House of Commons most laughable.

Sunday, 6*th.*—Had a long conversation with Mr S. Turner in my room on the subject of the report of the Bullion Committee. His ideas have on some points cleared up, and on some confirmed, my own. But the subject is more involved in difficulties than one at first imagines, from the very extraordinary circumstances in which the very extraordinary times have placed commerce, as well everything else, and therefore it requires a more steady and frequent recurrence to *first principles* to keep one's understanding clear.

Extract of a Letter from Charles Stuart, Esq., to Miss Berry.

Lisbon, 9th January, 1811.

. . . . I am sorry the public attention is directed rather to parish business in England than to the observation of the events which are going forward in this country. It is not Portugal merely we are defending, but we are training and forming an army accustomed to war on the great scale, and on whom we probably shall one day rely for the security of our firesides, though to most people that is a more interesting subject than it is to me, whose fireside is always in some other part of the world.

On this ground I should be sorry that any change in England induced people to give up the game here. We have a fair equal chance, and if the new or the old minister will allow us to fight it out, I am very well convinced that we shall get through the business, more honourably and more advantageously than we have any reason to expect. I hope you will not be uneasy about the brothers and husbands, and cousins, whose fate would depend on this determination: such considerations usually have more influence in ladies' politics than any calculations of the chances attendant on the different contingencies which may occur.

Saturday, 12*th*.—Dined at Mrs. Damer's with M. De Bréhan, the Frenchman who has brought her the present of a fine cup and saucer from the Empress Josephine.*

* In the work entitled 'Queens of Society,' before alluded to as misrepresenting the reception of Mrs. Damer at Paris in 1802, this gift of porcelain is also affixed to a wrong date. Mrs. Damer is there mentioned as visiting Paris in the year 1779, when 'she was introduced to the beautiful and witty Josephine Beauharnais, then a leader of fashion in that city, and their acquaintance had ripened into friendship,' that 'she heard no more of Josephine till one day a French gentleman called upon her with a fine piece of porcelain and a letter of introduction from the First Consul's wife; that Napoleon was anxious to conciliate the Whigs, and that Mrs. Damer set out

He appears by his conversation and manners, which are unaffected, to be something above the rank of an upper servant—a decent person employed in commissions, &c. He comes here with a great order to Lee and Kennedy, for plants for the said Empress; whether he brings a liquidation of her long account with them, I know not. He has a mother and an uncle settled here, who live together at Hampstead. The uncle is no other than that M. de Montier or Monstier, who was the first French agent to motive the peace of 1783, before Reyneval was sent here. He crossed from Dieppe to Gravesend as was intended, but by stress of weather was allowed to land at Margate. He, or anybody else leaving France for this country, must have a particular passport, signed twice by the Emperor's own hand.

Tuesday, 15*th*.—Found Miss C. Fanshawe at home; half her formality, I believe, depends upon the family to which she belongs. We are half of us the creatures of circumstances; or rather, the half-marred, half-made creatures of circumstance.

Wednesday, 16*th*.—Went to Little Strawberry.

Saturday, 19*th*.—Upon the terrace before my little green-house the sun was quite warm, and all the double violets upon the bank ready to blow; how occupied and happy I could be for many an hour in such a scene! but I am quite aware that in my particular circumstances I have nothing to do but to leave it, and forget it as soon as I can.

Monday, 21*st*.—Lady Charlotte Lindsay proposed from the Priory our acting with them, which I begged her in the most civil manner to refuse on my part, my health alone a more than sufficient apology: but if it were not,

for Paris after the Peace of Amiens, &c.' It appears that the French gentleman's visit was nine years after Mrs. Damer's visit in 1802, when she had little reason to be flattered by the reception given to her by the First Consul and his wife.

I should never think of enlisting in their troop for a thousand reasons—distance, time, expense, trouble, and exhibition to all London at Easter. Besides there is a time for every thing.

Friday, February 1*st.*—Went at nine o'clock to Kensington to the Princess of Wales'. Princess Charlotte had dined there, and I was anxious to see her. We found her, the Princess, the Lady Charlotte Campbell (in waiting), Miss Garth, Miss Hayman, Lady de Clifford, and Sir William Drummond,* playing at a round table at a foolish sort of game, of calling the cards by the name of Ninycumtwit, or something like that. Princess Charlotte was seated by her mother, who named us to her, and said to us, 'My daughter.' I sat down by the Princess; she whispered something to Princesss Charlotte about me; she answered immediately, 'I know it, I know it; she is a great friend of Mrs. Howe.'

A finer girl of fifteen one seldom sees, with an open lively countenance, and well-cut expressive features; fair, like all her family, but without having a fine complexion, or at present any colour, for by some inconceivable mismanagement at the time she had the small-pox, it has muddled her complexion, destroyed in part her eyebrows, and left several decided marks about the end of her nose. I dare say there is hardly another person in the kingdom, who within these last fifteen years has suffered as much by the small-pox, which only shows the old story, how much the children of princes are neglected and ill-treated. Her mouth is like the Prince of Wales's, without having however much sweetness, and her eyes are by no means as handsome as her mother's. She is lively, animated, and laughing; told Sir William Drummond, who was on

* Rt. Hon. Sir William Drummond, formerly Ambassador to the Court of Sicily, the author of a 'Review of the Governments of Sparta and Athens,' 'The Satires of Persius,' &c., also of a work, for private circulation, in which he treated some of the histories in the Old Testament as allegories.

the other side of her, to go on with what he was saying, for she liked nothing so much as politics; then got into a talk with Lady Charlotte Campbell, about being afraid of the dark and ghosts, and dismal stories; told a good one herself, and then made me tell her the story of Lillo's* 'Fatal Curiosity,' which Lady Charlotte mentioned, and which she had never heard of before. Soon after ten o'clock her carriage was announced, and away she went, very cheerfully, having kissed her mother, shook hands with Lady Charlotte, &c., and bowed to us. And thus is this girl, now a woman, who in three short years may be called to reign over this country, with all her senses awake, eager and curious about everything and everybody, sent away with her governess, and during the hours not spent with her, she has Mrs. —— to form her mind, manners, and disposition! Alas! poor Princes, one and all, can you ever be pitied enough, or even judged with common justice under all the disadvantages you labour? True, this poor thing is taught music, and taught Latin, neither of which will certainly be of *much service* to her in governing this country, in detecting folly and knavery, in surrounding herself with talents, and above all, in acquiring truth and stability of character. She knows no creature, but the Royal Family and their attendants; she has never yet seen a play or an opera; and whenever she is her own mistress, what must be her first idea but to satiate herself with pleasures, which every other girl of fifteen is beginning to appreciate at their just value, provided they are not entirely new to them.

We remained to supper; nobody joined the party, but Lord Aberdeen and the Hopes, who did not arrive till twelve o'clock, though asked at nine o'clock, which the Princess remarked. The Princess, though lively at supper,

* George Lillo, a dramatic writer, son of a Dutch jeweller; born 1693; died 1739.

and talking a great deal to me about her memoirs, which in joke she said I should publish, &c., is pensive, and not in her usual spirits, says she has the second-sight, and sees a great deal that is coming, nothing that anybody expects, and a great deal that nobody thinks of.

Saturday, 2nd.—Went to the play—'Cato'—in Mrs. Kemble's box. I have always particularly, and in spite of all abuse of it, loved the piece; it both interests and *affects* me, which magnanimity ever does. Kemble acted well. Young particularly so, in the short part of Portius; C. Kemble well in Juba; Syphax, by a man of the name of Egerton, who had no idea of the poetry he was repeating.

Friday, 8th.—To Mrs. Sotheby's, where was a sort of blue-stocking assembly, misses and their mammas without end, so pleased to carry them to a rational house, and unite pleasure and wisdom together!

Sunday, 10th.—Lady Charlotte Lindsay called for me in the Princess's carriage to go to dinner, and we took up Puységur at Monsieur's house in South Audley Street. The party at dinner were: Lord Gower,* Lord Charlemont, Mr. and Mrs. Hope, Mr. Lewis, and Sir H. England; Lady Glenbervie and Miss Hayman in waiting. The Princess did not look ill, but really was so. The men all went away sooner or later, and nobody remained to supper but myself and Lady Charlotte Lindsay. The Princess quiet and low, but, to give her her due, not out of humour.

From Sir W. Gell to Miss Berry.

Lisbon, Feb. 2, 1811.

My dear Friends,—If, as Plutarch says, you really wish for us back again in England, your hopes stand some chance of being realised, for we have this day taken measures for bringing about that desirable event—an event chiefly rendered necessary by the

* The late Duke of Sutherland.

total disorganization of the system of finance which seems to have affected us both at the same moment. . . . So many lies are invented on the subject of our situation here, and we are in general so completely in the dark on the subject of who, how many, where and when, that I shall give you what I have seen myself before I proceed to the reigning lies of the day. Romana is dead, and we went in the procession to his burial. He was, perhaps, the only learned man in his country, and I believe the only person in the Peninsula who had information sufficient to guide his judgment beyond the mere events of the day. He was a very good scholar—a thing quite unheard of in Spain; he was very well read in history, and if he was not a good general, which I very much doubt, there is no hope of a better among the survivors. Moreover, a person who with a small army and confined resources can preserve himself from any serious defeat, with 20,000 enemies in the country, for the space of two years, cannot be so very bad a commander as the English would represent him. I took particular pains to get acquainted with him, and think I never saw a person of whom one has heard so much, with so little of the humbug grandissima about him. The history of Romana being concluded, I shall proceed to inform you that the last lie from Cadiz says the French have so far raised the siege, that only 6,000 men remain there, and that we have it in contemplation to blow them and their works up together. It will be the first time since the revolution that the French have spent a whole year upon a siege and got nothing but their labour for their pains. A blind shell, that is a shell filled with lead to make it heavier, will just reach over the walls into the herb-market at Cadiz. This, however, requires so much powder, and burying the gun in the earth, that no gun can last long with such treatment, while the shell does little mischief, being directed, as Aristotle observes, so high in the air that it falls down perpendicularly, and can only kill at most one person at a time, and this, if indeed anyone is hit, is at the expense of five to six pounds a shot. It appears, however, very possible that our shipping might easily be annoyed in the harbour. As to Junot's death by a shot in the face, you may perhaps hear of it before this reaches you. It was at first certain; then quite false; then absolutely verified; then a lie again; and now remains uncertain, only this being known, that a person, supposed Junot, was hit in the face by a musket-ball, and fell from his horse. We have taken several letters which were to have been delivered to the French. One from Mrs. Junot, at Ciudad Rodrigo, says to Junot, 'I have just produced a son, which I am glad of, because it will please you. As to your ever establishing yourself at Abrantes, the hope does not seem likely ever to be realised, so I shall set off for Paris, as the sight of ten men per day carried past my window to their graves makes me melancholy; and if I go to Salamanca, as you recommend, they tell me I shall see not fewer than forty burials every day.' Some of those passages which relate to private concerns, Lord Wellington has copied for Junot in his own hand, and added congratulations on the birth of the son, so that Junot must answer in his own hand, which Lord Wellington knows well, and thus expects to find out whether he is killed or dangerously wounded, or unhurt. As to what you see in newspapers about the starvation of the French at Santarem a fortnight ago, that is all false; indeed, the event alone is a sufficient contradiction. Two or three days ago, however, it was suspected that the enemy was weakening his forces at Santarem by degrees, and Marshal Beresford went up the left bank of the Tagus to see that Abrantes was secure from any *coup-de-main* they might attempt if they retreated by that city. Upon the whole, though there is not *apparently* the smallest chance of any great overthrow of the French under Massena, they do not seem likely to be able to do anything against us, while they certainly are diminishing very rapidly in numbers throughout the Peninsula. Perhaps you have heard that since the war broke out 500,000 men have passed this way through Bayonne; and this account, compared with the statement of the French force in Spain up to December, 1810, shows that 280,000 have been somehow or other disposed of in this country, and this is their own account of the business, while they certainly have not a foot of land beyond what their army occupies, and even their armies have no communications unless it be on occasions where it is worth sending 5,000 or 6,000 men as an escort, for their letters are perpetually falling into our hands. Neither prisoners nor deserters now seem to come in to us quickly; indeed, desertion is difficult from the nature of the French position, but a great deal of this has been much magnified, as it appears that the French have lost only

1,500 men in the whole year by desertion, while we have lost 480 ourselves. I believe there are very few instances of the Portuguese deserting. This is I think all I know at present. As to climate, we have had sixty-four of bright sunshine and about twelve of heavy weather. We intend to be in England about the latter end of this month; indeed, I shall this day begin to pack up. . . . My health has so much improved by the assistance of M. Husson, that I am become an absolute nuisance in company from the riot I make. Indeed, Craven was asked the other day whether I was not an idiot. Luckily, my finances do not keep pace with my wits, and generally keep me down two or three steps lower than I should otherwise be, which saves me from becoming quite intolerable. I keep sighing for riches, but 'nobody coming to marry me, nobody going to die,' must be my motto. Tell Lady Char not to write, for I am coming to hear it all myself so soon as possible, and to take my waiting with her Ladyship. . . . You have spent the whole of the annuity I allowed you out of the rents of my estate in Eldorado.* Never mind, we are all ruined; we will fit up my sister Agnes's room this spring, and then we will make Mr. Berry perfectly miserable by effecting a thorough reform in his apartment.

Hope did very ill in not giving me a commission to buy old plate for him. We have it here for its weight in dollars, and beautifully solid in appearance, whereas the manufacture consists of a thin plate of silver, which is thumped and bumped into a variety of flowers and patterns with punches and mallets. Under these awful impressions I take my leave, assuring you all of my highest consideration, and of the delight with which I shall come again to set an example of morality and piety to your family in North Audley Street. There is no room for pictures, besides which an inundation of Vandals is now ascending the stairs. So adieu, my dear friends, with best love to dear Mrs. Damer, for whom I bring a little chip of marble, to see whether it is good for statuary, and of which there is plenty here.

Most affectionately yours,

ANACHARSIS.

* Mr. Gell alludes to some furniture procured by Miss Berry, either for their own use or for his, and about which they had corresponded.

JOURNAL.

Sunday, February 24th.—At three o'clock I went with Mrs. Apreece* to Mrs. Siddons', at Westbourne. Mrs. Siddons received me, as she always does, in a manner which flatters my internal vanity; for she has the germ of a superior nature in her, though burnt up by the long-continued dram of popular applause—'Datus in theatro'—which I know nobody who has ever withstood. Mrs. Apreece, in our journey there and back, entertaining.

Tuesday, 26th.—Augustus Foster† and Lord Morpeth called. They had been to the Prince's levée; great crowds, splendid liveries, and hussars of all colours. He very gracious, but speaking little to anybody. It began at or before two o'clock, and was over soon after four.

The following interesting correspondence between Professor Playfair and Miss Berry shows from whence sprang the suggestion of the work on a comparative state of manners; and, though not literally adopted by Miss Berry, was no doubt the origin of her future work on 'The Comparative View of Social Life in France and England.'

Edinburgh, 1st January.

My dear Madam,—It has long been determined that the letters of Mad. du Deffand shall be subjected to the ordeal of the 'Edinburgh Review,' but I do not believe that Rhadamanthus Smith will be the judge appealed to on that occasion. At all events, you may be sure that your note will be attended to. At one time I was afraid that the review of Mad. du D. must have come forward in the last No., which would have occasioned it to be done in a hurried way, and not nearly so well as I hope it may be in the next No. which comes out, or at least ought to come out, in February. You may expect to see your own work as an editor, meet with great commendation (indeed, I think it

* Afterwards married to Sir Humphry Davy.

† Son of Lady Elizabeth Foster.

cannot meet with too much); whether you will so much approve of the reviewer's opinion of Mad. du D. or of Lord O. I am not quite sure; this, however, I think I can say, that the tone of the review will not diminish the curiosity of the public, or their desire to be acquainted with the book.

To your questions about Scots law and Scots lawyers, I do not believe that I know enough of the matter to give any satisfactory answer. It is certainly to be regretted if the profligacy of English manners find a shelter or defence in the ruder and more imperfect legislation of another country, but it seems to me that it is not the *law* of this latter country that is so much to be blamed as the *morals* of the former.

That the laws of every country must be general rules, admitting of no exception, is unavoidable, and that the applications of such general rules to particular cases must often produce injustice, and must often shelter criminality, is a truth of which every country and every age have been unfortunate enough to afford many examples. I do not see any more than this in the instance of Lord ——, &c.

Your questions about —— refer to matters that I know nothing of, but they considerably awaken my curiosity, and will make me try to be informed. At all events, however, I think I know the answer that I would be disposed to make if you would draw from them or such like instances, any conclusions against Scotland in general. The sophistry by which people support their prejudices in the case of national character, and many others it were easy to name, seems to me to be this. (Do not be alarmed at the word sophistry; I do not think you are a person to be deceived by anybody's sophistry but your own, and against one's own sophistry I fear nobody is proof.) In every country there is a considerable quantity both of good and evil which it is impossible not to remark. When there are any prejudices already existing against the country, all the good is set down to the account of individual or personal character, and all the ill to the account of national and general character. Thus, by particularising the one and generalising the other, a picture is made out that seems to be quite like nature and perfectly copied from the truth, and at the same time quite conformable to all the prejudices already entertained. Now give me leave to say that I have often observed you doing exactly what I have now described; that is, when you met with good people or good things in this country, which might by chance now and then occur, you would immediately ascribe it, as you probably was very right in doing, to individual merit of some kind or other; but when the bad occurred, which it would do, God knows, but too often, you put all this down to the score of that unhappy nation, composed of Celts and Goths, which extends from the Tweed to the *Ultima Thule* of the North. The feelings of a good mind, that takes an interest in good people, and forms attachments to them, are thus gratified, and, at the same time, national prejudice is kept up and wars strengthened. You have a mind, give me leave to say, very superior to all the prejudices which it is of most importance to overcome. To the great idols, as Bacon calls them, to which so much worship is paid all over the world, you never bend the knee; but there are one or two smaller images which you seem to take pleasure in paying a little more respect to than is fairly their due. They are prejudices of no great account, I allow, and hardly of any moment at all in the estimation of the soundness of mental attainment; yet, even from these I would wish that *your mind* was entirely free. One is naturally most interested in the perfection of that which is already excellent.

You asked my opinion before on another subject—the manner in which you may employ your leisure in some literary occupation. When I received your former letter, in which this question was put, I happened to be with Lord W. Seymour, and I took the liberty of stating the matter to him. The idea that occurred, and that he was the first to suggest, was, that the *manners* of some Age distinguished in the history of our country, would make a good subject for you to study and give an account of. The manners, for example, in the reign of Queen Elizabeth as compared with those of the present day—I mean, of the fashionable world; or, perhaps the time of Queen Anne might be still better; there are ample materials for it, and the thing cannot be well done but by one who is properly acquainted with the fashionable world at present, and who has been in it, with all the observation and thorough acquaintance with it which we know you to possess. This seemed very good to us both, and the sort of reading into which it would lead you would be of a pleasant nature, not too intricate or laborious for enjoyment.

Since that, on thinking over all these things by myself, it has occurred that biography may offer good subjects for you. Eminent persons of either sex, who, though well known, are not so well known in the details of private life as they deserve to be, are good subjects for biographical memoirs or sketches, more or less particular, as circumstances might direct. What think you of some subject of this kind? Your short account of Mad. du Deffand is a proof of how well you would succeed in such a subject. It is written with a great deal of force, good sense, and good taste. I would be glad if you would write me on this subject.

R. Fergusson is here just now on his way to town. . . . I learn that he thinks of living at Raith; that he finds himself left with considerable encumbrances, and by no means rich. . . .

What a business in the political world! At last, it would seem that common sense is to prevail, but by a very small majority.

I understand Mrs. A. Apreece is either in London or is to be there soon, and I am very glad to think that you will certainly become acquainted.

I should like to know if you approve of either of the subjects above mentioned.

With best wishes, many years and happy ones, I remain, my dear Miss Berry, your respectful and affectionate Friend,

JOHN PLAYFAIR.

To Professor Playfair.

Feb., 1811.

How shall I thank you for so kindly taking the trouble of suggesting to me some employment for my useless time? I have thought much upon the two ideas you mention. But want your clear head to débrouiller them a little more before I can fix upon, or indeed fairly judge of either, and measure it with my own force, or rather, with my own weakness. Of reading and reference I am not afraid, as I read very quickly, and have several kind friends who would help me to the books I have not. But no biography at all within my sphere occurs to me. The other plan you mention might, I should think, in capable hands, be made very entertaining. . . . I have had for many years an idea, at times, wandering about in my head of something in English like *les caractères de la Bruyère.* I don't mean either a translation or an imitation, but merely an adoption of his arrangement, and I have by me a number of scraps written with a view to this, some arranged and more not arranged, under a selection of the heads into which he has divided his work. Whether any of this stuff could be worked up into something else, or if it be worth preserving at all, I have honestly and truly no idea. When you come to town in May (as we are led to hope), you will perhaps take the trouble of running over some of it and telling me; as it is a part of no whole, I have not yet a parent's partiality for it. I can myself see a thousand objections to anything built upon or recalling to memory *La Bruyère.* First, the perfection of the work itself, which one cannot hope to approach; next, the extreme facility with which the world would construe such a work into individual satire, and the difficulty which one might sometimes have oneself to avoid it. In short, I want somebody wiser than myself, both to tell me what to do, and how to do it; and then comes ever and anon headache, triumphant for two or three days together, and so absorbs my existence, as not only to make *all* occupation at the time impossible, but to damp all confidence, and destroy all projects for the employment of the hours left me. . . . Your friend Mrs. Apreece is to pass the evening with us to-morrow. Agnes was much pleased with her conversation and manner, and I hear of her agreeableness from all quarters. She will soon probably, like the rest of the world, be too much engaged in the dissipation of this great town to have as much time to bestow upon real society as she would wish.

The latest news of Robert is that he was this day elected of the Alfred Club, for which there were 314 candidates, and only eight vacancies; he was very desirous of filling one of them, and we were very glad to be able to secure him a number of votes.

Of politics it is quite impossible to speak. Come and see them: talking about them is in vain, for all arguments, and principles, and projects are overthrown. I feel myself convinced, by this last turn of the wheel for the present ministry, of two or three probabilities which all parties equally disclaim at present, but which, nevertheless, we shall see take place, except something much more wonderful should occur, than the Prince becoming attached to these people, who will flatter and wheedle him, and discover talents and virtues, and then such filial piety in him ! ! ! St. James's Square and Pall Mall to-day were full of the carriages of the Privy Council, who were in a body at Carleton House, to administer to him the oath prescribed by Parliament; and on Tuesday next, it is said, he opens the two Houses, but I have a bet he does it by commission. In the mean time the King is almost well again—that is to say, just mad enough to desire to reign, which he will do, so much like his son, and his son so much like him, that the happy country will never know the difference. Farewell! it is high time to recollect that you have something else to do than read my letters. . . . Remember me affectionately, and with many thanks, to Lord Webb, if near you; and believe me, with the sincerest regard and gratitude, your attached friend,

M. B.

P.S.—The admirable lesson you give on national prejudices, I really think will prevent me ever exposing myself on the subject again. It is no excuse to say that these prejudices were first instilled, and then strengthened by a chain of unfortunate circumstances. . . . But I ought to have known how to resist the series of unfavourable impressions to which I own, with shame, having yielded.

From the Hon. Keppel Craven to Miss Berry.

Lisbon, Thursday, March 7, 1811.

My dear Miss Berrys (for I mean to address you both at once),—I feel very reluctant in writing to you, being conscious that our friend Anacharsis must have told you everything that ever happened to us both while he was here, and nothing very much worth recording having occurred since his departure, unless it is the retreat of the French, which has actually begun, so much so that all our divisions are ordered to move, and Lord Wellington's head-quarters were yesterday morning at Santarem. Further we know not, but suppose that the news of the arrival of our reinforcements (which took place on Monday) must have urged the enemy to this step, or that of General Graham having arrived at Seville, which is said to be the case; but this last piece of intelligence I give you only as a report. I am the very worst person in the world to retail news, for I generally receive it incorrect and report it false. After this declaration you must judge what degree of credit you may attach to that I have given you. Sir J. Yorke and his fine squadron came in on Monday, and I fancy sail again to-morrow. He would not come and anchor under the town, as there is really scarcely *room* in the Tagus; but I wish he had, merely to surprise the Portuguese with the sight of seventeen sail of the line so near to them. We have had an exact representation of summer ever since Gell's departure, which has increased my stock of health to that degree that I am afraid of an apoplexy, but am going to guard against such an accident by a little sea discipline. My cousin Frederick Berkeley, who has lately been appointed to a troop ship, is going in a day or two to Oporto, to fetch some Portuguese recruits, and has asked me to be his companion in that cruise, which I have promised, as it will be a convenient opportunity of seeing Oporto, and there is at present nothing to be done at Lisbon, the theatres and balls having all closed since the commencement of Lent, and all my friends having galloped off to the army on Tuesday evening. Some were so kind as to leave me the charge of settling their accounts and packing up their baggage, by which agreeable employment I was taken up the whole of yesterday. I hope to be back in less than a fortnight, and then have a week to prepare for my own departure for England, which I mean, if possible, to take place by the first of next month, and, *Deo volente*, to embrace you (for that is a privilege of all travellers) by the 15th of April.

. . . Charles Stuart is a most delightful person, as you well know; he lets everybody turn his house topsy-turvy, and his dinners are quite delightful, as they possess the fundamental requisite for promoting agreeable conversation, I mean being well dressed; and then he never minds anyone's costume, so I indulge in the luxury of fancy dress, which is strictly forbidden at the Admiral's; besides which they last a very short time, and you may come in and go out whenever you please—in short, there never was so amiable a minister.

. . . Do you know St. Hermenegild? He was son to Leovigild, king of the Longobards, and brother to Prince Recavedus. He married Evarinta, a beautiful Catholic princess, and lived in the woods with her. His father, who followed the Arian Schism, sent a furious priest, called Ebbalinus, at the head of an army to seize him and bring him back, and the said minister found this holy pair in devout meditation on the top of a hill, which hill walked away the instant the soldiers tried to mount it, leaving in its stead a chasm full of flames. However, the prince returned of his own accord to his father, who, by the instigation of the priest, put him to death, which was announced to him by the Holy Ghost. At first it had been agreed to thrust him into the king's menagerie, but there the lions licked his feet, and quite treated him as a brother. So his head was cut off; notwithstanding which he went up to heaven with it on, dressed in a very handsome white robe, with a palm in his hand, in a cloud more beautiful and transparent than any of Mr. Orme's screens, surrounded by cherubims and angels playing on various instruments, and singing a chorus composed by Marus Portogallo. All this happened last Sunday, and you might see it to-night again were you going with me to the Portuguese Theatre, where these martyrdoms take place twice every week, in presence of a numerous and pious audience, who show their piety by clapping of hands and cries of Bravo.

. . . Pray have the kindness to remember me most particularly to Mrs. Damer. You cannot conceive how much I regret her giving up Strawberry Hill, for I must ever remember with pleasure the happy rainy days I occasionally passed there; our embarkations, disembarkations, eating strawberries, the wet grass that adorns the Bay of Biscay, and the terrific adventure of my boat, driven by a gale of wind into Mr. Somebody's garden. Let me live in hopes that the younger Strawberry will give me an opportunity of repeating those scenes of rural felicity. Oh dear! I had forgot among them the ready-made shoes of Richmond, the surviving pair of which I gave away a few days ago, in still a very serviceable state.

My kindest regards to Mr. Berry, whom I hope to find in excellent health. Do you know what *saudades* means? (don't read sausages) because it is the most comprehensive word in any language, and there is a flower called so in this place which I want to carry to England.

Adieu! expect to see me walk into your comfortable drawing-room some very cold Spring morning somewhere about a month hence.

Believe me, most sincerely and affectionately,

Your faithful

R. K. CRAVEN.

JOURNAL.

Saturday, March 9th.—A man standing in the pillory* in Oxford Street, at the end of our street, completely knocked me up, never having seen the operation before. I looked out of the window for the instant that the wretched man was putting in, and for one instant afterwards; when he was assailed by such a shower of every sort of mud, filth, and horrors, as to give every part of him and the machine one and the same hideous composition. The horror of seeing a wretched, degraded being, already exposed to the scorn and contempt of the multitude, thus treated by beings like himself; and to see the human form thus vilified, and human creatures—and those mostly women—thus treating it, seized upon my irritable nerves in such a manner as almost to give me what in my life I never had before—an hysterical affection between crying and screaming. We both fled from the window, and took refuge in my back room, to hear as little as we could of the noise of the crowd. It was over, thank heaven, at one o'clock, and nothing should ever bribe me to see such a sight again.

Sunday, 10th.—Went to church. Afterwards walked to Lady E. W., who is going, I think, fast into methodism, or melancholy of some sort or other. Afterwards to Mrs. Howe's. It is good, after having seen a mind like the first, to have the taste of it put out of one's mouth by such a mind as Mrs. Howe's at eighty-seven.

Monday, 11th.—Agnes called for me soon after ten, and we went together to Lady Elliot's; a true assembly, with all the 'my ladies,' and all their daughters in London,

* The pillory was abolished as a punishment in all cases except perjury, 56 George III., 1815–16. The pillory was totally abolished by Act 1 Vict. c. 30, June, 1837. The last who suffered this punishment at the Old Bailey was Peter James Bossy, for perjury, June 24, 1830.—*Haydn's Dict. of Dates*, p. 506–7.

on one side of the question at least; for of the opposition there was neither woman nor man, except one or two of the very young sprigs of assembly-goers.

Thursday, 14*th*.—In the evening to Mr. Grattan. Catalani, her husband, and a horrible sister of his, had dined there. She had sung a good deal before we came, and sung two little things afterwards, expressly for me. Mrs. Grattan always charming in her manner, and he, with whom I had a good deal of conversation about Haslem's* book on madness, &c., always entertaining and clever, in spite of his odd manner and still odder enunciation. But they don't understand society in their own house. She cannot move about to settle it, and he takes it as it comes. In this very small party all the women were sitting round the door of one of the two rooms, and all the men in the other.

Friday, 15*th*.—In the evening went to Lady Spencer's† before ten o'clock. An assembly in the drawing and billiard rooms of all the aristocracy of opposition, and of every Grenville, male and female, in the world. The rooms are uncommonly handsome; in the old style of carving, gilding, and crimson damask, than which nothing invented since is handsomer. Everybody seemed pleased. Everybody piqued themselves upon coming early, and it is to be repeated every Friday. Lord Hartington begged me to give him a little party on Wednesday next, the fast day. Agnes went to Mrs. Davenport's, where Tramazzini was singing.

Saturday, 16*th*.—I had heard from Lord Stafford, at Lady Spencer's the night before, that the 'Scotch Review,' with the criticism upon 'Madame du Deffand's Letters,' was out; and this morning, before I got my own, Lady

* William Saunders Haslem, M.D., author of the 'Inquiry into the Causes of the Extraordinary Addition to the Number of the Insane,' published in 1811.

† Lavinia, daughter of first Earl of Lucan, married, 1781, to George John, second Earl of Spencer, died 1831.

Donegall sent me a copy she had got early. I ought to be much content, and I am. Praise and blame often appear slight to me, which strike others in the light of very decided and satisfactory praise. Blame, or notice of faults, there is none; so of that I cannot complain. But I am fastidious, when I ought only to be thankful.

Miss Berry had certainly reason, on the whole, to be satisfied with the articles that appeared in the two leading reviews on her editorship of Madame du Deffand's Letters; yet it is not to be wondered at that she felt the praise by no means equal to the pains she had bestowed on her task, and the labour it had cost her. But such is the natural position of the editor of another person's writings. It may be a work of patience, of research, of candour, of judgment; but it is not an original work, and has no claim to the fame which may be attached to the author whose writings he has thus been the means of bringing to light. Such parts of the articles as related to the editor herself are here given, that the reader may see she had at least won the approbation and respect due to her diligence, discretion, and knowledge of the subjects required for her work.

Edinburgh Review, February 1811.

The circumstances of this publication are greatly in its favour, the editor having left nothing undone that could elucidate the text, or throw light on the persons and incidents to which it refers. This was highly necessary, and a task at the same time of no inconsiderable difficulty. The society of Madame du Deffand consisted of a great variety of persons, who though conspicuous and well known at the time when they lived, yet to us foreigners, at the distance of forty years, must many of them require to be introduced with some historical detail. In this respect, the editor has anticipated the wishes of the reader, and has furnished him, very concisely and clearly, with all the information he can desire, concerning the persons and events that are passing before him. This undertaking was in fact more arduous than at first appears, requiring qualifications which neither editors nor authors are always in possession of; as it could be executed by no person who had not lived in the best society both of France and England, and was not well acquainted with the history and manners of the fashionable world in both countries. One might have looked long in vain for one possessing these requisites among the grave and learned bodies from which the ranks of scholiasts and commentators are usually recruited.

Then follow extracts from the Letters, with the reviewer's comments, winding up with the concluding passage upon the work and its editor.

We must now take leave of Madame du Deffand, which however we cannot do without saying, that in our opinion her correspondence makes a valuable addition to the mass, not very considerable as yet of printed letters, perfectly natural and unaffected, and visibly never meant for publication. The editor deserves well of the public on this account, and still more on account of the judicious and enlightened observations with which the text is illustrated.

Quarterly Review, May 1811.

To the letters of the Marquise du Deffand and Mr. Horace Walpole are prefixed a preface, and a life of Madame du Deffand, by the editor. They are written in an excellent tone, and in a style temperate, chaste, and purely English. With much knowledge of the world, they evince a spirit of candour, corrected by a strong judgment and sound principle, and are evidently the production of a mind enlightened and vigorous, polished alike by extensive reading and by intercourse with the best society. The most important parts of Madame du Deffand's character are here accurately estimated, and placed in their just point of view. Her good qualities are not exaggerated, nor is the depravity of her heart disguised by a misplaced delicacy. On the whole, we have read these prefatory pieces with great satisfaction, and in offering this testimony to the merits of an anonymous writer, we cannot avoid expressing a hope, that a second opportunity may be soon given us of performing so agreeable a duty.

In spite of the just spirit in which Miss Berry was reviewed in the 'Edinburgh' and 'Quarterly,' it is clear that comments were passed upon her undertaking in the society in which she lived, which justified her view of the desire shown at that time to check all literary efforts in women. The extract from Mr. Mat. Lewis's letter, published by Lady Charlotte Bury, together with Lady Charlotte's own remarks, show that Miss Berry's view on this subject was shared by other ladies.

Extract from a Letter of M. G. Lewis to Lady Charlotte Bury.

Holland House, Dec. 9th, 1810.

I have galloped through two volumes of Madame du Deffand's Letters, and with much amusement, though the anecdotes are in themselves of no great value. . . . Have you read these letters? You know, of course, that they were edited by your friend Miss Berry, who has also written the preface, the life, and the notes, all of which are most outrageously abused by many persons, though, in my opinion, without any just grounds.*

* Note by Lady Charlotte Bury on Mr. Lewis's letter, written some years later, after the appearance of Miss Berry's later work:—'It would be difficult to account for this outrageous abuse were it not an established fact that all women who meddle with literature, especially those in the higher ranks of life, place themselves in a pillory, at which every impertinent idler conceives he has a right to throw his rotten eggs. Miss Berry has, however, established her reputation as an authoress in spite of all detraction. Her "Comparative View of Social Life in England and France" is assuredly one of the best written and most comprehensive views of the subject which can issue from the press, and combines all the tact of woman's feeling with the strength and terseness ascribed to male intellect alone. This work, so superior to the ephemeral fictions of the day, has obtained for her the sober and lasting suffrage of the public, the affection and admiration of a wide circle of friends, which it has ever been *her* privilege to call her own, and *their* pride to bestow.'

JOURNAL.

Friday, March 22nd, 1811.—Went, about eleven, to Lady Hertford's. We did not get in till near twelve, when the Regent had not arrived from dinner at Lord Cholmondeley's. He came soon afterwards, while we were in the outer room, and we saw the whole ceremony. A circle was immediately made, and the Regent, the Dukes of Clarence, Cumberland, Cambridge, and Gloucester, were all in it at the same time. The Regent looked wretchedly, swollen up with a muddled complexion, and was besides extremely tipsy—gravely and cautiously so. I happened to be a good while in the circle; and he at last gave me a formal grave bow, with *Kensington* legible on it.

In general, he speaks much less, both to men and women, than he did—it is the fashion of the day with him. Did not get away from Lady Hertford's till very near two o'clock—the Prince still there.

Thursday, April 4th.—Went to Lady Derby's. The same enormous crowd of all sorts of people that her assemblies always are—the Regent there; I was in his eye some time, but no notice taken.

Friday, 5th. — At three o'clock went to Devonshire House, to a practising of waltzes, as it was called. It was, in fact, a morning dance, with a cold dinner in one of the back drawing-rooms—the dancing in the saloon. It was pleasant enough.

Sunday, 7th.—In the morning I went to the Chapel Royal with Lady Tancred. After having been driven from post to pillar for places, we got two seats in the aisle, close by the singing boys, and heard the Bishop of London read the Communion Service very unimpressively, and the Archbishop of York preached a very gentlemanlike, sensible sermon, but one to which it was quite impossible to pin one's attention, for want of something to warm and interest one. The music excellent, though I think some part of the service better set in the York Cathedral. The Chapel Royal shamefully small for the domestic chapel to the King's first, and indeed only, palace in London; and the way in which money is not only taken, but extorted, by every doorkeeper, disgraceful.

Tuesday, 9*th*.—In the evening several people came. Sydney Smith's spirits at supper quite marvellous.

Wednesday, 10*th*.—Went to Mrs. Beauclerc's,* where was a small party — of women only ourselves, Lady Harriet [Leveson Gower] and Lady Georgiana [Morpeth,] Lady Harrowby, and Mrs. Locke. The old Duchess† was in one of the rooms. I had much talk with her about Madame du Deffand, with whose letters she is delighted, as having known all the society and persons mentioned.

Sunday, 14*th*.—I did not go to church in the morning, but had a long and interesting conversation with Thornton, about his views and plans, which I completely entered into, and should be too glad if I could anyhow second. After five, went to the Magdalen. We got there early, before the chapel was a third part full; but before the service began it was full in every part, containing, I suppose, at least six or seven hundred people. Everything about it very decent, and well kept and ordered. It was well lighted up with no less than ninety-six spermaceti candles. The preaching not good; the singing of the hymns and psalms from the women behind the high screen of green stuff, which entirely hides them from the audience, agreeable and affecting; indeed, I think the Evening Hymn always so. One or two of the voices were very sweet, and the rest did in chorus.

* Emily Charlotte, daughter of Sir William Ogilvy and the Duchess of Leicester; married, 1799, to Charles George Beauclerk, son of Topham and Lady Di Beauclerk.

† The old duchess was probably the Duchess of Leinster, daughter of Charles, second duke of Richmond.

From Professor Playfair.

Edinburgh, 17th April, 1811.

My dear Miss Berry,—. . . . I am very much disposed to think well of the work you propose to employ yourself in, and indeed to prefer it to either of the plans which had occurred to Lord W. and myself. Sketches of character of the kind you propose would give exercise to the powers of discrimination which (allow me to say it) you eminently possess, and to that turn for elegant and concise delineation of which you have lately furnished such good examples. I would, therefore, have you think seriously of this; it will afford you a pleasant occupation, and some day I hope afford pleasure and instruction to your friends and the public at large.

I am in the next place to make my confessions to you, and to tell you that I am the author of the review of M. du D. I am sorry that it did not fall into better hands, or what I regret more, that I could not do it better myself. Though I had a good deal of time allowed me, things turned out so that I was much hurried in the end. Then I was perplexed not a little by the great number of things that I admired in the letters, and in my wish to quote a great deal, became bewildered, and did not quote many of the things that are best. I have a greater admiration of the force, vivacity, and *nature* of the letters than I have anywhere expressed. I need not say that I very much admire the work of the editor; my admiration of that I thought it necessary to *keep down*, and to say much less than I felt. Soon after the publication of the letters, a review was sent from London, or rather a part of one, for it was not nearly complete, and though it was evidently the work of a person friendly to you, there seemed so little esteem of the book in general, and of the peculiar excellences of Mad. du D.'s style, that I instantly, on obtaining Jeffrey's consent, determined to try what I could do. I am conscious of having succeeded but very indifferently, but there was some danger that another person, at least not so *desirous* of succeeding well, might be employed. Nobody took a greater interest in the review than Professor Stewart: he suggested many remarks, and if I have after all produced a thing of so little value, that fault is my own, not that of my friends.

I hope you see a good deal of Mrs. Apreece, and like her society in London as well as we did in Edinburgh. I hear from her sometimes. She mentioned that you suspected me to be the author of the review.

My intention was to have been in London in the beginning of May; it answers better, however, for Lord John Russell, who lives with me, and means to go to town at the same time, that the journey should be put off to June. Early in that month I hope to have the pleasure of seeing you in North Audley Street. I shall request to be permitted to introduce Lord John Russell to you; he is one of the most promising young men I have ever met with. I shall not be able to make my stay in London so long as I would wish.

Farewell, my dear madam, and believe me to be, your sincere and attached friend,

JOHN PLAYFAIR.

Saturday, 20*th*.—I walked out with Lady Hardwicke in the shrubbery, to be told, by Catherine's desire, that her fate is fixed. I was surprised, having no idea that they had been much acquainted. I rejoice as it is pleasing them all, and as the person in question* is a man that Lady Hardwicke can marry, as well as her daughter —a thing absolutely necessary with her darling Catherine.

Monday, 22*nd*.—Tittenhanger. Drove to St. Albans, about three miles off. We called on Lady Spencer, who was not in the country. From thence we went to the Abbey church, for so it was, and as large as a cathedral. There is a great deal of very fine Gothic ornament applied to the walls of a very old Saxon church, a part of which remains in its primitive *Saxonity*. The tomb of Humphrey, the good Duke of Gloucester, very fine, but there is another much finer; and indeed, on the upper part, the most beautiful proportioned Gothic pierced work I ever saw, viz. the chapel tomb of an Abbot

* Lord Caledon.

Ramrudge. *Rams* are scattered all over the friezes, followed by the Gothic letters *rudge*, to give his name. The stone of this, and all the ornamented parts of this church, from Caen in Normandy. Why this? I know not.

Saturday, 27*th*.—Went at eleven o'clock, with my father, to Little Strawberry Hill. In spite of business I had to do or to think of, I took a melancholy round of the place by myself—recalling a thousand things and a thousand scenes to my memory. My melancholy at quitting this little place is always extreme; and now that I have no longer any hold in the neighbourhood, and that *this* is let for a twelvemonth, probably longer, in spite of all the trouble and expense it saves me, of which I must rejoice to be quit—the bidding adieu to a *home* at Twickenham can never be without a melancholy pang.

Sunday, 28*th*.—Went with Mrs. Locke to Kensington Gardens. They were as full as possible. Neither she nor I saw a single face that we knew, till we met Lord Aberdeen, and Mr. Ward, who joined us. The complexion of the company in these gardens is altered since I was there of a Sunday—always crowded with middling people, yet all the fine ladies used to come and show off their charms to the admiring mob; but now they have nothing to admire but one another.

I dined at Mrs. Apreece's; the party, Sydney Smith, Jeffrey, Malthus, Mr. Chinery, Mr. and Mrs. Tighe, and A. Turner. I sat by Malthus, and had a good deal of conversation with him—interesting, when one gets over his painful manner of speaking from wanting a palate to his mouth, and having had a hair-lip—not, however, at all unpleasant in appearance.

Tuesday, *May* 7*th*.—Dined at Rogers's. After dinner, Thomas Moore sung a good deal—his own Melalogue—a thing with words of his, set to old music, which had been rehearsed on the stage at Dublin—something in the style of Collins's Ode. . I thought little of it, although he both rehearses the words and plays the music admirably.

Sunday, 12*th*.—The finest summer day. I went to church; and, at three o'clock, to Kensington Gardens. Never went near the crowd, which was enormous, and gay and beautiful at a distance. The smell of the grass and flowering shrubs, from the recent rain, and the freshness and luxuriance of everything, perfectly beautiful. Such a lucky combination of weather and season does not often occur in an English spring. I have seen years without a single day and moment in them like this.

Tuesday, 14*th*.—Went to see West's picture at the British Institution in Pall Mall, and to the water-colour drawings in Bond Street, West's picture is a fine composition, and has very fine parts in it; in the back ground he comes in with his iron outline and his mistiness as usual. At the water-colours little real good, but Richter's things, which have twice the genius of Heaphy's in the same style.

Friday, 17*th*.—In the morning I went to Lady Charlemont, at Nollekens',* who is modelling a bust of her,—badly enough as to real taste and expression. Looked over all his things. The statue of Mr. Pitt, for the Senate House at Cambridge, very like. In the evening we went to the Marcets',† in Russell Square, where Racine's tragedy

* Joseph Nollekens, a celebrated sculptor, born 1737, R.A. in 1772, died 1823, in the eighty-sixth year of his age, leaving a fortune of nearly £200,000.—*Rose's Biog. Dict.*

† Dr. Marcet, a learned physician and experimental philosopher, born at Geneva, 1770, educated at Edinburgh, practised in London. He retired from his profession on coming into a fortune, in 1820 was elected Incumbent of the Council and Honorary Professor of Chemistry in the University of Geneva; died 1821.

Jane Marcet, wife to Dr. Marcet, daughter of Mr. Haldimand, a wealthy Swiss merchant settled in London, born 1769. Her earliest work was 'Conversations on Chemistry,' followed by 'Conversations on Political Economy,' 1816, pronounced by Mr. Maculloch to be 'on the whole the best of 'Berenice' was acted by a Mr. and Mrs. Lullin, and three other persons whose names I could not make out. None of them French. Mr. Lullin is a Genevois, and his wife an Englishwoman; consequently they all spoke with an accent, and none of them had the true recitation of French dramatic verse; but as they acted with a considerable degree of feeling and unction, and as Mrs. Lullin is a very pretty woman, with a charming speaking voice and a great expression of softness, it was interesting, and sufficiently well done to make one admire the beauty of Racine's most French tragedy.

This, I was glad to see, was the feeling of the whole English audience, which consisted principally of the most fashionable young people in town.

After 'Berenice,' Mr. and Mrs. Lullin gave us 'Defiance and Malice,' really very well.

Saturday, 18*th*.—I went with Joanna Baillie to Hampstead, to remain till Monday. Dined before four, and went out upon the Heath. Sat for above two hours in a delicious fine evening; afterwards read over together 'The Two Martius,'* and criticised them, and likewise some of my other scraps, which I think Joanna liked less than I expected.

Sunday, 19*th*.—Sat by the fire the whole day. Joanna Baillie gave us her drama upon Hope to read; it is only two acts, and I was soon through it. Very poetical, and much fancy, as all her things have; but this did not equal my expectation—how high it was I know not. It is certainly a sufficiently dramatic story, but not dramatically managed.

introduction to the science that has yet appeared.' Mrs. Marcet wrote on various other subjects, and is entitled to the lasting gratitude of her numerous readers for the patience and skill with which she disentangled the difficulties of various branches of science, and rendered their study comparatively easy. Died 1858.

* This piece, often alluded to in Miss Berry's Journal, was never published, and there is no trace of the MS. amongst her papers.—Ed.

Monday, 27th.—In the evening to Lady Hertford's; an enormous assembly; all the Princes.

Wednesday, 29th.—Went to Lady Stafford's. We got into chairs in St. James's Street, the string of carriages was so long. 1,500 cards had been issued, and yet it did not make a positive crowd in that great house,* except near the circles where the Prince stood.

Thursday, 30th.—Went with my sister to Kensington. A numerous ball; the Princess mighty gracious. I had a long and almost an affecting conversation with her, because for the first time she seemed to feel her own situation, while she continues very good-natured to others.

Saturday, June 1st.—In the evening to Mrs. Siddons's, at Westbourne Farm. Went before ten o'clock. The whole house was illuminated, on the outside with coloured lamps, and in the inside with candles, and every bush in the garden with lamps. In short, it was the prettiest little Vauxhall that could be, and a vast many people there. After staying very agreeably for about an hour, went to Kensington. Music at the Princess's, and about thirty people supped together.

Saturday, 8th.—Went to Lady Cork's.† A curious party, where, by way of something to do, she had had Thelwall ‡ reading Milton's 'Invocation to Light,' so abominably as to amuse or shock all the company.

* Cleveland House, since pulled down and replaced by Bridgewater House, the residence of the Earl of Ellesmere.

† Mary, daughter of first Viscount Galway, second wife of Edmund, seventh Earl of Cork. Lord Cork died 1798, Lady Cork, 1840.

‡ Thelwall, a miscellaneous writer, political agitator, and lecturer on elocution, born 1764, son of a silk mercer, apprenticed to a tailor, he was then articled to an attorney, but abandoned that profession and embraced literature as a profession. He became a member of the London Corresponding Society, and of that of the Friend of the People. He was tried for high treason with Horne Tooke and Thomas Hardy in 1794, defended by Mr. Erskine, and acquitted. In 1801 he became a lecturer on elocution, taking pupils to cure stammering and defects of speech. Amongst other works he

Sunday, 9th.—Dined with the Princess of Wales at Blackheath. Dining-room, *à la Gothique*, very pretty, but the rest of the house in abominable taste. After dinner, the Princess walked with me in the garden, and fell into talking of her own story, with which she began from her early youth, and continued in detail to the epoch of her marriage, and in still greater detail since. Every circumstance of the Prince's behaviour to her at and after their marriage; every circumstance of the contrivances for getting her out of Carlton House; his character, which she knows perfectly; the Queen's, which she abhors, and whom she believes to be her greatest enemy; her own father's and mother's, &c. &c. In short, after coming in to get some tea and put on a shawl, she resumed her walk and her talk to me till past one in the morning. Luckily, it was the finest moonlight night that ever was.

Thursday, 13th.—Dined at the Princess of Wales's, at Kensington. After dinner, the Princess walked out with me on the gravel walk before the windows, and resumed the conversation of Blackheath, drawing me into a window and asking me if I had thought upon the conversation we had the other day. I am not altogether so well satisfied with this one as with the other. It seems to me that she has more to fear.

Wednesday, 19th.—Promised to dine at Kensington. Found nobody but Lady Glenbervie ready dressed for the Regent's fête in the evening. At eight Lady Glenbervie set off, leaving us three alone with the Princess, and without any hope of being able to get away till she came back. I took upon myself the office of *Dragon*, and declared we must all four keep together the whole evening, for fear any stories were to be made of

wrote 'Poems in the Tower and in Newgate,' 'The Tribune,' 'Political Miscellanies,' 'A Letter on Stammering,' 'The Peripatetic,' and 'The Daughter of Adoption,' a novel; died 1834.—*Rose's Biog. Dict.*

any of us the next day, on the only evening in the year when the Princess was without any of her ladies.

We first walked in the gardens, which had a number of people in them; then the Princess played a great deal on the piano, in a manner to convince one she had played very well, but had been out of the habit of playing. Afterwards we talked of her and her education, and her various and curious governesses, &c. &c., till near twelve o'clock, when we supped, and in half-an-hour afterwards arrived Lady Glenbervie, who had very cleverly done her business at the fête, seen everything but the supper, and gave us a very good account of everything she had seen. But the Princess kept us so long hearing it that we were all exhausted, and it was past two o'clock before we got home.

Monday, 24th.—Went to see Carlton House, which remained with its decorations, and the servants in their state uniforms, and the Yeomen of the Guard in every room.

The crowd was great at the gateway, and we should have had much difficulty of getting in, if Lady Ellenborough had not sent for Sayer, one of the Bow Street officers, who was cap-in-hand to the chief-justice's lady.

Within the house, too, the crowd was great, but not such as to impede one another, except in the doorways; all the servants were uncommonly civil and attentive in accommodating the people, and making them go the right way. The house is magnificent, and the Gothic greenhouse or conservatory, where the Prince supped, though ridiculous for the purpose it was built for, certainly made a most beautiful and richly-ornamented supper room. All the plate was still upon the table, and all the magnificent gold plate upon the sideboard, in three ranks, at the top of the room, behind where the Prince sat; all the knives, forks, spoons, &c. &c., yet spread upon it, and so few people to guard and watch it, as really was creditable to the honesty of John Bull.

The temporary rooms in the garden are immense, and admirably contrived, and I dare say when lighted up must have been very handsome.

Wednesday, 26*th*.—To the ball at Devonshire House. The ball brilliant, from all the women having on their Carlton House gowns, and many their feathers. The Prince there; he passed me in the drawing-room when there were only a few people. I was standing by Lady Elizabeth Whitehead, and just behind Lady Melbourne, to whom he spoke, but avoided letting his eye fall upon me. So I am satisfied that Kensington sticks in his throat, and *qu'il se venge des grands sur les petites.*

Thursday, 27*th*.—Left London to go to Danesfield.

Saturday, 29*th*.—Went in Mrs. Scott's barouche to Park Place. Instead of driving up, as formerly, to the house to see Park Place, carriages turn up by the Horse Shoes, Lord Malmesbury having bought all the intervening land. It is impossible to describe the melancholy I felt at again finding myself at Park Place. We entered it by the kitchen garden, and from thence into the little flower-garden, where several recollections totally overcame me. They needed not the additional melancholy which the forlorn, the neglected, the ruined look of everything gave them. Had I known nothing of the inhabitants I could have sworn, only from seeing the place, that they cared little for the country. Poor Park Place! how changed in every particular! The alterations made in the inside of the house are, I think, not good. The furniture of the library is certainly improved, for there is a fine collection of books in it; a folio edition of all the Greek and Latin classics, probably having belonged to Hermes,* besides very fine copies of all the diplomatic books, dictionaries, foreign topography, &c. &c. I shall

* Mr. Harris, father of the first Lord Malmesbury.

probably never see it again, nor do I wish it; lest the image of it in its present state should derange and confuse my former recollections of its beauties, its comforts, its inhabitants, and my last winter visit there, when I vainly hoped for and looked forward to happiness within my grasp! We returned by Medenham Ferry. Close by the ferry house is the abbey, which belongs to Mrs. Scott. There is a good room for drinking tea in; the rest in a sort of ruin, except that inhabited by the woman who takes care of it. The rooms that are said to have been occupied by Wilkes, Paul Whitehead, &c., members of the famous or infamous club that met here forty or fifty years ago, are such rooms for size and convenience as no luxurious debauchers would condescend to inhabit now.* There are remains in the room called Wilkes's of a large cradle, in which it is said he slept. From Medenham a beautiful drive of a mile, through hayfields belonging to Danesfield. In the evening I read out to them, but my spirits had not at all recovered Park Place.

Extract of a Letter to Mrs. Damer.

Danesfield, June 30th, 1811.

I was at Park Place yesterday. It had rained much in the night, and was a gray, damp, melancholy day, suiting well with the feelings I carried to it. Never did I see a place which, without being much altered, is so perfectly changed, so *triste*, so comfortless! Everything is neglected: the seats all falling to pieces, the trees overgrown in some places and in others dead and left standing, the poor little flower garden with its fountain dry and its borders flowerless, its little arcades over-

* This club consisted of twelve members; the motto (from Rabelais) over the grand entrance was '*Ce que je voudras.*' Although the club became notorious, and their disgusting profanity was well known, it proved no bar either to the reception of the members in society or to the advancement in the State of Sir Francis Dashwood, the founder, who officiated as high Priest, and who became Chancellor of the Exchequer, Lord Sandwich, First Lord of the Admiralty, and Wilkes everything that the sober citizens of London could make of him.

grown and broke, and the thorn tree in the middle let to spread over the whole space. Oh, how every step of it affected me! I saw you and O'H. sitting under this thorn tree in its trim days, and myself having left you merely to enjoy the delicious sensation of knowing you were expressing for me every sentiment I could wish to inspire. I saw him following me into the laurel walk, and in giving me a letter (which I had accidentally dropped) in a joking manner, first convincing me of the seriousness of the sentiment I had inspired. I sat down at the end of the library, and saw your form at the bottom, on a ladder, arranging the new-placed books, and the look you gave and recalled, when you found us sitting at the other end of the room, just where you had left us when you returned again to your work . . . . I am so glad I have seen Park Place *once*, in spite of all the melancholy it inspired, but I should be sorry to see more of it.

JOURNAL.

Wednesday, July 3rd.—Returned to London.

Thursday, 11*th.*—Went to Lady Cork's; a great assembly in her upper rooms, which are very prettily furnished, particularly the boudoir, opening into the conservatory. The Prince there, and all the world; and a numerous world is still in London. There were some masks, and some people singing, and Mrs. Billington at a piano-forte.

Thursday, Aug. 1st.—I saw Mrs. Sheridan* by appointment in the morning, at her own house, about poor Richardson. Curious conversation on the subject of her husband and their pecuniary necessities. She cannot get 10*l.* to carry her out of London. Spoke and acts most kindly about poor Richardson.

Friday, 2*nd.*—Went to Mrs. Villiers', where was a regular ball of all that remained in London of dancers, and much the usual tapisserie of the walls of a ballroom; the Dowagers Rutland and Essex, Lady Clare, &c. Mrs.

* Miss Esther Jane Ogle, daughter of the Dean of Winchester, married to Mr. Sheridan, 1795.

Sheridan (to my utter amazement), after the conversation we had had the day before, was waltzing away there, the gayest among the gay. What happy versatility of mind! But, after all, what skin-deep gaiety!

Saturday, 3rd.—Sat for a long time with Lady Georgiana Morpeth; the first time I have seen her since her father's death. She was, as always, most right-feeling; and I parted with her, as I always do, with sincere affection and regret.

Sunday, 4th.—Went to Tunbridge Wells.

The following letter, addressed to Lady Georgiana Morpeth, on the subject of the position to which her brother had succeeded by his father's death, is one of the many proofs in Miss Berry's writings of how justly she appreciated the duties attached to the possession of honours and power:—

Tunbridge, 9th August, 1811.

MY DEAREST G——,—What you say is what the anxious mind of true, real and deep affection must necessarily feel of any person, however amiable, at his age, placed in his trying, or to use his own just expression, *awful* situation! for *awful* it is to the thinking mind, as comprising at once the power and the occasion of being nobly distinguished among men, or in spite of all the lace and fringe of life, to link to that order of beings, whose sentiments high birth cannot ennoble, whose heart the blessed power of doing good cannot warm, and whose character can never rise to their station. The more I think of my friend Hartington, the more I feel confirmed in my first ideas on his subject, that the being so early called to the performance of great, serious, and varied duties, will confirm all the good qualities we have already known in him, and steady and settle his character. But not to feel *anxious* about him for the next year or two, is to be either incapable of appreciating his present virtues, or insensible to his future success.

Saturday, 10th.—Dined at Mrs. Tighe's. The party consisted of Miss White,* Mr. Ward, Mr. Luttrell, and

* Miss Lydia White, well known in the literary society of her time.

myself. Mr. Luttrell entertaining, and Mr. Ward rather more serious, and therefore more agreeable than usual. But his manners are bad, and with a sort of affectation of *worldism*, smell most strongly of never having been in any other world than that of London.

Wednesday, Sept. 4th.—Tunbridge Wells. At twelve o'clock we set out for Hever Castle ten miles from hence. The view from the little castle (for it is small, surrounded by the moat in good preservation, and filled with water), is charming. Still more interesting is the inside, which, in spite of an ugly new staircase and other disfigurements, has remained as it was in the time of Sir Thomas Bulleyn, the father of Anne Bulleyn. It is now the habitation of a large farmer. The large dining-room is as it was, with its buttery, its large table, and some cupboards certainly contemporary. There is also a gallery at the top of the house, with the old woodwork and old ceiling. The little court remains unchanged; and the great oaken entrance-door under the tower is studded with thick nails, and is probably as old as the date of Edward III.

Extract of a Letter from Miss Berry to Mrs. Damer.

Tunbridge, 1811.

I read a great deal every morning, and indeed often of an evening; I don't know if any good will come of it, it does not seem yet to have cleared my head as to any use I can make of it. But in the meantime, I am more delighted with Mrs. Hutchinson * than with any book I have read for an age. She was a really superior woman, both as to head and heart. Her description and account of her husband's attachment to her, is the truest, the most elevated and admirable picture of love and true affection from and to a superior mind that can be imagined. It fills up every line of that ideal picture long ago traced by

* 'Memoirs of Colonel Hutchinson,' by his wife, Lucy, daughter of Sir Allan Apsley, born 1620. The Memoirs were not published till 1806.

imagination, and now engraved by reason on my heart. And in the sad certainty of never meeting with it, I feel better pleased with myself to suffer from its absence, than to be unable to comprehend or to deny its existence. Farewell, or I shall grow romantic.

Tuesday, 24th.—We set out for Mayfield with Lady Charlemont, Mrs. Abercrombie, Mrs. Gordon, and my sister. A pretty village, with a fine ruin of an ancient palace or residence of the archbishops of Canterbury; the most modern part is still inhabited by farmers. Mrs. Tighe, Miss White, Mr. Abercrombie, and Mr. Tierney accompanied us on horseback.

Wednesday, Oct. 2nd.—Drove, with Mr. and Mrs. Gordon and Lady Erroll, to Tunbridge Castle. I had no idea of the beauty of the ruin, nor of the goodness of the house that they have added or attached at the side of one of the towers, between which is the grand entrance-gate. The enclosure of the castle down to the river is a lawn and a shrubbery. It is at present to let; and we went all over it, Mr. Gordon having some idea of taking it.

Sunday, 27th.—Agnes and I went to Mr. Blake's,* to see his drawings, which are admirable. He sketches in every style, and always well. I never saw a more perfect amateur.

Wednesday, 30th.—Returned to London.

Sunday, Nov. 3rd.—In the evening with young Law, who talked to us with great intelligence of Sicily, where he has been spending five months.

Monday, 4th.—In the evening Mrs. Damer. I read Alfieri in Italian — but what Italian! so stuffed with Tuscanisms, so fraught with words immediately derived

* The late William Blake, Esq., of Portland Place and Danesbury Welwyn. His remarkable talent for drawing has been transmitted, and in a still higher degree, to his daughters, whose works have excited the greatest admiration, both in private and at the Amateur Exhibitions.

from the Latin, that it is hardly to be recognised as the language of Boccaccio, Machievelli, and other Italian classics.

From Professor Playfair.

Edinburgh, 21st October, 1811.

My dear Madam,—I intended to have written you a very long letter, but a problem I have been engaged on this morning has made me forget the time till it is hard on the hour when Sir John Sebright's frank will lose its efficacy. . . .

Have you been able to follow out anything of the plan of reading and writing that we talked of?

After leaving London, I stayed for a week at Woburn, and set out from thence with Lord J. Russell on a tour through the manufacturing and commercial towns in the West of England. This turned out very interesting, and took longer time than I had foreseen. Since I got home I have been kept so close at work printing a text-book of Natural Philosophy, that I only got leisure enough to visit Raith in the course of the last fortnight. Sir John Sebright and I, who have become great friends, went there together. The party we found there, though large, was exceeding pleasant, and I think, on the whole, there cannot be a pleasanter house than Raith now is. Every thing goes on well. . . .

I have been very much amused and entertained by Sir John Sebright; he is quite a singular man; of a powerful understanding, irregularly instructed, but possessed of much information, great knowledge of the world, and a familiar acquaintance with a vast number of subjects that lie quite out of the way of most people. . . .

I hope you have been admiring the comet, who is certainly one of the most splendid guests that ever made a visit to the solar system.

Yours, my dear Miss Berry, with the utmost affection and esteem,

John Playfair.

Wednesday, 13*th*.—Before four o'clock Lady C. Lindsay came to North Audley Street in the Princess of Wales's carriage, to carry me to Blackheath. We arrived there soon after five o'clock. The Princess received me with all possible kindness. After talking more than half an hour, Lady Charlotte took me to my apartments, consisting of two rooms, and a third for my maid. We dined before seven o'clock. The Princess, Lady Charlotte, and myself in a small dining-room. We afterwards went down stairs to the drawing-room, which opens into the greenhouse; a very warm and comfortable room. We talked a great deal, and separated before one o'clock.

Thursday, 14*th*.—I awoke with a bad headache. The Princess came to Lady Charlotte immediately after breakfast, and seeing that I was not well, begged I would remain quite quiet all the morning, telling me to ask for whatever I wished to have. I retired to my own comfortable room till seven o'clock, when I was well enough to go to dinner, and to spend the evening with the Princess, who was in good humour and very talkative.

Friday, 15*th*.—The Princess came in while we were breakfasting, and proposed a walk in the garden. Dr. Burney* dined and stayed here in the evening, and we had much good conversation. The Princess of Gloucester and her brother dined with the Duchess of Brunswick, and called upon the Princess in the afternoon.

Saturday, 16*th*.—The Duke of Brunswick came to see the Princess; she afterwards stayed talking for so long in Lady Charlotte's room, that we did not dine till eight o'clock. The evening, again, long conversation till half-past one o'clock.

Sunday, 17*th*.—Very fine winter's day. The Princess, Lady Charlotte, and I went to Lea Church; the parish of George Locke is a mile from here. Small country church, in a charming situation. After church we went into his house: the prettiest parsonage, with the gayest and most agreeable view. His wife was ill, and could

* Probably Dr. Charles Burney, son of Dr. Burney, well known for his works on music.

not see the Princess. From there we went to the Princess's kitchen garden on the Heath, where she has a pavilion with two or three rooms furnished, commanding a magnificent view on both sides. After luncheon we walked under the wall of Greenwich Park, which is a sort of Sunday promenade, where one sees a great many people—of common people the most part, not recognising the Princess.

Monday, 18*th*.—Next morning, after breakfast, I had by chance a *tête-à-tête* conversation with the Princess in Lady Charlotte's room. It was chiefly on the subject of idle frivolous correspondence that people would keep up with her. She had in her hand a letter of which she was speaking. We were all dressed before three o'clock for the reception of Princess Charlotte, who was to dine with her mother. Princess Sophia of Gloucester arrived just before, with Miss Dee: then Princess Charlotte with Lady de Clifford. She is very much grown and improved in figure since I saw her last January at Kensington. I don't know whether her face is improved; her mouth is less pleasing and less resembling her father's than it was; but her bust is perfect; her head not too large, and well placed; has much intelligence in her countenance, though the expression is not very agreeable; her walk is dreadful, but I think it is only girlish affectation, which will cure itself. We dined by daylight—seven women, and not one man; an unheard-of thing at the Princess's. After dinner we went down to the drawing-room, and there stayed till past seven o'clock, when the Princess Charlotte and her governess went away. Princess Sophia and her lady went with the Princess of Wales to the Duchess of Brunswick, and I departed for London.

Tuesday, *Dec.* 3*rd*.—We went, at two o'clock, to see Thornton's library, at which they are at this moment working. It is, of all the ideas of interior decoration, the most extraordinary; it is a Greek temple, like one of those at Pæstum, placed in the interior of a room, against the walls of which the books are arranged, and between which walls and the columns of the temple one can pass to the two ends. In short, it is the ideas of Gell, Hope, and Mr. Hopper (the architect employed), mixed and confused by the orders of our friend Thornton, who has not a single idea of his own upon these subjects.

Thursday, 5*th*.—Went to Brighton.

Friday, 13*th*.—Went with Lady Charlotte to hear the military band in the Prince's Pavilion. Luckily, we only heard two pieces, for the noise of so many loud instruments in a room (the dining-room) which could hardly hold them, was not a remedy for my headache. After the music, having an order, we saw the apartments of the Pavilion. All is Chinese, quite overloaded with china of all sorts and of all possible forms, many beautiful in themselves, but so overloaded one upon another, that the effect is more like a china shop baroquement arranged, than the abode of a Prince. All is gaudy, without looking gay; and all is crowded with ornaments, without being magnificent. The interior of the stables is imposing, though badly arranged for the comfort of the horses, and will only accommodate sixty beneath this large building. The riding house, which is attached to it, perfectly suits its purpose, and is, I think, likely not to be finished, though it is the only part of the habitation of the Prince which deserves preservation. He ought to have a tennis court of the same size, making a pendant to the riding house.

Saturday, 14*th*.—Returned to North Audley Street.

Tuesday, 24*th*.—Went to Wimpole with the Charlemonts.

Wednesday, 25*th*.—Went to the dairy, and to see the Gnu, the animal that Lord Caledon had brought for Lord Hardwicke from the Cape. It is the most singular animal that I have ever seen, larger than an ass of this country, resembling no other in particular; having two immense horns and a ferocious look, though doing no harm. It is a female, and comes from a mountainous country far in the interior of Africa, at the north of the Cape.

1812.

Wimpole.—Wednesday, January 1*st.*—Went with Elizabeth * to the school. The children have always a dinner on New Year's Day. It was in the school upon forms arranged as tables. The children behaved themselves very well, and after dinner we begged the schoolmistress to relax her discipline and allow a little talking. We made the children sing, and the most perfect happiness beamed upon forty-five young and innocent faces.†

Friday, 3*rd.*—Returned to London.

Tuesday, 14*th.*—Drove with Lady C. Campbell to Blackheath. We found the Princess, who received me in the most gracious manner possible. Poor Charlotte was so overcome with fatigue, that I was left *tête-à-tête* till half-past seven o'clock, when we separated to dress, I almost dead with so much talking. The toilette of the Princess is always so rapid, that it was impossible not to keep her waiting a few minutes. Lady Charlotte joined us at dinner, and the evening passed very agreeably.

Wednesday, 15*th.*—A fine winter's day. We did not see the Princess till luncheon at four o'clock, and from that time till seven o'clock we remained in conversation; then dinner, and again conversation till nearly one o'clock.

Thursday, 18*th.*—I remained quietly in my room till three o'clock, when the Princess sent for me to take a

* Lady Elizabeth Yorke.

† The desire to promote both the education and the recreation of the children of the poor has happily now become almost wholly universal in this country; but not the less honour is due to those who early in the century formed a small minority, but who set the example and took the lead in that good work.

walk to Mr. Angerstein's house. After luncheon went with the Princess to the Duchess of Brunswick, to whom she presented me, and with whom I had a long talk. The Duchess sat in her arm-chair in the middle of a fine large drawing-room, the Princess on one side, and I on the other. She invited me to dine with her the next day; but the Princess telling her that I was obliged to return home, insisted that we should dine there this day, to which the Princess consented, and there we were in our walking dress, talking till five o'clock, when dinner was served. It was a tolerable dinner, with German dishes, that they forced me to taste. At half past six we took coffee, and returned to the Princess's. After half an hour's conversation, separated to dress for the Princess's dinner, from which she did not excuse us, though it was an impossibility to eat again. Evening passed as usual.

Friday, 17*th*.—Returned to town.

Thursday, *February* 13*th*.—I had a long and very agreeable *tête-à-tête* with the Duke of Devonshire. He thinks so well, so sensibly, and has so good a heart, that he always gives me pleasure when he talks openly.

Sunday, 16*th*.—It is already known, and they were talking at dinner of the letter which the Prince of Wales has written to the Duke of York,* telling him that he should keep the same ministers after the 18th of this month, when all restrictions would cease, and he would govern completely as King.

Wednesday, 26*th*.—The morning at Devonshire House,

* The Prince's celebrated letter to the Duke of York, announcing his intention of retaining the Tory administration, and thus renouncing the Whig party, whom he had hitherto regarded as his own political friends, created great indignation, and amongst other satirical poems gave rise to Moore's Parody of the Letter, beginning—

> 'At length, dearest Freddy, the moment is nigh,
> When, with P-rc-v-l's leave, I may throw my chains by;
> And, as time now is precious, the first thing I do
> Is to sit down and write a wise letter to you.'

—*Moore's Works*, vol. v. p. 223.

where I found the Duke in his library with the Marquis Douglas and George Neville, who were looking over his beautiful books. The Duke accompanied us into the dining-room to see the new pictures, and he then told me of the legacy old Cavendish * had left him—nearly 7,000*l.* a year.

Tuesday, March 3rd.—In the evening I went in Kemble's box, where we found his wife, to see 'Julius Cæsar'—Kemble playing the part of Brutus, and Young, Cassius, admirably well.

Wednesday, 4th.—In the evening went to the Ancient Music. We found places near to Lord and Lady Derby, and were not far from the box where the Regent was, accompanied by the Dukes of Cumberland and Cambridge, and two or three other directors, and the faithful Lord Yarmouth. He only spoke to Lady Albemarle and Mrs. Howe.

To the Countess of Hardwicke from Miss Berry.

North Audley Street, Monday, March 16, 1812.

You will find me with a new friend in your Square, Lady Castlereagh, who has been so civil, and so successful in curing me of the toothache, that I am going to a small party to her

* Henry Cavendish, son of Lord Cavendish, cousin of the Duke of Devonshire, died March 1810. He left property to the amount of one million two hundred thousand pounds. Seven hundred thousand pounds he bequeathed to Lord G. Cavendish, two hundred thousand pounds to the Earl of Bessborough, and other legacies to the Cavendish family. He was a most eminent chemist and natural philosopher; he was conversant with every part of Sir J. Newton's philosophy, the principles of which he applied near forty (*now* ninety) years ago to an investigation of the laws on which the phenomena of electricity depend; he ascertained, in 1766, the extreme levity of inflammable gas, now called hydrogen gas; he discovered the composition of water by the union of two airs; laid the foundation of the modern system of chemistry, &c. &c. He died at the age of seventy-nine. Sir H. Davy, in pronouncing a high eulogium on him, said, 'Since the days of Sir J. Newton England has sustained no scientific loss so great as that of Cavendish. . . . His name will be an immortal honour to his house, to his age, and to his country.'—*Ann. Regis.* for 1810.

house this evening, and am asked to all her suppers. You see I am creeping over to the Ministerial side. However, to save appearances and my principles, if I can, I am going afterwards to your favourite Lady Caroline Lamb, who has some sort of a party down at Whitehall, to be in the way of hearing an early account of what is going on in the House of Peers on Lord Boringdon's motion, which, by the way, I believe, is put off. I have no time to talk to you about this motion. I was present when he started the first idea of it at dinner, at Devonshire House, on Monday se'nnight, which people smiled at, and nobody replied to. But however odd the motion, I should not be at all surprised, by what I have since heard, of it being completely a manœuvre of Lord Wellesley and Canning, and if it led to turning out Percival and his immediate adherents.

The author of the versification of the letter is little Anacreon, not avowedly, but certainly. You must see likewise a certain vision, said to be by Lord Byron, as well as some lines on the Princess Charlotte's tears at the *far-famed dinner,* and the *triumph of the whale* in the 'Examiner' of last Sunday. The prose squibs and abuse are endless. People begin to look grave about the license taken; but it is not yet, near as great as that at the end of Charles II.'s reign was! . . .

Thursday, 19*th.*—Went to Lady Castlereagh's, where there was an assembly entirely of ladies. There were only three men in the room when we arrived. All the male world was in the House of Lords to hear the motion of Lord Boringdon.* Near midnight we went to Melbourne House to Lady Caroline Lamb. They were at supper. Lady Holland with fifteen other ladies waiting the arrival

* Afterwards created Earl of Morley. The object of Lord Boringdon's motion was to move an address to the Prince Regent beseeching him to form an efficient administration that should be so composed as to unite the confidence and good will of all classes. He represented that in the present state of Ireland, no such confidence could be enjoyed by any administration whose characteristic principle was to resist a dispassionate consideration of the civil disabilities, under which His Majesty's Roman Catholic subjects there still laboured. Lord Grimstone moved an amendment which was in effect an expression of perfect satisfaction with the conduct of affairs since the commencement of the Regency. The amendment was carried by a majority of 93.—See *Annual Register,* 1812.

of the gentlemen from the Houses. An hour passed before they came. All opposition *en masse*, and all the Canning party, himself excepted, with a fallen look, after their *cheval de bataille*, Lord Wellesley, had entirely failed them at the hour of need, not having chosen to open his mouth.

Wednesday, 25*th*.—The Princess of Wales had settled, on Saturday last, to come and see us this morning in town. At four o'clock we sat down to table in the little drawing-room. It was a beautiful day. The sun shone out, and everything appeared very bright and very cheerful. The Princess seemed much pleased with the company and the luncheon, and fatigued no one, for at half-past five she returned to Blackheath.

Thursday, *April* 2*nd*.—Went to Lady Glenbervie's; Lord Byron was there, and I had a quarter of an hour's conversation, which, I own, gave me a great desire to know him better, and he seemed willing that I should do so.

Thursday, 9*th*.—I had a great deal of private conversation with the Princess, when I found her much more reasonable on her own affairs, and much more capable of listening to reason than usual. She begins to understand that she must be prudent, and that prudence alone will disarm her enemies—at least she has no other course to take.

Sunday, 12*th*.—I went to church, and afterwards took Lady Cornewall * to pay a visit to Catalani in her hermitage at Brompton. It is a small house with a drawing-room, decorated with French tapestry, and all the gilding, yellow, crimson, and looking-glasses that could be crammed into it.

Wednesday, 15*th*.—We went to Kensington; dinner of twenty-two people; Canning and several of his friends and his set. In the evening there was an assembly, many of whom, and we amongst others, were invited to supper. The Princess was melancholy; I never saw her so beat

* Wife of Sir George Cornewall.

down. She made me sit by her side for a long time; twice she tried to speak and could not, her voice always failing her. It was the recollections that were revived by the company, and not the public affairs, I am quite sure, by the answers she made upon what I said of the politics of the day.

Saturday, May 2nd.—Left 'The Two Martius' at Sir G. Beaumont's.

Sunday, 3rd.—Dined at Mr. Montague's with Lord and Lady Hardwicke, and Lady Elizabeth, Lord and Lady Elliott, &c., and Mr. Peel. The latter, he who spoke so well in the House of Commons, has a very agreeable countenance.

Thursday, 7th.—At the end of the evening I had half an hour's conversation with Lord Byron, principally on the subject of the Scotch Review, with which he is very much pleased. He is a singular man, and pleasant to me, but I very much fear that his head begins to be turned by all the adoration of the world, especially the women.

Friday, 8th.—Had a long conversation with Sir G. Beaumont in the morning upon poetry, &c. With all his natural taste, he is strangely misled by the dogmas of Coleridge, Wordsworth, &c.

Monday, 11th.—At dinner with my father and sister I received from Mrs. Locke a card which had been sent to her, and upon which was the wonderful news of the assassination of Mr. Percival in the lobby of the House of Commons. I began by doubting it, but a moment after our servant said he had heard it from Mr. Villiers's * valet. Directly after dinner Agnes went to Lady Donegall, and I wrote to ask Mrs. Villiers about it. The Villiers' had a large dinner, and I saw several persons arrive who ought to be well-informed. I received from them complete confirmation of the report. We went early to Mrs. G.

* Hon. J. C. Villiers, afterwards Earl of Clarendon, lived in North Audley Street.

Lamb's, where there was young Macdonald, Mr. Morrice, and two or three other people who had been in the House of Commons, and afterwards at the examination of the assassin,* who had not attempted to escape. Later in the evening Lords Lauderdale and Grey arrived, who had both been with the Address of the Lords to Carlton House. This deed, though horrible, is unfortunately one of all countries, and is not without its parallel even here. But that which is not so is the manner in which the populace took it, who surrounded the Houses of Parliament. They appeared so very little shocked.

Tuesday, 12*th*.—After breakfast I received a note from Lady Charlotte, asking me all I had heard and thought of the assassination.

Thursday, 14*th*.—Drove as far as Spring Gardens, having passed through the crowd of carriages from the two Houses, who were taking their Address to the Regent on the subject of the assassination of Percival.

Saturday, 16*th*.—Went to Mrs. Gordon, where there was an excellent assembly, and delightful music. The four sisters, † Naldi Tremazzani and two Portuguese.

Thursday, 21*st*.—I heard from Lady Grey ‡ herself that the Commons were up, and that they had left the Ministry in a minority of four upon the question of their own incapability. In all my life I had never been more astonished.

* Bellingham.

† The five sisters, Mrs. Peploe, Viscountess Hereford, Mrs. Frankland Lewis, Lady Duff Gordon, and Miss Cornewall, were all celebrated for their musical talents.

‡ Mr. Stuart Wortley submitted to the House a motion for an Address to the Prince Regent, praying his Royal Highness to take such measures as might be best calculated to form an efficient administration. The motion was in fact for a vote of want of confidence in the administration about to be formed. The previous question was moved and lost by four, and Mr. Wortley's motion was carried. Mr. Wortley then moved 'the Address should be carried by the whole House.' Mr. Yorke moved the previous question. Mr. Wortley then withdrew his motion, and moved that the Address should be presented by members of the Privy Council sitting in Parliament. A division ensued. Ministers had a majority of two.—*Hansard*.

Wednesday, 27th.—I got ready to go to Blackheath with Lady Charlotte Campbell. We found the Princess sitting under an elm tree near the house; there we remained talking nearly an hour. At dinner Sir James Mackintosh, Sir H. and Lady Davy, Mr. and Mrs. G. Locke, young Burney, and Campbell the poet.* The first and the last I saw for the first time. I am charmed with the first, and not at all with the latter; he appears to think too much of himself. Sir J. M. conversed very well upon literature, upon his travels, &c., has a quiet manner, and without the least affectation.

Thursday, 28th.—In the evening the Princess read to us 'Amelie de Mansfeldt.'†

Friday, 29th.—The Princess Charlotte and Lady de Clifford arrived just as we finished our drive. We all sat down to dinner without making any toilette. The young Princess was very gay, very talkative, in very good humour, and very —, all one could expect from a young girl of sixteen, very quick and very lively, and very ill brought up. After dinner she played all sorts of things upon the piano. Her musical memory is astonishing. As to her looks, she has grown and improved since I saw her in November; with rouge she would be really striking, but she does not walk any better, and has not dignified manners. She left between nine and ten o'clock. The Princess then continued reading 'Amelie de Mansfeldt.'

Tuesday, June 2nd.—Called on Lady Georgiana and then on Lady Harriet. I saw quite well from my conver-

* Thomas Campbell, the poet, born at Glasgow in 1767; author of 'Love and Madness,' 'Caroline,' 'Pleasures of Hope,' which latter work placed him at once in the front rank with the poets of the age, 'Lochiel's Warning,' 'Gertrude of Wyoming,' and many other poems. In 1802 he became secretary to Lord Minto. In 1806 the King granted him a pension of 200*l.* a year. He continued his literary labours till towards the close of his life. Died at Boulogne 1844.

† By Madame de Cottin.

sation with the latter how the political negotiation was going on.

Wednesday, 3rd.—Went to Lady Georgiana; met Lady Harriet and had a conversation with her in another room upon the politics of the day or rather the morning, because it changes two or three times a day.

Thursday, 4th.—We went at three o'clock to Sir H. Davy's house to meet the Princess of Wales, who was coming to take herself, and to see taken, the Imperial Gas. I had never before seen its wonderful effect, of which I had formed but a very imperfect idea. Davy had taken it, and Sydney Smith, Sir J. Mackintosh and Lady C. Campbell, and the Princess. The dose administered to the latter was so small that the effects were only visible in the eyes and upon the complexion, but upon the others it was an excitement, a vivacity, in fact a wonderful intoxication of three or more minutes, astonishing! and so delightful to themselves that they wished to retake it, and could not and would not desist from imbibing the dose which was destined for them, so long as the slightest breath remained.

Friday, 12th.—Went in the morning to Lady Harriet, where I found Lord Granville. We were all three agreed upon the conduct of the Ministers, or rather the opposition. Went to Lady Spencer's. A large party (for her). Lords Camden, Grey, and every one on the opposition side laughing with very bad grace.

Sunday, 14th.—At eleven o'clock we took Sir J. Mackintosh with us to Kensington to hear Sydney Smith preach in the Palace Chapel. The Princess had begged of us to come to her in her gallery; she was delighted to see Sir J, Mackintosh, whom she did not expect. After church Sydney Smith came in to luncheon, and then we went to see the great apartment, one part only being open and many of the pictures displaced. We all took leave of the Princess; Sydney Smith went to Holland House, Sir J.

Mackintosh walked with us across the garden. At half-past ten we went to Miss Johnstone's,* where there was good company and music. I found Mrs. Siddons there, who repeated to me in a corner alone the verses that she was going to recite on her farewell to the public; they are by her nephew Twiss,† and I thought them in good taste.

Monday, 15*th*.—Called by appointment on Sir G. Beaumont to meet Colman,‡ and read with him 'The Two Martius.' As Sir George had told him that it was written by a woman, I owned myself to be that woman, exacting at the same time the secrecy which every manager of a theatre grants and keeps faithfully. I read the piece: he stopped me each time where he thought something piquant could be added, and all his observations were like a master of the art. He took away the little piece, with full permission to make any alterations he liked: he proposed returning it to me with his ideas upon the alterations, so that I could make them myself. I went with Agnes to Lady Hertford: the crowd was as usual. The Regent and three or four of his brothers, only one or two of the Opposition; the greater part were not even asked.

Wednesday, 24*th*.—I went to Devonshire House to see the library of the late Dr. Dampier, Bishop of Ely, which the Duke had just bought of his heirs for 10,000*l*. The books are still on the floor in one of the drawing rooms. These books, with those which he is now buying at the

* Afterwards Countess St. Antonio and Duchesse Cannizzaro.

† Horace Twiss, Esq.

‡ George Colman the younger, born 1762. He was educated for the bar, but his father's affairs demanded his assistance, and he undertook the charge of the Haymarket Theatre: this brought him afterwards into serious difficulties. He lived for many years within the 'rules' of the Fleet, from which he was rescued through the interest of the Duke of York, who got for him the office of Licenser of Plays. He was the author of many plays, poems, &c.

Duke of Roxburgh's sale, will make one of the best libraries in the country.

Friday, 26th.—We dined with the Princess at Kensington. The company: Lady C. Lindsay, Lady C. Campbell, Mr. Lewis, Sir H. and Lady Davy, Sir J. Mackintosh, Sir H. Englefield, Mrs.* and Miss Pole, Lord Glenbervie and Campbell the poet, who was to read his first discourse upon Poetry, which he had delivered at the Institution; he did so during the evening with very good effect. At dinner, Lewis gave out a thousand *bêtises* upon the subject of poetry, pretending that he found Homer and Virgil wearisome. Campbell's discourse appeared to be made expressly to punish him and to expose the inaptitude of these heterodox opinions. Poor Lewis was in a very bad humour, and did not know where to hide his head during the reading, so he pretended to be sleeping.

Monday, 29th.—I went to the theatre in Lady Spencer's box, to see Mrs. Siddons take leave of the public.

Thursday, July 9th.—We went to Lady Buckinghamshire, to what she called a Venetian *déjeuner*, Heaven knows why! There were a great many masks, several hired, I think, from small theatres, because there were few, if any, masked as they ought to be. There were tents, lotteries, and fortune-tellers in the garden. In fact it was Bedlam let loose, but very amusing and very pretty—a hot summer's day.

Monday, 13th.—Walked at Chiswick with the Duke, from whom I obtained in part the papers † I wished for.

Wednesday, 15th.—At nine o'clock in the evening we went to Lady Hardwicke's for their play; I went to the green-room to assist in rouging, &c. The theatre was brilliant, really the prettiest private theatre I have ever

* Hon. Mrs. Wellesley Pole, afterwards Lady Maryborough.

† Lady Russell's letters.

seen. The audience numerous and very well placed. The Regent and the Princes, who were expected, did not come, except the Duke of Gloucester; the Regent sent to say that he hoped to be there by ten o'clock, but not to expect him.

Friday, 17*th*.—In the evening at Lady Hardwicke's, I to be audience, Agnes to be behind the scenes. There was a great deal of company. The Princess arrived before ten o'clock; also the Princess Sophia and the Duke of Gloucester. At half-past one o'clock we went down to a superb supper; 140 people supped there.

Saturday, 18*th*.—It was a beautiful day. The Princess had desired me to be at Kensington by two o'clock. Lady Hardwicke and her two daughters came on a visit of etiquette to the Princess, who received them in her dressing gown. She afterwards talked much and for a long time on the subject of her position *vis-à-vis* the Princess Charlotte, and of the ungracious reception she met with on her visit to her daughter at Windsor, this day week, the 11th of the month, and of the visit she had received the day before yesterday from Lord Liverpool, and of all that passed; but as I intend to put it all to paper, it is useless to write more here.*

Monday, 20*th*.—The Princess of Wales came at two o'clock to take me to Blackheath. We found young Burney to meet us. Before dinner, I had a long *tête-à-tête* conversation with the Princess about her situation, and what she will do, who she will choose for the new lady that she is going to take instead of Mrs. Lisle, who has resigned in a manner hardly fitting, as she has been only six weeks in service. At nine o'clock we set out, the Princess, Lady Charlotte Lindsay, Lord Henry [Fitzgerald], and I, in her landau, and returned to London, passing by the way of Lady C. Campbell's, which in-

* This paper is not to be found, and was perhaps never written.

creased the distance at least three or four miles. The lightning which began near Lewisham threatened a storm, and put me into a state of mind very little fit to amuse a Princess; but she knew my weakness, and without sharing it, showed me all possible attention to relieve my ridiculous fears.

Thursday, 23rd.—Lady Hardwicke and Elizabeth called, and we thought of many arrangements for the evening. I was tormented with a hundred notes to ask Lady Hardwicke for places. I showed them all to her, and always obtained what they asked. A quarter before ten o'clock we went to St. James's Square with Mrs. Tighe. She, I, and Mr. Ward were placed on the third form from the stage. Agnes behind the scenes. At ten o'clock the Regent came with the Duke of Clarence, the Duke of Cumberland, the Duc de Berri, and the Duc de Bourbon, with whom he had dined at the Prince de Condé's at Wimbledon. The Regent gave his arm to Lady Hardwicke, and sat in the first row beside her and his two brothers at his side. The two French Princes in the same row, on the other side of the middle. The Sultana was sitting behind, and would not come forward. The Regent, as well as his two brothers, was very attentive to the performance. The actors were so frightened at their august audience that they never acted so badly, and had recourse more than once to the prompter, which never happened to them before, and they were in despair behind the scenes—so my sister said; but nobody discovered it but those who had seen their more perfect acting on last Friday. At half past one o'clock the Regent and his brothers went to supper, followed by all the company, except the French Princes, who went away. Lady Hardwicke sat by the side of the Regent, then the Duke of Clarence next, then Lady Hertford, the Duke of Cumberland, and Lady Conyngham, &c. &c. The proportion of elderly ladies at the table was too large. At the end of the same table, by the side of Lord Hardwicke, sat the Duke of Norfolk and Lord Erskine. The Prince spoke to the Duke of Norfolk, but made no sign of recognition to Lord Erskine.

Tunbridge Wells.—Wednesday, August 5th.—I was at the hotel dining with Lady Milbanke, her daughter, Mrs. Hervey, and Mrs. and Miss Chaloner. Lady Milbanke's daughter * appears to have a great deal of mind, and she is said to have a good deal of information, and is not at all affected.

Monday, 10th.—I walked for nearly an hour with Miss Mercer † upon the Common, where we had a long conversation about the Princess Charlotte. She told me the manner in which the Prince conducted himself towards her, and upon the subject of her intimacy with Princess Charlotte. She has not put her foot in the Princess's house since Easter.

Monday, 17th.—The news of Lord Wellington's splendid victory,‡ which has been so much talked of, has at length arrived, Lord Buckingham § having received the despatches during the night, had sent one to each library on the Pantiles, where everybody saw them, and were talking of the news. In the evening there was a general illumination. The Pantiles were decorated very prettily with branches of oak mixed with flowers and laurels. I had often heard of the beauty of an illumination at Tunbridge, but it very much surpassed my expectations. The effect of Mount Sion from the Common, with its rows of houses raised one above another, and all lighted, would have been beautiful, but for the bonfires which they are in the habit here of making, by lighting furze upon

* Afterwards married to Lord Byron.

† Daughter of Lord Keith, now Comtesse de Flahault Baroness Nairne.

‡ Salamanca.

§ Marquess of Buckingham, born 1753, twice Viceroy of Ireland, in 1782 and 1787. Died 1813.

the Common in various places. It produces a grand effect of light, but the smoke prevented our seeing the illumination of the village. The evening was perfect for such a fête—quite fine, without a breath of wind.

Monday, 24*th.*—I went to Lady Wellington's,* the new Marchioness. She appeared to have suffered a great deal from the uncertainty which everybody had been in, for more than a fortnight, and she spoke with an enthusiasm and a worship of her hero which was truly edifying. She goes to London to-day to be present when the *Te Deum* is sung in the Portuguese ambassador's chapel in honour of the victory.

Worthing.—Friday, September 4*th.*—Drove to Broadwater, a village about a mile distant from Worthing. The church is very old, has belonged to an abbey, and there is also a fine monument erected to the family De la Warr, who formerly possessed a great deal of the country round. It is spoiled by *white-wash*, but deserves to be restored.

Sunday, 6*th.*—Drove with Lady Dudley† in her carriage and six horses as far as Shankbury. It is the highest of the South Downs, from which there is a splendid view on all sides. The extraordinary clearness of the day permitted us to see it in a manner that does not happen three times a year. We returned through the village of Sompting, the prettiest I have seen in these suburbs, situated upon the rising Downs, shaded by fine trees, and having a view of the sea across pretty meadows, terminating each side by woods.

Thursday, 10*th.*—Went to Tunbridge Wells.

Saturday, October 3*rd.*—I set out to see Knowle with Mrs. Pole in her landau and four horses, and with Lady

* Hon. Catherine Pakenham, third daughter of Edward Michael Lord Longford, married 1806; died 1831.

† Julia Lady Dudley, second daughter of Godfrey Boseville, Esq., of Gussthwaithe, Yorkshire.

Burghersh * and Charles Bagot.† The carriage took us to the door of the house. The outside is very beautiful, like Oxford Colleges; the first court much resembles Oriel College. All is well kept. The inside does not correspond with the outside, or rather does so, too much, because the inside too much resembles the interior of a college for a nobleman's house. Long narrow galleries, badly lighted, and small rooms not *en suite.* There is not a single room in which one felt it would be possible to establish oneself comfortably. The apartment which the family occupy, and which all the preceding families have occupied, is *au rez de chaussée*, and could perhaps be *snug*, but there is no comfortable furniture, nor even furniture enough. There are some very good portraits by Vandyke, by Sir A. More, and Jansen; but many to which they have given any names they pleased. There are several of Sir Joshua Reynolds' in the most perfect preservation. Amongst others, 'The Fortune-Teller' and 'The Counts Ugolino.' I had a higher idea of the latter than I have upon a second view. The figures do not group well. Ugolino and the second son are on one side the picture, and the three other sons on the other side. The painter has tried to unite them by a kind of wall or enclosure of stone, which, to my mind, has not succeeded; and the head of the old man is the head of the old beggar, of whom it is, in fact, the portrait, but it is a portrait and nothing else.

Friday, 9th.—Walked on the Pantiles, read the newspapers, which contained the extraordinary letter of Lord Cathcart announcing the great defeat of the French, and their nineteenth bulletin dated Moscow!!!‡ One might

* Daughter to Mrs. Wellesley Pole.

† Hon. Sir Charles Bagot, married, 1806, to Mrs. Wellesley Pole's daughter.

‡ The battle of Borodino (called by the French Moskwa) was claimed as a victory by both sides. Seven days after the Russians were singing *Te Deum* for their victory, the French entered Moscow.—*Ann. Reg.*

be almost amused at the Ministers being credulous enough to believe all, and then to let all their credulity appear. Their friends thought to make their excuse by saying that the French bulletin was false!!

Friday, 23*rd*.—Returned to North Audley Street.

Tuesday, *November* 10*th*.—I went to Lady Crewe's, who gave a sort of *luncheon dinner*, to which we were invited, to meet Dr. Burney and his sister Madame D'Arblay.* They were neither of them there. When we entered a dozen ladies were sitting around the fire with Miladi. Lawrence, the painter, the only gentleman. Dr. Burney was ill and could not come, but at last Madame D'Arblay arrived. I was very glad to see her again. She is wonderfully improved in good looks in ten years, which have usually a very different effect at an age when people begin to fall off. Her face has acquired expression and a charm which it never had before. She has gained an *embonpoint* very advantageous to her face. We did not talk much about France; but with her intelligence there was a great deal she could tell, and much she could not, having a husband and a French establishment, to which she was to return after the winter.

Monday, 23*rd*.—In the evening we went to the play at Drury Lane in Mr. Coutts's box. The new theatre has the finest form that I have seen here, or perhaps elsewhere. The *proscenium* is superb, though wide, for the arrangement of the scenes, and the exits and entries necessary on the English stage. The ornaments in front of the boxes are well devised—gay and brilliant without being *gaudy*.

Thursday, 28*th*.—The Princess's carriage came with Lady C. Lindsay. We set out on a thorough November day, and at four o'clock we found the Princess with the luncheon still before her. We stayed talking with her till

* Miss Burney, authoress of 'Evelina,' 'Cecilia,' &c.

seven o'clock, when she dismissed us to dress. I was ready in ten minutes, yet she was already at table when I went down. The evening passed as usual, talking till nearly one o'clock.

Friday, December 4th.—I went again with the Hardwickes to see the gas lights. The proprietor's house was all lighted with it for us to see. After having well studied the effects, we went down in the cellar, or rather the kitchen, of the house to examine the furnaces, &c. &c.

Sunday, 13th.—I have had a long visit from the Duke of Devonshire. I talked to him about his papers, and showed him the arrangement that I have made of those which are curious. He was so pleased, and so well understood the assistance that I could be of to him, whilst amusing myself in making the researches that I wish for now, that he has promised to entrust to me a quantity of letters of last century that have not been arranged.

Tuesday, 15th.—Went to Wimpole.

These letters, received during the year 1812, being a narrative of the tour to the East by Mr. Gell and Mr. Craven, have been placed in order at the end of the year, in preference to placing them according to the dates.

Eleusis, Atticshire, Thursday, Feb. 27, 1812.

MY DEAR FRIENDS,—You will be quite mistaken if you fancy that the pleasure of dating a letter from *Vaghi Colli, Ameni Prati,* is my chief inducement for writing, a very rainy day you will allow to be a much better occasion, but the best of all is that I have meant to do so for this long time past, and now that I see no immediate possibility of dispatching my performance to England, I can no longer refrain, and so I shall begin with informing you that the whole mission is at a dead standstill. We *are* at present at Athens waiting for our firman, which we expected to find there, and without which there is no balm in Gilead, or digging at Samos, Ephesus, Sardis, or poking for spangles in the Pactolus. We thought at first of going to Smyrna, and waiting for it there, but there are robbers at Sunium and French privateers throughout the Archipelago; so we have sent the vessel we had hired to know from the Smyrna consul what we are to do, and are now waiting its return in trembling expectation; and in the mean time are come to *Elucid*ate the mysteries of Ceres. I wish I could give you a bird's-eye view of our present apartment and also sketches of our different positions. Gell is sitting on the floor making a map of this place, and fighting the splashing of the rain that beats in upon his paper through the only window we can suffer to have open. I am sitting on the opposite side of the fire, on my own bed, my table consisting of a pair of blue trowsers bundled up into an inclined plane, that I may catch the few rays of light that are to be had, and at the same time the many fleas which appear inclined to read this letter. At my feet sits, or rather lies, Mr. Bedford, in one of those painful attitudes that make one feel the cruel inconvenience of one's own legs. He is mending the fractures of broken columns, architraves, which are scattered in all directions about this village, by drawing them in a perfect state, such as you will see them in when published by the Society of Dilettanti. Then our other artist, Mr. Gandy, is in the distance, trying in vain to make a large writing desk lie flat and steady on the top of a small round trunk. The perspective is filled up by avenues of pots and pans, garlands of onions, and draperies of dusty cobwebs. The Albanian peasant to whom the mansion belongs occasionally comes in to see what he can steal, under pretence of making up the fire, in doing which he generally involves us in a cloud of smoke and dust for some minutes; but think not it was always thus; for till this day the weather was so fine, that I shaved every morning on the flat roof of our neighbour's house, where we also had our breakfast; and we found it so warm in our perambulations, that a sudden thought struck us, and we spontaneously left off cravats, and I have had some notion of dismissing other cumbersome articles of dress. Anacharsis will have it that this place is very pretty: I maintain it is only agreeable and cheerful, and gives one perfectly the idea of Proserpine gathering anemones, the beauty and quantity of which is to this present time something quite astonishing.

I conclude that you are all in London, and if so, Sir Harry or Lady Charlotte have probably told you all our adventures previous to our arrival at Athens—such as the festivities of Zante, our risks and perils in a gunboat, our shipwreck on a desolate island, our being shot at by an Ętolian savage, our bathing at Patras, our visit to the Bay of Corinth, and finally, our eating pancakes for breakfast. We are the only Englishmen just now in the town of Minerva, but there are four Northern artists, that is Germen, as Gell calls them, two of which call themselves Barons. *Ils mangent un coffre et rotent autour de la table* with great effect, especially in Italian, where *molto* *Pelo*/*bello* and *molto* *Pene*/*bene* stand always for much *skin* and *pain*; but they are very unassuming urbane persons in other respects. We have besides Mr. Fauval, the French Consul, who is the original *c'est moi qui l'ai découvert*, and consequently very entertaining. The country about Athens is by no means so beautiful as most of the other parts of Greece which I have yet seen, and the present town is, moreover, placed on the wrong side of the citadel, but it is worth coming all the way from England to see the temple of Theseus only. In point of landscape, nothing can exceed Zante in all its parts, which is an eternal garden, but will soon be spoilt by the English—I mean as a residence. You have both been enough abroad to know what nuisances one's countrymen are unless they are as agreeable as one's own self, which never happens; which reminds me of what rascals the Greeks are. Oh! you can imagine nothing like their lying, thieving, cheating, overreaching, intriguing, caballing and plotting. With that it is very difficult to keep angry with them long, as they are never ashamed or enraged at being detected in their iniquities, and their gaiety is never at all impaired by your reproaches, and as they are all equally bad, you cannot help employing them the next time they come with a smiling face.

Gell is quite furious at my finding time to write, never considering that he passes whole mornings in taking angles to form half a map, while I scramble about doing absolutely nothing; though I believe I have really found out the gap through which, as my servant calls it, *the devil took away that Princess to h—l.* It is quite surprising what an enthusiasm has seized all our *Drumsticks* for antiquities, and with what avidity they undertake the most laborious journeys over rocks and precipices in search of broken columns, when they perhaps would grudge carrying a note from Albany to Portland Place. One of them passes his life in digging for our artists, and was so overjoyed at having part of a *peppermint*, which you would never guess to mean a *pediment*.

By the bye, I believe Ceres, or her descendants the Greek saints, have great objections to have their monuments examined and turned about by English hands, for Gell and his servant were stopped in a research of that kind by an unknown but threatening voice which bade them 'dig no more;' and the latter dreamt of it, and woke us all by hallooing aloud: for my part I have seen the shades of Ceres and Proserpine, and I expect more visions. Talking of visions, I am tormented by bad dreams, and one of them is that Lady C. Campbell is dead; it has returned so often that it begins to make me unhappy, and I long to return to Athens for no other reason than the hope of getting rid of it.

This place is entirely inhabited by Albanians or their grandsons, and these have the prettiest dresses you can imagine. I went into one of their cottages yesterday to see a boy that was ill of an intermittent fever, and the child of the house, about a year and a half old, seeing something strange in a dark dress (their's are always white), began to scream; when its grandmother, to pacify it, told it I was *a dog*, and began patting and coaxing me, which so encouraged the brat that it came up to me and made doggish noises at me, and wanted to put some bread into my mouth, which you will allow was quite a new adventure and mentioned in nobody's travels.

Gell has had two fits of the gout since we left England; but the Eau Médicinale has cured him. As to me, I never was so well in all my life, not even when I wrote my name so often on the wall at Florence, which you afterwards saw, which was the beginning of our acquaintance.

Eleusis, Sunday, March 1.

Good fortune has sent the Frederickstein frigate into the Piræus, not to take us to Smyrna as we expected, but to carry this to Malta, where it is going with dispatches; so to-morrow morning I ride off to Athens to see the captain and commit my letter to his care. We learn that Frederick North is at Chio, his nephew, Mr. Douglas, gone to Russia, and Cockerell the architect reaping Ionian antiquities long before us. Poor Gell is not quite as well as I wish, and I apprehend a return of gout. It is quite English March weather, with rain and hail, but though in a mud cottage, we have excellent fires, and when it holds up, it is so fine and summery that I walked yesterday eight miles to the top of a horned mountain, and bathed in the sea when I returned, finding it so hot.

I must now take my leave of you, quite delighted at finding a chance of the letter going. Anacharsis sends all manner of loves to both of you and Mr. Berry, to whom you will please to give my kindest regards. Also say a thousand kind things for us both to dear Mrs. Damer, and if you ever meet the 'moderate horror,' tell her I often think of her.

And believe me, dearest friends,

Yours most sincerely and affectionately,

R. K. CRAVEN.

From Sir Wm. Gell to the Miss Berrys.

Smyrna, May 7, 1812.

MOST AGREEABLE PEOPLE,—You are always so kind and so amiable to me that you stand instead of father, mother, and family to me, and your house instead of an at-home in the country, and that is my excuse for writing to you as if by my writing I prevented you from forgetting me amidst the gaieties of London. We are at length arrived at Smyrna, not, indeed, much the worse for wear, but some three months later than we intended, on account of the horrors we have been submitting to on account of the pirates and Mainiote thieves, who cut off noses and ears by way of the least harm that can happen to you, and who have, except for armed vessels, completely cleared the Archipelago from everything like a sail or an oar. We have done, however, a great deal, though we have not done one single thing we were sent about; for instance, we have entirely discovered and put on a new footing the Temple of Ceres at Eleusis, we have restored a Temple of Diana Propylæa, which people never dreamed of, and we have completely arranged the Propylæa as large as those of Athens, without wanting a single member. All this is much better than the Asiatic business in point of interest; so this is a plan of it, for you and Mrs. Damer:—1, Temple of Ceres, about 180 feet square, with a portico of twelve columns in front; what think you of that? 5, a portal of the Corinthian order; 2, the Propylæa, the inner ranges of which are Ionic; 3, a great pavement; 4, the Temple of Diana Propylæa; 6, 6, 6, wall of the peribolus. All these things are of white marble, and we are ready in between thirty nd forty plates. There is something for you. We think of

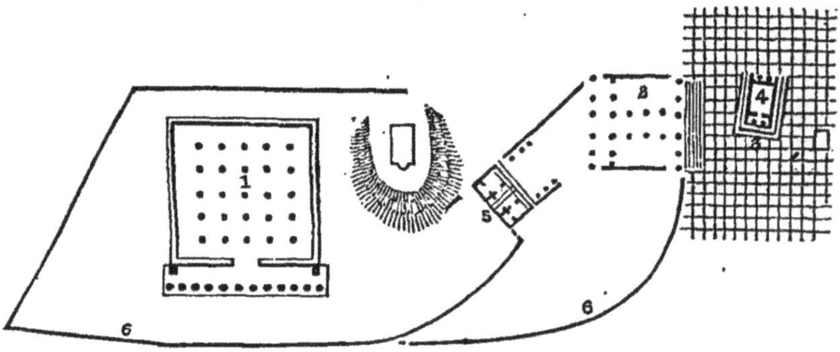

going hence to Sardis in a few days, but the Turks are levying troops, and therefore the shops are shut for fear of the said gentlemen helping themselves to what suits them, and all for nothing, so we cannot get what we want. We have reports of plagues, which I don't, however, see much reason to believe in, though I am certain Sir Harry will send for a doctor the instant he hears of anything from Turkey. The worst thing I now hear of, is of the Aga of Denislen, who commands the cities of Laodicæa, their Apolis and Aphrodisias, and who is now in so violent and outrageous a state of rebellion that nothing can touch his feelings. We are now trying to negociate him through other rebels, his friends, but I have as yet heard of no results. At all events I shall do something, and have not the least doubt of Samos and Sardis, Patara and Telmissus. They threaten me with the plague at Tralles, in addition to the terrible Aga of Denislen, who, if he cannot be calmed, will jockey me out of four of my places. I must inform you, however, that the restorers of temples, as they thought after Vitruvius, who have published the Dilettanti work, are considerably blown up, and are accused of having searched so little that they have falsified the temples, particularly that of Bacchus at Teos, most cruelly. Mr. Cockerell, I understand, says the building is quite of another shape from that represented. The truth is, the thing was not understood in those days; however, we shall probably see what truth there is in this. We know that the Dilly have published Ceres at Eleusis with six columns, and we know that we find twelve, and that it was like a Moorish mosque, all supported with pillars, dotted about like the mosque at Cordova. This country is exquisitely beautiful and well wooded; the town I do not much patronise. The English are, I think, rather gone down in the world since my last visit to these countries. The Dardanelles expedition and Egyptian have done us no good, though Miss Agnes and the Talents planned them. And I shall seal to you with a seal I bought, which was that of one of the Persian satraps slain at the battle of Talavera —I mean Marathon. I don't think we shall be home before March 1813, when I hope you will all have good fires to receive us. We have had here the worst winter ever known; it snowed three or four hours one day at Athens, and was cold for six or seven. I have had ninety gouts, and drunk half my cellar of Husson. Moreover, I got it three or four times by going up mountains to make a map of the sacred way from Athens to Eleusis, which 'though I say it as should not,' is by far the best map ever yet seen of any country, which I mention to you in private, that you may have the penetration of discovering its merit, for of course among the fine architectural drawings, an unfortunate map will make no figure at all, though it cost me a great deal of trouble and gout, and, moreover, between sleeping and waking, always gave me deep ravines and glens in my knees and ancles all the time I was laid up. I hope you will not be wicked enough to omit writing to me at this place, which I see by my instructions are our head-quarters; and as Lady Hardwicke has recovered the art of speaking, and is therefore no longer fit to represent the sign of the 'good woman,' I beg you will present me most piously to said Lady and her Lord. Pray don't suffer Mr. Berry to set the room to rights, or to prevent the lighting of the fire, for I am sure you are all dying of cold. Adieu! my dears; I kiss Miss Agnes between the eyes, and salute the curls which adorn your head when you are in a gala dress. I would send something kind to the Marchioness of Davies St[t], and to Mr. Moore, who would have lent me his carriage if I dared. Ah, Mrs. Harrot, who came from the garret when your mistress laughed at the Italian

A THERMIAN LADY.*

in my letter, remember how you cheated us out of the Yorkshire pudding twice, and expect not a fig from Smyrna.

Your ever affectionate,

ANACHARSIS.

Pray remember me most cordially to the Daughter of Phidias.

* 'What is beauty but a name?'—that is, observe the beautiful Lady of Thermia, an island at which we anchored. 'Beauty when unadorned 's adorn'd the most,'—that is, if people wear red silk stockings stuffed at the ancles with cotton, put on fifteen jackets and flounces all of different colours, they must look like feather-beds and walk like geese. There is a beauty for you who enslaves all beholders at Thermia.

From the Same to the Same.

Cnidos, July 3, 1812.

This letter ought to be addressed to all lovers of retirement, for there is not a soul except our own party or its adherents within three hours, which may indeed be all the better for us, as the whole country has the plague, from Pergamo to Attalia. We have voyaged in pursuit of Dillydandyisms, sometimes with and sometimes without success, for the last two months, in little boats; and as our course was southward, and a strong N. wind called Meltame blows all the summer, we have always terminated our trips in a very short time; but that is not all: the Asiatic terrà firma is plagued, the islands will not receive you for fear of the plague, you have French privateers in all the gulphs, and behind every rock you are in danger of pouncing upon the Mainiote pirates,—so that I don't know whether it will be possible to avoid such a series of plagues, or jockey such a variety of thieves. At Samos, one of our objects of research, we lived three weeks in a magazine near the ruins, but the temple has only half of one column standing, and the brutes of the place would not let us dig; in spite of which, however, we have a temple about 350 feet long, ten columns by twenty of the Ionic order, near seven feet diameter; we have a sacred way from it to the city; and we have a large city, the walls of which are very perfect, with an agora, of which we have made out something with ornaments, something new, and the remains of the great mole which was 120 feet high. We came to Samos from Scio, where, oh! ye gods, what millions of gardens and picturesque towers in them, and orange and lemon flowers without end! Thence Craven departed to Constantinople, where he will be lucky enough to be presented by or with Mr. Liston, who just arrived in time. We should now expect him to return to us, but think between all the crossings and jostlings we have had in a very zigzag course, the pirates, privateers, and the plague, he will be a full month in finding us out. From Samos we took our boat and sailed towards Cos, with a strong wind, which would have just carried us to Gaithronisi, into the mouths of the thieves, had we not met with a boat which had just escaped them. We immediately turned about, and were going to give up Asia entirely, and retire to Delos till the plague was over, but we had scarcely reached the Cape of Trogylium, under Mt Mycale, when a strong breeze sprang up again and tore us along to windward of the robbers, across the mouth of the Meander, to the port of the Jeronta, or the oracle of the Branchidæ, near Miletus. This was a little corner peopled by Athenians and Salaminians, where they kept a kind of guard against infection, though not very strictly. There we examined the temple of Apollo Didymæus, of which the ruins are stupendous; the columns are Ionic, but the Dilettanti have published their capitals; however the height, and plan, and almost everything else were wanting. How the late mission did not manage to give more details we could not conceive. We set to work, therefore, and can now give you views, a map of the place, a plan, section, elevation, and the order complete; besides digging up all but one of the statues, which are the oldest specimen of sculpture in Greece, with the Boustrophedon inscription, which is this, on one of them.

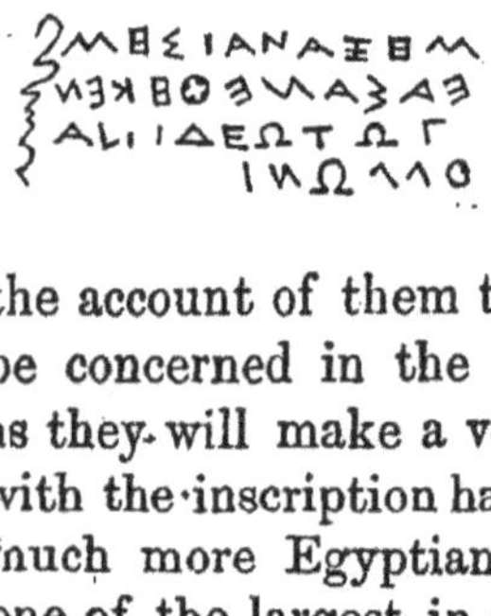

We have drawn and measured the whole set of these gentry, and as they are invaluable in point of style, I shall be much obliged to you to communicate the account of them to Mr. Knight, and those who are or may be concerned in the second volume of Statues by the Dilly's, as they will make a very prominent figure in the same. That with the inscription has lost its body, but there are several others much more Egyptian than Greek. As to the temple, it was one of the largest in the world, and the heap of ruins, though only three columns are standing, is wonderful. It had ten columns by twenty-one, was not quite so broad as that at Samos, but a little longer; there were five or six rows of columns sixty-four feet high, between the front and the Pronaos, all which we have established, and the whole disposition of the pilasters within; some of the same are given in the first volume of the 'Ionian Antiquities.' The columns are about seven feet diameter, but being so very tall one can only wonder that any remain. The ornaments are very elegant, but the marble is not so fine as the Athenian, and the whole gives one the idea of being built for the benefit of the first earthquake instead of being erected for eternity, like those of European Greece. We sailed from Jeronta to Cos, where we remained only two days, and then went to Halicarnassus (Budrom) on the opposite coast of Caria, where the Bey kept guard against the plague. It is a most beautiful spot, and the tomb of Mausolus I have no doubt is now converted into the foundations of the castle, which is a picturesque building of the time of the Knights of Rhodes. From Halicarnassus we sailed in about three hours to this place, Cnidos, Capo Crio, or Takir Boroun. One would not have expected that anything dedicated to Venus should have so completely changed its nature as to have become the Cold Cape, as it is now called. The place is the most curious one ever saw, but very convenient for trade or defence, if its inhabitants could have lived without eating, for there is no cultivable ground in sight, yet the city must have been very large. The island is defended toward the sea by the most magnificent precipices I ever saw. The walls and towers are tremendously strong, and nothing can exceed the beauty of the ports or the magnificence of the city seen from the island; where, besides many terraces of the most ponderous masonry, you have in sight a theatre of white marble between two terraces, on one of which we have a Doric portico of more than fifty columns, 300 feet long, overlooked by a Corinthian temple of white marble, and on the other side a terrace, with what I have not yet discovered. We are living in holes and corners, among ruined Greek churches and bushes; but upon the whole the place is not unpleasant, as the wind is constant and furious, so that we don't die of heat, as we otherwise should do. In the winter Capo Crio must be the devil of a place; and certainly the sea which flies over it now, must then have draggled poor Venus most woefully. She really might be said to rise out of the froth of the sea here, for the spray almost reaches us, and coming round the corner, I never saw anything so frightful as the rocks, so terrible as the whirlwind, or so torn into dust as the waves.

July 6.

Animals, which the sun invigorates at first, die of too large a dose—a moral reflection upon the grasshoppers, and locusts, and fleas. The former have lived upon my pantaloons, and the latter upon me for some days; but the sun has now silenced completely the singing and skipping of the whole party, and they are giving up the ghost and drying up, post haste, in all quarters. Yesterday we broiled to the tombs which adorned the sacred way. The great people must have had the plague, there are so many; and a great deal of money, they are so solid; and have been very fine fellows, for most of them are styled heroes.

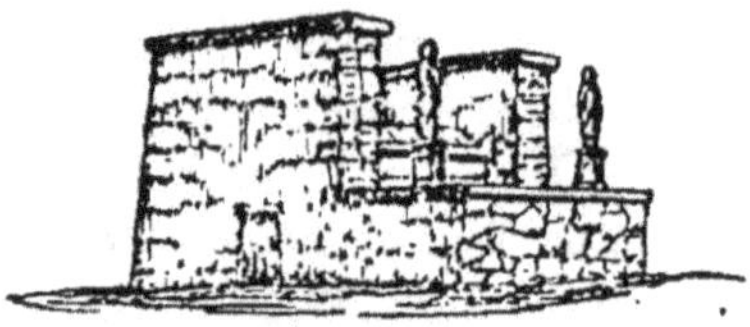

It saves a great deal of expense in paper to say they were some thus, and others plain towers, with massy cornices and the sarcophagus within. We have found a temple of the Ionic order, very small but very beautiful; but upon the whole we have every reason to believe ourselves cruelly indebted to the Romans for our specimens of architecture here. We have had a visit from the Aga, and as he fell in love with my sword, which I could not spare, I gave him some pistol barrels, with which he rode off on a mule, too happy, having disentangled with much labour his Tartar pantaloons from the bushes and stones. They are made of about forty ells of thick sky-blue cloth. He brought us two or three lambs; some yaunti or sour milk, like milk and lemons; some Kaimak, which is a thick edition of the film on boil'd milk, very good in tea; and he sent us as many people as we want to dig at Venus, Apollo, and Neptune, so that upon the whole he was of great use; besides telling all his people to bring us what we wanted. The natives are all Turks; they are very quiet, and sit at the distance of fifty yards from our dens or tents to see us, not rushing in as the Greeks do. There have been people from a great distance to see the Milords, and they all bring a present of cucumbers, melons, or whatever they are possessed of, for which presents, however, we are glad to pay them, for the nearest village is an hour and a-half, and the Agao village, who makes good Kaimak, is four or five. The Cnidian post not being regular since the battles of Issus and Arbela, I shall, I hope, send this from Rhodes. N.B.—On the 16th I had the gout, and was laid up; the consequence was an earthquake; so as it was very doubtful whether my ruin would stand without any assistance at all, I bounced out at the first shock. The jackals eat up the sheep, Mr. Bedford fell ill of an ague, and so we proceeded to Rhodes, where I now write this on the 19th. No news of Craven, so I give him up for the voyage, as we shall proceed to Maori, and to consult the oracle at Patara immediately.

From the Hon. R. K. Craven to Miss Berry.

Constantinople, Wednesday, July 8.

My dear Friends,—I am much tempted to defer the writing to you for some days, in order that I may impress your minds with awe by dating from Mount Olympus, where I am going; but I reflected that you might, at the same time, be alarmed by an idea that I might have become an eternal inhabitant of that elevated region, and I prefer addressing you as an humble Christian to the vanity of shamming demigod. This letter *ought* to be very classical, for it will be conveyed by the 'Argo,' but I fear I can only make it commonplace, being induced to write by the certainty of its reaching you in safety, and not costing much more than it is worth. I have been here exactly three weeks, which are more than enough to satisfy curiosity, and perhaps too much to be pleasant, as there is no place I should so much dislike as a residence, notwithstanding its natural beauties, which I acknowledge to be unique. Mr. and Mrs. Liston made their *entrée* about ten days since, and the ex-minister, Mr. Canning,* returns to England in the ship that brought them out, which was not allow'd to come up higher than the *Darningneedles*; the rest of their voyage being perform'd in open boats, in which Her Excellency slept every night with the common sailors; but don't think I mean to be scandalous, her august spouse being also of the party. That is the only mode of conveyance at this time of year, and is probably the most eligible as well as agreeable, for the north wind prevails so constantly, that a voyage in anything but row boats would be a never-ending undertaking, and this only lasts four or five days.

I have been divorced from the learned mission ever since the 26th of May, when they sail'd from Scio to Samos, and are since gone to Rhodes and such parts of the coast of Asia Minor as the plague will allow them to examine. This said plague broke out at Smyrna the very day after we left it, and there are some feeble reports of its being here—that is, there have been what are term'd a few *accidents* in the Turkish town; that is,

* Now Lord Stratford de Redcliffe.

people dying without any apparent cause but the will of God. You need, however, not be the least alarm'd, for this letter will be quarantin'd, and fumigated very often before it reaches North Audley Street, which I calculate to be in about three months. The moment I have visited the abode of the gods, I shall set off in quest of my earthly companions, though I have not the smallest idea where I shall light upon them. I visited Mitylene and the Troad in my way here. At the former place, I was all but stoned to death by Sappho's descendants, who would insist upon it I came from Smyrna with the plague; and I was obliged to fly for protection to the Bishop, who was very gracious, and gave me a wooden spoon to scratch my back; which reminds me that Mrs. Forasti, a great lady at Zante, when Mrs. Airey, the Governor's wife, complain'd of cold, stirr'd the coals of the brazier with a silver tea-spoon she drew from her pocket. Such are the primitive manners of Ionian dames. I have seen the Sultan twice. He is like Lord Aberdeen, and looks dignified in pale melancholy. You would long to steal all his horse's trappings to make sofa-covers of the saddle-cloths, and necklaces of the bridles; but what Miss Agnes would absolutely die of, in a transport of embroidery is the bazaar for handkerchiefs, which is, indeed, enough to turn the most stoic brain. I have never ventur'd but once in it. You may hear of the Seraglio and St. Sophia, and the Seven Towers; but nothing is to be compared to the said bazaar, except it is the two caps which are always carried immediately after the Grand Signor when he rides out. You must not imagine that I am deck'd out in Oriental finery, like Lady Hester Stanhope. I preserve my independence and European over-alls. She displays hers by Turkish trowsers, and rides *à la Mameluke* on a fine Arabian given her by the Pacha of Cairo, with an alarming number of pistols in her girdle. The fashionable place here for the summer is a village call'd Buyukdere, which is anything but retired; at the same time better than this, and with some sort of society, as there are the Foreign Ministers, two of which, the Spanish and Neapolitan, are really extremely pleasant, though the former talks of the *bagues de la mer*. Here there are nothing but Dragowomen, very ill calculated to support the credit of their husbands' employments, if one is to judge from their silence. Count Italinsky is arrived by way of Russian

Minister; but peace is not yet signed, and the prisoners of war not released from the arsenal here, so there are some sceptics on the subject. Our ambassadress is a very good-natur'd sort of person; but I am very much alarm'd about her, since I have read that there is a fountain on the sea-shore in Thrace which has the singular property of causing the ewes that drink of it to produce *black lambs*. The boats that come from the Dardanelles usually stop at every fountain they come to, and should Her Excellency have tasted of this prolific stream, I leave you to judge of the consequences; for, putting aside Mr. Liston's feelings on the subjects, it will be such an example to the *corps diplomatique*. I wish you were here, that I might take you to the Cumberland tea-gardens, under the shape of a shiosque at a spot call'd *les Eaux douces*, which I think you would admire almost as much as the original, and where you would get some very thick coffee without cream or sugar, and some pipes, both which are acknowledged to be infinitely superior to tea and bread and butter. Mr. Liston's private secretary is a Mr. Turner, whom I wanted to be brother to your Miss Turner, though not agreeable enough to belong to her. Pray tell her so, with my kind remembrance and wishes that she were here to nurse me under the sufferings of a red-hot coal, which Miss Agnes once had on her back, but which is fixed on the back of my neck, and yields not to poultice or plaster. People say it has saved my life, and that I ought to be very glad; but I really am very sorry, for I don't sleep, and I wish you would cure it. After Brousa I am going to Mt. Athos, and fancy I am going to Thessalian Tempe and Thermopylæ; but the fact is, I am going to hunt for Gell, without whom I am a fish out of water. If a mouse eats your bag of salt, it is a bad omen; also if you have two bags of gall, or your liver is meagre and unusual, you will wage war with great energy and violence; but if you meet a person with one eye bigger than the other, you must spit three times in his bosom. These are the results of my present studies, which you may communicate to any antiquarian you please. My best regards wait upon Mr. Berry, and pray, pray say a thousand kind things for me to Mrs. Damer, and believe that I am ever your very affec^{te} and sincere

R. K. CRAVEN.

From Sir Wm. Gell to the Miss Berrys.

Vathi, Samos, Nov. 26, 1812.

Of all people I really think the amiable Queens of North Audley Street were the very last from whom I expected a letter, when my bug-puzzlers or curtains were untied this morning to admit a packet of letters from Smyrna, where the plague is not furious at present. It is probable that, when I wrote last to you, it was from Capo Crio or Cnidus, and in that letter I must have given you the history of the pranks of the Dilettanti up to that time. We have left nothing to be done at Patara; but tombs, and not temples, and theatres of Roman times (Vespasian) are the chief objects of curiosity there. As to the Oracle of Apollo, there is nothing by which it can be traced, nor are there any remains of sufficient antiquity. Telmissus was certainly no more than a fortress, nevertheless it was a large one, and the theatre of great size. There are no other remains except tombs cut in the rocks, which are curious, but I can tell you little of it, as I was so ill I could not stand when I was there, and kept my bed for two months afterwards at Rhodes, to my sorrow and the irreparable loss of the learned world. It was in vain we tried to get inland; the plague always prevented us, and the privateers kept the sea so well, that with the north wind, which did not change till the middle of October, it would have been impossible to escape. However, no time was really lost, for Messrs. Bedford and Gandy made a voyage to Myra in Lycia, whence they brought home the richest collection of tombs, good, bad, quizzical, and *clockcasical* ever seen, which I hope we shall have published. At length, however, we got to Samos, and having discovered an opening on the continent without the plague, though it was only three hours off, we resolved on a push for Aphrodisias, if possible, as well as Magnesia on the Meander. In order to effect this, and not to have our return intercepted by this happy malady, I found the only way would be to send one of the artists one way, and one the other. It fell to Mr. Gandy's lot, therefore, to procure the true and genuine Aphrodisiacs for the Society. To mine and Mr. Bedford's the introduction to the world of the celebrated and much-longed-for temple of Diana Leucophryne at Magnesia Neckclothia Pennytrumpettata ad Mæandrum. I do assure you there is not a grain of magnesia on the spot at present. The temple, however, is beautiful, and only the greatest treasure possible to artists, being cited for certain peculiarities by Vitruvius. It is about 100 feet by 200, 8 columns in front and 15 in flanks of a most beautiful Ionic, 4 feet 7 in. in diameter. Among the novelties are the Amazonian Ladies on the frieze. The Amazons are ridiculously little till they jump from their steeds, when they become the most strapping heroines possible. As these ladies are perishing entirely by their own ambition, one is not so much concerned to see them generally torn off their horses by the hair, as if they had been more civilized personages.

Now, I shall tell you neither how we lived in a mill and then in a baker's shop in the rainy season, neither of which had tight roofs, nor will I regale you with an attempt to substitute curricles for horses, which were drawn by two black buffaloes, which I suppose are yet on their way home, as they went so slow. I never saw them but at first setting out, for all these things either become known, or are not worth knowing. I shall give you an account of Aphrodisias. First of all, you pass through Guzel Hissar, where only 30,000 people died of the plague last year, and then going twice as far to the crossing the Meander as the distance hitherto given by travellers, you go four times as far as they have called it from thence to Aphrodisias. The people are great drunkards, both Mussulmen and Mussulwomen, and there are 400 houses among the ruins of as many more.. They care neither for the devil or Dr. Solomon, so that the Mission had to pay for whatever they measured. The situation is a pretty plain watered by a river, which, from an inscription, I suppose the Timilus. In the middle of the city is a small hill, round the base of which run walls, built of odds and ends of temples, Cupids, giants, Glauci, columns, festoons, and common stones. This beautifully regular work was, I conclude also from an inscription, the work of Constans or some of those tasteful emperors whose medals show their zeal for the arts. The temple of Venus is destroyed, but of white marble equal to, if not really Parian. The order Ionic, with 6 columns in front by 13. N.B. The names of the subscribers on each. It would be good if you could get rid of certain plinths under the bases; but it was built in Roman days, when plinths were thought improvements. In front of the temple is a Propylæum of the Corinthian order, but alas! this has twisted columns. Round the temple is an enclosure about 700 feet long, by half that breadth. This is also formed of Ionic columns, but full of defects. There is a theatre very much ruined, and a circus very perfect. Inscriptions of athletæ and conquerors at all kinds of nose-pulling, from all parts of the world, abound. The place must have grown up from some extraordinary miracle committed by the goddess, and by some knowing priest contriving the games. The fact is *poca cosa vale per le'arte*, though people have said so much of it. Nevertheless, a great number of columns yet standing justify the accounts of travellers who have called it magnificent. From what I see of the country, the more you go inland, the less of Greek and more of Roman will be your fate; so that I regret but little that the Plague and Co. prevent our seeing Hierapolis, and as to Laodicæa, it was entirely Romanissimo. Every fragment Mr. Gandy found at Guzel Hissar (Tralles) was decidedly Roman; and as to Sardis, though there is a great temple, the columns are buried more than half, so that to make out plan, order, or elevation would have cost twice the capital of the Dandy's. Magnesia is worth all Asia. Indeed, we are now very rich in drawings, really richissimi. We are coming home post haste, if that can be haste which talks of 3,000 miles by sea, and a certain quarantine of forty days, wherever we go. We believe we shall manage, through Zante, to cheat some of the imprisonment, and to find a passage. Our business is over, and we are only here till H.M. brig 'Kite' comes to know our fate. In the meantime, I have the pleasure of an ague for my amusement, in consequence of our last trip and more of one cold day here. The bustle in the clouds seems, however, now over, and serenity is, I hope, reestablished in the atmosphere for some weeks. We were above six months without rain, but of course we have now had a good dose of it, which, I suppose, will do till February or March. Pray remember me most kindly to the Daughter of Phidias. I shall walk in to your house one very cold day in March, till which time, believe me, my dear good friends,

Your most affectionate

ANACHARSIS.

Mr. Craven sends his duty.

JOURNAL.

1813.

Wimpole, Friday, Jan. 1st.—I went to the school-feast at two o'clock with Lady Hardwicke's two daughters, and assisted in helping fify-three mortals, boys and girls, from three years old to twelve, with plum-pudding, meat pies, and roast beef. The quantity that the children eat is astonishing! After dinner the prize for work done by each child in the course of the year was given,—the girls for needlework and boys for knitting stockings, &c. In my life I never saw a happier assembly; the little ones who had done nothing received each of them a penny. There were also prizes for those who wrote the best, and who hemmed the best, to which I had the honour of contributing.

Thursday, 7th.—The little Krumpholz left this morning for London, where she is going to be married very suitably. She was much overcome last night at leaving this house, which has been her home ever since she was thirteen years old, when Lady Hardwicke took charge of her, for the sake of music and speaking French with her daughters. She was the daughter of the husband of the famous harpist, Madame Krumpholz, by a former marriage. An orphan, without father or mother, the Duchess of Bourbon took charge of her, had her educated in a convent, and at the commencement of the Revolution wisely found her another protectress.

Tuesday, 19th.—Returned to London.

From Sir U. Price to Miss Berry.

Foxley, January 19, 1813

Here is a most flaming ode on the burning of Moscow, &c., which the author humbly lays at your feet. When you have recovered from your first enthusiasm, I beg you will exercise your cooler judgment, and send me your criticisms. It will be a strange thing if there should be one spark of fire in this ode of mine, considering the time and circumstances of its birth: it was composed almost entirely *sub Dio* and *sub Jove frigido*, and ancle deep in snow; for it was exactly during the fortnight or three weeks that the snow lay on the ground before Christmas. I was then very busy, marking and cutting in a wood at some distance; and sometimes I drew forth my hacker (for I carry my Durindana in a scabbard), and sometimes my paper; now gave a *coup de hache*, and then a *coup de crayon*; and in this manner 'I built the lofty rhyme.' Thus far, indeed, the state of the weather and the ground might be of use to me, as I could paint *dal vero* (tho' heaven be praised, from a very diminutive scale), the icy blast, the trackless snow, the piercing cold, &c. You will immediately see that as far as metre goes, I had Gray's Bard in my eye, 'Numeros,'—I wish I could add, 'animosque secutur.' This subject is certainly a very fine one; the principal actor one of the most extraordinary men 'that ever lived on the tide of times,' the burning of Moscow one of the most extraordinary, unexpected, and striking events that ever took place, and the motives and consequences not less so. Had Gray been living, and in the full possession of his powers, he could have made a noble ode; but you know that poetry is not my *metier*, and that, as Voltaire once chose to say of himself, 'Je ne fais que de la vile prose.' After all, if I did not think this bold attempt of mine had some merit, I should not send it to you; and if you should think it worth showing to any of your poetical and critical friends, do not at first tell them whose it is, but let them guess. I may, perhaps, be well taken in by this request, and you may write me word that one guessed Parvus Pybus, another, Sir James Bland Burges, and a third did not think the thing worth guessing at at all. You will, of course, show it to Mrs. Damer, and I hope she will not be displeased with the *Finale*; which, by the by, will confine the guessers, should there be any, to a narrow choice. I sent an early copy to Fitzpatrick; and Rogers happening to come in at the moment, he could not resist showing it him: I have since altered it a good deal, and as Rogers had seen the first sketch, I have sent him this new, and I hope improved, edition. He and Fitzpatrick are the only persons out of my own family to whom the secret (which indeed is none), has been told. One circumstance mentioned in these verses is strikingly confirmed by what my nephew L[d] Tyrconnel was an eye-witness of: he saw the late governor of Moscow set fire to his own magnificent palace. You may happen to have seen in the papers that L[d] Tyrconnel has been with Admiral Tchesagoff: it is an odd circumstance, though certainly not of a lyrical kind, that the parson of my parish was the man who married this amphibious hero to a daughter of Commissioner Proby's; and, to finish the history, the ceremony was performed at Paddington. The only person, besides Mrs. Damer, to whom I *wish* you to show my verses, is my friend Sir Harry Englefield: make him guess and criticise.

Most truly yours,

U. PRICE.

From Miss Berry to the Countess of Hardwicke.

North Audley Street, Sunday, 21st February, 1813.

. . . . I wish what you say upon the letter of the Princess of Wales had been on any other subject; it is so just, so clever, so well expressed, that I should like to have given you the credit of it with a certain number of people and *passed it off as my own* with others; but upon *this* subject I hear as much and say as little as I can (I mean without any affectation of silence), for fear of being supposed to know more than I do. It was reported yesterday that at the Council held on Friday, to which many Privy Counsellors not Cabinet Ministers were summoned, among others, little Abbot, that it had been determined not to adopt *any* measures upon the Princess's letter. That the Chancellor* had absolutely refused going over the old business again. One shall know in the course of to-day if this is true. If it is (I mean that no fresh investigation is to be proceeded on), the Princess may well consider it as a triumph (pray Heaven she bears it with moderation!); for after the manner that all the

* Lord Eldon.

ministerial people, and all the people speaking their language, have lately expressed themselves of her, and of their own difficulties, for these last two years, in restraining the Prince from taking active measures against her, it is quite impossible to suppose they would not now indulge the P. *if* it were in their power. . . . The report is, that all idea of proceeding against her, either upon old or new griefs, is abandoned; and that the Prince's ill-humour is such, that neither ministers nor servants know what to do with him. . . .

P.S.—Sir H. Davy, who was here last night, desires me to tell you that the nymph *Florina*, whom he was expecting to arrive from Wimpole to his longing arms by the waggon on Saturday (what a sinking in poetry!) is not yet come, and he begins to be uneasy about her. . . .

Sunday, March 21st.—Lieutenant-Colonel Campbell and I set out for Blackheath: we found Miss Knight with the Princess. She was visibly touched by the manner in which we met her and kissed her hand: the tears were in her eyes. Afterwards she reseated herself and was very cheerful.

Monday, 22nd.—In the evening we had a little party of seventeen people for music, which passed off very agreeably. After the music they waltzed; they imitated the opera-dancers, and then acted proverbs in pantomime: in short, it so chanced they were really gay and amused themselves.

Saturday, 27th.—We arrived at Blackheath at five o'clock. I saw the Princess in the garden. We walked a little while; she perceived that I was not well, and begged I would not dress. On going down to dinner I was surprised to find Lady Percival and her son, a boy of fourteen years old. Whilst we were at dinner the Duke of Brunswick came to speak with his sister about their mother's will. They retired to the drawing-room, and we remained with the second course before us for nearly an hour. Afterwards the Princess and Lady Clara were engaged in making a sketch of a letter and an envelope to all the executors of the late Duchess, as she had named seven.

From the Hon. R. K. Craven to the Miss Berrys.

From durance vile
In Malta's isle. 3rd of April, 1813.

DEAREST FRIENDS,—The inclosed should have charmed your longing eyes some two months ago, as you will see by its date, but only arrived here a few days since; Gell will not write it over again, indeed, he has not time, though people in quarantine have a tolerable share of that commodity on their hands; but there are maps to correct, sketches to finish, journals to revise, for this is, we hope, our last resting place, and to-morrow sails the packet; so I have burnt my former envelope, and hastily substitute this scrawl: the other was more legible and more worthy of being read, as it contained an account of Mr. Curius' house at Samos, with all its concomitant horrors in the shape of bugs, Greeks, spoilt children, and tame rabbits, all things unknown in our present abode, where there is but one engine of terror, viz., the plague, but that terrifies the people in the town much more than us its next-door neighbours. We shall be about a week longer, and then let loose upon the streets of Valetta to find a passage to England. Frederick North says being in quarantine is the pleasantest state of existence in the world, that it is like the gout without the pain of it, which is a refinement I don't understand. You must not mind Gell's letters being stabbed, it is the fashion with all epistles from the Levant. I need not say we are in all haste to get home, and throw ourselves at your feet; we think of you every day at dinner, because they send us so few peas from the inn, and you are always so lavish of them. We have been delayed everywhere—at Athens very pleasantly; at Corinth, very much the contrary; at Patras, odiously; at Zante, very well, because there is a most amiable Governor, and an elysium of orange groves: that Zante is a spot of peculiar grace and loveliness, and makes one long to be romantic and very young, neither of which I have felt for many years. I have no news, except the Queen of Sicily's pranks, which the papers will tell you of. The Concannons are here—did you know them? They have wandered over Italy, of which their account would make you weep. Imagine no carriages at Naples, and every soul in Florence drowned in tears. . . . I hope you mean to be very kind to us, for we shall feel very shy at reappearing in the world, especially me, who am undergoing the noviciate of a downright entire wig, which makes me feel as if I had sham calves.

I find I can talk of nothing but myself, but consider we are in the lazaretto, dans cet affreux palais de la vengeance, où respirent à la fois le crime et l'innocence, that is, perfect health and all manner of pestilence, with which

I ever remain, your very obliged and affectionate friend,

R. K. CRAVEN.

Monday, April 12th.—At one o'clock Agnes and I went to the Bayswater Gate, in Kensington Gardens, to see the City bringing their address to the Princess.* The crowd around the palace was great and kept increasing every moment, people here flocking through all the walks of the garden in file and in crowds, all coming to increase the enormous circle around the palace on the side of the Princess's apartment. Seeing the impossibility of getting nearer before it was too late, we left the garden by the little gate of the palace, and passing through the Duke of Kent's court, got into Lady Charlotte Lindsay's apartment. Arrived as far as the little drawing.room, we found nothing but preparations for a dinner of eight or ten people, but hearing sounds in the next room, I knocked at the door, and a voice, which I recognised to be that of the Princess, called out to us to come in. We found the Princess with her three ladies and Miss Hayman, all dressed and eating in haste, awaiting the arrival of the Lord Mayor.

* At a Common Hall convoked on the 2nd of April, an Address to the Princess was moved, and, notwithstanding some opposition, carried almost unanimously. It stated 'the indignation and abhorrence' with which the Livery of London viewed 'the foul conspiracy against the honour and life of Her Royal Highness, and their admiration at her moderation, frankness, and magnanimity under her long persecution.' This address sprang from the report of certain members of the Privy Council upon the conduct of the Princess, and the discussion to which this report gave rise in Parliament. *Ann. Reg.*

When the Vice-Chancellor St. Leger announced that the Lord Mayor was approaching, the Princess went down with the ladies, and we at their tail, to the dining-room of her apartment, where she was to receive. After she was placed with her ladies, and Miss Hayman, and her Chamberlain, they opened all the shutters to allow the Princess to be seen by the immense crowd collected in the gardens. They applauded tremendously, and showed every possible mark of good-will towards her. At last, after a good half hour, the Lord Mayor and four Aldermen, accompanied by more than 150 Liverymen, came in and advanced towards the Princess. The applause at this moment was so great and so noisy, that they were obliged to threaten the crowd outside to shut the windows if they were not more quiet: this threat obtained a respectful silence. The town clerk (in the absence of the recorder) read the address very well; and the Princess read her answer also very well, though at the beginning the sentences were rather too long and difficult for her to pronounce well. She began in a low voice, which afterwards grew stronger. In the last part, where she spoke of her daughter, &c., she expressed herself with a good deal of feeling, and seemed to be moved, which had a very good effect, as well as the deliberate manner with which she dwelt upon that part in which she spoke of the rest of the Royal Family. After the address and answer, the Lord Mayor, the Aldermen, and the Liverymen kissed her hand, and went out by the little room (where we were) to join their carriages in the Duke of Kent's court. When they were all gone, the crowd outside called so loudly for the Princess, that her ladies begged of her to show herself at the middle window, and then at the doors, and then at the two ends of the apartment: this she did, accompanied by her ladies and conducted by her chamberlain, and, having curtsied to the people, immediately retired. I never saw a crowd that better deserved to have its wishes gratified, for it was not a common mob, but workmen, small tradespeople, mixed with well-dressed people, and conducting themselves perfectly. After this ceremony, which was really touching from the ardour of the people to show their good-will towards her, the Princess crossed the apartment, taking me by the arm to go back to Lady Charlotte's little drawing-room. We there found dinner, the guests being her four ladies and we two, Mr. St. Leger and Mr. Fox, who arrived during the speeches. After dinner took leave of the Princess, finding the carriage at Bayswater Gate; sorry only to leave the gardens so soon on such a fine evening, enlivened as they were by groups of people, in addition to the crowd which had surrounded the palace.

Wednesday, May 12th.—I went to Lady Davy's in the evening. There were seventy or eighty people there: amongst others Miss Edgeworth,* who was my object. She is very small, with a countenance which promises nothing at first sight, or as one sees her in society. She has very winning manners. She received with much warmth what I said of my desire to see the author of her works, and of all the obligations that I felt in common with all our sex towards one of her genius. She said a great many pretty things of all she had heard of me, and of my society; but feeling that I did not deserve them, it had little effect upon me, and had hardly the power of raising me for a moment from the depression into which I have fallen.

Monday, 24th.—In the evening was the question of the Catholic Emancipation Bill, the first clause, which gave the Catholics admission into Parliament, was lost by a majority of four votes.

Tuesday, 25th.—Went with Lord and Lady Charle-

* Maria Edgeworth, daughter of Richard Lovell Edgeworth; born 1767. The well-known author of many popular works adapted to the understanding of all ages, and whose memory is entitled to the gratitude of those who in their childhood have profited by her power of combining and conveying to others instruction and amusement; died 1849.

mont * to Blackheath to see the Princess. She was much more lively than the last time I saw her; spoke with the greatest pleasure and impatience of being established in town, and of her certainty now of having a house there.

Wednesday, 26*th*.—We went to Mrs. Marcet's to see 'Spartacus' played by the Lullins and Regnier, who alone remained of the last year's troup. 'Spartacus' has all the defects with which we reproach French tragedy: long expositions, recitals of the effect of passions rather than the effects themselves, though there are some fine parts, strong sentiments, some striking couplets, and the denoûment, which has a grand effect. Madame Lullin played even better than last year. They gave afterwards 'Défiance et Malice' very well.

Saturday, 29*th*.—Supped at Lady Davy's with the Princess; there was only Lady Charlemont and Lady Charlotte Lindsay, besides ourselves, and the gentlemen were Lord Byron, Mr. Grattan, Lord Lansdowne, Sir J. Mackintosh, Mr. Mackenzie, Mr. Stuart of Glasserton, and Lord Charlemont. The Princess was tired body and mind, and as she confessed herself, nothing less than intoxicated with the applause that she had received at the Opera.†

Tuesday, *June* 1*st*.—Drove with the Duke of Devonshire, in his curricle, to Chiswick, where he showed me all the alterations that he was about to make, in adding the gardens of Lady M. Coke's house to his. The house is down, and in the gardens he has constructed a magnificent hot-house, with a conservatory for flowers, the middle under a cupola. Altogether it is 300 feet long. The communication between the two gardens is through

* Earl of Charlemont; married, in 1802, to Anne, daughter of William Bermingham, Esq., of Ross Hill, Galway.

† 'At the Opera the other night, every person stood up when the Princess entered the house, and there was a burst of applause.'—*Lady C. Bury's Diary*.

what was the old greenhouse, of which they have made a double arcade, making the prettiest effect possible.

Thursday, 3*rd*.—Walked to Miss Edgeworth's, who we found sitting at breakfast with her father* and stepmother.† We heard he would not allow his daughter to go to see the Princess of Wales Tuesday last, because he and his wife were not invited. The little woman herself is always amiable, always natural, intelligent, and sensible.

Tuesday, 29*th*.—In the evening we had a few people at home; and Madame de Staël, who came, talked, questioned, and went away again like a flash of lightning, or rather like a torrent.

Monday, *July* 5*th*.—The grand breakfast at Carlton House was given to-day, so all the world was out of doors. The largest part of the company assembled at three o'clock, not to separate till four o'clock to-morrow morning—that is to say, having been present at a fête which will last thirteen hours.

Wednesday, 7*th*.—I went to see the illumination‡ of Lord Dudley's house,§ which was very beautiful. All these three days, or rather nights' of illumination have been in the finest weather; a rare thing in this country.

Friday, 8*th*.—Went in the morning to see the Indians, who performed some juggling tricks in Pall Mall. I was very much amused. The figures, dress, language, and the movements of these two men, all transport one into another quarter of the globe; their skill seemed almost supernatural.

Tuesday, 20*th*.—To-day is to be the grand fête at Vauxhall, so much talked of, in honour of Lord Wellington's victories. At ten o'clock I started with Mrs.

* Richard Lovell Edgeworth, born 1744, died 1817. He wrote with his daughter Essays on Irish Bulls, on Education, and various other works.

† Mr. Edgeworth's fourth wife.

‡ For the battle of Vittoria.

§ Dudley House, in Park Lane.

Montague in a coach, and Mr. Knutzen, the Norwegian, for my cavalier, and Mr. Tisdale* as her's. Before Carlton House the carriage stopped, and what was my horror when I saw that we had already got to the tail of the carriages, which extended from Pall Mall to Vauxhall! We were obliged to be patient; I was too thankful to think I was not in our own carriage, and to know that the horses and the coachman that we had were amongst the best in London. All the skill of the coachman and the strength of the horses were necessary to draw us out: there never was such a confusion of carriages, without order, without soldiers, or any precaution whatever against the accidents which must inevitably happen in such an assemblage. At length, after two hours on the road, and many very perilous moments, we got out of the carriage, about half a mile from Vauxhall, as the only means of getting there at all. There never was a fête (even in this country) at which it was so difficult to arrive, with so little to tempt one to stay, and from which it was so impossible to get away.† The stewards who had dined there, and were walking about with their wands of office, could do nothing for those that belonged to them. For the most part of the people there was no means of eating, drinking, or sitting down. We were able to do the latter; but when at half-past three in the morning we wished to leave, the crowd was for a few minutes terrible, and after getting through it, we had to walk for more than a mile to join the carriage. They will not catch me at such a fête in this country again. This has cost more than 10,000*l.*, and they had either the carelessness or the meanness not to pay the toll-gate,

* Son of the Countess of Charleville by a former marriage.

† This account affords a striking contrast to the arrangements now made when large crowds are expected to assemble, and particularly on that remarkable occasion, within the memory of all, the opening of the Crystal Palace in Hyde Park, 1851.

so that each carriage was stopped for fourpence. They say that 13,000 persons were present—I do not believe that. The decoration was brilliant, without much taste; the fireworks not better than usual, but repeated three times during the evening.

Wednesday, 21*st*.—We saw Madame de Staël this morning at her own house, who very much amused us with her ideas of English society. She will soon be disgusted with it: I have always prophesied that.

Thursday, 22*nd*.—Went to Little Strawberry.

Friday, 23*rd*.—We went in the morning for a short time to the late Mr. Walter's* house, where they were selling all off by auction. The magnificence of the drawing-room furniture is very great. It is only in this country that the editor of a paper could live at such an expense.

Sir William Gell had just returned at this time to England, and was thus cordially welcomed by the Miss Berrys:—

From Miss Berry to Sir William Gell.

Twickenham, 24th July, 1813.

You can never be half so glad to see us as we shall be to see you. In short, all your particular friends have agreed among themselves that they cannot do without you; so never think of being allowed to go to Phigalia again, except you travel like a Tartar prince, with your whole horde about you.

When we shall see you here Heaven knows, for you will be one of the great lions of London yourself; and you have just come in time to save Mde. de Staël's life, who certainly would have *roared* herself to death in another week.

When you will be allowed to go and show yourself at the country fairs I know not, but I am not without hopes that you will, ere it be very long, break away from your keepers, and give us a look of you here.

We have a snug little den prepared for you. I am ready with a hearty embrace, Agnes with another, accompanied by a continuation of the old dispute, as good as new, Penelope's

* Editor of the *Times* newspaper.

suitors, and endless, like her own web—and 'then Mrs. Harrot descends from her garret,' to make you such a pudding as shall put all other puddings to the blush, not to mention an Alderney cow, which we have hired on purpose to give you as much milk and cream as you like, hot and hot.

And now farewell, for lions have as little time for reading as for writing letters.

JOURNAL.

Sunday, 25*th*.—About four o'clock the Princess arrived very unexpectedly with Lady Charlotte. She had luncheon, stayed and talked till nearly five o'clock, when she was obliged to take Gell to Brandenberg House to dinner. The Princess is melancholy, and almost in ill humour, now seeing more nearly the truth as to her position.

Saturday, 31*st*.—We dined early, to go on the water from six till past nine o'clock: it was a delicious evening, and the scene at Richmond in great beauty. Here the large ship, the Navigation Barge, filled with people, stopped for some time. We rowed, with a hundred other boats also filled with people, around the barge, on board of which they were dancing and playing music.

Tuesday, August 3rd.—Whilst Agnes and my father were taking tea, the Princess of Wales arrived, with Lady Charlotte Lindsay, Gell, his sister, and the little Willy. There was nothing to be done but to give them some tea and coffee. The Princess is always in good humour, and takes all in good part when she falls in like a shot. She took a short walk in the garden, and returned about ten o'clock to Kensington.

Thursday, 19*th*.—Lady Glenbervie and Lady Charlotte Lindsay came this afternoon. We were under the beeches with them when the Duchess of Devonshire arrived, with Madame de Staël, her daughter, and Mr. Foster, in a barouche. We sat together under the trees, and after Lady Glenbervie and Charlotte were gone, Madame de

Staël related to us for nearly an hour the works that she thought of writing, three to be published during her lifetime, and one after her death; all that with a detail and a rapidity truly amusing.

Miss Berry's letter to Lady Hardwicke gives a lively description of the last few weeks spent at Little Strawberry.

Letter to Lady Hardwicke.

September 11th, 1813.

Where are we, and what have we been about? Why we have been keeping a guingette (Anglicè, a hedge ale-house), to which I have *assigned* the *sign* of the 'Cat and Bagpipes,' where everybody has seemed to take it for granted that they were sure to find 'Tea and coffee,' 'Hot roast and boiled every day,' and 'Dinners dressed on the shortest notice.' Certainly our custom in the *chance line* has been great, to say nothing of our beds having been always 'slept in *the night before*.'

Thus have passed the six or eight weeks which I had destined to quiet reading, to Charles the Second, the Duchess of Cleveland, and many such worthies!

But we are now shortly going to a retreat which we shall certainly find sufficiently retired—I mean N. Audley St. Our business here in the *public line*, however great, has not, as you may suspect, been *profitable*, so that we cannot make any further excursions *en famille* this year. We have, however, much enjoyed our sojourn at this pretty little place, which was never in greater beauty.

Parting with it, however necessary, and however I have wished it, will be a pang—parting with it for seven years!—for more, much more, than *ever* to me! N'en parlons plus. 'Quite the contrary.' Let me tell you that Madame de Staël sticks to her intention of coming to you the middle of November—that I stick to *my* intention of meeting her, and that Sir J. Mackintosh, who in October is going, not fox-hunting, but paper-hunting, to the Duke of Leeds, in Yorkshire, intends meeting us both at Wimpole on his return,—if you and Lord Hardwicke do not forbid these banns. Long before that time I trust you will have drunk your fill of Malvern. By the bye, drinking puts me in mind of four ridiculous lines, being an account of the travels of the learned Porson, which Sir J. Mackintosh repeated to us the other day, and which I send to Lord Hardwicke:—

'I went to Strasbourg to get drunk
With that learned Grecian Brouncke;
And then to Leipzig to get drunker
With that more learned Grecian Brouncker.'

Upon which Madame de Staël exclaimed, '*Ah! que c'est joli!*' an application of the word which amused me almost as much as the lines.

The said Staël is still at Richmond till the end of the month, when her torrent of words and ideas will no longer flow into the Thames, but turn its course towards London, and then to Lord Lansdowne's, and then into Staffordshire, and then—'To Nova Zembla and the Lord knows where;' but still she sticks to being at Wimpole the middle of November.

I trust and hope long before that time to have better accounts of your voice; but if you must still be deprived of it, there cannot certainly be a more convenient visitor to a *dumb* woman than Madame de Staël.

The Dowager Duchess of M. is very much one of the women whom a friend of ours calls *virtuous by patent.* But she has very much the manners of a lady, which neither her patent for virtue, nor even that of nobility, gives.

The following letter from Madame de Staël to Miss Berry appears to have been written from some country house:—

Jeudi, 23 Sept.

Je vous dirai bien sincèrement que votre lettre m'a fait un grand bien. J'ai besoin de vous donner toute la confiance de mon cœur; et cette amitié, qui n'a point de secrets ni de soupçons, est tout à fait nécessaire à mon bonheur. Je préfère votre esprit, votre caractère, tout vous enfin, aux autres, et je vous prie de me permettre de compter sur vous comme vous devez compter sur moi. Cette déclaration, plus franche que celle des Alliés, étant faite, je reviens à mes intérêts du jour. Vous dînez chez moi dimanche, et je reviens demain. Je ne sais pas si ma fille communiera ou non samedi, c'est le ministre de la paroisse qui doit en décider. Il y a ici Lady Cowper, Lady

Caroline, les maris de ces dames, Mr. Nugent, Mr. Ward. Lady Besborough est partie ce matin, et Lord Melburne nous a quitté, quoiqu'il fut assez bien apprivoisé avec moi. Y a-t-il des nouvelles de la paix ou de la guerre? Vous concevez de quel intérêt cela est pour moi. Entre les Cosaques et le Corse, je vois bien peu d'espoir de liberté pour la France, et je ne sais que souhaiter, mais je sais très-bien que craindre. Aimez-moi, je vous prie, avec indulgence à de certains égards, parce que vous avez su faire plus de sacrifices que moi; mais ce qui ajoute à votre mérite c'est que nos caractères ont plus d'analogie que nos actions. Adieu. Tâchez donc de guérir ces maux de tête. Voyez Farquhar; il me traite. Adieu.

JOURNAL.

Saturday, September 18*th.*—We signed with Alderman Wood the agreement for our pretty little house for seven years at one hundred and fifty guineas a year, he paying the taxes, repairs, and every other expense. It is very little for property in this neighbourhood, and in such a good situation. After going round the garden, &c., we told him he could take possession after Wednesday next. I wish that the Wednesday were passed, because adieux are always sad.

Wednesday, 22*nd.*—Removed to London. It was fine —I was very glad, bad weather would have increased the sadness of our adieu to Little Strawberry. I took a turn round the enclosure quite alone. The recollections that my walk brought to mind were all melancholy. During twenty-two years that I had owned it, I had been but little happy; still though I left it with regret, I told myself that this separation was necessary: I had long wished for it, as that would save us from an expense and from cares which weighed down upon us, and which increased more and more every day. That the last two months had perhaps been the greatest enjoyment that I had ever had in the place, because I was almost sure of being quit of it. I said to myself all that, I felt the truth of it, but notwithstanding I suffered, and should have felt sorry if I had not suffered.

Saturday, October 2nd.—In the evening Agnes and I went to Sir J. Mackintosh's, where Madame de Staël had dined; we found there the Davys, Ward, Lord Byron, Malthus, Curran * the famous Irish advocate, and some other men. Madame de Staël appropriated as usual Curran, though Sir James tried and succeeded in making the conversation more general. Curran's conversation is eloquent, but without taste.

Tuesday, 5th.—Saw Lord Webb Seymour. In the evening we went to Madame de Staël, where there was a very agreeable society of about half-a-dozen ladies and twenty gentlemen. One should never have said, in looking at the company yesterday, that one was in London in the month of October. London would be really delightful if it was never fuller than at the present time.

Wednesday, 6th.—Dined at the Princess's. The Princess joined less in the conversation than I ever saw her before.

Saturday, 9th.—At dinner we had Sir H. and Lady Davy, Mrs. Damer, Lord W. Seymour, and Frederick Douglas. In the evening, Madame de Staël and her daughter, the two Rawdons, Mr. and Mrs. Gordon, Mr. Mercer, Mr. Ward, Dr. Kinnaird, Mr. Boswell, the Countesse de Palmella. A very good little society, where Madame de Staël and Ward talked a great deal and very well.

Monday, 11th.—I went to Madame de Staël † in the

* James Curran, born 1750. He was regarded as one of the leading Irish patriots; greatly distinguished by his oratory in the stormy debates of the Irish House of Commons, and by his strong opposition to the union of Ireland with England; died 1817.

† '. . . S'il fait mauvais, ne sortez pas, et donnez-moi seulement la consolation de votre société dès que vous le pourrez. Ma fille est aussi bien qu'une rougeole puisse la permettre.'

morning, knowing that her daughter had the measles. I conversed quietly and agreeably with her for half an hour.

Tuesday, 19*th*.—Returning home from dinner with Madame de Staël, I found a man sleeping upon the door-steps; our servants called to the watchman to take charge of him. The threshold of the door was all covered with blood, which had been running from the wounds in his head. The poor man had been ill-treated in the streets, he had knocked loudly at our door for assistance, having seen a light. At last the watchmen carried him away upon a stretcher, that I made them make of a door which our men had given them.

Sunday, 31*st*.—Dined at Kensington with Lady Glenbervie and Lady Charlotte; the other visitors were Douglas Kinnaird and Mr. Lewis. The Princess was in good humour, but not very cheerful, and appearing to find her situation more hopeless, without the death of *one of the two*,—which is very true.

Saturday, *November* 6*th*.—I have seen the best of the illuminations for the great success of the allies in Germany. Carlton House was very brilliant, the Admiralty and all the Government Offices, the Ministers' houses, and the houses of other official men, but the illumination is not at all general, and though this evening (Saturday) there were a great number of people in the streets, towards Pall Mall and Whitehall there was not the least confusion, and in our quarter perfect tranquillity.

Wednesday, 17*th*.—In the morning I saw Ward for a moment, and afterwards I was with the Princess for an hour at her house.* It is anything but a palace, but the situation is good, and she is certainly better lodged than I have ever seen her elsewhere.

Wednesday, 24*th*.—They fired the guns for the re-establishment of the British Government at Hanover, and

* Connaught Place.

in the evening we heard the news of the taking of St. Fé in France by Lord Wellington.

Thursday, 25*th*.—At nine o'clock in the morning the guns were fired for the news of the preceding evening, and again between three and four, for the arrival of the news of the taking of Dresden by the Allies. No one ever remembered the guns being fired three times in thirty-six hours, as it has now happened.

From Miss Berry to Lady Georgiana Morpeth.

November 25th, 1813.

MY DEAR G.,—I have appeared very ungrateful in not sooner thanking you for your letter of the 30th from Castle Howard; but I have the old, tiresome, but alas! too *real* excuse of such health, as actually eats up three parts of my existence. I am consequently left with but a fourth part of the time which people possess for the business, the amusements, and the idlenesses of life. This makes me live in a perpetual vain attempt to do *more* than is possible.

The retirement of London, in which I thought I was going to do so much after the dissipation of Twickenham, has turned out, as London always does to me (except during what is called *the season*), so agreeable, so much good society, and one could so well enjoy it, that I have had just as little time to myself as I had in the country.

The Staël left Richmond much about the same time that we left Twickenham, and wherever she is, there will society be also —if it is to be had within ten miles *à la ronde*. Except during her visit to Bowood, and now that she is for a week at Middleton,* she has been constantly in town, giving very agreeable dinners and soirées, with two or three women and half-a-dozen men—*dont elle se charge toute seule.*

She is always entertaining, and I, who know her so much and so well, will add always good-natured, and never *méchante*. Ward and she will amuse you. She thinks him handsome, and *d'un joli tourneur*. I tell her she has undertaken two miracles,

* Seat of the Earl of Jersey, in Oxfordshire.

to make him *poli envers les femmes, et pieux envers Dieu.* And there is no saying, if they go on, what her success may be. *En attendant,* they make very good company for other people.

Among the agreeables, we have had Lady Harrowby in town for some weeks.

JOURNAL.

Wednesday, Dec. 1*st.*—We both of us dined with the Princess in Connaught Place, the first time that she has given a dinner in her new house, which is still all upside down. The company consisted only of Gell and Craven, who arrived in town to-day. Lady C. Campbell and Lady C. Lindsay in waiting. The Princess was particularly melancholy, wept when speaking to me of herself, confessing herself entirely overwhelmed with her situation and her prospects for the future.

Tuesday, 7*th.*—Dined at Lord Stafford's with Madame de Stäel, her daughter, and her son, Sir James and Lady Mackintosh, &c. In the evening more guests, making a very agreeable soirée. At dinner the conversation rather flagged. Madame de Stäel was not excited enough; it appeared to me that she only wanted that to be as brilliant as usual, though she had to-day received the news of the death of Comte Louis de Narbonne. One must acknowledge that one could not lose an old lover more gaily, as it was said of Charles the VIIth of his kingdom.

Saturday, 11*th.*—At nine o'clock in the evening I went to Madame de Stäel's. The Duke of Sussex, Lord and Lady Liverpool, Lord Harrowby, and several diplomats, had dined there. In the evening other ladies arrived, Lady Stafford and her daughter Mrs. G. Lamb, &c.

Sunday, 26*th.*—Dined at Madame de Stäel's with Sir James and Lady Mackintosh, Mr. Ward, The Comte Palmilla, Mr. Sharp, and her own family. A very agreeable dinner: two or three artists in the evening.

Wednesday, 29*th.*—Dined at the Princess's: there were

only Mr. Craven, Little Willy,* and a young playfellow of his, and Lady Orme: these dinners become insupportable; the dulness makes me almost ill in the course of a long evening, only interrupted by the Princess singing with Mr. Craven, which is a screeching of which no idea can be formed without hearing it.

From Sir Uvedale Price to Miss Berry.

Foxley, December 18th, 1813.

. . . . I want your assistance in making some inquiries, which, as you may suppose, relate to the work about which I am very busily employed. I have never told you exactly what it was to be, and as I feel sure that you take the same interest in my productions that I do in yours—scribetur tibi formâ loquacitur; and, indeed, something of the kind is necessary by way of preface to the inquiries. If our two publications should happen to come out at the same time, we shall produce them under similar titles, for mine is intended to be a 'Comparative View' of the different opinions respecting *visible* beauty; other kinds of beauty will of course be often considered, but chiefly in the way of illustration. Hogarth's 'Analysis of Beauty' is, I believe, the first book written in our language on the subject, and, as far as I know, in any other. Many things in it have been laughed at, and are open to ridicule; but it contains a number of just and original observations, and Burke's theory is in a great degree taken from it, though he has not acknowledged his obligations. The principal writers, after these two, are Knight, Dugald Stewart, and Alison, at least I know of no others. Alison's theory is at present the most popular; partly I believe from its being very flattering to the spiritual part of our nature, and partly from its having been very highly spoken of, and very ingeniously explained and illustrated, in the 'Edinburgh Review' of 1811. I will not say, as Knight said to me in one of his letters about Burke's theory (giving one a strong hint that he should serve mine the same sauce), 'If I do not cut up "The Sublime and Beautiful" root and branch, set me down for a blockhead.' The risk is too great in case of failure; for an author of nice sensibility should be less afraid of having his head

* William Austen.

laid on the block, than of having the block fixed to his head. I will venture to say, however, that, if I am not strangely mistaken, Mr. Alison's theory will be found on examination, in many essential points, more like the baseless fabric of a vision than the strong-based promontory. You will not suppose from this that I deny, or do not feel and acknowledge in its fullest extent, the powerful influence of association; I only question the exclusive influence which has been attributed to it, and by that, something may be allowed, where visible beauty is concerned, to form colour and physical qualities. Fitzpatrick, in that exquisite poem I once read to you, has settled the matter most judiciously, and one might almost think that he had these metaphysicians in view when he makes the Soul say to the Body,

> Yet trust me, I'm willing to waive all dispute;
> For though certain grave doctors, by few understood,
> Think they flatter me much when they call you a brute,
> Those who wish to divide us can mean us no good.

So much for my preface; now for the inquiries. The review was made on a late edition of Alison; my remarks on the first in 1790; and I *believe* that there was none between the two. This I could wish you to inquire; and also whether in the last edition there is much that is entirely new, or whether there are many essential alterations. The other inquiry I wish you to make is of a more extensive kind. I believe I am acquainted with most of the English authors who have written on the subject in question; but I do not know of any who have expressly written on it in French. You are likely to know whether there be any such treatise, or anything worth notice mixed with other matter; and if you should not, your friend Madame de Staël, though she may not have turned her mind particularly to objects of that kind, is very likely to know what has been written on them, and perhaps you will get what information you can for me. I never happened to be in company with her, and I thought myself very unlucky, particularly as Spencer asked me to meet her one evening at his house. I remember that Mdme. Moreau was likewise to be there. You may very well ask what could keep me away. I am almost ashamed of saying it was a concert, which, in spite of my passion for music, I should have given up, but it was not only a very choice one, but one to which

Lady Douglas was, as a great favour, allowed to carry me. In the way there she gave me an excellent account of a conversation she had overheard between Madame de Staël and Lord Erskine. I have not yet seen 'L'Allemagne;' but your letter is full of it, and Lord Holland, in one of his, asks me, Have you read 'L'Allemagne'? 'Du bruit de Bajazet mon âme importunée' can have no rest till I have read it, and I have no doubt of the pleasure it will give me. She is certainly a very extraordinary woman, even when one considers the stock she comes from, and how highly bred she is, for thinking and writing.

Upon reading a few days ago in the papers an account of the Queen of Naples' magnificent reception at the Ottoman court, it occurred to me that the Grand Signior might have taken a fancy for her. She carries me back to Naples, and brings to my mind her last exploit there, and the blot, the only blot in Nelson's character, when he gave his sanction to such abominations,

> Against his better knowledge, not deceived,
> But fondly overcome with female charm.

END OF THE SECOND VOLUME.

CPSIA information can be obtained
at www.ICGtesting.com
Printed in the USA
LVHW112143080422
715402LV00007B/90

9 783752 588330